THE BROADVIEW ANTHOLOGY OF
SHORT FICTION

Fourth Canadian Edition

Edited by Laura Buzzard and Marjorie Mather

broadview press

BROADVIEW PRESS – www.broadviewpress.com
Peterborough, Ontario, Canada

Founded in 1985, Broadview Press remains a wholly independent publishing house. Broadview's focus is on academic publishing; our titles are accessible to university and college students as well as scholars and general readers. With 800 titles in print, Broadview has become a leading international publisher in the humanities, with world-wide distribution. Broadview is committed to environmentally responsible publishing and fair business practices.

Library and Archives Canada Cataloguing in Publication

Title: The Broadview anthology of short fiction / edited by Laura Buzzard and Marjorie Mather.
Names: Buzzard, Laura, editor. | Mather, Marjorie, editor.
Description: Fourth Canadian edition.
Identifiers: Canadiana 2020017858X | ISBN 9781554813834 (softcover)
Subjects: LCSH: Short stories, English. | LCSH: Short stories, American. | CSH: Short stories, Canadian (English) | LCGFT: Short stories.
Classification: LCC PS648.S5 B76 2020 | DDC 823/.0108—dc23

Broadview Press handles its own distribution in North America:
PO Box 1243, Peterborough, Ontario K9J 7H5, Canada
555 Riverwalk Parkway, Tonawanda, NY 14150, USA
Tel: (705) 743-8990; Fax: (705) 743-8353
email: customerservice@broadviewpress.com

For all territories outside of North America, distribution is handled by Eurospan Group.

Broadview Press acknowledges the financial support
of the Government of Canada for our publishing activities.

Canadä

Typeset by Eileen Eckert
Cover design by Lisa Brawn

PRINTED IN CANADA

CONTENTS

ACKNOWLEDGEMENTS

The editors owe a debt of gratitude to Julia Gaunce and Suzette Mayr, who edited the first edition of this anthology in 2004. They did not work directly on this edition, but their vision for the anthology continues to inform our decisions.

We also wish to thank the instructors who provided feedback and suggestions for the new edition:

Laura Davis
Deborah Torkko
Jeffrey Donaldson
Michael Helm
Audrey Barkman Hill
Matthew Zantingh

Contributing Writers and Editors

Tara Bodie
Don LePan
Andrew Reszitnyk
Nora Ruddock
Helena Snopek

NATHANIEL HAWTHORNE

Among Nathaniel Hawthorne's paternal ancestors was one of the judges who participated in the 1692 Salem witch trials; on his mother's side, rumours of incest and public shaming that occurred generations before circulated in the family. According to critic Thomas E. Connolly, a "deep family guilt settled upon [Hawthorne], and this guilt undoubtedly prompted him to critical attacks in his literary works on the rigours of Puritanism." Whether or not it was Hawthorne's "family guilt" that drove him to write what he did, the theme of exposing the hypocrisy of Puritan culture does appear in several of his works.

Following the death of his father, Hawthorne's mother moved him and his two sisters to her family home, where he was raised among his eight unmarried aunts and uncles, and where he had a substantial library at his disposal. When he was nine years old, an injury to his foot required him to stop attending school; he spent his recovery reading his favourite authors, who included Edmund Spenser and William Shakespeare. From 1821 to 1825, Hawthorne attended Bowdoin College. He was not a brilliant student—he came in eighteenth in a class of 38 and was once fined for playing cards.

Hawthorne married Sophia Peabody in 1842, and they moved to Concord, Massachusetts. While living here, Hawthorne completed a volume of short pieces entitled *Mosses from an Old Manse* (1846). After Sophia gave birth to their first two children in rapid succession, the Hawthornes struggled to meet the financial demands of their new family. During this time of financial hardship, Hawthorne concentrated his efforts on writing *The Scarlet Letter*, a book that was to guarantee his literary reputation. Two more novels quickly followed—beginning with *The House of the Seven Gables* in 1851—as well as a collection of short stories, two works for children, and a biography of his politician friend Franklin Pierce.

When Pierce became president in 1853, he gave Hawthorne a job as American consul in Liverpool. Hawthorne, now supporting three children, needed the steady income, but this appointment slowed his writing career. He did, however, publish one more novel, *The Marble Faun* (1860), the same year he returned to the United States. Hawthorne died four years later and was buried at Sleepy Hollow Cemetery in Concord, Massachusetts.

The Minister's Black Veil: A Parable

THE SEXTON[1] stood in the porch of Milford meeting-house, pulling busily at the bell-rope. The old people of the village came stooping along the street. Children, with bright faces, tripped merrily beside their parents, or mimicked a graver gait, in the conscious dignity of their Sunday clothes. Spruce bachelors looked sidelong at the pretty maidens, and fancied that the Sabbath sunshine made them prettier than on week days. When the throng had mostly streamed into the porch, the sexton began to toll the bell, keeping his eye on the Reverend Mr. Hooper's door. The first glimpse of the clergyman's figure was the signal for the bell to cease its summons.

"But what has good Parson Hooper got upon his face?" cried the sexton in astonishment.

All within hearing immediately turned about, and beheld the semblance of Mr. Hooper, pacing slowly his meditative way towards the meeting-house. With one accord they started, expressing more wonder than if some strange minister were coming to dust the cushions of Mr. Hooper's pulpit.

"Are you sure it is our parson?" inquired Goodman Gray of the sexton.

"Of a certainty it is good Mr. Hooper," replied the sexton. "He was to have exchanged pulpits with Parson Shute, of Westbury; but Parson Shute sent to excuse himself yesterday, being to preach a funeral sermon."

The cause of so much amazement may appear sufficiently slight. Mr. Hooper, a gentlemanly person, of about thirty, though still a bachelor, was dressed with due clerical neatness, as if a careful wife had starched his band, and brushed the weekly dust from his Sunday's garb. There was but one thing remarkable in his appearance. Swathed about his forehead, and hanging down over his face, so low as to be shaken by his breath, Mr. Hooper had on a black veil. On a nearer view it seemed to consist of two folds of crape, which entirely concealed his features, except the mouth and chin, but probably did not intercept his sight, further than to give a darkened aspect to all living and inanimate things. With this gloomy shade before him, good Mr. Hooper walked onward, at a slow and quiet pace, stooping somewhat, and looking on the ground, as is customary with abstracted men, yet nodding kindly to those of his parishioners who still

---

1   An officer responsible for maintaining a church.

waited on the meeting-house steps. But so wonder-struck were they that his greeting hardly met with a return.

"I can't really feel as if good Mr. Hooper's face was behind that piece of crape," said the sexton.

"I don't like it," muttered an old woman, as she hobbled into the meeting-house. "He has changed himself into something awful, only by hiding his face."

"Our parson has gone mad!" cried Goodman Gray, following him across the threshold. A rumor of some unaccountable phenomenon had preceded Mr. Hooper into the meeting-house, and set all the congregation astir. Few could refrain from twisting their heads towards the door; many stood upright, and turned directly about; while several little boys clambered upon the seats, and came down again with a terrible racket. There was a general bustle, a rustling of the women's gowns and shuffling of the men's feet, greatly at variance with that hushed repose which should attend the entrance of the minister. But Mr. Hooper appeared not to notice the perturbation of his people. He entered with an almost noiseless step, bent his head mildly to the pews on each side, and bowed as he passed his oldest parishioner, a white-haired great-grandsire, who occupied an arm-chair in the centre of the aisle. It was strange to observe how slowly this venerable man became conscious of something singular in the appearance of his pastor. He seemed not fully to partake of the prevailing wonder, till Mr. Hooper had ascended the stairs, and showed himself in the pulpit, face to face with his congregation, except for the black veil. That mysterious emblem was never once withdrawn. It shook with his measured breath, as he gave out the psalm; it threw its obscurity between him and the holy page, as he read the Scriptures; and while he prayed, the veil lay heavily on his uplifted countenance. Did he seek to hide it from the dread Being whom he was addressing?

Such was the effect of this simple piece of crape, that more than one woman of delicate nerves was forced to leave the meeting-house. Yet perhaps the pale-faced congregation was almost as fearful a sight to the minister, as his black veil to them.

Mr. Hooper had the reputation of a good preacher, but not an energetic one: he strove to win his people heavenward by mild, persuasive influences, rather than to drive them thither by the thunders of the Word. The sermon which he now delivered was marked by the same characteristics of style and manner as the general series of his pulpit oratory. But there was something, either in the sentiment of the discourse itself, or in the imagination of the auditors, which made it greatly the most powerful effort that they had ever heard from their pastor's lips. It was tinged, rather more darkly than usual, with the gentle gloom of Mr. Hooper's temperament. The subject had reference to secret sin, and those sad mysteries which we hide from our nearest and dearest, and would fain conceal from our own consciousness, even forgetting that the Omniscient can detect them. A subtle power was breathed into his words. Each member of the congregation, the most innocent girl, and the man of hardened breast, felt as if the preacher had crept upon them, behind his awful veil, and discovered their hoarded iniquity of deed or thought. Many spread their clasped hands on their bosoms. There was nothing terrible in what Mr. Hooper said, at least, no violence; and yet, with every tremor of his melancholy voice, the hearers quaked. An unsought pathos came hand in hand with awe. So sensible were the audience of some unwonted attribute in their minister, that they longed for a breath of wind to blow aside the veil, almost believing that a stranger's visage would be discovered, though the form, gesture, and voice were those of Mr. Hooper.

At the close of the services, the people hurried out with indecorous confusion, eager to communicate their pent-up amazement, and conscious of lighter spirits the moment they lost sight of the black veil. Some gathered in little circles, huddled closely together, with their mouths all whispering in the centre; some went homeward alone, wrapt in silent meditation; some talked loudly, and profaned the Sabbath day with ostentatious laughter. A few shook their sagacious heads, intimating that they could penetrate the mystery; while one or two affirmed that there was no mystery at all, but only that Mr. Hooper's eyes were so weakened by the midnight lamp, as to require a shade. After a brief interval, forth came good Mr. Hooper also, in the rear of his flock. Turning his veiled face from one group to another, he paid due reverence to the hoary heads, saluted the middle aged with kind dignity as their friend and spiritual guide, greeted the young with mingled authority and love, and laid his hands on the little children's heads to bless them. Such was always his custom on the Sabbath day. Strange and bewildered looks repaid him for his courtesy. None, as on former occasions, aspired to the honor of walking by their pastor's side. Old Squire Saunders, doubtless by an accidental lapse of memory, neglected to invite Mr. Hooper to his table, where the good clergyman had been wont to bless the food, almost every Sunday since his settlement. He returned, therefore, to the parsonage, and, at the moment of closing the door, was observed to look back upon the people, all of whom had their eyes fixed upon the minister. A sad smile gleamed faintly from beneath the black veil, and flickered about his mouth, glimmering as he disappeared.

"How strange," said a lady, "that a simple black veil, such as any woman might wear on her bonnet, should become such a terrible thing on Mr. Hooper's face!"

"Something must surely be amiss with Mr. Hooper's intellects," observed her husband, the physician of the village. "But the strangest part of the affair is the effect of this vagary, even on a sober-minded man like myself. The black veil, though it covers only our pastor's face, throws its influence over his whole person, and makes him ghostlike from head to foot. Do you not feel it so?"

"Truly do I," replied the lady; "and I would not be alone with him for the world. I wonder he is not afraid to be alone with himself!"

"Men sometimes are so," said her husband.

The afternoon service was attended with similar circumstances. At its conclusion, the bell tolled for the funeral of a young lady. The relatives and friends were assembled in the house, and the more distant acquaintances stood about the door, speaking of the good qualities of the deceased, when their talk was interrupted by the appearance of Mr. Hooper, still covered with his black veil. It was now an appropriate emblem. The clergyman stepped into the room where the corpse was laid, and bent over the coffin, to take a last farewell of his deceased parishioner. As he stooped, the veil hung straight down from his forehead, so that, if her eyelids had not been closed forever, the dead maiden might have seen his face. Could Mr. Hooper be fearful of her glance, that he so hastily caught back the black veil? A person who watched the interview between the dead and living, scrupled not to affirm, that, at the instant when the clergyman's features were disclosed, the corpse had slightly shuddered, rustling the shroud and muslin cap, though the countenance retained the composure of death. A superstitious old woman was the only witness of this prodigy. From the coffin Mr. Hooper passed into the chamber of the mourners, and thence to the head of the staircase, to make the funeral prayer. It was a tender and heart-dissolving prayer, full of sorrow, yet so imbued with celestial hopes, that the music of a heavenly harp, swept by the fingers of the dead, seemed faintly to be heard among the saddest accents of the minister. The people trembled, though they but darkly understood him when he prayed that they, and himself, and all of mortal race, might be ready, as he trusted this young maiden had been, for the dreadful hour that should snatch the veil from their faces. The bearers went heavily forth, and the mourners followed, saddening all the street, with the dead before them, and Mr. Hooper in his black veil behind.

"Why do you look back?" said one in the procession to his partner.

"I had a fancy," replied she, "that the minister and the maiden's spirit were walking hand in hand."

"And so had I, at the same moment," said the other.

That night, the handsomest couple in Milford village were to be joined in wedlock. Though reckoned a melancholy man, Mr. Hooper had a placid cheerfulness for such occasions, which often excited a sympathetic smile where livelier merriment would have been thrown away. There was no quality of his disposition which made him more beloved than this. The company at the wedding awaited his arrival with impatience, trusting that the strange awe, which had gathered over him throughout the day, would now be dispelled. But such was not the result. When Mr. Hooper came, the first thing that their eyes rested on was the same horrible black veil, which had added deeper gloom to the funeral, and could portend nothing but evil to the wedding. Such was its immediate effect on the guests that a cloud seemed to have rolled duskily from beneath the black crape, and dimmed the light of the candles. The bridal pair stood up before the minister. But the bride's cold fingers quivered in the tremulous hand of the bridegroom, and her deathlike paleness caused a whisper that the maiden who had been buried a few hours before was come from her grave to be married. If ever another wedding were so dismal, it was that famous one where they tolled the wedding knell. After performing the ceremony, Mr. Hooper raised a glass of wine to his lips, wishing happiness to the new-married couple in a strain of mild pleasantry that ought to have brightened the features of the guests, like a cheerful gleam from the hearth. At that instant, catching a glimpse of his figure in the looking-glass, the black veil involved his own spirit in the horror with which it overwhelmed all others. His frame shuddered, his lips grew white, he spilt the untasted wine upon the carpet, and rushed forth into the darkness. For the Earth, too, had on her Black Veil.

The next day, the whole village of Milford talked of little else than Parson Hooper's black veil. That, and the mystery concealed behind it, supplied a topic for discussion between acquaintances meeting in the street, and good women gossiping at their open windows. It was the first item of news that the tavern-keeper told to his guests. The children babbled of it on their way to school. One imitative little imp covered his face with an old black handkerchief, thereby so affrighting his playmates that the panic seized himself, and he well-nigh lost his wits by his own waggery.

It was remarkable that of all the busybodies and impertinent people in the parish, not one ventured to put the plain question to Mr. Hooper, wherefore he did this thing. Hitherto, whenever there appeared the slightest call for such interference, he had never lacked advisers, nor shown himself averse to be guided by their judgment. If he erred at all, it was by so painful a degree of self-distrust, that even the mildest censure would lead him to consider an indifferent action as a crime. Yet, though so well acquainted with this amiable weakness, no individual among his parishioners chose to make the black veil a subject of friendly remonstrance. There was a feeling of dread, neither plainly confessed nor carefully concealed, which caused each to shift the responsibility upon another, till at length it was found expedient to send a deputation to the church, in order to deal with Mr. Hooper about the mystery, before it should grow into a scandal. Never did an embassy so ill discharge its duties. The minister received them with friendly courtesy, but became silent, after they were seated, leaving to his visitors, the whole burden of introducing their important business. The topic, it might be supposed, was obvious enough. There was the black veil swathed round Mr. Hooper's forehead, and concealing every feature above his placid mouth, on which, at times, they could perceive the glimmering of a melancholy smile. But that piece of crape, to their imagination, seemed to hang down before his heart, the symbol of a fearful secret between him and them. Were the veil but cast aside, they might speak freely of it, but not till then. Thus they sat a considerable time, speechless, confused, and shrinking uneasily from Mr. Hooper's eye, which they felt to be fixed upon them with an invisible glance. Finally, the deputies returned abashed to their constituents, pronouncing the matter too weighty to be handled, except by a council of the churches, if, indeed, it might not require a general synod.

But there was one person in the village unappalled by the awe with which the black veil had impressed all beside herself. When the deputies returned without an explanation, or even venturing to demand one, she, with the calm energy of her character, determined to chase away the strange cloud that appeared to be settling round Mr. Hooper, every moment more darkly than before. As his plighted wife, it should be her privilege to know what the black veil concealed. At the minister's first visit, therefore, she entered upon the subject with a direct simplicity, which made the task easier both for him and her. After he had seated himself, she fixed her eyes steadfastly upon the veil, but could discern nothing of the dreadful gloom that had so overawed the multitude: it was but a double fold of crape, hanging down from his forehead to his mouth, and slightly stirring with his breath.

"No," she said aloud, and smiling, "there is nothing terrible in this piece of crape, except that it hides a face which I am always glad to look upon. Come, good sir, let the sun shine from behind the cloud. First lay aside your black veil: then tell me why you put it on."

Mr. Hooper's smile glimmered faintly.

"There is an hour to come," said he, "when all of us shall cast aside our veils. Take it not amiss, beloved friend, if I wear this piece of crape till then."

"Your words are a mystery, too," returned the young lady. "Take away the veil from them, at least."

"Elizabeth, I will," said he, "so far as my vow may suffer me. Know, then, this veil is a type and a symbol, and I am bound to wear it ever, both in light and darkness, in solitude and before the gaze of multitudes, and as with strangers, so with my familiar friends. No mortal eye will see it withdrawn. This dismal shade must separate me from the world: even you, Elizabeth, can never come behind it!"

"What grievous affliction hath befallen you," she earnestly inquired, "that you should thus darken your eyes forever?"

"If it be a sign of mourning," replied Mr. Hooper, "I, perhaps, like most other mortals, have sorrows dark enough to be typified by a black veil."

"But what if the world will not believe that it is the type of an innocent sorrow?" urged Elizabeth. "Beloved and respected as you are, there may be whispers that you hide your face under the consciousness of secret sin. For the sake of your holy office, do away this scandal!"

The color rose into her cheeks as she intimated the nature of the rumors that were already abroad in the village. But Mr. Hooper's mildness did not forsake him. He even smiled again—that same sad smile, which always appeared like a faint glimmering of light, proceeding from the obscurity beneath the veil.

"If I hide my face for sorrow, there is cause enough," he merely replied; "and if I cover it for secret sin, what mortal might not do the same?"

And with this gentle, but unconquerable obstinacy did he resist all her entreaties. At length Elizabeth sat silent. For a few moments she appeared lost in thought, considering, probably, what new methods might be tried to withdraw her lover from so dark a fantasy, which, if it had no other meaning, was perhaps a symptom of mental disease. Though of a firmer character than his own, the tears rolled down her cheeks. But, in an instant, as it were, a new feeling took the place of sorrow: her eyes were fixed insensibly on the black veil, when, like a sudden twilight in the air, its terrors fell around her. She arose, and stood trembling before him.

"And do you feel it then, at last?" said he mournfully.

She made no reply, but covered her eyes with her hand, and turned to leave the room. He rushed forward and caught her arm.

"Have patience with me, Elizabeth!" cried he, passionately. "Do not desert me, though this veil must be between us here on earth. Be mine, and hereafter there shall be no veil over my face, no darkness between our souls! It is but a mortal veil—it is not for eternity! O! you know not how lonely I am, and how frightened, to be alone behind my black veil. Do not leave me in this miserable obscurity forever!"

"Lift the veil but once, and look me in the face," said she.

"Never! It cannot be!" replied Mr. Hooper.

"Then farewell!" said Elizabeth.

She withdrew her arm from his grasp, and slowly departed, pausing at the door, to give one long shuddering gaze, that seemed almost to penetrate the mystery of the black veil. But, even amid his grief, Mr. Hooper smiled to think that only a material emblem had separated him from happiness, though the horrors, which it shadowed forth, must be drawn darkly between the fondest of lovers.

From that time no attempts were made to remove Mr. Hooper's black veil, or, by a direct appeal, to discover the secret which it was supposed to hide. By persons who claimed a superiority to popular prejudice, it was reckoned merely an eccentric whim, such as often mingles with the sober actions of men otherwise rational, and tinges them all with its own semblance of insanity. But with the multitude, good Mr. Hooper was irreparably a bugbear.[2] He could not walk the street with any peace of mind, so conscious was he that the gentle and timid would turn aside to avoid him, and that others would make it a point of hardihood to throw themselves in his way. The impertinence of the latter class compelled him to give up his customary walk at sunset to the burial ground; for when he leaned pensively over the gate, there would always be faces behind the gravestones, peeping at his black veil. A fable went the rounds that the stare of the dead people drove him thence. It grieved him, to the very depth of his kind heart, to observe how the children fled from his approach, breaking up their merriest sports, while his melancholy figure was yet afar off. Their instinctive dread caused him to feel more strongly than aught else, that a preternatural horror was interwoven with the threads of the black crape. In truth, his own antipathy to the veil was known to be so great, that he never willingly passed before a mirror, nor stooped to drink at a still fountain, lest, in its peaceful bosom, he should be affrighted by himself. This was what gave plausibility to the whispers, that Mr. Hooper's conscience tortured him for some great crime too horrible to be entirely concealed, or otherwise than so obscurely intimated. Thus, from beneath the black veil, there rolled a cloud into the sunshine, an ambiguity of sin or sorrow, which enveloped the poor minister, so that love or sympathy could never reach him. It was said that ghost and fiend consorted with him there. With self-shudderings and outward terrors, he walked continually in its shadow, groping darkly within his own soul, or gazing through a medium that saddened the whole world. Even the lawless wind, it was believed, respected his dreadful secret, and never blew aside the veil. But still good Mr. Hooper sadly smiled at the pale visages of the worldly throng as he passed by.

Among all its bad influences, the black veil had one desirable effect, of making its wearer a very efficient clergyman. By the aid of his mysterious emblem—for there was no other apparent cause—he became a man of awful power over souls that were in agony for sin. His converts always regarded him with a dread peculiar to themselves, affirming, though but figuratively, that, before he brought them to celestial light, they had been with him behind the black veil. Its gloom, indeed, enabled him to sympathize with all dark affections. Dying sinners cried aloud for Mr. Hooper, and would not yield their breath till he

---

2   A creature that causes great fear or anxiety.

appeared; though ever, as he stooped to whisper consolation, they shuddered at the veiled face so near their own. Such were the terrors of the black veil, even when Death had bared his visage! Strangers came long distances to attend service at his church, with the mere idle purpose of gazing at his figure, because it was forbidden them to behold his face. But many were made to quake ere they departed! Once, during Governor Belcher's administration,[3] Mr. Hooper was appointed to preach the election sermon. Covered with his black veil, he stood before the chief magistrate, the council, and the representatives, and wrought so deep an impression, that the legislative measures of that year were characterized by all the gloom and piety of our earliest ancestral sway.

In this manner Mr. Hooper spent a long life, irreproachable in outward act, yet shrouded in dismal suspicions; kind and loving, though unloved, and dimly feared; a man apart from men, shunned in their health and joy, but ever summoned to their aid in mortal anguish. As years wore on, shedding their snows above his sable veil, he acquired a name throughout the New England churches, and they called him Father Hooper. Nearly all his parishioners, who were of mature age when he was settled, had been borne away by many a funeral: he had one congregation in the church, and a more crowded one in the churchyard; and having wrought so late into the evening, and done his work so well, it was now good Father Hooper's turn to rest.

Several persons were visible by the shaded candle-light, in the death chamber of the old clergyman. Natural connections he had none. But there was the decorously grave, though unmoved physician, seeking only to mitigate the last pangs of the patient whom he could not save. There were the deacons, and other eminently pious members of his church. There, also, was the Reverend Mr. Clark, of Westbury, a young and zealous divine, who had ridden in haste to pray by the bedside of the expiring minister. There was the nurse, no hired handmaiden of death, but one whose calm affection had endured thus long in secrecy, in solitude, amid the chill of age, and would not perish, even at the dying hour. Who, but Elizabeth! And there lay the hoary head of good Father Hooper upon the death pillow, with the black veil still swathed about his brow, and reaching down over his face, so that each more difficult gasp of his faint breath caused it to stir. All through life that piece of crape had hung between him and the world: it had separated him from cheerful brotherhood and woman's love, and kept him in that saddest of all prisons, his own heart; and still it lay upon his face, as if to deepen the gloom of his darksome chamber, and shade him from the sunshine of eternity.

---

3   Jonathan Belcher was governor of the British colonies of Massachusetts, New Hampshire, and New Jersey from 1730 to 1741.

For some time previous, his mind had been confused, wavering doubtfully between the past and the present, and hovering forward, as it were, at intervals, into the indistinctness of the world to come. There had been feverish turns, which tossed him from side to side, and wore away what little strength he had. But in his most convulsive struggles, and in the wildest vagaries of his intellect, when no other thought retained its sober influence, he still showed an awful solicitude lest the black veil should slip aside. Even if his bewildered soul could have forgotten, there was a faithful woman at his pillow, who, with averted eyes, would have covered that aged face, which she had last beheld in the comeliness of manhood. At length the death-stricken old man lay quietly in the torpor of mental and bodily exhaustion, with an imperceptible pulse, and breath that grew fainter and fainter, except when a long, deep, and irregular inspiration seemed to prelude the flight of his spirit.

The minister of Westbury approached the bedside.

"Venerable Father Hooper," said he, "the moment of your release is at hand. Are you ready for the lifting of the veil that shuts in time from eternity?"

Father Hooper at first replied merely by a feeble motion of his head; then, apprehensive, perhaps, that his meaning might be doubtful, he exerted himself to speak.

"Yea," said he, in faint accents, "my soul hath a patient weariness until that veil be lifted."

"And is it fitting," resumed the Reverend Mr. Clark, "that a man so given to prayer, of such a blameless example, holy in deed and thought, so far as mortal judgment may pronounce; is it fitting that a father in the church should leave a shadow on his memory, that may seem to blacken a life so pure? I pray you, my venerable brother, let not this thing be! Suffer us to be gladdened by your triumphant aspect as you go to your reward. Before the veil of eternity be lifted, let me cast aside this black veil from your face!"

And thus speaking, the Reverend Mr. Clark bent forward to reveal the mystery of so many years. But, exerting a sudden energy, that made all the beholders stand aghast, Father Hooper snatched both his hands from beneath the bedclothes, and pressed them strongly on the black veil, resolute to struggle, if the minister of Westbury would contend with a dying man.

"Never!" cried the veiled clergyman. "On earth, never!"

"Dark old man!" exclaimed the affrighted minister, "with what horrible crime upon your soul are you now passing to the judgment?"

Father Hooper's breath heaved; it rattled in his throat; but, with a mighty effort, grasping forward with his hands, he caught hold of life, and held it back till he should speak. He even raised himself in bed; and there he sat, shivering with the arms of death around him, while the black veil hung down, awful, at that last moment, in the gathered terrors of a lifetime. And yet the faint, sad smile, so often there, now seemed to glimmer from its obscurity, and linger on Father Hooper's lips.

"Why do you tremble at me alone?" cried he, turning his veiled face round the circle of pale spectators. "Tremble also at each other! Have men avoided me, and women shown no pity, and children screamed and fled, only for my black veil? What, but the mystery which it obscurely typifies, has made this piece of crape so awful? When the friend shows his inmost heart to his friend; the lover to his best beloved; when man does not vainly shrink from the eye of his Creator, loathsomely treasuring up the secret of his sin; then deem me a monster for the symbol beneath which I have lived, and die! I look around me, and lo! on every visage a Black Veil!"

While his auditors shrank from one another, in mutual affright, Father Hooper fell back upon his pillow, a veiled corpse, with a faint smile lingering on his lips. Still veiled, they laid him in his coffin, and a veiled corpse they bore him to the grave. The grass of many years has sprung up and withered on that grave; the burial stone is moss-grown, and good Mr. Hooper's face is dust; but awful is still the thought that it mouldered beneath the Black Veil!

—1836

EDGAR ALLAN POE

Edgar Allan Poe was born in 1809 in Boston, Massachusetts, the son of itinerant stage actors. His father disappeared when Poe was two, and his mother died of tuberculosis two years later. Poe and his brother and sister were split up and sent to live with three different families; Poe went to live with Frances and John Allan, a Virginian couple. By all accounts he was a happy child, and it was not until his adolescence that he began to experience conflict with his foster father, a well-to-do tobacco and dry goods merchant who refused to provide the degree of financial support that most of Poe's fellow students at the University of Virginia received from their families. Poe's education was terminated when he was unable to pay the significant gambling debts he had accumulated. He ran away to Boston and published his first poetry collection, *Tamerlane and Other Poems*, in 1827 under the pseudonym "a Bostonian." He enlisted in the army in 1827, using a false name to hide himself from his creditors, and managed to publish a second collection entitled *Al Aaraaf, Tamerlane, and Minor Poems* in 1829. In 1830 he was accepted into the US Military Academy at West Point but was soon expelled for carousing and irresponsible behaviour.

Shortly afterward, Poe went to live in Baltimore with some of his father's extended family. He continued to struggle for financial security, often taking on editorial jobs for various periodicals in order to pay the bills. He achieved some level of comfort in this way, but his drinking and subsequent unreliability often made him unable to maintain a job for an extended period of time. Many of the dark stories for which he is best remembered appeared in *Tales of the Grotesque and Arabesque* (1840), while "The Raven," his only true popular success during his lifetime, appeared in *The Raven and Other Poems* (1845).

In 1836, Poe married his cousin Virginia Clemm. In spite of recurring bouts of grinding poverty—and despite the fact that Virginia was only 13 at the time of their wedding—the marriage was reported to be a happy one. In 1845, she died of tuberculosis, and four years later Poe became engaged to Sarah Elmira Royster, a widow who had been a childhood love. In October 1849, while travelling, he was found delirious on the street in Baltimore,

Maryland, and died soon afterward. There has been much speculation about the cause of Poe's death, but no medical records survive, and his death remains a mystery.

During his lifetime, Poe was well known as a critic, but his poems and stories did not sell widely (with the exception of "The Raven," which garnered him fame but little profit). The extent of his influence on genre fiction, and on American short fiction in general, was appreciated only after his death. He is sometimes referred to as the inventor of the detective story and as a major contributor to the development of science fiction and gothic stories; according to Alberto Manguel, Poe "set out the laws that govern a tale of horror."

The Cask of Amontillado

THE THOUSAND injuries of Fortunato I had borne as I best could, but when he ventured upon insult I vowed revenge. You, who so well know the nature of my soul, will not suppose, however, that I gave utterance to a threat. *At length* I would be avenged; this was a point definitely settled—but the very definitiveness with which it was resolved precluded the idea of risk. I must not only punish but punish with impunity. A wrong is unredressed when retribution overtakes its redresser. It is equally unredressed when the avenger fails to make himself felt as such to him who has done the wrong.

It must be understood that neither by word nor deed had I given Fortunato cause to doubt my good will. I continued, as was my wont, to smile in his face, and he did not perceive that my smile *now* was at the thought of his immolation.

He had a weak point—this Fortunato—although in other regards he was a man to be respected and even feared. He prided himself on his connoisseurship in wine. Few Italians have the true virtuoso spirit. For the most part their enthusiasm is adopted to suit the time and opportunity, to practise imposture upon the British and Austrian millionaires. In painting and gemmary, Fortunato, like his countrymen, was a quack, but in the matter of old wines he was sincere. In this respect I did not differ from him materially;—I was skilful in the Italian vintages myself, and bought largely whenever I could.

It was about dusk, one evening during the supreme madness of the carnival season, that I encountered my friend. He accosted me with excessive warmth, for he had been drinking much. The man wore motley. He had on a tight-fitting parti-striped dress, and his head was surmounted by the conical cap and bells. I was so pleased to see him that I thought I should never have done wringing his hand.

I said to him—"My dear Fortunato, you are luckily met. How remarkably well you are looking today. But I have received a pipe of what passes for Amontillado, and I have my doubts."

"How?" said he. "Amontillado? A pipe? Impossible! And in the middle of the carnival!"

"I have my doubts," I replied; "and I was silly enough to pay the full Amontillado price without consulting you in the matter. You were not to be found, and I was fearful of losing a bargain."

"Amontillado!"

"I have my doubts."

"Amontillado!"

"And I must satisfy them."

"Amontillado!"

"As you are engaged, I am on my way to Luchresi. If any one has a critical turn it is he. He will tell me—"

"Luchresi cannot tell Amontillado from Sherry."

"And yet some fools will have it that his taste is a match for your own."

"Come, let us go."

"Whither?"

"To your vaults."

"My friend, no; I will not impose upon your good nature. I perceive you have an engagement. Luchresi—"

"I have no engagement;—come."

"My friend, no. It is not the engagement, but the severe cold with which I perceive you are afflicted. The vaults are insufferably damp. They are encrusted with nitre."

"Let us go, nevertheless. The cold is merely nothing. Amontillado! You have been imposed upon. And as for Luchresi, he cannot distinguish Sherry from Amontillado."

Thus speaking, Fortunato possessed himself of my arm; and putting on a mask of black silk and drawing a *roquelaire*[1] closely about my person, I suffered him to hurry me to my palazzo.

There were no attendants at home; they had absconded to make merry in honour of the time. I had told them that I should not return until the morning, and had given them explicit orders not to stir from the house. These orders were sufficient, I well knew, to insure their immediate disappearance, one and all, as soon as my back was turned.

I took from their sconces two flambeaux, and giving one to Fortunato, bowed him through several suites of rooms to the archway that led into the vaults. I

---

1   A knee-length cloak.

passed down a long and winding staircase, requesting him to be cautious as he followed. We came at length to the foot of the descent, and stood together upon the damp ground of the catacombs of the Montresors.

The gait of my friend was unsteady, and the bells upon his cap jingled as he strode.

"The pipe," he said.

"It is farther on," said I; "but observe the white web-work which gleams from these cavern walls."

He turned towards me, and looked into my eyes with two filmy orbs that distilled the rheum of intoxication.

"Nitre?" he asked, at length.

"Nitre," I replied. "How long have you had that cough?"

"Ugh! ugh! ugh!—ugh! ugh! ugh!—ugh! ugh! ugh!—ugh! ugh! ugh!—ugh! ugh! ugh!"

My poor friend found it impossible to reply for many minutes.

"It is nothing," he said, at last.

"Come," I said, with decision, "we will go back; your health is precious. You are rich, respected, admired, beloved; you are happy, as once I was. You are a man to be missed. For me it is no matter. We will go back; you will be ill, and I cannot be responsible. Besides, there is Luchresi—"

"Enough," he said; "the cough is a mere nothing; it will not kill me. I shall not die of a cough."

"True—true," I replied; "and, indeed, I had no intention of alarming you unnecessarily—but you should use all proper caution. A draught of this Medoc will defend us from the damps."

Here I knocked off the neck of a bottle which I drew from a long row of its fellows that lay upon the mould.

"Drink," I said, presenting him the wine.

He raised it to his lips with a leer. He paused and nodded to me familiarly, while his bells jingled.

"I drink," he said, "to the buried that repose around us."

"And I to your long life."

He again took my arm, and we proceeded.

"These vaults," he said, "are extensive."

"The Montresors," I replied, "were a great and numerous family."

"I forget your arms."

"A huge human foot d'or, in a field azure;[2] the foot crushes a serpent rampant whose fangs are imbedded in the heel."

---

2   A golden foot upon a blue background.

"And the motto?"

"*Nemo me impune lacessit.*"[3]

"Good!" he said.

The wine sparkled in his eyes and the bells jingled. My own fancy grew with the Medoc. We had passed through long walls of piled skeletons, with casks and puncheons intermingling, into the inmost recesses of the catacombs. I paused again, and this time I made bold to seize Fortunato by an arm above the elbow.

"The nitre!" I said; "see, it increases. It hangs like moss upon the vaults. We are below the river's bed. The drops of moisture trickle among the bones. Come, we will go back ere it is too late. Your cough—"

"It is nothing," he said; "let us go on. But first, another draught of the Medoc."

I broke and reached him a flagon of De Grave. He emptied it at a breath. His eyes flashed with a fierce light. He laughed and threw the bottle upwards with a gesticulation I did not understand.

I looked at him in surprise. He repeated the movement—a grotesque one.

"You do not comprehend?" he said.

"Not I," I replied.

"Then you are not of the brotherhood."

"How?"

"You are not of the masons."

"Yes, yes," I said; "yes, yes."

"You? Impossible! A mason?"

"A mason," I replied.

"A sign," he said, "a sign."

"It is this," I answered, producing from beneath the folds of my *roquelaire* a trowel.

"You jest," he exclaimed, recoiling a few paces. "But let us proceed to the Amontillado."

"Be it so," I said, replacing the tool beneath the cloak and again offering him my arm. He leaned upon it heavily. We continued our route in search of the Amontillado. We passed through a range of low arches, descended, passed on, and descending again, arrived at a deep crypt, in which the foulness of the air caused our flambeaux rather to glow than flame.

At the most remote end of the crypt there appeared another less spacious. Its walls had been lined with human remains, piled to the vault overhead, in the fashion of the great catacombs of Paris. Three sides of this interior crypt were still ornamented in this manner. From the fourth side the bones had been thrown down, and lay promiscuously upon the earth, forming at one point

---

3   Latin: "No one may insult me without being punished."

a mound of some size. Within the wall thus exposed by the displacing of the bones, we perceived a still interior crypt or recess, in depth about four feet, in width three, in height six or seven. It seemed to have been constructed for no especial use within itself, but formed merely the interval between two of the colossal supports of the roof of the catacombs, and was backed by one of their circumscribing walls of solid granite.

It was in vain that Fortunato, uplifting his dull torch, endeavoured to pry into the depth of the recess. Its termination the feeble light did not enable us to see.

"Proceed," I said; "herein is the Amontillado. As for Luchresi—"

"He is an ignoramus," interrupted my friend, as he stepped unsteadily forward, while I followed immediately at his heels. In an instant he had reached the extremity of the niche, and finding his progress arrested by the rock, stood stupidly bewildered. A moment more and I had fettered him to the granite. In its surface were two iron staples, distant from each other about two feet, horizontally. From one of these depended a short chain, from the other a padlock. Throwing the links about his waist, it was but the work of a few seconds to secure it. He was too much astounded to resist. Withdrawing the key I stepped back from the recess.

"Pass your hand," I said, "over the wall; you cannot help feeling the nitre. Indeed, it is *very* damp. Once more let me *implore* you to return. No? Then I must positively leave you. But I must first render you all the little attentions in my power."

"The Amontillado!" ejaculated my friend, not yet recovered from his astonishment.

"True," I replied; "the Amontillado."

As I said these words I busied myself among the pile of bones of which I have before spoken. Throwing them aside, I soon uncovered a quantity of building stone and mortar. With these materials and with the aid of my trowel, I began vigorously to wall up the entrance of the niche.

I had scarcely laid the first tier of the masonry when I discovered that the intoxication of Fortunato had in a great measure worn off. The earliest indication I had of this was a low moaning cry from the depth of the recess. It was *not* the cry of a drunken man. There was then a long and obstinate silence. I laid the second tier, and the third, and the fourth; and then I heard the furious vibrations of the chain. The noise lasted for several minutes, during which, that I might hearken to it with the more satisfaction, I ceased my labours and sat down upon the bones. When at last the clanking subsided, I resumed the trowel, and finished without interruption the fifth, the sixth, and the seventh tier. The wall was now nearly upon a level with my breast. I again paused, and holding the flambeaux over the mason-work, threw a few feeble rays upon the figure within.

A succession of loud and shrill screams, bursting suddenly from the throat of the chained form, seemed to thrust me violently back. For a brief moment I hesitated, I trembled. Unsheathing my rapier, I began to grope with it about the recess; but the thought of an instant reassured me. I placed my hand upon the solid fabric of the catacombs, and felt satisfied. I reapproached the wall; I replied to the yells of him who clamoured. I re-echoed, I aided, I surpassed them in volume and in strength. I did this, and the clamourer grew still.

It was now midnight, and my task was drawing to a close. I had completed the eighth, the ninth and the tenth tier. I had finished a portion of the last and the eleventh; there remained but a single stone to be fitted and plastered in. I struggled with its weight; I placed it partially in its destined position. But now there came from out the niche a low laugh that erected the hairs upon my head. It was succeeded by a sad voice, which I had difficulty in recognizing as that of the noble Fortunato. The voice said—

"Ha! ha! ha!—he! he! he!—a very good joke, indeed—an excellent jest. We will have many a rich laugh about it at the palazzo—he! he! he!—over our wine—he! he! he!"

"The Amontillado!" I said.

"He! he! he!—he! he! he!—yes, the Amontillado. But is it not getting late? Will not they be awaiting us at the palazzo, the Lady Fortunato and the rest? Let us be gone."

"Yes," I said, "let us be gone."

"*For the love of God, Montresor!*"

"Yes," I said, "for the love of God!"

But to these words I hearkened in vain for a reply. I grew impatient. I called aloud—

"Fortunato!"

No answer. I called again—

"Fortunato!"

No answer still. I thrust a torch through the remaining aperture and let it fall within. There came forth in return only a jingling of the bells. My heart grew sick; it was the dampness of the catacombs that made it so. I hastened to make an end of my labour. I forced the last stone into its position; I plastered it up. Against the new masonry I re-erected the old rampart of bones. For the half of a century no mortal has disturbed them. *In pace requiescat!*[4]

—*1846*

---

4   Latin: "Rest in peace!"

THOMAS HARDY

Although Thomas Hardy once said that he considered poetry a more serious genre than fiction and calculated that he had spent more years writing the former, it is as the author of novels such as *Tess of the D'Urbervilles* (1891) and *Jude the Obscure* (1896) that he is regarded as one of the greatest writers of the Victorian era. Hardy was born in 1840, the son of a stonemason and his wife who lived in Higher Bockhampton in Dorset, near Dorchester. Growing up in a working-class family, Hardy was made very aware of the social divisions that determined the hierarchy of the rich and the working classes. This awareness of divisions and hierarchies would later inform his work as a writer.

Hardy worked as an architect and pursued writing simultaneously. In 1868 he submitted to several publishers the manuscript for a novel, *The Poor Man and the Lady*. The manuscript was unanimously rejected; it would be a few more years before the world would see his first published novel, *Desperate Remedies* (1871). The serializing of his fourth novel, *Far from the Madding Crowd*, in *Cornhill Magazine* (1874) and its subsequent publication in book form established Hardy as a serious writer.

An agnostic himself, Hardy married the evangelical Emma Lavinia Gifford, the daughter of a church rector, in 1874; they travelled to France shortly after the marriage and returned to England to settle in London. By this time, Hardy had given up architecture in order to write full time, and by 1878 his publications had established him as a major figure in the literary world. In 1885, he and his wife moved to Dorchester and into a house Hardy had designed himself, called Max Gate.

The publication of *Jude the Obscure* in 1896 served as a major turning point in Hardy's literary career, as his frank engagement with sexuality and his critical approach to religion and marriage scandalized many readers. Reviews of the book were so vicious (one reviewer re-titled the novel "Jude the Obscene") that some Hardy scholars believe the criticism prompted Hardy to cease writing novels for the rest of his life and concentrate almost exclusively on poetry. By this time, however, Hardy's reputation as one of the foremost novelists of the nineteenth century had already been well established. After Emma Lavinia's death in 1912, Hardy married Florence Emily Dugdale in 1914. When he died in 1928, his heart was buried with his first wife; his ashes were interred at Westminster Abbey.

The Son's Veto

TO THE EYES of a man viewing it from behind, the nut-brown hair was a wonder and a mystery. Under the black beaver hat, surmounted by its tuft of black feathers, the long locks, braided and twisted and coiled like the rushes of a basket, composed a rare, if somewhat barbaric, example of ingenious art. One could understand such weavings and coilings being wrought to last intact for a year, or even a calendar month; but that they should be all demolished regularly at bedtime, after a single day of permanence, seemed a reckless waste of successful fabrication.

And she had done it all herself, poor thing. She had no maid, and it was almost the only accomplishment she could boast of. Hence the unstinted pains.

She was a young invalid lady—not so very much of an invalid—sitting in a wheeled chair, which had been pulled up in the front part of a green enclosure, close to a band-stand, where a concert was going on, during a warm June afternoon. It had place in one of the minor parks or private gardens that are to be found in the suburbs of London, and was the effort of a local association to raise money for some charity. There are worlds within worlds in the great city, and though nobody outside the immediate district had ever heard of the charity, or the band, or the garden, the enclosure was filled with an interested audience sufficiently informed on all these.

As the strains proceeded many of the listeners observed the chaired lady, whose back hair, by reason of her prominent position, so challenged inspection. Her face was not easily discernible, but the aforesaid cunning tress-weavings, the white ear and poll, and the curve of a cheek which was neither flaccid nor sallow, were signals that led to the expectation of good beauty in front. Such expectations are not infrequently disappointed as soon as the disclosure comes; and in the present case, when the lady, by a turn of the head, at length revealed herself, she was not so handsome as the people behind her had supposed, and even hoped—they did not know why.

For one thing (alas! the commonness of this complaint), she was less young than they had fancied her to be. Yet attractive her face unquestionably was, and not at all sickly. The revelation of its details came each time she turned to talk to a boy of twelve or thirteen who stood beside her, and the shape of whose hat and jacket implied that he belonged to a well-known public school. The immediate by-standers could hear that he called her "Mother."

When the end of the programme was reached, and the audience withdrew, many chose to find their way out by passing at her elbow. Almost all turned their heads to take a full and near look at the interesting woman, who remained stationary in the chair till the way should be clear enough for her to be wheeled out without obstruction. As if she expected their glances, and did not mind gratifying their curiosity, she met the eyes of several of her observers by lifting her own, showing these to be soft, brown, and affectionate orbs, a little plaintive in their regard.

She was conducted out of the garden, and passed along the pavement till she disappeared from view, the school-boy walking beside her. To inquiries made by some persons who watched her away, the answer came that she was the second wife of the incumbent of a neighboring parish, and that she was lame. She was generally believed to be a woman with a story—an innocent one, but a story of some sort or other.

In conversing with her on their way home the boy who walked at her elbow said that he hoped his father had not missed them.

"He have been so comfortable these last few hours that I am sure he cannot have missed us," she replied.

"*Has*, dear mother—not *have!*" exclaimed the public-school boy, with an impatient fastidiousness that was almost harsh. "Surely you know that by this time!"

His mother hastily adopted the correction, and did not resent his making it, or retaliate, as she might well have done, by bidding him to wipe that crumby mouth of his, whose condition had been caused by surreptitious attempts to eat a piece of cake without taking it out of the pocket wherein it lay concealed. After this the pretty woman and the boy went onward in silence.

That question of grammar bore upon her history, and she fell into reverie, of a somewhat sad kind to all appearance. It might have been assumed that she was wondering if she had done wisely in shaping her life as she had shaped it, to bring out such a result as this.

In a remote nook in North Wessex, forty miles from London, near the thriving county-town of Aldbrickham, there stood a pretty village with its church and parsonage, which she knew well enough, but her son had never seen. It was her native village, Gaymead, and the first event bearing upon her present situation had occurred at that place when she was only a girl of nineteen.

How well she remembered it, that first act in her little tragi-comedy, the death of her reverend husband's first wife. It happened on a spring evening, and she who now and for many years had filled that first wife's place was then parlor-maid in the parson's house.

When everything had been done that could be done, and the death was announced, she had gone out in the dusk to visit her parents, who were living in the same village, to tell them the sad news. As she opened the white swing-gate and looked towards the trees which rose westward, shutting out the pale light of the evening sky, she discerned, without much surprise, the figure of a man standing in the hedge, though she roguishly exclaimed, as a matter of form, "Oh, Sam, how you frightened me!"

He was a young gardener of her acquaintance. She told him the particulars of the late event, and they stood silent, these two young people, in that elevated, calmly philosophic mind which is engendered when a tragedy has happened close at hand, and has not happened to the philosophers themselves. But it had its bearings upon their relations.

"And will you stay on now at the Vicarage, just the same?" asked he.

She had hardly thought of that. "Oh yes—I suppose," she said. "Everything will be just as usual, I imagine."

He walked beside her towards her mother's. Presently his arm stole round her waist. She gently removed it; but he placed it there again, and she yielded the point. "You see, dear Sophy, you don't know that you'll stay on; you may want a home; and I shall be ready to offer one some day, though I may not be ready just yet."

"Why, Sam, how can you be so fast? I've never even said I liked 'ee; and it is all your own doing, coming after me."

"Still, it is nonsense to say I am not to have a try at you, like the rest." He stooped to kiss her a farewell, for they had reached her mother's door.

"No, Sam; you sha'n't!" she cried, putting her hand over his mouth. "You ought to be more serious on such a night as this." And she bade him adieu without allowing him to kiss her or to come indoors.

The vicar just left a widower was at this time a man about forty years of age, of good family, and childless. He had led a secluded existence in this college living, partly because there were no resident landowners; and his loss now intensified his habit of withdrawal from outward observation. He was still less seen than heretofore, kept himself still less in time with the rhythm and racket of the movements called progress in the world without. For many months after his wife's decease the economy of his household remained as before; the cook, the house-maid, the parlor-maid, and the man out-of-doors performed their duties or left them undone, just as nature prompted them—the vicar knew not which. It was then represented to him that his servants seemed to have nothing to do in his small family of one. He was struck with the truth of this representation, and decided to cut down his establishment. But he was forestalled by Sophy, the parlor-maid, who said one evening that she wished to leave him.

"And why?" said the parson.

"Sam Hobson has asked me to marry him, sir."

"Well—do you want to marry?"

"Not much. But it would be a home for me. And we have heard that one of us will have to leave."

A day or two after she said: "I don't want to leave just yet, sir, if you don't wish it. Sam and I have quarrelled."

He looked at her. He had hardly ever observed her before, though he had been frequently conscious of her soft presence in the room. What a kitten-like, flexuous, tender creature she was! She was the only one of the servants with whom he came into immediate and continuous relation. What should he do if Sophy were gone?

Sophy did not go, but one of the others did, and things proceeded quietly again.

When Mr. Twycott, the vicar, was ill, Sophy brought up his meals to him, and she had no sooner left the room one day than he heard a noise on the stairs. She had slipped down with the tray, and so twisted her foot that she could not stand. The village surgeon was called in; the vicar got better, but Sophy was incapacitated for a long time; and she was informed that she must never again walk much or engage in any occupation which required her to stand long on her feet. As soon as she was comparatively well she spoke to him alone. Since she was forbidden to walk and bustle about, and, indeed, could not do so, it became her duty to leave. She could very well work at something sitting down, and she had an aunt a seamstress.

The parson had been very greatly moved by what she had suffered on his account, and he exclaimed, "No, Sophy; lame or not lame, I cannot let you go. You must never leave me again."

He came close to her, and, though she could never exactly tell how it happened, she became conscious of his lips upon her cheek. He then asked her to marry him. Sophy did not exactly love him, but she had a respect for him which almost amounted to veneration. Even if she had wished to get away from him she hardly dared refuse a personage so reverend and august in her eyes, and she assented forthwith to be his wife.

Thus it happened that one fine morning, when the doors of the church were naturally open for ventilation, and the singing birds fluttered in and alighted on the tie-beams of the roof, there was a marriage-service at the communion rails which hardly a soul knew of. The parson and a neighboring curate had entered at one door, and Sophy at another, followed by two necessary persons, where-upon in a short time there emerged a newly-made husband and wife.

Mr. Twycott knew perfectly well that he had committed social suicide by this step, despite Sophy's spotless character, and he had taken his measures accordingly. An exchange of livings had been arranged with an acquaintance who was incumbent of a church in the south of London, and as soon as possible the couple removed thither, abandoning their pretty country home with trees and shrubs and glebe[1] for a narrow, dusty house in a long, straight street, and their fine peal of bells for the wretchedest one-tongue clangor that ever tortured mortal ears. It was all on her account. They were, however, away from every one who had known her former position, and also under less observation from without than they would have had to put up with in any country parish.

Sophy the woman was as charming a partner as a man could possess, though Sophy the lady had her deficiencies. She showed a natural aptitude for little domestic refinements, so far as related to things and manners; but in what is called culture she was less intuitive. She had now been married more than fourteen years, and her husband had taken much trouble with her education; but she still held confused ideas on the use of "was" and "were," which did not beget a respect for her among the few acquaintances she made. Her great grief in this relation was that her only child, on whose education no expense had been or would be spared, was now old enough to perceive these deficiencies in his mother, and not only to see them but to feel irritated at their existence.

Thus she lived on in the city, and wasted hours in braiding her beautiful hair, till her once apple cheeks waned to pink of the very faintest. Her foot had never regained its natural strength after the accident, and she was mostly obliged to avoid walking altogether. Her husband had grown to like London for its freedom and its domestic privacy; but he was twenty years his Sophy's senior, and had latterly been seized with a serious illness. On this day, however, he had seemed to be well enough to justify her accompanying her son Randolph to the concert.

II

The next time we get a glimpse of her is when she appears in the mournful attire of a widow.

Mr. Twycott had never rallied, and now lay in a well-packed cemetery to the south of the great city, where, if all the dead it contained had stood erect and alive, not one would have known him or recognized his name. The boy had dutifully followed him to the grave, and was now again at school.

---

1   Land granted to a member of the clergy.

Throughout these changes Sophy had been treated like the child she was in nature though not in years. She was left with no control over anything that had been her husband's beyond her modest personal income. In his anxiety lest her inexperience should be overreached he had safeguarded with trustees all he possibly could. The completion of the boy's course at the public school, to be followed in due time by Oxford and ordination, had been all previsioned and arranged, and she really had nothing to occupy her in the world but to eat and drink, and make a business of indolence, and go on weaving and coiling the nut-brown hair, merely keeping a home open for the son whenever he came to her during vacations.

Foreseeing his probable decease long years before her, her husband in his lifetime had purchased for her use a semi-detached villa in the same long, straight road whereon the church and parsonage faced, which was to be hers as long as she chose to live in it. Here she now resided, looking out upon the fragment of lawn in front, and through the railings at the ever-flowing traffic; or, bending forward over the window-sill on the first floor, stretching her eyes far up and down the vista of sooty trees, hazy air, and drab house façades, along which echoed the noises common to a suburban main thoroughfare.

Somehow, her boy, with his aristocratic school-knowledge, his grammars, and his aversions, was losing those wide infantine sympathies, extending as far as to the sun and moon themselves, with which he, like other children, had been born, and which his mother, a child of nature herself, had loved in him; he was reducing their compass to a population of a few thousand wealthy and titled people, the mere veneer of a thousand million or so of others who did not interest him at all. He drifted further and further away from her. Sophy's *milieu* being a suburb of minor tradesmen and under-clerks, and her almost only companions the two servants of her own house, it was not surprising that after her husband's death she soon lost the little artificial tastes she had acquired from him, and became—in her son's eyes—a mother whose mistakes and origin it was his painful lot as a gentleman to blush for. As yet he was far from being man enough—if he ever would be—to rate these sins of hers at their true infinitesimal value beside the yearning fondness that welled up and remained penned in her heart till it should be more fully accepted by him, or by some other person or thing. If he had lived at home with her he would have had all of it; but he seemed to require so very little in present circumstances, and it remained stored.

Her life became insupportably dreary; she could not take walks, and had no interest in going for drives, or, indeed, in travelling anywhere. Nearly two years passed without an event, and still she looked on that suburban road, thinking of the village in which she had been born, and whither she would have gone back—oh, how gladly!—even to work in the fields.

Taking no exercise, she often could not sleep, and would rise in the night or early morning and look out upon the then vacant thoroughfare, where the lamps stood like sentinels waiting for some procession to go by. An approximation to such a procession was indeed made every early morning about one o'clock, when the country vehicles passed up with loads of vegetables for Covent Garden market. She often saw them creeping along at this silent and dusky hour—wagon after wagon, bearing green bastions of cabbages nodding to their fall, yet never falling; walls of baskets enclosing masses of beans and peas; pyramids of snow-white turnips, swaying howdahs[2] of mixed produce—creeping along behind aged night-horses, who seemed ever patiently wondering between their hollow coughs why they had always to work at that still hour when all other sentient creatures were privileged to rest. Wrapped in a cloak, it was soothing to watch and sympathize with them when depression and nervousness hindered sleep, and to see how the fresh green-stuff brightened to life as it came opposite the lamp, and how the sweating animals steamed and shone with their miles of travel.

They had an interest, almost a charm, for Sophy, these semi-rural people and vehicles moving in an urban atmosphere, leading a life quite distinct from that of the daytime toilers on the same road. One morning a man who accompanied a wagon-load of potatoes gazed rather hard at the house fronts as he passed, and with a curious emotion she thought his form was familiar to her. She looked out for him again. His being an old-fashioned conveyance with a yellow front, it was easily recognizable, and on the third night after she saw it a second time. The man alongside was, as she had fancied, Sam Hobson, formerly gardener at Gaymead, who would at one time have married her.

She had occasionally thought of him, and wondered if life in a cottage with him would not have been a happier lot than the life she had accepted. She had not thought of him passionately, but her now dismal situation lent an interest to his resurrection—a tender interest which it is impossible to exaggerate. She went back to bed, and began thinking. When did these market-gardeners, who travelled up to town so regularly at one or two in the morning, come back? She dimly recollected seeing their empty wagons, hardly noticeable among the ordinary day-traffic, passing down at some hour before noon.

It was only April, but that morning, after breakfast, she had the window opened, and sat looking out, the feeble sun shining full upon her. She affected to sew, but her eyes never left the street. Between ten and eleven the desired wagon, now unladen, reappeared on its return journey. But Sam was not looking round him then, and drove on in a reverie.

---

2   Platforms placed on the backs of work horses.

"Sam!" cried she.

Turning with a start, his face lighted up. He called to him a little boy to hold the horse, alighted, and came and stood under her window.

"I can't come down easily, Sam, or I would!" she said. "Did you know I lived here?"

"Well, Mrs. Twycott, I knew you lived along here somewhere. I have often looked out for 'ee."

He briefly explained his own presence on the scene. He had long since given up his gardening in the village near Aldbrickham, and was now manager at a market-gardener's on the south side of London, it being part of his duty to go up to Covent Garden with wagon-loads of produce two or three times a week. In answer to her curious inquiry, he admitted that he had come to this particular district because he had seen in the Aldbrickham paper a year or two before the announcement of the death in South London of the aforetime vicar of Gaymead, which had revived an interest in her dwelling-place that he could not extinguish, leading him to hover about the locality till his present post had been secured. They spoke of their native village in dear old North Wessex, the spots in which they had played together as children. She tried to feel that she was a dignified personage now, that she must not be too confidential with Sam. But she could not keep it up, and the tears hanging in her eyes were indicated in her voice.

"You are not happy, Mrs. Twycott, I'm afraid," he said.

"Oh, of course not! I lost my husband only the year before last."

"Ah! I meant in another way. You'd like to be home again?"

"This is my home—for life. The house belongs to me. But I understand"—She let it out then. "Yes, Sam. I long for home—*our* home! I *should* like to be there, and never leave it, and die there." But she remembered herself. "That's only a momentary feeling. I have a son, you know, a dear boy. He's at school now."

"Somewhere handy, I suppose? I see there's lots of 'em along this road."

"Oh no! Not in one of these wretched holes! At a public school—one of the most distinguished in England."

"Chok it all! of course! I forgot, ma'am, that you've been a lady for so many years."

"No, I am not a lady," she said, sadly. "I never shall be. But he's a gentleman, and that—makes it—oh, how difficult for me!"

III

The acquaintance thus oddly reopened proceeded apace. She often looked out to get a few words with him, by night or by day. Her sorrow was that she could not accompany her one old friend on foot a little way, and talk more freely than she could do while he paused before the house. One night, at the beginning of June, when she was again on the watch after an absence of some days from the window, he entered the gate and said, softly, "Now, wouldn't some air do you good? I've only half a load this morning. Why not ride up to Covent Garden with me? There's a nice seat on the cabbages, where I've spread a sack. You can be home again in a cab before anybody is up."

She refused at first, and then, trembling with excitement, hastily finished her dressing, and wrapped herself up in cloak and veil, afterwards sidling downstairs by the aid of the handrail, in a way she could adopt on an emergency. When she had opened the door she found Sam on the step, and he lifted her bodily on his strong arm across the little forecourt into his vehicle. Not a soul was visible or audible in the infinite length of the straight, flat highway, with its ever-waiting lamps converging to points in each direction. The air was fresh as country air at this hour, and the stars shone, except to the north-eastward; where there was a whitish light—the dawn. Sam carefully placed her in the seat and drove on.

They talked as they had talked in old days, Sam pulling himself up now and then, when he thought himself too familiar. More than once she said with misgiving that she wondered if she ought to have indulged in the freak. "But I am so lonely in my house," she added, "and this makes me so happy!"

"You must come again, dear Mrs. Twycott. There is no time o' day for taking the air like this."

It grew lighter and lighter. The sparrows became busy in the streets, and the city waxed denser around them. When they approached the river it was day, and on the bridge they beheld the full blaze of morning sunlight in the direction of St. Paul's, the river glistening towards it, and not a craft stirring.

Near Covent Garden he put her into a cab, and they parted, looking into each other's faces like the very old friends they were. She reached home without adventure, limped to the door, and let herself in with her latch-key unseen.

The air and Sam's presence had revived her; her cheeks were quite pink—almost beautiful. She had something to live for in addition to her son. A woman of pure instincts, she knew there had been nothing really wrong in the journey, but supposed it conventionally to be very wrong indeed.

Soon, however, she gave way to the temptation of going with him again, and on this occasion their conversation was distinctly tender, and Sam said he never should forget her, notwithstanding that she had served him rather badly at one time. After much hesitation he told her of a plan it was in his power to carry out, and one he should like to take in hand, since he did not care for London work; it was to set up as a master greengrocer down at Aldbrickham, the county-town of their native place. He knew of an opening—a shop kept by aged people who wished to retire.

"And why don't you do it, then, Sam?" she asked, with a slight heart-sinking.

"Because I'm not sure if—you'd join me. I know you wouldn't—couldn't! Such a lady as ye've been so long, you couldn't be a wife to a man like me."

"I hardly suppose I could!" she assented, also frightened at the idea.

"If you could," he said, eagerly, "you'd on'y have to sit in the back parlor and look through the glass partition when I was away sometimes—just to keep an eye on things. The lameness wouldn't hinder that. I'd keep you as genteel as ever I could, dear Sophy—if I might think of it," he pleaded.

"Sam, I'll be frank," she said, putting her hand on his. "If it were only myself I would do it, and gladly, though everything I possess would be lost to me by marrying again."

"I don't mind that. It's more independent."

"That's good of you, dear, dear Sam. But there's something else. I have a son. I almost fancy when I am miserable sometimes that he is not really mine, but one I hold in trust for my late husband. He seems to belong so little to me personally, so entirely to his dead father. He is so much educated and I so little that I do not feel dignified enough to be his mother. Well, he would have to be told."

"Yes. Unquestionably." Sam saw her thought and her fear. "Still, you can do as you like, Sophy—Mrs. Twycott," he added. "It is not you who are the child, but he."

"Ah, you don't know! Sam, if I could, I would marry you, some day. But you must wait awhile, and let me think."

It was enough for him, and he was blithe at their parting. Not so she. To tell Randolph seemed impossible. She could wait till he had gone up to Oxford, when what she did would affect his life but little. But would he ever tolerate the idea? And if not, could she defy him?

She had not told him a word when the yearly cricket-match came on at Lord's between the public schools, though Sam had already gone back to Aldbrickham. Mrs. Twycott felt stronger than usual. She went to the match with Randolph, and was able to leave her chair and walk about occasionally. The bright idea occurred to her that she could casually broach the subject while moving round among the spectators, when the boy's spirits were high with interest in the game, and he would weigh domestic matters as feathers in the scale beside the day's victory. They promenaded under the lurid July sun, this pair, so wide apart, yet so near, and Sophy saw the large proportion of boys like her own, in their broad white collars and dwarf hats, and all around the rows of great coaches under which was jumbled the debris of luxurious luncheons—bones, pie-crusts, champagne-bottles, glasses, plates, napkins, and the family silver; while on the coaches sat the proud fathers and mothers; but never a poor mother like her. If Randolph had not appertained to these, had not centred all his interests in them, had not cared exclusively for the class they belonged to, how happy would things have been! A great huzza at some small performance with the bat burst from the multitude of relatives, and Randolph jumped wildly into the air to see what had happened. Sophy fetched up the sentence that had been already shaped; but she could not get it out. The occasion was, perhaps, an inopportune one. The contrast between her story and the display of fashion to which Randolph had grown to regard himself as akin would be fatal. She awaited a better time.

It was on an evening when they were alone in their plain suburban residence, where life was not blue but brown, that she ultimately broke silence, qualifying her announcement of a probable second marriage by assuring him that it would not take place for a long time to come, when he would be living quite independently of her.

The boy thought the idea a very reasonable one, and asked if she had chosen anybody. She hesitated; and he seemed to have a misgiving. He hoped his step-father would be a gentleman, he said.

"Not what you call a gentleman," she answered, timidly. "He'll be much as I was before I knew your father;" and by degrees she acquainted him with the whole. The youth's face remained fixed for a moment; then he flushed, leaned on the table, and burst into passionate tears.

His mother went up to him, kissed all of his face that she could get at, and patted his back as if he were still the baby he once had been, crying herself the while. When he had somewhat recovered from his paroxysm he went hastily to his own room and fastened the door.

Parleyings were attempted through the key-hole, outside which she waited and listened. It was long before he would reply, and when he did it was to say sternly at her from within: "I am ashamed of you! It will ruin me! A miserable boor! a churl! a clown! It will degrade me in the eyes of all the gentlemen of England!"

"Say no more—perhaps I am wrong! I will struggle against it!" she cried, miserably.

Before Randolph left her that summer a letter arrived from Sam to inform her that he had been unexpectedly fortunate in obtaining the shop. He was in possession; it was the largest in the town, combining fruit with vegetables, and he thought it would form a home worthy even of her some day. Might he not run up to town to see her?

She met him by stealth, and said he must still wait for her final answer. The autumn dragged on, and when Randolph was home at Christmas for the holidays she broached the matter again. But the young gentleman was inexorable.

It was dropped for months; renewed again; abandoned under his repugnance; again attempted, and thus the gentle creature reasoned and pleaded till four or five long years had passed. Then the faithful Sam revived his suit with some peremptoriness. Sophy's son, now an undergraduate, was down from Oxford one Easter, when she again opened the subject. As soon as he was ordained, she argued, he would have a home of his own, wherein she, with her bad grammar and her ignorance, would be an encumbrance to him. Better obliterate her as much as possible.

He showed a more manly anger now, but would not agree. She on her side was more persistent, and he had doubts whether she could be trusted in his absence. But by indignation and contempt for her taste he completely maintained his ascendency; and finally taking her before a little cross and shrine that he had erected in his bedroom for his private devotions, there bade her kneel, and swear that she would not wed Samuel Hobson without his consent. "I owe this to my father!" he said.

The poor woman swore, thinking he would soften as soon as he was ordained and in full swing of clerical work. But he did not. His education had by this time sufficiently ousted his humanity to keep him quite firm; though his mother might have led an idyllic life with her faithful fruiterer and green-grocer, and nobody have been anything the worse in the world.

Her lameness became more confirmed as time went on, and she seldom or never left the house in the long southern thoroughfare, where she seemed to be pining her heart away. "Why mayn't I say to Sam that I'll marry him? Why mayn't I?" she would murmur plaintively to herself when nobody was near.

Some four years after this date a middle-aged man was standing at the door of the largest fruiterer's shop in Aldbrickham. He was the proprietor, but to-day, instead of his usual business attire, he wore a neat suit of black; and his window was partly shuttered. From the railway station a funeral procession was seen approaching; it passed his door and went out of the town towards the village of Gaymead. The man, whose eyes were wet, held his hat in his hand as the vehicles moved by; while from the mourning coach a young smooth-shaven priest in a high waistcoat looked black as a cloud at the shopkeeper standing there.

—1891

KATE CHOPIN

Katherine Chopin was born in St. Louis, Missouri, in 1850. She was one of three children and the only child to reach adulthood in a family presided over by an Irish immigrant father and a mother who belonged to an aristocratic family of French descent. Her father died in a train wreck in 1855 and Kate, with her mother, went to live with her widowed maternal grandmother and great-grandmother. She graduated in 1868 from the Catholic St. Louis Academy of the Sacred Heart, and in 1870 made her debut into St. Louis society. During a trip to New Orleans, she met Oscar Chopin, a cotton trader and plantation owner; they were married in 1871. The couple moved to Cloutierville, Louisiana, where Oscar owned several plantations.

She became a writer late in life, beginning her career only after the death of her husband in 1882. Her short stories and two published novels were often considered transgressive in her day, addressing the subjects of race and class, marriage and divorce, sexuality, and female autonomy. Through her provocative writing, Chopin sought to expose the nature of truth as tied to the limited perspective of the individual, showing that, in her words, "truth rests upon a shifting basis and is apt to be kaleidoscopic."

The controversy that Chopin's ideas incited is perhaps best exemplified by the reception to her most recognized work, *The Awakening* (1899). The novel, which depicts one woman's sensual awakening and her defiance of societal expectations of women, received high praise from a few reviewers, but a larger number dismissed it as "morbid," "sordid," and "sex fiction." It took scholars roughly 50 years after Chopin's death to acknowledge *The Awakening* as a novel of enduring importance—a work of historical value for its critical engagement with the role of women at the turn of the nineteenth century, but also a work that would continue to resonate for generations of readers.

The Story of an Hour

KNOWING THAT Mrs. Mallard was afflicted with a heart trouble, great care was taken to break to her as gently as possible the news of her husband's death.

It was her sister Josephine who told her, in broken sentences; veiled hints that revealed in half concealing. Her husband's friend Richards was there, too, near her. It was he who had been in the newspaper office when intelligence of the railroad disaster was received, with Brently Mallard's name leading the list of "killed." He had only taken the time to assure himself of its truth by a second telegram, and had hastened to forestall any less careful, less tender friend in bearing the sad message.

She did not hear the story as many women have heard the same, with a paralyzed inability to accept its significance. She wept at once, with sudden, wild abandonment, in her sister's arms. When the storm of grief had spent itself she went away to her room alone. She would have no one follow her.

There stood, facing the open window, a comfortable, roomy armchair. Into this she sank, pressed down by a physical exhaustion that haunted her body and seemed to reach into her soul.

She could see in the open square before her house the tops of trees that were all aquiver with the new spring life. The delicious breath of rain was in the air. In the street below a peddler was crying his wares. The notes of a distant song which someone was singing reached her faintly, and countless sparrows were twittering in the eaves.

There were patches of blue sky showing here and there through the clouds that had met and piled one above the other in the west facing her window.

She sat with her head thrown back upon the cushion of the chair, quite motionless, except when a sob came up into her throat and shook her, as a child who has cried itself to sleep continues to sob in its dreams.

She was young, with a fair, calm face, whose lines bespoke repression and even a certain strength. But now there was a dull stare in her eyes, whose gaze was fixed away off yonder on one of those patches of blue sky. It was not a glance of reflection, but rather indicated a suspension of intelligent thought.

There was something coming to her and she was waiting for it, fearfully. What was it? She did not know; it was too subtle and elusive to name. But she felt it, creeping out of the sky, reaching toward her through the sounds, the scents, the color that filled the air.

Now her bosom rose and fell tumultuously. She was beginning to recognize this thing that was approaching to possess her, and she was striving to beat it back with her will—as powerless as her two white slender hands would have been.

When she abandoned herself a little whispered word escaped her slightly parted lips. She said it over and over under her breath: "free, free, free!" The vacant stare and the look of terror that had followed it went from her eyes. They stayed keen and bright. Her pulses beat fast, and the coursing blood warmed and relaxed every inch of her body.

She did not stop to ask if it were or were not a monstrous joy that held her. A clear and exalted perception enabled her to dismiss the suggestion as trivial.

She knew that she would weep again when she saw the kind, tender hands folded in death; the face that had never looked save with love upon her, fixed and gray and dead. But she saw beyond that bitter moment a long procession of years to come that would belong to her absolutely. And she opened and spread her arms out to them in welcome.

There would be no one to live for her during those coming years; she would live for herself. There would be no powerful will bending hers in that blind persistence with which men and women believe they have a right to impose a private will upon a fellow-creature. A kind intention or a cruel intention made the act seem no less a crime as she looked upon it in that brief moment of illumination.

And yet she had loved him—sometimes. Often she had not. What did it matter! What could love, the unsolved mystery, count for in face of this possession of self-assertion which she suddenly recognized as the strongest impulse of her being!

"Free! Body and soul free!" she kept whispering.

Josephine was kneeling before the closed door with her lips to the keyhole, imploring for admission. "Louise, open the door! I beg; open the door—you will make yourself ill. What are you doing, Louise? For heaven's sake open the door."

"Go away. I am not making myself ill." No; she was drinking in a very elixir of life through that open window.

Her fancy was running riot along those days ahead of her. Spring days, and summer days, and all sorts of days that would be her own. She breathed a quick prayer that life might be long. It was only yesterday she had thought with a shudder that life might be long.

She arose at length and opened the door to her sister's importunities. There was a feverish triumph in her eyes, and she carried herself unwittingly like a goddess of Victory. She clasped her sister's waist, and together they descended the stairs. Richards stood waiting for them at the bottom.

Some one was opening the front door with a latchkey. It was Brently Mallard who entered, a little travel-stained, composedly carrying his grip-sack and umbrella. He had been far from the scene of accident, and did not even know there had been one. He stood amazed at Josephine's piercing cry; at Richards' quick motion to screen him from the view of his wife.

But Richards was too late.

When the doctors came they said she had died of heart disease—of joy that kills.

—*1894*

ANTON PAVLOVICH CHEKHOV

Although well-known as the author of four major plays, *The Seagull* (1896), *Uncle Vanya* (1897), *Three Sisters* (1901), and *The Cherry Orchard* (1904), Anton Chekhov was also highly acclaimed as a writer of short stories. Raised in the small Russian city of Taganrog, he moved to Moscow after his father's death to attend medical school and to help support his family. He began his writing career while he was still a student—to earn extra money, he sent stories to humour magazines—and continued to write short stories throughout his life, producing over 500 pieces in total. Many of his stories were translated into English in the early twentieth century, and their publication has been described by novelist James T. Farrell as "one of the greatest single literary influences at work in the short story of America, England, and Ireland" in that it encouraged authors in those traditions to "seek in simple and realistic terms to make of the story a form that more seriously reflects life."

Chekhov experimented extensively with narrative voice; in a typical Chekhov story, the governing narrative voice is objective and aloof, but at times also adopts the point of view of one or more of the characters. This technique, which has come to be known as "free indirect discourse," anticipates the more extended "stream of consciousness" narrative techniques adopted by James Joyce and other modernist writers. Chekhov also practised medicine. He said that his experience as a physician was integral to his writing: "My study of medicine significantly broadened the scope of my observations and enriched me with knowledge whose value for me as a writer only a doctor can appreciate.... It seems to me that as a doctor I have described the sicknesses of the soul correctly."

Late in 1884, Chekhov began to suffer from tuberculosis. As a doctor he must have recognized the disease, but he denied it and continued to work. He won the Pushkin Prize in 1888 and continued writing stories. He settled on his own estate at Melikhovo, where he stayed until 1898, continuing to write and practice medicine. He ran a free clinic for peasants, organized relief during cholera and famine outbreaks, and travelled for miles to visit the sick.

Chekhov's last years were spent in Nice and Yalta, as he sought better climates to help his worsening illness. He wrote some of his greatest short stories in this period, among them "The Little Trilogy" (1898), "The Lady with a Dog" (1899), "In the Ravine" (1900), and "The Bishop" (1902). In 1904, Chekhov went to Badenweiler, Germany with his wife Olga, where he died on July 15.

An Upheaval[1]

MASHENKA Pavletsky, a young girl who had only just finished her studies at a boarding school, returning from a walk to the house of the Kushkins, with whom she was living as a governess, found the household in a terrible turmoil. Mihailo, the porter who opened the door to her, was excited and red as a crab.

Loud voices were heard from upstairs.

"Madame Kushkin is in a fit, most likely, or else she has quarreled with her husband," thought Mashenka.

In the hall and in the corridor she met maid-servants. One of them was crying. Then Mashenka saw, running out of her room, the master of the house himself, Nikolay Sergeitch, a little man with a flabby face and a bald head, though he was not old. He was red in the face and twitching all over. He passed the governess without noticing her, and throwing up his arms, exclaimed:

"Oh, how horrible it is! How tactless! How stupid! How barbarous! Abominable!"

Mashenka went into her room, and then, for the first time in her life, it was her lot to experience in all its acuteness the feeling that is so familiar to persons in dependent positions, who eat the bread of the rich and powerful, and cannot speak their minds. There was a search going on in her room. The lady of the house, Fedosya Vassilyevna, a stout, broad-shouldered, uncouth woman with thick black eyebrows, a faintly perceptible moustache, and red hands, who was exactly like a plain, illiterate cook in face and manners, was standing, without her cap on, at the table, putting back into Mashenka's workbag balls of wool, scraps of materials, and bits of paper.... Evidently the governess's arrival took her by surprise, since, on looking round and seeing the girl's pale and astonished face, she was a little taken aback, and muttered:

"*Pardon.* I ... I upset it accidentally.... My sleeve caught in it...."

And saying something more, Madame Kushkin rustled her long skirts and went out. Mashenka looked round her room with wondering eyes, and, unable

---

1   Translation by Constance Garnett.

to understand it, not knowing what to think, shrugged her shoulders, and turned cold with dismay. What had Fedosya Vassilyevna been looking for in her work-bag? If she really had, as she said, caught her sleeve in it and upset everything, why had Nikolay Sergeitch dashed out of her room so excited and red in the face? Why was one drawer of the table pulled out a little way? The money-box, in which the governess put away ten kopeck[2] pieces and old stamps, was open. They had opened it, but did not know how to shut it, though they had scratched the lock all over. The whatnot with her books on it, the things on the table, the bed—all bore fresh traces of a search. Her linen-basket, too. The linen had been carefully folded, but it was not in the same order as Mashenka had left it when she went out. So the search had been thorough, most thorough. But what was it for? Why? What had happened? Mashenka remembered the excited porter, the general turmoil which was still going on, the weeping servant-girl; had it not all some connection with the search that had just been made in her room? Was not she mixed up in something dreadful? Mashenka turned pale, and feeling cold all over, sank on to her linen-basket.

A maid-servant came into the room.

"Liza, you don't know why they have been rummaging in my room?" the governess asked her.

"Mistress has lost a brooch worth two thousand," said Liza.

"Yes, but why have they been rummaging in my room?"

"They've been searching every one, miss. They've searched all my things, too. They stripped us all naked and searched us.... God knows, miss, I never went near her toilet-table, let alone touching the brooch. I shall say the same at the police-station."

"But ... why have they been rummaging here?" the governess still wondered.

"A brooch has been stolen, I tell you. The mistress has been rummaging in everything with her own hands. She even searched Mihailo, the porter, herself. It's a perfect disgrace! Nikolay Sergeitch simply looks on and cackles like a hen. But you've no need to tremble like that, miss. They found nothing here. You've nothing to be afraid of if you didn't take the brooch."

"But, Liza, it's vile ... it's insulting," said Mashenka, breathless with indignation. "It's so mean, so low! What right had she to suspect me and to rummage in my things?"

"You are living with strangers, miss," sighed Liza. "Though you are a young lady, still you are ... as it were ... a servant.... It's not like living with your papa and mamma."

---

2   Russian currency. One hundred kopecks equals one rouble.

Mashenka threw herself on the bed and sobbed bitterly. Never in her life had she been subjected to such an outrage, never had she been so deeply insulted.... She, well-educated, refined, the daughter of a teacher, was suspected of theft; she had been searched like a street-walker! She could not imagine a greater insult. And to this feeling of resentment was added an oppressive dread of what would come next. All sorts of absurd ideas came into her mind. If they could suspect her of theft, then they might arrest her, strip her naked, and search her, then lead her through the street with an escort of soldiers, cast her into a cold, dark cell with mice and woodlice, exactly like the dungeon in which Princess Tarakanov[3] was imprisoned. Who would stand up for her? Her parents lived far away in the provinces; they had not the money to come to her. In the capital she was as solitary as in a desert, without friends or kindred. They could do what they liked with her.

"I will go to all the courts and all the lawyers," Mashenka thought, trembling. "I will explain to them, I will take an oath.... They will believe that I could not be a thief!"

Mashenka remembered that under the sheets in her basket she had some sweetmeats, which, following the habits of her schooldays, she had put in her pocket at dinner and carried off to her room. She felt hot all over, and was ashamed at the thought that her little secret was known to the lady of the house; and all this terror, shame, resentment, brought on an attack of palpitation of the heart, which set up a throbbing in her temples, in her heart, and deep down in her stomach.

"Dinner is ready," the servant summoned Mashenka.

"Shall I go, or not?"

Mashenka brushed her hair, wiped her face with a wet towel, and went into the dining-room. There they had already begun dinner. At one end of the table sat Fedosya Vassilyevna with a stupid, solemn, serious face; at the other end Nikolay Sergeitch. At the sides there were the visitors and the children. The dishes were handed by two footmen in swallowtails and white gloves. Every-one knew that there was an upset in the house, that Madame Kushkin was in trouble, and everyone was silent. Nothing was heard but the sound of munching and the rattle of spoons on the plates.

The lady of the house, herself, was the first to speak.

"What is the third course?" she asked the footman in a weary, injured voice.

---

3   Yelizaveta Alekseyevna (1753–75), an impostor who claimed to be a Russian princess. She was captured in 1775 and died of tuberculosis while in prison.

"*Esturgeon à la russe*,"[4] answered the footman.

"I ordered that, Fenya," Nikolay Sergeitch hastened to observe. "I wanted some fish. If you don't like it, *ma chère*,[5] don't let them serve it. I just ordered it...."

Fedosya Vassilyevna did not like dishes that she had not ordered herself, and now her eyes filled with tears.

"Come, don't let us agitate ourselves," Mamikov, her household doctor, observed in a honeyed voice, just touching her arm, with a smile as honeyed. "We are nervous enough as it is. Let us forget the brooch! Health is worth more than two thousand roubles!"

"It's not the two thousand I regret," answered the lady, and a big tear rolled down her cheek. "It's the fact itself that revolts me! I cannot put up with thieves in my house. I don't regret it—I regret nothing; but to steal from me is such ingratitude! That's how they repay me for my kindness...."

They all looked into their plates, but Mashenka fancied after the lady's words that everyone was looking at her. A lump rose in her throat; she began crying and put her handkerchief to her lips.

"*Pardon*," she muttered. "I can't help it. My head aches. I'll go away."

And she got up from the table, scraping her chair awkwardly, and went out quickly, still more overcome with confusion.

"It's beyond everything!" said Nikolay Sergeitch, frowning. "What need was there to search her room? How out of place it was!"

"I don't say she took the brooch," said Fedosya Vassilyevna, "but can you answer for her? To tell the truth, I haven't much confidence in these learned paupers."

"It really was unsuitable, Fenya.... Excuse me, Fenya, but you've no kind of legal right to make a search."

"I know nothing about your laws. All I know is that I've lost my brooch. And I will find the brooch!" She brought her fork down on the plate with a clatter, and her eyes flashed angrily. "And you eat your dinner, and don't interfere in what doesn't concern you!"

Nikolay Sergeitch dropped his eyes mildly and sighed. Meanwhile Mashenka, reaching her room, flung herself on her bed. She felt now neither alarm nor shame, but she felt an intense longing to go and slap the cheeks of this hard, arrogant, dull-witted, prosperous woman.

---

4   Russian preparation of sturgeon, a large, freshwater fish; "à la russe" translates literally to "in the Russian style."

5   French: my dear.

Lying on her bed she breathed into her pillow and dreamed of how nice it would be to go and buy the most expensive brooch and fling it into the face of this bullying woman. If only it were God's will that Fedosya Vassilyevna should come to ruin and wander about begging, and should taste all the horrors of poverty and dependence, and that Mashenka, whom she had insulted, might give her alms! Oh, if only she could come in for a big fortune, could buy a carriage, and could drive noisily past the windows so as to be envied by that woman!

But all these were only dreams, in reality there was only one thing left to do—to get away as quickly as possible, not to stay another hour in this place. It was true it was terrible to lose her place, to go back to her parents, who had nothing; but what could she do? Mashenka could not bear the sight of the lady of the house nor of her little room; she felt stifled and wretched here. She was so disgusted with Fedosya Vassilyevna, who was so obsessed by her illnesses and her supposed aristocratic rank, that everything in the world seemed to have become coarse and unattractive because this woman was living in it. Mashenka jumped up from the bed and began packing.

"May I come in?" asked Nikolay Sergeitch at the door; he had come up noiselessly to the door, and spoke in a soft, subdued voice. "May I?"

"Come in."

He came in and stood still near the door. His eyes looked dim and his red little nose was shiny. After dinner he used to drink beer, and the fact was perceptible in his walk, in his feeble, flabby hands.

"What's this?" he asked, pointing to the basket.

"I am packing. Forgive me, Nikolay Sergeitch, but I cannot remain in your house. I feel deeply insulted by this search!"

"I understand.... Only you are wrong to go. Why should you? They've searched your things, but you ... what does it matter to you? You will be none the worse for it."

Mashenka was silent and went on packing. Nikolay Sergeitch pinched his moustache, as though wondering what he should say next, and went on in an ingratiating voice:

"I understand, of course, but you must make allowances. You know my wife is nervous, headstrong; you mustn't judge her too harshly."

Mashenka did not speak.

"If you are so offended," Nikolay Sergeitch went on, "well, if you like, I'm ready to apologise. I ask your pardon."

Mashenka made no answer, but only bent lower over her box. This exhausted, irresolute man was of absolutely no significance in the household. He stood in the pitiful position of a dependent and hanger-on, even with the servants, and his apology meant nothing either.

"H'm! ... You say nothing! That's not enough for you. In that case, I will apologise for my wife. In my wife's name.... She behaved tactlessly, I admit it as a gentleman...."

Nikolay Sergeitch walked about the room, heaved a sigh, and went on: "Then you want me to have it rankling here, under my heart.... You want my conscience to torment me...."

"I know it's not your fault, Nikolay Sergeitch," said Mashenka, looking him full in the face with her big tear-stained eyes. "Why should you worry yourself?"

"Of course, no.... But still, don't you ... go away. I entreat you."

Mashenka shook her head. Nikolay Sergeitch stopped at the window and drummed on the pane with his finger-tips.

"Such misunderstandings are simply torture to me," he said. "Why, do you want me to go down on my knees to you, or what? Your pride is wounded, and here you've been crying and packing up to go; but I have pride, too, and you do not spare it! Or do you want me to tell you what I would not tell as Confession? Do you? Listen; you want me to tell you what I won't tell the priest on my deathbed?"

Mashenka made no answer.

"I took my wife's brooch," Nikolay Sergeitch said quickly. "Is that enough now? Are you satisfied? Yes, I ... took it.... But, of course, I count on your discretion.... For God's sake, not a word, not half a hint to any one!"

Mashenka, amazed and frightened, went on packing; she snatched her things, crumpled them up, and thrust them anyhow into the box and the basket. Now, after this candid avowal on the part of Nikolay Sergeitch, she could not remain another minute, and could not understand how she could have gone on living in the house before.

"And it's nothing to wonder at," Nikolay Sergeitch went on after a pause. "It's an everyday story! I need money, and she ... won't give it to me. It was my father's money that bought this house and everything, you know! It's all mine, and the brooch belonged to my mother, and ... it's all mine! And she took it, took possession of everything.... I can't go to law with her, you'll admit.... I beg you most earnestly, overlook it ... stay on. *Tout comprendre, tout pardonner.*[6] Will you stay?"

"No!" said Mashenka resolutely, beginning to tremble. "Let me alone, I entreat you!"

"Well, God bless you!" sighed Nikolay Sergeitch, sitting down on the stool near the box. "I must own I like people who still can feel resentment, contempt, and so on. I could sit here forever and look at your indignant face.... So you

---

6   French: To understand all is to forgive all.

won't stay, then? I understand.... It's bound to be so ... Yes, of course.... It's all right for you, but for me—wo-o-o-o! ... I can't stir a step out of this cellar. I'd go off to one of our estates, but in every one of them there are some of my wife's rascals ... stewards, experts, damn them all! They mortgage and remortgage.... You mustn't catch fish, must keep off the grass, mustn't break the trees."

"Nikolay Sergeitch!" his wife's voice called from the drawing-room. "Agnia, call your master!"

"Then you won't stay?" asked Nikolay Sergeitch, getting up quickly and going towards the door. "You might as well stay, really. In the evenings I could come and have a talk with you. Eh? Stay! If you go, there won't be a human face left in the house. It's awful!"

Nikolay Sergeitch's pale, exhausted face besought her, but Mashenka shook her head, and with a wave of his hand he went out.

Half an hour later she was on her way.

—*1886*

CHARLOTTE PERKINS GILMAN

Charlotte Perkins Gilman was born into a family prominent in activism and reform; her great aunt was Harriet Beecher Stowe, author of *Uncle Tom's Cabin*. As a young woman she embraced the idea that a single woman could be a useful member of society and she resolved to dedicate her life to her work. Circumstances intervened, however: she fell in love, married, and plunged into a severe depression after the birth of her only child in 1885. She received treatment from the "nerve doctor" S. Weir Mitchell, who prescribed his famous "rest cure"—isolation, quiet domesticity, and abstention from intellectual endeavours—which greatly worsened her condition. In 1892, she published the short story "The Yellow Wallpaper," in which the protagonist is treated according to similar principles.

By this time, Gilman had left her husband, moved to California, and began again to work outside the home, forging a career as a feminist writer and lecturer. For the remainder of her life Gilman lectured widely, and she published seven novels including the feminist utopian novel *Herland*, several collections of poetry, her monthly magazine *The Forerunner*, and numerous essays on topics relevant to feminism and socialism. In 1900 she married her first cousin George Houghton Gilman after an extended courtship. The marriage was regarded as a relatively happy one—unlike the experience of her first marriage, Perkins Gilman did not give up her career plans or sense of independence for her husband—but George Gilman died in 1934 of a cerebral hemorrhage. In 1932 she learned that she had breast cancer, and in 1935 she committed suicide by chloroform after months of careful planning because of her conviction—as she states in her posthumously published autobiography *The Living of Charlotte Perkins Gilman*—that it is "the simplest of human rights to choose a quick and easy death in place of a slow and horrible one."

She won admiration from women reformers such as Jane Addams (1860–1935) and Elizabeth Cady Stanton (1815–1902). Her non-fiction work, *Women and Economics* (1898), was a bestseller. From 1909 to 1916, she wrote for and edited her own magazine, *The Forerunner*; in 1915, the magazine serialized her novel, *Herland*, about a utopia populated solely by women. In a statement that she made about the composition of "The Yellow Wallpaper," Gilman expressed the belief that informs all of her writing: "Work, in which is joy and growth and service, without which one is a pauper and a parasite," was essential for women.

The Yellow Wallpaper

IT IS VERY seldom that mere ordinary people like John and myself secure ancestral halls for the summer.

A colonial mansion, a hereditary estate, I would say a haunted house and reach the height of romantic felicity—but that would be asking too much of fate!

Still I will proudly declare that there is something queer about it.

Else, why should it be let so cheaply? And why have stood so long untenanted?

John laughs at me, of course, but one expects that.

John is practical in the extreme. He has no patience with faith, an intense horror of superstition, and he scoffs openly at any talk of things not to be felt and seen and put down in figures.

John is a physician, and *perhaps*—(I would not say it to a living soul, of course, but this is dead paper and a great relief to my mind)—*perhaps* that is one reason I do not get well faster.

You see, he does not believe I am sick! And what can one do?

If a physician of high standing, and one's own husband, assures friends and relatives that there is really nothing the matter with one but temporary nervous depression—a slight hysterical tendency—what is one to do?

My brother is also a physician, and also of high standing, and he says the same thing.

So I take phosphates or phosphites—whichever it is—and tonics, and air and exercise, and journeys, and am absolutely forbidden to "work" until I am well again.

Personally, I disagree with their ideas.

Personally, I believe that congenial work, with excitement and change, would do me good.

But what is one to do?

I did write for a while in spite of them, but it *does* exhaust me a good deal—having to be so sly about it, or else meet with heavy opposition.

I sometimes fancy that in my condition, if I had less opposition and more society and stimulus—but John says the very worst thing I can do is to think about my condition, and I confess it always makes me feel bad.

So I will let it alone and talk about the house.

The most beautiful place! It is quite alone, standing well back from the road, quite three miles from the village. It makes me think of English places that you read about, for there are hedges and walls and gates that lock, and lots of separate little houses for the gardeners and people.

There is a *delicious* garden! I never saw such a garden—large and shady, full of box-bordered paths, and lined with long grape-covered arbors with seats under them.

There were greenhouses, but they are all broken now.

There was some legal trouble, I believe, something about the heirs and co-heirs; anyhow, the place has been empty for years.

That spoils my ghostliness, I am afraid, but I don't care—there is something strange about the house—I can feel it.

I even said so to John one moonlight evening, but he said what I felt was a draught, and shut the window.

I get unreasonably angry with John sometimes. I'm sure I never used to be so sensitive. I think it is due to this nervous condition.

But John says if I feel so, I shall neglect proper self-control; so I take pains to control myself—before him, at least, and that makes me very tired.

I don't like our room a bit. I wanted one downstairs that opened on the piazza and had roses all over the window, and such pretty old-fashioned chintz hangings! But John would not hear of it.

He said there was only one window and not room for two beds, and no near room for him if he took another.

He is very careful and loving, and hardly lets me stir without special direction.

I have a schedule prescription for each hour in the day; he takes all care from me, and so I feel basely ungrateful not to value it more.

He said we came here solely on my account, that I was to have perfect rest and all the air I could get. "Your exercise depends on your strength, my dear," said he, "and your food somewhat on your appetite; but air you can absorb all the time." So we took the nursery at the top of the house.

It is a big, airy room, the whole floor nearly, with windows that look all ways, and air and sunshine galore. It was nursery first and then playroom and gymnasium, I should judge; for the windows are barred for little children, and there are rings and things in the walls.

The paint and paper look as if a boys' school had used it. It is stripped off—the paper—in great patches all around the head of my bed, about as far as I can reach, and in a great place on the other side of the room low down. I never saw a worse paper in my life. One of those sprawling flamboyant patterns committing every artistic sin.

It is dull enough to confuse the eye in following, pronounced enough to constantly irritate and provoke study, and when you follow the lame uncertain curves for a little distance they suddenly commit suicide—plunge off at outrageous angles, destroy themselves in unheard-of contradictions.

The color is repellent, almost revolting; a smouldering unclean yellow, strangely faded by the slow-turning sunlight. It is a dull yet lurid orange in some places, a sickly sulphur tint in others.

No wonder the children hated it! I should hate it myself if I had to live in this room long.

There comes John, and I must put this away—he hates to have me write a word.

We have been here two weeks, and I haven't felt like writing before, since that first day.

I am sitting by the window now, up in this atrocious nursery, and there is nothing to hinder my writing as much as I please, save lack of strength.

John is away all day, and even some nights when his cases are serious.

I am glad my case is not serious!

But these nervous troubles are dreadfully depressing.

John does not know how much I really suffer. He knows there is no reason to suffer, and that satisfies him.

Of course it is only nervousness. It does weigh on me so not to do my duty in any way!

I mean to be such a help to John, such a real rest and comfort, and here I am a comparative burden already!

Nobody would believe what an effort it is to do what little I am able—to dress and entertain, and order things.

It is fortunate Mary is so good with the baby. Such a dear baby!

And yet I *cannot* be with him, it makes me so nervous.

I suppose John never was nervous in his life. He laughs at me so about this wallpaper!

At first he meant to repaper the room, but afterwards he said that I was letting it get the better of me, and that nothing was worse for a nervous patient than to give way to such fancies.

He said that after the wallpaper was changed it would be the heavy bedstead, and then the barred windows, and then that gate at the head of the stairs, and so on.

"You know the place is doing you good," he said, "and really, dear, I don't care to renovate the house just for a three months' rental."

"Then do let us go downstairs," I said. "There are such pretty rooms there."

Then he took me in his arms and called me a blessed little goose, and said he would go down cellar, if I wished, and have it whitewashed into the bargain.

But he is right enough about the beds and windows and things.

It is as airy and comfortable a room as anyone need wish, and, of course, I would not be so silly as to make him uncomfortable just for a whim.

I'm really getting quite fond of the big room, all but that horrid paper.

Out of one window I can see the garden—those mysterious deep-shaded arbors, the riotous old-fashioned flowers, and bushes and gnarly trees.

Out of another I get a lovely view of the bay and a little private wharf belonging to the estate. There is a beautiful shaded lane that runs down there from the house. I always fancy I see people walking in these numerous paths and arbors, but John has cautioned me not to give way to fancy in the least. He says that with my imaginative power and habit of story-making, a nervous weakness like mine is sure to lead to all manner of excited fancies, and that I ought to use my will and good sense to check the tendency. So I try.

I think sometimes that if I were only well enough to write a little it would relieve the press of ideas and rest me.

But I find I get pretty tired when I try.

It is so discouraging not to have any advice and companionship about my work. When I get really well, John says we will ask Cousin Henry and Julia down for a long visit; but he says he would as soon put fireworks in my pillow-case as to let me have those stimulating people about now.

I wish I could get well faster.

But I must not think about that. This paper looks to me as if it *knew* what a vicious influence it had!

There is a recurrent spot where the pattern lolls like a broken neck and two bulbous eyes stare at you upside down.

I get positively angry with the impertinence of it and the everlastingness. Up and down and sideways they crawl, and those absurd unblinking eyes are everywhere. There is one place where two breadths didn't match, and the eyes go all up and down the line, one a little higher than the other.

I never saw so much expression in an inanimate thing before, and we all know how much expression they have! I used to lie awake as a child and get more entertainment and terror out of blank walls and plain furniture than most children could find in a toy-store.

I remember what a kindly wink the knobs of our big old bureau used to have, and there was one chair that always seemed like a strong friend.

I used to feel that if any of the other things looked too fierce I could always hop into that chair and be safe.

The furniture in this room is no worse than inharmonious, however, for we had to bring it all from downstairs. I suppose when this was used as a playroom they had to take the nursery things out, and no wonder! I never saw such ravages as the children have made here.

The wallpaper, as I said before, is torn off in spots, and it sticketh closer than a brother[1]—they must have had perseverance as well as hatred.

Then the floor is scratched and gouged and splintered, the plaster itself is dug out here and there, and this great heavy bed which is all we found in the room, looks as if it had been through the wars.

But I don't mind it a bit—only the paper.

There comes John's sister. Such a dear girl as she is, and so careful of me! I must not let her find me writing.

She is a perfect and enthusiastic housekeeper, and hopes for no better profession. I verily believe she thinks it is the writing which made me sick!

But I can write when she is out, and see her a long way off from these windows.

There is one that commands the road, a lovely shaded winding road, and one that just looks off over the country. A lovely country, too, full of great elms and velvet meadows.

This wallpaper has a kind of sub-pattern in a different shade, a particularly irritating one, for you can only see it in certain lights, and not clearly then.

But in the places where it isn't faded and where the sun is just so—I can see a strange, provoking, formless sort of figure that seems to skulk about behind that silly and conspicuous front design.

There's sister on the stairs!

Well, the Fourth of July is over! The people are all gone, and I am tired out. John thought it might do me good to see a little company, so we just had Mother and Nellie and the children down for a week.

Of course I didn't do a thing. Jennie sees to everything now.

But it tired me all the same.

John says if I don't pick up faster he shall send me to Weir Mitchell in the fall.

But I don't want to go there at all. I had a friend who was in his hands once, and she says he is just like John and my brother, only more so!

Besides, it is such an undertaking to go so far.

I don't feel as if it was worthwhile to turn my hand over for anything, and I'm getting dreadfully fretful and querulous.

I cry at nothing, and cry most of the time.

Of course I don't when John is here, or anybody else, but when I am alone.

1　*sticketh ... brother* See Proverbs 18.24.

And I am alone a good deal just now. John is kept in town very often by serious cases, and Jennie is good and lets me alone when I want her to.

So I walk a little in the garden or down that lovely lane, sit on the porch under the roses, and lie down up here a good deal.

I'm getting really fond of the room in spite of the wallpaper. Perhaps because of the wallpaper.

It dwells in my mind so!

I lie here on this great immovable bed—it is nailed down, I believe—and follow that pattern about by the hour. It is as good as gymnastics, I assure you. I start, we'll say, at the bottom, down in the corner over there where it has not been touched, and I determine for the thousandth time that I *will* follow that pointless pattern to some sort of conclusion.

I know a little of the principle of design, and I know this thing was not arranged on any laws of radiation, or alternation, or repetition, or symmetry, or anything else that I ever heard of.

It is repeated, of course, by the breadths, but not otherwise.

Looked at in one way, each breadth stands alone; the bloated curves and flourishes—a kind of "debased Romanesque"[2] with delirium tremens[3]—go waddling up and down in isolated columns of fatuity.

But, on the other hand, they connect diagonally, and the sprawling outlines run off in great slanting waves of optic horror, like a lot of wallowing sea-weeds in full chase.

The whole thing goes horizontally, too, at least it seems so, and I exhaust myself trying to distinguish the order of its going in that direction.

They have used a horizontal breadth for a frieze, and that adds wonderfully to the confusion.

There is one end of the room where it is almost intact, and there, when the crosslights fade and the low sun shines directly upon it, I can almost fancy radiation after all—the interminable grotesque seems to form around a common center and rush off in headlong plunges of equal distraction.

It makes me tired to follow it. I will take a nap, I guess.

I don't know why I should write this.

I don't want to.

I don't feel able.

---

2   Medieval architectural style involving columns and round arches similar to those found in Roman architecture.

3   Condition resulting from extreme alcohol withdrawal; its symptoms include tremors, hallucinations, and random physical movements.

And I know John would think it absurd. But I *must* say what I feel and think in some way—it is such a relief!

But the effort is getting to be greater than the relief.

Half the time now I am awfully lazy, and lie down ever so much.

John says I mustn't lose my strength, and has me take cod liver oil and lots of tonics and things, to say nothing of the ale and wine and rare meat.

Dear John! He loves me very dearly, and hates to have me sick. I tried to have a real earnest reasonable talk with him the other day, and tell him how I wish he would let me go and make a visit to Cousin Henry and Julia.

But he said I wasn't able to go, nor able to stand it after I got there; and I did not make out a very good case for myself, for I was crying before I had finished.

It is getting to be a great effort for me to think straight. Just this nervous weakness, I suppose.

And dear John gathered me up in his arms, and just carried me upstairs and laid me on the bed, and sat by me and read to me till it tired my head.

He said I was his darling and his comfort and all he had, and that I must take care of myself for his sake, and keep well.

He says no one but myself can help me out of it, that I must use my will and self-control and not let any silly fancies run away with me.

There's one comfort—the baby is well and happy, and does not have to occupy this nursery with the horrid wallpaper.

If we had not used it, that blessed child would have! What a fortunate escape! Why, I wouldn't have a child of mine, an impressionable little thing, live in such a room for worlds.

I never thought of it before, but it is lucky that John kept me here after all, I can stand it so much easier than a baby, you see.

Of course I never mention it to them any more—I am too wise—but I keep watch for it all the same.

There are things in that paper that nobody knows about but me, or ever will.

Behind that outside pattern the dim shapes get clearer every day.

It is always the same shape, only very numerous.

And it is like a woman stooping down and creeping about behind that pattern. I don't like it a bit. I wonder—I begin to think—I wish John would take me away from here!

It is so hard to talk with John about my case, because he is so wise, and because he loves me so.

But I tried it last night.

It was moonlight. The moon shines in all around just as the sun does.

I hate to see it sometimes, it creeps so slowly, and always comes in by one window or another.

John was asleep and I hated to waken him, so I kept still and watched the moonlight on that undulating wallpaper till I felt creepy.

The faint figure behind seemed to shake the pattern, just as if she wanted to get out.

I got up softly and went to feel and see if the paper *did* move, and when I came back John was awake.

"What is it, little girl?" he said. "Don't go walking about like that—you'll get cold."

I thought it was a good time to talk, so I told him that I really was not gaining here, and that I wished he would take me away.

"Why, darling!" said he. "Our lease will be up in three weeks, and I can't see how to leave before.

"The repairs are not done at home, and I cannot possibly leave town just now. Of course if you were in any danger, I could and would, but you really are better, dear, whether you can see it or not. I am a doctor, dear, and I know. You are gaining flesh and color, your appetite is better, I feel really much easier about you."

"I don't weigh a bit more," said I, "nor as much; and my appetite may be better in the evening when you are here but it is worse in the morning when you are away!"

"Bless her little heart!" said he with a big hug. "She shall be as sick as she pleases! But now let's improve the shining hours[4] by going to sleep, and talk about it in the morning!"

"And you won't go away?" I asked gloomily.

"Why, how can I, dear? It is only three weeks more and then we will take a nice little trip of a few days while Jennie is getting the house ready. Really, dear, you are better!"

"Better in body perhaps—" I began, and stopped short, for he sat up straight and looked at me with such a stern, reproachful look that I could not say another word.

"My darling," said he, "I beg of you, for my sake and for our child's sake, as well as your own, that you will never for one instant let that idea enter your mind! There is nothing so dangerous, so fascinating, to a temperament like yours. It is a false and foolish fancy. Can you not trust me as a physician when I tell you so?"

---

4   See Isaac Watts's popular children's poem "Against Idleness and Mischief" (1715): "How doth the little busy bee / Improve each shining hour."

So of course I said no more on that score, and we went to sleep before long. He thought I was asleep first, but I wasn't, and lay there for hours trying to decide whether that front pattern and the back pattern really did move together or separately.

On a pattern like this, by daylight, there is a lack of sequence, a defiance of law, that is a constant irritant to a normal mind.

The color is hideous enough, and unreliable enough, and infuriating enough, but the pattern is torturing.

You think you have mastered it, but just as you get well under way in following, it turns a back-somersault and there you are. It slaps you in the face, knocks you down, and tramples upon you. It is like a bad dream.

The outside pattern is a florid arabesque,[5] reminding one of a fungus. If you can imagine a toadstool in joints, an interminable string of toadstools, budding and sprouting in endless convolutions—why, that is something like it.

That is, sometimes!

There is one marked peculiarity about this paper, a thing nobody seems to notice but myself, and that is that it changes as the light changes.

When the sun shoots in through the east window—I always watch for that first long, straight ray—it changes so quickly that I never can quite believe it.

That is why I watch it always.

By moonlight—the moon shines in all night when there is a moon—I wouldn't know it was the same paper.

At night in any kind of light, in twilight, candlelight, lamplight, and worst of all by moonlight, it becomes bars! The outside pattern, I mean, and the woman behind it is as plain as can be.

I didn't realize for a long time what the thing was that showed behind, that dim sub-pattern, but now I am quite sure it is a woman.

By daylight she is subdued, quiet. I fancy it is the pattern that keeps her so still. It is so puzzling. It keeps me quiet by the hour.

I lie down ever so much now. John says it is good for me, and to sleep all I can.

Indeed he started the habit by making me lie down for an hour after each meal.

It is a very bad habit I am convinced, for you see, I don't sleep.

And that cultivates deceit, for I don't tell them I'm awake—O no!

The fact is I am getting a little afraid of John.

He seems very queer sometimes, and even Jennie has an inexplicable look.

---

5   Complex decorative design.

It strikes me occasionally, just as a scientific hypothesis, that perhaps it is the paper!

I have watched John when he did not know I was looking, and come into the room suddenly on the most innocent excuses, and I've caught him several times *looking at the paper*! And Jennie too. I caught Jennie with her hand on it once.

She didn't know I was in the room, and when I asked her in a quiet, a very quiet voice, with the most restrained manner possible, what she was doing with the paper—she turned around as if she had been caught stealing, and looked quite angry—asked me why I should frighten her so!

Then she said that the paper stained everything it touched, that she had found yellow smooches on all my clothes and John's, and she wished we would be more careful!

Did not that sound innocent? But I know she was studying that pattern, and I am determined that nobody shall find it out but myself!

Life is very much more exciting now than it used to be. You see I have something more to expect, to look forward to, to watch. I really do eat better, and am more quiet than I was.

John is so pleased to see me improve! He laughed a little the other day, and said I seemed to be flourishing in spite of my wallpaper.

I turned it off with a laugh. I had no intention of telling him it was *because* of the wallpaper—he would make fun of me. He might even want to take me away.

I don't want to leave now until I have found it out. There is a week more, and I think that will be enough.

I'm feeling so much better!

I don't sleep much at night, for it is so interesting to watch developments; but I sleep a good deal during the daytime.

In the daytime it is tiresome and perplexing.

There are always new shoots on the fungus, and new shades of yellow all over it. I cannot keep count of them, though I have tried conscientiously.

It is the strangest yellow, that wallpaper! It makes me think of all the yellow things I ever saw—not beautiful ones like buttercups, but old, foul, bad yellow things.

But there is something else about that paper—the smell! I noticed it the moment we came into the room, but with so much air and sun it was not bad. Now we have had a week of fog and rain, and whether the windows are open or not, the smell is here.

It creeps all over the house.

I find it hovering in the dining-room, skulking in the parlor, hiding in the hall, lying in wait for me on the stairs.

It gets into my hair.

Even when I go to ride, if I turn my head suddenly and surprise it—there is that smell!

Such a peculiar odor, too! I have spent hours in trying to analyze it, to find what it smelled like.

It is not bad—at first—and very gentle, but quite the subtlest, most enduring odor I ever met.

In this damp weather it is awful, I wake up in the night and find it hanging over me.

It used to disturb me at first. I thought seriously of burning the house—to reach the smell.

But now I am used to it. The only thing I can think of that it is like is the *color* of the paper! A yellow smell.

There is a very funny mark on this wall, low down, near the mopboard. A streak that runs round the room. It goes behind every piece of furniture, except the bed, a long, straight, even *smooch*, as if it had been rubbed over and over.

I wonder how it was done and who did it, and what they did it for. Round and round and round—round and round and round—it makes me dizzy!

I really have discovered something at last.

Through watching so much at night, when it changes so, I have finally found out.

The front pattern *does* move—and no wonder! The woman behind shakes it!

Sometimes I think there are a great many women behind, and sometimes only one, and she crawls around fast, and her crawling shakes it all over.

Then in the very bright spots she keeps still, and in the very shady spots she just takes hold of the bars and shakes them hard.

And she is all the time trying to climb through. But nobody could climb through that pattern—it strangles so; I think that is why it has so many heads.

They get through, and then the pattern strangles them off and turns them upside down, and makes their eyes white!

If those heads were covered or taken off it would not be half so bad.

I think that woman gets out in the daytime!

And I'll tell you why—privately—I've seen her!

I can see her out of every one of my windows!

It is the same woman, I know, for she is always creeping, and most women do not creep by daylight.

I see her in that long shaded lane, creeping up and down. I see her in those dark grape arbors, creeping all around the garden.

I see her on that long road under the trees, creeping along, and when a carriage comes she hides under the blackberry vines.

I don't blame her a bit. It must be very humiliating to be caught creeping by daylight!

I always lock the door when I creep by daylight. I can't do it at night, for I know John would suspect something at once.

And John is so queer now that I don't want to irritate him. I wish he would take another room! Besides, I don't want anybody to get that woman out at night but myself.

I often wonder if I could see her out of all the windows at once.

But, turn as fast as I can, I can only see out of one at one time.

And though I always see her, she *may* be able to creep faster than I can turn! I have watched her sometimes away off in the open country, creeping as fast as a cloud shadow in a wind.

If only that top pattern could be gotten off from the under one! I mean to try it, little by little.

I have found out another funny thing, but I shan't tell it this time! It does not do to trust people too much.

There are only two more days to get this paper off, and I believe John is beginning to notice. I don't like the look in his eyes.

And I heard him ask Jennie a lot of professional questions about me. She had a very good report to give.

She said I slept a good deal in the daytime.

John knows I don't sleep very well at night, for all I'm so quiet!

He asked me all sorts of questions, too, and pretended to be very loving and kind.

As if I couldn't see through him!

Still, I don't wonder he acts so, sleeping under this paper for three months.

It only interests me, but I feel sure John and Jennie are affected by it.

Hurrah! This is the last day, but it is enough. John is to stay in town over night, and won't be out until this evening.

Jennie wanted to sleep with me—the sly thing; but I told her I should undoubtedly rest better for a night all alone.

That was clever, for really I wasn't alone a bit! As soon as it was moonlight and that poor thing began to crawl and shake the pattern, I got up and ran to help her.

I pulled and she shook, I shook and she pulled, and before morning we had peeled off yards of that paper.

A strip about as high as my head and half around the room.

And then when the sun came and that awful pattern began to laugh at me, I declared I would finish it today!

We go away tomorrow, and they are moving all my furniture down again to leave things as they were before.

Jennie looked at the wall in amazement, but I told her merrily that I did it out of pure spite at the vicious thing.

She laughed and said she wouldn't mind doing it herself, but I must not get tired.

How she betrayed herself that time!

But I am here, and no person touches this paper but Me—not *alive*!

She tried to get me out of the room—it was too patent! But I said it was so quiet and empty and clean now that I believed I would lie down again and sleep all I could; and not to wake me even for dinner—I would call when I woke.

So now she is gone, and the servants are gone, and the things are gone, and there is nothing left but that great bedstead nailed down, with the canvas mattress we found on it.

We shall sleep downstairs tonight, and take the boat home tomorrow.

I quite enjoy the room, now it is bare again.

How those children did tear about here!

This bedstead is fairly gnawed!

But I must get to work.

I have locked the door and thrown the key down into the front path.

I don't want to go out, and I don't want to have anybody come in, till John comes.

I want to astonish him.

I've got a rope up here that even Jennie did not find. If that woman does get out, and tries to get away, I can tie her!

But I forgot I could not reach far without anything to stand on!

This bed will *not* move!

I tried to lift and push it until I was lame, and then I got so angry I bit off a little piece at one corner—but it hurt my teeth.

Then I peeled off all the paper I could reach standing on the floor. It sticks horribly and the pattern just enjoys it! All those strangled heads and bulbous eyes and waddling fungus growths just shriek with derision!

I am getting angry enough to do something desperate. To jump out of the window would be admirable exercise, but the bars are too strong even to try.

Besides I wouldn't do it. Of course not. I know well enough that a step like that is improper and might be misconstrued.

I don't like to *look* out of the windows even—there are so many of those creeping women, and they creep so fast.

I wonder if they all come out of that wallpaper as I did?

But I am securely fastened now by my well-hidden rope—you don't get me out in the road there!

I suppose I shall have to get back behind the pattern when it comes night, and that is hard!

It is so pleasant to be out in this great room and creep around as I please!

I don't want to go outside. I won't, even if Jennie asks me to.

For outside you have to creep on the ground, and everything is green instead of yellow.

But here I can creep smoothly on the floor, and my shoulder just fits in that long smooch around the wall, so I cannot lose my way.

Why there's John at the door!

It is no use, young man, you can't open it!

How he does call and pound!

Now he's crying to Jennie for an axe.

It would be a shame to break down that beautiful door!

"John dear!" said I in the gentlest voice. "The key is down by the front steps, under a plantain leaf!"

That silenced him for a few moments.

Then he said—very quietly indeed, "Open the door, my darling!"

"I can't," said I. "The key is down by the front door under a plantain leaf!"

And then I said it again, several times, very gently and slowly, and said it so often that he had to go and see, and he got it of course, and came in. He stopped short by the door.

"What is the matter?" he cried. "For God's sake, what are you doing!"

I kept on creeping just the same, but I looked at him over my shoulder.

"I've got out at last," said I, "in spite of you and Jane! And I've pulled off most of the paper, so you can't put me back!"

Now why should that man have fainted? But he did, and right across my path by the wall, so that I had to creep over him every time!

—*1892*

JAMES JOYCE

James Joyce was born in Dublin, and although he left the city for good in 1904, it provided the background for all his major works. His best-known novel, *Ulysses* (1922), describes a day in the life of three of the city's inhabitants, with the various incidents paralleling episodes from Homer's *Odyssey*. It is written in an intricately constructed combination of literary styles, including long sections of stream-of-consciousness.

Joyce and Nora Barnacle, a woman whom he met on a Dublin street and who would become his wife and lifelong companion, lived in Trieste, Zurich, and Paris, where Joyce made his living by teaching English. In 1914, the modernist poet Ezra Pound arranged for Joyce's autobiographical novel, *A Portrait of the Artist as a Young Man*, to be serialized in *The Egoist*, a British magazine. The same year, Joyce's collection of short stories, *Dubliners*, was published. Joyce had submitted and resubmitted to various publishers, but their squeamishness over the subject matter prevented the collection from being published for almost 10 years. Even the collection's eventual publisher worried that the negative portrayal of Dublin and its inhabitants in the collection would provoke charges of libel. In a letter to his publisher, Joyce states his reason for leaving the stories as he originally wrote them:

> My intention was to write a chapter of the moral history of my country and I chose Dublin for the scene because the city seemed to me the centre of paralysis.... I have written it for the most part in a style of scrupulous meanness and with the conviction that he is a very bold man who dares to alter in the presentment, still more to deform, whatever he has seen and heard. I cannot do any more than this.

Joyce now began work on *Ulysses*. In 1918, *The Egoist* and an American magazine, *The Little Review*, began serializing the work, but charges that passages were obscene led to the suspension of serialization. Joyce is said to have retorted, "If *Ulysses* isn't fit to read, life isn't fit to live." It was finally published in book form in Paris in 1922.

By this time, friends and admirers were supporting Joyce financially, allowing him to concentrate on his writing; he began work on his last book, *Finnegans Wake*, an extremely complex work of dream imaginings and linguistic invention, which was published in 1939.

Araby[1]

NORTH RICHMOND Street, being blind,[2] was a quiet street except at the hour when the Christian Brothers' School set the boys free. An uninhabited house of two storeys stood at the blind end, detached from its neighbours in a square ground. The other houses of the street, conscious of decent lives within them, gazed at one another with brown imperturbable faces.

The former tenant of our house, a priest, had died in the back drawing-room. Air, musty from having been long enclosed, hung in all the rooms, and the waste room behind the kitchen was littered with old useless papers. Among these I found a few paper-covered books, the pages of which were curled and damp: *The Abbot*,[3] by Walter Scott, *The Devout Communicant*[4] and *The Memoirs of Vidocq*.[5] I liked the last best because its leaves were yellow. The wild garden behind the house contained a central apple-tree and a few straggling bushes under one of which I found the late tenant's rusty bicycle-pump. He had been a very charitable priest; in his will he had left all his money to institutions and the furniture of his house to his sister.

When the short days of winter came dusk fell before we had well eaten our dinners. When we met in the street the houses had grown sombre. The space of sky above us was the colour of ever-changing violet and towards it the lamps of the street lifted their feeble lanterns. The cold air stung us and we played till our bodies glowed. Our shouts echoed in the silent street. The career of our play brought us through the dark muddy lanes behind the houses where we ran the gantlet of the rough tribes from the cottages, to the back doors of the dark dripping gardens where odours arose from the ash-pits, to the dark odorous

---

1   Charity bazaar held in Dublin in 1894.

2   I.e., being a dead-end street.

3   1820 historical novel by Sir Walter Scott about Mary, Queen of Scots.

4   Title common to several nineteenth-century religious tracts.

5   Autobiography of François Vidocq, a nineteenth-century Parisian criminal turned police detective.

stables where a coachman smoothed and combed the horse or shook music from the buckled harness. When we returned to the street light from the kitchen windows had filled the areas.[6] If my uncle was seen turning the corner we hid in the shadow until we had seen him safely housed. Or if Mangan's sister came out on the doorstep to call her brother in to his tea we watched her from our shadow peer up and down the street. We waited to see whether she would remain or go in and, if she remained, we left our shadow and walked up to Mangan's steps resignedly. She was waiting for us, her figure defined by the light from the half-opened door. Her brother always teased her before he obeyed and I stood by the railings looking at her. Her dress swung as she moved her body and the soft rope of her hair tossed from side to side.

Every morning I lay on the floor in the front parlour watching her door. The blind was pulled down to within an inch of the sash so that I could not be seen. When she came out on the doorstep my heart leaped. I ran to the hall, seized my books and followed her. I kept her brown figure always in my eye and, when we came near the point at which our ways diverged, I quickened my pace and passed her. This happened morning after morning. I had never spoken to her, except for a few casual words, and yet her name was like a summons to all my foolish blood.

Her image accompanied me even in places the most hostile to romance. On Saturday evenings when my aunt went marketing I had to go to carry some of the parcels. We walked through the flaring streets, jostled by drunken men and bargaining women, amid the curses of labourers, the shrill litanies of shop-boys who stood on guard by the barrels of pigs' cheeks, the nasal chanting of street-singers, who sang a *come-all-you*[7] about O'Donovan Rossa,[8] or a ballad about the troubles in our native land. These noises converged in a single sensation of life for me: I imagined that I bore my chalice safely through a throng of foes. Her name sprang to my lips at moments in strange prayers and praises which I myself did not understand. My eyes were often full of tears (I could not tell why) and at times a flood from my heart seemed to pour itself out into my bosom. I thought little of the future. I did not know whether I would ever speak to her or not or, if I spoke to her, how I could tell her of my confused adoration. But my body was like a harp and her words and gestures were like fingers running upon the wires.

One evening I went into the back drawing-room in which the priest had died. It was a dark rainy evening and there was no sound in the house. Through

---

6   Spaces between the railings and the fronts of houses, below street level.

7   Ballad, so called because many ballads started with this phrase.

8   Jeremiah O'Donovan Rossa (1831–1915), an activist for Irish independence.

one of the broken panes I heard the rain impinge upon the earth, the fine incessant needles of water playing in the sodden beds. Some distant lamp or lighted
window gleamed below me. I was thankful that I could see so little. All my
senses seemed to desire to veil themselves and, feeling that I was about to slip
from them, I pressed the palms of my hands together until they trembled, murmuring: *O love! O love!* many times.

At last she spoke to me. When she addressed the first words to me I was
so confused that I did not know what to answer. She asked me was I going to
Araby. I forget whether I answered yes or no. It would be a splendid bazaar, she
said; she would love to go.

—And why can't you? I asked.

While she spoke she turned a silver bracelet round and round her wrist. She
could not go, she said, because there would be a retreat that week in her convent.[9] Her brother and two other boys were fighting for their caps and I was
alone at the railings. She held one of the spikes, bowing her head towards me.
The light from the lamp opposite our door caught the white curve of her neck,
lit up her hair that rested there and, falling, lit up the hand upon the railing. It
fell over one side of her dress and caught the white border of a petticoat, just
visible as she stood at ease.

—It's well for you, she said.

—If I go, I said, I will bring you something.

What innumerable follies laid waste my waking and sleeping thoughts after that evening! I wished to annihilate the tedious intervening days. I chafed
against the work of school. At night in my bedroom and by day in the classroom
her image came between me and the page I strove to read. The syllables of the
word *Araby* were called to me through the silence in which my soul luxuriated
and cast an Eastern enchantment over me. I asked for leave to go to the bazaar
on Saturday night. My aunt was surprised and hoped it was not some Freema-
son[10] affair. I answered few questions in class. I watched my master's face pass
from amiability to sternness; he hoped I was not beginning to idle. I could not
call my wandering thoughts together. I had hardly any patience with the serious
work of life which, now that it stood between me and my desire, seemed to me
child's play, ugly monotonous child's play.

On Saturday morning I reminded my uncle that I wished to go to the bazaar
in the evening. He was fussing at the hallstand, looking for the hat-brush, and
answered me curtly:

9 I.e., convent school.
10 In reference to the Freemasons, a secret society believed by many in Ireland to be
   anti-Catholic.

—Yes, boy, I know.

As he was in the hall I could not go into the front parlour and lie at the window. I left the house in bad humour and walked slowly towards the school. The air was pitilessly raw and already my heart misgave me.

When I came home to dinner my uncle had not yet been home. Still it was early. I sat staring at the clock for some time and, when its ticking began to irritate me, I left the room. I mounted the staircase and gained the upper part of the house. The high cold empty gloomy rooms liberated me and I went from room to room singing. From the front window I saw my companions playing below in the street. Their cries reached me weakened and indistinct and, leaning my forehead against the cool glass, I looked over at the dark house where she lived. I may have stood there for an hour, seeing nothing but the brown-clad figure cast by my imagination, touched discreetly by the lamplight at the curved neck, at the hand upon the railings and at the border below the dress.

When I came downstairs again I found Mrs. Mercer sitting at the fire. She was an old garrulous woman, a pawnbroker's widow, who collected used stamps for some pious purpose. I had to endure the gossip of the tea-table. The meal was prolonged beyond an hour and still my uncle did not come. Mrs. Mercer stood up to go: she was sorry she couldn't wait any longer, but it was after eight o'clock and she did not like to be out late, as the night air was bad for her. When she had gone I began to walk up and down the room, clenching my fists. My aunt said:

—I'm afraid you may put off your bazaar for this night of Our Lord.

At nine o'clock I heard my uncle's latchkey in the halldoor. I heard him talking to himself and heard the hallstand rocking when it had received the weight of his overcoat. I could interpret these signs. When he was midway through his dinner I asked him to give me the money to go to the bazaar. He had forgotten.

—The people are in bed and after their first sleep now, he said.

I did not smile. My aunt said to him energetically:

—Can't you give him the money and let him go? You've kept him late enough as it is.

My uncle said he was very sorry he had forgotten. He said he believed in the old saying: *All work and no play makes Jack a dull boy.* He asked where I was going and, when I had told him a second time he asked me did I know *The Arab's Farewell to his Steed.*[11] When I left the kitchen he was about to recite the opening lines of the piece to my aunt.

I held a florin tightly in my hand as I strode down Buckingham Street towards the station. The sight of the streets thronged with buyers and glaring with gas

---

11   Popular Romantic poem by Caroline Norton (1808–77).

recalled to me the purpose of my journey. I took my seat in a third-class carriage of a deserted train. After an intolerable delay the train moved out of the station slowly. It crept onward among ruinous houses and over the twinkling river. At Westland Row Station a crowd of people pressed to the carriage doors; but the porters moved them back, saying that it was a special train for the bazaar. I remained alone in the bare carriage. In a few minutes the train drew up beside an improvised wooden platform. I passed out on to the road and saw by the lighted dial of a clock that it was ten minutes to ten. In front of me was a large building which displayed the magical name.

I could not find any sixpenny entrance and, fearing that the bazaar would be closed, I passed in quickly through a turnstile, handing a shilling to a weary-looking man. I found myself in a big hall girdled at half its height by a gallery. Nearly all the stalls were closed and the greater part of the hall was in darkness. I recognized a silence like that which pervades a church after a service. I walked into the centre of the bazaar timidly. A few people were gathered about the stalls which were still open. Before a curtain, over which the words *Café Chantant*[12] were written in coloured lamps, two men were counting money on a salver.[13] I listened to the fall of the coins.

Remembering with difficulty why I had come I went over to one of the stalls and examined porcelain vases and flowered tea-sets. At the door of the stall a young lady was talking and laughing with two young gentlemen. I remarked their English accents and listened vaguely to their conversation.

—O, I never said such a thing!

—O, but you did!

—O, but I didn't!

—Didn't she say that?

—Yes. I heard her.

—O, there's a ... fib!

Observing me the young lady came over and asked me did I wish to buy anything. The tone of her voice was not encouraging; she seemed to have spoken to me out of a sense of duty. I looked humbly at the great jars that stood like eastern guards at either side of the dark entrance to the stall and murmured:

—No, thank you.

The young lady changed the position of one of the vases and went back to the two young men. They began to talk of the same subject. Once or twice the young lady glanced at me over her shoulder.

---

12 Café that provides musical entertainment.

13 Tray.

I lingered before her stall, though I knew my stay was useless, to make my interest in her wares seem the more real. Then I turned away slowly and walked down the middle of the bazaar. I allowed the two pennies to fall against the sixpence in my pocket. I heard a voice call from one end of the gallery that the light was out. The upper part of the hall was now completely dark.

Gazing up into the darkness I saw myself as a creature driven and derided by vanity; and my eyes burned with anguish and anger.

—1914

Eveline

SHE SAT at the window watching the evening invade the avenue. Her head was leaned against the window curtains and in her nostrils was the odour of dusty cretonne.[14] She was tired.

Few people passed. The man out of the last house passed on his way home; she heard his footsteps clacking along the concrete pavement and afterwards crunching on the cinder path before the new red houses. One time there used to be a field there in which they used to play every evening with other people's children. Then a man from Belfast bought the field and built houses in it—not like their little brown houses but bright brick houses with shining roofs. The children of the avenue used to play together in that field—the Devines, the Waters, the Dunns, little Keogh the cripple, she and her brothers and sisters. Ernest, however, never played: he was too grown up. Her father used often to hunt them in out of the field with his blackthorn stick; but usually little Keogh used to keep *nix*[15] and call out when he saw her father coming. Still they seemed to have been rather happy then. Her father was not so bad then; and besides, her mother was alive. That was a long time ago; she and her brothers and sisters were all grown up; her mother was dead. Tizzie Dunn was dead, too, and the Waters had gone back to England. Everything changes. Now she was going to go away like the others, to leave her home.

Home! She looked round the room, reviewing all its familiar objects which she had dusted once a week for so many years, wondering where on earth all the dust came from. Perhaps she would never see again those familiar objects from which she had never dreamed of being divided. And yet during all those years

---

14   Thick cotton fabric often used for chair coverings or curtains.
15   Keep watch.

she had never found out the name of the priest whose yellowing photograph hung on the wall above the broken harmonium[16] beside the coloured print of the promises made to Blessed Margaret Mary Alacoque.[17] He had been a school friend of her father. Whenever he showed the photograph to a visitor her father used to pass it with a casual word:

—He is in Melbourne now.

She had consented to go away, to leave her home. Was that wise? She tried to weigh each side of the question. In her home anyway she had shelter and food; she had those whom she had known all her life about her. Of course she had to work hard both in the house and at business. What would they say of her in the Stores when they found out that she had run away with a fellow? Say she was a fool, perhaps; and her place would be filled up by advertisement. Miss Gavan would be glad. She had always had an edge on her, especially whenever there were people listening.

—Miss Hill, don't you see these ladies are waiting?

—Look lively, Miss Hill, please.

She would not cry many tears at leaving the Stores.

But in her new home, in a distant unknown country, it would not be like that. Then she would be married—she, Eveline. People would treat her with respect then. She would not be treated as her mother had been. Even now, though she was over nineteen, she sometimes felt herself in danger of her father's violence. She knew it was that that had given her the palpitations. When they were growing up he had never gone for her, like he used to go for Harry and Ernest, because she was a girl; but latterly he had begun to threaten her and say what he would do to her only for her dead mother's sake. And now she had nobody to protect her. Ernest was dead and Harry, who was in the church decorating business, was nearly always down somewhere in the country. Besides, the invariable squabble for money on Saturday nights had begun to weary her unspeakably. She always gave her entire wages—seven shillings—and Harry always sent up what he could but the trouble was to get any money from her father. He said she used to squander the money, that she had no head, that he wasn't going to give her his hard-earned money to throw about the streets, and much more, for he was usually fairly bad of a Saturday night. In the end he would give her the money and ask her had she any intention of buying Sunday's dinner. Then she had to rush out as quickly as she could and do her marketing, holding her black leather purse tightly in her hand as she elbowed her way through the crowds

---

16 Reed instrument similar to an organ.

17 Marguerite Marie Alacoque (1647–90), a French Catholic nun and religious mystic who had visions of Christ. She was made a saint in 1920.

and returning home late under her load of provisions. She had hard work to keep the house together and to see that the two young children who had been left to her charge went to school regularly and got their meals regularly. It was hard work—a hard life—but now that she was about to leave it she did not find it a wholly undesirable life.

She was about to explore another life with Frank. Frank was very kind, manly, open-hearted. She was to go away with him by the night-boat to be his wife and to live with him in Buenos Ayres where he had a home waiting for her. How well she remembered the first time she had seen him; he was lodging in a house on the main road where she used to visit. It seemed a few weeks ago. He was standing at the gate, his peaked cap pushed back on his head and his hair tumbled forward over a face of bronze. Then they had come to know each other. He used to meet her outside the Stores every evening and see her home. He took her to see *The Bohemian Girl*[18] and she felt elated as she sat in an unaccustomed part of the theatre with him. He was awfully fond of music and sang a little. People knew that they were courting and, when he sang about the lass that loves a sailor, she always felt pleasantly confused. He used to call her Poppens out of fun. First of all it had been an excitement for her to have a fellow and then she had begun to like him. He had tales of distant countries. He had started as a deck boy at a pound a month on a ship of the Allan Line[19] going out to Canada. He told her the names of the ships he had been on and the names of the different services. He had sailed through the Straits of Magellan and he told her stories of the terrible Patagonians.[20] He had fallen on his feet in Buenos Ayres, he said, and had come over to the old country just for a holiday. Of course, her father had found out the affair and had forbidden her to have anything to say to him.

—I know these sailor chaps, he said.

One day he had quarrelled with Frank and after that she had to meet her lover secretly.

The evening deepened in the avenue. The white of two letters in her lap grew indistinct. One was to Harry; the other was to her father. Ernest had been her favourite but she liked Harry too. Her father was becoming old lately, she noticed; he would miss her. Sometimes he could be very nice. Not long before, when she had been laid up for a day, he had read her out a ghost story and made toast

---

18   1843 opera by Irish composer Michael Balfe.

19   Steamship company that made weekly sailings between Liverpool and western Canada via South America.

20   Sea route near the tip of South America; terrible Patagonians Refers either to the strong, unpredictable Patagonian winds in the Strait of Magellan, or to a group of South American natives that early explorers had claimed were giants. By the beginning of the nineteenth century, this rumour had been discredited.

for her at the fire. Another day, when their mother was alive, they had all gone for a picnic to the Hill of Howth.[21] She remembered her father putting on her mother's bonnet to make the children laugh.

Her time was running out but she continued to sit by the window, leaning her head against the window curtain, inhaling the odour of dusty cretonne. Down far in the avenue she could hear a street organ playing. She knew the air. Strange that it should come that very night to remind her of the promise to her mother, her promise to keep the home together as long as she could. She remembered the last night of her mother's illness; she was again in the close dark room at the other side of the hall and outside she heard a melancholy air of Italy. The organ-player had been ordered to go away and given sixpence. She remembered her father strutting back into the sickroom saying:

—Damned Italians! coming over here!

As she mused the pitiful vision of her mother's life laid its spell on the very quick of her being—that life of commonplace sacrifices closing in final craziness. She trembled as she heard again her mother's voice saying constantly with foolish insistence:

—Derevaun Seraun! Derevaun Seraun![22]

She stood up in a sudden impulse of terror. Escape! She must escape! Frank would save her. He would give her life, perhaps love, too. But she wanted to live. Why should she be unhappy? She had a right to happiness. Frank would take her in his arms, fold her in his arms. He would save her.

She stood among the swaying crowd in the station at the North Wall. He held her hand and she knew that he was speaking to her, saying something about the passage over and over again. The station was full of soldiers with brown baggages. Through the wide doors of the sheds she caught a glimpse of the black mass of the boat, lying in beside the quay wall, with illumined portholes. She answered nothing. She felt her cheek pale and cold and, out of a maze of distress, she prayed to God to direct her, to show her what was her duty. The boat blew a long mournful whistle into the mist. If she went, to-morrow she would be on the sea with Frank, steaming towards Buenos Ayres. Their passage had been booked. Could she still draw back after all he had done for her? Her distress awoke a nausea in her body and she kept moving her lips in silent fervent prayer.

A bell clanged upon her heart. She felt him seize her hand:

—Come!

---

21 Hill located northeast of Dublin, on the Howth peninsula.
22 The meaning of this phrase is uncertain; it may be garbled Irish or simply gibberish.

All the seas of the world tumbled about her heart. He was drawing her into them: he would drown her. She gripped with both hands at the iron railing.

—Come!

No! No! No! It was impossible. Her hands clutched the iron in frenzy. Amid the seas she sent a cry of anguish!

—Eveline! Evvy!

He rushed beyond the barrier and called to her to follow. He was shouted at to go on but he still called to her. She set her white face to him, passive, like a helpless animal. Her eyes gave him no sign of love or farewell or recognition.

—1914

VIRGINIA WOOLF

It is no accident that the life of Virginia Woolf, one of the most innovative writers of the twentieth century, coincides very nearly with the emergence and flourishing of literary modernism. Many of her highly experimental novels—notably *Mrs Dalloway* (1925), *To the Lighthouse* (1927), and *The Waves* (1931)—are key landmarks in the modernist revolt against conventional modes of literary representation. In contrast to what she described as the superficial, "materialist" fixation of Edwardian novelists on external details, Woolf set out to convey the essence of lived experience, the incessant influx of impressions—"trivial, fantastic, evanescent, or engraved with the sharpness of steel"—that stream through and light up the mind from moment to crowded moment with all manner of fugitive, seemingly random images, thoughts, feelings, memories, and associations.

For Woolf, life does not form an orderly, linear chronicle of events, like "a series of gig lamps symmetrically arranged." Rather, "life is a luminous halo, a semi-transparent envelope surrounding us from the beginning of consciousness to the end." In order to faithfully render some semblance of this "uncircumscribed spirit," Woolf followed writers like James Joyce in developing a fluid stream-of-consciousness technique that subordinates the action of plot to the subjective interplay of perception, recollection, emotion, and understanding. This essentially lyrical method is used to great effect in stories like "Kew Gardens" (1919).

The circumstances of Woolf's own life were often deeply troubled. Although born into an illustrious British family with an impressive literary pedigree, Woolf received no formal education, an injustice that occupies a central place in much of her social and political writing. The loss of her parents and several siblings exacted a heavy emotional and psychological toll, and periodic fits of madness and depression ultimately led her to suicide. But though her hauntingly beautiful, intricately crafted novels and stories are written in a predominantly elegiac key, they also explore the rich multiplicity of connections between individuals, memories, and moments in time that persist across the years.

Kew Gardens[1]

FROM THE oval-shaped flower-bed there rose perhaps a hundred stalks spreading into heart-shaped or tongue-shaped leaves half way up and unfurling at the tip red or blue or yellow petals marked with spots of colour raised upon the surface; and from the red, blue or yellow gloom of the throat emerged a straight bar, rough with gold dust and slightly clubbed at the end. The petals were voluminous enough to be stirred by the summer breeze, and when they moved, the red, blue, and yellow lights passed one over the other, staining an inch of the brown earth beneath with a spot of the most intricate colour. The light fell either upon the smooth grey back of a pebble, or the shell of a snail with its brown circular veins, or, falling into a raindrop, it expanded with such intensity of red, blue, and yellow the thin walls of water that one expected them to burst and disappear. Instead, the drop was left in a second silver grey once more, and the light now settled upon the flesh of a leaf, revealing the branching thread of fibre beneath the surface, and again it moved on and spread its illumination in the vast green spaces beneath the dome of the heart-shaped and tongue-shaped leaves. Then the breeze stirred rather more briskly overhead and the colour was flashed into the air above, into the eyes of the men and women who walk in Kew Gardens in July.

The figures of these men and women straggled past the flower-bed with a curiously irregular movement not unlike that of the white and blue butterflies who crossed the turf in zig-zag flights from bed to bed. The man was about six inches in front of the woman, strolling carelessly, while she bore on with greater purpose, only turning her head now and then to see that the children were not too far behind. The man kept this distance in front of the woman purposely, though perhaps unconsciously, for he wanted to go on with his thoughts.

"Fifteen years ago I came here with Lily," he thought. "We sat somewhere over there by a lake, and I begged her to marry me all through the hot afternoon. How the dragon-fly kept circling round us: how clearly I see the dragon-fly and her shoe with the square silver buckle at the toe. All the time I spoke I saw her shoe and when it moved impatiently I knew without looking up what she was going to say: the whole of her seemed to be in her shoe. And my love, my desire, were in the dragon-fly; for some reason I thought that if it settled there, on that leaf, the broad one with the red flower in the middle of it, if the dragonfly settled on the leaf she would say 'Yes' at once. But the dragon-fly went round and round: it never settled anywhere—of course not, happily not, or I shouldn't be

---

1   Royal Botanic Gardens in Kew, a district of Greater London.

walking here with Eleanor and the children—Tell me, Eleanor, d'you ever think of the past?"

"Why do you ask, Simon?"

"Because I've been thinking of the past. I've been thinking of Lily, the woman I might have married ... Well, why are you silent? Do you mind my thinking of the past?"

"Why should I mind, Simon? Doesn't one always think of the past, in a garden with men and women lying under the trees? Aren't they one's past, all that remains of it, those men and women, those ghosts lying under the trees ... one's happiness, one's reality?"

"For me, a square silver shoe-buckle and a dragon-fly—"

"For me, a kiss. Imagine six little girls sitting before their easels twenty years ago, down by the side of a lake, painting the water-lilies, the first red water-lilies I'd ever seen. And suddenly a kiss, there on the back of my neck. And my hand shook all the afternoon so that I couldn't paint. I took out my watch and marked the hour when I would allow myself to think of the kiss for five minutes only—it was so precious—the kiss of an old grey-haired woman with a wart on her nose, the mother of all my kisses all my life. Come Caroline, come Hubert."

They walked on past the flower-bed, now walking four abreast, and soon diminished in size among the trees and looked half transparent as the sunlight and shade swam over their backs in large trembling irregular patches.

In the oval flower-bed the snail, whose shell had been stained red, blue, and yellow for the space of two minutes or so, now appeared to be moving very slightly in its shell, and next began to labour over the crumbs of loose earth which broke away and rolled down as it passed over them. It appeared to have a definite goal in front of it, differing in this respect from the singular high-stepping angular green insect who attempted to cross in front of it, and waited for a second with its antennae trembling as if in deliberation, and then stepped off as rapidly and strangely in the opposite direction. Brown cliffs with deep green lakes in the hollows, flat blade-like trees that waved from root to tip, round boulders of grey stone, vast crumpled surfaces of a thin crackling texture—all these objects lay across the snail's progress between one stalk and another to his goal. Before he had decided whether to circumvent the arched tent of a dead leaf or to breast it there came past the bed the feet of other human beings.

This time they were both men. The younger of the two wore an expression of perhaps unnatural calm; he raised his eyes and fixed them very steadily in front of him while his companion spoke, and directly his companion had done speaking he looked on the ground again and sometimes opened his lips only after a long pause and sometimes did not open them at all. The elder man had a curiously uneven and shaky method of walking, jerking his hand forward and throwing up his head abruptly, rather in the manner of an impatient carriage horse tired of waiting outside a house; but in the man these gestures were irresolute and pointless. He talked almost incessantly; he smiled to himself and again began to talk, as if the smile had been an answer. He was talking about spirits—the spirits of the dead, who, according to him, were even now telling him all sorts of odd things about their experiences in Heaven.

"Heaven was known to the ancients as Thessaly,[2] William, and now, with this war,[3] the spirit matter is rolling between the hills like thunder." He paused, seemed to listen, smiled, jerked his head and continued:—

"You have a small electric battery and a piece of rubber to insulate the wire— isolate?—insulate?—well, we'll skip the details, no good going into details that wouldn't be understood—and in short the little machine stands in any convenient position by the head of the bed, we will say, on a neat mahogany stand. All arrangements being properly fixed by workmen under my direction, the widow applies her ear and summons the spirit by sign as agreed. Women! Widows! Women in black—"

Here he seemed to have caught sight of a woman's dress in the distance, which in the shade looked a purple black. He took off his hat, placed his hand upon his heart, and hurried towards her muttering and gesticulating feverishly. But William caught him by the sleeve and touched a flower with the tip of his walking-stick in order to divert the old man's attention. After looking at it for a moment in some confusion the old man bent his ear to it and seemed to answer a voice speaking from it, for he began talking about the forests of Uruguay which he had visited hundreds of years ago in company with the most beautiful young woman in Europe. He could be heard murmuring about forests of Uruguay blanketed with the wax petals of tropical roses, nightingales, sea beaches, mermaids and women drowned at sea, as he suffered himself to be moved on by William, upon whose face the look of stoical patience grew slowly deeper and deeper.

Following his steps so closely as to be slightly puzzled by his gestures came two elderly women of the lower middle class, one stout and ponderous, the other rosy-cheeked and nimble. Like most people of their station[4] they were frankly fascinated by any signs of eccentricity betokening a disordered brain, especially in the well-to-do; but they were too far off to be certain whether the gestures were merely eccentric or genuinely mad. After they had scrutinised the

---

2　Region of ancient Greece.
3　I.e., World War I (1914–18).
4　I.e., their position in English society.

old man's back in silence for a moment and given each other a queer, sly look, they went on energetically piecing together their very complicated dialogue:

> "Nell, Bert, Lot, Cess, Phil, Pa, he says, I says, she says, I says, I says,
> I says—"
> "My Bert, Sis, Bill, Grandad, the old man, sugar,
>   Sugar, flour, kippers, greens
>   Sugar, sugar, sugar."

The ponderous woman looked through the pattern of falling words at the flowers standing cool, firm and upright in the earth, with a curious expression. She saw them as a sleeper waking from a heavy sleep sees a brass candlestick reflecting the light in an unfamiliar way, and closes his eyes and opens them, and seeing the brass candlestick again, finally starts broad awake and stares at the candlestick with all his powers. So the heavy woman came to a standstill opposite the oval-shaped flower-bed, and ceased even to pretend to listen to what the other woman was saying. She stood there letting the words fall over her, swaying the top part of her body slowly backwards and forwards, looking at the flowers. Then she suggested that they should find a seat and have their tea.

The snail had now considered every possible method of reaching his goal without going round the dead leaf or climbing over it. Let alone the effort needed for climbing a leaf, he was doubtful whether the thin texture which vibrated with such an alarming crackle when touched even by the tip of his horns would bear his weight; and this determined him finally to creep beneath it, for there was a point where the leaf curved high enough from the ground to admit him. He had just inserted his head in the opening and was taking stock of the high brown roof and was getting used to the cool brown light when two other people came past outside on the turf. This time they were both young, a young man and a young woman. They were both in the prime of youth, or even in that season which precedes the prime of youth, the season before the smooth pink folds of the flower have burst their gummy case, when the wings of the butterfly, though fully grown, are motionless in the sun.

"Lucky it isn't Friday," he observed.

"Why? D'you believe in luck?"

"They make you pay sixpence on Friday."

"What's sixpence anyway? Isn't it worth sixpence?"

"What's 'it'—what do you mean by 'it'?"

"O anything—I mean—you know what I mean."

Long pauses came between each of these remarks: they were uttered in toneless and monotonous voices. The couple stood still on the edge of the flower-bed, and together pressed the end of her parasol deep down into the soft earth. The action and the fact that his hand rested on the top of hers expressed their feelings in a strange way, as these short insignificant words also expressed something, words with short wings for their heavy body of meaning, inadequate to carry them far and thus alighting awkwardly upon the very common objects that surrounded them and were to their inexperienced touch so massive: but who knows (so they thought as they pressed the parasol into the earth) what precipices aren't concealed in them, or what slopes of ice don't shine in the sun on the other side? Who knows? Who has ever seen this before? Even when she wondered what sort of tea they gave you at Kew, he felt that something loomed up behind her words, and stood vast and solid behind them; and the mist very slowly rose and uncovered—O Heavens,—what were those shapes?—little white tables, and waitresses who looked first at her and then at him; and there was a bill that he would pay with a real two shilling piece, and it was real, all real, he assured himself, fingering the coin in his pocket, real to everyone except to him and to her; even to him it began to seem real; and then—but it was too exciting to stand and think any longer, and he pulled the parasol out of the earth with a jerk and was impatient to find the place where one had tea with other people, like other people.

"Come along, Trissie; it's time we had our tea."

"Wherever does one have one's tea?" she asked with the oddest thrill of excitement in her voice, looking vaguely round and letting herself be drawn on down the grass path, trailing her parasol, turning her head this way and that way, forgetting her tea, wishing to go down there and then down there, remembering orchids and cranes among wild flowers, a Chinese pagoda and a crimson-crested bird; but he bore her on.

Thus one couple after another with much the same irregular and aimless movement passed the flower-bed and were enveloped in layer after layer of green-blue vapour, in which at first their bodies had substance and a dash of colour, but later both substance and colour dissolved in the green-blue atmosphere. How hot it was! So hot that even the thrush chose to hop, like a mechanical bird, in the shadow of the flowers, with long pauses between one movement and the next; instead of rambling vaguely the white butterflies danced one above another, making with their white shifting flakes the outline of a shattered marble column above the tallest flowers; the glass roofs of the palm house shone as if a whole market full of shiny green umbrellas had opened in the sun; and in the drone of the aeroplane the voice of the summer sky murmured its fierce soul. Yellow and black, pink and snow white, shapes of all these colours, men, women, and children, were spotted for a second upon the horizon, and then, seeing the breadth of yellow that lay upon the grass, they wavered and sought shade beneath the trees, dissolving like drops of water in the yellow and green atmosphere, staining it faintly with red and blue. It seemed as if all gross and heavy bodies had sunk down in the heat motionless and lay huddled upon the ground, but their voices went wavering from them as if they were flames lolling from the thick waxen bodies of candles. Voices, yes, voices, wordless voices, breaking the silence suddenly with such depth of contentment, such passion of desire, or, in the voices of children, such freshness of surprise; breaking the silence? But there was no silence; all the time the motor omnibuses were turning their wheels and changing their gear; like a vast nest of Chinese boxes[5] all of wrought steel turning ceaselessly one within another the city murmured; on the top of which the voices cried aloud and the petals of myriads of flowers flashed their colours into the air.

—1921

---

5   Boxes that fit inside each other.

KATHERINE MANSFIELD

Kathleen Mansfield Beauchamp was the daughter of a businessman who later became the affluent director of the Bank of New Zealand. She was born in 1888 in Wellington, New Zealand, the setting for a large part of her fiction. At 15, she travelled with her family to England, where she studied music for three years at Queen's College. There she met Ida Baker (later known as Leslie Moore or L.M.), with whom she would form a lifelong relationship.

Upon completing her education, Mansfield made London her home. Over the course of 10 years, she had relationships with men (one of whom she married) and continued to maintain her connection with L.M. (her mother committed her to "cold water therapy" in a small Bavarian town in order to "cure" her of her attraction to L.M.). In 1911, she met John Middleton Murry, an Oxford undergraduate and literary editor of the new review *Rhythm*, when he visited her in order to discuss a story she had submitted to him; soon afterward they became lovers, and they married in 1918, after her divorce from her first husband was completed.

Two of Mansfield's most important friendships were with the writers D.H. Lawrence and Virginia Woolf. Although she occasionally criticized Mansfield's bohemian behaviour and attitudes, Woolf was a great admirer of Mansfield, and each influenced the other's work. Mansfield's friendship with Lawrence was less stable, and Lawrence may have drawn on aspects of her life and personality in his sometimes unflattering fictional portrait of Gudrun Brangwen in the novel *Women in Love* (1920). During World War I, Mansfield's only brother Leslie was killed in a training accident. After this tragedy, she wrote *Prelude* (1918) and *At the Bay* (1921), both of which reconstruct the childhood she had shared with her brother.

In the final years of her life, Mansfield suffered from a number of illnesses, the most serious of which was tuberculosis. She still, however, managed to produce critically celebrated works such as *Bliss and Other Stories* (1920) and *The Garden Party and Other Stories* (1922). Throughout this time she was faithfully attended by L.M. Mansfield was only 35 when she died of a hemorrhage, but her reputation as a major figure in literary Modernism was already well established.

Murry collected Mansfield's loose papers and notebooks together after her death, and published them under the titles *The Journal of Katherine Mansfield* (1927) and *The Scrapbook of Katherine Mansfield* (1939). Also published posthumously were two collections of fiction, *The Dove's Nest* (1923) and *Something Childish* (1924).

The Doll's House

WHEN DEAR old Mrs. Hay went back to town after staying with the Burnells she sent the children a doll's house. It was so big that the carter and Pat carried it into the courtyard, and there it stayed, propped up on two wooden boxes beside the feed-room door. No harm could come to it; it was summer. And perhaps the smell of paint would have gone off by the time it had to be taken in. For, really, the smell of paint coming from that doll's house ('Sweet of old Mrs. Hay, of course; most sweet and generous!')—but the smell of paint was quite enough to make anyone seriously ill, in Aunt Beryl's opinion. Even before the sacking was taken off. And when it was ...

There stood the Doll's house, a dark, oily, spinach green, picked out with bright yellow. Its two solid little chimneys, glued on to the roof, were painted red and white, and the door, gleaming with yellow varnish, was like a little slab of toffee. Four windows, real windows, were divided into panes by a broad streak of green. There was actually a tiny porch, too, painted yellow, with big lumps of congealed paint hanging along the edge.

But perfect, perfect little house! Who could possibly mind the smell. It was part of the joy, part of the newness.

"Open it quickly, someone!"

The hook at the side was stuck fast. Pat prized it open with his penknife, and the whole house front swung back, and—there you were, gazing at one and the same moment into the drawing-room and dining-room, the kitchen and two bedrooms. That is the way for a house to open! Why don't all houses open like that? How much more exciting than peering through the slit of a door into a mean little hall with a hat-stand and two umbrellas! That is—isn't it?—what you long to know about a house when you put your hand on the knocker. Perhaps it is the way God opens houses at the dead of night when He is taking a quiet turn with an angel ...

"O-oh!" The Burnell children sounded as though they were in despair. It was too marvellous; it was too much for them. They had never seen anything like it in their lives. All the rooms were papered. There were pictures on the walls, painted on the paper, with gold frames complete. Red carpet covered all the floors except the kitchen; red plush chairs in the drawing-room, green in the dining-room; tables, beds with real bedclothes, a cradle, a stove, a dresser with tiny plates and one big jug. But what Kezia liked more than anything, what she liked frightfully, was the lamp. It stood in the middle of the dining-room table, an exquisite little amber lamp with a white globe. It was even filled all ready for lighting, though, of course, you couldn't light it. But there was something inside that looked like oil and moved when you shook it.

The father and mother dolls, who sprawled very stiff as though they had fainted in the drawing-room, and their two little children asleep upstairs, were really too big for the doll's house. They didn't look as though they belonged. But the lamp was perfect. It seemed to smile at Kezia, to say, "I live here." The lamp was real.

The Burnell children could hardly walk to school fast enough the next morning. They burned to tell everybody, to describe, to—well—to boast about their doll's house before the school-bell rang.

"I'm to tell," said Isabel, "because I'm the eldest. And you two can join in after. But I'm to tell first."

There was nothing to answer. Isabel was bossy, but she was always right, and Lottie and Kezia knew too well the powers that went with being eldest. They brushed through the thick buttercups at the road edge and said nothing.

"And I'm to choose who's to come and see it first. Mother said I might."

For it had been arranged that while the doll's house stood in the courtyard they might ask the girls at school, two at a time, to come and look. Not to stay to tea, of course, or to come traipsing through the house. But just to stand quietly in the courtyard while Isabel pointed out the beauties, and Lottie and Kezia looked pleased ...

But hurry as they might, by the time they had reached the tarred palings of the boys' playground the bell had begun to jangle. They only just had time to whip off their hats and fall into line before the roll was called. Never mind. Isabel tried to make up for it by looking very important and mysterious and by whispering behind her hand to the girls near her, "Got something to tell you at playtime."

Playtime came and Isabel was surrounded. The girls of her class nearly fought to put their arms round her, to walk away with her, to beam flatteringly, to be her special friend. She held quite a court under the huge pine trees at the side of the playground. Nudging, giggling together, the little girls pressed up close. And the only two who stayed outside the ring were the two who were always outside, the little Kelveys. They knew better than to come anywhere near the Burnells.

For the fact was, the school the Burnell children went to was not at all the kind of place their parents would have chosen if there had been any choice. But there was none. It was the only school for miles. And the consequence was all the children of the neighbourhood, the Judge's little girls, the doctor's daughters, the store-keeper's children, the milkman's, were forced to mix together. Not to speak of there being an equal number of rude, rough little boys as well. But the line had to be drawn somewhere. It was drawn at the Kelveys. Many of the children, including the Burnells, were not allowed even to speak to them. They walked past the Kelveys with their heads in the air, and as they set the fashion in all matters of behaviour, the Kelveys were shunned by everybody. Even the teacher had a special voice for them, and a special smile for the other children when Lil Kelvey came up to her desk with a bunch of dreadfully common-looking flowers.

They were the daughters of a spry, hard-working little washerwoman, who went about from house to house by the day. This was awful enough. But where was Mr. Kelvey? Nobody knew for certain. But everybody said he was in prison. So they were the daughters of a washerwoman and a gaolbird. Very nice company for other people's children! And they looked it. Why Mrs. Kelvey made them so conspicuous was hard to understand. The truth was they were dressed in "bits" given to her by the people for whom she worked. Lil, for instance, who was a stout, plain child, with big freckles, came to school in a dress made from a green art-serge table-cloth of the Burnells', with red plush sleeves from the Logans' curtains. Her hat, perched on top of her high forehead, was a grown-up woman's hat, once the property of Miss Lecky, the postmistress. It was turned up at the back and trimmed with a large scarlet quill. What a little guy she looked! It was impossible not to laugh. And her little sister, our Else, wore a long white dress, rather like a nightgown, and a pair of little boy's boots. But whatever our Else wore she would have looked strange. She was a tiny wishbone of a child, with cropped hair and enormous solemn eyes—a little white owl. Nobody had ever seen her smile; she scarcely ever spoke. She went through life holding on to Lil, with a piece of Lil's skirt screwed up in her hand. Where Lil went, our Else followed. In the playground, on the road going to and from school, there was Lil marching in front and our Else holding on behind. Only when she wanted anything, or when she was out of breath, our Else gave Lil a tug, a twitch, and Lil stopped and turned round. The Kelveys never failed to understand each other.

Now they hovered at the edge; you couldn't stop them listening. When the little girls turned round and sneered, Lil, as usual, gave her silly, shamefaced smile, but our Else only looked.

And Isabel's voice, so very proud, went on telling. The carpet made a great sensation, but so did the beds with real bedclothes, and the stove with an oven door.

When she finished Kezia broke in. "You've forgotten the lamp, Isabel."

"Oh, yes," said Isabel, "and there's a teeny little lamp, all made of yellow glass, with a white globe that stands on the dining-room table. You couldn't tell it from a real one."

"The lamp's best of all," cried Kezia. She thought Isabel wasn't making half enough of the little lamp. But nobody paid any attention. Isabel was choosing the two who were to come back with them that afternoon and see it. She chose Emmie Cole and Lena Logan. But when the others knew they were all to have a chance, they couldn't be nice enough to Isabel. One by one they put their arms round Isabel's waist and walked her off. They had something to whisper to her, a secret. "Isabel's *my* friend."

Only the little Kelveys moved away forgotten; there was nothing more for them to hear.

Days passed, and as more children saw the doll's house, the fame of it spread. It became the one subject, the rage. The one question was, "Have you seen Burnells' doll's house? Oh, ain't it lovely!" "Haven't you seen it? Oh, I say!"

Even the dinner hour was given up to talking about it. The little girls sat under the pines eating their thick mutton sandwiches and big slabs of johnny cake spread with butter. While always, as near as they could get, sat the Kelveys, our Else holding on to Lil, listening too, while they chewed their jam sandwiches out of a newspaper soaked with large red blobs.

"Mother," said Kezia, "can't I ask the Kelveys just once?"

"Certainly not, Kezia."

"But why not?"

"Run away, Kezia; you know quite well why not."

At last everybody had seen it except them. On that day the subject rather flagged. It was the dinner hour. The children stood together under the pine trees, and suddenly, as they looked at the Kelveys eating out of their paper, always by themselves, always listening, they wanted to be horrid to them. Emmie Cole started the whisper.

"Lil Kelvey's going to be a servant when she grows up."

"O-oh, how awful!" said Isabel Burnell, and she made eyes at Emmie.

Emmie swallowed in a very meaning way and nodded to Isabel as she'd seen her mother do on those occasions.

"It's true—it's true—it's true," she said.

Then Lena Logan's little eyes snapped. "Shall I ask her?" she whispered.

"Bet you don't," said Jessie May.

"Pooh, I'm not frightened," said Lena. Suddenly she gave a little squeal and danced in front of the other girls. "Watch! Watch me! Watch me now!" said Lena. And sliding, gliding, dragging one foot, giggling behind her hand, Lena went over to the Kelveys.

Lil looked up from her dinner. She wrapped the rest quickly away. Our Else stopped chewing. What was coming now?

"Is it true you're going to be a servant when you grow up, Lil Kelvey?" shrilled Lena.

Dead silence. But instead of answering, Lil only gave her silly, shamefaced smile. She didn't seem to mind the question at all. What a sell for Lena! The girls began to titter.

Lena couldn't stand that. She put her hands on her hips; she shot forward. "Yah, yer father's in prison!" she hissed, spitefully.

This was such a marvellous thing to have said that the little girls rushed away in a body, deeply, deeply excited, wild with joy. Someone found a long rope, and they began skipping. And never did they skip so high, run in and out so fast, or do such daring things as on that morning.

In the afternoon Pat called for the Burnell children with the buggy and they drove home. There were visitors. Isabel and Lottie, who liked visitors, went upstairs to change their pinafores. But Kezia thieved out at the back. Nobody was about; she began to swing on the big white gates of the courtyard. Presently, looking along the road, she saw two little dots. They grew bigger, they were coming towards her. Now she could see that one was in front and one close behind. Now she could see that they were the Kelveys. Kezia stopped swinging. She slipped off the gate as if she was going to run away. Then she hesitated. The Kelveys came nearer, and beside them walked their shadows, very long, stretching right across the road with their heads in the buttercups. Kezia clambered back on the gate; she had made up her mind; she swung out.

"Hullo," she said to the passing Kelveys.

They were so astounded that they stopped. Lil gave her silly smile. Our Else stared.

"You can come and see our doll's house if you want to," said Kezia, and she dragged one toe on the ground. But at that Lil turned red and shook her head quickly.

"Why not?" asked Kezia.

Lil gasped, then she said, "Your ma told our ma you wasn't to speak to us."

"Oh, well," said Kezia. She didn't know what to reply. "It doesn't matter. You can come and see our doll's house all the same. Come on. Nobody's looking."

But Lil shook her head still harder.

"Don't you want to?" asked Kezia.

Suddenly there was a twitch, a tug at Lil's skirt. She turned round. Our Else was looking at her with big, imploring eyes; she was frowning; she wanted to go. For a moment Lil looked at Else very doubtfully. But then our Else twitched her skirt again. She started forward. Kezia led the way. Like two little stray cats they followed across the courtyard to where the doll's house stood.

"There it is," said Kezia.

There was a pause. Lil breathed loudly, almost snorted; our Else was still as stone.

"I'll open it for you," said Kezia kindly. She undid the hook and they looked inside.

"There's the drawing-room and the dining-room, and that's the—"

"Kezia!"

Oh, what a start they gave!

"Kezia!"

It was Aunt Beryl's voice. They turned round. At the back door stood Aunt Beryl, staring as if she couldn't believe what she saw.

"How dare you ask the little Kelveys into the courtyard?" said her cold, furious voice. "You know as well as I do, you're not allowed to talk to them. Run away, children, run away at once. And don't come back again," said Aunt Beryl. And she stepped into the yard and shooed them out as if they were chickens.

"Off you go immediately!" she called, cold and proud.

They did not need telling twice. Burning with shame, shrinking together, Lil huddling along like her mother, our Else dazed, somehow they crossed the big courtyard and squeezed through the white gate.

"Wicked, disobedient little girl!" said Aunt Beryl bitterly to Kezia, and she slammed the doll's house to.

The afternoon had been awful. A letter had come from Willie Brent, a terrifying, threatening letter, saying if she did not meet him that evening in Pulman's Bush, he'd come to the front door and ask the reason why! But now that she had frightened those little rats of Kelveys and given Kezia a good scolding, her heart felt lighter. That ghastly pressure was gone. She went back to the house humming.

When the Kelveys were well out of sight of Burnells', they sat down to rest on a big red drainpipe by the side of the road. Lil's cheeks were still burning; she took off the hat with the quill and held it on her knee. Dreamily they looked over the hay paddocks, past the creek, to the group of wattles where Logan's cows stood waiting to be milked. What were their thoughts?

Presently our Else nudged up close to her sister. But now she had forgotten the cross lady. She put out a finger and stroked her sister's quill; she smiled her rare smile.

"I seen the little lamp," she said, softly.

Then both were silent once more.

—1922

ERNEST HEMINGWAY

Ernest Hemingway's influence can be seen in the objective style of writing he propagated, characterized by sparse sentences devoid of embellishment. Hemingway famously argues for his technique in *Death in the Afternoon* (1932): "If a writer of prose knows enough about what he is writing about he may omit things that he knows and the reader, if the writer is writing truly enough, will have a feeling of those things as strongly as though the writer had stated them. The dignity of movement of an iceberg is due to only one-eighth of it being above water." In 1952, Hemingway was awarded the Pulitzer Prize for his novel *The Old Man and the Sea*, the story of a Cuban fisherman's quest to reel in a giant marlin. In 1954, he was awarded the Nobel Prize in Literature for his "mastery of the art of narrative, most recently demonstrated in *The Old Man and the Sea*, and for the influence that he has exerted on contemporary style."

In 1918, Hemingway travelled to Italy as an ambulance driver for the American Red Cross. His injury and recuperation later that year removed him from service, but the experience inspired his 1929 novel, *A Farewell to Arms*. His first novel, *The Sun Also Rises* (1926), drew from his life as an expatriate in Paris in the 1920s. During the Spanish Civil War (1936–39), Hemingway raised money for the Republican cause and travelled throughout Spain as a journalist. This inspired his greatest commercial success, the 1939 novel *For Whom the Bell Tolls*, a semi-autobiographical story of a young American who fights fascism.

Hemingway's writing reflects his passion for pursuits such as bullfighting, fishing, and hunting, and often examines the cruel legacy of war. In presenting the Nobel Prize to Hemingway, Anders Osterling said: "It may be true that Hemingway's earlier writings display brutal, cynical, and callous sides which may be considered at variance with the Nobel Prize's requirement for a work of an ideal tendency. But on the other hand, he also possesses a heroic pathos which forms the basic element in his awareness of life, a manly love of danger and adventure with a natural admiration for every individual who fights the good fight in a world of reality overshadowed by violence and death."

Hemingway died by suicide in Idaho in 1961, after a period of serious depression.

Hills Like White Elephants

THE HILLS across the valley of the Ebro[1] were long and white. On this side there was no shade and no trees and the station was between two lines of rails in the sun. Close against the side of the station there was the warm shadow of the building and a curtain, made of strings of bamboo beads, hung across the open door into the bar, to keep out flies. The American and the girl with him sat at a table in the shade, outside the building. It was very hot and the express from Barcelona would come in forty minutes. It stopped at this junction for two minutes and went on to Madrid.

"What should we drink?" the girl asked. She had taken off her hat and put it on the table.

"It's pretty hot," the man said.

"Let's drink beer."

"Dos cervezas," the man said into the curtain.

"Big ones?" a woman asked from the doorway.

"Yes. Two big ones."

The woman brought two glasses of beer and two felt pads. She put the felt pads and the beer glasses on the table and looked at the man and the girl. The girl was looking off at the line of hills. They were white in the sun and the country was brown and dry.

"They look like white elephants," she said.

"I've never seen one," the man drank his beer.

"No, you wouldn't have."

"I might have," the man said. "Just because you say I wouldn't have doesn't prove anything."

The girl looked at the bead curtain. "They've painted something on it," she said. "What does it say?"

"Anis del Toro. It's a drink."

"Could we try it?"

---

1   Second largest river in Spain, rising in the Cantabrian Mountains and flowing to the Mediterranean Sea.

The man called "Listen" through the curtain. The woman came out from the bar.

"Four reales."[2]

"We want two Anis del Toro."

"With water?"

"Do you want it with water?"

"I don't know," the girl said. "Is it good with water?"

"It's all right."

"You want them with water?" asked the woman.

"Yes, with water."

"It tastes like licorice," the girl said and put the glass down.

"That's the way with everything."

"Yes," said the girl. "Everything tastes of licorice. Especially all the things you've waited so long for, like absinthe."[3]

"Oh, cut it out."

"You started it," the girl said. "I was being amused. I was having a fine time."

"Well, let's try and have a fine time."

"All right. I was trying. I said the mountains looked like white elephants. Wasn't that bright?"

"That was bright."

"I wanted to try this new drink. That's all we do, isn't it—look at things and try new drinks?"

"I guess so."

The girl looked across at the hills.

"They're lovely hills," she said. "They don't really look like white elephants. I just meant the coloring of their skin through the trees."

"Should we have another drink?"

"All right."

The warm wind blew the bead curtain against the table.

"The beer's nice and cool," the man said.

"It's lovely," the girl said.

---

2   Obsolete units of Spanish currency. Eight reales made up one Spanish dollar.

3   Liquor made in part from the anise plant. Like other liquors made with anise (anis, sambuka, ouzo, raki, etc.), absinthe tastes similar to licorice, and turns from clear to cloudy when water is added to it. Unlike other anise-flavoured drinks, absinthe also contains the herb grande wormwood, which is toxic when consumed in large quantities; the drink was widely believed to enhance creativity, and became associated with bohemian culture. Absinthe was banned in North America and much of Europe—though not in Spain—in the early twentieth century.

"It's really an awfully simple operation, Jig," the man said. "It's not really an operation at all."

The girl looked at the ground the table legs rested on.

"I know you wouldn't mind it, Jig. It's really not anything. It's just to let the air in."

The girl did not say anything.

"I'll go with you and I'll stay with you all the time. They just let the air in and then it's all perfectly natural."

"Then what will we do afterward?"

"We'll be fine afterward. Just like we were before."

"What makes you think so?"

"That's the only thing that bothers us. It's the only thing that's made us unhappy."

The girl looked at the bead curtain, put her hand out and took hold of two of the strings of beads.

"And you think then we'll be all right and be happy."

"I know we will. You don't have to be afraid. I've known lots of people that have done it."

"So have I," said the girl. "And afterwards they were all so happy."

"Well," the man said, "if you don't want to you don't have to. I wouldn't have you do it if you didn't want to. But I know it's perfectly simple."

"And you really want to?"

"I think it's the best thing to do. But I don't want you to do it if you don't really want to."

"And if I do it you'll be happy and things will be like they were and you'll love me?"

"I love you now. You know I love you."

"I know. But if I do it, then it will be nice again if I say things are like white elephants, and you'll like it?"

"I'll love it. I love it now but I just can't think about it. You know how I get when I worry."

"If I do it you won't ever worry?"

"I won't worry about that because it's perfectly simple."

"Then I'll do it. Because I don't care about me."

"What do you mean?"

"I don't care about me."

"Well, I care about you."

"Oh, yes. But I don't care about me. And I'll do it and then everything will be fine."

"I don't want you to do it if you feel that way."

The girl stood up and walked to the end of the station. Across, on the other side, were fields of grain and trees along the banks of the Ebro. Far away, beyond the river, were mountains. The shadow of a cloud moved across the field of grain and she saw the river through the trees.

"And we could have all this," she said. "And we could have everything and every day we make it more impossible."

"What did you say?"

"I said we could have everything."

"We can have everything."

"No, we can't."

"We can have the whole world."

"No, we can't."

"We can go everywhere."

"No, we can't. It isn't ours any more."

"It's ours."

"No, it isn't. And once they take it away, you never get it back."

"But they haven't taken it away."

"We'll wait and see."

"Come on back in the shade," he said. "You mustn't feel that way."

"I don't feel any way," the girl said. "I just know things."

"I don't want you to do anything that you don't want to do—"

"Nor that isn't good for me," she said. "I know. Could we have another beer?"

"All right. But you've got to realize—"

"I realize," the girl said. "Can't we maybe stop talking?"

They sat down at the table and the girl looked across at the hills on the dry side of the valley and the man looked at her and at the table.

"You've got to realize," he said, "that I don't want you to do it if you don't want to. I'm perfectly willing to go through with it if it means anything to you."

"Doesn't it mean anything to you? We could get along."

"Of course it does. But I don't want anybody but you. I don't want any one else. And I know it's perfectly simple."

"Yes, you know it's perfectly simple."

"It's all right for you to say that, but I do know it."

"Would you do something for me now?"

"I'd do anything for you."

"Would you please please please please please please please stop talking?"

He did not say anything but looked at the bags against the wall of the station. There were labels on them from all the hotels where they had spent nights.

"But I don't want you to," he said, "I don't care anything about it."

"I'll scream," the girl said.

The woman came out through the curtains with two glasses of beer and put them down on the damp felt pads. "The train comes in five minutes," she said.

"What did she say?" asked the girl.

"That the train is coming in five minutes."

The girl smiled brightly at the woman, to thank her.

"I'd better take the bags over to the other side of the station," the man said. She smiled at him.

"All right. Then come back and we'll finish the beer."

He picked up the two heavy bags and carried them around the station to the other tracks. He looked up the tracks but could not see the train. Coming back, he walked through the barroom, where people waiting for the train were drinking. He drank an Anis at the bar and looked at the people. They were all waiting reasonably for the train. He went out through the bead curtain. She was sitting at the table and smiled at him.

"Do you feel better?" he asked.

"I feel fine," she said. "There's nothing wrong with me. I feel fine."

—1927

HISAYE YAMAMOTO

Hisaye Yamamoto's life as a second-generation Japanese American (or *nisei*) was drastically altered when, in 1942, the American government relocated and incarcerated over 100,000 Japanese nationals and Americans of Japanese heritage who lived on the west coast of the United States. Along with her family, Yamamoto was forced to move from Redondo Beach, California, where she was born in 1921, to live in internment camps in Poston, Arizona. Yamamoto had begun publishing in newspapers as a teenager, and, in spite of the hardship, she continued writing. She was a journalist for the internment camp newspaper, the *Poston Chronicle*, which also published her serial mystery "Death Rides the Rails to Poston."

After World War II ended and the camps were dissolved, Yamamoto moved to Los Angeles. There, she worked from 1945–48 as a columnist for the *Los Angeles Tribune*, a weekly newspaper with a primarily African American readership; it was the only newspaper in Los Angeles that would hire a Japanese writer. In 1948, she sold her first story, "The High-Heeled Shoes," to *Partisan Review*; in 1950 she was awarded a John Hay Whitney Foundation Opportunity Fellowship, which gave her the financial freedom to write full-time for a year. She then turned down a fellowship from Stanford to volunteer with the Catholic Worker religious movement at a rehabilitation farm in Staten Island, New York.

In 1955, Yamamoto married, returned to Los Angeles, and began having children; for a time she listed her profession as "housewife." She continued writing short stories, however, which were published in periodicals such as *Harper's Bazaar*, *Kenyon Review*, and *Arizona Quarterly*. As her stories accumulated, they received more and more critical attention, resulting in accolades such as an American Book Award for Lifetime Achievement from the Before Columbus foundation in 1986.

Yamamoto's stories were eventually collected in *Seventeen Syllables: 5 Stories of Japanese American Life* (published in Japan in 1985); the works in the collection have been described by the scholar Charles L. Crow as "rich, emotionally complex and tightly controlled." An expanded edition with four more stories was released in 2001. Yamamoto died in 2011 at the age of 89, a year after receiving the 2010 Asian American Writers' Workshop's Lifetime Achievement Award. In its announcement of the award, the AAWW acclaimed her "brutal, efficient fables of race, saturated with the social subtext of the American small town." While her work captures the specific experiences of twentieth-century Japanese Americans, the committee wrote, "Yamamoto's stories always feel relevant to the present."

Seventeen Syllables

THE FIRST Rosie knew that her mother had taken to writing poems was one evening when she finished one and read it aloud for her daughter's approval. It was about cats, and Rosie pretended to understand it thoroughly and appreciate it no end, partly because she hesitated to disillusion her mother about the quantity and quality of Japanese she had learned in all the years now that she had been going to Japanese school every Saturday (and Wednesday, too, in the summer). Even so, her mother must have been skeptical about the depth of Rosie's understanding, because she explained afterwards about the kind of poem she was trying to write.

See, Rosie, she said, it was a *haiku*, a poem in which she must pack all her meaning into seventeen syllables only, which were divided into three lines of five, seven, and five syllables. In the one she had just read, she had tried to capture the charm of a kitten, as well as comment on the superstition that owning a cat of three colors meant good luck.

"Yes, yes, I understand. How utterly lovely," Rosie said, and her mother, either satisfied or seeing through the deception and resigned, went back to composing.

The truth was that Rosie was lazy; English lay ready on the tongue but Japanese had to be searched for and examined, and even then put forth tentatively (probably to meet with laughter). It was so much easier to say yes, yes, even when one meant no, no. Besides, this was what was in her mind to say: I was looking through one of your magazines from Japan last night, Mother, and towards the back I found some *haiku* in English that delighted me. There was one that made me giggle off and on until I fell asleep—

> *It is morning, and lo!*
> *I lie awake, comme il faut,*[1]
> *sighing for some dough.*

---

1   French: As it should be; in keeping with social norms.

Now, how to reach her mother, how to communicate the melancholy song? Rosie knew formal Japanese by fits and starts, her mother had even less English, no French. It was much more possible to say yes, yes.

It developed that her mother was writing the *haiku* for a daily newspaper, the *Mainichi Shimbun*, that was published in San Francisco. Los Angeles, to be sure, was closer to the farming community in which the Hayashi family lived and several Japanese vernaculars were printed there, but Rosie's parents said they preferred the tone of the northern paper. Once a week, the *Mainichi* would have a section devoted to *haiku*, and her mother became an extravagant contributor, taking for herself the blossoming pen name, Ume Hanazono.

So Rosie and her father lived for awhile with two women, her mother and Ume Hanazono. Her mother (Tome Hayashi by name) kept house, cooked, washed, and along with her husband and the Carrascos, the Mexican family hired for the harvest, did her ample share of picking tomatoes out in the sweltering fields and boxing them in tidy strata in the cool packing shed. Ume Hanazono, who came to life after the dinner dishes were done, was an earnest, muttering stranger who often neglected speaking when spoken to and stayed busy at the parlor table as late as midnight scribbling with pencil on scratch paper or carefully copying characters on good paper with her fat, pale green Parker.

The new interest had some repercussions on the household routine. Before, Rosie had been accustomed to her parents and herself taking their hot baths early and going to bed almost immediately afterwards, unless her parents challenged each other to a game of flower cards or unless company dropped in. Now if her father wanted to play cards, he had to resort to solitaire (at which he always cheated fearlessly), and if a group of friends came over, it was bound to contain someone who was also writing *haiku*, and the small assemblage would be split in two, her father entertaining the nonliterary members and her mother comparing ecstatic notes with the visiting poet.

If they went out, it was more of the same thing. But Ume Hanazono's life span, even for a poet's, was very brief—perhaps three months at most.

One night they went over to see the Hayano family in the neighboring town to the west, an adventure both painful and attractive to Rosie. It was attractive because there were four Hayano girls, all lovely and each one named after a season of the year (Haru, Natsu, Aki, Fuyu), painful because something had been wrong with Mrs. Hayano ever since the birth of her first child. Rosie would sometimes watch Mrs. Hayano, reputed to have been the belle of her native village, making her way about a room, stooped, slowly shuffling, violently trembling (*always* trembling), and she would be reminded that this woman, in this same condition, had carried and given issue to three babies. She would look wonderingly at Mr. Hayano, handsome, tall, and strong, and she would look at her four pretty friends. But it was not a matter she could come to any decision about.

On this visit, however, Mrs. Hayano sat all evening in the rocker, as motionless and unobtrusive as it was possible for her to be, and Rosie found the greater part of the evening practically anesthetic. Too, Rosie spent most of it in the girls' room, because Haru, the garrulous one, said almost as soon as the bows and other greetings were over, "Oh, you must see my new coat!"

It was a pale plaid of grey, sand, and blue, with an enormous collar, and Rosie, seeing nothing special in it, said, "Gee, how nice."

"Nice?" said Haru, indignantly. "Is that all you can say about it? It's gorgeous! And so cheap, too. Only seventeen-ninety eight, because it was a sale. The saleslady said it was twenty-five dollars regular."

"Gee," said Rosie. Natsu, who never said much and when she said anything said it shyly, fingered the coat covetously and Haru pulled it away.

"Mine," she said, putting it on. She minced in the aisle between the two large beds and smiled happily. "Let's see how your mother likes it."

She broke into the front room and the adult conversation and went to stand in front of Rosie's mother, while the rest watched from the door. Rosie's mother was properly envious. "May I inherit it when you're through with it?"

Haru, pleased, giggled and said yes, she could, but Natsu reminded gravely from the door, "You promised me, Haru."

Everyone laughed but Natsu, who shamefacedly retreated into the bedroom. Haru came in laughing, taking off the coat. "We were only kidding, Natsu," she said. "Here, you try it on now."

After Natsu buttoned herself into the coat, inspected herself solemnly in the bureau mirror, and reluctantly shed it, Rosie, Aki, and Fuyu got their turns, and Fuyu, who was eight, drowned in it while her sisters and Rosie doubled up in amusement. They all went into the front room later, because Haru's mother quaveringly called to her to fix the tea and rice cakes and open a can of sliced peaches for everybody. Rosie noticed that her mother and Mr. Hayano were talking together at the little table—they were discussing a *haiku* that Mr. Hayano was planning to send to the *Mainichi*, while her father was sitting at one end of the sofa looking through a copy of *Life*, the new picture magazine. Occasionally, her father would comment on a photograph, holding it toward Mrs. Hayano and speaking to her as he always did—loudly, as though he thought someone such as she must surely be at least a trifle deaf also.

The five girls had their refreshments at the kitchen table, and it was while Rosie was showing the sisters her trick of swallowing peach slices without chewing (she chased each slippery crescent down with a swig of tea) that her father brought his empty teacup and untouched saucer to the sink and said, "Come on, Rosie, we're going home now."

"Already?" asked Rosie.

"Work tomorrow," he said.

He sounded irritated, and Rosie, puzzled, gulped one last yellow slice and stood up to go, while the sisters began protesting, as was their wont.

"We have to get up at five-thirty," he told them, going into the front room quickly, so that they did not have their usual chance to hang onto his hands and plead for an extension of time.

Rosie, following, saw that her mother and Mr. Hayano were sipping tea and still talking together, while Mrs. Hayano concentrated, quivering, on raising the handleless Japanese cup to her lips with both her hands and lowering it back to her lap. Her father, saying nothing, went out the door, onto the bright porch, and down the steps. Her mother looked up and asked, "Where is he going?"

"Where is he going?" Rosie said. "He said we were going home now."

"Going home?" Her mother looked with embarrassment at Mr. Hayano and his absorbed wife and then forced a smile. "He must be tired," she said.

Haru was not giving up yet. "May Rosie stay overnight?" she asked, and Natsu, Aki, and Fuyu came to reinforce their sister's plea by helping her make a circle around Rosie's mother. Rosie, for once having no desire to stay was relieved when her mother, apologizing to the perturbed Mr. and Mrs. Hayano for her father's abruptness at the same time, managed to shake her head no at the quartet, kindly but adamant, so that they broke their circle and let her go.

Rosie's father looked ahead into the windshield as the two joined him. "I'm sorry," her mother said. "You must be tired." Her father, stepping on the starter, said nothing. "You know how I get when it's *haiku*," she continued, "I forget what time it is." He only grunted.

As they rode homeward silently, Rosie, sitting between, felt a rush of hate for both—for her mother for begging, for her father for denying her mother. I wish this old Ford would crash, right now, she thought, then immediately, no, no, I wish my father would laugh, but it was too late: already the vision had passed through her mind of the green pick-up crumpled in the dark against one of the mighty eucalyptus trees they were just riding past, of the three contorted, bleeding bodies, one of them hers.

Rosie ran between two patches of tomatoes, her heart working more rambunctiously than she had ever known it to. How lucky it was that Aunt Taka and Uncle Gimpachi had come tonight, though, how very lucky. Otherwise she might not have really kept her half-promise to meet Jesus Carrasco. Jesus was going to be a senior in September at the same school she went to, and his parents were the ones helping with the tomatoes this year. She and Jesus, who hardly remembered seeing each other at Cleveland High where there were so many other people and two whole grades between them, had become great friends this summer—he always had a joke for her when he periodically drove the loaded pick-up up from the fields to the shed where she was usually sorting while her mother and father did the packing, and they laughed a great deal together over infinitesimal repartee during the afternoon break for chilled watermelon or ice cream in the shade of the shed.

What she enjoyed most was racing him to see who could finish picking a double row first. He, who could work faster, would tease her by slowing down until she thought she would surely pass him this time, then speeding up furiously to leave her several sprawling vines behind. Once he had made her screech hideously by crossing over, while her back was turned, to place atop the tomatoes in her green-stained bucket a truly monstrous, pale green worm (it had looked more like an infant snake). And it was when they had finished a contest this morning, after she had pantingly pointed a green finger at the immature tomatoes evident in the lugs at the end of his row and he had returned the accusation (with justice), that he had startlingly brought up the matter of their possibly meeting outside the range of both their parents' dubious eyes.

"What for?" she had asked.

"I've got a secret I want to tell you," he said.

"Tell me now," she demanded.

"It won't be ready till tonight," he said.

She laughed. "Tell me tomorrow then."

"It'll be gone tomorrow," he threatened.

"Well, for seven hakes, what is it?" she had asked, more than twice, and when he had suggested that the packing shed would be an appropriate place to find out, she had cautiously answered maybe. She had not been certain she was going to keep the appointment until the arrival of mother's sister and her husband. Their coming seemed a sort of signal of permission, of grace, and she had definitely made up her mind to lie and leave as she was bowing them welcome.

So as soon as everyone appeared settled back for the evening, she announced loudly that she was going to the privy outside, "I'm going to the *benjo*!" and slipped out the door. And now that she was actually on her way, her heart pumped in such an undisciplined way that she could hear it with her ears. It's because I'm running, she told herself, slowing to a walk. The shed was up ahead, one more patch away, in the middle of the fields. Its bulk, looming in the dimness, took on a sinisterness that was funny when Rosie reminded herself that it was only a wooden frame with a canvas roof and three canvas walls that made a slapping noise on breezy days.

Jesus was sitting on the narrow plank that was the sorting platform and she went around to the other side and jumped backwards to seat herself on the rim of a packing stand. "Well, tell me," she said without greeting, thinking her voice sounded reassuringly familiar.

"I saw you coming out the door," Jesus said. "I heard you running part of the way, too."

"Uh-huh," Rosie said. "Now tell me the secret."

"I was afraid you wouldn't come," he said.

Rosie delved around the chicken-wire bottom of the stall for number two tomatoes, ripe, which she was sitting beside, and came up with a left-over that felt edible. She bit into it and began sucking out the pulp and seeds. "I'm here," she pointed out.

"Rosie, are you sorry you came?"

"Sorry? What for?" she said. "You said you were going to tell me something."

"I will, I will," Jesus said, but his voice contained disappointment, and Rosie fleetingly felt the older of the two, realizing a brand-new power which vanished without category under her recognition.

"I have to go back in a minute," she said. "My aunt and uncle are here from Wintersburg. I told them I was going to the privy."

Jesus laughed. "You funny thing," he said. "You slay me!"

"Just because you have a bathroom *inside*," Rosie said. "Come on, tell me."

Chuckling, Jesus came around to lean on the stand facing her. They still could not see each other very clearly, but Rosie noticed that Jesus became very sober again as he took the hollow tomato from her hand and dropped it back into the stall. When he took hold of her empty hand, she could find no words to protest; her vocabulary had become distressingly constricted and she thought desperately that all that remained intact now was yes and no and oh, and even these few sounds would not easily out. Thus, kissed by Jesus, Rosie fell for the first time entirely victim to a helplessness delectable beyond speech. But the terrible, beautiful sensation lasted no more than a second, and the reality of Jesus' lips and tongue and teeth and hands made her pull away with such strength that she nearly tumbled.

Rosie stopped running as she approached the lights from the windows of home. How long since she had left? She could not guess, but gasping yet, she went to the privy in back and locked herself in. Her own breathing deafened her in the dark, close space, and she sat and waited until she could hear at last the nightly calling of the frogs and crickets. Even then, all she could think to say was oh, my, and the pressure of Jesus' face against her face would not leave.

No one had missed her in the parlor, however, and Rosie walked in and through quickly, announcing that she was next going to take a bath. "Your father's in the bathhouse," her mother said, and Rosie, in her room, recalled that she had not seen him when she entered. There had been only Aunt Taka and Uncle Gimpachi with her mother at the table, drinking tea. She got her robe and straw sandals and crossed the parlor again to go outside. Her mother was telling them about the *haiku* competition in the *Mainichi* and the poem she had entered.

Rosie met her father coming out of the bathhouse. "Are you through, Father?" she asked. "I was going to ask you to scrub my back."

"Scrub your own back," he said shortly, going toward the main house.

"What have I done now?" she yelled after him. She suddenly felt like doing a lot of yelling. But he did not answer, and she went into the bathhouse. Turning on the dangling light, she removed her denims and T-shirt and threw them in the big carton for dirty clothes standing next to the washing machine. Her other things she took with her into the bath compartment to wash after her bath. After she had scooped a basin of hot water from the square wooden tub, she sat on the grey cement of the floor and soaped herself at exaggerated leisure, singing "Red Sails in the Sunset" at the top of her voice and using da-da-da where she suspected her words. Then, standing up, still singing, for she was possessed by the notion that any attempt now to analyze would result in spoilage and she believed that the larger her volume the less she would be able to hear herself think, she obtained more hot water and poured it on until she was free of lather. Only then did she allow herself to step into the steaming vat, one leg first, then the remainder of her body inch by inch until the water no longer stung and she could move around at will.

She took a long time soaking, afterwards remembering to go around outside to stoke the embers of the tin-lined fireplace beneath the tub and to throw on a few more sticks so that the water might keep its heat for her mother, and when she finally returned to the parlor, she found her mother still talking *haiku* with her aunt and uncle, the three of them on another round of tea. Her father was nowhere in sight.

At Japanese school the next day (Wednesday, it was), Rosie was grave and giddy by turns. Preoccupied at her desk in the row for students on Book Eight, she made up for it at recess by performing wild mimicry for the benefit of her friend Chizuko. She held her nose and whined a witticism or two in what she considered was the manner of Fred Allen; she assumed intoxication and a British accent to go over the climax of the Rudy Vallee recording of the pub conversation about William Ewart Gladstone; she was the child Shirley Temple piping, "On the Good Ship Lollipop"; she was the gentleman soprano of the Four Inkspots trilling, "If I Didn't Care."[2] And she felt reasonably satisfied when Chizuko wept and gasped, "Oh, Rosie, you ought to be in the movies!"

Her father came after her at noon, bringing her sandwiches of minced ham and two nectarines to eat while she rode, so that she could pitch right into the sorting when they got home. The lugs were piling up, he said, and the ripe tomatoes in them would probably have to be taken to the cannery tomorrow if they were not ready for the produce haulers tonight. "This heat's not doing them any good. And we've got no time for a break today."

It *was* hot, probably the hottest day of the year, and Rosie's blouse stuck damply to her back even under the protection of the canvas. But she worked as efficiently as a flawless machine and kept the stalls heaped, with one part of her mind listening in to the parental murmuring about the heat and the tomatoes and with another part planning the exact words she would say to Jesus when he drove up with the first load of the afternoon. But when at last she saw that the pick-up was coming, her hands went berserk and the tomatoes started falling in the wrong stalls, and her father said, "Hey, hey! Rosie, watch what you're doing!"

"Well, I have to go to the *benjo*," she said, hiding panic.

"Go in the weeds over there," he said, only half-joking.

"Oh, Father!" she protested.

"Oh, go on home," her mother said. "We'll make out for awhile."

In the privy Rosie peered through a knothole toward the fields, watching as much as she could of Jesus. Happily she thought she saw him look in the direction of the house from time to time before he finished unloading and went back toward the patch where his mother and father worked. As she was heading for the shed, a very presentable black car purred up the dirt driveway to the house and its driver motioned to her. Was this the Hayashi home, he wanted to know. She nodded. Was she a Hayashi? Yes, she said, thinking that he was a good-looking man. He got out of the car with a huge, flat package and she saw that he warmly wore a business suit. "I have something here for your mother then," he said, in a more elegant Japanese than she was used to.

---

2   Fred Allen (1894–1956) was a popular radio comedian; Rudy Vallee (1901–86) was a popular singer in the 1920s; William E. Gladstone (1809–98) led the Liberal Party in Britain and was prime minister for many years; Shirley Temple (1928–2014) was a famous Hollywood child actor; The Ink Spots were a vocal quartet popular in the 1930s and 1940s.

She told him where her mother was and he came along with her, patting his face with an immaculate white handkerchief and saying something about the coolness of San Francisco. To her surprised mother and father, he bowed and introduced himself as, among other things, the *haiku* editor of the *Mainichi Shimbun*, saying that since he had been coming as far as Los Angeles anyway, he had decided to bring her the first prize she had won in the recent contest.

"First prize?" her mother echoed, believing and not believing, pleased and overwhelmed. Handed the package with a bow, she bobbed her head up and down numerous times to express her utter gratitude.

"It is nothing much," he added, "but I hope it will serve as a token of our great appreciation for your contributions and our great admiration of your considerable talent."

"I am not worthy," she said, falling easily into his style. "It is I who should make some sign of my humble thanks for being permitted to contribute."

"No, no, to the contrary," he said, bowing again.

But Rosie's mother insisted, and then saying that she knew she was being unorthodox, she asked if she might open the package because her curiosity was so great. Certainly she might. In fact, he would like her reaction to it, for personally, it was one of his favorite *Hiroshiges*.[3]

Rosie thought it was a pleasant picture, which looked to have been sketched with delicate quickness. There were pink clouds, containing some graceful calligraphy, and a sea that was a pale blue except at the edges, containing four sampans[4] with indications of people in them. Pines edged the water and on the far-off beach there was a cluster of thatched huts towered over by pine-dotted mountains of grey and blue. The frame was scalloped and gilt.

After Rosie's mother pronounced it without peer and somewhat prodded her father into nodding agreement, she said Mr. Kuroda must at least have a cup of tea after coming all this way, and although Mr. Kuroda did not want to impose, he soon agreed that a cup of tea would be refreshing and went along with her to the house, carrying the picture for her.

"Ha, your mother's crazy!" Rosie's father said, and Rosie laughed uneasily as she resumed judgment on the tomatoes. She had emptied six lugs when he broke into an imaginary conversation with Jesus to tell her to go and remind her mother of the tomatoes, and she went slowly.

Mr. Kuroda was in his shirtsleeves expounding some *haiku* theory as he munched a rice cake, and her mother was rapt. Abashed in the great man's

---

3   Japanese artist Ando Hiroshige (1797–1858) is perhaps best-known for his colour woodblock prints of landscapes.

4   A type of small boat propelled by oars or a sail.

presence, Rosie stood next to her mother's chair until her mother looked up inquiringly, and then she started to whisper the message, but her mother pushed her gently away and reproached, "You are not being very polite to our guest."

"Father says the tomatoes ..." Rosie said aloud, smiling foolishly.

"Tell him I shall only be a minute," her mother said, speaking the language of Mr. Kuroda.

When Rosie carried the reply to her father, he did not seem to hear and she said again, "Mother says she'll be back in a minute."

"All right, all right," he nodded, and they worked again in silence. But suddenly, her father uttered an incredible noise, exactly like the cork of a bottle popping, and the next Rosie knew, he was stalking angrily toward the house, almost running in fact, and she chased after him crying, "Father! Father! What are you going to do?"

He stopped long enough to order her back to the shed. "Never mind!" he shouted. "Get on with the sorting!"

And from the place in the fields where she stood, frightened and vacillating, Rosie saw her father enter the house. Soon Mr. Kuroda came out alone, putting on his coat. Mr. Kuroda got into his car and backed out down the driveway onto the highway. Next her father emerged, also alone, something in his arms (it was the picture, she realized), and, going over to the bathhouse woodpile, he threw the picture on the ground and picked up the axe. Smashing the picture, glass and all (she heard the explosion faintly), he reached over for the kerosene that was used to encourage the bath fire and poured it over the wreckage. I am dreaming, Rosie said to herself, I am dreaming, but her father, having made sure that his act of cremation was irrevocable, was even then returning to the fields.

Rosie ran past him and toward the house. What had become of her mother? She burst into the parlor and found her mother at the back window watching the dying fire. They watched together until there remained only a feeble smoke under the blazing sun. Her mother was very calm.

"Do you know why I married your father?" she said without turning.

"No," said Rosie. It was the most frightening question she had ever been called upon to answer. Don't tell me now, she wanted to say, tell me tomorrow, tell me next week, don't tell me today. But she knew she would be told now, that the telling would combine with the other violence of the hot afternoon to level her life, her world to the very ground.

It was like a story out of the magazines illustrated in sepia, which she had consumed so greedily for a period until the information had somehow reached her that those wretchedly unhappy autobiographies, offered to her as the testimonials of living men and women, were largely inventions: Her mother, at nineteen, had come to America and married her father as an alternative to suicide.

At eighteen she had been in love with the first son of one of the well-to-do families in her village. The two had met whenever and wherever they could, secretly, because it would not have done for his family to see him favor her—her father had no money; he was a drunkard and a gambler besides. She had learned she was with child; an excellent match had already been arranged for her lover. Despised by her family, she had given premature birth to a stillborn son, who would be seventeen now. Her family did not turn her out, but she could no longer project herself in any direction without refreshing in them the memory of her indiscretion. She wrote to Aunt Taka, her favorite sister in America, threatening to kill herself if Aunt Taka would not send for her. Aunt Taka hastily arranged a marriage with a young man of whom she knew, but lately arrived from Japan, a young man of simple mind, it was said, but of kindly heart. The young man was never told why his unseen betrothed was so eager to hasten the day of meeting.

The story was told perfectly, with neither groping for words nor untoward passion. It was as though her mother had memorized it by heart, reciting it to herself so many times over that its nagging vileness had long since gone.

"I had a brother then?" Rosie asked, for this was what seemed to matter now; she would think about the other later, she assured herself, pushing back the illumination which threatened all that darkness that had hitherto been merely mysterious or even glamorous. "A half-brother?"

"Yes."

"I would have liked a brother," she said.

Suddenly, her mother knelt on the floor and took her by the wrists. "Rosie," she said urgently, "Promise me you will never marry!" Shocked more by the request than the revelation, Rosie stared at her mother's face. Jesus, Jesus, she called silently, not certain whether she was invoking the help of the son of Carrascos or of God, until there returned sweetly the memory of Jesus' hand, how it had touched her and where. Still her mother waited for an answer, holding her wrists so tightly that her hands were going numb. She tried to pull free. Promise, her mother whispered fiercely, promise. Yes, yes, I promise, Rosie said. But for an instant she turned away, and her mother, hearing the familiar glib agreement, released her. Oh, you, you, you, her eyes and twisted mouth said, you fool. Rosie, covering her face, began at last to cry, and the embrace and consoling hand came much later than she expected.

—1949

JAMES BALDWIN

Celebrated for his achievements as a prose stylist and for his incisive examinations of American society, James Baldwin had a controversial career as a novelist and essayist and as a prominent contributor to the American Civil Rights Movement of the 1950s and 1960s. Born in New York City in 1924, Baldwin was the eldest child in a family of nine children. His family suffered from severe poverty, and Baldwin took on a large portion of the responsibility for the care of his siblings. From junior high school onward, Baldwin was writing, contributing to student publications, and fervently reading and re-reading Harriet Beecher Stowe's *Uncle Tom's Cabin* and works by Charles Dickens.

Upon graduating from high school, Baldwin moved to Greenwich Village in 1943, and for five years worked by day and wrote by night. In 1948, he published his first short story, "Previous Condition," and, on the strength of his writing, won a Rosenwald Fellowship. Hoping to escape the oppression he experienced in America both as a Black man and as a gay man, Baldwin decided to move to Paris with "holes in his socks and $40 in his pocket."[1]

Baldwin never returned to live permanently in America again, but visited often, living, in his own words, as a "commuter" for the rest of his life. He quickly became part of the expatriate Black Paris community known as "la Rive Noire." His first novel, *Go Tell It on the Mountain* (1953), was a critical success but not a financial one, and he worked as a journalist in order to support himself. In 1957, he returned to the United States to report on the American South. His essays and journalistic pieces catapulted him to national prominence; he lectured and was present at major Civil Rights events including the 1963 March on Washington. He came in contact with major Civil Rights figures such as Martin Luther King, Jr., and later Malcolm X,

---

1 James Campbell, *Exiled in Paris: Richard Wright, James Baldwin, Samuel Beckett, and Others on the Left Bank* (Berkeley: U of California P, 2003) 23.

Angela Davis, and Huey Newton, and for a time was regarded as one of the most important intellectuals of the Civil Rights Movement.

His political presence and literary career reached a high point in 1963 with the publication of *The Fire Next Time*, a non-fiction examination of race, religion, and American history that remains one of the most influential works of the Civil Rights era. This work's success allowed him financial stability for the first time. His work in later decades, however, was not immediately as well received, in part because it openly explored the uneasy complexities of racial oppression and the subject of love between men. Baldwin lived the remainder of his life primarily in Turkey and France, where in 1986 he received the French Legion of Honour. In 1987, in St. Paul de Vence, France, he died of cancer.

Sonny's Blues

I READ about it in the paper, in the subway, on my way to work. I read it, and I couldn't believe it, and I read it again. Then perhaps I just stared at it, at the newsprint spelling out his name, spelling out the story. I stared at it in the swinging lights of the subway car, and in the faces and bodies of the people, and in my own face, trapped in the darkness which roared outside.

It was not to be believed and I kept telling myself that, as I walked from the subway station to the high school. And at the same time I couldn't doubt it. I was scared, scared for Sonny. He became real to me again. A great block of ice got settled in my belly and kept melting there slowly all day long, while I taught my classes algebra. It was a special kind of ice. It kept melting, sending trickles of ice water all up and down my veins, but it never got less. Sometimes it hardened and seemed to expand until I felt my guts were going to come spilling out or that I was going to choke or scream. This would always be at a moment when I was remembering some specific thing Sonny had once said or done.

When he was about as old as the boys in my classes his face had been bright and open, there was a lot of copper in it; and he'd had wonderfully direct brown eyes, and great gentleness and privacy. I wondered what he looked like now. He had been picked up, the evening before, in a raid on an apartment downtown, for peddling and using heroin.

I couldn't believe it but what I mean by that is that I couldn't find any room for it anywhere inside me, I had kept it outside me for a long time. I hadn't wanted to know. I had had suspicions, but I didn't name them. I kept putting them away. I told myself that Sonny was wild, but he wasn't crazy. And he'd always been a good boy, he hadn't ever turned hard or evil or disrespectful, the way kids can, so quick, so quick, especially in Harlem. I didn't want to believe that I'd ever see my brother going down, coming to nothing, all that light in his face gone out, in the condition I'd already seen so many others. Yet it had happened and here I was, talking about algebra to a lot of boys who might, every one of them for all I knew, be popping off needles every time they went to the head. Maybe it did more for them than algebra could.

I was sure that the first time Sonny had ever had horse,[2] he couldn't have been much older than these boys were now. These boys, now, were living as we'd been living then, they were growing up with a rush and their heads bumped abruptly against the low ceiling of their actual possibilities. They were filled with rage. All they really knew were two darknesses, the darkness of their lives, which was now closing in on them, and the darkness of the movies, which had blinded them to that other darkness, and in which they now, vindictively, dreamed, at once more together than they were at any other time, and more alone.

When the last bell rang, the last class ended, I let out my breath. It seemed I'd been holding it for all that time. My clothes were wet—I may have looked as though I'd been sitting in a steam bath, all dressed up, all afternoon. I sat alone in the classroom a long time. I listened to the boys outside, downstairs, shouting and cursing and laughing. Their laughter struck me for perhaps the first time. It was not the joyous laughter which—God knows why—one associates with children. It was mocking and insular, its intent was to denigrate. It was disenchanted, and in this, also, lay the authority of their curses. Perhaps I was listening to them because I was thinking about my brother and in them I heard my brother. And myself.

One boy was whistling a tune, at once very complicated and very simple, it seemed to be pouring out of him as though he were a bird, and it sounded very cool and moving through all that harsh, bright air, only just holding its own through all those other sounds.

I stood up and walked over to the window and looked down into the courtyard. It was the beginning of the spring and the sap was rising in the boys. A teacher passed through them every now and again, quickly, as though he or she couldn't wait to get out of that courtyard, to get those boys out of their sight and off their minds. I started collecting my stuff. I thought I'd better get home and talk to Isabel.

The courtyard was almost deserted by the time I got downstairs. I saw this boy standing in the shadow of a doorway looking just like Sonny. I almost called

---

2   Heroin.

his name. Then I saw that it wasn't Sonny, but somebody we used to know, a boy from around our block. He'd been Sonny's friend. He'd never been mine, having been too young for me, and, anyway, I'd never liked him. And now, even though he was a grown-up man, he still hung around that block, still spent hours on the street corners, was always high and raggy. I used to run into him from time to time and he'd often work around to asking me for a quarter or fifty cents. He always had some real good excuse, too, and I always gave it to him. I don't know why.

But now, abruptly, I hated him. I couldn't stand the way he looked at me, partly like a dog, partly like a cunning child. I wanted to ask him what the hell he was doing in the school courtyard.

He sort of shuffled over to me, and he said, "I see you got the papers. So you already know about it."

"You mean about Sonny? Yes, I already know about it. How come they didn't get you?"

He grinned. It made him repulsive and it also brought to mind what he'd looked like as a kid. "I wasn't there. I stay away from them people."

"Good for you." I offered him a cigarette and I watched him through the smoke. "You come all the way down here just to tell me about Sonny?"

"That's right." He was sort of shaking his head and his eyes looked strange, as though they were about to cross. The bright sun deadened his damp dark brown skin and it made his eyes look yellow and showed up the dirt in his kinked hair. He smelled funky. I moved a little away from him and I said, "Well, thanks. But I already know about it and I got to get home."

"I'll walk you a little ways," he said. We started walking. There were a couple of kids still loitering in the courtyard and one of them said goodnight to me and looked strangely at the boy beside me.

"What're you going to do?" he asked me. "I mean, about Sonny?"

"Look. I haven't seen Sonny for over a year, I'm not sure I'm going to do anything. Anyway, what the hell *can* I do?"

"That's right," he said quickly, "ain't nothing you can do. Can't much help old Sonny no more, I guess."

It was what I was thinking and so it seemed to me he had no right to say it.

"I'm surprised at Sonny, though," he went on—he had a funny way of talking, he looked straight ahead as though he were talking to himself—"I thought Sonny was a smart boy. I thought he was too smart to get hung."

"I guess he thought so too," I said sharply, "and that's how he got hung. And how about you? You're pretty goddamn smart, I bet."

Then he looked directly at me, just for a minute. "I ain't smart," he said. "If I was smart, I'd have reached for a pistol a long time ago."

"Look. Don't tell *me* your sad story, if it was up to me, I'd give you one." Then I felt guilty—guilty, probably, for never having supposed that the poor bastard *had* a story of his own, much less a sad one, and I asked, quickly, "What's going to happen to him now?"

He didn't answer this. He was off by himself some place.

"Funny thing," he said, and from his tone we might have been discussing the quickest way to get to Brooklyn, "when I saw the papers this morning, the first thing I asked myself was if I had anything to do with it. I felt sort of responsible."

I began to listen more carefully. The subway station was on the corner, just before us, and I stopped. He stopped, too. We were in front of a bar and he ducked slightly, peering in, but whoever he was looking for didn't seem to be there. The juke box was blasting away with something black and bouncy and I half watched the barmaid as she danced her way from the juke box to her place behind the bar. And I watched her face as she laughingly responded to something someone said to her, still keeping time to the music. When she smiled one saw the little girl, one sensed the doomed, still-struggling woman beneath the battered face of the semi-whore.

"I never *give* Sonny nothing," the boy said finally, "but a long time ago I come to school high and Sonny asked me how it felt." He paused, I couldn't bear to watch him, I watched the barmaid, and I listened to the music which seemed to be causing the pavement to shake. "I told him it felt great." The music stopped, the barmaid paused and watched the juke box until the music began again. "It did."

All this was carrying me some place I didn't want to go. I certainly didn't want to know how it felt. It filled everything, the people, the houses, the music, the dark quicksilver barmaid, with menace; and this menace was their reality.

"What's going to happen to him now?" I asked again.

"They'll send him away some place and they'll try to cure him." He shook his head. "Maybe he'll even think he's kicked the habit. Then they'll let him loose"—he gestured, throwing his cigarette into the gutter. "That's all."

"What do you mean, that's *all*?"

But I knew what he meant.

"I *mean*, that's *all*." He turned his head and looked at me, pulling down the corners of his mouth. "Don't you know what I mean?" he asked, softly.

"How the hell *would* I know what you mean?" I almost whispered it, I don't know why.

"That's right," he said to the air, "how would *he* know what I mean?" He turned toward me again, patient and calm, and yet I somehow felt him shaking, shaking as though he were going to fall apart. I felt that ice in my guts again, the dread I'd felt all afternoon; and again I watched the barmaid, moving about the bar, washing glasses, and singing. "Listen. They'll let him out and then it'll just start all over again. That's what I mean."

"You mean—they'll let him out. And then he'll just start working his way back in again. You mean he'll never kick the habit. Is that what you mean?"

"That's right," he said, cheerfully. "*You* see what I mean."

"Tell me," I said at last, "why does he want to die? He must want to die, he's killing himself, why does he want to die?"

He looked at me in surprise. He licked his lips. "He don't want to die. He wants to live. Don't nobody want to die, ever."

Then I wanted to ask him—too many things. He could not have answered, or if he had, I could not have borne the answers. I started walking. "Well, I guess it's none of my business."

"It's going to be rough on old Sonny," he said. We reached the subway station. "This is your station?" he asked. I nodded. I took one step down. "Damn!" he said, suddenly. I looked up at him. He grinned again. "Damn it if I didn't leave all my money home. You ain't got a dollar on you, have you? Just for a couple of days, is all."

All at once something inside gave and threatened to come pouring out of me. I didn't hate him any more. I felt that in another moment I'd start crying like a child.

"Sure," I said. "Don't sweat." I looked in my wallet and didn't have a dollar, I only had a five. "Here," I said. "That hold you?"

He didn't look at it—he didn't want to look at it. A terrible, closed look came over his face, as though he were keeping the number on the bill a secret from him and me. "Thanks," he said, and now he was dying to see me go. "Don't worry about Sonny. Maybe I'll write him or something."

"Sure," I said. "You do that. So long."

"Be seeing you," he said. I went on down the steps.

And I didn't write Sonny or send him anything for a long time. When I finally did, it was just after my little girl died, and he wrote me back a letter which made me feel like a bastard.

Here's what he said:

Dear brother,

You don't know how much I needed to hear from you. I wanted to write you many a time but I dug how much I must have hurt you and so I didn't write. But now I feel like a man who's been trying to climb up out of some deep, real deep and funky hole and just saw the sun up there, outside. I got to get outside.

I can't tell you much about how I got here. I mean I don't know how to tell you. I guess I was afraid of something or I was trying to escape from something and you know I have never been very strong in the head (smile). I'm glad Mama and Daddy are dead and can't see what's happened to their son and I swear if I'd known what I was doing I would never have hurt you so, you and a lot of other fine people who were nice to me and who believed in me.

I don't want you to think it had anything to do with me being a musician. It's more than that. Or maybe less than that. I can't get anything straight in my head down here and I try not to think about what's going to happen to me when I get outside again. Sometime I think I'm going to flip and *never* get outside and sometime I think I'll come straight back. I tell you one thing, though, I'd rather blow my brains out than go through this again. But that's what they all say, so they tell me. If I tell you when I'm coming to New York and if you could meet me, I sure would appreciate it. Give my love to Isabel and the kids and I was sure sorry to hear about little Gracie. I wish I could be like Mama and say the Lord's will be done, but I don't know it seems to me that trouble is the one thing that never does get stopped and I don't know what good it does to blame it on the Lord. But maybe it does some good if you believe it.
Your brother,
Sonny

Then I kept in constant touch with him and I sent him whatever I could and I went to meet him when he came back to New York. When I saw him many things I thought I had forgotten came flooding back to me. This was because I had begun, finally, to wonder about Sonny, about the life that Sonny lived inside. This life, whatever it was, had made him older and thinner and it had deepened the distant stillness in which he had always moved. He looked very unlike my baby brother. Yet, when he smiled, when we shook hands, the baby brother I'd never known looked out from the depths of his private life, like an animal waiting to be coaxed into the light.

"How you been keeping?" he asked me.

"All right. And you?"

"Just fine." He was smiling all over his face. "It's good to see you again."

"It's good to see you."

The seven years' difference in our ages lay between us like a chasm: I wondered if these years would ever operate between us as a bridge. I was remembering, and it made it hard to catch my breath, that I had been there when he was born; and I had heard the first words he had ever spoken. When he started to walk, he walked from our mother straight to me. I caught him just before he fell when he took the first steps he ever took in this world.

"How's Isabel?"

"Just fine. She's dying to see you."

"And the boys?"

"They're fine, too. They're anxious to see their uncle."

"Oh, come on. You know they don't remember me."

"Are you kidding? Of course they remember you."

He grinned again. We got into a taxi. We had a lot to say to each other, far too much to know how to begin.

As the taxi began to move, I asked, "You still want to go to India?"

He laughed. "You still remember that. Hell, no. This place is Indian enough for me."

"It used to belong to them," I said.

And he laughed again. "They damn sure knew what they were doing when they got rid of it."

Years ago, when he was around fourteen, he'd been all hipped on the idea of going to India. He read books about people sitting on rocks, naked, in all kinds of weather, but mostly bad, naturally, and walking barefoot through hot coals and arriving at wisdom. I used to say that it sounded to me as though they were getting away from wisdom as fast as they could. I think he sort of looked down on me for that.

"Do you mind," he asked, "if we have the driver drive alongside the park? On the west side—I haven't seen the city in so long."

"Of course not," I said. I was afraid that I might sound as though I were humoring him, but I hoped he wouldn't take it that way.

So we drove along, between the green of the park and the stony, lifeless elegance of hotels and apartment buildings, toward the vivid, killing streets of our childhood. These streets hadn't changed, though housing projects jutted up out of them now like rocks in the middle of a boiling sea. Most of the houses in which we had grown up had vanished, as had the stores from which we had stolen, the basements in which we had first tried sex, the rooftops from which we had hurled tin cans and bricks. But houses exactly like the houses of our past yet dominated the landscape, boys exactly like the boys we once had been found themselves smothering in these houses, came down into the streets for light and air and found themselves encircled by disaster. Some escaped the trap, most didn't. Those who got out always left something of themselves behind, as some animals amputate a leg and leave it in the trap. It might be said, perhaps, that I had escaped, after all, I was a school teacher; or that Sonny had, he hadn't lived in Harlem for years. Yet, as the cab moved uptown through streets which seemed, with a rush, to darken with dark people, and as I covertly studied Sonny's face, it came to me that what we both were seeking through our separate cab windows was that part of ourselves which had been left behind. It's always at the hour of trouble and confrontation that the missing member aches.

We hit 110th Street and started rolling up Lenox Avenue. And I'd known this avenue all my life, but it seemed to me again, as it had seemed on the day I'd first heard about Sonny's trouble, filled with a hidden menace which was its very breath of life.

"We almost there," said Sonny.

"Almost." We were both too nervous to say anything more.

We live in a housing project. It hasn't been up long. A few days after it was up it seemed uninhabitably new, now, of course, it's already rundown. It looks like a parody of the good, clean, faceless life—God knows the people who live in it do their best to make it a parody. The beat-looking grass lying around isn't enough to make their lives green, the hedges will never hold out the streets, and they know it. The big windows fool no one, they aren't big enough to make space out of no space. They don't bother with the windows, they watch the TV screen instead. The playground is most popular with the children who don't play at jacks, or skip rope, or roller skate, or swing, and they can be found in it after dark. We moved in partly because it's not too far from where I teach, and partly for the kids; but it's really just like the houses in which Sonny and I grew up. The same things happen, they'll have the same things to remember. The moment Sonny and I started into the house I had the feeling that I was simply bringing him back into the danger he had almost died trying to escape.

Sonny had never been talkative. So I don't know why I was sure he'd be dying to talk to me when supper was over the first night. Everything went fine, the oldest boy remembered him, and the youngest boy liked him, and Sonny had remembered to bring something for each of them; and Isabel, who is really much nicer than I am, more open and giving, had gone to a lot of trouble about dinner and was genuinely glad to see him. And she's always been able to tease Sonny in a way that I haven't. It was nice to see her face so vivid again and to hear her laugh and watch her make Sonny laugh. She wasn't, or, anyway, she didn't seem to be, at all uneasy or embarrassed. She chatted as though there were no subject which had to be avoided and she got Sonny past his first, faint stiffness. And thank God she was there, for I was filled with that icy dread again. Everything I did seemed awkward to me, and everything I said sounded freighted with hidden meaning. I was trying to remember everything I'd heard about dope addiction and I couldn't help watching Sonny for signs. I wasn't doing it out of malice. I was trying to find out something about my brother. I was dying to hear him tell me he was safe.

"Safe!" my father grunted, whenever Mama suggested trying to move to a neigh-borhood which might be safer for children. "Safe, hell! Ain't no place safe for kids, nor nobody."

He always went on like this, but he wasn't, ever, really as bad as he sounded, not even on weekends, when he got drunk. As a matter of fact, he was always on the lookout for "something a little better," but he died before he found it. He died suddenly during a drunken weekend in the middle of the war, when Sonny was fifteen. He and Sonny hadn't ever got on too well. And this was partly because Sonny was the apple of his father's eye. It was because he loved Sonny so much and was frightened for him, that he was always fighting with him. It doesn't do any good to fight with Sonny. Sonny just moves back, inside himself, where he can't be reached. But the principal reason that they never hit it off is that they were so much alike. Daddy was big and rough and loud-talking, just the op-posite of Sonny, but they both had—that same privacy.

Mama tried to tell me something about this, just after Daddy died. I was home on leave from the army.

This was the last time I ever saw my mother alive. Just the same, this picture gets all mixed up in my mind with pictures I had of her when she was younger. The way I always see her is the way she used to be on a Sunday afternoon, say, when the old folks were talking after the big Sunday dinner. I always see her wearing pale blue. She'd be sitting on the sofa. And my father would be sitting in the easy chair, not far from her. And the living room would be full of church folks and relatives. There they sit, in chairs all around the living room, and the night is creeping up outside, but nobody knows it yet. You can see the darkness growing against the windowpanes and you hear the street noises every now and again, or maybe the jangling beat of a tambourine from one of the churches close by, but it's real quiet in the room. For a moment nobody's talking, but every face looks darkening, like the sky outside. And my mother rocks a little from the waist, and my father's eyes are closed. Everyone is looking at something a child can't see. For a minute they've forgotten the children. Maybe a kid is lying on the rug, half asleep. Maybe somebody's got a kid in his lap and is absent-mindedly stroking the kid's head. Maybe there's a kid, quiet and big-eyed, curled up in a big chair in the corner. The silence, the darkness coming, and the darkness in the faces frighten the child obscurely. He hopes that the hand which strokes his forehead will never stop—will never die. He hopes that there will never come a time when the old folks won't be sitting around the living room, talking about where they've come from, and what they've seen, and what's happened to them and their kinfolk.

But something deep and watchful in the child knows that this is bound to end, is already ending. In a moment someone will get up and turn on the light.

Then the old folks will remember the children and they won't talk any more that day. And when light fills the room, the child is filled with darkness. He knows that every time this happens he's moved just a little closer to that darkness outside. The darkness outside is what the old folks have been talking about. It's what they've come from. It's what they endure. The child knows that they won't talk any more because if he knows too much about what's happened to *them*, he'll know too much too soon, about what's going to happen to *him*.

The last time I talked to my mother, I remember I was restless. I wanted to get out and see Isabel. We weren't married then and we had a lot to straighten out between us.

There Mama sat, in black, by the window. She was humming an old church song, *Lord, you brought me from a long ways off.* Sonny was out somewhere. Mama kept watching the streets.

"I don't know," she said, "if I'll ever see you again, after you go off from here. But I hope you'll remember the things I tried to teach you."

"Don't talk like that," I said, and smiled. "You'll be here a long time yet."

She smiled, too, but she said nothing. She was quiet for a long time. And I said, "Mama, don't you worry about nothing. I'll be writing all the time, and you be getting the checks ..."

"I want to talk to you about your brother," she said, suddenly. "If anything happens to me he ain't going to have nobody to look out for him."

"Mama," I said, "ain't nothing going to happen to you *or* Sonny. Sonny's all right. He's a good boy and he's got good sense."

"It ain't a question of his being a good boy," Mama said, "nor of his having good sense. It ain't only the bad ones, nor yet the dumb ones that gets sucked under." She stopped, looking at me. "Your Daddy once had a brother," she said, and she smiled in a way that made me feel she was in pain. "You didn't never know that, did you?"

"No," I said, "I never knew that," and I watched her face.

"Oh, yes," she said, "your Daddy had a brother." She looked out of the window again. "I know you never saw your Daddy cry. But *I* did—many a time, through all these years."

I asked her, "What happened to his brother? How come nobody's ever talked about him?"

This was the first time I ever saw my mother look old.

"His brother got killed," she said, "when he was just a little younger than you are now. I knew him. He was a fine boy. He was maybe a little full of the devil, but he didn't mean nobody no harm."

Then she stopped and the room was silent, exactly as it had sometimes been on those Sunday afternoons. Mama kept looking out into the streets.

"He used to have a job in the mill," she said, "and, like all young folks, he just liked to perform on Saturday nights. Saturday nights, him and your father would drift around to different places, go to dances and things like that, or just sit around with people they knew, and your father's brother would sing, he had a fine voice, and play along with himself on his guitar. Well, this particular Saturday night, him and your father was coming home from some place, and they were both a little drunk and there was a moon that night, it was bright like day. Your father's brother was feeling kind of good, and he was whistling to himself, and he had his guitar slung over his shoulder. They was coming down a hill and beneath them was a road that turned off from the highway. Well, your father's brother, being always kind of frisky, decided to run down this hill, and he did, with that guitar banging and clanging behind him, and he ran across the road, and he was making water behind a tree. And your father was sort of amused at him and he was still coming down the hill, kind of slow. Then he heard a car motor and that same minute his brother stepped from behind the tree, into the road, in the moonlight. And he started to cross the road. And your father started to run down the hill, he says he don't know why. This car was full of white men. They was all drunk, and when they seen your father's brother they let out a great whoop and holler and they aimed the car straight at him. They was having fun, they just wanted to scare him, the way they do sometimes, you know. But they was drunk. And I guess the boy being drunk, too, and scared, kind of lost his head. By the time he jumped it was too late. Your father says he heard his brother scream when the car rolled over him, and he heard the wood of that guitar when it give, and he heard them strings go flying, and he heard them white men shouting, and the car kept on a-going and it ain't stopped till this day. And, time your father got down the hill, his brother weren't nothing but blood and pulp."

Tears were gleaming on my mother's face. There wasn't anything I could say.

"He never mentioned it," she said, "because I never let him mention it before you children. Your Daddy was like a crazy man that night and for many a night thereafter. He says he never in his life seen anything as dark as that road after the lights of that car had gone away. Weren't nothing, weren't nobody on that road, just your Daddy and his brother and that busted guitar. Oh, yes. Your Daddy never did really get right again. Till the day he died he weren't sure but that every white man he saw was the man that killed his brother."

She stopped and took out her handkerchief and dried her eyes and looked at me.

"I ain't telling you all this," she said, "to make you scared or bitter or to make you hate nobody. I'm telling you this because you got a brother. And the world ain't changed."

I guess I didn't want to believe this. I guess she saw this in my face. She turned away from me, toward the window again, searching those streets.

"But I praise my Redeemer," she said at last, "that He called your Daddy home before me. I ain't saying it to throw no flowers at myself, but, I declare, it keeps me from feeling too cast down to know I helped your father get safely through this world. Your father always acted like he was the roughest, strongest man on earth. And everybody took him to be like that. But if he hadn't had me there—to see his tears!"

She was crying again. Still, I couldn't move. I said, "Lord, Lord, Mama, I didn't know it was like that."

"Oh, honey," she said, "there's a lot that you don't know. But you are going to find out." She stood up from the window and came over to me. "You got to hold on to your brother," she said, "and don't let him fall, no matter what it looks like is happening to him and no matter how evil you gets with him. You going to be evil with him many a time. But don't you forget what I told you, you hear?"

"I won't forget," I said. "Don't you worry, I won't forget. I won't let nothing happen to Sonny."

My mother smiled as though she was amused at something she saw in my face. Then, "You may not be able to stop nothing from happening. But you got to let him know you's *there*."

Two days later I was married, and then I was gone. And I had a lot of things on my mind and I pretty well forgot my promise to Mama until I got shipped home on a special furlough for her funeral.

And, after the funeral, with just Sonny and me alone in the empty kitchen, I tried to find out something about him.

"What do you want to do?" I asked him.

"I'm going to be a musician," he said.

For he had graduated, in the time I had been away, from dancing to the juke box to finding out who was playing what, and what they were doing with it, and he had bought himself a set of drums.

"You mean, you want to be a drummer?" I somehow had the feeling that being a drummer might be all right for other people but not for my brother Sonny.

"I don't think," he said, looking at me very gravely, "that I'll ever be a good drummer. But I think I can play a piano."

I frowned. I'd never played the role of the oldest brother quite so seriously before, had scarcely ever, in fact, *asked* Sonny a damn thing. I sensed myself in the presence of something I didn't really know how to handle, didn't understand. So I made my frown a little deeper as I asked: "What kind of musician do you want to be?"

He grinned. "How many kinds do you think there are?"

"Be *serious*," I said.

He laughed, throwing his head back, and then looked at me. "I *am* serious."

"Well, then, for Christ's sake, stop kidding around and answer a serious question. I mean, do you want to be a concert pianist, you want to play classical music and all that, or—or what?" Long before I finished he was laughing again.

"For Christ's *sake*, Sonny!"

He sobered, but with difficulty. "I'm sorry. But you sound so—*scared*!" and he was off again.

"Well, you may think it's funny now, baby, but it's not going to be so funny when you have to make your living at it, let me tell you *that*." I was furious because I knew he was laughing at me and I didn't know why.

"No," he said, very sober now, and afraid, perhaps, that he'd hurt me, "I don't want to be a classical pianist. That isn't what interests me. I mean"—he paused, looking hard at me, as though his eyes would help me to understand, and then gestured helplessly, as though perhaps his hand would help—"I mean, I'll have a lot of studying to do, and I'll have to study *everything*, but, I mean, I want to play *with*—jazz musicians." He stopped. "I want to play jazz," he said.

Well, the word had never before sounded as heavy, as real, as it sounded that afternoon in Sonny's mouth. I just looked at him and I was probably frowning a real frown by this time. I simply couldn't see why on earth he'd want to spend his time hanging around nightclubs, clowning around on bandstands, while people pushed each other around a dance floor. It seemed—beneath him, somehow. I had never thought about it before, had never been forced to, but I suppose I had always put jazz musicians in a class with what Daddy called "good-time people."

"Are you *serious*?"

"Hell, *yes*, I'm serious."

He looked more helpless than ever, and annoyed, and deeply hurt.

I suggested, helpfully: "You mean—like Louis Armstrong?"

His face closed as though I'd struck him. "No. I'm not talking about none of that old-time, down home crap."

"Well, look, Sonny, I'm sorry, don't get mad. I just don't altogether get it, that's all. Name somebody—you know, a jazz musician you admire."

"Bird."

"Who?"

"Bird! Charlie Parker! Don't they teach you nothing in the goddamn army?"

I lit a cigarette. I was surprised and then a little amused to discover that I was trembling. "I've been out of touch," I said. "You'll have to be patient with me. Now. Who's this Parker character?"

"He's just one of the greatest jazz musicians alive," said Sonny, sullenly, his hands in his pockets, his back to me. "Maybe *the* greatest," he added, bitterly, "that's probably why *you* never heard of him."

"All right," I said. "I'm ignorant. I'm sorry. I'll go out and buy all the cat's records right away, all right?"

"It don't," said Sonny, with dignity, "make any difference to me. I don't care what you listen to. Don't do me no favors."

I was beginning to realize that I'd never seen him so upset before. With another part of my mind I was thinking that this would probably turn out to be one of those things kids go through and that I shouldn't make it seem important by pushing it too hard. Still, I didn't think it would do any harm to ask: "Doesn't all this take a lot of time? Can you make a living at it?"

He turned back to me and half leaned, half sat, on the kitchen table. "Everything takes time," he said, "and—well, yes, sure, I can make a living at it. But what I don't seem to be able to make you understand is that it's the only thing I want to do."

"Well, Sonny," I said gently, "you know people can't always do exactly what they *want* to do—"

"*No*, I don't know that," said Sonny, surprising me. "I think people *ought* to do what they want to do, what else are they alive for?"

"You getting to be a big boy," I said desperately, "it's time you started thinking about your future."

"I'm thinking about my future," said Sonny, grimly. "I think about it all the time."

I gave up. I decided, if he didn't change his mind, that we could always talk about it later. "In the meantime," I said, "you got to finish school." We had already decided that he'd have to move in with Isabel and her folks. I knew this wasn't the ideal arrangement because Isabel's folks are inclined to be dicty[3] and they hadn't especially wanted Isabel to marry me. But I didn't know what else to do. "And we have to get you fixed up at Isabel's."

There was a long silence. He moved from the kitchen table to the window. "That's a terrible idea. You know it yourself."

"Do you have a *better* idea?"

He just walked up and down the kitchen for a minute. He was as tall as I was. He had started to shave. I suddenly had the feeling that I didn't know him at all.

He stopped at the kitchen table and picked up my cigarettes. Looking at me with a kind of mocking, amused defiance, he put one between his lips. "You mind?"

---

3   Bossy or snobbish.

"You smoking already?"

He lit the cigarette and nodded, watching me through the smoke. "I just wanted to see if I'd have the courage to smoke in front of you." He grinned and blew a great cloud of smoke to the ceiling. "It was easy." He looked at my face. "Come on, now. I bet you was smoking at my age, tell the truth."

I didn't say anything but the truth was on my face, and he laughed. But now there was something very strained in his laugh. "Sure. And I bet that ain't all you was doing."

He was frightening me a little. "Cut the crap," I said. "We already decided that you was going to go and live at Isabel's. Now what's got into you all of a sudden?"

"*You* decided it," he pointed out. "*I* didn't decide nothing." He stopped in front of me, leaning against the stove, arms loosely folded. "Look, brother, I don't want to stay in Harlem no more, I really don't." He was very earnest. He looked at me, then over toward the kitchen window. There was something in his eyes I'd never seen before, some thoughtfulness, some worry all his own. He rubbed the muscle of one arm. "It's time I was getting out of here."

"Where do you want to *go*, Sonny?"

"I want to join the army. Or the navy, I don't care. If I say I'm old enough, they'll believe me."

Then I got mad. It was because I was so scared. "You must be crazy. You god-damn fool, what the hell do you want to go and join the *army* for?"

"I just told you. To get out of Harlem."

"Sonny, you haven't even finished *school*. And if you really want to be a musi-cian, how do you expect to study if you're in the *army*?"

He looked at me, trapped, and in anguish. "There's ways. I might be able to work out some kind of deal. Anyway, I'll have the G.I. Bill when I come out."

"*If* you come out." We stared at each other. "Sonny, please. Be reasonable. I know the setup is far from perfect. But we got to do the best we can."

"I ain't learning nothing in school," he said. "Even when I go." He turned away from me and opened the window and threw his cigarette out into the narrow al-ley. I watched his back. "At least, I ain't learning nothing you'd want me to learn." He slammed the window so hard I thought the glass would fly out, and turned back to me. "And I'm sick of the stink of these garbage cans!"

"Sonny," I said, "I know how you feel. But if you don't finish school now, you're going to be sorry later that you didn't." I grabbed him by the shoulders. "And you only got another year. It ain't so bad. And I'll come back and I swear I'll help you do *whatever* you want to do. Just try to put up with it till I come back. Will you please do that? For me?"

He didn't answer and he wouldn't look at me.

"Sonny. You hear me?"

He pulled away. "I hear you. But you never hear anything *I* say."

I didn't know what to say to that. He looked out the window and then back at me. "OK," he said, and sighed. "I'll try."

Then I said, trying to cheer him up a little, "They got a piano at Isabel's. You can practice on it."

And as a matter of fact, it did cheer him up for a minute. "That's right," he said to himself. "I forgot that." His face relaxed a little. But the worry, the thoughtfulness, played on it still, the way shadows play on a face which is staring into the fire.

But I thought I'd never hear the end of that piano. At first, Isabel would write me, saying how nice it was that Sonny was so serious about his music and how, as soon as he came in from school, or wherever he had been when he was supposed to be at school, he went straight to that piano and stayed there until suppertime. And, after supper, he went back to that piano and stayed there until everybody went to bed. He was at the piano all day Saturday and all day Sunday. Then he bought a record player and started playing records. He'd play one record over and over again, all day long sometimes, and he'd improvise along with it on the piano. Or he'd play one section of the record, one chord, one change, one progression, then he'd do it on the piano. Then back to the record. Then back to the piano.

Well, I really don't know how they stood it. Isabel finally confessed that it wasn't like living with a person at all, it was like living with sound. And the sound didn't make any sense to her, didn't make any sense to any of them— naturally. They began, in a way, to be afflicted by this presence that was living in their home. It was as though Sonny were some sort of god, or monster. He moved in an atmosphere which wasn't like theirs at all. They fed him and he ate, he washed himself, he walked in and out of their door; he certainly wasn't nasty or unpleasant or rude. Sonny isn't any of those things; but it was as though he were all wrapped up in some cloud, some fire, some vision all his own; and there wasn't any way to reach him.

At the same time, he wasn't really a man yet, he was still a child, and they had to watch out for him in all kinds of ways. They certainly couldn't throw him out. Neither did they dare to make a great scene about that piano because even they dimly sensed, as I sensed, from so many thousands of miles away, that Sonny was at that piano playing for his life.

But he hadn't been going to school. One day a letter came from the school board and Isabel's mother got it—there had, apparently, been other letters but Sonny had torn them up. This day, when Sonny came in, Isabel's mother showed him the letter and asked where he'd been spending his time. And she finally got it out of him that he'd been down in Greenwich Village, with musicians and other characters, in a white girl's apartment. And this scared her and she started to scream at him and what came up, once she began—though she denies it to this day—was what sacrifices they were making to give Sonny a decent home and how little he appreciated it.

Sonny didn't play the piano that day. By evening, Isabel's mother had calmed down but then there was the old man to deal with, and Isabel herself. Isabel says she did her best to be calm but she broke down and started crying. She says she just watched Sonny's face. She could tell, by watching him, what was happening with him. And what was happening was that they penetrated his cloud, they had reached him. Even if their fingers had been a thousand times more gentle than human fingers ever are, he could hardly help feeling that they had stripped him naked and were spitting on that nakedness. For he also had to see that his presence, that music, which was life or death to him, had been torture for them and that they had endured it, not at all for his sake, but only for mine. And Sonny couldn't take that. He can take it a little better today than he could then but he's still not very good at it and, frankly, I don't know anybody who is.

The silence of the next few days must have been louder than the sound of all the music ever played since time began. One morning, before she went to work, Isabel was in his room for something and she suddenly realized that all of his records were gone. And she knew for certain that he was gone. And he was. He went as far as the navy would carry him. He finally sent me a postcard from some place in Greece and that was the first I knew that Sonny was still alive. I didn't see him any more until we were both back in New York and the war had long been over.

He was a man by then, of course, but I wasn't willing to see it. He came by the house from time to time, but we fought almost every time we met. I didn't like the way he carried himself, loose and dreamlike all the time, and I didn't like his friends, and his music seemed to be merely an excuse for the life he led. It sounded just that weird and disordered.

Then we had a fight, a pretty awful fight, and I didn't see him for months. By and by I looked him up, where he was living, in a furnished room in the Village, and I tried to make it up. But there were lots of other people in the room and Sonny just lay on his bed, and he wouldn't come downstairs with me, and he treated these other people as though they were his family and I weren't. So I got mad and then he got mad, and then I told him that he might just as well be dead as live the way he was living. Then he stood up and he told me not to worry about him any more in life, that he *was* dead as far as I was concerned. Then he pushed me to the door and the other people looked on as though nothing were happening, and he slammed the door behind me. I stood in the hallway, staring at the door. I heard somebody laugh in the room and then the tears came to my eyes. I started down the steps, whistling to keep from crying, I kept whistling to myself, *You going to need me, baby, one of these cold, rainy days.*

I read about Sonny's trouble in the spring. Little Grace died in the fall. She was a beautiful little girl. But she only lived a little over two years. She died of polio and she suffered. She had a slight fever for a couple of days, but it didn't seem like anything and we just kept her in bed. And we would certainly have called the doctor, but the fever dropped, she seemed to be all right. So we thought it had just been a cold. Then, one day she was up, playing, Isabel was in the kitchen fixing lunch for the two boys when they'd come in from school, and she heard Grace fall down in the living room. When you have a lot of children you don't always start running when one of them falls, unless they start screaming or something. And, this time, Gracie was quiet. Yet, Isabel says that when she heard that *thump* and then that silence, something happened to her to make her afraid. And she ran to the living room and there was little Grace on the floor, all twisted up, and the reason she hadn't screamed was that she couldn't get her breath. And when she did scream, it was the worst sound, Isabel says, that she'd ever heard in all her life, and she still hears it sometimes in her dreams. Isabel will sometimes wake me up with a low, moaning, strangling sound and I have to be quick to awaken her and hold her to me and where Isabel is weeping against me seems a mortal wound.

I think I may have written Sonny the very day that little Grace was buried. I was sitting in the living room in the dark, by myself, and I suddenly thought of Sonny. My trouble made his real.

One Saturday afternoon, when Sonny had been living with us, or anyway, been in our house, for nearly two weeks, I found myself wandering aimlessly about the living room, drinking from a can of beer, and trying to work up courage to search Sonny's room. He was out, he was usually out whenever I was home, and Isabel had taken the children to see their grandparents. Suddenly I was standing still in front of the living room window, watching Seventh Avenue. The idea of searching Sonny's room made me still. I scarcely dared to admit to myself what I'd be searching for. I didn't know what I'd do if I found it. Or if I didn't.

On the sidewalk across from me, near the entrance to a barbecue joint, some people were holding an old-fashioned revival meeting. The barbecue cook, wearing a dirty white apron, his conked hair reddish and metallic in the pale sun, and a cigarette between his lips, stood in the doorway, watching them. Kids and older people paused in their errands and stood there, along with some older men and a couple of very tough-looking women who watched everything that happened on the avenue, as though they owned it, or were maybe owned by it. Well, they were watching this, too. The revival was being carried on by three sisters in black, and a brother. All they had were their voices and their Bibles and a tambourine. The brother was testifying and while he testified two of the sisters stood together, seeming to say amen, and the third sister walked around with the tambourine outstretched and a couple of people dropped coins into it. Then the brother's testimony ended and the sister who had been taking up the collection dumped the coins into her palm and transferred them to the pocket of her long black robe. Then she raised both hands, striking the tambourine against the air, and then against one hand, and she started to sing. And the two other sisters and the brother joined in.

It was strange, suddenly, to watch, though I had been seeing these meetings all my life. So, of course, had everybody else down there. Yet, they paused and watched and listened and I stood still at the window. "*'Tis the old ship of Zion,*" they sang, and the sister with the tambourine kept a steady, jangling beat, "*it has rescued many a thousand!*" Not a soul under the sound of their voices was hearing this song for the first time, not one of them had been rescued. Nor had they seen much in the way of rescue work being done around them. Neither did they especially believe in the holiness of the three sisters and the brother, they knew too much about them, knew where they lived, and how. The woman with the tambourine, whose voice dominated the air, whose face was bright with joy, was divided by very little from the woman who stood watching her, a cigarette between her heavy, chapped lips, her hair a cuckoo's nest, her face scarred and swollen from many beatings, and her black eyes glittering like coal. Perhaps they both knew this, which was why, when, as rarely, they addressed each other, they addressed each other as Sister. As the singing filled the air the watching, listening faces underwent a change; the eyes focusing on something within; the music seemed to soothe a poison out of them; and time seemed, nearly, to fall away from the sullen, belligerent, battered faces, as though they were fleeing back to their first condition, while dreaming of their last. The barbecue cook half shook his head and smiled, and dropped his cigarette and disappeared into his joint. A man fumbled in his pockets for change and stood holding it in his hand impatiently, as though he had just remembered a pressing appointment further up the avenue. He looked furious. Then I saw Sonny, standing on the edge of the crowd. He was carrying a wide, flat notebook, with a green cover, and it made him look, from where I was standing, almost like a schoolboy. The coppery sun brought out the copper in his skin, he was very faintly smiling, standing very still. Then the singing stopped, the tambourine turned into a collection plate again. The furious man dropped in his coins and vanished, so did a couple of the women, and Sonny dropped some change in the plate, looking directly at the woman with a little smile. He started across the avenue, toward the house. He has a slow, loping walk, something like the way Harlem hipsters walk, only he's imposed on this his own half-beat. I had never really noticed it before.

I stayed at the window, both relieved and apprehensive. As Sonny disappeared from my sight, they began singing again. And they were still singing when his key turned in the lock.

"Hey," he said.

"Hey, yourself. You want some beer?"

"No. Well maybe." But he came up to the window and stood beside me, looking out. "What a warm voice," he said.

They were singing *If I could only hear my mother pray again!*

"Yes," I said, "and she can sure beat that tambourine."

"But what a terrible song," he said, and laughed. He dropped his notebook on the sofa and disappeared into the kitchen. "Where's Isabel and the kids?"

"I think they went to see their grandparents. You hungry?"

"No." He came back into the living room with his can of beer. "You want to come some place with me tonight?"

I sensed, I don't know how, that I couldn't possibly say no. "Sure. Where?"

He sat down on the sofa and picked up his notebook and started leafing through it. "I'm going to sit in with some fellows in a joint in the Village."

"You mean, you're going to play, tonight?"

"That's right." He took a swallow of his beer and moved back to the window. He gave me a sidelong look. "If you can stand it."

"I'll try," I said.

He smiled to himself and we both watched as the meeting across the way broke up. The three sisters and the brother, heads bowed, were singing *God be with you till we meet again*. The faces around them were very quiet. Then the song ended. The small crowd dispersed. We watched the three women and the lone man walk slowly up the avenue.

"When she was singing before," said Sonny, abruptly, "her voice reminded me for a minute of what heroin feels like sometimes—when it's in your veins. It makes you feel sort of warm and cool at the same time. And distant. And—and sure." He sipped his beer, very deliberately not looking at me. I watched his face. "It makes you feel—in control. Sometimes you've got to have that feeling."

"Do you?" I sat down slowly in the easy chair.

"Sometimes." He went to the sofa and picked up his notebook again. "Some people do."

"In order," I asked, "to play?" And my voice was very ugly, full of contempt and anger.

"Well"—he looked at me with great, troubled eyes, as though, in fact, he hoped his eyes would tell me things he could never otherwise say—"they *think* so. And *if* they think so—!"

"And what do *you* think?" I asked.

He sat on the sofa and put his can of beer on the floor. "I don't know," he said, and I couldn't be sure if he were answering my question or pursuing his thoughts. His face didn't tell me. "It's not so much to *play*. It's to *stand* it, to be able to make it at all. On any level." He frowned and smiled: "In order to keep from shaking to pieces."

"But these friends of yours," I said, "they seem to shake themselves to pieces pretty goddamn fast."

"Maybe." He played with the notebook. And something told me that I should curb my tongue, that Sonny was doing his best to talk, that I should listen. "But of course you only know the ones that've gone to pieces. Some don't—or at least they haven't *yet* and that's just about all *any* of us can say." He paused. "And then there are some who just live, really, in hell, and they know it and they see what's happening and they go right on. I don't know." He sighed, dropped the notebook, folded his arms. "Some guys, you can tell from the way they play they on something *all* the time. And you can see that, well, it makes something real for them. But of course," he picked up his beer from the floor and sipped it and put the can down again, "they *want* to, too, you've got to see that. Even some of them that say they don't—*some*, not all."

"And what about you?" I asked—I couldn't help it. "What about you? Do *you* want to?"

He stood up and walked to the window and I remained silent for a long time. Then he sighed. "Me," he said. Then: "While I was downstairs before, on my way here, listening to that woman sing, it struck me all of a sudden how much suffering she must have had to go through—to sing like that. It's *repulsive* to think you have to suffer that much."

I said: "But there's no way not to suffer—is there, Sonny?"

"I believe not," he said and smiled, "but that's never stopped anyone from trying." He looked at me. "Has it?" I realized, with this mocking look, that there stood between us, forever, beyond the power of time or forgiveness, the fact that I had held silence—so long!—when he had needed human speech to help him. He turned back to the window. "No, there's no way not to suffer. But you try all kinds of ways to keep from drowning in it, to keep on top of it, and to make it seem—well, like *you*. Like you did something, all right, and now you're suffering for it. You know?" I said nothing. "Well, you know," he said, impatiently, "why *do* people suffer? Maybe it's better to do something to give it a reason, *any* reason."

"But we just agreed," I said, "that there's no way not to suffer. Isn't it better, then, just to—take it?"

"But nobody just takes it," Sonny cried, "that's what I'm telling you! *Everybody* tries not to. You're just hung up on the *way* some people try—it's not *your* way!"

The hair on my face began to itch, my face felt wet. "That's not true," I said, "that's not true. I don't give a damn what other people do, I don't even care how they suffer. I just care how *you* suffer." And he looked at me. "Please believe me," I said, "I don't want to see you—die—trying not to suffer."

"I won't," he said flatly, "die trying not to suffer. At least, not any faster than anybody else."

"But there's no need," I said, trying to laugh, "is there? in killing yourself."

I wanted to say more, but I couldn't. I wanted to talk about will power and how life could be—well, beautiful. I wanted to say that it was all within; but was it? or, rather, wasn't that exactly the trouble? And I wanted to promise that I would never fail him again. But it would all have sounded—empty words and lies.

So I made the promise to myself and prayed that I would keep it.

"It's terrible sometimes, inside," he said, "that's what's the trouble. You walk these streets, black and funky and cold, and there's not really a living ass to talk to, and there's nothing shaking, and there's no way of getting it out—that storm inside. You can't talk it and you can't make love with it, and when you finally try to get with it and play it, you realize *nobody's* listening. So *you've* got to listen. You got to find a way to listen."

And then he walked away from the window and sat on the sofa again, as though all the wind had suddenly been knocked out of him. "Sometimes you'll do *anything* to play, even cut your mother's throat." He laughed and looked at me. "Or your brother's." Then he sobered. "Or your own." Then: "Don't worry. I'm all right now and I think I'll *be* all right. But I can't forget—where I've been. I don't mean just the physical place I've been, I mean where I've *been*. And *what* I've been."

"What have you been, Sonny?" I asked.

He smiled—but sat sideways on the sofa, his elbow resting on the back, his fingers playing with his mouth and chin, not looking at me. "I've been something I didn't recognize, didn't know I could be. Didn't know anybody could be." He stopped, looking inward, looking helplessly young, looking old. "I'm not talking about it now because I feel *guilty* or anything like that—maybe it would be better if I did, I don't know. Anyway, I can't really talk about it. Not to you, not to anybody," and now he turned and faced me. "Sometimes, you know, and it was actually when I was most *out* of the world, I felt that I was in it, that I was *with* it, really, and I could play or I didn't really have to *play*, it just came out of me, it was there. And I don't know how I played, thinking about it now, but I know I did awful things, those times, sometimes to people. Or it wasn't that I *did* anything to them—it was that they weren't real." He picked up the beer can; it was empty; he rolled it between his palms: "And other times—well, I needed a fix, I needed to find a place to lean. I needed to clear a space to *listen*—and I couldn't find it, and I went *crazy*. I did terrible things to *me*, I was terrible *for me*." He began pressing the beer can between his hands, I watched the metal begin to give. It glittered, as he played with it like a knife, and I was afraid he would cut himself, but I said nothing. "Oh well. I can never tell you. I was all by myself at the bottom of something, stinking and sweating and crying and shaking, and I smelled it, you know? *my* stink, and I thought I'd die if I couldn't get away from it and yet, all the same, I knew that everything I was doing was just locking me in with it. And I didn't know," he paused, still flattening the beer can, "I didn't know, I still *don't* know, something kept telling me that maybe it was good to smell your own stink, but I didn't think that *that* was what I'd been trying to do—and—who can stand it?" and he abruptly dropped the ruined beer can, looking at me with a small, still smile, and then rose, walking to the window as though it were the lodestone rock. I watched his face, he watched the avenue. "I couldn't tell you when Mama died—but the reason I wanted to leave Harlem so bad was to get away from drugs. And then, when I ran away, that's what I was running from—really. When I came back, nothing had changed, *I* hadn't changed, I was just—older." And he stopped, drumming with his fingers on the windowpane. The sun had vanished, soon darkness would fall. I watched his face. "It can come again," he said, almost as though speaking to himself. Then he turned to me. "It can come again," he repeated. "I just want you to know that."

"All right," I said, at last. "So it can come again. All right."

He smiled, but the smile was sorrowful. "I had to try to tell you," he said.

"Yes," I said. "I understand that."

"You're my brother," he said, looking straight at me, and not smiling at all.

"Yes," I repeated, "yes, I understand that."

He turned back to the window, looking out. "All that hatred down there," he said, "all that hatred and misery and love. It's a wonder it doesn't blow the avenue apart."

We went to the only nightclub on a short, dark street, downtown. We squeezed through the narrow, chattering, jampacked bar to the entrance of the big room, where the bandstand was. And we stood there for a moment, for the lights were very dim in this room and we couldn't see. Then, "Hello, boy," said the voice and an enormous black man, much older than Sonny or myself, erupted out of all that atmospheric lighting and put an arm around Sonny's shoulder. "I been sitting right here," he said, "waiting for you."

He had a big voice, too, and heads in the darkness turned toward us.

Sonny grinned and pulled a little away, and said, "Creole, this is my brother. I told you about him."

Creole shook my hand. "I'm glad to meet you, son," he said, and it was clear that he was glad to meet me *there*, for Sonny's sake. And he smiled, "You got a real musician in *your* family," and he took his arm from Sonny's shoulder and slapped him, lightly, affectionately, with the back of his hand.

"Well. Now I've heard it all," said a voice behind us. This was another musician, and a friend of Sonny's, a coal-black, cheerful-looking man, built close to the ground. He immediately began confiding to me, at the top of his lungs, the most terrible things about Sonny, his teeth gleaming like a lighthouse and his laugh coming up out of him like the beginning of an earthquake. And it turned out that everyone at the bar knew Sonny, or almost everyone, some were musicians, working there, or nearby, or not working, some were simply hangers-on, and some were there to hear Sonny play. I was introduced to all of them and they were all very polite to me. Yet, it was clear that, for them, I was only Sonny's brother. Here, I was in Sonny's world. Or, rather, his kingdom. Here, it was not even a question that his veins bore royal blood.

They were going to play soon and Creole installed me, by myself, at a table in a dark corner. Then I watched them, Creole, and the little black man, and Sonny, and the others, while they horsed around, standing just below the bandstand. The light from the bandstand spilled just a little short of them and, watching them laughing and gesturing and moving about, I had the feeling that they, nevertheless, were being most careful not to step into that circle of light too suddenly; that if they moved into the light too suddenly without thinking, they would perish in flame. Then, while I watched, one of them, the small black man, moved into the light and crossed the bandstand and started fooling around with his drums. Then—being funny and being, also, extremely ceremonious—Creole took Sonny by the arm and led him to the piano. A woman's voice called Sonny's name and a few hands started clapping. And Sonny, also being funny and being ceremonious, and so touched, I think, that he could have cried, but neither hiding it nor showing it, riding it like a man, grinned, and put both hands to his heart and bowed from the waist.

Creole then went to the bass fiddle and a lean, very bright-skinned brown man jumped up on the bandstand and picked up his horn. So there they were, and the atmosphere on the bandstand and in the room began to change and tighten. Someone stepped up to the microphone and announced them. Then there were all kinds of murmurs. Some people at the bar shushed others. The waitress ran around, frantically getting in the last orders, guys and chicks got closer to each other, and the lights on the bandstand, on the quartet, turned to a kind of indigo. Then they all looked different there. Creole looked about him for the last time, as though he were making certain that all his chickens were in the coop, and then he—jumped and struck the fiddle. And there they were.

All I know about music is that not many people ever really hear it. And even then, on the rare occasions when something opens within, and the music enters, what we mainly hear, or hear corroborated, are personal, private, vanishing evocations. But the man who creates the music is hearing something else, is dealing with the roar rising from the void and imposing order on it as it hits the air. What is evoked in him, then, is of another order, more terrible because it has no words, and triumphant, too, for that same reason. And his triumph, when he triumphs, is ours. I just watched Sonny's face. His face was troubled, he was working hard, but he wasn't with it. And I had the feeling that, in a way, everyone on the bandstand was waiting for him, both waiting for him and pushing him along. But as I began to watch Creole, I realized that it was Creole who held them all back. He had them on a short rein. Up there, keeping the beat with his whole body, waiting on the fiddle, with his eyes half closed, he was listening to everything, but he was listening to Sonny. He was having a dialogue with Sonny. He wanted Sonny to leave the shoreline and strike out for the deep water. He was Sonny's witness that deep water and drowning were not the same thing—he had been there, and he knew. And he wanted Sonny to know. He was waiting for Sonny to do the things on the keys which would let Creole know that Sonny was in the water.

And, while Creole listened, Sonny moved, deep within, exactly like someone in torment. I had never before thought of how awful the relationship must be between the musician and his instrument. He has to fill it, this instrument, with the breath of life, his own. He has to make it do what he wants it to do. And a piano is just a piano. It's made out of so much wood and wires and little hammers and big ones, and ivory. While there's only so much you can do with it, the only way to find this out is to try: to try and make it do everything.

And Sonny hadn't been near a piano for over a year. And he wasn't on much better terms with his life, not the life that stretched before him now. He and the piano stammered, started one way, got scared, stopped; started another way, panicked, marked time, started again; then seemed to have found a direction, panicked again, got stuck. And the face I saw on Sonny I'd never seen before. Everything had been burned out of it, and, at the same time, things usually hidden were being burned in, by the fire and fury of the battle which was occurring in him up there.

Yet, watching Creole's face as they neared the end of the first set, I had the feeling that something had happened, something I hadn't heard. Then they finished, there was scattered applause, and then, without an instant's warning, Creole started into something else, it was almost sardonic, it was *Am I Blue*. And, as though he commanded, Sonny began to play. Something began to happen. And Creole let out the reins. The dry, low, black man said something awful on the drums. Creole answered, and the drums talked back. Then the horn insisted, sweet and high, slightly detached perhaps, and Creole listened, commenting now and then, dry and driving, beautiful and calm and old. Then they all came together again, and Sonny was part of the family again. I could tell this from his face. He seemed to have found, right there beneath his fingers, a damn brand-new piano. It seemed that he couldn't get over it. Then, for a while, just being happy with Sonny, they seemed to be agreeing with him that brand-new pianos certainly were a gas.

Then Creole stepped forward to remind them that what they were playing was the blues. He hit something in all of them, he hit something in me, myself, and the music tightened and deepened, apprehension began to beat the air. Creole began to tell us what the blues were all about. They were not about anything very new. He and his boys up there were keeping it new, at the risk of ruin, destruction, madness, and death, in order to find new ways to make us listen. For, while the tale of how we suffer, and how we are delighted, and how we may triumph is never new, it always must be heard. There isn't any other tale to tell, it's the only light we've got in all this darkness.

And this tale, according to that face, that body, those strong hands on those strings, has another aspect in every country, and a new depth in every generation. Listen, Creole seemed to be saying, listen. Now these are Sonny's blues. He made the little black man on the drums know it, and the bright, brown man on the horn. Creole wasn't trying any longer to get Sonny in the water. He was wishing him Godspeed. Then he stepped back, very slowly, filling the air with the immense suggestion that Sonny speak for himself.

Then they all gathered around Sonny and Sonny played. Every now and again one of them seemed to say amen. Sonny's fingers filled the air with life, his life. But that life contained so many others. And Sonny went all the way back, he really began with the spare, flat statement of the opening phrase of the song. Then he began to make it his. It was very beautiful because it wasn't hurried and it was no longer a lament. I seemed to hear with what burning he had made it his, and what burning we had yet to make it ours, how we could cease lamenting. Freedom lurked around us and I understood, at last, that he could help us to be free if we would listen, that he would never be free until we did. Yet, there was no battle in his face now, I heard what he had gone through, and would continue to go through until he came to rest in earth. He had made it his: that long line, of which we knew only Mama and Daddy. And he was giving it back, as everything must be given back, so that, passing through death, it can live forever. I saw my mother's face again, and felt, for the first time, how the stones of the road she had walked on must have bruised her feet. I saw the moonlit road where my father's brother died. And it brought something else back to me, and carried me past it, I saw my little girl again and felt Isabel's tears again, and I felt my own tears begin to rise. And I was yet aware that this was only a moment, that the world waited outside, as hungry as a tiger, and that trouble stretched above us, longer than the sky.

Then it was over. Creole and Sonny let out their breath, both soaking wet, and grinning. There was a lot of applause and some of it was real. In the dark, the girl came by and I asked her to take drinks to the bandstand. There was a long pause, while they talked up there in the indigo light and after awhile I saw the girl put a Scotch and milk on top of the piano for Sonny. He didn't seem to notice it, but just before they started playing again, he sipped from it and looked toward me, and nodded. Then he put it back on top of the piano. For me, then, as they began to play again, it glowed and shook above my brother's head like the very cup of trembling.[4]

—*1957*

---

4   See Isaiah 51:22.

FLANNERY O'CONNOR

Born in Savannah, Georgia, Mary Flannery O'Connor spent most of her life in the American South, where her novels and most of her short stories are set. Participating in the tradition of the "Southern grotesque," her writing blends humour and Gothic horror, often incorporating bleak or violent events and physically deformed or morally twisted characters. O'Connor approached the "Southern grotesque" through the lens of her intensely deep Catholic faith; indeed, she writes that "the meaning of life is centered in our Redemption by Christ and what I see in the world I see in its relation to that."

After graduating from the Georgia State College for Women in 1945, O'Connor spent three years at the prestigious Writers' Workshop at Iowa State University. She probably would have remained in the northern United States had she not been struck in 1950 by the first signs of lupus. Weakened by the disease and the debilitating cortisone treatments it required, she went to live with her mother in Milledgeville, Georgia, where she would remain for the rest of her life.

Although O'Connor was a deeply committed Catholic, her fiction is set in the Southern "Bible Belt" where Protestantism was predominant, and her characters are often Protestant fundamentalists who are both materially and spiritually poor. Her stories focus on terrible events befalling such characters, she said, in order to portray "the action of grace in territory held largely by the devil." She described her short story collection *A Good Man Is Hard to Find* (1955), which received the O. Henry Award for short fiction, as a book of "stories about original sin."

In addition to *A Good Man Is Hard to Find*, O'Connor published two novels—*Wise Blood* (1952) and *The Violent Bear It Away* (1960)—before her early death in 1964 as a result of lupus. Her last short story collection, *Everything that Rises Must Converge*, was published posthumously the following year.

A Good Man Is Hard to Find

THE GRANDMOTHER didn't want to go to Florida. She wanted to visit some of her connections in east Tennessee and she was seizing at every chance to change Bailey's mind. Bailey was the son she lived with, her only boy. He was sitting on the edge of his chair at the table, bent over the orange sports section of the *Journal*. "Now look here, Bailey," she said, "see here, read this," and she stood with one hand on her thin hip and the other rattling the newspaper at his bald head. "Here this fellow that calls himself The Misfit is aloose from the Federal Pen and headed toward Florida and you read here what it says he did to these people. Just you read it. I wouldn't take my children in any direction with a criminal like that aloose in it. I couldn't answer to my conscience if I did."

Bailey didn't look up from his reading so she wheeled around then and faced the children's mother, a young woman in slacks, whose face was as broad and innocent as a cabbage and was tied around with a green head-kerchief that had two points on the top like rabbit's ears. She was sitting on the sofa, feeding the baby his apricots out of a jar. "The children have been to Florida before," the old lady said. "You all ought to take them somewhere else for a change so they would see different parts of the world and be broad. They never have been to east Tennessee."

The children's mother didn't seem to hear her but the eight-year-old boy, John Wesley, a stocky child with glasses, said, "If you don't want to go to Florida, why dontcha stay at home?" He and the little girl, June Star, were reading the funny papers on the floor.

"She wouldn't stay at home to be queen for a day," June Star said without raising her yellow head.

"Yes and what would you do if this fellow, The Misfit, caught you?" the grandmother asked.

"I'd smack his face," John Wesley said.

"She wouldn't stay at home for a million bucks," June Star said. "Afraid she'd miss something. She has to go everywhere we go."

"All right, Miss," the grandmother said. "Just remember that the next time you want me to curl your hair."

June Star said her hair was naturally curly.

The next morning the grandmother was the first one in the car, ready to go. She had her big black valise that looked like the head of a hippopotamus in one corner, and underneath it she was hiding a basket with Pitty Sing, the cat, in it. She didn't intend for the cat to be left alone in the house for three days because he would miss her too much and she was afraid he might brush against one of the gas burners and accidentally asphyxiate himself. Her son, Bailey, didn't like to arrive at a motel with a cat.

She sat in the middle of the back seat with John Wesley and June Star on either side of her. Bailey and the children's mother and the baby sat in front and they left Atlanta at eight forty-five with the mileage on the car at 55890. The grandmother wrote this down because she thought it would be interesting to say how many miles they had been when they got back. It took them twenty minutes to reach the outskirts of the city.

The old lady settled herself comfortably, removing her white cotton gloves and putting them up with her purse on the shelf in front of the back window. The children's mother still had on slacks and still had her head tied up in a green kerchief, but the grandmother had on a navy blue straw sailor hat with a bunch of white violets on the brim and a navy blue dress with a small white dot in the print. Her collars and cuffs were white organdy trimmed with lace and at her neckline she had pinned a purple spray of cloth violets containing a sachet. In case of an accident, anyone seeing her dead on the highway would know at once that she was a lady.

She said she thought it was going to be a good day for driving, neither too hot nor too cold, and she cautioned Bailey that the speed limit was fifty-five miles an hour and that the patrolmen hid themselves behind billboards and small clumps of trees and sped out after you before you had a chance to slow down. She pointed out interesting details of the scenery: Stone Mountain; the blue granite that in some places came up to both sides of the highway; the brilliant red clay banks slightly streaked with purple; and the various crops that made rows of green lace-work on the ground. The trees were full of silver-white sunlight and the meanest of them sparkled. The children were reading comic magazines and their mother had gone back to sleep.

"Let's go through Georgia fast so we won't have to look at it much," John Wesley said.

"If I were a little boy," said the grandmother, "I wouldn't talk about my native state that way. Tennessee has the mountains and Georgia has the hills."

"Tennessee is just a hillbilly dumping ground," John Wesley said, "and Georgia is a lousy state too."

"You said it," June Star said.

"In my time," said the grandmother, folding her thin veined fingers, "children were more respectful of their native states and their parents and everything else. People did right then. Oh look at the cute little pickaninny!"[1] she said and

---

1 Derogatory term for an African American child.

pointed to a Negro child standing in the door of a shack. "Wouldn't that make a picture, now?" she asked and they all turned and looked at the little Negro out of the back window. He waved.

"He didn't have any britches on," June Star said.

"He probably didn't have any," the grandmother explained. "Little niggers[2] in the country don't have things like we do. If I could paint, I'd paint that picture," she said.

The children exchanged comic books.

The grandmother offered to hold the baby and the children's mother passed him over the front seat to her. She set him on her knee and bounced him and told him about the things they were passing. She rolled her eyes and screwed up her mouth and stuck her leathery thin face into his smooth bland one. Occasionally he gave her a faraway smile. They passed a large cotton field with five or six graves fenced in the middle of it, like a small island. "Look at the graveyard!" the grandmother said, pointing it out. "That was the old family burying ground. That belonged to the plantation."

"Where's the plantation?" John Wesley asked.

"Gone With the Wind," said the grandmother. "Ha. Ha."

When the children finished all the comic books they had brought, they opened the lunch and ate it. The grandmother ate a peanut butter sandwich and an olive and would not let the children throw the box and the paper napkins out the window. When there was nothing else to do they played a game by choosing a cloud and making the other two guess what shape it suggested. John Wesley took one the shape of a cow and June Star guessed a cow and John Wesley said, no, an automobile, and June Star said he didn't play fair, and they began to slap each other over the grandmother.

The grandmother said she would tell them a story if they would keep quiet. When she told a story, she rolled her eyes and waved her head and was very dramatic. She said once when she was a maiden lady she had been courted by a Mr. Edgar Atkins Teagarden from Jasper, Georgia. She said he was a very good-looking man and a gentleman and that he brought her a watermelon every Saturday afternoon with his initials cut in it, E.A.T. Well, one Saturday, she said, Mr. Teagarden brought the watermelon and there was nobody at home and he left it on the front porch and returned in his buggy to Jasper, but she never got the watermelon, she said, because a nigger boy ate it when he saw the initials, E.A.T.! This story tickled John Wesley's funny bone and he giggled and giggled but June Star didn't think it was any good. She said she wouldn't marry a

---

2   This pejorative term remained in frequent use by many white Americans in the South until well into the 1960s.

man that just brought her a watermelon on Saturday. The grandmother said she would have done well to marry Mr. Teagarden because he was a gentleman and had bought Coca-Cola stock when it first came out and that he had died only a few years ago, a very wealthy man.

They stopped at The Tower for barbecued sandwiches. The Tower was a part stucco and part wood filling station and dance hall set in a clearing outside of Timothy. A fat man named Red Sammy Butts ran it and there were signs stuck here and there on the building and for miles up and down the highway saying, TRY RED SAMMY'S FAMOUS BARBECUE. NONE LIKE FAMOUS RED SAMMY'S! RED SAM! THE FAT BOY WITH THE HAPPY LAUGH. A VETERAN! RED SAMMY'S YOUR MAN!

Red Sammy was lying on the bare ground outside The Tower with his head under a truck while a gray monkey about a foot high, chained to a small chinaberry tree, chattered nearby. The monkey sprang back into the tree and got on the highest limb as soon as he saw the children jump out of the car and run toward him.

Inside, The Tower was a long dark room with a counter at one end and tables at the other and dancing space in the middle. They all sat down at a board table next to the nickelodeon and Red Sam's wife, a tall burnt-brown woman with hair and eyes lighter than her skin, came and took their order. The children's mother put a dime in the machine and played "The Tennessee Waltz," and the grandmother said that tune always made her want to dance. She asked Bailey if he would like to dance but he only glared at her. He didn't have a naturally sunny disposition like she did and trips made him nervous. The grandmother's brown eyes were very bright. She swayed her head from side to side and pretended she was dancing in her chair. June Star said play something she could tap to so the children's mother put in another dime and played a fast number and June Star stepped out onto the dance floor and did her tap routine.

"Ain't she cute?" Red Sam's wife said, leaning over the counter. "Would you like to come be my little girl?"

"No I certainly wouldn't," June Star said. "I wouldn't live in a broken-down place like this for a million bucks!" and she ran back to the table.

"Ain't she cute?" the woman repeated, stretching her mouth politely.

"Ain't you ashamed?" hissed the grandmother.

Red Sam came in and told his wife to quit lounging on the counter and hurry up with these people's order. His khaki trousers reached just to his hip bones and his stomach hung over them like a sack of meal swaying under his shirt. He came over and sat down at a table nearby and let out a combination sigh and yodel. "You can't win," he said. "You can't win," and he wiped his sweating red face off with a gray handkerchief. "These days you don't know who to trust," he said. "Ain't that the truth?"

"People are certainly not nice like they used to be," said the grandmother.

"Two fellers come in here last week," Red Sammy said, "driving a Chrysler. It was a old beat-up car but it was a good one and these boys looked all right to me. Said they worked at the mill and you know I let them fellers charge the gas they bought? Now why did I do that?"

"Because you're a good man!" the grandmother said at once.

"Yes'm, I suppose so," Red Sam said as if he were struck with this answer.

His wife brought the orders, carrying the five plates all at once without a tray, two in each hand and one balanced on her arm. "It isn't a soul in this green world of God's that you can trust," she said. "And I don't count nobody out of that, not nobody," she repeated, looking at Red Sammy.

"Did you read about that criminal, The Misfit, that's escaped?" asked the grandmother.

"I wouldn't be a bit surprised if he didn't attact this place right here," said the woman. "If he hears about it being here, I wouldn't be none surprised to see him. If he hears it's two cent in the cash register, I wouldn't be a tall surprised if he...."

"That'll do," Red Sam said. "Go bring these people their Co'-Colas," and the woman went off to get the rest of the order.

"A good man is hard to find," Red Sammy said. "Everything is getting terrible. I remember the day you could go off and leave your screen door unlatched. Not no more."

He and the grandmother discussed better times. The old lady said that in her opinion Europe was entirely to blame for the way things were now. She said the way Europe acted you would think we were made of money and Red Sam said it was no use talking about it, she was exactly right. The children ran outside into the white sunlight and looked at the monkey in the lacy chinaberry tree. He was busy catching fleas on himself and biting each one carefully between his teeth as if it were a delicacy.

They drove off again into the hot afternoon. The grandmother took cat naps and woke up every few minutes with her own snoring. Outside of Toombsboro she woke up and recalled an old plantation that she had visited in this neighborhood once when she was a young lady. She said the house had six white columns across the front and that there was an avenue of oaks leading up to it and two little wooden trellis arbors on either side in front where you sat down with your suitor after a stroll in the garden. She recalled exactly which road to turn off to get to it. She knew that Bailey would not be willing to lose any time looking at an old house, but the more she talked about it, the more she wanted to see it once again and find out if the little twin arbors were still standing. "There was a secret panel in this house," she said craftily, not telling the truth but wishing that she were, "and the story went that all the family silver was hidden in it when Sherman[3] came through but it was never found ..."

"Hey!" John Wesley said. "Let's go see it! We'll find it! We'll poke all the woodwork and find it! Who lives there? Where do you turn off at? Hey Pop, can't we turn off there?"

"We never have seen a house with a secret panel!" June Star shrieked. "Let's go to the house with the secret panel! Hey, Pop, can't we go see the house with the secret panel!"

"It's not far from here, I know," the grandmother said. "It wouldn't take over twenty minutes."

Bailey was looking straight ahead. His jaw was as rigid as a horseshoe. "No," he said.

The children began to yell and scream that they wanted to see the house with the secret panel. John Wesley kicked the back of the front seat and June Star hung over her mother's shoulder and whined desperately into her ear that they never had any fun even on their vacation, that they could never do what THEY wanted to do. The baby began to scream and John Wesley kicked the back of the seat so hard that his father could feel the blows in his kidney.

"All right!" he shouted and drew the car to a stop at the side of the road. "Will you all shut up? Will you all just shut up for one second? If you don't shut up, we won't go anywhere."

"It would be very educational for them," the grandmother murmured.

"All right," Bailey said, "but get this: this is the only time we're going to stop for anything like this. This is the one and only time."

"The dirt road that you have to turn down is about a mile back," the grandmother directed. "I marked it when we passed."

"A dirt road," Bailey groaned.

After they had turned around and were headed toward the dirt road, the grandmother recalled other points about the house, the beautiful glass over the front doorway and the candle-lamp in the hall. John Wesley said that the secret panel was probably in the fireplace.

"You can't go inside this house," Bailey said. "You don't know who lives there."

"While you all talk to the people in front, I'll run around behind and get in a window," John Wesley suggested.

"We'll all stay in the car," his mother said.

---

3   American Union commander William Tecumseh Sherman (1820–91). Near the end of the American Civil War in 1864 Sherman marched his troops through Georgia, often ransacking homes and confiscating property.

They turned onto the dirt road and the car raced roughly along in a swirl of pink dust. The grandmother recalled the times when there were no paved roads and thirty miles was a day's journey. The dirt road was hilly and there were sudden washes in it and sharp curves on dangerous embankments. All at once they would be on a hill, looking down over the blue tops of trees for miles around, then the next minute, they would be in a red depression with the dust-coated trees looking down on them.

"This place had better turn up in a minute," Bailey said, "or I'm going to turn around."

The road looked as if no one had traveled on it in months.

"It's not much farther," the grandmother said and just as she said it, a horrible thought came to her. The thought was so embarrassing that she turned red in the face and her eyes dilated and her feet jumped up, upsetting her valise in the corner. The instant the valise moved, the newspaper top she had over the basket under it rose with a snarl and Pitty Sing, the cat, sprang onto Bailey's shoulder.

The children were thrown to the floor and their mother, clutching the baby, was thrown out the door onto the ground; the old lady was thrown into the front seat. The car turned over once and landed right-side-up in a gulch off the side of the road. Bailey remained in the driver's seat with the cat—gray-striped with a broad white face and an orange nose—clinging to his neck like a caterpillar.

As soon as the children saw they could move their arms and legs, they scrambled out of the car, shouting, "We've had an ACCIDENT!" The grandmother was curled up under the dashboard, hoping she was injured so that Bailey's wrath would not come down on her all at once. The horrible thought she had had before the accident was that the house she had remembered so vividly was not in Georgia but in Tennessee.

Bailey removed the cat from his neck with both hands and flung it out the window against the side of a pine tree. Then he got out of the car and started looking for the children's mother. She was sitting against the side of the red gutted ditch, holding the screaming baby, but she only had a cut down her face and a broken shoulder. "We've had an ACCIDENT!" the children screamed in a frenzy of delight.

"But nobody's killed," June Star said with disappointment as the grandmother limped out of the car, her hat still pinned to her head but the broken front brim standing up at a jaunty angle and the violet spray hanging off the side. They all sat down in the ditch, except the children, to recover from the shock. They were all shaking.

"Maybe a car will come along," said the children's mother hoarsely.

"I believe I have injured an organ," said the grandmother, pressing her side, but no one answered her. Bailey's teeth were clattering. He had on a yellow sport shirt with bright blue parrots designed in it and his face was as yellow as the shirt. The grandmother decided that she would not mention that the house was in Tennessee.

The road was about ten feet above and they could see only the tops of the trees on the other side of it. Behind the ditch they were sitting in there were more woods, tall and dark and deep. In a few minutes they saw a car some distance away on top of a hill, coming slowly as if the occupants were watching them. The grandmother stood up and waved both arms dramatically to attract their attention. The car continued to come on slowly, disappeared around a bend and appeared again, moving even slower, on top of the hill they had gone over. It was a big black battered hearse-like automobile. There were three men in it.

It came to a stop just over them and for some minutes, the driver looked down with a steady expressionless gaze to where they were sitting, and didn't speak. Then he turned his head and muttered something to the other two and they got out. One was a fat boy in black trousers and a red sweat shirt with a silver stallion embossed on the front of it. He moved around on the right side of them and stood staring, his mouth partly open in a kind of loose grin. The other had on khaki pants and a blue striped coat and a gray hat pulled down very low, hiding most of his face. He came around slowly on the left side. Neither spoke.

The driver got out of the car and stood by the side of it, looking down at them. He was an older man than the other two. His hair was just beginning to gray and he wore silver-rimmed spectacles that gave him a scholarly look. He had a long creased face and didn't have on any shirt or undershirt. He had on blue jeans that were too tight for him and was holding a black hat and a gun. The two boys also had guns.

"We've had an ACCIDENT!" the children screamed.

The grandmother had the peculiar feeling that the bespectacled man was someone she knew. His face was as familiar to her as if she had known him all her life but she could not recall who he was. He moved away from the car and began to come down the embankment, placing his feet carefully so that he wouldn't slip. He had on tan and white shoes and no socks, and his ankles were red and thin. "Good afternoon," he said. "I see you all had you a little spill."

"We turned over twice!" said the grandmother.

"Oncet," he corrected. "We seen it happen. Try their car and see will it run, Hiram," he said quietly to the boy with the gray hat.

"What you got that gun for?" John Wesley asked. "Whatcha gonna do with that gun?"

"Lady," the man said to the children's mother, "would you mind calling them children to sit down by you? Children make me nervous. I want all you all to sit down right together there where you're at."

"What are you telling US what to do for?" June Star asked.

Behind them the line of woods gaped like a dark open mouth. "Come here," said their mother.

"Look here now," Bailey began suddenly, "we're in a predicament! We're in...."

The grandmother shrieked. She scrambled to her feet and stood staring. "You're The Misfit!" she said. "I recognized you at once!"

"Yes'm," the man said, smiling slightly as if he were pleased in spite of himself to be known, "but it would have been better for all of you, lady, if you hadn't of reckernized me."

Bailey turned his head sharply and said something to his mother that shocked even the children. The old lady began to cry and The Misfit reddened.

"Lady," he said, "don't you get upset. Sometimes a man says things he don't mean. I don't reckon he meant to talk to you thataway."

"You wouldn't shoot a lady, would you?" the grandmother said and removed a clean handkerchief from her cuff and began to slap at her eyes with it.

The Misfit pointed the toe of his shoe into the ground and made a little hole and then covered it up again. "I would hate to have to," he said.

"Listen," the grandmother almost screamed, "I know you're a good man. You don't look a bit like you have common blood. I know you must come from nice people!"

"Yes mam," he said, "finest people in the world." When he smiled he showed a row of strong white teeth. "God never made a finer woman than my mother and my daddy's heart was pure gold," he said. The boy with the red sweat shirt had come around behind them and was standing with his gun at his hip. The Misfit squatted down on the ground. "Watch them children, Bobby Lee," he said. "You know they make me nervous." He looked at the six of them huddled together in front of him and he seemed to be embarrassed as if he couldn't think of anything to say. "Ain't a cloud in the sky," he remarked, looking up at it. "Don't see no sun but don't see no cloud neither."

"Yes, it's a beautiful day," said the grandmother. "Listen," she said, "you shouldn't call yourself The Misfit because I know you're a good man at heart. I can just look at you and tell."

"Hush!" Bailey yelled. "Hush! Everybody shut up and let me handle this!" He was squatting in the position of a runner about to sprint forward but he didn't move.

"I pre-chate that, lady," The Misfit said and drew a little circle in the ground with the butt of his gun.

"It'll take a half a hour to fix this here car," Hiram called, looking over the raised hood of it.

"Well, first you and Bobby Lee get him and that little boy to step over yonder with you," The Misfit said, pointing to Bailey and John Wesley. "The boys want to ast you something," he said to Bailey. "Would you mind stepping back in them woods there with them?"

"Listen," Bailey began, "we're in a terrible predicament! Nobody realizes what this is," and his voice cracked. His eyes were as blue and intense as the parrots in his shirt and he remained perfectly still.

The grandmother reached up to adjust her hat brim as if she were going to the woods with him but it came off in her hand. She stood staring at it and after a second she let it fall on the ground. Hiram pulled Bailey up by the arm as if he were assisting an old man. John Wesley caught hold of his father's hand and Bobby Lee followed. They went off toward the woods and just as they reached the dark edge, Bailey turned and supporting himself against a gray naked pine trunk, he shouted, "I'll be back in a minute, Mamma, wait on me!"

"Come back this instant!" his mother shrilled but they all disappeared into the woods.

"Bailey Boy!" the grandmother called in a tragic voice but she found she was looking at The Misfit squatting on the ground in front of her. "I just know you're a good man," she said desperately. "You're not a bit common!"

"Nome, I ain't a good man," The Misfit said after a second as if he had considered her statement carefully, "but I ain't the worst in the world neither. My daddy said I was a different breed of dog from my brothers and sisters. 'You know,' Daddy said, 'it's some that can live their whole life out without asking about it and it's others has to know why it is, and this boy is one of the latters. He's going to be into everything!'" He put on his black hat and looked up suddenly and then away deep into the woods as if he were embarrassed again. "I'm sorry I don't have on a shirt before you ladies," he said, hunching his shoulders slightly. "We buried our clothes that we had on when we escaped and we're just making do until we can get better. We borrowed these from some folks we met," he explained.

"That's perfectly all right," the grandmother said. "Maybe Bailey has an extra shirt in his suitcase."

"I'll look and see terrectly," The Misfit said.

"Where are they taking him?" the children's mother screamed.

"Daddy was a card himself," The Misfit said. "You couldn't put anything over on him. He never got in trouble with the Authorities though. Just had the knack of handling them."

"You could be honest too if you'd only try," said the grandmother. "Think how wonderful it would be to settle down and live a comfortable life and not have to think about somebody chasing you all the time."

The Misfit kept scratching in the ground with the butt of his gun as if he were thinking about it. "Yes'm, somebody is always after you," he murmured.

The grandmother noticed how thin his shoulder blades were just behind his hat because she was standing up looking down on him. "Do you ever pray?" she asked.

He shook his head. All she saw was the black hat wiggle between his shoulder blades. "Nome," he said.

There was a pistol shot from the woods, followed closely by another. Then silence. The old lady's head jerked around. She could hear the wind move through the tree tops like a long satisfied insuck of breath. "Bailey Boy!" she called.

"I was a gospel singer for a while," The Misfit said. "I been most everything. Been in the arm service, both land and sea, at home and abroad, been twict married, been an undertaker, been with the railroads, plowed Mother Earth, been in a tornado, seen a man burnt alive oncet," and he looked up at the children's mother and the little girl who were sitting close together, their faces white and their eyes glassy; "I even seen a woman flogged," he said.

"Pray, pray," the grandmother began, "pray, pray...."

"I never was a bad boy that I remember of," The Misfit said in an almost dreamy voice, "but somewheres along the line I done something wrong and got sent to the penitentiary. I was buried alive," and he looked up and held her attention to him by a steady stare.

"That's when you should have started to pray," she said. "What did you do to get sent to the penitentiary that first time?"

"Turn to the right, it was a wall," The Misfit said, looking up again at the cloudless sky. "Turn to the left, it was a wall. Look up it was a ceiling, look down it was a floor. I forget what I done, lady. I set there and set there, trying to remember what it was I done and I ain't recalled it to this day. Oncet in a while, I would think it was coming to me, but it never come."

"Maybe they put you in by mistake," the old lady said vaguely.

"Nome," he said. "It wasn't no mistake. They had the papers on me."

"You must have stolen something," she said.

The Misfit sneered slightly. "Nobody had nothing I wanted," he said. "It was a head-doctor at the penitentiary said what I had done was kill my daddy but I known that for a lie. My daddy died in nineteen ought nineteen of the epidemic flu and I never had a thing to do with it. He was buried in the Mount Hopewell Baptist churchyard and you can go there and see for yourself."

"If you would pray," the old lady said, "Jesus would help you."

"That's right," The Misfit said.

"Well then, why don't you pray?" she asked trembling with delight suddenly.

"I don't want no hep," he said. "I'm doing all right by myself."

Bobby Lee and Hiram came ambling back from the woods. Bobby Lee was dragging a yellow shirt with bright blue parrots in it.

"Thow me that shirt, Bobby Lee," The Misfit said. The shirt came flying at him and landed on his shoulder and he put it on. The grandmother couldn't name what the shirt reminded her of. "No, lady," The Misfit said while he was buttoning it up, "I found out the crime don't matter. You can do one thing or you can do another, kill a man or take a tire off his car, because sooner or later you're going to forget what it was you done and just be punished for it."

The children's mother had begun to make heaving noises as if she couldn't get her breath. "Lady," he asked, "would you and that little girl like to step off yonder with Bobby Lee and Hiram and join your husband?"

"Yes, thank you," the mother said faintly. Her left arm dangled helplessly and she was holding the baby, who had gone to sleep, in the other. "Hep that lady up, Hiram," The Misfit said as she struggled to climb out of the ditch, "and Bobby Lee, you hold onto that little girl's hand."

"I don't want to hold hands with him," June Star said. "He reminds me of a pig."

The fat boy blushed and laughed and caught her by the arm and pulled her into the woods after Hiram and her mother.

Alone with The Misfit, the grandmother found that she had lost her voice. There was not a cloud in the sky nor any sun. There was nothing around her but woods. She wanted to tell him that he must pray. She opened and closed her mouth several times before anything came out. Finally she found herself saying, "Jesus. Jesus," meaning, Jesus will help you, but the way she was saying it, it sounded as if she might be cursing.

"Yes'm," The Misfit said as if he agreed. "Jesus thown everything off balance. It was the same case with Him as with me except He hadn't committed any crime and they could prove I had committed one because they had the papers on me. Of course," he said, "they never shown me my papers. That's why I sign myself now. I said long ago, you get you a signature and sign everything you do and keep a copy of it. Then you'll know what you done and you can hold up the crime to the punishment and see do they match and in the end you'll have something to prove you ain't been treated right. I call myself The Misfit," he said, "because I can't make what all I done wrong fit what all I gone through in punishment."

There was a piercing scream from the woods, followed closely by a pistol report. "Does it seem right to you, lady, that one is punished a heap and another ain't punished at all?"

"Jesus!" the old lady cried. "You've got good blood! I know you wouldn't shoot a lady! I know you come from nice people! Pray! Jesus, you ought not to shoot a lady. I'll give you all the money I've got!"

"Lady," The Misfit said, looking beyond her far into the woods, "there never was a body that give the undertaker a tip."

There were two more pistol reports and the grandmother raised her head like a parched old turkey hen crying for water and called, "Bailey Boy, Bailey Boy!" as if her heart would break.

"Jesus was the only One that ever raised the dead," The Misfit continued, "and He shouldn't have done it. He thown everything off balance. If He did what He said, then it's nothing for you to do but thow away everything and follow Him, and if He didn't, then it's nothing for you to do but enjoy the few minutes you got left the best way you can—by killing somebody or burning down his house or doing some other meanness to him. No pleasure but meanness," he said and his voice had become almost a snarl.

"Maybe He didn't raise the dead," the old lady mumbled, not knowing what she was saying and feeling so dizzy that she sank down in the ditch with her legs twisted under her.

"I wasn't there so I can't say He didn't," The Misfit said. "I wisht I had of been there," he said, hitting the ground with his fist. "It ain't right I wasn't there because if I had of been there I would of known. Listen lady," he said in a high voice, "if I had of been there I would of known and I wouldn't be like I am now." His voice seemed about to crack and the grandmother's head cleared for an instant. She saw the man's face twisted close to her own as if he were going to cry and she murmured, "Why you're one of my babies. You're one of my own children!" She reached out and touched him on the shoulder. The Misfit sprang back as if a snake had bitten him and shot her three times through the chest. Then he put his gun down on the ground and took off his glasses and began to clean them.

Hiram and Bobby Lee returned from the woods and stood over the ditch, looking down at the grandmother who half sat and half lay in a puddle of blood with her legs crossed under her like a child's and her face smiling up at the cloudless sky.

Without his glasses, The Misfit's eyes were red-rimmed and pale and defenseless-looking. "Take her off and thow her where you thown the others," he said, picking up the cat that was rubbing itself against his leg.

"She was a talker, wasn't she?" Bobby Lee said, sliding down the ditch with a yodel.

"She would of been a good woman," The Misfit said, "if it had been somebody there to shoot her every minute of her life."

"Some fun!" Bobby Lee said.

"Shut up, Bobby Lee," The Misfit said. "It's no real pleasure in life."

—1953

URSULA K. LE GUIN

Few writers have done more to elevate the standing of science fiction as a recognized literary pursuit than Ursula K. Le Guin. Together with fellow American authors Philip K. Dick and Samuel R. Delany, Le Guin was instrumental in the emergence of New Wave science fiction, a movement that distinguished itself from the genre's so-called Golden Age of the 1940s and 1950s by a greater attention to style, increasingly nuanced characterization, a mounting interest in experimental narrative, and a more forthright engagement with political and gender issues. Le Guin's finest works—among them the Hugo and Nebula Award-winning novels *The Left Hand of Darkness* (1969) and *The Dispossessed* (1974)—are remarkable not only for the fluent evenness of their prose and the conceptual seriousness of their subject matter but also for their political astuteness and the minutely observed social and cultural details of the worlds they imagine into being.

The daughter of a noted anthropologist and psychologist, Le Guin was educated at Radcliffe College and Columbia. Her early interest in cultural anthropology, Jungian psychology, and Taoist philosophy would eventually come to provide a unifying conceptual framework for her writing. In the tradition of J.R.R. Tolkien's world-building, many of Le Guin's novels and stories dramatize a conflict between vividly realized alien cultures that the protagonist—frequently a traveller—observes and participates in as a quasi-anthropologist. Archetypal figures and settings such as those psychologist Carl Jung believed to symbolize humanity's shared psychic heritage also figure prominently in her work, which often has a richly allegorical dimension. Taoism, a third key element in Le Guin's intellectual framework, is likewise central to many of her texts, particularly the doctrine of inaction, which urges passivity over aggression, and the principle of the relativity of opposites, which posits the interdependence of light and darkness, good and evil, and male and female.

More than a master storyteller, Le Guin has done much to advance the place of science fiction as a literature of ideas. In affirming the importance of imagination to human experience, her work demonstrates that science fiction can reflect the world more faithfully than what conventionally passes for realism.

The Ones Who Walk Away from Omelas

WITH A clamor of bells that set the swallows soaring, the Festival of Summer came to the city. Omelas, bright-towered by the sea. The rigging of the boats in harbor sparkled with flags. In the streets between houses with red roofs and painted walls, between old moss-grown gardens and under avenues of trees, past great parks and public buildings, processions moved. Some were decorous: old people in long stiff robes of mauve and grey, grave master workmen, quiet, merry women carrying their babies and chatting as they walked. In other streets the music beat faster, a shimmering of gong and tambourine, and the people went dancing, the procession was a dance. Children dodged in and out, their high calls rising like the swallows' crossing flights over the music and the singing. All the processions wound towards the north side of the city, where on the great water-meadow called the Green Fields boys and girls, naked in the bright air, with mud-stained feet and ankles and long, lithe arms, exercised their restive horses before the race. The horses wore no gear at all but a halter without bit. Their manes were braided with streamers of silver, gold, and green. They flared their nostrils and pranced and boasted to one another; they were vastly excited, the horse being the only animal who has adopted our ceremonies as his own. Far off to the north and west the mountains stood up half encircling Omelas on her bay. The air of morning was so clear that the snow still crowning the Eighteen Peaks burned with white-gold fire across the miles of sunlit air, under the dark blue of the sky. There was just enough wind to make the banners that marked the racecourse snap and flutter now and then. In the silence of the broad green meadows one could hear the music winding through the city streets, farther and nearer and ever approaching, a cheerful faint sweetness of the air that from time to time trembled and gathered together and broke out into the great joyous clanging of the bells.

Joyous! How is one to tell about joy? How describe the citizens of Omelas?

They were not simple folk, you see, though they were happy. But we do not say the words of cheer much any more. All smiles have become archaic.[1]

---

1   Reference to the "archaic smile," an expression found on the faces of many sculpted figures from Ancient Greece.

Given a description such as this one tends to make certain assumptions. Given a description such as this one tends to look next for the King, mounted on a splendid stallion and surrounded by his noble knights, or perhaps in a golden litter borne by great-muscled slaves. But there was no king. They did not use swords, or keep slaves. They were not barbarians. I do not know the rules and laws of their society, but I suspect that they were singularly few. As they did without monarchy and slavery, so they also got on without the stock exchange, the advertisement, the secret police, and the bomb. Yet I repeat that these were not simple folk, not dulcet shepherds, noble savages, bland utopians. They were not less complex than us. The trouble is that we have a bad habit, encouraged by pedants and sophisticates, of considering happiness as something rather stupid. Only pain is intellectual, only evil interesting. This is the treason of the artist: a refusal to admit the banality of evil and the terrible boredom of pain. If you can't lick 'em, join 'em. If it hurts, repeat it. But to praise despair is to condemn delight, to embrace violence is to lose hold of everything else. We have almost lost hold; we can no longer describe a happy man, nor make any celebration of joy. How can I tell you about the people of Omelas? They were not naive and happy children—though their children were, in fact, happy. They were mature, intelligent, passionate adults whose lives were not wretched. O miracle! but I wish I could describe it better. I wish I could convince you. Omelas sounds in my words like a city in a fairy tale, long ago and far away, once upon a time. Perhaps it would be best if you imagined it as your own fancy bids, assuming it will rise to the occasion, for certainly I cannot suit you all. For instance, how about technology? I think that there would be no cars or helicopters in and above the streets; this follows from the fact that the people of Omelas are happy people. Happiness is based on a just discrimination of what is necessary, what is neither necessary nor destructive, and what is destructive. In the middle category, however—that of the unnecessary but undestructive, that of comfort, luxury, exuberance, etc.—they could perfectly well have central heating, subway trains, washing machines, and all kinds of marvelous devices not yet invented here, floating light-sources, fuelless power, a cure for the common cold. Or they could have none of that: it doesn't matter. As you like it. I incline to think that people from towns up and down the coast have been coming in to Omelas during the last days before the Festival on very fast little trains and double-decked trains and that the train station of Omelas is actually the handsomest building in town, though plainer than the magnificent Farmers' Market. But even granted trains, I fear that Omelas so far strikes some of you as goody-goody. Smiles, bells, parades, horses, bleh. If so, please add an orgy. If an orgy would help, don't hesitate. Let us not, however, have temples from which issue beautiful nude priests and priestesses already half in ecstasy and ready to copulate with any man or woman, lover or stranger, who desires union with the deep godhead of the blood, although that was my first idea. But really it would be better not to have any temples in Omelas—at least, not manned temples. Religion yes, clergy no. Surely the beautiful nudes can just wander about, offering themselves like divine soufflés to the hunger of the needy and the rapture of the flesh. Let them join the processions. Let tambourines be struck above the copulations, and the glory of desire be proclaimed upon the gongs, and (a not unimportant point) let the offspring of these delightful rituals be beloved and looked after by all. One thing I know there is none of in Omelas is guilt. But what else should there be? I thought at first there were no drugs, but that is puritanical. For those who like it, the faint insistent sweetness of *drooz* may perfume the ways of the city, *drooz* which first brings a great lightness and brilliance to the mind and limbs, and then after some hours a dreamy languor, and wonderful visions at last of the very arcana and inmost secrets of the Universe, as well as exciting the pleasure of sex beyond all belief; and it is not habit-forming. For more modest tastes I think there ought to be beer. What else, what else belongs in the joyous city? The sense of victory, surely, the celebration of courage. But as we did without clergy, let us do without soldiers. The joy built upon successful slaughter is not the right kind of joy; it will not do; it is fearful and it is trivial. A boundless and generous contentment, a magnanimous triumph felt not against some outer enemy but in communion with the finest and fairest in the souls of all men everywhere and the splendor of the world's summer: this is what swells the hearts of the people of Omelas, and the victory they celebrate is that of life. I really don't think many of them need to take *drooz*.

Most of the processions have reached the Green Fields by now. A marvelous smell of cooking goes forth from the red and blue tents of the provisioners. The faces of small children are amiably sticky; in the benign grey beard of a man a couple of crumbs of rich pastry are entangled. The youths and girls have mounted their horses and are beginning to group around the starting line of the course. An old woman, small, fat, and laughing, is passing out flowers from a basket, and tall young men wear her flowers in their shining hair. A child of nine or ten sits at the edge of the crowd, alone, playing on a wooden flute. People pause to listen, and they smile, but they do not speak to him, for he never ceases playing and never sees them, his dark eyes wholly rapt in the sweet, thin magic of the tune.

He finishes, and slowly lowers his hands holding the wooden flute.

As if that little private silence were the signal, all at once a trumpet sounds from the pavilion near the starting line: imperious, melancholy, piercing. The horses rear on their slender legs, and some of them neigh in answer. Sober-faced, the young riders stroke the horses' necks and soothe them, whispering,

"Quiet, quiet, there my beauty, my hope...." They begin to form in rank along the starting line. The crowds along the racecourse are like a field of grass and flowers in the wind. The Festival of Summer has begun.

Do you believe? Do you accept the festival, the city, the joy? No? Then let me describe one more thing.

In a basement under one of the beautiful public buildings of Omelas, or perhaps in the cellar of one of its spacious private homes, there is a room. It has one locked door, and no window. A little light seeps in dustily between cracks in the boards, secondhand from a cobwebbed window somewhere across the cellar. In one corner of the little room a couple of mops, with stiff, clotted, foul-smelling heads, stand near a rusty bucket. The floor is dirt, a little damp to the touch, as cellar dirt usually is. The room is about three paces long and two wide: a mere broom closet or disused tool room. In the room a child is sitting. It could be a boy or a girl. It looks about six, but actually is nearly ten. It is feeble-minded. Perhaps it was born defective, or perhaps it has become imbecile through fear, malnutrition, and neglect. It picks its nose and occasionally fumbles vaguely with its toes or genitals, as it sits hunched in the corner farthest from the bucket and the two mops. It is afraid of the mops. It finds them horrible. It shuts its eyes, but it knows the mops are still standing there; and the door is locked; and nobody will come. The door is always locked; and nobody ever comes, except that sometimes—the child has no understanding of time or interval—sometimes the door rattles terribly and opens, and a person, or several people, are there. One of them may come in and kick the child to make it stand up. The others never come close, but peer in at it with frightened, disgusted eyes. The food bowl and the water jug are hastily filled, the door is locked, the eyes disappear. The people at the door never say anything, but the child, who has not always lived in the tool room, and can remember sunlight and its mother's voice, sometimes speaks. "I will be good," it says. "Please let me out. I will be good!" They never answer. The child used to scream for help at night, and cry a good deal, but now it only makes a kind of whining, "eh-haa, eh-haa," and it speaks less and less often. It is so thin there are no calves to its legs; its belly protrudes; it lives on a half-bowl of corn meal and grease a day. It is naked. Its buttocks and thighs are a mass of festered sores, as it sits in its own excrement continually.

They all know it is there, all the people of Omelas. Some of them have come to see it, others are content merely to know it is there. They all know that it has to be there. Some of them understand why, and some do not, but they all understand that their happiness, the beauty of their city, the tenderness of their friendships, the health of their children, the wisdom of their scholars, the skill of their makers, even the abundance of their harvest and the kindly weathers of their skies, depend wholly on this child's abominable misery.

This is usually explained to children when they are between eight and twelve, whenever they seem capable of understanding; and most of those who come to see the child are young people, though often enough an adult comes, or comes back, to see the child. No matter how well the matter has been explained to them, these young spectators are always shocked and sickened at the sight. They feel disgust, which they had thought themselves superior to. They feel anger, outrage, impotence, despite all the explanations. They would like to do something for the child. But there is nothing they can do. If the child were brought up into the sunlight out of that vile place, if it were cleaned and fed and comforted, that would be a good thing, indeed; but if it were done, in that day and hour all the prosperity and beauty and delight of Omelas would wither and be destroyed. Those are the terms. To exchange all the goodness and grace of every life in Omelas for that single, small improvement: to throw away the happiness of thousands for the chance of the happiness of one: that would be to let guilt within the walls indeed.

The terms are strict and absolute; there may not even be a kind word spoken to the child.

Often the young people go home in tears, or in a tearless rage, when they have seen the child and faced this terrible paradox. They may brood over it for weeks or years. But as time goes on they begin to realize that even if the child could be released, it would not get much good of its freedom: a little vague pleasure of warmth and food, no doubt, but little more. It is too degraded and imbecile to know any real joy. It has been afraid too long ever to be free of fear. Its habits are too uncouth for it to respond to humane treatment. Indeed, after so long it would probably be wretched without walls about it to protect it, and darkness for its eyes, and its own excrement to sit in. Their tears at the bitter injustice dry when they begin to perceive the terrible justice of reality and to accept it. Yet it is their tears and anger, the trying of their generosity and the acceptance of their helplessness, which are perhaps the true source of the splendor of their lives. Theirs is no vapid, irresponsible happiness. They know that they, like the child, are not free. They know compassion. It is the existence of the child, and their knowledge of its existence, that makes possible the nobility of their architecture, the poignancy of their music, the profundity of their science. It is because of the child that they are so gentle with children. They know that if the wretched one were not there snivelling in the dark, the other one, the flute-player, could make no joyful music as the young riders line up in their beauty for the race in the sunlight of the first morning of summer.

Now do you believe in them? Are they not more credible? But there is one more thing to tell, and this is quite incredible.

At times one of the adolescent girls or boys who go to see the child does not go home to weep or rage, does not, in fact, go home at all. Sometimes also a man or woman much older falls silent for a day or two, and then leaves home. These people go out into the street, and walk down the street alone. They keep walking, and walk straight out of the city of Omelas, through the beautiful gates. They keep walking across the farmlands of Omelas. Each one goes alone, youth or girl, man or woman. Night falls; the traveller must pass down village streets, between the houses with yellow-lit windows, and on out into the darkness of the fields. Each alone, they go west or north, towards the mountains. They go on. They leave Omelas, they walk ahead into the darkness, and they do not come back. The place they go towards is a place even less imaginable to most of us than the city of happiness. I cannot describe it at all. It is possible that it does not exist. But they seem to know where they are going, the ones who walk away from Omelas.

—1973

CHINUA ACHEBE

Chinua Achebe was born in Nigeria when the country was still a colonial territory of the British Empire. As a boy he went to the Church Mission Society School, yet was simultaneously immersed in Igbo culture and tradition. In 1948 he began attending University College, Ibadan, initially to study medicine. He decided to quit medicine and take a degree in literature: "I was abandoning the realm of stories and they would not let me go." He established his place as an important figure in world literature with the publication of his first novel, *Things Fall Apart*, in 1958. It remains, perhaps, the work for which he is best known, but Achebe was a prolific and wide-ranging writer who steadily published novels, short stories, poetry, essays, and children's books until his death in 2013.

While still a student, Achebe read literary accounts of Africa written by Europeans, many of which he found "appalling." This experience taught him that more African voices should represent Africans; Achebe writes that he "decided that the story we had to tell could not be told by anyone else no matter how gifted or well intentioned." For Achebe, telling such stories accurately was of political as well as artistic importance because his writing was "concerned with universal human communication across racial and cultural boundaries as a means of fostering respect for all people" and, he believed, "such respect can only issue from understanding." Though Achebe wrote in English, he forged a unique style that attempted to give voice to Nigerian experience in its own terms, weaving Igbo proverbs, terms, speech patterns, and images into his prose.

As in the selection here, as well as in novels such as *No Longer at Ease* (1960) and *Arrow of God* (1964), Achebe's protagonists are often flawed individuals, recalling the characters of the classical tragedies. He resisted simple tales of good and evil, attempting instead to represent the complexity and uncertainty of the human experience.

Dead Men's Path

MICHAEL OBI'S hopes were fulfilled much earlier than he had expected. He was appointed headmaster of Ndume Central School in January 1949. It had always been an unprogressive school, so the Mission authorities[1] decided to send a young and energetic man to run it. Obi accepted this responsibility with enthusiasm. He had many wonderful ideas and this was an opportunity to put them into practice. He had had sound secondary school education which designated him a "pivotal teacher" in the official records and set him apart from the other headmasters in the mission field. He was outspoken in his condemnation of the narrow views of these older and often less-educated ones.

"We shall make a good job of it, shan't we?" he asked his young wife when they first heard the joyful news of his promotion.

"We shall do our best," she replied. "We shall have such beautiful gardens and everything will be just *modern* and delightful...." In their two years of married life she had become completely infected by his passion for "modern methods" and his denigration of "these old and superannuated people in the teaching field who would be better employed as traders in the Onitsha[2] market." She began to see herself already as the admired wife of the young headmaster, the queen of the school.

The wives of the other teachers would envy her position. She would set the fashion in everything.... Then, suddenly, it occurred to her that there might not be other wives. Wavering between hope and fear, she asked her husband, looking anxiously at him.

"All our colleagues are young and unmarried," he said with enthusiasm which for once she did not share. "Which is a good thing," he continued.

"Why?"

"Why? They will give all their time and energy to the school."

Nancy was downcast. For a few minutes she became skeptical about the new school; but it was only for a few minutes. Her little personal misfortune could not blind her to her husband's happy prospects. She looked at him as he sat folded up in a chair. He was stoop-shouldered and looked frail. But he sometimes surprised people with sudden bursts of physical energy. In his present posture, however, all his bodily strength seemed to have retired behind his deep-set eyes, giving them an extraordinary power of penetration. He was only twenty-six, but looked thirty or more. On the whole, he was not unhandsome.

---

1   Many schools in African countries formerly colonized by the British were run by Christian missionary organizations.

2   City in southeastern Nigeria; the Onitsha market is one of the largest in West Africa.

"A penny for your thoughts, Mike," said Nancy after a while, imitating the woman's magazine she read.

"I was thinking what a grand opportunity we've got at last to show these people how a school should be run."

Ndume School was backward in every sense of the word. Mr. Obi put his whole life into the work, and his wife hers too. He had two aims. A high standard of teaching was insisted upon, and the school compound was to be turned into a place of beauty. Nancy's dream-gardens came to life with the coming of the rains, and blossomed. Beautiful hibiscus and allamanda hedges in brilliant red and yellow marked out the carefully tended school compound from the rank neighborhood bushes.

One evening as Obi was admiring his work he was scandalized to see an old woman from the village hobble right across the compound, through a marigold flower-bed and the hedges. On going up there he found faint signs of an almost disused path from the village across the school compound to the bush on the other side.

"It amazes me," said Obi to one of his teachers who had been three years in the school, "that you people allowed the villagers to make use of this footpath. It is simply incredible." He shook his head.

"The path," said the teacher apologetically, "appears to be very important to them. Although it is hardly used, it connects the village shrine with their place of burial."

"And what has that got to do with the school?" asked the headmaster.

"Well, I don't know," replied the other with a shrug of the shoulders. "But I remember there was a big row some time ago when we attempted to close it."

"That was some time ago. But it will not be used now," said Obi as he walked away. "What will the Government Education Officer think of this when he comes to inspect the school next week? The villagers might, for all I know, decide to use the schoolroom for a pagan ritual during the inspection."

Heavy sticks were planted closely across the path at the two places where it entered and left the school premises. These were further strengthened with barbed wire.

Three days later the village priest of *Ani*[3] called on the headmaster. He was an old man and walked with a slight stoop. He carried a stout walking-stick which he usually tapped on the floor, by way of emphasis, each time he made a new point in his argument.

---

3   Traditional belief system of the Igbo people of Nigeria, often called Odinani.

"I have heard," he said after the usual exchange of cordialities, "that our ancestral footpath has recently been closed...."

"Yes," replied Mr. Obi. "We cannot allow people to make a highway of our school compound."

"Look here, my son," said the priest bringing down his walking-stick, "this path was here before you were born and before your father was born. The whole life of this village depends on it. Our dead relatives depart by it and our ancestors visit us by it. But most important, it is the path of children coming in to be born...."

Mr. Obi listened with a satisfied smile on his face.

"The whole purpose of our school," he said finally, "is to eradicate just such beliefs as that. Dead men do not require footpaths. The whole idea is just fantastic. Our duty is to teach your children to laugh at such ideas."

"What you say may be true," replied the priest, "but we follow the practices of our fathers. If you reopen the path we shall have nothing to quarrel about. What I always say is: let the hawk perch and let the eagle perch." He rose to go.

"I am sorry," said the young headmaster. "But the school compound cannot be a thoroughfare. It is against our regulations. I would suggest your constructing another path, skirting our premises. We can even get our boys to help in building it. I don't suppose the ancestors will find the little detour too burdensome."

"I have no more words to say," said the old priest, already outside.

Two days later a young woman in the village died in childbed. A diviner was immediately consulted and he prescribed heavy sacrifices to propitiate ancestors insulted by the fence.

Obi woke up next morning among the ruins of his work. The beautiful hedges were torn up not just near the path but right round the school, the flowers trampled to death and one of the school buildings pulled down ... That day, the white Supervisor came to inspect the school and wrote a nasty report on the state of the premises but more seriously about the "tribal-war situation developing between the school and the village, arising in part from the misguided zeal of the new headmaster."

—*1953*

ALICE MUNRO

Alice Munro is acclaimed as a writer with a keen eye for detail and a fine sense of emotional nuance. In 2009, when she received the Man Booker International Prize, the award panel commented that "she brings as much depth, wisdom, and precision to every story as most novelists bring to a lifetime of novels."

Alice Laidlaw was born into a farming community in Huron County, Ontario. After graduating from high school, she won a partial scholarship to attend the University of Western Ontario. She completed two years towards a degree in English, but she was unable to continue her studies due to strained finances. In 1951, she married James Munro; they moved to Vancouver and then to Victoria, British Columbia, where the couple opened a bookstore. They eventually had three daughters, and the demands of motherhood affected Munro's writing in significant ways. She put it this way in a 1973 interview with Graeme Gibson: "In twenty years I've never had a day when I didn't have to think about somebody else's needs. And this means the writing has to be fitted in around it." In 1973, Munro and her husband divorced, and she moved back to Ontario.

Though Munro has set her stories in a wide variety of locations, from Scotland to Illinois to British Columbia, much of her fiction is set in Huron County—often referred to by readers and scholars as "Alice Munro country." The regional focus of Southern Gothic writing by American authors such as Flannery O'Connor was influential for Munro, because, as she explains, she "felt there a country being depicted that was like my own ... the part of the country I come from is absolutely gothic." The "Ontario Gothic" in Munro's work touches on the complexity that underlies the domestic—what the main character Del Jordan in *Lives of Girls and Women* describes as "dull, simple, amazing and unfathomable—deep caves paved with kitchen linoleum."

Munro has published 14 original collections of short stories and several compilations, and has received the Governor General's Literary Award and the Giller Prize, among many other honours. On October 10, 2013, she was awarded the Nobel Prize in Literature.

Gravel

AT THAT TIME we were living beside a gravel pit. Not a large one, hollowed out by monster machinery, just a minor pit that a farmer must have made some money from years before. In fact, the pit was shallow enough to lead you to think that there might have been some other intention for it—foundations for a house, maybe, that never made it any further.

My mother was the one who insisted on calling attention to it. "We live by the old gravel pit out the service-station road," she'd tell people, and laugh, because she was so happy to have shed everything connected with the house, the street—the husband—with the life she'd had before.

I barely remember that life. That is, I remember some parts of it clearly, but without the links you need to form a proper picture. All that I retain in my head of the house in town is the wallpaper with Teddy bears in my old room. In this new house, which was really a trailer, my sister, Caro, and I had narrow cots, stacked one above the other. When we first moved there, Caro talked to me a lot about our old house, trying to get me to remember this or that. It was when we were in bed that she talked like this, and generally the conversation ended with me failing to remember and her getting cross. Sometimes I thought I did remember, but out of contrariness or fear of getting things wrong I pretended not to.

It was summer when we moved to the trailer. We had our dog with us. Blitzee. "Blitzee loves it here," my mother said, and it was true. What dog wouldn't love to exchange a town street, even one with spacious lawns and big houses, for the wide-open countryside? She took to barking at every car that went past, as if she owned the road, and now and then she brought home a squirrel or a groundhog she'd killed. At first Caro was quite upset by this, and Neal would have a talk with her, explaining about a dog's nature and the chain of life in which some things had to eat other things.

"She gets her dog food," Caro argued, but Neal said, "Suppose she didn't? Suppose someday we all disappeared and she had to fend for herself?"

"I'm not going to," Caro said. "I'm not going to disappear, and I'm always going to look after her."

"You think so?" Neal said, and our mother stepped in to deflect him. Neal was always ready to get on the subject of the Americans and the atomic bomb, and our mother didn't think we were ready for that yet. She didn't know that when he brought it up I thought he was talking about an atomic bun. I knew that there was something wrong with this interpretation, but I wasn't about to ask questions and get laughed at.

Neal was an actor. In town there was a professional summer theatre, a new thing at the time, which some people were enthusiastic about and others worried about, fearing that it would bring in riffraff. My mother and father had been among those in favor, my mother more actively so, because she had more time. My father was an insurance agent and travelled a lot. My mother had got busy with various fund-raising schemes for the theatre and donated her services as an usher. She was good-looking and young enough to be mistaken for an actress. She'd begun to dress like an actress, too, in shawls and long skirts and dangling necklaces. She'd left her hair wild and stopped wearing makeup. Of course, I had not understood or even particularly noticed these changes at the time. My mother was my mother. But no doubt Caro had. And my father. Though, from all that I know of his nature and his feelings for my mother, I think he may have been proud to see how good she looked in these liberating styles and how well she fit in with the theatre people. When he spoke about this time later on, he said that he had always approved of the arts. I can imagine now how embarrassed my mother would have been, cringing and laughing to cover up her cringing, if he'd made this declaration in front of her theatre friends.

Well, then came a development that could have been foreseen and probably was, but not by my father. I don't know if it happened to any of the other volunteers. I do know, though I don't remember it, that my father wept and for a whole day followed my mother around the house, not letting her out of his sight and refusing to believe her. And, instead of telling him anything to make him feel better, she told him something that made him feel worse.

She told him that the baby was Neal's.

Was she sure?

Absolutely. She had been keeping track.

What happened then?

My father gave up weeping. He had to get back to work. My mother packed up our things and took us to live with Neal in the trailer he had found, out in the country. She said afterward that she had wept, too. But she said also that she had felt alive. Maybe for the first time in her life, truly alive. She felt as if she had been given a chance; she had started her life all over again. She'd walked out on her silver and her china and her decorating scheme and her flower garden and even on the books in her bookcase. She would live now, not read. She'd left her clothes hanging in the closet and her high-heeled shoes in their shoe trees. Her diamond ring and her wedding ring on the dresser. Her silk nightdresses in their drawer. She meant to go around naked at least some of the time in the country, as long as the weather stayed warm.

That didn't work out, because when she tried it Caro went and hid in her cot and even Neal said he wasn't crazy about the idea.

What did he think of all this? Neal. His philosophy, as he put it later, was to welcome whatever happened. Everything is a gift. We give and we take.

I am suspicious of people who talk like this, but I can't say that I have a right to be.

He was not really an actor. He had got into acting, he said, as an experiment. To see what he could find out about himself. In college, before he dropped out, he had performed as part of the chorus in "Oedipus Rex."[1] He had liked that— the giving yourself over, blending with others. Then one day, on the street in Toronto, he ran into a friend who was on his way to try out for a summer job with a new small-town theatre company. He went along, having nothing better to do, and ended up getting the job, while the other fellow didn't. He would play Banquo.[2] Sometimes they make Banquo's ghost visible, sometimes not. This time they wanted a visible version and Neal was the right size. An excellent size. A solid ghost. He had been thinking of wintering in our town anyway, before my mother sprang her surprise. He had already spotted the trailer. He had enough carpentry experience to pick up work renovating the theatre, which would see him through till spring. That was as far ahead as he liked to think.

Caro didn't even have to change schools. She was picked up by the school bus at the end of the short lane that ran alongside the gravel pit. She had to make friends with the country children, and perhaps explain some things to the town children who had been her friends the year before, but if she had any difficulty with that I never heard about it.

Blitzee was always waiting by the road for her to come home.

I didn't go to kindergarten, because my mother didn't have a car. But I didn't mind doing without other children. Caro, when she got home, was enough for me. And my mother was often in a playful mood. As soon as it snowed that winter she and I built a snowman and she asked, "Shall we call it Neal?" I said O.K., and we stuck various things on it to make it funny. Then we decided that I would run out of the house when his car came and say, "Here's Neal, here's Neal!" but be pointing up at the snowman. Which I did, but Neal got out of the car mad and yelled that he could have run me over.

---

1   *Oedipus the King* (c. 429 BCE): a Greek tragedy written by Sophocles. A chorus of Theban Elders advise Oedipus throughout the play.

2   From *Macbeth* (1606), a tragedy by William Shakespeare: Macbeth has Banquo murdered when he perceives him as a threat to his rise to power. Banquo's ghost appears before Macbeth later in the play.

That was one of the few times that I saw him act like a father.

Those short winter days must have seemed strange to me—in town, the lights came on at dusk. But children get used to changes. Sometimes I wondered about our other house. I didn't exactly miss it or want to live there again—I just wondered where it had gone.

My mother's good times with Neal went on into the night. If I woke up and had to go to the bathroom, I'd call for her. She would come happily but not in any hurry, with some piece of cloth or a scarf wrapped around her—also a smell that I associated with candlelight and music. And love.

Something did happen that was not so reassuring, but I didn't try to make much sense of it at the time. Blitzee, our dog, was not very big, but she didn't seem small enough to fit under Caro's coat. I don't know how Caro managed to do it. Not once but twice. She hid the dog under her coat on the school bus, and then, instead of going straight to school, she took Blitzee back to our old house in town, which was less than a block away. That was where my father found the dog, on the winter porch, which was not locked, when he came home for his solitary lunch. There was great surprise that she had got there, found her way home like a dog in a story. Caro made the biggest fuss, and claimed not to have seen the dog at all that morning. But then she made the mistake of trying it again, maybe a week later, and this time, though nobody on the bus or at school suspected her, our mother did.

I can't remember if our father brought Blitzee back to us. I can't imagine him in the trailer or at the door of the trailer or even on the road to it. Maybe Neal went to the house in town and picked her up. Not that that's any easier to imagine.

If I've made it sound as though Caro was unhappy or scheming all the time, that isn't the truth. As I've said, she did try to make me talk about things, at night in bed, but she wasn't constantly airing grievances. It wasn't her nature to be sulky. She was far too keen on making a good impression. She liked people to like her; she liked to stir up the air in a room with the promise of something you could even call merriment. She thought more about that than I did.

She was the one who most took after our mother, I think now.

There must have been some probing about what she'd done with the dog. I think I can remember some of it.

"I did it for a trick."

"Do you want to go and live with your father?"

I believe that was asked, and I believe she said no.

I didn't ask her anything. What she had done didn't seem strange to me. That's probably how it is with younger children—nothing that the strangely powerful older child does seems out of the ordinary.

Our mail was deposited in a tin box on a post, down by the road. My mother and I would walk there every day, unless it was particularly stormy, to see what had been left for us. We did this after I got up from my nap. Sometimes it was the only time we went outside all day. In the morning, we watched children's television shows—or she read while I watched. (She had not given up reading for very long.) We heated up some canned soup for lunch, then I went down for my nap while she read some more. She was quite big with the baby now and it stirred around in her stomach, so that I could feel it. Its name was going to be Brandy—already was Brandy—whether it was a boy or a girl.

One day when we were going down the lane for the mail, and were in fact not far from the box, my mother stopped and stood quite still.

"Quiet," she said to me, though I hadn't said a word or even played the shuffling game with my boots in the snow.

"I was being quiet," I said.

"Shush. Turn around."

"But we didn't get the mail."

"Never mind. Just walk."

Then I noticed that Blitzee, who was always with us, just behind or ahead of us, wasn't there anymore. Another dog was, on the opposite side of the road, a few feet from the mailbox.

My mother phoned the theatre as soon as we got home and let in Blitzee, who was waiting for us. Nobody answered. She phoned the school and asked someone to tell the bus driver to drive Caro up to the door. It turned out that the driver couldn't do that, because it had snowed since Neal last plowed the lane, but he did watch until she got to the house. There was no wolf to be seen by that time.

Neal was of the opinion that there never had been one. And if there had been, he said, it would have been no danger to us, weak as it was probably from hibernation.

Caro said that wolves did not hibernate. "We learned about them in school."

Our mother wanted Neal to get a gun.

"You think I'm going to get a gun and go and shoot a goddam poor mother wolf who has probably got a bunch of babies back in the bush and is just trying to protect them, the way you're trying to protect yours?" he said quietly.

Caro said, "Only two. They only have two at a time."

"O.K. O.K. I'm talking to your mother."

"You don't know that," my mother said. "You don't know if it's got hungry cubs or anything."

I had never thought she'd talk to him like that.

He said, "Easy. Easy. Let's just think a bit. Guns are a terrible thing. If I went and got a gun, then what would I be saying? That Vietnam[3] was O.K.? That I might as well have gone to Vietnam?"

"You're not an American."

"You're not going to rile me."

This is more or less what they said, and it ended up with Neal not having to get a gun. We never saw the wolf again, if it was a wolf. I think my mother stopped going to get the mail, but she may have become too big to be comfortable doing that anyway.

The snow dwindled magically. The trees were still bare of leaves and my mother made Caro wear her coat in the mornings, but she came home after school dragging it behind her.

My mother said that the baby had got to be twins, but the doctor said it wasn't.

"Great. Great," Neal said, all in favor of the twins idea. "What do doctors know."

The gravel pit had filled to its brim with melted snow and rain, so that Caro had to edge around it on her way to catch the school bus. It was a little lake, still and dazzling under the clear sky. Caro asked with not much hope if we could play in it.

Our mother said not to be crazy. "It must be twenty feet deep," she said.

Neal said, "Maybe ten."

Caro said, "Right around the edge it wouldn't be."

Our mother said yes it was. "It just drops off," she said. "It's not like going in at the beach, for fuck's sake. Just stay away from it."

She had started saying "fuck" quite a lot, perhaps more than Neal did, and in a more exasperated tone of voice.

"Should we keep the dog away from it, too?" she asked him.

Neal said that that wasn't a problem. "Dogs can swim."

A Saturday. Caro watched "The Friendly Giant"[4] with me and made comments that spoiled it. Neal was lying on the couch, which unfolded into his and my mother's bed. He was smoking his kind of cigarettes, which could not be smoked at work so had to be made the most of on weekends. Caro sometimes bothered him, asking to try one. Once he had let her, but told her not to tell our mother.

---

3   The Vietnam War (1955–75) was between communist North Vietnam and the anticommunist South Vietnam; America's role as an ally of South Vietnam was (and still is) a source of much controversy.

4   A popular Canadian television show for children that aired from 1958 to 1985.

I was there, though, so I told.

There was alarm, though not quite a row.

"You know he'd have those kids out of here like a shot," our mother said. "Never again."

"Never again," Neal said agreeably. "So what if he feeds them poison Rice Krispies crap?"

In the beginning, we hadn't seen our father at all. Then, after Christmas, a plan had been worked out for Saturdays. Our mother always asked afterward if we had had a good time. I always said yes, and meant it, because I thought that if you went to a movie or to look at Lake Huron or ate in a restaurant, that meant that you had had a good time. Caro said yes, too, but in a tone of voice that suggested that it was none of our mother's business. Then my father went on a winter holiday to Cuba (my mother remarked on this with some surprise and maybe approval) and came back with a lingering sort of flu that caused the visits to lapse. They were supposed to resume in the spring, but so far they hadn't.

After the television was turned off, Caro and I were sent outside to run around, as our mother said, and get some fresh air. We took the dog with us.

When we got outside, the first thing we did was loosen and let trail the scarves our mother had wrapped around our necks. (The fact was, though we may not have put the two things together, the deeper she got into her pregnancy the more she slipped back into behaving like an ordinary mother, at least when it was a matter of scarves we didn't need or regular meals. There was not so much championing of wild ways as there had been in the fall.) Caro asked me what I wanted to do, and I said I didn't know. This was a formality on her part but the honest truth on mine. We let the dog lead us, anyway, and Blitzee's idea was to go and look at the gravel pit. The wind was whipping the water up into little waves, and very soon we got cold, so we wound our scarves back around our necks.

I don't know how much time we spent just wandering around the water's edge, knowing that we couldn't be seen from the trailer. After a while, I realized that I was being given instructions.

I was to go back to the trailer and tell Neal and our mother something.

That the dog had fallen into the water.

The dog had fallen into the water and Caro was afraid she'd be drowned.

Blitzee. Drownded.

Drowned.

But Blitzee wasn't in the water.

She could be. And Caro could jump in to save her.

I believe I still put up some argument, along the lines of she hasn't, you haven't, it could happen but it hasn't. I also remembered that Neal had said dogs didn't drown.

Caro instructed me to do as I was told.

Why?

I may have said that, or I may have just stood there not obeying and trying to work up another argument.

In my mind I can see her picking up Blitzee and tossing her, though Blitzee was trying to hang on to her coat. Then backing up, Caro backing up to take a run at the water. Running, jumping, all of a sudden hurling herself at the water. But I can't recall the sound of the splashes as they, one after the other, hit the water. Not a little splash or a big one. Perhaps I had turned toward the trailer by then—I must have done so.

When I dream of this, I am always running. And in my dreams I am running not toward the trailer but back toward the gravel pit. I can see Blitzee floundering around and Caro swimming toward her, swimming strongly, on the way to rescue her. I see her light-brown checked coat and her plaid scarf and her proud successful face and reddish hair darkened at the end of its curls by the water. All I have to do is watch and be happy—nothing required of me, after all.

What I really did was make my way up the little incline toward the trailer. And when I got there I sat down. Just as if there had been a porch or a bench, though in fact the trailer had neither of these things. I sat down and waited for the next thing to happen.

I know this because it's a fact. I don't know, however, what my plan was or what I was thinking. I was waiting, maybe, for the next act in Caro's drama. Or in the dog's.

I don't know if I sat there for five minutes. More? Less? It wasn't too cold.

I went to see a professional person about this once and she convinced me—for a time, she convinced me—that I must have tried the door of the trailer and found it locked. Locked because my mother and Neal were having sex and had locked it against interruptions. If I'd banged on the door they would have been angry. The counsellor was satisfied to bring me to this conclusion, and I was satisfied, too. For a while. But I no longer think that was true. I don't think they would have locked the door, because I know that once they didn't and Caro walked in and they laughed at the look on her face.

Maybe I remembered that Neal had said that dogs did not drown, which meant that Caro's rescue of Blitzee would not be necessary. Therefore she herself wouldn't be able to carry out her game. So many games, with Caro.

Did I think she could swim? At nine, many children can. And in fact it turned out that she'd had one lesson the summer before, but then we had moved to the trailer and she hadn't taken any more. She may have thought she could manage well enough. And I may indeed have thought that she could do anything she wanted to.

The counsellor did not suggest that I might have been sick of carrying out Caro's orders, but the thought did occur to me. It doesn't quite seem right, though. If I'd been older, maybe. At the time, I still expected her to fill my world.

How long did I sit there? Likely not long. And it's possible that I did knock. After a while. After a minute or two. In any case, my mother did, at some point, open the door, for no reason. A presentiment.

Next thing, I am inside. My mother is yelling at Neal and trying to make him understand something. He is getting to his feet and standing there speaking to her, touching her, with such mildness and gentleness and consolation. But that is not what my mother wants at all and she tears herself away from him and runs out the door. He shakes his head and looks down at his bare feet. His big helpless-looking toes.

I think he says something to me with a singsong sadness in his voice. Strange. Beyond that I have no details.

My mother didn't throw herself into the water. She didn't go into labor from the shock. My brother, Brent, was not born until a week or ten days after the funeral, and he was a full-term infant. Where she was while she waited for the birth to happen I do not know. Perhaps she was kept in the hospital and sedated as much as possible under the circumstances.

I remember the day of the funeral quite well. A very pleasant and comfortable woman I didn't know—her name was Josie—took me on an expedition. We visited some swings and a sort of doll's house that was large enough for me to go inside, and we ate a lunch of my favorite treats, but not enough to make me sick. Josie was somebody I got to know very well later on. She was a friend my father had made in Cuba, and after the divorce she became my stepmother, his second wife.

My mother recovered. She had to. There was Brent to look after and, most of the time, me. I believe I stayed with my father and Josie while she got settled in the house that she planned to live in for the rest of her life. I don't remember being there with Brent until he was big enough to sit up in his high chair.

My mother went back to her old duties at the theatre. At first she may have worked as she had before, as a volunteer usher, but by the time I was in school she had a real job, with pay, and year-round responsibilities. She was the business manager. The theatre survived, through various ups and downs, and is still going now.

Neal didn't believe in funerals, so he didn't attend Caro's. He never saw Brent. He wrote a letter—I found this out much later—saying that since he did not intend to act as a father it would be better for him to bow out at the start. I never mentioned him to Brent, because I thought it would upset my mother. Also because Brent showed so little sign of being like him—like Neal—and seemed, in fact, so much more like my father that I really wondered about what was going on around the time he was conceived. My father has never said anything about this and never would. He treats Brent just as he treats me, but he is the kind of man who would do that anyway.

He and Josie have not had any children of their own, but I don't think that bothers them. Josie is the only person who ever talks about Caro, and even she doesn't do it often. She does say that my father doesn't hold my mother responsible. He has also said that he must have been sort of a stick-in-the-mud when my mother wanted more excitement in her life. He needed a shaking-up, and he got one. There's no use being sorry about it. Without the shaking-up, he would never have found Josie and the two of them would not have been so happy now.

"Which two?" I might say, just to derail him, and he would staunchly say, "Josie. Josie, of course."

My mother cannot be made to recall any of those times, and I don't bother her with them. I know that she has driven down the lane we lived on, and found it quite changed, with the sort of trendy houses you see now, put up on unproductive land. She mentioned this with the slight scorn that such houses evoke in her. I went down the lane myself but did not tell anyone. All the eviscerating that is done in families these days strikes me as a mistake.

Even where the gravel pit was a house now stands, the ground beneath it levelled.

I have a partner, Ruthann, who is younger than I am but, I think, somewhat wiser. Or at least more optimistic about what she calls routing out my demons. I would never have got in touch with Neal if it had not been for her urging. Of course, for a long time I had no way, just as I had no thought, of getting in touch. It was he who finally wrote to me. A brief note of congratulations, he said, after seeing my picture in the *Alumni Gazette*. What he was doing looking through the *Alumni Gazette* I have no idea. I had received one of those academic honors that mean something in a restricted circle and little anywhere else.

He was living hardly fifty miles away from where I teach, which also happens to be where I went to college. I wondered if he had been there at that time. So close. Had he become a scholar?

At first I had no intention of replying to the note, but I told Ruthann and she said that I should think about writing back. So the upshot was that I sent him an e-mail, and arrangements were made. I was to meet him in his town, in the unthreatening surroundings of a university cafeteria. I told myself that if he looked unbearable—I did not quite know what I meant by this—I could just walk on through.

He was shorter than he used to be, as adults we remember from childhood usually are. His hair was thin, and trimmed close to his head. He got me a cup of tea. He was drinking tea himself.

What did he do for a living?

He said that he tutored students in preparation for exams. Also, he helped them write their essays. Sometimes, you might say, he wrote those essays. Of course, he charged.

"It's no way to get to be a millionaire, I can tell you."

He lived in a dump. Or a semi-respectable dump. He liked it. He looked for clothes at the Sally Ann. That was O.K., too.

"Suits my principles."

I did not congratulate him on any of this, but, to tell the truth, I doubt that he expected me to.

"Anyway, I don't think my life style is so interesting. I think you might want to know how it happened."

I could not figure out how to speak.

"I was stoned," he said. "And, furthermore, I'm not a swimmer. Not many swimming pools around where I grew up. I'd have drowned, too. Is that what you wanted to know?"

I said that he was not really the one that I was wondering about.

Then he became the third person I'd asked, "What do you think Caro had in mind?"

The counsellor had said that we couldn't know. "Likely she herself didn't know what she wanted. Attention? I don't think she meant to drown herself. Attention to how bad she was feeling?"

Ruthann had said, "To make your mother do what she wanted? Make her smarten up and see that she had to go back to your father?"

Neal said, "It doesn't matter. Maybe she thought she could paddle better than she could. Maybe she didn't know how heavy winter clothes can get. Or that there wasn't anybody in a position to help her."

He said to me, "Don't waste your time. You're not thinking what if you had hurried up and told, are you? Not trying to get in on the guilt?"

I said that I had considered what he was saying, but no.

"The thing is to be happy," he said. "No matter what. Just try that. You can. It gets to be easier and easier. It's nothing to do with circumstances. You wouldn't believe how good it is. Accept everything and then tragedy disappears. Or tragedy lightens, anyway, and you're just there, going along easy in the world."

Now, goodbye.

I see what he meant. It really is the right thing to do. But, in my mind, Caro keeps running at the water and throwing herself, as if in triumph, and I'm still caught, waiting for her to explain to me, waiting for the splash.

—2011

Tricks

"I'LL DIE," said Robin, on an evening years ago. "I'll die if they don't have that dress ready."

They were in the screen porch of the dark-green clapboard house on Isaac Street. Willard Greig, who lived next door, was playing rummy at the card table with Robin's sister, Joanne. Robin was sitting on the couch, frowning at a magazine. The smell of nicotiana[5] fought with a smell of ketchup simmering in some kitchen along the street.

Willard watched Joanne barely smile, before she inquired in a neutral voice, "What did you say?"

"I said, I'll die." Robin was defiant. "I'll die if they don't have that dress ready by tomorrow. The cleaners."

"That's what I thought you said. You'd die?"

You could never catch Joanne on any remark of that sort.

Her tone was so mild, her scorn so immensely quiet, her smile—now vanished—was just the tiny lifting of a corner of her mouth.

"Well, I will," said Robin defiantly. "I need it."

"She *needs* it, she'll *die*, she's going to the *play*," said Joanne to Willard, in a confidential tone.

Willard said, "Now, Joanne." His parents, and he himself, had been friends of the girls' parents—he still thought of these two as *the girls*—and now that all of the parents were dead he felt it was his duty to keep the daughters, as much as possible, out of each other's hair.

Joanne was now thirty years old, Robin twenty-six. Joanne had a childish body, a narrow chest, a long sallow face, and straight, fine, brown hair. She never tried to pretend she was anything but an unlucky person, stunted halfway between childhood and female maturity. Stunted, crippled in a way, by severe and persisting asthma from childhood on. You didn't expect a person who looked like that, a person who couldn't step outside in winter or be left alone at night,

---

5 Tobacco.

to have such a devastating way of catching on to other, more fortunate people's foolishness. Or to have such a fund of contempt. All their lives, it seemed to Willard, he'd been watching Robin's eyes fill up with tears of wrath, and hearing Joanne say, "What's the matter with you *now*?"

Tonight Robin had felt only a slight sting. Tomorrow was her day to go to Stratford, and she felt herself already living outside Joanne's reach.

"What's the play, Robin?" Willard asked, to smooth things as much as he could. "Is it by Shakespeare?"

"Yes. *As You Like It*."

"And can you follow him all right? Shakespeare?" Robin said she could.

"You're a wonder."

***

For five years Robin had been doing this. One play every summer. It had started when she was living in Stratford, training to be a nurse. She went with a fellow student who had a couple of free tickets from her aunt, who worked on costumes. The girl who had the tickets was bored sick—it was *King Lear*—so Robin had kept quiet about how she felt. She could not have expressed it anyway—she would rather have gone away from the theater alone, and not had to talk to anybody for at least twenty-four hours. Her mind was made up then to come back. And to come by herself.

It wouldn't be difficult. The town where she had grown up, and where, later, she had to find her work because of Joanne, was only thirty miles away. People there knew that the Shakespeare plays were being put on in Stratford, but Robin had never heard of anybody going to see one. People like Willard were afraid of being looked down on by the people in the audience, as well as having the problem of not following the language. And people like Joanne were sure that nobody, ever, could really like Shakespeare, and so if anybody from here went, it was because they wanted to mix with the higher-ups, who were not enjoying it themselves but only letting on they were. Those few people in town who made a habit of seeing stage productions preferred to go to Toronto, to the Royal Alex, when a Broadway musical was on tour.

Robin liked to have a good seat, so she could only afford a Saturday matinee. She picked a play that was being done on one of her weekends off from the hospital. She never read it beforehand, and she didn't care whether it was a tragedy or a comedy. She had yet to see a single person there that she knew; in the theater or out on the streets, and that suited her very well. One of the nurses she worked with had said to her, "I'd never have the nerve to do that all on my own," and that had made Robin realize how different she herself must be from most people. She never felt more at ease than at these times, surrounded by strangers. After the play she would walk downtown, along the river, and find some inexpensive place to eat—usually a sandwich, as she sat on a stool at the counter. And at twenty to eight she would catch the train home. That was all. Yet those few hours filled her with an assurance that the life she was going back to, which seemed so makeshift and unsatisfactory, was only temporary and could easily be put up with. And there was a radiance behind it, behind that life, behind everything, expressed by the sunlight seen through the train windows. The sunlight and long shadows on the summer fields, like the remains of the play in her head.

Last year, she saw *Antony and Cleopatra*. When it was over she walked along the river, and noticed that there was a black swan—the first she had ever seen—a subtle intruder gliding and feeding at a short distance from the white ones. Perhaps it was the glisten of the white swans' wings that made her think of eating at a real restaurant this time, not at a counter. White tablecloth, a few fresh flowers, a glass of wine, and something unusual to eat, like mussels, or Cornish hen. She made a move to check in her purse, to see how much money she had.

And her purse was not there. The seldom-used little paisley-cloth bag on its silver chain was not slung over her shoulder as usual, it was gone. She had walked alone nearly all the way downtown from the theater without noticing that it was gone. And of course her dress had no pockets. She had no return ticket, no lipstick, no comb, and no money. Not a dime.

She remembered that throughout the play she had held the purse on her lap, under her program. She did not have the program now, either. Perhaps both had slipped to the floor? But no—she remembered having the bag in the toilet cubicle of the Ladies Room. She had hung it by the chain on the hook that was on the back of the door. But she had not left it there. No. She had looked at herself in the mirror over the washbasin, she had got the comb out to fiddle with her hair. Her hair was dark, and fine, and though she visualized it puffed up like Jackie Kennedy's, and did it up in rollers at night, it had a tendency to go flat. Otherwise she had been pleased with what she saw. She had greenish-gray eyes and black eyebrows and a skin that tanned whether she tried or not, and all this was set off well by her tight-waisted, full-skirted dress of avocado-green polished cotton, with the rows of little tucks around the hips.

That was where she had left it. On the counter by the washbasin. Admiring herself, turning and looking over her shoulder to catch sight of the V of the dress at the back—she believed she had a pretty back—and checking that there was no bra strap showing anywhere.

And on a tide of vanity, of silly gratification, she had sallied out of the Ladies Room, leaving the purse behind.

She climbed the bank to the street and started back to the theater by the straightest route. She walked as fast as she could. There was no shade along the street, and there was busy traffic. In the heat of the late afternoon. She was almost running. That caused the sweat to leak out from under the shields in her dress. She trekked across the baking parking lot—now empty—and up the hill. No more shade up there, and nobody in sight around the theater building.

But it was not locked. In the empty lobby she stood a moment to get her sight back after the outdoor glare. She could feel her heart thumping, and the drops of moisture popping out on her upper lip. The ticket booths were closed, and so was the refreshment counter. The inner theater doors were locked. She took the stairway down to the washroom, her shoes clattering on the marble steps.

Let it be open, let it be open, let it be there.

No. There was nothing on the smooth veined counter, nothing in the waste-baskets, nothing on any hook on the back of any door.

A man was mopping the floor of the lobby when she came upstairs. He told her that it might have been turned in to the Lost and Found, but the Lost and Found was locked. With some reluctance he left his mopping and led her down another stairs to a cubbyhole containing several umbrellas, parcels, and even jackets and hats and a disgusting-looking brownish fox scarf. But no paisley-cloth shoulder purse.

"No luck," he said.

"Could it be under my seat?" she begged, though she was sure it could not be.

"Already been swept in there."

There was nothing for her to do then but climb the stairs, walk through the lobby, and go out onto the street.

She walked in the other direction from the parking lot, seeking shade. She could imagine Joanne saying that the cleaning man had already stashed her purse away to take home to his wife or his daughter, that is what they were like in a place like this. She looked for a bench or a low wall to sit down on while she figured things out. She didn't see such a thing anywhere.

A large dog came up behind her and knocked against her as it passed. It was a dark-brown dog, with long legs and an arrogant, stubborn expression.

"Juno. Juno," a man called. "Watch where you're going."

"She is just young and rude," he said to Robin. "She thinks she owns the sidewalk. She's not vicious. Were you afraid?"

Robin said, "No." The loss of her purse had preoccupied her and she had not thought of an attack from a dog being piled on top of that.

"When people see a Doberman they are often frightened. Dobermans have a reputation to be fierce, and she is trained to be fierce when she's a watchdog, but not when she's walking."

Robin hardly knew one breed of dog from another. Because of Joanne's asthma, they never had dogs or cats around the house.

"It's all right," she said.

Instead of going ahead to where the dog Juno was waiting, her owner called her back. He fixed the leash he was carrying onto her collar.

"I let her loose down on the grass. Down below the theater. She likes that. But she ought to be on the leash up here. I was lazy. Are you ill?"

Robin did not even feel surprised at this change in the conversation's direction. She said, "I lost my purse. It was my own fault. I left it by the washbasin in the Ladies Room at the theater and I went back to look but it was gone. I just walked away and left it there after the play."

"What play was it today?"

"*Antony and Cleopatra*," she said. "My money was in it and my train ticket home."

"You came on the train? To see *Antony and Cleopatra*?"

"Yes."

She remembered the advice their mother had given to her and to Joanne about travelling on the train, or travelling anywhere. Always have a couple of bills folded and pinned to your underwear. Also, don't get into a conversation with a strange man.

"What are you smiling at?" he said.

"I don't know."

"Well, you can go on smiling," he said, "because I will be happy to lend you some money for the train. What time does it go?"

She told him, and he said, "All right. But before that you should have some food. Or you will be hungry and not enjoy the train ride. I haven't anything with me, because when I go to take Juno on her walk I do not bring any money. But it isn't far to my shop. Come with me and I'll get it out of the till."

She had been too preoccupied, until now, to notice that he spoke with an accent. What was it? It was not French or Dutch—the two accents that she thought she could recognize, French from school and Dutch from the immigrants who were sometimes patients in the hospital. And the other thing she took note of was that he spoke of her enjoying the train ride. Nobody she knew would speak of a grown person doing that. But he spoke of it as being quite natural and necessary.

At the corner of Downie Street, he said, "We turn this way. My house is just along here."

He said *house*, when he had said *shop* before. But it could be that his shop was in his house.

She was not worried. Afterwards she wondered about that. Without a moment's hesitation she had accepted his offer of help, allowed him to rescue her, found it entirely natural that he should not carry money with him on his walks but could get it from the till in his shop.

A reason for this might have been his accent. Some of the nurses mocked the accents of the Dutch farmers and their wives—behind their backs, of course. So Robin had got into the habit of treating such people with special consideration, as if they had speech impediments, or even some mental slowness, though she knew that this was nonsense. An accent, therefore, roused in her a certain benevolence and politeness.

And she had not looked at him at all closely. At first she was too upset, and then it was not easy, because they were walking side by side. He was tall, long-legged, and walked quickly. One thing she had noticed was the sunlight glinting on his hair, which was cut short as stubble, and it seemed to her that it was bright silver. That is, gray. His forehead, being broad and high, also shone in the sun, and she had somehow got the impression that he was a generation beyond her—a courteous, yet slightly impatient, schoolteacherly, high-handed sort of person, who demanded respect, never intimacy. Later, indoors, she was able to see that the gray hair was mixed with a rusty red—though his skin had an olive tint unusual for a redhead—and that his indoor movements were sometimes awkward, as if he wasn't used to having company in his living space. He was probably not more than ten years older than she was.

She had trusted him for faulty reasons. But she had not been mistaken to do so.

The shop really was in a house. A narrow brick house left over from earlier days, on a street otherwise lined with buildings built to be shops. There was the sort of front door and step and window that a regular house would have, and in the window was an elaborate clock. He unlocked the door, but did not turn around the sign that said *Closed*. Juno crowded in ahead of them both, and again he apologized for her.

"She thinks it's her job to check that there's nobody in here who shouldn't be, and not anything different from when she went out."

The place was full of clocks. Dark wood and light wood, painted figures and gilded domes. They sat on shelves and on the floor and even on the counter across which business could be transacted. Beyond that, some sat on benches with their insides exposed. Juno slipped between them neatly, and could be heard thumping up a stairs.

"Are you interested in clocks?"

Robin said "No," before she thought of being polite.

"All right, then I do not have to go into my spiel," he said, and led her along the path Juno had taken, past the door of what was probably a toilet, and up the steep stairway. Then they were in a kitchen where all was clean and bright and tidy, and Juno was waiting beside a red dish on the floor, flopping her tail.

"You just wait," he said. "Yes. Wait. Don't you see we have a guest?"

He stood aside for Robin to enter the big front room, which had no rug on the wide painted floorboards and no curtains, only shades, on the windows. There was a hi-fi system taking up a good deal of space along one wall, and a sofa along the wall opposite, of the sort that would pull out to make a bed. A couple of canvas chairs, and a bookcase with books on one shelf and magazines on the others, tidily stacked. No pictures or cushions or ornaments in sight. A bachelor's room, with everything deliberate and necessary and proclaiming a certain austere satisfaction. Very different from the only other bachelor premises Robin was familiar with—Willard Greig's, which seemed more like a forlorn encampment established casually in the middle of his dead parents' furniture.

"Where would you like to sit?" he said. "The sofa? It is more comfortable than the chairs. I will make you a cup of coffee and you sit here and drink it while I make some supper. What do you do other times, between when the play is over and the train is going home?"

Foreigners talked differently, leaving a bit of space around the words, the way actors do.

"Walk," Robin said. "And I get something to eat."

"The same today, then. Are you bored when you eat alone?"

"No. I think about the play."

The coffee was very strong, but she got used to it. She did not feel that she should offer to help him in the kitchen, as she would have done with a woman. She got up and crossed the room almost on tiptoe and helped herself to a magazine. And even as she picked it up she knew this would be useless—the magazines were all printed on cheap brown paper in a language she could neither read nor identify.

In fact she realized, once she had it open on her lap, that she could not even identify all the letters.

He came in with more coffee.

"Ah," he said. "So do you read my language?"

That sounded sarcastic, but his eyes avoided her. It was almost as if, inside his own place, he had turned shy.

"I don't even know what language it is," she answered.

"It is Serbian. Some people say Serbo-Croatian."

"Is that where you come from?"

"I am from Montenegro."

Now she was stumped. She did not know where Montenegro was. Beside Greece? No—that was Macedonia.

"Montenegro is in Yugoslavia," he said. "Or that is what they tell us. But we don't think so."

"I didn't think you could get out of those countries," she said. "Those Communist countries. I didn't think you could just leave like ordinary people and get out into the West."

"Oh, you can." He spoke as if this did not interest him very much, or as if he had forgotten about it. "You can get out if you really want to. I left nearly five years ago. And now it is easier. Very soon I am going back there and then I expect I will be leaving again. Now I must cook your dinner. Or you will go away hungry."

"Just one thing," said Robin. "Why can't I read these letters? I mean, what letters are they? Is this the alphabet where you come from?"

"The Cyrillic alphabet. Like Greek. Now I'm cooking."

She sat with the strangely printed pages open in her lap and thought that she had entered a foreign world. A small piece of a foreign world on Downie Street in Stratford. Montenegro. Cyrillic alphabet. It was rude, she supposed, to keep asking him things. To make him feel like a specimen. She would have to control herself, though now she could come up with a host of questions.

All the clocks below—or most of them—began to chime the hour. It was already seven o'clock.

"Is there any later train?" he called from the kitchen.

"Yes. At five to ten."

"Will that be all right? Will anybody worry about you?"

She said no. Joanne would be displeased, but you could not exactly call that being worried.

Supper was a stew or thick soup, served in a bowl, with bread and red wine.

"Stroganoff," he said. "I hope you like it."

"It's delicious," she said truthfully. She was not so sure about the wine—she would have liked it sweeter. "Is this what you eat in Montenegro?"

"Not exactly. Montenegrin food is not very good. We are not famous for our food."

So then it was surely all right to say, "What are you famous for?"

"What are you?"

"Canadian."

"No. What are you famous for?"

That vexed her, she felt stupid. Yet she laughed.

"I don't know. I guess nothing."

"What Montenegrins are famous for is yelling and screaming and fighting. They're like Juno. They need discipline."

He got up to put on some music. He did not ask what she wanted to hear, and that was a relief. She did not want to be asked which composers she preferred, when the only two she could think of were Mozart and Beethoven and she was not sure she could tell their work apart. She really liked folk music, but she thought he might find that preference tiresome and condescending, linking it up to some idea she had of Montenegro.

He put on a kind of jazz.

Robin had never had a lover, or even a boyfriend. How had this happened, or not happened? She did not know. There was Joanne, of course, but there were other girls, similarly burdened, who had managed. A reason might have been that she had not given the matter enough attention, soon enough. In the town she lived in, most girls were seriously attached to somebody before they finished high school, and some didn't finish high school, but dropped out to get married. The girls of the better class, of course—the few girls whose parents could afford to send them to college—were expected to detach themselves from any high school boyfriend before going off to look for better prospects. The discarded boys were soon snapped up, and the girls who had not moved quickly enough then found themselves with slim pickings. Beyond a certain age, any new man who arrived was apt to come equipped with a wife.

But Robin had had her opportunity. She had gone away to train to be a nurse, which should have given her a fresh start. Girls who trained to be nurses got a chance at doctors. There too, she had failed. She didn't realize it at the time. She was too serious, maybe that was the problem. Too serious about something like *King Lear* and not about making use of dances and tennis games. A certain kind of seriousness in a girl could cancel out looks. But it was hard to think of a single case in which she envied any other girl the man she had got. In fact she couldn't yet think of anybody she wished she had married.

Not that she was against marriage altogether. She was just waiting, as if she was a girl of fifteen, and it was only now and then that she was brought up against her true situation. Occasionally one of the women she worked with would arrange for her to meet somebody, and then she would be shocked at the prospect that had been considered suitable. And recently even Willard had frightened her, by making a joke about how he should move in someday, and help her look after Joanne.

Some people were already excusing her, even praising her, taking it for granted that she had planned from the beginning to devote her life to Joanne.

When they had finished eating he asked her if she would like to take a walk along the river before she caught her train. She agreed, and he said that they could not do that unless he knew her name.

"I might want to introduce you," he said.

She told him.

"Robin like the bird?"

"Like Robin Redbreast," she said, as she had often said before, without thinking about it. Now she was so embarrassed that all she could do was go on speaking recklessly.

"It's your turn now to tell me yours."

His name was Daniel. "Danilo. But Daniel here."

"So here is here," she said, still in this saucy tone which was the result of embarrassment at Robin Redbreast. "But where is there? In Montenegro—do you live in a town or the country?"

"I lived in the mountains."

While they were sitting in the room above his shop there had been a distance, and she had never feared—and never hoped—that the distance would be altered by any brusque or clumsy or sly movement of his. On the few occasions when this had happened with other men she had felt embarrassed for them. Now of necessity she and this man walked fairly close to each other and if they met someone their arms might brush together. Or he would move slightly behind her to get out of the way and his arm or chest knocked for a second against her back. These possibilities, and the knowledge that the people they met must see them as a couple, set up something like a hum, a tension, across her shoulders and down that one arm.

He asked her about *Antony and Cleopatra*, had she liked it (yes) and what part she had liked best. What came into her mind then were various bold and convincing embraces, but she could not say so.

"The part at the end," she said, "where she is going to put the asp on her body"—she had been going to say *breast*, then changed it, but *body* did not sound much better—"and the old man comes in with the basket of figs that the asp is in and they joke around, sort of. I think I liked it because you didn't expect that then. I mean, I liked other things too, I liked it all, but that was different."

"Yes," he said. "I like that too."

"Did you see it?"

"No. I'm saving my money now. But I read a lot of Shakespeare once, students read it when they were learning English. In the daytime I learned about clocks, in the nighttime I learned English. What did you learn?"

"Not so much," she said. "Not in school. After that I learned what you have to, to be a nurse."

"That's a lot to learn, to be a nurse. I think so."

After that they spoke about the coolness of the evening, how welcome it was, and how the nights had lengthened noticeably, though there was still all August to get through. And about Juno, how she had wanted to come with them but had settled down immediately when he reminded her that she had to stay and guard the shop. This talk felt more and more like an agreed-upon subterfuge, like a conventional screen for what was becoming more inevitable all the time, more necessary, between them.

But in the light of the railway depot, whatever was promising, or mysterious, was immediately removed. There were people lined up at the window, and he stood behind them, waiting his turn, and bought her ticket. They walked out onto the platform, where passengers were waiting.

"If you will write your full name and address on a piece of paper," she said, "I'll send you the money right away."

Now it will happen, she thought. And *it* was nothing. Now nothing will happen. Good-bye. Thank you. I'll send the money. No hurry. Thank you. It was no trouble. Thank you just the same. Good-bye.

"Let's walk along here," he said, and they walked along the platform away from the light.

"Better not to worry about the money. It is so little and it might not get here anyway, because I am going away so soon. Sometimes the mail is slow."

"Oh, but I must pay you back."

"I'll tell you how to pay me back, then. Are you listening?"

"Yes."

"I will be here next summer in the same place. The same shop. I will be there by June at the latest. Next summer. So you will choose your play and come here on the train and come to the shop."

"I will pay you back then?"

"Oh yes. And I will make dinner and we'll drink wine and I will tell you all about what has happened in the year and you will tell me. And I want one other thing."

"What?"

"You will wear the same dress. Your green dress. And your hair the same."

She laughed. "So you'll know me."

"Yes."

They were at the end of the platform, and he said, "Watch here," then, "All right?" as they stepped down on the gravel.

"All right," said Robin with a lurch in her voice, either because of the uncertain surface of the gravel or because by now he had taken hold of her at the shoulders, then was moving his hands down her bare arms.

"It is important that we have met," he said. "I think so. Do you think so?"

She said, "Yes."

"Yes. Yes."

He slid his hands under her arms to hold her closer, around the waist, and they kissed again and again.

The conversation of kisses. Subtle, engrossing, fearless, transforming. When they stopped they were both trembling, and it was with an effort that he got his voice under control, tried to speak matter-of-factly.

"We will not write letters, letters are not a good idea. We will just remember each other and next summer we will meet. You don't have to let me know, just come. If you still feel the same, you will just come."

They could hear the train. He helped her up to the platform, then did not touch her anymore, but walked briskly beside her, feeling for something in his pocket.

Just before he left her, he handed her a folded piece of paper. "I wrote on it before we left the shop," he said.

On the train she read his name. *Danilo Adzic*. And the words *Bjelojevici. My village.*

She walked from the station, under the dark full trees. Joanne had not gone to bed. She was playing solitaire.

"I'm sorry I missed the early train," Robin said. "I've had my supper. I had Stroganoff."

"So that's what I'm smelling."

"And I had a glass of wine."

"I can smell that too."

"I think I'll go right up to bed."

"I think you'd better."

Trailing clouds of glory, thought Robin on her way upstairs. From God, who is our home.[6]

How silly that was, and even sacrilegious, if you could believe in sacrilege. Being kissed on a railway platform and told to report in a year's time. If Joanne knew about it, what would she say? A foreigner. Foreigners pick up girls that nobody else will have.

---

6   A reference to William Wordsworth's 1807 poem "Ode: Intimations of Immortality."

For a couple of weeks the two sisters hardly spoke. Then, seeing that there were no phone calls or letters, and that Robin went out in the evenings only to go to the library, Joanne relaxed. She knew that something had changed, but she didn't think it was serious. She began to make jokes to Willard.

In front of Robin she said, "You know that our girl here has started having mysterious adventures in Stratford? Oh yes. I tell you. Came home smelling of drink and goulash. You know what that smells like? Vomit."

What she probably thought was that Robin had gone to some weird restaurant, with some European dishes on the menu, and ordered a glass of wine with her meal, thinking herself to be sophisticated.

Robin was going to the library to read about Montenegro. "For more than two centuries," she read, "the Montenegrins maintained the struggle against the Turks and the Albanians, which for them was almost the whole duty of man. (Hence the Montenegrins' reputation for dignity, bellicosity,[7] and aversion to work, which last is a standing Yugoslav joke.)"

Which two centuries these were, she could not discover. She read about kings, bishops, wars, assassinations, and the greatest of all Serbian poems, called "The Mountain Garland," written by a Montenegrin king. She hardly retained a word of what she read. Except the name, the real name of Montenegro, which she did not know how to pronounce. *Crna Gora.*

She looked at maps, where it was hard enough to find the country itself, but possible finally, with a magnifying glass, to become familiar with the names of various towns (none of them Bjelojevici) and with the rivers Moraca and Tara, and the shaded mountain ranges, which seemed to be everywhere but in the Zeta Valley.

Her need to follow this investigation was hard to explain, and she did not try to explain it (though of course her presence in the library was noted, and her absorption). What she must have been trying to do—and what she at least half succeeded in doing—was to settle Danilo into some real place and a real past, to think that these names she was learning must have been known to him, this history must have been what he learned in school, some of these places must have been visited by him as a child or as a young man. And were being visited, perhaps, by him now. When she touched a printed name with her finger, she might have touched the very place he was in.

She tried also to learn from books, from diagrams, about clock making, but there she was not successful.

He remained with her. The thought of him was there when she woke up, and in lulls at work. The Christmas celebrations brought her thoughts round to

---

7   Aggression.

ceremonies in the Orthodox Church, which she had read about, bearded priests in gold vestments, candles and incense and deep mournful chanting in a foreign tongue. The cold weather and the ice far out into the lake made her think of winter in the mountains. She felt as if she had been chosen to be connected to that strange part of the world, chosen for a different sort of fate. Those were words she used to herself. *Fate. Lover.* Not *boyfriend. Lover.* Sometimes she thought of the casual, reluctant way he had spoken about getting in and out of that country, and she was afraid for him, imagining him involved in dark schemes, cinematic plots and dangers. It was probably a good thing that he had decided there should be no letters. Her life would have been drained entirely into composing them and waiting for them. Writing and waiting, waiting and writing. And of course worrying, if they didn't arrive.

She had something now to carry around with her all the time. She was aware of a shine on herself, on her body, on her voice and all her doings. It made her walk differently and smile for no reason and treat the patients with uncommon tenderness. It was her pleasure to dwell on one thing at a time and she could do that while she went about her duties, while she ate supper with Joanne. The bare wall of the room, with the rectangles of streaked light reflected on it through the slatted blinds. The rough paper of the magazines, with their old-fashioned sketched illustrations, instead of photographs. The thick crockery bowl, with a yellow band around it, in which he served the Stroganoff. The chocolate color of Juno's muzzle, and her lean strong legs. Then the cooling air in the streets, and the fragrance from the municipal flower beds and the streetlamps by the river, around which a whole civilization of tiny bugs darted and circled.

The sinking in her chest, then the closing down, when he came back with her ticket. But after that the walk, the measured steps, the descent from the platform to the gravel. Through the thin soles of her shoes she had felt pain from the sharp pebbles.

Nothing faded for her, however repetitive this program might be. Her memories, and the embroidery on her memories, just kept wearing a deeper groove.

It is important that we have met.

Yes. Yes.

Yet when June came, she delayed. She had not yet decided on which play, or sent away for her ticket. Finally she thought it best to choose the anniversary day, the same day as last year. The play on that day was *As You Like It*. It struck her that she could just go on to Downie Street, and not bother with the play, because she would be too preoccupied or excited to notice much of it. She was superstitious, however, about altering the day's pattern. She got her ticket. And she took her green dress to the cleaners. She had not worn it since that day, but she wanted it to be perfectly fresh, crisp as new.

The woman who did the pressing, at the cleaners, had missed some days that week. Her child was sick. But it was promised that she would be back, the dress would be ready on Saturday morning.

"I'll die," said Robin. "I'll die if they don't have that dress ready for tomorrow."

She looked at Joanne and Willard, playing rummy at the table. She had seen them in this pose so often, and now it was possible she might never see them again. How far they were from the tension and defiance, the risk of her life.

The dress was not ready. The child was still sick. Robin considered taking the dress home and ironing it herself, but she thought she would be too nervous to make a good job of it. Especially with Joanne looking on. She went immediately downtown, to the only possible dress shop, and was lucky enough, she thought, to find another green dress, just as good a fit but made along straight lines, and sleeveless. The color was not avocado, but lime, green. The woman in the store said that was the color this year, and that full skirts and pinched waists had gone out.

Through the train window she saw rain starting. She did not even have an umbrella. And in the seat across from her was a passenger she knew, a woman who had had her gallbladder out just a few months ago, at the hospital. This woman had a married daughter in Stratford. She was a person who thought that two people known to each other, meeting on the train and headed for the same place, should keep up a conversation.

"My daughter's meeting me," she said. "We can take you where you're going. Especially when it's raining."

It was not raining when they got to Stratford, the sun was out and it was very hot. Nevertheless Robin saw nothing for it but to accept the ride. She sat in the back seat with two children who were eating Popsicles. It seemed a miracle that she did not get some orange or strawberry liquid dripped onto her dress.

She was not able to wait for the play to be over. She was shivering in the air-conditioned theater because this dress was made of such light material and had no sleeves. Or it might have been from nervousness. She made her apologetic way to the end of the row, and climbed up the aisle with its irregular steps and went out into the daylight of the lobby. Raining again, very hard. Alone in the Ladies Room, the same one where she had lost her purse, she worked at her hair. The damp was destroying her pouf, the hair she had rolled to be smooth was falling into wispy curly black strands around her face. She should have brought hairspray. She did as good a job as she could, backcombing.

The rain had stopped when she came out, and again the sun was shining, glaring on the wet pavement. Now she set out. Her legs felt weak, as on those occasions when she had to go to the blackboard, at school, to demonstrate a math problem, or had to stand in front of the class to recite memory work. Too soon, she was at the corner of Downie Street. Within a few minutes now, her life would be changed. She was not ready, but she could not stand any delay.

In the second block she could see ahead of her that odd little house, held in place by the conventional shop buildings on either side.

Closer she came, closer. The door stood open, as was the case with most shops along the street—not many of them had put in air-conditioning. There was just a screen door in place to keep out the flies.

Up the two steps, then she stood outside the door. But did not push it open for a moment, so that she could get her eyes used to the half-dark interior, and not stumble when she went in.

He was there, in the work space beyond the counter, busy under a single bulb. He was bent forward, seen in profile, engrossed in the work he was doing on a clock. She had feared a change. She had feared in fact that she was not remembering him accurately. Or that Montenegro might have altered something—given him a new haircut, a beard. But no—he was the same. The work light shining on his head showed the same bristle of hair, glinting as before, silver with its red-brown tarnish. A thick shoulder, slightly hunched, sleeve rolled up to bare the muscled forearm. An expression on his face of concentration, keenness, perfect appreciation of whatever he was doing, of the mechanism he was working with. The same look that had been in her mind, though she had never seen him working on his clocks before. She had been imagining that look bent on herself.

No. She didn't want to walk in. She wanted him to get up, come towards her, open the door. So she called to him. Daniel. Being shy at the last moment of calling him Danilo, for fear she might pronounce the foreign syllables in a clumsy way.

He had not heard—or probably, because of what he was doing, he delayed looking up. Then he did look up, but not at her—he appeared to be searching for something he needed at the moment. But in raising his eyes he caught sight of her. He carefully moved something out of his way, pushed back from the worktable, stood up, came reluctantly towards her.

He shook his head at her slightly.

Her hand was ready to push the door open, but she did not do it. She waited for him to speak, but he did not. He shook his head again. He was perturbed. He stood still. He looked away from her, looked around the shop—looked at the array of clocks, as if they might give him some information or some support.

When he looked again at her face, he shivered, and involuntarily—but perhaps not—he bared his front teeth. As if the sight of her gave him a positive fright, an apprehension of danger.

And she stood there, frozen, as if there was a possibility still that this might be a joke, a game.

Now he came towards her again, as if he had made up his mind what to do. Not looking at her anymore, but acting with determination and—so it seemed to her—revulsion, he put a hand against the wooden door, the shop door which stood open, and pushed it shut in her face.

This was a shortcut. With horror she understood what he was doing. He was putting on this act because it was an easier way to get rid of her than making an explanation, dealing with her astonishment and female carrying-on, her wounded feelings and possible collapse and tears.

***

Shame, terrible shame, was what she felt. A more confident, a more experienced, woman would have felt anger and walked away in a fine fury. *Piss on him.* Robin had heard a woman at work talk about a man who had abandoned her. *You can't trust anything in trousers.* That woman had acted as if she was not surprised. And deep down, Robin now was not surprised, either, but the blame was for herself. She should have understood those words of last summer, the promise and farewell at the station, as a piece of folly, unnecessary kindness to a lonely female who had lost her purse and came to plays by herself. He would have regretted that before he got home, and prayed that she wouldn't take him seriously.

It was quite possible that he had brought back a wife from Montenegro, a wife upstairs—that would explain the alarm in his face, the shudder of dismay. If he had thought of Robin it would be in fear of her doing just what she had been doing—dreaming her dreary virginal dreams, fabricating her silly plans. Women had probably made fools of themselves over him before now, and he would have found ways to get rid of them. This was a way. Better cruel than kind. No apologies, no explanations, no hope. Pretend you don't recognize her, and if that doesn't work, slam a door in her face. The sooner you can get her to hate you, the better.

Though with some of them it's uphill work.

Exactly. And here she was, weeping. She had managed to hold it back along the street, but on the path by the river, she was weeping. The same black swan swimming alone, the same families of ducklings and their quacking parents, the sun on the water. It was better not to try to escape, better not to ignore this blow.

If you did that for a moment, you had to put up with its hitting you again, a great crippling whack in the chest.

***

"Better timing this year," Joanne said. "How was your play?"

"I didn't see all of it. Just when I was going into the theater some bug flew into my eye. I blinked and blinked but I couldn't get rid of it and I had to get up and go to the Ladies and try to wash it out. And then I must've got part of it on the towel and rubbed it into the other eye too."

"You look as if you'd been bawling your eyes out. When you came in I thought that must've been a whale of a sad play. You better wash your face in salt water."

"I was going to."

There were other things she was going to do, or not do. Never go to Stratford, never walk on those streets, never see another play. Never wear the green dresses, neither the lime nor the avocado. Avoid hearing any news of Montenegro, which should not be too difficult.

II

Now the real winter has set in and the lake is frozen over almost all the way to the breakwater. The ice is rough, in some places it looks as if big waves had been frozen in place. Workmen are out taking down the Christmas lights. Flu is reported. People's eyes water from walking against the wind. Most women are into their winter uniform of sweatpants and ski jackets.

But not Robin. When she steps off the elevator to visit the third and top floor of the hospital, she is wearing a long black coat, gray wool skirt, and a lilac-gray silk blouse. Her thick, straight, charcoal-gray hair is cut shoulder-length, and she has tiny diamonds in her ears. (It is still noted, just as it used to be, that some of the best-looking, best-turned-out women in town are those who did not marry.) She does not have to dress like a nurse now, because she works part-time and only on this floor.

You can take the elevator up to the third floor in the usual way, but it's more difficult to get down. The nurse behind the desk has to push a hidden button to release you. This is the Psychiatric Ward, though it is seldom called that. It looks west over the lake, like Robin's apartment, and so it is often called Sunset Hotel. And some older people refer to it as the Royal York. The patients there are short-term, though with some of them the short terms keep recurring. Those whose delusions or withdrawals or miseries become permanent are housed elsewhere, in the County Home, properly called the Long Term Care Facility, just outside of town.

In forty years the town has not grown a great deal, but it has changed. There are two shopping malls, though the stores on the square struggle on. There are new houses—an adult community—out on the bluffs, and two of the big old houses overlooking the lake have been converted to apartments. Robin has been lucky enough to get one of these. The house on Isaac Street where she and Joanne used to live has been smartened up with vinyl and turned into a real estate office. Willard's house is still the same, more or less. He had a stroke a few years ago but made a good recovery, though he has to walk with two canes. When he was in the hospital Robin saw quite a lot of him. He talked about what good neighbors she and Joanne had been, and what fun they had playing cards.

Joanne has been dead for eighteen years, and after selling the house Robin has moved away from old associations. She doesn't go to church anymore, and except for those who become patients in the hospital, she hardly ever sees the people she knew when she was young, the people she went to school with.

The prospects of marriage have opened up again, in a limited way, at her time of life. There are widowers looking around, men left on their own. Usually they want a woman experienced at marriage—though a good job doesn't come amiss either. But Robin has made it clear that she isn't interested. The people she has known since she was young say she never has been interested, that's just the way she is. Some of the people she knows now think she must be a lesbian, but that she has been brought up in an environment so primitive and crippling that she can't acknowledge it.

There are different sorts of people in town now, and these are the people she has made friends with. Some of them live together without being married. Some of them were born in India and Egypt and the Philippines and Korea. The old patterns of life, the rules of earlier days, persist to some extent, but a lot of people go their own way without even knowing about such things. You can buy almost any kind of food you want, and on a fine Sunday morning you can sit at a sidewalk table drinking fancy coffee and enjoying the sound of church bells, without any thought of worship. The beach is no longer surrounded by railway sheds and warehouses—you can walk on a boardwalk for a mile along the lake. There is a Choral Society and a Players Society. Robin is still very active in the Players Society, though not onstage so much as she once was. Several years ago she played Hedda Gabler. The general response was that it was an unpleasant play but that she played Hedda splendidly. An especially good job as the character—so people said—was so much the opposite of herself in real life.

Quite a number of people from here go to Stratford these days. She goes instead to see plays at Niagara-on-the-Lake.

Robin notes the three cots lined up against the opposite wall.

"What's up?" she says to Coral, the nurse at the desk.

"Temporary," says Coral, in a dubious tone. "It's the redistribution."

Robin goes to hang her coat and bag up in the closet behind the desk, and Coral tells her that these cases are from Perth County. It's some kind of switch on account of overcrowding there, she says. Only somebody got their wires crossed and the county facility here isn't ready for them yet, so it's been decided to park them here for the time being.

"Should I go over and say hello?"

"Up to you. Last I looked they were all out of it."

The three cots have their sides up, the patients lying flat. And Coral was right, they all seem to be sleeping. Two old women and one old man. Robin turns away, and then turns back. She stands looking down at the old man. His mouth is open and his false teeth, if he has any, have been removed. He has his hair yet, white and cropped short. Flesh fallen away, cheeks sunken, but still a face broad at the temples, retaining some look of authority and—as when she last saw it— of perturbation. Patches of shrivelled, pale, almost silvery skin, probably where cancerous spots have been cut away. His body worn down, legs almost disappearing under the covers, but still some breadth in the chest and shoulders, very much as she remembers.

She reads the card attached to the foot of his bed.

Alexander Adzic.

Danilo. Daniel.

Perhaps that is his second name. Alexander. Or else he has lied, taken the precaution of telling a lie or half a lie, right from the start and nearly to the end.

She goes back to the desk and speaks to Coral.

"Any info on that man?"

"Why? Do you know him?"

"I think I might."

"I'll see what there is. I can call it up."

"No hurry," Robin says. "Just when you have time. It's only curiosity. I better go now and see my people."

It is Robin's job to talk to these patients twice a week, to write reports on them, as to how their delusions or depressions are clearing up, whether the pills are working, and how their moods are affected by the visits they have had from their relatives or their partners. She has worked on this floor for years, ever since the practice of keeping psychiatric patients close to home was introduced back in the seventies, and she knows many of the people who keep coming back. She took some extra courses to qualify herself for treating psychiatric cases, but it's something she had a feeling for anyway. Sometime after she came back from Stratford, not having seen *As You Like It*, she had begun to be drawn to this work. Something—though not what she was expecting—*had* changed her life.

She saves Mr. Wray till the last, because he generally wants the most time. She isn't always able to give him as much as he would like—it depends on the problems of the others. Today the rest of them are generally on the mend, thanks to their pills, and all they do is apologize about the fuss they have caused. But Mr. Wray, who believes that his contributions to the discovery of DNA have never been rewarded or acknowledged, is on the rampage about a letter to James Watson.[8] Jim, he calls him.

"That letter I sent Jim," he says. "I know enough not to send a letter like that and not keep a copy. But yesterday I went looking through my files and guess what? You tell me what."

"You better tell me," says Robin.

"Not there. Not there. Stolen."

"It could be misplaced. I'll have a look around."

"I'm not surprised. I should have given up long ago. I'm fighting the Big Boys and who ever wins when you fight Them? Tell me the truth. Tell me. Should I give up?"

"You have to decide. Only you."

He begins to recite to her, once more, the particulars of his misfortune. He has not been a scientist, he has worked as a surveyor, but he must have followed scientific progress all his life. The information he has given her, and even the drawings he has managed with a dull pencil, are no doubt correct. Only the story of his being cheated is clumsy and predictable, and probably owes a lot to the movies or television.

But she always loves the part of the story where he describes how the spiral unzips and the two strands float apart. He shows her how, with such grace, such appreciative hands. Each strand setting out on its appointed journey to double itself according to its own instructions.

He loves that too, he marvels at it, with tears in his eyes. She always thanks him for his explanation, and wishes that he could stop there, but of course he can't.

Nevertheless, she believes he's getting better. When he begins to root around in the byways of the injustice, to concentrate on something like the stolen letter, it means he's probably getting better.

With a little encouragement, a little shift in his attention, he could perhaps fall in love with her. This has happened with a couple of patients, before now.

---

8   James Watson and Francis Crick were credited with discovering DNA in 1953.

Both were married. But that did not keep her from sleeping with them, after they were discharged. By that time, however, feelings were altered. The men felt gratitude, she felt goodwill, both of them felt some sort of misplaced nostalgia.

Not that she regrets it. There's very little now that she regrets. Certainly not her sexual life, which has been sporadic and secret but, on the whole, comforting. The effort she put into keeping it secret was perhaps hardly necessary, seeing how people had made up their minds about her—the people she knew now had done that just as thoroughly and mistakenly as the people she knew long ago.

***

Coral hands her a printout.

"Not much," she says.

Robin thanks her and folds it and takes it to the closet, to put it into her purse. She wants to be alone when she reads it. But she can't wait till she gets home. She goes down to the Quiet Room, which used to be the Prayer Room. Nobody was in there being quiet at the moment.

> Adzic, Alexander. Born July 3, 1924, Bjelojevici, Yugoslavia. Emigrated Canada, May 29, 1962, care of brother Danilo Adzic, born Bjelojevici, July 3, 1924, Canadian citizen.
>
> Alexander Adzic lived with his brother Danilo until the latter's death Sept 7, 1995. He was admitted to Perth County Long Term Care Facility Sept 25, 1995, and has been a patient there since that date.
>
> Alexander Adzic apparently has been deaf-mute since birth or from illness shortly after. No Special Education Facilities available as a child. I.Q. never determined but he was trained to work at clock repairs. No training in sign language. Dependent on brother and to all appearances emotionally inaccessible otherwise. Apathy, no appetite, occasional hostility, general regression since admission.

Outrageous.

Brothers.

Twins.

Robin wants to set this piece of paper in front of someone, some authority. This is ridiculous. This I do not accept.

Nevertheless.

Shakespeare should have prepared her. Twins are often the reason for mix-ups and disasters in Shakespeare. A means to an end, those tricks are supposed to be. And in the end the mysteries are solved, the pranks are forgiven, true love or something like it is rekindled, and those who were fooled have the good grace not to complain.

He must have gone out on an errand. A brief errand. He would not leave that brother in charge for very long. Perhaps the screen door was hooked—she had never tried to push it open. Perhaps he had told his brother to hook it and not open it while he himself was giving Juno a walk around the block. She had wondered why Juno wasn't there.

If she had come a little later. A little earlier. If she had stayed till the play was over or skipped the play altogether. If she had not bothered with her hair.

And then? How could they have managed, he with Alexander and she with Joanne? By the way Alexander behaved on that day, it did not look as if he would have put up with any intrusion, any changes. And Joanne would certainly have suffered. Less perhaps from having the deaf-mute Alexander in the house than from Robin's marriage to a foreigner.

Hard now to credit, the way things were then.

It was all spoiled in one day, in a couple of minutes, not by fits and starts, struggles, hopes and losses, in the long-drawn-out way that such things are more often spoiled. And if it's true that things are usually spoiled, isn't the quick way the easier way to bear?

But you don't really take that view, not for yourself. Robin doesn't. Even now she can yearn for her chance. She is not going to spare a moment's gratitude for the trick that has been played. But she'll come round to being grateful for the discovery of it. That, at least—the discovery which leaves everything whole, right up to the moment of frivolous intervention. Leaves you outraged, but warmed from a distance, clear of shame.

That was another world they had been in, surely. As much as any world concocted on the stage. Their flimsy arrangement, their ceremony of kisses, the foolhardy faith enveloping them that everything would sail ahead as planned. Move an inch this way or that, in such a case, and you're lost.

Robin has had patients who believe that combs and toothbrushes must lie in the right order, shoes must face in the right direction, steps must be counted, or some sort of punishment will follow.

If she has failed in that department, it would be in the matter of the green dress. Because of the woman at the cleaners, the sick child, she wore the wrong green dress.

She wished she could tell somebody. Him.

—2004

ALISTAIR MACLEOD

Alistair MacLeod was a Canadian short-story writer and novelist. Born in North Battleford, Saskatchewan, to Nova Scotian parents, he was raised in Cape Breton, Nova Scotia, from the age of 10. MacLeod began publishing short stories in journals in the 1960s and 1970s, and attracted international recognition following the publication of "The Boat" in the *Massachusetts Review* in 1968. This story was republished in the annual volume of *Best American Short Stories* the following year. His first collection, *The Lost Salt Gift of Blood*, was published to critical acclaim in 1976. His novel, *No Great Mischief* (1999), made him the first Canadian to win the International IM-PAC Dublin Literary Award in 2001.

After finishing high school, MacLeod attended St. Francis Xavier University, graduating with a BA and BEd in 1960. He then went on to receive an MA in 1961 from the University of New Brunswick, and a PhD in 1968 from Notre Dame, specializing in early nineteenth-century British literature. His own work has strong affinities with the fiction of that period, particularly in its focus on local landscape, rural life, folk traditions, and the changes imposed by industrialism and urbanization on small communities.

Much of MacLeod's fiction depicts the psychological, physical, and emotional experience of the mining and fishing communities of Nova Scotia, set against the natural cycles of the seasons, of the sea, and of life and death. He often uses first-person present-tense narration, which lends immediacy to his subjects and themes and foregrounds the experience of memory; Joyce Carol Oates writes that the "single underlying motive" for the stories "is the urge to memorialize, the urge to sanctify." This elegiac tone is reminiscent of the Scottish and English traditions of oral literature, and the lyrical power of MacLeod's prose underscores this association, as does the natural ease of the storytelling.

For much of his career, MacLeod taught literature and creative writing at the University of Windsor. Each summer, he and his family returned to Inverness in Cape Breton, where he wrote his stories. MacLeod died of a stroke in 2014.

In the Fall

"WE'LL JUST have to sell him," I remember my mother saying with finality. "It will be a long winter and I will be alone here with only these children to help me. Besides, he eats too much and we will not have enough feed for the cattle as it is."

It is the second Saturday of November and already the sun seems to have vanished for the year. Each day dawns duller and more glowering and the waves of the grey Atlantic are sullen and almost yellow at their peaks as they pound relentlessly against the round smooth boulders that lie scattered as if by a careless giant at the base of the ever-resisting cliffs. At night, when we lie in our beds, we can hear the waves rolling in and smashing, rolling in and smashing, so relentless and regular that it is possible to count rhythmically between the thunder of each: one, two, three, four; one, two, three, four.

It is hard to realize that this is the same ocean that is the crystal blue of summer when only the thin oil-slicks left by the fishing boats or the startling whiteness of the riding seagulls mar its azure sameness. Now it is roiled and angry, and almost anguished; hurling up the brown dirty balls of scudding foam, the sticks of pulpwood from some lonely freighter, the caps of unknown men, buoys from mangled fishing nets and the inevitable bottles that contain no messages. And always also the shreds of blackened and stringy seaweed that it has ripped and torn from its own lower regions, as if this is the season for self-mutilation—the puffing out of the secret, private, unseen hair.

We are in the kitchen of our house and my mother is speaking as she energetically pokes at the wood and coal within her stove. The smoke escapes, billows upward and flattens itself out against the ceiling. Whenever she speaks she does something with her hands. It is as if the private voice within her can only be liberated by some kind of physical action. She is tall and dark with high cheekbones and brown eyes. Her hair, which is very long and very black, is pulled back severely and coiled in a bun at the base of her neck, where it is kept in place by combs of coral.

My father is standing with his back toward us and is looking out the window to where the ocean pounds against the cliffs. His hands are clasped behind his back. He must be squeezing them together very tightly because they are almost white—especially the left. My father's left hand is larger than his right and his left arm is about three inches longer than normal. That is because he holds his stevedore's hook in his left hand when he works upon the waterfront in Halifax. His complexion is lighter than my mother's and his eyes are grey, which is also the predominant colour of his thinning hair.

We have always lived on the small farm between the ocean and the coal mining town. My father has always worked on his land in the summer and at one time he would spend his winters working within the caverns of the coal mine. Later when he could bear the underground no longer he had spent the time from November to April as an independent coal-hauler, or working in his woodlot where he cut timbers for the mine roof's support. But it must have been a long time ago, for I can scarcely remember a time when the mine worked steadily or a winter when he has been with us, and I am almost fourteen. Now each winter he goes to Halifax but he is often a long time in going. He will stand as he does now, before the window, for perhaps a week or more and then he will be gone and we will see him only at Christmas and on the odd weekend; for he will be over two hundred miles away and the winter storms will make travelling difficult and uncertain. Once, two years ago, he came home for a weekend and the blizzard came so savagely and with such intensity that he could not return until Thursday. My mother told him he was a fool to make such a journey and that he had lost a week's wages for nothing—a week's wages that she and six children could certainly use. After that he did not come again until it was almost spring.

"It wouldn't hurt to keep him another winter," he says now, still looking out the window. "We've kept him through all of them before. He doesn't eat much now since his teeth have gone bad."

"He was of some use before," says my mother shortly and rattling the lids of her stove. "When you were home you used him in the woods or to haul coal—not that it ever got us much. These last years he's been worthless. It would be cheaper to rent a horse for the summer or perhaps even hire a tractor. We don't need a horse any more, not even a young one, let alone one that will probably die in March after we've fed him all that time." She replaces the stove-lids—all in their proper places.

They are talking about our old horse Scott, who has been with us all of my life. My father had been his driver for two winters in the underground and they had become fond of one another and in the time of the second spring, when he left the mine forever, the man had purchased the horse from the Company so that they might both come out together to see the sun and walk upon the grass. And that the horse might be saved from the blindness that would inevitably come if he remained within the deeps; the darkness that would make him like itself.

At one time he had even looked like coal, when his coat was black and shiny strong, relieved by only a single white star in the centre of his forehead; but that too was a long time ago and now he is very grey about the eyes, and his legs are stiff when he first begins to walk.

"Oh, he won't die in March," says my father, "he'll be okay. You said the same thing last fall and he came through okay. Once he was on the grass again he was like a two-year-old."

For the past three or four years Scott has had heaves. I guess heaves come to horses from living too near the ocean and its dampness; like asthma comes to people, making them cough and sweat and struggle for breath. Or perhaps from eating dry and dusty hay for too many winters in the prison of a narrow stall. Perhaps from old age too. Perhaps from all of them. I don't know. Someone told my little brother David who is ten that dampening the hay would help, and last winter from early January when Scott began to cough really bad, David would take a dipper of water and sprinkle it on the hay after we'd put it in the manger. Then David would say the coughing was much better and I would say so too.

"He's not a two-year-old," says my mother shortly and begins to put on her coat before going out to feed her chickens. "He's old and useless and we're not running a rest home for retired horses. I am alone here with six children and I have plenty to do."

Long ago when my father was a coal-hauler and before he was married he would sometimes become drunk, perhaps because of his loneliness, and during a short February day and a long February night he had drunk and talked and slept inside the bootlegger's, oblivious to the frozen world without, until in the next morning's dehydrated despair he had staggered to the door and seen both horse and sleigh where he had left them and where there was no reason for them to be. The coal was glowing black on the sleigh beneath the fine powdered snow that seems to come even when it is coldest, seeming more to form like dew than fall like rain, and the horse was standing like a grey ghostly form in the early morning's darkness. His own black coat was covered with the hoar frost that had formed of yesterday's sweat, and tiny icicles hung from his nose.

My father could not believe that the horse had waited for him throughout the night of bitter cold, untied and unnecessary, shifting his feet on the squeaking snow, and flickering his muscles beneath the frozen harness. Before that night he had never been waited for by any living thing and he had buried his face in the hoar-frost mane and stood there quietly for a long, long time, his face in the heavy black hair and the ice beading on his cheeks.

He has told us this story many times, even though it bores my mother. When he tells it David sits on his lap and says that he would have waited too, no matter how long and no matter how cold. My mother says she hopes David would have more sense.

"Well, I have called MacRae and he is to come for him today," my mother says as she puts on her coat and prepares to feed her chickens. "I wanted to get it over with while you were still here. The next thing I know you'll be gone and we'll be stuck with him for another winter. Grab the pail, James," she says to me, "come and help me feed the chickens. At least there's some point in feeding them."

"Just a minute," he says, "just a goddamn minute." He turns quickly from the window and I see his hands turn into fists and his knuckles white and cold. My mother points to the younger children and shakes her head. He is temporarily stymied because she has so often told him he must not swear before them and while he hesitates we take our pails and escape.

As we go to where the chickens are kept, the ocean waves are even higher, and the wind has risen so that we have to use our bodies to shield the pails that we carry. If we do not, their contents will be scooped out and scattered wildly to the skies. It is beginning to rain and the drops are so driven by the fierceness of the wind that they ping against the galvanized sides of the pails and sting and then burn upon our cheeks.

Inside the chicken-house it is warm and acrid as the chickens press around us. They are really not chickens any more but full grown capons[1] which my mother has been raising all summer and will soon sell on the Christmas market. Each spring she gets day-old chicks and we feed them ground-up hardboiled eggs and chick-starter. Later we put them into outside pens and then in the fall into this house where they are fattened. They are Light Sussex which is the breed my mother favours because they are hardy and good weight-producers. They are very, very white now with red combs and black and gold glittering eyes and with a ring of startling black at the base of their white, shining necks. It is as if a white fluid had been poured over their heads and cascaded down their necks to where it suddenly and magically changed to black after exposure to the air. The opposite in colour but the same in lustre. Like piano keys.

My mother moves about them with ease and they are accustomed to her and jostle about her as she fills their troughs with mash and the warm water we have brought. Sometimes I like them and sometimes I do not. The worst part seems to be that it doesn't really matter. Before Christmas they will all be killed and dressed and then in the spring there will be another group and they will always look and act and end in the same way. It is hard to really like what you are planning to kill and almost as hard to feel dislike, and when there are many instead of one they begin to seem almost as the blueberries and strawberries we pick in summer. Just a whole lot of them to be alive in their way for a little while and then to be picked and eaten, except it seems the berries would be there anyway but the capons we are responsible for and encourage them to eat a great deal, and try our best to make them warm and healthy and strong so that we may kill them in the end. My father is always uncomfortable around them and avoids

---

1   Castrated roosters.

them as much as possible. My friend Henry Van Dyken says that my father feels that way because he is Scottish, and that Scotsmen are never any good at raising poultry or flowers because they think such tasks are for women and that they make a man ashamed. Henry's father is very good at raising both.

As we move about the closeness of the chicken-house the door bangs open and David is almost blown in upon us by the force of the wind and the rain. "There's a man with a big truck that's got an old bull on it," he says, "he just went in the house."

When we enter the kitchen MacRae is standing beside the table, just inside the door. My father is still at the window although now with his back to it. It does not seem that they have said anything.

MacRae, the drover, is in his fifties. He is short and heavy-set with a red face and a cigar in the corner of his mouth. His eyes are small and bloodshot. He wears Wellington boots with his trousers tucked inside them, a broad western-style belt, and a brown suede jacket over a flannel shirt which is open at the neck exposing his reddish chest-hair. He carries a heavy stock whip in his hand and taps it against the side of his boot. Because of his short walk in the wind-driven rain, his clothes are wet and now in the warmth of the kitchen they give off a steamy, strong odour that mingles uncomfortably with that of his cigar. An odour that comes of his jostling and shoving the countless frightened animals that have been carried on the back of his truck, an odour of manure and sweat and fear.

"I hear you've got an old knacker," he says now around the corner of his cigar. "Might get rid of him for mink-feed if I'm lucky. The price is twenty dollars."

My father says nothing, but his eyes, which seem the grey of the ocean behind him, remind me of a time when the log which Scott was hauling seemed to ricochet wildly off some half-submerged obstacle, catching the man's legs beneath its onrushing force and dragging and grinding him beneath it until it smashed into a protruding stump, almost uprooting it and knocking Scott back upon his haunches. And his eyes then in their greyness had reflected fear and pain and almost a mute wonder at finding himself so painfully trapped by what seemed all too familiar.

And it seemed now that we had, all of us, conspired against him, his wife and six children and the cigar-smoking MacRae, and that we had almost brought him to bay with his back against the ocean-scarred window so pounded by the driving rain and with all of us ringed before him. But still he says nothing, although I think his mind is racing down all the possible avenues of argument, and rejecting them all because he knows the devastating truth that awaits him at the end of each: "There is no need of postponing it; the truck is here and there will never be a better opportunity; you will soon be gone; he will never be any younger; the price will never be any higher; he may die this winter and we will get nothing at all; we are not running a rest home for retired horses; I am alone here with six children and I have more than enough to do; the money for his feed could be spent on your children; don't your children mean more to you than a horse; it is unfair to go and leave us here with him to care for."

Then with a nod he moves from the window and starts toward the door. "You're not ..." begins David, but he is immediately silenced by his mother. "Be quiet," she says, "go and finish feeding the chickens," and then, as if she cannot help it, "at least there is some point in feeding them." Almost before my father stops, I know she is sorry about the last part. That she fears that she has reached for too much and perhaps even now has lost all she had before. It is like when you attempt to climb one of the almost vertical sea-washed cliffs, edging upward slowly and groping with blue-tipped fingers from one tiny crevice to the next and then seeing the tantalizing twig which you cannot resist seizing, although even as you do, you know it can be grounded in nothing, for there is no vegetation there nor soil to support it and the twig is but a reject tossed up there by the sea, and even then you are tensing yourself for the painful, bruising slide that must inevitably follow. But this time for my mother, it does not. He only stops and looks at her for a moment before forcing open the door and going out into the wind. David does not move.

"I think he's going to the barn," says my mother then with surprising softness in her voice, and telling me with her eyes that I should go with him. By the time MacRae and I are outside he is already halfway to the barn; he has no hat nor coat and is walking sideways and leaning and knifing himself into the wind which blows his trousers taut against the outlines of his legs.

As MacRae and I pass the truck I cannot help but look at the bull. He is huge and old and is an Ayrshire.[2] He is mostly white except for the almost cherry-red markings of his massive shoulders and on his neck and jowls. His heavy head is forced down almost to the truck's floor by a reinforced chain halter and by a rope that has been doubled through his nose ring and fastened to an iron bar bolted to the floor. He has tried to turn his back into the lashing wind and rain, and his bulk is pressed against the truck's slatted side at an unnatural angle to his grotesquely fastened head. The floor of the truck is greasy and slippery with a mixture of the rain and his own excrement, and each time he attempts to move, his feet slide and threaten to slip from under him. He is trembling with the strain, and the muscles in his shoulders give involuntary little twitches and his eyes roll upward in their sockets. The rain mingles with his sweat and courses down his flanks in rivulets of grey.

---

2   Breed of dairy cattle, originally from Ayrshire, Scotland.

"How'd you like to have a pecker on you like that fella?" shouts MacRae into the wind. "Bet he's had his share and driven it into them little heifers a good many times. Boy, you get hung like that, you'll have all them horny little girls squealin' for you to take 'em behind the bushes. No time like it with them little girls, just when the juice starts runnin' in em and they're findin' out what it's for." He runs his tongue over his lips appreciatively and thwacks his whip against the sodden wetness of his boot.

Inside the barn it is still and sheltered from the storm. Scott is in the first stall and then there is a vacant one and then those of the cattle. My father has gone up beside Scott and is stroking his nose but saying nothing. Scott rubs his head up and down against my father's chest. Although he is old he is still strong and the force of his neck as he rubs almost lifts my father off his feet and pushes him against the wall.

"Well, no time like the present," says MacRae, as he unzips his fly and begins to urinate in the alleyway behind the stalls.

The barn is warm and close and silent, and the odour from the animals and from the hay is almost sweet. Only the sound of MacRae's urine and the faint steam that rises from it disturb the silence and the scene. "Ah, sweet relief," he says, rezipping his trousers and giving his knees a little bend for adjustment as he turns toward us. "Now let's see what we've got here."

He puts his back against Scott's haunches and almost heaves him across the stall before walking up beside him to where my father stands. The inspection does not take long; I suppose because not much is expected of future mink-feed. "You've got a good halter on him there," says MacRae, "I'll throw in a dollar for it, you won't be needin' it anyway." My father looks at him for what seems a very long time and then almost imperceptibly nods his head. "Okay," says MacRae, "twenty-one dollars, a deal's a deal." My father takes the money, still without saying anything, opens the barn door and without looking backward walks through the rain toward his house. And I follow him because I do not know what else to do.

Within the house it is almost soundless. My mother goes to the stove and begins rinsing her teapot and moving her kettle about. Outside we hear MacRae starting the engine of his truck and we know he is going to back it against the little hill beside the barn. It will be easier to load his purchase from there. Then it is silent again, except for the hissing of the kettle which is now too hot and which someone should move to the back of the stove; but nobody does.

And then all of us are drawn with a strange fascination to the window, and, yes, the truck is backed against the little hill as we knew and MacRae is going into the barn with his whip still in his hand. In a moment he reappears, leading Scott behind him.

As he steps out of the barn the horse almost stumbles but regains his balance quickly. Then the two ascend the little hill, both of them turning their faces from the driving rain. Scott stands quietly while MacRae lets down the tailgate of his truck. When the tailgate is lowered it forms a little ramp from the hill to the truck and MacRae climbs it with the halter-shank in his hand, tugging it impatiently. Scott places one foot on the ramp and we can almost hear, or perhaps I just imagine it, the hollow thump of his hoof upon the wet planking; but then he hesitates, withdraws his foot and stops. MacRae tugs at the rope but it has no effect. He tugs again. He comes halfway down the little ramp, reaches out his hand, grasps the halter itself and pulls; we can see his lips moving and he is either coaxing or cursing or both; he is facing directly into the rain now and it is streaming down his face. Scott does not move. MacRae comes down from the truck and leads Scott in a wide circle through the wet grass. He goes faster and faster, building up speed and soon both man and horse are almost running. Through the greyness of the blurring, slanting rain they look almost like a black-and-white movie that is badly out of focus. Suddenly without changing speed, MacRae hurries up the ramp of the truck and the almost-trotting horse follows him, until his hoof strikes the tailboard. Then he stops suddenly. As the rope jerks taut, MacRae, who is now in the truck and has been carried forward by his own momentum, is snapped backward; he bounces off the side of the bull, loses his footing on the slimy planking and falls into the wet filth of the truck box's floor. Almost before we can wonder if he is hurt, he is back upon his feet; his face is livid and his clothes are smeared with manure and running brown rivulets; he brings the whip, which he has somehow never relinquished even in his fall, down savagely between the eyes of Scott, who is still standing rigidly at the tailgate. Scott shakes his head as if dazed and backs off into the wet grass trailing the rope behind him.

It has all happened so rapidly that we in the window do not really know what to do, and are strangely embarrassed by finding ourselves where we are. It is almost as if we have caught ourselves and each other doing something that is shameful. Then David breaks the spell. "He is not going to go," he says, and then almost shouts, "he is just not going to go—ever. Good for him. Now that he's hit him, it's for sure. He'll never go and he'll have to stay." He rushes toward my father and throws his arms around his legs.

And then the door is jerked open and MacRae is standing there angrily with his whip still in his hand. His clothes are still soggy from his fall and the water trails from them in brown drops upon my mother's floor. His face is almost purple as he says, "Unless I get that fuckin' horse on the truck in the next five minutes, the deal's off and you'll be a goddamn long time tryin' to get anybody else to pay that kinda money for the useless old cocksucker."

It is as if all of the worst things one imagines happening suddenly have. But it is not at all as you expected. And I think I begin to understand for the first time how difficult and perhaps how fearful it is to be an adult and I am suddenly and selfishly afraid not only for myself now but for what it seems I am to be. For I had somehow always thought that if one talked like that before women or small children or perhaps even certain men, the earth would open up or lightning would strike or that at least many people would scream and clap their hands over their ears in horror or that the offender, if not turned to stone, would certainly be beaten by a noble, clean-limbed hero. But it does not happen that way at all. All that happens is the deepening of the thundercloud greyness in my father's eyes and the heightening of the colour in my mother's cheeks. And I realize also with a sort of shock that in spite of Scott's refusal to go on the truck, nothing has really changed. I mean not really; and that all of the facts remain awfully and simply the same: that Scott is old and that we are poor and that my father must soon go away and that he must leave us either with Scott or without him. And that it is somehow like my mother's shielding her children from "swearing" for so many years, only to find one day that it too is there in its awful reality, in spite of everything that she had wished and wanted. And even as I am thinking this, my father goes by MacRae, who is still standing in the ever-widening puddles of brown, seeming like some huge growth that is nourished by the foul-smelling waters that he himself has brought.

David, who had released my father's legs with the entrance of MacRae, makes a sort of flying tackle for them now, but I intercept him and find myself saying as if from a great distance my mother's phrases in something that sounds almost like her voice, "Let's go and finish feeding the chickens." I tighten my grip on his arm and we almost have to squeeze past MacRae whose bulk is blocking the doorway and who has not yet made a motion to leave.

Out of doors my father is striding directly into the slashing rain to where Scott is standing in something like puzzlement with his back to the rain and his halter-shank dangling before him. When he sees my father approach he cocks his ears and nickers in recognition. My father who looks surprisingly slight with his wet clothes plastered to his body takes the rope in his hand and moves off with the huge horse following him eagerly. Their movement seems almost that of the small tug docking the huge ocean freighter, except that they are so individually and collectively alive. As they approach the truck's ramp, it is my father who hesitates and seems to flinch, and it is his foot which seems to recoil as it touches the planking; but on the part of Scott there is no hesitation at all; his hooves echo firmly and confidently on the strong wet wood and his head is almost pressed into the small of my father's back; he is so eager to get to wherever they are going.

He follows him as I have remembered them all of my life and imagined them even before. Following wildly through the darkened caverns of the mine in its dryness as his shoes flashed sparks from the tracks and the stone; and in its wet-ness with both of them up to their knees in water, feeling rather than seeing the landing of their splashing feet and with the coal cars thundering behind them with such momentum that were the horse to stumble, the very cars he had set in motion would roll over him, leaving him mangled and grisly to be hauled above ground only as carrion for the wheeling gulls. And on the surface, following, in the summer's heat with the jolting haywagon and the sweat churned to froth between his legs and beneath his collar, fluttering white on the blackness of his glistening coat. And in the winter, following, over the semi-frozen swamps as the snapping, whistling logs snaked behind him, grunting as he broke through the shimmering crystal ice which slashed his fetlocks and caused a scarlet trail of bloodied perforations on the whiteness of the snow. And in the winter, too, with the ton of coal upon the sleigh, following, even over the snowless stretches, driven bare by the wind, leaning low with his underside parallel and almost touching the ground, grunting, and swinging with violent jolts to the right and then to the left, moving the sleigh forward only by moving it sideways, which he had learned was the only way it would move at all.

Even as my father is knotting the rope, MacRae is hurrying past us and slam-ming shut the tailgate and dropping down the iron bolts that will hold it in its place. My father climbs over the side of the box and down as MacRae steps onto the running-board and up into the cab. The motor roars and the truck lurches forward. It leaves two broad wet tracks in the grass like the trails of two slimy giant slugs and the smell of its exhaust hangs heavy on the air. As it takes the turn at the bottom of the lane Scott tries to turn his head and look back but the rope has been tied very short and he is unable to do so. The sheets of rain come down like so many slanted, beaded curtains, making it impossible to see what we know is there, and then there is only the receding sound of the motor, the wet trails on the grass and the exhaust fumes in the air.

It is only then that I realize that David is no longer with me, but even as the question comes to the surface so also does its answer and I run toward the squawking of the chicken-house.

Within the building it is difficult to see and difficult to breathe and difficult to believe that so small a boy could wreak such havoc in so short a time. The air is thick with myriad dust particles from the disturbed floor, and bits of straw and tiny white scarlet-flecked feathers eddy and dip and swirl. The frightened capons, many of them already bloodied and mangled, attempt short and un-gainly flights, often colliding with each other in midair. Their overfed bodies are too heavy for their weak and unused wings and they are barely able to get off the floor and flounder for a few feet before thumping down to dusty crippled landings. They are screaming with terror and their screams seem as unnatural as their flights, as if they had been terribly miscast in the most unsuitable of roles. Many of them are already lifeless and crumpled and dustied and bloodied on the floor, like sad, grey wadded newspapers that have been used to wipe up blood. The sheen of their feathers forever gone.

In the midst of it all David moves like a small blood-spattered dervish, swinging his axe in all directions and almost unknowingly as if he were blind-folded. Dust has settled on the dampness of his face and the tears make tiny trails through its greyness, like lonely little rivers that have really nothing to water. A single tiny feather is plastered to his forehead and he is coughing and sobbing, both at the same time.

When my father appears beside me in the doorway he seems to notice for the first time that he is not alone. With a final exhausted heave he throws the axe at my father. "Cocksucker," he says in some kind of small, sad parody of MacRae, and bolts past us through the door, almost colliding with my mother, who now comes from out of the rain. He has had very little strength with which to throw the axe and it clatters uselessly off the wall and comes to rest against my father's boot, wet and bloodied, with feathers and bits of flesh still clinging to its blade.

I am tremendously sorry for the capons, now so ruined and so useless, and for my mother and for all the time and work she has put into them for all of us. But I do not know what to do and I know not what to say.

As we leave the melancholy little building the wind cuts in from the ocean with renewed fury. It threatens to lift you off your feet and blow you to the skies and your crotch is numb and cold as your clothes are flattened hard against the front of your body, even as they tug and snap at your back in insistent, billowing balloons. Unless you turn or lower your head it is impossible to breathe, for the air is blown back almost immediately into your lungs, and your throat convulses and heaves. The rain is now a stinging sleet which is rapidly becoming the win-ter's first snow. It is impossible to see into it, and the ocean off which it rushes is lost in the swirling whiteness, although it thunders and roars in its invisible nearness like the heavy bass blending with the shrieking tenor of the wind. You hear so much that you can hardly hear at all. And you are almost immobile and breathless and blind and deaf. Almost but not quite. For by turning and leaning your body and your head, you can move and breathe and see and hear a little at a time. You do not gain much but you can hang on to what little you have and your toes curl almost instinctively within your shoes as if they are trying to grasp the earth.

I stop and turn my face from the wind and look back the way I have come. My parents are there, blown together behind me. They are not moving, either, only trying to hold their place. They have turned sideways to the wind and are facing and leaning into each other with their shoulders touching, like the end-timbers of a gabled roof. My father puts his arms around my mother's waist and she does not remove them as I have always seen her do. Instead she reaches up and removes the combs of coral from the heaviness of her hair. I have never seen her hair in all its length before and it stretches out now almost parallel to the earth, its shining blackness whipped by the wind and glistening like the snow that settles and melts upon it. It surrounds and engulfs my father's head and he buries his face within its heavy darkness, and draws my mother closer toward him. I think they will stand there for a long, long time, leaning into each other and into the wind-whipped snow and with the ice freezing to their cheeks. It seems that perhaps they should be left alone, so I turn and take one step and then another and move forward a little at a time. I think I will try to find David, that perhaps he may understand.

—*1976*

RAYMOND CARVER

Born in Clatskanie, Oregon, to working-poor parents, Raymond Carver was raised in an abusive and unstable alcoholic home. By the age of 20, he was married with two children, working menial jobs, and drinking heavily. Struggling to pay the family's bills, he began writing poetry and short stories to earn extra money. Carver's experiences provided him with an intimate understanding of the hard-fought lives of America's struggling classes and he wrote about them with honesty and respect. "They're my people," said Carver. "I could never write down to them."

1977 marked the beginning of what Carver called his "second life." First, his collection of short stories, *Will You Please Be Quiet, Please?* (1976), was nominated for a National Book Award; then he quit drinking and remained sober for the rest of his life. His subsequent collection *What We Talk about When We Talk about Love* (1981), which was an enormous success, moved critic Michael Wood to praise Carver's work for its "edges and silences" in which "a good deal of the unsayable gets said." Even greater success followed with the publication of *Cathedral* (1983), a collection that broke from the minimalism of Carver's previous work in favour of a new expansiveness. Together with Alice Munro, Carver is often credited with rejuvenating the genre of the short story in the last quarter of the twentieth century. Some literary scholars have named him as second only to Ernest Hemingway in terms of his stylistic influence on the contemporary short story.

Carver's final collection, *Where I'm Calling From* (1988), appeared only months before his death. A heavy smoker who once referred to himself as "a cigarette with a body attached to it," Carver succumbed to lung cancer at the age of 50. His grave lies in Port Angeles, Washington, and overlooks the Strait of Juan de Fuca.

Cathedral

THIS BLIND man, an old friend of my wife's, he was on his way to spend the night. His wife had died. So he was visiting the dead wife's relatives in Connecticut. He called my wife from his in-laws'. Arrangements were made. He would come by train, a five-hour trip, and my wife would meet him at the station. She hadn't seen him since she worked for him one summer in Seattle ten years ago. But she and the blind man had kept in touch. They made tapes and mailed them back and forth. I wasn't enthusiastic about his visit. He was no one I knew. And his being blind bothered me. My idea of blindness came from the movies. In the movies, the blind moved slowly and never laughed. Sometimes they were led by seeing-eye dogs. A blind man in my house was not something I looked forward to.

That summer in Seattle she had needed a job. She didn't have any money. The man she was going to marry at the end of the summer was in officers' training school. He didn't have any money, either. But she was in love with the guy, and he was in love with her, etc. She'd seen something in the paper: HELP WANTED—*Reading to Blind Man*, and a telephone number. She phoned and went over, was hired on the spot. She'd worked with this blind man all summer. She read stuff to him, case studies, reports, that sort of thing. She helped him organize his little office in the county social-service department. They'd become good friends, my wife and the blind man. How do I know these things? She told me. And she told me something else. On her last day in the office, the blind man asked if he could touch her face. She agreed to this. She told me he touched his fingers to every part of her face, her nose—even her neck! She never forgot it. She even tried to write a poem about it. She was always trying to write a poem. She wrote a poem or two every year, usually after something really important had happened to her.

When we first started going out together, she showed me the poem. In the poem, she recalled his fingers and the way they had moved around over her face. In the poem, she talked about what she had felt at the time, about what went through her mind when the blind man touched her nose and lips. I can remember I didn't think much of the poem. Of course, I didn't tell her that. Maybe I just don't understand poetry. I admit it's not the first thing I reach for when I pick up something to read.

Anyway, this man who'd first enjoyed her favors, the officer-to-be, he'd been her childhood sweetheart. So okay. I'm saying that at the end of the summer she let the blind man run his hands over her face, said goodbye to him, married her childhood etc., who was now a commissioned officer, and she moved away from Seattle. But they'd kept in touch, she and the blind man. She made the first contact after a year or so. She called him up one night from an Air Force base in Alabama. She wanted to talk. They talked. He asked her to send him a tape and tell him about her life. She did this. She sent the tape. On the tape, she told the blind man about her husband and about their life together in the military. She told the blind man she loved her husband but she didn't like it where they lived and she didn't like it that he was a part of the military-industrial thing. She told the blind man she'd written a poem about what it was like to be an Air Force officer's wife. The poem wasn't finished yet. She was still writing it. The blind man made a tape. He sent her the tape. She made a tape. This went on for years. My wife's officer was posted to one base and then another. She sent tapes from Moody AFB, McGuire, McConnell, and finally Travis, near Sacramento, where one night she got to feeling lonely and cut off from people she kept losing in that moving-around life. She got to feeling she couldn't go it another step. She went in and swallowed all the pills and capsules in the medicine chest and washed them down with a bottle of gin. Then she got into a hot bath and passed out.

But instead of dying, she got sick. She threw up. Her officer—why should he have a name? he was the childhood sweetheart, and what more does he want?—came home from somewhere, found her, and called the ambulance. In time, she put it all on a tape and sent the tape to the blind man. Over the years, she put all kinds of stuff on tapes and sent the tapes off lickety-split. Next to writing a poem every year, I think it was her chief means of recreation. On one tape, she told the blind man she'd decided to live away from her officer for a time. On another tape, she told him about her divorce. She and I began going out, and of course she told her blind man about it. She told him everything, or so it seemed to me. Once she asked me if I'd like to hear the latest tape from the blind man. This was a year ago. I was on the tape, she said. So I said okay, I'd listen to it. I got us drinks and we settled down in the living room. We made ready to listen. First she inserted the tape into the player and adjusted a couple of dials. Then she pushed a lever. The tape squeaked and someone began to talk in this loud voice. She lowered the volume. After a few minutes of harmless chitchat, I heard my own name in the mouth of this stranger, this blind man I didn't even know! And then this: "From all you've said about him, I can only conclude—" But we were interrupted, a knock at the door, something, and we didn't ever get back to the tape. Maybe it was just as well. I'd heard all I wanted to.

Now this same blind man was coming to sleep in my house.

"Maybe I could take him bowling," I said to my wife. She was at the draining board doing scalloped potatoes. She put down the knife she was using and turned around.

"If you love me," she said, "you can do this for me. If you don't love me, okay. But if you had a friend, any friend, and the friend came to visit, I'd make him feel comfortable." She wiped her hands with the dish towel.

"I don't have any blind friends," I said.

"You don't have *any* friends," she said. "Period. Besides," she said, "goddamn it, his wife's just died! Don't you understand that? The man's lost his wife!"

I didn't answer. She'd told me a little about the blind man's wife. Her name was Beulah. Beulah! That's a name for a colored woman.

"Was his wife a Negro?" I asked.

"Are you crazy?" my wife said. "Have you just flipped or something?" She picked up a potato. I saw it hit the floor, then roll under the stove. "What's wrong with you?" she said. "Are you drunk?"

"I'm just asking," I said.

Right then my wife filled me in with more detail than I cared to know. I made a drink and sat at the kitchen table to listen. Pieces of the story began to fall into place.

Beulah had gone to work for the blind man the summer after my wife had stopped working for him. Pretty soon Beulah and the blind man had themselves a church wedding. It was a little wedding—who'd want to go to such a wedding in the first place?—just the two of them, plus the minister and the minister's wife. But it was a church wedding just the same. It was what Beulah had wanted, he'd said. But even then Beulah must have been carrying the cancer in her glands. After they had been inseparable for eight years—my wife's word, *inseparable*—Beulah's health went into a rapid decline. She died in a Seattle hospital room, the blind man sitting beside the bed and holding on to her hand. They'd married, lived and worked together, slept together—had sex, sure—and then the blind man had to bury her. All this without his having ever seen what the goddamned woman looked like. It was beyond my understanding. Hearing this, I felt sorry for the blind man for a little bit. And then I found myself thinking what a pitiful life this woman must have led. Imagine a woman who could never see herself as she was seen in the eyes of her loved one. A woman who could go on day after day and never receive the smallest compliment from her beloved. A woman whose husband could never read the expression on her face, be it misery or something better. Someone who could wear makeup or not—what difference to him? She could, if she wanted, wear green eye-shadow around one eye, a straight pin in her nostril, yellow slacks and purple shoes, no matter. And then to slip off into death, the blind man's hand on her hand, his blind eyes streaming tears—I'm imagining now—her last thought maybe this: that he never even knew what she looked like, and she on an express to the grave. Robert was left with a small insurance policy and half of a twenty-peso Mexican coin. The other half of the coin went into the box with her. Pathetic.

So when the time rolled around, my wife went to the depot to pick him up. With nothing to do but wait—sure, I blamed him for that—I was having a drink and watching the TV when I heard the car pull into the drive. I got up from the sofa with my drink and went to the window to have a look.

I saw my wife laughing as she parked the car. I saw her get out of the car and shut the door. She was still wearing a smile. Just amazing. She went around to the other side to where the blind man was already starting to get out. This blind man, feature this, he was wearing a full beard! A beard on a blind man! Too much, I say. The blind man reached into the back seat and dragged out a suitcase. My wife took his arm, shut the car door, and, talking all the way, moved him down the drive and then up the steps to the front porch. I turned off the TV. I finished my drink, rinsed the glass, dried my hands. Then I went to the door.

My wife said, "I want you to meet Robert. Robert, this is my husband. I've told you all about him." She was beaming. She had this blind man by his coat sleeve.

The blind man let go of his suitcase and up came his hand.

I took it. He squeezed hard, held my hand, and then he let it go.

"I feel like we've already met," he boomed.

"Likewise," I said. I didn't know what else to say. Then I said, "Welcome. I've heard a lot about you." We began to move then, a little group, from the porch into the living room, my wife guiding him by the arm. The blind man was carrying his suitcase in his other hand. My wife said things like, "To your left here, Robert. That's right. Now watch it, there's a chair. That's it. Sit down right here. This is the sofa. We just bought this sofa two weeks ago."

I started to say something about the old sofa. I'd liked that old sofa. But I didn't say anything. Then I wanted to say something else, small-talk, about the scenic ride along the Hudson. How going *to* New York, you should sit on the right-hand side of the train, and coming *from* New York, the left-hand side.

"Did you have a good train ride?" I said. "Which side of the train did you sit on, by the way?"

"What a question, which side!" my wife said. "What's it matter which side?" she said.

"I just asked," I said.

"Right side," the blind man said. "I hadn't been on a train in nearly forty years. Not since I was a kid. With my folks. That's been a long time. I'd nearly forgotten the sensation. I have winter in my beard now," he said. "So I've been told, anyway. Do I look distinguished, my dear?" the blind man said to my wife.

"You look distinguished, Robert," she said. "Robert," she said. "Robert, it's just so good to see you."

My wife finally took her eyes off the blind man and looked at me. I had the feeling she didn't like what she saw. I shrugged.

I've never met, or personally known, anyone who was blind. This blind man was late forties, a heavy-set, balding man with stooped shoulders, as if he carried a great weight there. He wore brown slacks, brown shoes, a light-brown shirt, a tie, a sports coat. Spiffy. He also had this full beard. But he didn't use a cane and he didn't wear dark glasses. I'd always thought dark glasses were a must for the blind. Fact was, I wished he had a pair. At first glance, his eyes looked like anyone else's eyes. But if you looked close, there was something different about them. Too much white in the iris, for one thing, and the pupils seemed to move around in the sockets without his knowing it or being able to stop it. Creepy. As I stared at his face, I saw the left pupil turn in toward his nose while the other made an effort to keep in one place. But it was only an effort, for that eye was on the roam without his knowing it or wanting it to be.

I said, "Let me get you a drink. What's your pleasure? We have a little of everything. It's one of our pastimes."

"Bub, I'm a Scotch man myself," he said fast enough in this big voice.

"Right," I said. Bub! "Sure you are. I knew it."

He let his fingers touch his suitcase, which was sitting alongside the sofa. He was taking his bearings. I didn't blame him for that.

"I'll move that up to your room," my wife said.

"No, that's fine," the blind man said loudly. "It can go up when I go up."

"A little water with the Scotch?" I said.

"Very little," he said.

"I knew it," I said.

He said, "Just a tad. The Irish actor, Barry Fitzgerald? I'm like that fellow. When I drink water, Fitzgerald said, I drink water. When I drink whiskey, I drink whiskey." My wife laughed. The blind man brought his hand up under his beard. He lifted his beard slowly and let it drop.

I did the drinks, three big glasses of Scotch with a splash of water in each. Then we made ourselves comfortable and talked about Robert's travels. First the long flight from the West Coast to Connecticut, we covered that. Then from Connecticut up here by train. We had another drink concerning that leg of the trip.

I remembered having read somewhere that the blind didn't smoke because, as speculation had it, they couldn't see the smoke they exhaled. I thought I knew that much and that much only about blind people. But this blind man smoked his cigarette down to the nubbin and then lit another one. This blind man filled his ashtray and my wife emptied it.

When we sat down at the table for dinner, we had another drink. My wife heaped Robert's plate with cube steak, scalloped potatoes, green beans. I buttered him up two slices of bread. I said, "Here's bread and butter for you." I swallowed some of my drink. "Now let us pray," I said, and the blind man lowered his head. My wife looked at me, her mouth agape. "Pray the phone won't ring and the food doesn't get cold," I said.

We dug in. We ate everything there was to eat on the table. We ate like there was no tomorrow. We didn't talk. We ate. We scarfed. We grazed that table. We were into serious eating. The blind man had right away located his foods, he knew just where everything was on his plate. I watched with admiration as he used his knife and fork on the meat. He'd cut two pieces of meat, fork the meat into his mouth, and then go all out for the scalloped potatoes, the beans next, and then he'd tear off a hunk of buttered bread and eat that. He'd follow this up with a big drink of milk. It didn't seem to bother him to use his fingers once in a while, either.

We finished everything, including half a strawberry pie. For a few moments, we sat as if stunned. Sweat beaded on our faces. Finally, we got up from the table and left the dirty plates. We didn't look back. We took ourselves into the living room and sank into our places again. Robert and my wife sat on the sofa. I took the big chair. We had us two or three more drinks while they talked about the major things that had come to pass for them in the past ten years. For the most part, I just listened. Now and then I joined in. I didn't want him to think I'd left the room, and I didn't want her to think I was feeling left out. They talked of things that had happened to them—to them!—these past ten years. I waited in vain to hear my name on my wife's sweet lips: "And then my dear husband came into my life"—something like that. But I heard nothing of the sort. More talk of Robert. Robert had done a little of everything, it seemed, a regular blind jack-of-all-trades. But most recently he and his wife had had an Amway[1] distributorship, from which, I gathered, they'd earned their living, such as it was. The blind man was also a ham radio operator. He talked in his loud voice about conversations he'd had with fellow operators in Guam, in the Philippines, in Alaska, and even in Tahiti. He said he'd have a lot of friends there if he ever wanted to go visit those places. From time to time, he'd turn his blind face toward me, put his hand under his beard, ask me something. How long had I been in my present position? (Three years.) Did I like my work? (I didn't.) Was I going to stay with it? (What were the options?) Finally, when I thought he was beginning to run down, I got up and turned on the TV.

---

1   Large multi-level sales company.

My wife looked at me with irritation. She was heading toward a boil. Then she looked at the blind man and said, "Robert, do you have a TV?"

The blind man said, "My dear, I have two TVs. I have a color set and a black-and-white thing, an old relic. It's funny, but if I turn the TV on, and I'm always turning it on, I turn on the color set. It's funny, don't you think?"

I didn't know what to say to that. I had absolutely nothing to say to that. No opinion. So I watched the news program and tried to listen to what the announcer was saying.

"This is a color TV," the blind man said. "Don't ask me how, but I can tell."

"We traded up a while ago." I said.

The blind man had another taste of his drink. He lifted his beard, sniffed it, and let it fall. He leaned forward on the sofa. He positioned his ashtray on the coffee table, then put the lighter to his cigarette. He leaned back on the sofa and crossed his legs at the ankles.

My wife covered her mouth, and then she yawned. She stretched. She said, "I think I'll go upstairs and put on my robe. I think I'll change into something else. Robert, you make yourself comfortable," she said.

"I'm comfortable," the blind man said.

"I want you to feel comfortable in this house," she said.

"I am comfortable," the blind man said.

After she'd left the room, he and I listened to the weather report and then to the sports roundup. By that time, she'd been gone so long I didn't know if she was going to come back. I thought she might have gone to bed. I wished she'd come back downstairs. I didn't want to be left alone with a blind man. I asked him if he wanted to smoke some dope with me. I said I'd just rolled a number. I hadn't, but I planned to do so in about two shakes.

"I'll try some with you," he said.

"Damn right," I said. "That's the stuff."

I got our drinks and sat down on the sofa with him. Then I rolled us two fat numbers. I lit one and passed it. I brought it to his fingers. He took it and inhaled.

"Hold it as long as you can," I said. I could tell he didn't know the first thing.

My wife came back downstairs wearing her pink robe and her pink slippers.

"What do I smell?" she said.

"We thought we'd have us some cannabis," I said.

My wife gave me a savage look. Then she looked at the blind man and said, "Robert, I didn't know you smoked."

He said, "I do now, my dear. There's a first time for everything. But I don't feel anything yet."

"This stuff is pretty mellow," I said. "This stuff is mild. It's dope you can reason with," I said. "It doesn't mess you up."

"Not much it doesn't, bub," he said, and laughed.

My wife sat on the sofa between the blind man and me. I passed her the number. She took it and toked and then passed it back to me. "Which way is this going?" she said. Then she said, "I shouldn't be smoking this. I can hardly keep my eyes open as it is. That dinner did me in. I shouldn't have eaten so much."

"It was the strawberry pie," the blind man said. "That's what did it," he said, and he laughed his big laugh. Then he shook his head.

"There's more strawberry pie," I said.

"Do you want some more, Robert?" my wife said.

"Maybe in a little while," he said.

We gave our attention to the TV. My wife yawned again. She said, "Your bed is made up when you feel like going to bed, Robert. I know you must have had a long day. When you're ready to go to bed, say so." She pulled his arm. "Robert?"

He came to and said, "I've had a real nice time. This beats tapes, doesn't it?"

I said, "Coming at you," and I put the number between his fingers. He inhaled, held the smoke, and then let it go. It was like he'd been doing it since he was nine years old.

"Thanks, bub," he said. "But I think this is all for me. I think I'm beginning to feel it," he said. He held the burning roach out for my wife.

"Same here," she said. "Ditto. Me, too." She took the roach and passed it to me. "I may just sit here for a while between you two guys with my eyes closed. But don't let me bother you, okay? Either one of you. If it bothers you, say so. Otherwise, I may just sit here with my eyes closed until you're ready to go to bed," she said. "Your bed's made up, Robert, when you're ready. It's right next to our room at the top of the stairs. We'll show you up when you're ready. You wake me up now, you guys, if I fall asleep." She said that and then she closed her eyes and went to sleep.

The news program ended. I got up and changed the channel. I sat back down on the sofa. I wished my wife hadn't pooped out. Her head lay across the back of the sofa, her mouth open. She'd turned so that her robe had slipped away from her legs, exposing a juicy thigh. I reached to draw her robe back over her, and it was then that I glanced at the blind man. What the hell! I flipped the robe open again.

"You say when you want some strawberry pie," I said.

"I will," he said.

I said, "Are you tired? Do you want me to take you up to your bed? Are you ready to hit the hay?"

"Not yet," he said. "No, I'll stay up with you, bub. If that's all right. I'll stay up until you're ready to turn in. We haven't had a chance to talk. Know what I mean? I feel like me and her monopolized the evening." He lifted his beard and he let it fall. He picked up his cigarettes and lighter.

"That's all right," I said. Then I said, "I'm glad for the company."

And I guess I was. Every night I smoked dope and stayed up as long as I could before I fell asleep. My wife and I hardly ever went to bed at the same time. When I did go to sleep, I had these dreams. Sometimes I'd wake up from one of them, my heart going crazy.

Something about the church and the Middle Ages was on the TV. Not your run-of-the-mill TV fare. I wanted to watch something else. I turned to the other channels. But there was nothing on them, either. So I turned back to the first channel and apologized.

"Bub, it's all right," the blind man said. "It's fine with me. Whatever you want to watch is okay. I'm always learning something. Learning never ends. It won't hurt me to learn something tonight. I got ears," he said.

We didn't say anything for a time. He was leaning forward with his head turned at me, his right ear aimed in the direction of the set. Very disconcerting. Now and then his eyelids dropped and then they snapped open again. Now and then he put his fingers into his beard and tugged, like he was thinking about something he was hearing on the television.

On the screen, a group of men wearing cowls was being set upon and tormented by men dressed in skeleton costumes and men dressed as devils. The men dressed as devils wore devil masks, horns, and long tails. This pageant was part of a procession. The Englishman who was narrating the thing said it took place in Spain once a year. I tried to explain to the blind man what was happening.

"Skeletons," he said. "I know about skeletons," he said and he nodded.

The TV showed this one cathedral. Then there was a long, slow look at another one. Finally, the picture switched to the famous one in Paris, with its flying buttresses and its spires reaching up to the clouds. The camera pulled away to show the whole of the cathedral rising above the skyline.

There were times when the Englishman who was telling the thing would shut up, would simply let the camera move around over the cathedrals. Or else the camera would tour the countryside, men in fields walking behind oxen. I waited as long as I could. Then I felt I had to say something. I said, "They're showing the outside of this cathedral now. Gargoyles. Little statues carved to look like monsters. Now I guess they're in Italy. Yeah, they're in Italy. There's paintings on the walls of this one church."

"Are those fresco paintings, bub?" he asked, and he sipped from his drink.

I reached for my glass. But it was empty. I tried to remember what I could remember. "You're asking me are those frescoes?" I said. "That's a good question. I don't know."

The camera moved to a cathedral outside Lisbon. The differences in the Portuguese cathedral compared with the French and Italian were not that great. But they were there. Mostly the interior stuff. Then something occurred to me, and I said, "Something has occurred to me. Do you have any idea what a cathedral is? What they look like, that is? Do you follow me? If somebody says cathedral to you, do you have any notion what they're talking about? Do you know the difference between that and a Baptist church, say?"

He let the smoke dribble from his mouth. "I know they took hundreds of workers fifty or a hundred years to build," he said. "I just heard the man say that, of course. I know generations of the same families worked on a cathedral. I heard him say that, too. The men who began their life's work on them, they never lived to see the completion of their work. In that wise, bub, they're no different from the rest of us, right?" He laughed. Then his eyelids drooped again. His head nodded. He seemed to be snoozing. Maybe he was imagining himself in Portugal. The TV was showing another cathedral now. This one was in Germany. The Englishman's voice droned on. "Cathedrals," the blind man said. He sat up and rolled his head back and forth. "If you want the truth, bub, that's about all I know. What I just said. What I heard him say. But maybe you could describe one to me? I wish you'd do it. I'd like that. If you want to know, I really don't have a good idea."

I stared hard at the shot of the cathedral on the TV. How could I even begin to describe it? But say my life depended on it. Say my life was being threatened by an insane guy who said I had to do it or else.

I stared some more at the cathedral before the picture flipped off into the countryside. There was no use. I turned to the blind man and said, "To begin with, they're very tall." I was looking around the room for clues. "They reach way up. Up and up. Toward the sky. They're so big, some of them, they have to have these supports. To help hold them up, so to speak. These supports are called buttresses. They remind me of viaducts, for some reason. But maybe you don't know viaducts, either? Sometimes the cathedrals have devils and such carved into the front. Sometimes lords and ladies. Don't ask me why this is," I said.

He was nodding. The whole upper part of his body seemed to be moving back and forth.

"I'm not doing so good, am I?" I said.

He stopped nodding and leaned forward on the edge of the sofa. As he listened to me, he was running his fingers through his beard. I wasn't getting through to him, I could see that. But he waited for me to go on just the same. He nodded, like he was trying to encourage me. I tried to think what else to say. "They're really big," I said. "They're massive. They're built of stone. Marble, too, sometimes. In those olden days, when they built cathedrals, men wanted to be close to God. In those olden days, God was an important part of everyone's life. You could tell this from their cathedral-building. I'm sorry," I said, "but it looks like that's the best I can do for you. I'm just no good at it."

"That's all right, bub," the blind man said. "Hey, listen, I hope you don't mind my asking you. Can I ask you something? Let me ask you a simple question, yes or no. I'm just curious and there's no offense. You're my host. But let me ask if you are in any way religious? You don't mind my asking?"

I shook my head. He couldn't see that, though. A wink is the same as a nod to a blind man. "I guess I don't believe in it. In anything. Sometimes it's hard. You know what I'm saying?"

"Sure, I do," he said.

"Right," I said.

The Englishman was still holding forth. My wife sighed in her sleep. She drew a long breath and went on with her sleeping.

"You'll have to forgive me," I said. "But I can't tell you what a cathedral looks like. It just isn't in me to do it. I can't do any more than I've done."

The blind man sat very still, his head down, as he listened to me.

I said, "The truth is, cathedrals don't mean anything special to me. Nothing. Cathedrals. They're something to look at on late-night TV. That's all they are."

It was then that the blind man cleared his throat. He brought something up. He took a handkerchief from his back pocket. Then he said, "I get it, bub. It's okay. It happens. Don't worry about it," he said. "Hey, listen to me. Will you do me a favor? I got an idea. Why don't you find us some heavy paper? And a pen. We'll do something. We'll draw one together. Get us a pen and some heavy paper. Go on, bub, get the stuff," he said.

So I went upstairs. My legs felt like they didn't have any strength in them. They felt like they did after I'd done some running. In my wife's room, I looked around. I found some ballpoints in a little basket on her table. And then I tried to think where to look for the kind of paper he was talking about.

Downstairs, in the kitchen, I found a shopping bag with onion skins at the bottom of the bag. I emptied the bag and shook it. I brought it into the living room and sat down with it near his legs. I moved some things, smoothed the wrinkles from the bag, spread it out on the coffee table.

The blind man got down from the sofa and sat next to me on the carpet.

He ran his fingers over the paper. He went up and down the sides of the paper. The edges, even the edges. He fingered the corners.

"All right," he said. "All right, let's do her."

He found my hand, the hand with the pen. He closed his hand over my hand. "Go ahead, bub, draw," he said. "Draw. You'll see. I'll follow along with you. It'll be okay. Just begin now like I'm telling you. You'll see. Draw," the blind man said.

So I began. First I drew a box that looked like a house. It could have been the house I lived in. Then I put a roof on it. At either end of the roof, I drew spires. Crazy.

"Swell," he said. "Terrific. You're doing fine," he said. "Never thought anything like this could happen in your lifetime, did you, bub? Well, it's a strange life, we all know that. Go on now. Keep it up."

I put in windows with arches. I drew flying buttresses. I hung great doors. I couldn't stop. The TV station went off the air. I put down the pen and closed and opened my fingers. The blind man felt around over the paper. He moved the tips of his fingers over the paper, all over what I had drawn, and he nodded.

"Doing fine," the blind man said.

I took up the pen again, and he found my hand. I kept at it. I'm no artist. But I kept drawing just the same.

My wife opened up her eyes and gazed at us. She sat up on the sofa, her robe hanging open. She said, "What are you doing? Tell me, I want to know."

I didn't answer her.

The blind man said, "We're drawing a cathedral. Me and him are working on it. Press hard," he said to me. "That's right. That's good," he said. "Sure. You got it, bub. I can tell. You didn't think you could. But you can, can't you? You're cooking with gas now. You know what I'm saying? We're going to really have us something here in a minute. How's the old arm?" he said. "Put some people in there now. What's a cathedral without people?"

My wife said, "What's going on? Robert, what are you doing? What's going on?"

"It's all right," he said to her. "Close your eyes now," the blind man said to me.

I did it. I closed them just like he said.

"Are they closed?" he said. "Don't fudge."

"They're closed," I said.

"Keep them that way," he said. He said, "Don't stop now. Draw."

So we kept on with it. His fingers rode my fingers as my hand went over the paper. It was like nothing else in my life up to now.

Then he said, "I think that's it. I think you got it," he said. "Take a look. What do you think?"

But I had my eyes closed. I thought I'd keep them that way for a little longer. I thought it was something I ought to do.

"Well?" he said. "Are you looking?"

My eyes were still closed. I was in my house. I knew that. But I didn't feel like I was inside anything.

"It's really something," I said.

—1983

MARGARET ATWOOD

Margaret Atwood is a writer who defies traditional categories. Her internationally renowned novels, short stories, and poems span and splice together a multitude of genres and have established her as a germinal figure in Canadian literature.

Born in Ottawa in 1939, Atwood spent her childhood living with her family in Ottawa in the winters and spending the remaining parts of the year in northern Quebec and Ontario while her entomologist father conducted his research on bees, spruce budworms, and tent caterpillars. In an interview with Eleanor Wachtel, Atwood has described the wild landscape of her childhood:

> [I]f you are watching a figure in that landscape, one minute you see it and the next minute you don't. It disappears among the trees, it goes around the corner, people dive. There is a constant metamorphosis going on between human figures, foliage and water surfaces in that sort of landscape ... it's easy to get lost and there is always the possibility that something may come out of the woods.

Atwood examined Canadian literary history and its relation to landscape in her first scholarly book, *Survival: A Thematic Guide to Canadian Literature* (1972). The work became a landmark in Canadian literary criticism, sparking a charged debate about marginalized figures in Canadian writing. Atwood's career has also been notable for her literary and political activism; she is a co-founder and past president of the Writers' Union of Canada, and has been president of PEN International's Canadian English-speaking branch and vice-president of PEN International. Political issues are close to the surface in much of her fiction—as well as in *Payback: Debt and the Shadow Side of Wealth* (2008), which became a non-fiction bestseller.

Although it was the stark, terse, eerily detached poetry in collections like *The Journals of Susanna Moodie* (1970) that made her reputation, Atwood's fiction is astonishing for its variety of tone, mingling seriousness, playful irony, sardonic humour, and even Gothic terror. Her fiction spans a similarly diverse range of genres, from the dystopian "speculative fiction" of *The Handmaid's Tale* (1985) and its Booker Prize-winning sequel *The Testaments* (2019) to historical novels such as *Alias Grace* (1996).

For Atwood, every art form is enclosed by a "set of brackets," conventions that check "the deviousness and inventiveness and audacity and perversity of the creative spirit." In her work she aims to "expand the brackets," rewriting traditions to deliver the creative spirit from restraint. Though she has written a good deal of realist fiction, her fascination with storytelling has also led her to experiment widely with metafictional techniques. Of all the labels critics have applied to her, perhaps "trickster" suits Atwood best, for she is a master fabricator of great wit and imagination whose work refashions the rules to prove that, in the end, "art is what you can get away with."

Stone Mattress

AT THE OUTSET Verna had not intended to kill anyone. What she had in mind was a vacation, pure and simple. Take a breather, do some inner accounting, shed worn skin. The Arctic suits her: there's something inherently calming in the vast cool sweeps of ice and rock and sea and sky, undisturbed by cities and highways and trees and the other distractions that clutter up the landscape to the south.

Among the clutter she includes other people, and by other people she means men. She's had enough of men for a while. She's made an inner memo to renounce flirtations and any consequences that might result from them. She doesn't need the cash, not anymore. She's not extravagant or greedy, she tells herself: all she ever wanted was to be protected by layer upon layer of kind, soft, insulating money, so that nobody and nothing could get close enough to harm her. Surely she has at last achieved this modest goal.

But old habits die hard, and it's not long before she's casting an appraising eye over her fleece-clad fellow-travellers dithering with their wheely bags in the lobby of the first-night airport hotel. Passing over the women, she ear-tags the male members of the flock. Some have females attached to them, and she eliminates these on principle: why work harder than you need to? Prying a spouse loose can be arduous, as she discovered via her first husband: discarded wives stick like burrs.

It's the solitaries who interest her, the lurkers at the fringes. Some of these are too old for her purposes; she avoids eye contact with them. The ones who cherish the belief that there's life in the old dog yet: these are her game. Not that she'll do anything about it, she tells herself, but there's nothing wrong with a little warmup practice, if only to demonstrate to herself that she can still knock one off if she wishes to.

For that evening's meet-and-greet she chooses her cream-colored pullover, perching the Magnetic Northward nametag just slightly too low on her left breast. Thanks to Aquacize and core strength training, she's still in excellent shape for her age, or indeed for any age, at least when fully clothed and buttressed with carefully fitted underwiring. She wouldn't want to chance a deck chair in a bikini—superficial puckering has set in, despite her best efforts—which is one reason for selecting the Arctic over, say, the Caribbean. Her face is what it is, and certainly the best that money can buy at this stage: with a little bronzer and pale eyeshadow and mascara and glimmer powder and low lighting, she can finesse ten years.

"Though much is taken, much remains,"[1] she murmurs to her image in the mirror. Her third husband had been a serial quotation freak with a special penchant for Tennyson. "Come into the garden, Maud,"[2] he'd been in the habit of saying just before bedtime. It had driven her mad at the time.

She adds a dab of cologne—an understated scent, floral, nostalgic—then she blots it off, leaving a mere whiff. It's a mistake to overdo it: though elderly noses aren't as keen as they may once have been, it's best to allow for allergies; a sneezing man is not an attentive man.

She makes her entrance slightly late, smiling a detached but cheerful smile—it doesn't do for an unaccompanied woman to appear too eager—accepts a glass of the passable white wine they're doling out, and drifts among the assembled nibblers and sippers. The men will be retired professionals: doctors, lawyers, engineers, stockbrokers, interested in Arctic exploration, polar bears, archeology, birds, Inuit crafts, perhaps even Vikings or plant life or geology. Magnetic Northward attracts serious punters, with an earnest bunch of experts laid on to herd them around and lecture to them. She's investigated the two other outfits that tour the region, but neither appeals. One features excessive hiking and attracts the under-fifties—not her target market—and the other goes in for singsongs and dressing up in silly outfits, so she's stuck with Magnetic Northward, which offers the comfort of familiarity. She travelled with this company once before, after the death of her third husband, five years ago, so she knows pretty much what to expect.

---

1   A reference to the line "Though much is taken, much abides" in the poem "Ulysses" by Alfred, Lord Tennyson (1809–92).

2   A poem by Alfred, Lord Tennyson.

There's a lot of sportswear in the room, much beige among the men, many plaid shirts, vests with multiple pockets. She notes the nametags: a Fred, a Dan, a Rick, a Norm, a Bob. Another Bob, then another: there are a lot of Bobs on this trip. Several appear to be flying solo. Bob: a name once of heavy significance to her, though surely she's rid herself of that load of luggage by now. She selects one of the thinner but still substantial Bobs, glides close to him, raises her eyelids, and lowers them again. He peers down at her chest.

"Verna," he says. "That's a lovely name."

"Old-fashioned," she says. "From the Latin word for 'spring.' When everything springs to life again." That line, so filled with promises of phallic renewal, had been effective in helping to secure her second husband. To her third husband she'd said that her mother had been influenced by the eighteenth-century Scottish poet James Thomson and his vernal breezes, which was a preposterous but enjoyable lie: she had, in fact, been named after a lumpy, bun-faced dead aunt. As for her mother, she'd been a strict Presbyterian with a mouth like a vise grip, who despised poetry and was unlikely to have been influenced by anything softer than a granite wall.

During the preliminary stages of netting her fourth husband, whom she'd flagged as a kink addict, Verna had gone even further. She'd told him she'd been named for "The Rite of Spring," a highly sexual ballet that ended with torture and human sacrifice. He'd laughed, but he'd also wriggled: a sure sign of the hook going in.

Now she says, "And you're ... Bob." It's taken her years to perfect the small breathy intake, a certified knee-melter.

"Yes," Bob says. "Bob Goreham," he adds, with a diffidence he surely intends to be charming. Verna smiles widely to disguise her shock. She finds herself flushing with a combination of rage and an almost reckless mirth. She looks him full in the face: yes, underneath the thinning hair and the wrinkles and the obviously whitened and possibly implanted teeth, it's the same Bob—the Bob of fifty-odd years before. Mr. Heartthrob, Mr. Senior Football Star, Mr. Astounding Catch, from the rich, Cadillac-driving end of town where the mining-company big shots lived. Mr. Shit, with his looming bully's posture and his lopsided joker's smile.

How amazing to everyone, back then—not only everyone in school but everyone, for in that armpit of a town they'd known to a millimetre who drank and who didn't and who was no better than she should be and how much change you kept in your back pocket—how amazing that golden-boy Bob had singled out insignificant Verna for the Snow Queen's Palace winter formal. Pretty Verna, three years younger; studious, grade-skipping, innocent Verna, tolerated but not included, clawing her way toward a scholarship as her ticket out of town. Gullible Verna, who'd believed she was in love.

Or who *was* in love. When it came to love, wasn't believing the same as the real thing? Such beliefs drain your strength and cloud your vision. She's never allowed herself to be skewered in that tiger trap again.

What had they danced to that night? "Rock Around the Clock." "Hearts Made of Stone." "The Great Pretender." Bob had steered Verna around the edges of the gym, holding her squashed up against his carnation buttonhole, for the unskilled, awkward Verna of those days had never been to a dance before and was no match for Bob's strenuous and flamboyant moves. For meek Verna, life was church and studies and household chores and her weekend job clerking in the drugstore, with her grim-faced mother regulating every move. No dates; those wouldn't have been allowed, not that she'd been asked on any. But her mother had permitted her to go to the well-supervised high-school dance with Bob Goreham, for wasn't he a shining light from a respectable family? She'd even allowed herself a touch of smug gloating, silent though it had been. Holding her head up after the decampment of Verna's father had been a full-time job, and had given her a very stiff neck. From this distance Verna could understand it.

So out the door went Verna, starry-eyed with hero worship, wobbling on her first high heels. She was courteously inserted into Bob's shiny red convertible with the treacherous Mickey of rye[3] already lurking in the glove compartment, where she sat bolt upright, almost catatonic with shyness, smelling of Prell shampoo and Jergens lotion, wrapped in her mother's mothbally out-of-date rabbit stole and an ice-blue tulle-skirted dress that looked as cheap as it was.

Cheap. Cheap and disposable. Use and toss. That was what Bob had thought about her, from the very first.

Now Bob grins a little. He looks pleased with himself: maybe he thinks Verna is blushing with desire. But he doesn't recognize her! He really doesn't! How many fucking Vernas can he have met in his life?

Get a grip, she tells herself. She's not invulnerable after all, it appears. She's shaking with anger, or is it mortification? To cover herself she takes a gulp of her wine, and immediately chokes on it. Bob springs into action, giving her a few brisk but caressing thumps on the back.

"Excuse me," she manages to gasp. The crisp, cold scent of carnations envelops her. She needs to get away from him; all of a sudden she feels quite sick. She hurries to the ladies' room, which is fortunately empty, and throws up her white wine and her cream-cheese-and-olive canapé into a cubicle toilet. She wonders if it's too late to cancel the trip. But why should she run from Bob again?

---

3   A 375 mL bottle of alcohol.

Back then she'd had no choice. By the end of that week, the story was all over town. Bob had spread it himself, in a farcical version that was very different from what Verna herself remembered. Slutty, drunken, willing Verna, what a joke. She'd been followed home from school by groups of leering boys, hooting and calling out to her: *Easy out! Can I have a ride*? *Candy's dandy but liquor's quicker!* Those were some of the milder slogans. She'd been shunned by girls, fearful that the disgrace—the ludicrous, hilarious smuttiness of it all—would rub off on them.

Then there was her mother. It hadn't taken long for the scandal to hit church circles. What little her mother had to say through her clamp of a mouth was to the point: Verna had made her own bed, and now she would have to lie in it. No, she could not wallow in self-pity—she would just have to face the music, not that she would ever live it down, because one false step and you fell, that's how life was. When it was evident that the worst had happened, she bought Verna a bus ticket and shipped her off to a church-run Home for Unwed Mothers on the outskirts of Toronto.

There Verna spent the days peeling potatoes and scrubbing floors and scouring toilets along with her fellow-delinquents. They wore gray maternity dresses and gray wool stockings and clunky brown shoes, all paid for by generous donations, they were informed. In addition to their scouring and peeling chores, they were treated to bouts of prayer and self-righteous hectoring. What had happened to them was justly deserved, the speeches went, because of their depraved behavior, but it was never too late to redeem themselves through hard work and self-restraint. They were cautioned against alcohol, tobacco, and gum chewing, and were told that they should consider it a miracle of God if any decent man ever wanted to marry them.

Verna's labor was long and difficult. The baby was taken away from her immediately so that she would not get attached to it. There was an infection, with complications and scarring, but it was all for the best, she overheard one brisk nurse telling another, because those sorts of girls made unfit mothers anyway. Once she could walk, Verna was given five dollars and a bus ticket and instructed to return to the guardianship of her mother, because she was still a minor.

But she could not face that—that or the town in general—so she headed for downtown Toronto. What was she thinking? No actual thoughts, only feelings: mournfulness, woe, and, finally, a spark of defiant anger. If she was as trashy and worthless as everyone seemed to think, she might as well act that way, and, in between rounds of waitressing and hotel-room cleaning, she did.

It was only by great good luck that she stumbled upon an older married man who took an interest in her. She traded three years of noontime sex with him for the price of her education. A fair exchange, to her mind—she bore him no ill will. She learned a lot from him, how to walk in high heels being the least of it—and pulled herself up and out. Little by little she jettisoned the crushed image of Bob that she still carried like a dried flower—incredibly!—next to her heart.

She pats her face back into place and repairs her mascara, which has bled down her cheeks despite its waterproof claims. Courage, she tells herself. She will not be chased away, not this time. She'll tough it out; she's more than a match for five Bobs now. And she has the advantage, because Bob doesn't have a clue who she is. Does she really look that different? Yes, she does. She looks better. There's her silver-blond hair, and the various alterations, of course. But the real difference is in the attitude—the confident way she carries herself. It would be hard for Bob to see through that façade to the shy, mousy-haired, snivelling idiot she'd been at fourteen.

After adding a last film of powder, she rejoins the group and lines up at the buffet for roast beef and salmon. She won't eat much of it, but then she never does, not in public: a piggy, gobbling woman is not a creature of mysterious allure. She refrains from scanning the crowd to pinpoint Bob's position—he might wave to her, and she needs time to think—and selects a table at the far end of the room. But presto, Bob is sliding in beside her without so much as a may-I-join-you. He assumes he's already pissed on this fire hydrant, she thinks. Spray-painted this wall. Cut the head off this trophy and got his picture taken with his foot on the body. As he did once before, not that he realizes it. She smiles.

He's solicitous. Is Verna all right? Oh, yes, she replies. It's just that something went down the wrong way. Bob launches straight into the preliminaries. What does Verna do? Retired, she says, though she had a rewarding career as a physiotherapist, specializing in the rehabilitation of heart and stroke victims. "That must have been interesting," Bob says. Oh, yes, Verna says. So fulfilling to help people.

It had been more than interesting. Wealthy men recovering from life-threatening episodes had recognized the worth of an attractive younger woman with deft hands, an encouraging manner, and an intuitive knowledge of when to say nothing. Or, as her third husband put it in his Keatsian mode, heard melodies are sweet, but those unheard are sweeter.[4] There was something about the intimacy of the relationship—so physical—that led to other intimacies, though Verna had always stopped short of sex: it was a religious thing, she'd said. If no marriage proposal was forthcoming, she would extricate herself, citing her duty to patients who needed her more. That had forced the issue twice.

She'd chosen her acceptances with an eye to the medical condition involved, and once married she'd done her best to provide value for money.

---

4   A reference to the poem "Ode on a Grecian Urn" by John Keats (1795–1821).

Each husband had departed not only happy but grateful, if a little sooner than might have been expected. But each had died of natural causes—a lethal recurrence of the heart attack or stroke that had hit him in the first place. All she'd done was give them tacit permission to satisfy every forbidden desire: to eat artery-clogging foods, to drink as much as they liked, to return to their golf games too soon. She'd refrained from commenting on the fact that, strictly speaking, they were being too zealously medicated. She'd wondered about the dosages, she'd say later, but who was she to set her own opinion up against a doctor's?

And if a man happened to forget that he'd already taken his pills for that evening and found them neatly laid out in their usual place and took them again, wasn't that to be expected? Blood thinners could be so hazardous, in excess. You could bleed into your own brain.

Then there was sex: the terminator, the coup de grâce. Verna herself had no interest in sex as such, but she knew what was likely to work. "You only live once," she'd been in the habit of saying, lifting a champagne glass during a candlelit supper and then setting out the Viagra, a revolutionary breakthrough but so troubling to the blood pressure. It was essential to call the paramedics in promptly, though not too promptly. "He was like this when I woke up" was an acceptable thing to say. So was "I heard a strange sound in the bathroom, and then when I went to look ..."

She has no regrets. She did those men a favor: surely better a swift exit than a lingering decline.

With two of the husbands, there'd been difficulties with the grownup children over the will. Verna had graciously said that she understood how they must feel, then she'd paid them off, more than was strictly fair considering the effort she'd put in. Her sense of justice has remained Presbyterian: she doesn't want much more than her due, but she doesn't want much less, either. She likes balanced accounts.

Bob leans in toward her, sliding his arm along the back of her chair. Is her husband along for the cruise? he asks, closer to her ear than he should be, breathing in. No, she says, she is recently widowed—here she looks down at the table, hoping to convey muted grief—and this is a sort of healing voyage. Bob says he's very sorry to hear it, but what a coincidence, for his own wife passed away just six months ago. It had been a blow—they'd been really looking forward to the golden years together. She'd been his college sweetheart—it was love at first sight. Does Verna believe in love at first sight? Yes, Verna says, she does.

Bob confides further: they'd waited until after his law degree to get married and then they'd had three kids, and now there are five grandkids—he's so proud of them all. If he shows me any baby pictures, Verna thinks, I'll hit him.

"It does leave an empty space, doesn't it?" Bob says. "A sort of blank." Verna admits that it does. Would Verna care to join Bob in a bottle of wine?

You crap artist, Verna thinks. So you went on to get married and have children and a normal life, just as if nothing ever happened. Whereas for me ... She feels queasy.

"I'd love to," she says. "But let's wait until we're on the ship. That would be more leisurely." She gives him the eyelids again. "Now I'm off to my beauty sleep." She smiles, rises from the table.

"Oh, surely you don't need that," Bob says gallantly. The asshole actually pulls out her chair for her. He hadn't shown such fine manners back then. Nasty, brutish, and short, as her third husband had said, quoting Hobbes on the subject of natural man.[5] Nowadays a girl would know to call the police. Nowadays Bob would go to jail no matter what lies he might tell, because Verna was underage. But there had been no true words for the act then: rape was what occurred when some maniac jumped on you out of a bush, not when your formal-dance date drove you to a side road in the mangy twice-cut forest surrounding a tin-pot mining town and told you to drink up like a good girl and then took you apart, layer by torn layer. To make it worse, Bob's best friend, Ken, had turned up in his own car to help out. The two of them had been laughing. They'd kept her panty girdle as a souvenir.

Afterward, Bob had pushed her out of the car halfway back, surly because she was crying. "Shut up or walk home," he'd said. She has a picture of herself limping along the icy roadside with her bare feet stuck in her dyed-to-match ice-blue heels, dizzy and raw and shivering and—a further ridiculous humiliation—hiccupping. What had concerned her most at that moment was her nylons—where were her nylons? She'd bought them with her own drugstore money. She must have been in shock.

Did she remember correctly? Had Bob stuck her panty girdle upside down on his head and danced about in the snow with the garter tabs flopping around like jesters' bells?

Panty girdle, she thinks. How prehistoric. It, and all the long-gone archeology that went with it. Now a girl would be on the pill or have an abortion without a backward glance. How Paleolithic to still feel wounded by any of it.

It was Ken—not Bob—who'd come back for her, told her brusquely to get in, driven her home. He, at least, had had the grace to be shamefaced. "Don't say anything," he'd muttered. And she hadn't, but her silence had done her no good.

---

5   Thomas Hobbes (1588–1679) was an English philosopher who famously said, in his book *Leviathan*, that in a natural state the lives of individuals would be "solitary, poor, nasty, brutish, and short."

Why should she be the only one to have suffered for that night? She'd been stupid, granted, but Bob had been vicious. And he'd gone scot-free, without consequences or remorse, whereas her entire life had been distorted. The Verna of the day before had died, and a different Verna had solidified in her place: stunted, twisted, mangled. It was Bob who'd taught her that only the strong can win, that weakness should be mercilessly exploited. It was Bob who'd turned her into—why not say the word?—a murderer.

The next morning, during the chartered flight north to where the ship is floating on the Beaufort Sea, she considers her choices. She could play Bob like a fish right up to the final moment, then leave him cold with his pants around his ankles: a satisfaction, but a minor one. She could avoid him throughout the trip and leave the equation where it's been for the past fifty-some years: unresolved. Or she could kill him. She contemplates this third option with theoretical calm. Just say, for instance, if she were to murder Bob, how might she do it during the cruise without getting caught? Her meds-and-sex formula would be far too slow and might not work anyway, since Bob did not appear to suffer from any ailments. Pushing him off the ship is not a viable option. Bob is too big, the railings are too high, and she knows from her previous trip that there will always be people on deck, enjoying the breathtaking views and taking pictures. A corpse in a cabin would attract police and set off a search for DNA and fabric hairs and so forth, as on television. No, she would have to arrange the death during one of the onshore visits. But how? Where? She consults the itinerary and the map of the proposed route. An Inuit settlement will not do: dogs will bark, children will follow. As for the other stops, the land they'll be visiting is bare of concealing features. Staff with guns will accompany them to protect against polar bears. Maybe an accident with one of the guns? For that she'd need split-second timing.

Whatever the method, she'd have to do it early in the voyage, before he had time to make any new friends—people who might notice he was missing. Also, the possibility that Bob will suddenly recognize her is ever present. And if that happens it will be game over. Meanwhile, it would be best not to be seen with him too much. Enough to keep his interest up, but not enough to start rumors of, for instance, a budding romance. On a cruise, word of mouth spreads like the flu.

***

Once on board the ship—it's the *Resolute II*, familiar to Verna from her last voyage—the passengers line up to deposit their passports at Reception. Then they assemble in the forward lounge for a talk on procedure given by three of the discouragingly capable staff members. Every time they go ashore, the first one says with a severe Viking frown, they must turn their tags on the tag board from green to red. When they come back to the ship, they must turn their tags back to green. They must always wear life jackets for the Zodiac trips to shore; the life jackets are the new, thin kind that inflate once in water. They must deposit their life jackets on the shore when landing, in the white canvas bags provided, and put them back on when departing. If there are any tags unturned or any life jackets left in the bags, the staff will know that someone is still ashore. They do not want to be left behind, do they? And now a few housekeeping details. They will find laundry bags in their cabins. Bar bills will be charged to their accounts, and tips will be settled at the end. The ship runs on an open-door policy, to facilitate the work of the cleaning staff, but of course they can lock their rooms if they wish. There is a lost-and-found at Reception. All clear? Good.

The second speaker is the archeologist, who, to Verna, looks about twelve. They will be visiting sites of many kinds, she says, including Independence 1, Dorset, and Thule, but they must never, never take anything. No artifacts, and especially no bones. Those bones might be human, and they must be very careful not to disturb them. But even animal bones are an important source of scarce calcium for ravens and lemmings and foxes and, well, the entire food chain, because the Arctic recycles everything. All clear? Good.

Now, says the third speaker, a fashionably bald individual who looks like a personal trainer, a word about the guns. Guns are essential, because polar bears are fearless. But the staff will always fire into the air first, to scare the bear away. Shooting a bear is a last resort, but bears can be dangerous, and the safety of passengers is the first priority. There is no need to fear the guns: the bullets will be taken out during the Zodiac trips to and from shore, and it will not be possible for anyone to get shot. All clear? Good.

Clearly a gun accident won't do, Verna thinks. No passenger is going to get near those guns.

After lunch, there's a lecture on walruses. There are rumors of rogue walruses that prey on seals, puncturing them with their tusks, then sucking out the fat with their powerful mouths. The women on either side of Verna are knitting. One of them says, "Liposuction." The other laughs.

Once the talks are over, Verna goes out on deck. The sky is clear, with a flight of lenticular clouds hovering in it like spaceships; the air is warm; the sea is aqua. There's a classic iceberg on the port side, with a center so blue it looks dyed, and ahead of them is a mirage—a fata morgana, towering like an ice castle on the horizon, completely real except for the faint shimmering at its edges. Sailors have been lured to their deaths by those; they've drawn mountains on maps where no mountains were.

"Beautiful, isn't it?" Bob says, materializing at her side. "How about that bottle of wine tonight?"

"Stunning," Verna says, smiling. "Perhaps not tonight—I promised some of the girls." True enough—she's made a date with the knitting women.

"Maybe tomorrow?" Bob grins, and shares the fact that he has a single cabin: "No. 222, like the painkiller," he quips, and comfortably amidships.[6] "Hardly any rock and roll at all," he adds. Verna says that she, too, has a single: worth the extra expense, because that way you can really relax. She draws out "relax" until it sounds like a voluptuous writhe on satin sheets.

Glancing at the tag board while strolling around the ship after dinner, Verna notes Bob's tag—close enough to her own. Then she buys a pair of cheap gloves in the gift shop. She's read a lot of crime novels.

The next day starts with a talk on geology by an energetic young scientist who has been arousing some interest among the passengers, especially the female ones. By great good fortune, he tells them, and because of a change in itinerary owing to ice pack, they'll be making an unanticipated stop, where they'll be able to view a wonder of the geological world, a sight permitted to very few. They'll be privileged to see the world's earliest fossilized stromatolites, clocking in at an astonishing 1.9 billion years old—before fish, before dinosaurs, before mammals—the very first preserved form of life on this planet. What is a stromatolite? he asks rhetorically, his eyes gleaming. The word comes from the Greek *stroma*, a mattress, coupled with the root word for "stone." Stone mattress: a fossilized cushion, formed by layer upon layer of blue-green algae building up into a mound or dome. It was this very same blue-green algae that created the oxygen they are now breathing. Isn't that astonishing?

A wizened, elflike man at Verna's lunchtime table grumbles that he hopes they'll be seeing something more exciting than rocks. He's one of the other Bobs: Verna's been taking an inventory. An extra Bob may come in handy. "I'm looking forward to them," she says. "The stone mattresses." She gives the word *mattress* the tiniest hint of suggestiveness, and gets an approving twinkle out of Bob the Second. Really, they're never too old to flirt.

Out on deck after coffee, she surveys the approaching land through her binoculars. It's autumn here: the leaves on the miniature trees that snake along the ground like vines are red and orange and yellow and purple, with rock surging out of them in waves and folds. There's a ridge, a higher ridge, then a higher one. It's on the second ridge that the best stromatolites are to be found, the geologist has told them.

---

6   In the middle of the ship.

Will someone who has slipped behind the third ridge be visible from the second one? Verna doesn't think so.

Now they're all stuffed into their waterproof pants and their rubber boots; now they're being zipped and buckled into their life jackets like outsized kindergarten kids; now they're turning their tags from green to red; now they're edging down the gangway and being whisked into the black inflatable Zodiacs. Bob has made it into Verna's Zodiac. He lifts his camera, snaps her picture.

Verna's heart is beating more rapidly. If he recognizes me spontaneously, I won't kill him, she thinks. If I tell him who I am and he recognizes me and then apologizes, I still won't kill him. That's two more escape chances than he gave her. It will mean forgoing the advantage of surprise, a move that could be hazardous—Bob is much bigger than she is—but she wishes to be more than fair.

They've landed and have shed their life jackets and rubber footwear and are lacing up their hiking boots. Verna strolls closer to Bob, notes that he hasn't bothered with the rubber boots. He's wearing a red baseball cap; as she watches, he turns it backward.

Now they're all scattering. Some stay by the shore; some move up to the first ridge. The geologist is standing there with his hammer, a twittering cluster already gathered around him. He's in full lecture mode: they will please not take any of the stromatolites, but the ship has a sampling permit, so if anyone finds a particularly choice fragment, especially a cross section, check with him first and they can put it on the rock table he'll set up on board, where everyone can see it. Here are some examples, for those who may not want to tackle the second ridge ...

Heads go down; cameras come out. Perfect, Verna thinks. The more distraction the better. She feels without looking that Bob is close by. Now they're at the second ridge, which some are climbing more easily than others. Here are the best stromatolites, a whole field of them. There are unbroken ones, like bubbles or boils, small ones, ones as big as half a soccer ball. Some have lost their tops, like eggs in the process of hatching. Still others have been ground down, so that all that's left of them is a series of raised concentric oblongs, like a cinnamon bun or the growth rings on a tree.

And here's one shattered into four, like a Dutch cheese sliced into wedges. Verna picks up one of the quarters, examines the layers, each year black, gray, black, gray, black, and at the bottom the featureless core. The piece is heavy, and sharp at the edges. Verna lifts it into her backpack.

Here comes Bob as if on cue, lumbering slowly as a zombie up the hill toward her. He's taken off his outer jacket, tucked it under his backpack straps. He's out of breath. She has a moment of compunction: he's over the hill; frailty is gaining on him. Shouldn't she let bygones be bygones? Boys will be boys. Aren't they all just hormone puppets at that age? Why should any human being be judged by something that was done in another time, so long ago it might be centuries?

A raven flies overhead, circles around. Can it tell? Is it waiting? She looks down through its eyes, sees an old woman—because, face it, she is an old woman now—on the verge of murdering an even older man because of an anger already fading into the distance of used-up time. It's paltry. It's vicious. It's normal. It's what happens in life.

"Great day," Bob says. "It's good to have a chance to stretch your legs."

"Isn't it?" Verna says. She moves toward the far side of the second ridge. "Maybe there's something better over there. But weren't we told not to go that far? Out of sight?"

Bob gives a rules-are-for-peasants laugh. "We're paying for this," he says. He actually takes the lead, not up the third ridge but around behind it. Out of sight is where he wants to be.

The gun bearer on the second ridge is yelling at some people straying off to the left. He has his back turned. A few more steps and Verna glances over her shoulder: she can't see anyone, which means that no one can see her. They squelch over a patch of boggy ground. She takes her thin gloves out of her pocket, slips them on. Now they're at the far side of the third ridge, at the sloping base.

"Come over here," Bob says, patting the rock. His backpack is beside him. "I brought us a few drinks." All around him is a tattered gauze of black lichen.

"Terrific," Verna says. She sits down, unzips her backpack. "Look," she says. "I found a perfect specimen." She turns, positioning the stromatolite between them, supporting it with both hands. She takes a breath. "I think we've known each other before," she says. "I'm Verna Pritchard. From high school."

Bob doesn't miss a beat. "I thought there was something familiar about you," he says. He's actually smirking.

She remembers that smirk. She has a vivid picture of Bob capering triumphantly in the snow, sniggering like a ten-year-old. Herself wrecked and crumpled.

She knows better than to swing widely. She brings the stromatolite up hard, a short sharp jab right underneath Bob's lower jaw. There's a crunch, the only sound. His head snaps back. Now he's sprawled on the rock. She holds the stromatolite over his forehead, lets it drop. Again. Once again. There. That seems to have done it.

Bob looks ridiculous, with his eyes open and fixed and his forehead mashed in and blood running down both sides of his face. "You're a mess," she says. He looks laughable, so she laughs. As she suspected, the front teeth are implants.

She takes a moment to steady her breathing. Then she retrieves the stromato-lite, being careful not to let any of the blood touch her or even her gloves, and slides it into a pool of bog water. Bob's baseball cap has fallen off; she stuffs it into her pack, along with his jacket. She empties out his backpack: nothing in there but the camera, a pair of woollen mitts, a scarf, and six miniature bottles of Scotch—how pathetically hopeful of him. She rolls the pack up, stuffs it inside her own, adds the camera, which she'll toss into the sea later. Then she dries the stromatolite off on the scarf, checking to make sure there's no visible blood, and stows it in her pack. She leaves Bob to the ravens and the lemmings and the rest of the food chain.

Then she hikes back around the base of the third ridge, adjusting her jacket. Anyone looking will assume she's just been having a pee. People do sneak off like that, on shore visits. But no one is looking.

She finds the young geologist—he's still on the second ridge, along with his coterie of admirers—and produces the stromatolite.

"May I take it back to the ship?" she asks sweetly. "For the rock table?"

"Fantastic sample!" he says.

Travellers are making their way shoreward, back to the Zodiacs. When she reaches the bags with the life jackets, Verna fumbles with her shoelaces until all eyes are elsewhere and she can cram an extra life jacket into her backpack. The pack is a lot bulkier than it was when she left the ship, but it would be odd if anyone noticed that.

Once up the gangway, she diddles around with her pack until everyone else has moved past the tag board, then flips Bob's tag from red to green. And her own tag, too, of course.

On the way to her cabin she waits till the corridor is clear, then slips through Bob's unlocked door. The room key is on the dresser; she leaves it there. She hangs up the life jacket and Bob's waterproof and baseball cap, runs some water in the sink, messes up a towel. Then she goes to her own cabin along the still-empty corridor, takes off her gloves, washes them, and hangs them up to dry. She's broken a nail, worse luck, but she can repair that. She checks her face: a touch of sunburn, but nothing serious. For dinner, she dresses in pink and makes an effort to flirt with Bob the Second, who gamely returns her serves but is surely too decrepit to be a serious prospect. Just as well—her adrenaline level is plummeting. If there are northern lights, they've been told, there will be an announcement, but Verna doesn't intend to get up for them.

So far she's in the clear. All she has to do now is maintain the mirage of Bob, faithfully turning his tag from green to red, from red to green. He'll move objects around in his cabin, wear different items from his beige-and-plaid ward-robe, sleep in his bed, take showers, leaving the towels on the floor. He will receive a first-name-only invitation to have dinner at a staff table, which will then quietly appear under the door of one of the other Bobs, and no one will spot the substitution. He will brush his teeth. He will adjust his alarm clock. He will send in laundry, without, however, filling out the slip: that would be too risky. The cleaning staff won't care—a lot of older people forget to fill out their laundry slips.

Meanwhile, the stromatolite will sit on the geological samples table and will be picked up and examined and discussed, acquiring many fingerprints. At the end of the trip it will be jettisoned. The *Resolute II* will travel for fourteen days; it will stop for shore visits eighteen times. It will sail past ice caps and sheer cliffs, and mountains of gold and copper and ebony black and silver gray; it will glide through pack ice; it will anchor off long, implacable beaches and explore fjords gouged by glaciers over millions of years. In the midst of such rigorous and demanding splendor, who will remember Bob?

There will be a moment of truth at the end of the voyage, when Bob will not appear to pay his bill and pick up his passport; nor will he pack his bags. There will be a flurry of concern, followed by a staff meeting—behind closed doors, so as not to alarm the passengers. Ultimately, there will be a news item: Bob, tragically, must have fallen off the ship on the last night of the voyage while leaning over to get a better camera angle on the northern lights. No other explanation is possible.

Meanwhile, the passengers will have scattered to the winds, Verna among them. If, that is, she pulls it off. Will she or won't she? She ought to care more about that—she ought to find it an exciting challenge—but right now she just feels tired and somewhat empty.

Though at peace, though safe. Calm of mind all passion spent, as her third husband used to say so annoyingly after his Viagra sessions. Those Victorians always coupled sex with death. Who was that poet anyway? Keats? Tennyson? Her memory isn't what it was. But the details will come back to her later.

—*2011*

TOBIAS WOLFF

Tobias Wolff is an American writer, born in Alabama in 1945. Best known for his short stories and memoirs, he has also written two novels. Wolff's stories belong to the tradition of Maupassant, Joyce, Hemingway, and Chekhov; they are highly crafted, realistic, and focused on the psychological dimensions of character.

In 1949 Wolff's parents separated, and he moved with his mother to Washington State, where they settled first in Seattle and then in the small town of Concrete. His early years are chronicled in his memoir, *This Boy's Life* (1989), a book which received wide critical acclaim; many credited it with helping to revive the genre of memoir in America. *This Boy's Life* was made into a film in 1993, starring Robert De Niro and Leonardo DiCaprio.

One of Wolff's earliest creative endeavours was to escape his domestic situation by gaining a scholarship to a Pennsylvania prep school, The Hill School. He won the scholarship by means of forged documents attesting to his academic and athletic prowess. He spent two idyllic years there, before being expelled for his failures in mathematics. After a short period working at sea, he joined the American army, serving for four years in Vietnam; his second memoir, *In Pharaoh's Army* (1994), describes the horror and absurdity of his experiences during that time.

After the war, Wolff attended Oxford University. He graduated in 1975; that same year he published his first work of fiction, the novel *Ugly Rumors*. His first short story collection, *In the Garden of the North American Martyrs* (1981), was a critical success, and his novella *The Barracks Thief* (1984) won the Pen/Faulkner award. He has since published numerous acclaimed short story collections, and for many years he taught writing at Stanford University. In 2015 he received a National Medal of Arts.

Wolff has been cited as a contributor to the "modern renaissance" of the American short story, which many critics see as beginning in the 1970s and continuing until the present. Wolff rejects such categorizations; he claims instead that there has been an unbroken line of great short stories in America, from Edgar Allan Poe onward. He says that "the short story ... is the perfect

American form," capturing the nomadic, fragmented experience of modern American life.

Powder

JUST BEFORE Christmas my father took me skiing at Mount Baker. He'd had to fight for the privilege of my company, because my mother was still angry with him for sneaking me into a nightclub during his last visit, to see Thelonious Monk.[1]

He wouldn't give up. He promised, hand on heart, to take good care of me and have me home for dinner on Christmas Eve, and she relented. But as we were checking out of the lodge that morning it began to snow, and in this snow he observed some rare quality that made it necessary for us to get in one last run. We got in several last runs. He was indifferent to my fretting. Snow whirled around us in bitter, blinding squalls, hissing like sand, and still we skied. As the lift bore us to the peak yet again, my father looked at his watch and said, "Criminy. This'll have to be a fast one."

By now I couldn't see the trail. There was no point in trying. I stuck to him like white on rice and did what he did and somehow made it to the bottom without sailing off a cliff. We returned our skis and my father put chains on the Austin-Healey while I swayed from foot to foot, clapping my mittens and wishing I was home. I could see everything. The green tablecloth, the plates with the holly pattern, the red candles waiting to be lit.

We passed a diner on our way out. "You want some soup?" my father asked. I shook my head. "Buck up," he said. "I'll get you there. Right, doctor?"

I was supposed to say, "Right, doctor," but I didn't say anything.

A state trooper waved us down outside the resort. A pair of sawhorses were blocking the road. The trooper came up to our car and bent down to my father's window. His face was bleached by the cold. Snowflakes clung to his eyebrows and to the fur trim of his jacket and cap.

"Don't tell me," my father said.

The trooper told him. The road was closed. It might get cleared, it might not. Storm took everyone by surprise. So much, so fast. Hard to get people moving. Christmas Eve. What can you do.

My father said, "Look. We're talking about five, six inches. I've taken this car through worse than that."

---

1   Thelonious Monk (1917–82) was a famous jazz musician.

The trooper straightened up. His face was out of sight but I could hear him. "The road is closed."

My father sat with both hands on the wheel, rubbing the wood with his thumbs. He looked at the barricade for a long time. He seemed to be trying to master the idea of it. Then he thanked the trooper, and with a weird, old-maidy show of caution turned the car around. "Your mother will never forgive me for this," he said.

"We should have left before," I said. "Doctor."

He didn't speak to me again until we were in a booth at the diner, waiting for our burgers. "She won't forgive me," he said. "Do you understand? Never."

"I guess," I said, but no guesswork was required; she wouldn't forgive him.

"I can't let that happen." He bent toward me. "I'll tell you what I want. I want us all to be together again. Is that what you want?"

"Yes, sir."

He bumped my chin with his knuckles. "That's all I needed to hear."

When we finished eating he went to the pay phone in the back of the diner, then joined me in the booth again. I figured he'd called my mother, but he didn't give a report. He sipped at his coffee and stared out the window at the empty road. "Come on, come on," he said, though not to me. A little while later he said it again. When the trooper's car went past, lights flashing, he got up and dropped some money on the check. "Okay. Vamanos."[2]

The wind had died. The snow was falling straight down, less of it now and lighter. We drove away from the resort, right up to the barricade. "Move it," my father told me. When I looked at him he said, "What are you waiting for?" I got out and dragged one of the sawhorses aside, then put it back after he drove through. He pushed the door open for me. "Now you're an accomplice," he said. "We go down together." He put the car into gear and gave me a look. "Joke, son."

Down the first long stretch I watched the road behind us, to see if the trooper was on our tail. The barricade vanished. Then there was nothing but snow: snow on the road, snow kicking up from the chains, snow on the trees, snow in the sky; and our trail in the snow. Then I faced forward and had a shock. The lay of the road behind us had been marked by our own tracks, but there were no tracks ahead of us. My father was breaking virgin snow between a line of tall trees. He was humming "Stars Fell on Alabama."[3] I felt snow brush along the floorboards under my feet. To keep my hands from shaking I clamped them between my knees.

My father grunted in a thoughtful way and said, "Don't ever try this yourself."

---

2   A mispronunciation of *vámonos*, Spanish for "Let's go."

3   1934 jazz song.

"I won't."

"That's what you say now, but someday you'll get your license and then you'll think you can do anything. Only you won't be able to do this. You need, I don't know—a certain instinct."

"Maybe I have it."

"You don't. You have your strong points, but not this. I only mention it because I don't want you to get the idea this is something just anybody can do. I'm a great driver. That's not a virtue, okay? It's just a fact, and one you should be aware of. Of course you have to give the old heap some credit, too. There aren't many cars I'd try this with. Listen!"

I did listen. I heard the slap of the chains, the stiff, jerky rasp of the wipers, the purr of the engine. It really did purr. The old heap was almost new. My father couldn't afford it, and kept promising to sell it, but here it was.

I said, "Where do you think that policeman went to?"

"Are you warm enough?" He reached over and cranked up the blower. Then he turned off the wipers. We didn't need them. The clouds had brightened. A few sparse, feathery flakes drifted into our slipstream and were swept away. We left the trees and entered a broad field of snow that ran level for a while and then tilted sharply downward. Orange stakes had been planted at intervals in two parallel lines and my father steered a course between them, though they were far enough apart to leave considerable doubt in my mind as to exactly where the road lay. He was humming again, doing little scat riffs around the melody.

"Okay then. What are my strong points?"

"Don't get me started," he said. "It'd take all day."

"Oh, right. Name one."

"Easy. You always think ahead."

True. I always thought ahead. I was a boy who kept his clothes on numbered hangers to insure proper rotation. I bothered my teachers for homework assignments far ahead of their due dates so I could draw up schedules. I thought ahead, and that was why I knew that there would be other troopers waiting for us at the end of our ride, if we even got there. What I did not know was that my father would wheedle and plead his way past them—he didn't sing "O Tannenbaum," but just about—and get me home for dinner, buying a little more time before my mother decided to make the split final. I knew we'd get caught; I was resigned to it. And maybe for this reason I stopped moping and began to enjoy myself.

Why not? This was one for the books. Like being in a speedboat, only better. You can't go downhill in a boat. And it was all ours. And it kept coming, the laden trees, the unbroken surface of snow, the sudden white vistas. Here and there I saw hints of the road, ditches, fences, stakes, but not so many that I could have found my way. But then I didn't have to. My father was driving. My father in his forty-eighth year, rumpled, kind, bankrupt of honor, flushed with certainty. He was a great driver. All persuasion, no coercion. Such subtlety at the wheel, such tactful pedalwork. I actually trusted him. And the best was yet to come—switchbacks and hairpins impossible to describe. Except maybe to say this: if you haven't driven fresh powder, you haven't driven.

—*1996*

TIM O'BRIEN

Tim O'Brien was born in 1946 in Austin, Minnesota, but lived the majority of his youth in Worthington, Minnesota, which he refers to as the "Turkey capital of the world." Upon graduating with his BA in political science from Macalester College in 1968, he received his draft notice for the Vietnam War. In a 1990 New York Times interview he spoke of the summer before his departure for Vietnam: "It was the most terrible summer of my life, worse than being in the war. My conscience kept telling me not to go, but my whole upbringing told me I had to. That horrible summer made me a writer." O'Brien resisted the impulse to either flee to Canada or go to jail (the other options available to men drafted for service at this time), and from February 1969 until March 1970, he served as an infantry foot soldier in Vietnam, an experience that informs much of his work.

Upon his return from the war, he studied American foreign policy at Harvard's School of Government. Starting in 1972, he interned at the *Washington Post*, then briefly worked for the paper full-time. O'Brien's first book was a memoir entitled *If I Die in a Combat Zone, Box Me Up and Send Me Home* (1973). His novels include *Going After Cacciato* (1978), recipient of the National Book Award for fiction, and *In the Lake of the Woods* (1994), winner of the James Fenimore Cooper Prize and *Time* magazine's best novel of the year. Among his other novels are *Tomcat in Love* (1998) and *July, July* (2002). He lives in Texas and teaches at Texas State University.

His fifth book, *The Things They Carried* (1990), a collection of interrelated stories, won France's Prix du Meilleur Livre Etranger and was a finalist for the Pulitzer Prize and the National Book Critics Circle Award. The collection chronicles the experiences of an infantry soldier in Alpha Company during and after the war in Vietnam. The stories reveal O'Brien's interest in the complex nature of fiction: the narratives are often interrupted by "true" stories that are made up, and by similar stories told from different points of view. They also feature a character—one the author insists is not autobiographical—named Tim O'Brien. "I believe in stories," O'Brien said in 1990, "in their incredible power to keep people alive, to keep the living alive, and the dead. And if I have started now to play with the stories, inside the stories themselves, well, that's what people do all the time. Storytelling is the essential human activity."

The Things They Carried.

FIRST LIEUTENANT Jimmy Cross carried letters from a girl named Martha, a junior at Mount Sebastian College in New Jersey. They were not love letters, but Lieutenant Cross was hoping, so he kept them folded in plastic at the bottom of his rucksack. In the late afternoon, after a day's march, he would dig his foxhole, wash his hands under a canteen, unwrap the letters, hold them with the tips of his fingers, and spend the last hour of light pretending. He would imagine romantic camping trips into the White Mountains in New Hampshire. He would sometimes taste the envelope flaps, knowing her tongue had been there. More than anything, he wanted Martha to love him as he loved her, but the letters were mostly chatty, elusive on the matter of love. She was a virgin, he was almost sure. She was an English major at Mount Sebastian, and she wrote beautifully about her professors and roommates and midterm exams, about her respect for Chaucer and her great affection for Virginia Woolf. She often quoted lines of poetry; she never mentioned the war, except to say, Jimmy, take care of yourself. The letters weighed 10 ounces. They were signed Love, Martha, but Lieutenant Cross understood that Love was only a way of signing and did not mean what he sometimes pretended it meant. At dusk, he would carefully return the letters to his rucksack. Slowly, a bit distracted, he would get up and move among his men, checking the perimeter, then at full dark he would return to his hole and watch the night and wonder if Martha was a virgin.

The things they carried were largely determined by necessity. Among the necessities or near-necessities were P-38 can openers, pocket knives, heat tabs, wristwatches, dog tags, mosquito repellent, chewing gum, candy, cigarettes, salt tablets, packets of Kool-Aid, lighters, matches, sewing kits, Military Payment Certificates, C rations, and two or three canteens of water. Together, these items weighed between 15 and 20 pounds, depending upon a man's habits or rate of metabolism. Henry Dobbins, who was a big man, carried extra rations; he was especially fond of canned peaches in heavy syrup over pound cake. Dave Jensen, who practiced field hygiene, carried a toothbrush, dental floss, and several hotel-sized bars of soap he'd stolen on R&R in Sydney, Australia. Ted Lavender, who was scared, carried tranquilizers until he was shot in the head outside the village of Than Khe in mid-April. By necessity, and because it was SOP,[1] they all carried steel helmets that weighed 5 pounds including the liner and camouflage cover. They carried the standard fatigue jackets and trousers. Very few carried underwear. On their feet they carried jungle boots—2.1 pounds—and Dave Jensen carried three pairs of socks and a can of Dr. Scholl's foot powder as a precaution against trench foot. Until he was shot, Ted Lavender carried six or seven ounces of premium dope, which for him was a necessity. Mitchell Sanders, the RTO,[2] carried condoms. Norman Bowker carried a diary. Rat Kiley carried comic books. Kiowa, a devout Baptist, carried an illustrated New Testament that had been presented to him by his father, who taught Sunday school in Oklahoma City, Oklahoma. As a hedge against bad times, however, Kiowa also carried his grandmother's distrust of the white man, his grandfather's old hunting hatchet. Necessity dictated. Because the land was mined and booby-trapped, it was SOP for each man to carry a steel-centered, nylon-covered flak jacket, which weighed 6.7 pounds, but which on hot days seemed much heavier. Because you could die so quickly, each man carried at least one large compress bandage, usually in the helmet band for easy access. Because the nights were cold, and because the monsoons were wet, each carried a green plastic poncho that could be used as a raincoat or groundsheet or makeshift tent. With its quilted liner, the poncho weighed almost two pounds, but it was worth every ounce. In April, for instance, when Ted Lavender was shot, they used his poncho to wrap him up, then to carry him across the paddy, then to lift him into the chopper that took him away.

They were called legs or grunts.

To carry something was to hump it, as when Lieutenant Jimmy Cross humped his love for Martha up the hills and through the swamps. In its intransitive form, to hump meant to walk, or to march, but it implied burdens far beyond the intransitive.

Almost everyone humped photographs. In his wallet, Lieutenant Cross carried two photographs of Martha. The first was a Kodacolor snapshot signed Love, though he knew better. She stood against a brick wall. Her eyes were gray and neutral, her lips slightly open as she stared straight-on at the camera. At night, sometimes, Lieutenant Cross wondered who had taken the picture, because he knew she had boyfriends, because he loved her so much, and because he could see the shadow of the picture-taker spreading out against the brick wall. The second photograph had been clipped from the 1968 Mount

---

1   Standard operating procedure.
2   Radio telephone operator.

Sebastian yearbook. It was an action shot—women's volleyball—and Martha was bent horizontal to the floor, reaching, the palms of her hands in sharp focus, the tongue taut, the expression frank and competitive. There was no visible sweat. She wore white gym shorts. Her legs, he thought, were almost certainly the legs of a virgin, dry and without hair, the left knee cocked and carrying her entire weight, which was just over one hundred pounds. Lieutenant Cross remembered touching that left knee. A dark theater, he remembered, and the movie was *Bonnie and Clyde*, and Martha wore a tweed suit, and during the final scene, when he touched her knee, she turned and looked at him in a sad, sober way that made him pull his hand back, but he would always remember the feel of the tweed skirt and the knee beneath it and the sound of the gunfire that killed Bonnie and Clyde, how embarrassing it was, how slow and oppressive. He remembered kissing her good night at the dorm door. Right then, he thought, he should've done something brave. He should've carried her up the stairs to her room and tied her to the bed and touched that left knee all night long. He should've risked it. Whenever he looked at the photographs, he thought of new things he should've done.

What they carried was partly a function of rank, partly of field specialty.

As a first lieutenant and platoon leader, Jimmy Cross carried a compass, maps, code books, binoculars, and a .45-caliber pistol that weighed 2.9 pounds fully loaded. He carried a strobe light and the responsibility for the lives of his men.

As an RTO, Mitchell Sanders carried the PRC-25 radio, a killer, 26 pounds with its battery.

As a medic, Rat Kiley carried a canvas satchel filled with morphine and plasma and malaria tablets and surgical tape and comic books and all the things a medic must carry, including M&M's for especially bad wounds, for a total weight of nearly 20 pounds.

As a big man, therefore a machine gunner, Henry Dobbins carried the M-60, which weighed 23 pounds unloaded, but which was almost always loaded. In addition, Dobbins carried between 10 and 15 pounds of ammunition draped in belts across his chest and shoulders.

As PFCs[3] or Spec 4s, most of them were common grunts and carried the standard M-16 gas-operated assault rifle. The weapon weighed 7.5 pounds unloaded, 8.2 pounds with its full 20-round magazine. Depending on numerous factors, such as topography and psychology, the riflemen carried anywhere from 12 to 20 magazines, usually in cloth bandoliers, adding on another 8.4

---

3   Privates first class.

pounds at minimum, 14 pounds at maximum. When it was available, they also carried M-16 maintenance gear—rods and steel brushes and swabs and tubes of LSA oil—all of which weighed about a pound. Among the grunts, some carried the M-79 grenade launcher, 5.9 pounds unloaded, a reasonably light weapon except for the ammunition, which was heavy. A single round weighed 10 ounces. The typical load was 25 rounds. But Ted Lavender, who was scared, carried 34 rounds when he was shot and killed outside Than Khe, and he went down under an exceptional burden, more than 20 pounds of ammunition, plus the flak jacket and helmet and rations and water and toilet paper and tranquilizers and all the rest, plus the unweighed fear. He was dead weight. There was no twitching or flopping. Kiowa, who saw it happen, said it was like watching a rock fall, or a big sandbag or something—just boom, then down—not like the movies where the dead guy rolls around and does fancy spins and goes ass over teakettle—not like that, Kiowa said, the poor bastard just flat-fuck fell. Boom. Down. Nothing else. It was a bright morning in mid-April. Lieutenant Cross felt the pain. He blamed himself. They stripped off Lavender's canteens and ammo, all the heavy things, and Rat Kiley said the obvious, the guy's dead, and Mitchell Sanders used his radio to report one U.S. KIA[4] and to request a chopper. Then they wrapped Lavender in his poncho. They carried him out to a dry paddy, established security, and sat smoking the dead man's dope until the chopper came. Lieutenant Cross kept to himself. He pictured Martha's smooth young face, thinking he loved her more than anything, more than his men, and now Ted Lavender was dead because he loved her so much and could not stop thinking about her. When the dustoff arrived, they carried Lavender aboard. Afterward they burned Than Khe. They marched until dusk, then dug their holes, and that night Kiowa kept explaining how you had to be there, how fast it was, how the poor guy just dropped like so much concrete. Boom-down, he said. Like cement.

In addition to the three standard weapons—the M-60, M-16, and M-79—they carried whatever presented itself, or whatever seemed appropriate as a means of killing or staying alive. They carried catch-as-catch-can. At various times, in various situations, they carried M-14s and CAR-15s and Swedish Ks and grease guns and captured AK-47s and Chi-Coms and RPGs and Simonov carbines and black market Uzis and .38-caliber Smith & Wesson handguns and 66 mm LAWs[5] and shotguns and silencers and blackjacks and bayonets and C-4 plastic explosives. Lee Strunk carried a slingshot; a weapon of last resort, he called it. Mitchell Sanders carried brass knuckles. Kiowa carried his grandfather's

---

4   Killed in action.
5   A kind of shoulder-fired rocket.

feathered hatchet. Every third or fourth man carried a Claymore antipersonnel mine—3.5 pounds with its firing device. They all carried fragmentation grenades—14 ounces each. They all carried at least one M-18 colored smoke grenade—24 ounces. Some carried CS[6] or tear gas grenades. Some carried white phosphorus grenades. They carried all they could bear, and then some, including a silent awe for the terrible power of the things they carried.

In the first week of April, before Lavender died, Lieutenant Jimmy Cross received a good-luck charm from Martha. It was a simple pebble, an ounce at most. Smooth to the touch, it was a milky white color with flecks of orange and violet, oval-shaped, like a miniature egg. In the accompanying letter, Martha wrote that she had found the pebble on the Jersey shoreline, precisely where the land touched water at high tide, where things came together but also separated. It was this separate-but-together quality, she wrote, that had inspired her to pick up the pebble and to carry it in her breast pocket for several days, where it seemed weightless, and then to send it through the mail, by air, as a token of her truest feelings for him. Lieutenant Cross found this romantic. But he wondered what her truest feelings were, exactly, and what she meant by separate-but-together. He wondered how the tides and waves had come into play on that afternoon along the Jersey shoreline when Martha saw the pebble and bent down to rescue it from geology. He imagined bare feet. Martha was a poet, with the poet's sensibilities, and her feet would be brown and bare, the toenails unpainted, the eyes chilly and somber like the ocean in March, and though it was painful, he wondered who had been with her that afternoon. He imagined a pair of shadows moving along the strip of sand where things came together but also separated. It was phantom jealousy, he knew, but he couldn't help himself. He loved her so much. On the march, through the hot days of early April, he carried the pebble in his mouth, turning it with his tongue, tasting sea salt and moisture. His mind wandered. He had difficulty keeping his attention on the war. On occasion he would yell at his men to spread out the column, to keep their eyes open, but then he would slip away into daydreams, just pretending, walking barefoot along the Jersey shore, with Martha, carrying nothing. He would feel himself rising. Sun and waves and gentle winds, all love and lightness.

What they carried varied by mission.

When a mission took them to the mountains, they carried mosquito netting, machetes, canvas tarps, and extra bug juice.

---

6   Type of tear gas.

If a mission seemed especially hazardous, or if it involved a place they knew to be bad, they carried everything they could. In certain heavily mined AOs,[7] where the land was dense with Toe Poppers and Bouncing Betties, they took turns humping a 28-pound mine detector. With its headphones and big sensing plate, the equipment was a stress on the lower back and shoulders, awkward to handle, often useless because of the shrapnel in the earth, but they carried it anyway, partly for safety, partly for the illusion of safety.

On ambush, or other night missions, they carried peculiar little odds and ends, Kiowa always took along his New Testament and a pair of moccasins for silence. Dave Jensen carried night-sight vitamins high in carotene. Lee Strunk carried his slingshot; ammo, he claimed, would never be a problem. Rat Kiley carried brandy and M&M's candy. Until he was shot, Ted Lavender carried the starlight scope, which weighed 6.3 pounds with its aluminum carrying case. Henry Dobbins carried his girlfriend's pantyhose wrapped around his neck as a comforter. They all carried ghosts. When dark came, they would move out single file across the meadows and paddies to their ambush coordinates, where they would quietly set up the Claymores and lie down and spend the night waiting.

Other missions were more complicated and required special equipment. In mid-April, it was their mission to search out and destroy the elaborate tunnel complexes in the Than Khe area south of Chu Lai. To blow the tunnels, they carried one-pound blocks of pentrite high explosives, four blocks to a man, 68 pounds in all. They carried wiring, detonators, and battery-powered clackers. Dave Jensen carried earplugs. Most often, before blowing the tunnels, they were ordered by higher command to search them, which was considered bad news, but by and large they just shrugged and carried out orders. Because he was a big man, Henry Dobbins was excused from tunnel duty. The others would draw numbers. Before Lavender died there were 17 men in the platoon, and whoever drew the number 17 would strip off his gear and crawl in headfirst with a flashlight and Lieutenant Cross's .45-caliber pistol. The rest of them would fan out as security. They would sit down or kneel, not facing the hole, listening to the ground beneath them, imagining cobwebs and ghosts, whatever was down there—the tunnel walls squeezing in—how the flashlight seemed impossibly heavy in the hand and how it was tunnel vision in the very strictest sense, compression in all ways, even time, and how you had to wiggle in—ass and elbows—a swallowed-up feeling—and how you found yourself worrying about odd things: Will your flashlight go dead? Do rats carry rabies? If you screamed, how far would the sound carry? Would your buddies hear it? Would they have

---

7   Area of operations.

the courage to drag you out? In some respects, though not many, the waiting was worse than the tunnel itself. Imagination was a killer.

On April 16, when Lee Strunk drew the number 17, he laughed and muttered something and went down quickly. The morning was hot and very still. Not good, Kiowa said. He looked at the tunnel opening, then out across a dry paddy toward the village of Than Khe. Nothing moved. No clouds or birds or people. As they waited, the men smoked and drank Kool-Aid, not talking much, feeling sympathy for Lee Strunk but also feeling the luck of the draw. You win some, you lose some, said Mitchell Sanders, and sometimes you settle for a rain check. It was a tired line and no one laughed.

Henry Dobbins ate a tropical chocolate bar. Ted Lavender popped a tranquilizer and went off to pee.

After five minutes, Lieutenant Jimmy Cross moved to the tunnel, leaned down, and examined the darkness. Trouble, he thought—a cave-in maybe. And then suddenly, without willing it, he was thinking about Martha. The stresses and fractures, the quick collapse, the two of them buried alive under all that weight. Dense, crushing love. Kneeling, watching the hole, he tried to concentrate on Lee Strunk and the war, all the dangers, but his love was too much for him, he felt paralyzed, he wanted to sleep inside her lungs and breathe her blood and be smothered. He wanted her to be a virgin and not a virgin, all at once. He wanted to know her. Intimate secrets: Why poetry? Why so sad? Why that grayness in her eyes? Why so alone? Not lonely, just alone—riding her bike across campus or sitting off by herself in the cafeteria—even dancing, she danced alone—and it was the aloneness that filled him with love. He remembered telling her that one evening. How she nodded and looked away. And how, later, when he kissed her, she received the kiss without returning it, her eyes wide open, not afraid, not a virgin's eyes, just flat and uninvolved.

Lieutenant Cross gazed at the tunnel. But he was not there. He was buried with Martha under the white sand at the Jersey shore. They were pressed together, and the pebble in his mouth was her tongue. He was smiling. Vaguely, he was aware of how quiet the day was, the sullen paddies, yet he could not bring himself to worry about matters of security. He was beyond that. He was just a kid at war, in love. He was twenty-four years old. He couldn't help it.

A few moments later Lee Strunk crawled out of the tunnel. He came up grinning, filthy but alive. Lieutenant Cross nodded and closed his eyes while the others clapped Strunk on the back and made jokes about rising from the dead.

Worms, Rat Kiley said. Right out of the grave. Fuckin' zombie.

The men laughed. They all felt great relief.

Spook city, said Mitchell Sanders.

Lee Strunk made a funny ghost sound, a kind of moaning, yet very happy, and right then, when Strunk made that high happy moaning sound, when he went *Ahhooooo*, right then Ted Lavender was shot in the head on his way back from peeing. He lay with his mouth open. The teeth were broken. There was a swollen black bruise under his left eye. The cheekbone was gone. Oh shit, Rat Kiley said, the guy's dead. The guy's dead, he kept saying, which seemed profound—the guy's dead. I mean really.

The things they carried were determined to some extent by superstition. Lieutenant Cross carried his good-luck pebble. Dave Jensen carried a rabbit's foot. Norman Bowker, otherwise a very gentle person, carried a thumb that had been presented to him as a gift by Mitchell Sanders. The thumb was dark brown, rubbery to the touch, and weighted four ounces at most. It had been cut from a VC[8] corpse, a boy of fifteen or sixteen. They'd found him at the bottom of an irrigation ditch, badly burned, flies in his mouth and eyes. The boy wore black shorts and sandals. At the time of his death he had been carrying a pouch of rice, a rifle, and three magazines of ammunition.

You want my opinion, Mitchell Sanders said, there's a definite moral here.

He put his hand on the dead boy's wrist. He was quiet for a time, as if counting a pulse, then he patted the stomach, almost affectionately, and used Kiowa's hunting hatchet to remove the thumb.

Henry Dobbins asked what the moral was.

Moral?

You know. *Moral.*

Sanders wrapped the thumb in toilet paper and handed it across to Norman Bowker. There was no blood. Smiling, he kicked the boy's head, watched the flies scatter, and said, It's like with that old TV show—Paladin. Have gun, will travel.[9]

Henry Dobbins thought about it.

Yeah, well, he finally said. I don't see no moral.

There it *is*, man.

Fuck off.

They carried USO stationery and pencils and pens. They carried Sterno, safety pins, trip flares, signal flares, spools of wire, razor blades, chewing tobacco, liberated joss sticks and statuettes of the smiling Buddha, candles, grease pencils, *The Stars and Stripes*, fingernail clippers, Psy Ops leaflets, bush hats, bolos, and

---

8   Viet Cong.

9   *Have Gun, Will Travel* was a television show set in the wild American west. The show's protagonist, a gun-for-hire, was named Paladin.

much more. Twice a week, when the resupply choppers came in, they carried hot chow in green mermite cans and large canvas bags filled with iced beer and soda pop. They carried plastic water containers, each with a two-gallon capacity. Mitchell Sanders carried a set of starched tiger fatigues for special occasions. Henry Dobbins carried Black Flag insecticide. Dave Jensen carried empty sandbags that could be filled at night for added protection. Lee Strunk carried tanning lotion. Some things they carried in common. Taking turns, they carried the big PRC-77 scrambler radio, which weighed 30 pounds with its battery. They shared the weight of memory. They took up what others could no longer bear. Often, they carried each other, the wounded or weak. They carried infections. They carried chess sets, basketballs, Vietnamese-English dictionaries, insignia of rank, Bronze Stars and Purple Hearts, plastic cards imprinted with the Code of Conduct. They carried diseases, among them malaria and dysentery. They carried lice and ringworm and leeches and paddy algae and various rots and molds. They carried the land itself—Vietnam, the place, the soil—a powdery orange-red dust that covered their boots and fatigues and faces. They carried the sky. The whole atmosphere, they carried it, the humidity, the monsoons, the stink of fungus and decay, all of it, they carried gravity. They moved like mules. By daylight they took sniper fire, at night they were mortared, but it was not battle, it was just the endless march, village to village, without purpose, nothing won or lost. They marched for the sake of the march. They plodded along slowly, dumbly, leaning forward against the heat, unthinking, all blood and bone, simple grunts, soldiering with their legs, toiling up the hills and down into the paddies and across the rivers and up again and down, just humping, one step and then the next and then another, but no volition, no will, because it was automatic, it was anatomy, and the war was entirely a matter of posture and carriage, the hump was everything, a kind of inertia, a kind of emptiness, a dullness of desire and intellect and conscience and hope and human sensibility. Their principles were in their feet. Their calculations were biological. They had no sense of strategy or mission. They searched the villages without knowing what to look for, not caring, kicking over jars of rice, frisking children and old men, blowing tunnels, sometimes setting fires and sometimes not, then forming up and moving on to the next village, then other villages, where it would always be the same. They carried their own lives. The pressures were enormous. In the heat of early afternoon, they would remove their helmets and flak jackets, walking bare, which was dangerous but which helped ease the strain. They would often discard things along the route of march. Purely for comfort, they would throw away rations, blow their Claymores and grenades, no matter, because by nightfall the resupply choppers would arrive with more of the same, then a day or two later still more, fresh watermelons and crates of ammunition and sunglasses and woolen sweaters—the resources were stunning—sparklers for the Fourth of July, colored eggs for Easter—it was the great American war chest—the fruits of science, the smokestacks, the canneries, the arsenals at Hartford, the Minnesota forests, the machine shops, the vast fields of corn and wheat—they carried like freight trains; they carried it on their backs and shoulders—and for all the ambiguities of Vietnam, all the mysteries and unknowns, there was at least the single abiding certainty that they would never be at a loss for things to carry.

After the chopper took Lavender away, Lieutenant Jimmy Cross led his men into the village of Than Khe. They burned everything. They shot chickens and dogs, they trashed the village well, they called in artillery and watched the wreckage, then they marched for several hours through the hot afternoon, and then at dusk, while Kiowa explained how Lavender died, Lieutenant Cross found himself trembling.

He tried not to cry. With his entrenching tool, which weighed five pounds, he began digging a hole in the earth.

He felt shame. He hated himself. He had loved Martha more than his men, and as a consequence Lavender was now dead, and this was something he would have to carry like a stone in his stomach for the rest of the war.

All he could do was dig. He used his entrenching tool like an ax, slashing, feeling both love and hate, and then later, when it was full dark, he sat at the bottom of his foxhole and wept. It went on for a long while. In part, he was grieving for Ted Lavender, but mostly it was for Martha, and for himself, because she belonged to another world, which was not quite real, and because she was a junior at Mount Sebastian College in New Jersey, a poet and a virgin and uninvolved, and because he realized she did not love him and never would.

Like cement, Kiowa whispered in the dark. I swear to God—boom, down. Not a word.

I've heard this, said Norman Bowker.

A pisser, you know? Still zipping himself up. Zapped while zipping.

All right, fine. That's enough.

Yeah, but you had to see it, the guy just—

I *heard*, man. Cement. So why not shut the fuck *up*?

Kiowa shook his head sadly and glanced over at the hole where Lieutenant Jimmy Cross sat watching the night. The air was thick and wet. A warm dense fog had settled over the paddies and there was the stillness that precedes rain.

After a time Kiowa sighed.

One thing for sure, he said. The lieutenant's in some deep hurt. I mean that crying jag—the way he was carrying on—it wasn't fake or anything, it was real heavy-duty hurt. The man cares.

Sure, Norman Bowker said.

Say what you want, the man does care.

We all got problems.

Not Lavender.

No, I guess not, Bowker said. Do me a favor, though.

Shut up?

That's a smart Indian. Shut up.

Shrugging, Kiowa pulled off his boots. He wanted to say more, just to lighten up his sleep, but instead he opened his New Testament and arranged it beneath his head as a pillow. The fog made things seem hollow and unattached. He tried not to think about Ted Lavender, but then he was thinking how fast it was, no drama, down and dead, and how it was hard to feel anything except surprise. It seemed unchristian. He wished he could find some great sadness, or even anger, but the emotion wasn't there and he couldn't make it happen. Mostly he felt pleased to be alive. He liked the smell of the New Testament under his cheek, the leather and ink and paper and glue, whatever the chemicals were. He liked hearing the sounds of night. Even his fatigue, it felt fine, the stiff muscles and the prickly awareness of his own body, a floating feeling. He enjoyed not being dead. Lying there, Kiowa admired Lieutenant Jimmy Cross's capacity for grief. He wanted to share the man's pain, he wanted to care as Jimmy Cross cared. And yet when he closed his eyes, all he could think, was Boom-down, and all he could feel was the pleasure of having his boots off and the fog curling in around him and the damp soil and the Bible smells and the plush comfort of night.

After a moment Norman Bowker sat up in the dark.

What the hell, he said. You want to talk, *talk*. Tell it to me.

Forget it.

No, man, go on. One thing I hate, it's a silent Indian.

For the most part they carried themselves with poise, a kind of dignity. Now and then, however, there were times of panic, when they squealed or wanted to squeal but couldn't, when they twitched and made moaning sounds and covered their heads and said Dear Jesus and flopped around on the earth and fired their weapons blindly and cringed and sobbed and begged for the noise to stop and went wild and made stupid promises to themselves and to God and to their mothers and fathers, hoping not to die. In different ways, it happened to all of them. Afterward, when the firing ended, they would blink and peek up. They would touch their bodies, feeling shame, then quickly hiding it.

They would force themselves to stand. As if in slow motion, frame by frame, the world would take on the old logic—absolute silence, then the wind, then sunlight, then voices. It was the burden of being alive. Awkwardly, the men would reassemble themselves, first in private, then in groups, becoming soldiers again. They would repair the leaks in their eyes. They would check for casualties, call in dustoffs, light cigarettes, try to smile, clear their throats and spit and begin cleaning their weapons. After a time someone would shake his head and say, No lie, I almost shit my pants, and someone else would laugh, which meant it was bad, yes, but the guy had obviously not shit his pants, it wasn't that bad, and in any case nobody would ever do such a thing and then go ahead and talk about it. They would squint into the dense, oppressive sunlight. For a few moments, perhaps, they would fall silent, lighting a joint and tracking its passage from man to man, inhaling, holding in the humiliation. Scary stuff, one of them might say. But then someone else would grin or flick his eyebrows and say, Roger-dodger, almost cut me a new asshole, *almost*.

There were numerous such poses. Some carried themselves with a sort of wistful resignation, others with pride or stiff soldierly discipline or good humor or macho zeal. They were afraid of dying but they were even more afraid to show it.

They found jokes to tell.

They used a hard vocabulary to contain the terrible softness. *Greased* they'd say. *Offed, lit up, zapped while zipping.* It wasn't cruelty, just stage presence. They were actors. When someone died, it wasn't quite dying, because in a curious way it seemed scripted, and because they had their lines mostly memorized, irony mixed with tragedy, and because they called it by other names, as if to encyst and destroy the reality of death itself. They kicked corpses. They cut off thumbs. They talked grunt lingo. They told stories about Ted Lavender's supply of tranquilizers, how the poor guy didn't feel a thing, how incredibly tranquil he was.

There's a moral here, said Mitchell Sanders.

They were waiting for Lavender's chopper, smoking the dead man's dope.

The moral's pretty obvious, Sanders said, and winked. Stay away from drugs. No joke, they'll ruin your day every time.

Cute, said Henry Dobbins.

Mind blower, get it? Talk about wiggy. Nothing left, just blood and brains.

They made themselves laugh.

There it is, they'd say. Over and over—there it is, my friend, there it is—as if the repetition itself were an act of poise, a balance between crazy and almost crazy, knowing without going, there it is, which meant be cool, let it ride, because Oh yeah, man, you can't change what can't be changed, there it is, there it absolutely and positively and fucking well *is*.

They were tough.

They carried all the emotional baggage of men who might die. Grief, terror, love, longing—these were intangibles, but the intangibles had their own mass and specific gravity, they had tangible weight. They carried shameful memories. They carried the common secret of cowardice barely restrained, the instinct to run or freeze or hide, and in many respects this was the heaviest burden of all, for it could never be put down, it required perfect balance and perfect posture. They carried their reputations. They carried the soldier's greatest fear, which was the fear of blushing. Men killed, and died, because they were embarrassed not to. It was what had brought them to the war in the first place, nothing positive, no dreams of glory or honor, just to avoid the blush of dishonor. They died so as not to die of embarrassment. They crawled into tunnels and walked point and advanced under fire. Each morning, despite the unknowns, they made their legs move. They endured. They kept humping. They did not submit to the obvious alternative, which was simply to close the eyes and fall. So easy, really. Go limp and tumble to the ground and let the muscles unwind and not speak and not budge until your buddies picked you up and lifted you into the chopper that would roar and dip its nose and carry you off to the world. A mere matter of falling, yet no one ever fell. It was not courage, exactly; the object was not valor. Rather, they were too frightened to be cowards.

By and large they carried these things inside, maintaining the masks of composure. They sneered at sick call. They spoke bitterly about guys who had found release by shooting off their own toes or fingers. Pussies, they'd say. Candy-asses. It was fierce, mocking talk, with only a trace of envy or awe, but even so the image played itself out behind their eyes.

They imagined the muzzle against flesh. So easy: squeeze the trigger and blow away a toe. They imagined it. They imagined the quick, sweet pain, then the evacuation to Japan, then a hospital with warm beds and cute geisha nurses.

And they dreamed of freedom birds.

At night, on guard, staring into the dark, they were carried away by jumbo jets. They felt the rush of takeoff. *Gone!* they yelled. And then velocity—wings and engines—a smiling stewardess—but it was more than a plane, it was a real bird, a big sleek silver bird with feathers and talons and high screeching. They were flying. The weights fell off; there was nothing to bear. They laughed and held on tight, feeling the cold slap of wind and altitude, soaring, thinking *It's over, I'm gone!*—they were naked, they were light and free—it was all lightness, bright and fast and buoyant, light as light, a helium buzz in the brain, a giddy bubbling in the lungs as they were taken up over the clouds and the war, beyond duty, beyond gravity and mortification and global entanglements—*Sin loi!*[10]

---

10 Vietnamese: "Pardon me."

they yelled. *I'm sorry, motherfuckers, but I'm out of it, I'm goofed, I'm on a space cruise, I'm gone!*—and it was a restful, unencumbered sensation, just riding the light waves, sailing that big silver freedom bird over the mountains and oceans, over America, over the farms and great sleeping cities and cemeteries and highways and the golden arches of McDonald's, it was flight, a kind of fleeing, a kind of falling, falling higher and higher, spinning off the edge of the earth and beyond the sun and through the vast, silent vacuum where there were no burdens and where everything weighed exactly nothing—*Gone!* they screamed. *I'm sorry but I'm gone!*—and so at night, not quite dreaming, they gave themselves over to lightness, they were carried, they were purely borne.

On the morning after Ted Lavender died, First Lieutenant Jimmy Cross crouched at the bottom of his foxhole and burned Martha's letters. Then he burned the two photographs. There was a steady rain falling, which made it difficult, but he used heat tabs and Sterno to build a small fire, screening it with his body, holding the photographs over the tight blue flame with the tips of his fingers.

He realized it was only a gesture. Stupid, he thought. Sentimental, too, but mostly just stupid.

Lavender was dead. You couldn't burn the blame.

Besides, the letters were in his head. And even now, without photographs, Lieutenant Cross could see Martha playing volleyball in her white gym shorts and yellow T-shirt. He could see her moving in the rain.

When the fire died out, Lieutenant Cross pulled his poncho over his shoulders and ate breakfast from a can.

There was no great mystery, he decided.

In those burned letters Martha had never mentioned the war, except to say, Jimmy, take care of yourself. She wasn't involved. She signed the letters Love, but it wasn't love, and all the fine lines and technicalities did not matter. Virginity was no longer an issue. He hated her. Yes, he did. He hated her. Love, too, but it was a hard, hating kind of love.

The morning came up wet and blurry. Everything seemed part of everything else, the fog and Martha and the deepening rain.

He was a soldier, after all.

Half smiling, Lieutenant Jimmy Cross took out his maps. He shook his head hard, as if to clear it, then bent forward and began planning the day's march. In ten minutes, or maybe twenty, he would rouse the men and they would pack up and head west, where the maps showed the country to be green and inviting. They would do what they had always done. The rain might add some weight, but otherwise it would be one more day layered upon all the other days.

He was realistic about it. There was that new hardness in his stomach. He loved her but he hated her.

No more fantasies, he told himself.

Henceforth, when he thought about Martha, it would be only to think that she belonged elsewhere. He would shut down the daydreams. This was not Mount Sebastian, it was another world, where there were no pretty poems or mid-term exams, a place where men died because of carelessness and gross stupidity. Kiowa was right. Boom-down, and you were dead, never partly dead.

Briefly, in the rain, Lieutenant Cross saw Martha's gray eyes gazing back at him.

He understood.

It was very sad, he thought. The things men carried inside. The things men did or felt they had to do.

He almost nodded at her, but didn't.

Instead he went back to his maps. He was now determined to perform his duties firmly and without negligence. It wouldn't help Lavender, he knew that, but from this point on he would comport himself as an officer. He would dispose of his good-luck pebble. Swallow it, maybe, or use Lee Strunk's slingshot, or just drop it along the trail. On the march he would impose strict field discipline. He would be careful to send out flank security, to prevent straggling or bunching up, to keep his troops moving at the proper pace and at the proper interval. He would insist on clean weapons. He would confiscate the remainder of Lavender's dope. Later in the day, perhaps, he would call the men together and speak to them plainly. He would accept the blame for what had happened to Ted Lavender. He would be a man about it. He would look them in the eyes, keeping his chin level, and he would issue the new SOPs in a calm, impersonal tone of voice, a lieutenant's voice, leaving no room for argument or discussion. Commencing immediately, he'd tell them, they would no longer abandon equipment along the route of march. They would police up their acts. They would get their shit together, and keep it together, and maintain it neatly and in good working order.

He would not tolerate laxity. He would show strength, distancing himself.

Among the men there would be grumbling, of course, and maybe worse, because their days would seem longer and their loads heavier, but Lieutenant Jimmy Cross reminded himself that his obligation was not to be loved but to lead. He would dispense with love; it was not now a factor. And if anyone quarreled or complained, he would simply tighten his lips and arrange his shoulders in the correct command posture. He might give a curt little nod. Or he might not. He might just shrug and say, Carry on, then they would saddle up and form into a column and move out toward the villages west of Than Khe.

—1990

LYDIA DAVIS

Lydia Davis is an American writer and translator. She is widely recognized as a contemporary master of micro (or "flash") fiction, a genre that has steadily increased in prominence since the 1980s. In a review of Davis's *Collected Stories* (2009), James Wood describes her work as "unique in American writing, in its combination of lucidity, aphoristic brevity, formal originality, sly comedy, metaphysical bleakness, philosophical pressure, and human wisdom." Davis won a MacArthur Fellowship in 2003 and the Man Booker International Prize in 2013.

Davis was born in 1947 in Northampton, Massachusetts, where her parents taught at Smith College. Her father was a writer and a professor of English literature, her mother a prominent feminist and communist. The family moved to New York when Davis was ten. Her earliest influences include Franz Kafka, John Dos Passos, Samuel Beckett, and Vladimir Nabokov. In an interview, Davis has said that "My father would go to the dictionary all the time and look up a word to see not only exactly what it meant but where it came from and its different, possibly more obscure, meanings. So you couldn't speak carelessly without someone noticing. Not that they were pedantic, but just that they noticed. It was like the scenery. Language was something that you paid attention to all the time."

When Davis was 15, she went to study music in Vermont at the Putney School, and afterwards attended Barnard College. While there, she met the future novelist Paul Auster, and the two of them married in 1974. They settled in France, during which time they both took up translation as a means to support themselves, work that Davis would continue throughout her career. Davis published her first collection, *The Thirteenth Woman*, in 1976, followed by *Sketches for a Life of Wassilly* in 1981. In that same year, Davis and Auster divorced; she would marry the painter Arthur Cote in 1987. Davis continued to publish stories, but it wasn't until her 1986 collection *Break It Down* that she received widespread recognition.

Although Davis's reputation rests primarily on her "short short fiction," she has also written a well-respected novel, *The End of the Story* (1995).

Davis published her *Collected Stories* in 2009 to widespread acclaim, followed by the collection *Can't and Won't* in 2014.

Lydia Davis's formal experimentation, precise prose style, and her gift, according to critic Martin Clancy, "of making our unconscious or semi-conscious struggles visible," have earned her a place among the foremost writers of her generation.

The Brother-in-Law

HE WAS SO quiet, so small and thin, that he was hardly there. The brother-in-law. Whose brother-in-law they did not know. Or where he came from, or if he would leave.

They could not guess where he slept at night, though they searched for a depression on the couch or a disorder among the towels. He left no smell behind him.

He did not bleed, he did not cry, he did not sweat. He was dry. Even his urine divorced itself from his penis and entered the toilet almost before it had left him, like a bullet from a gun.

They hardly saw him: if they entered a room, he was gone like a shadow, sliding around the door frame, slipping over the sill. A breath was all they ever heard from him, and even then they could not be sure it hadn't been a small breeze passing over the gravel outside.

He could not pay them. He left money every week, but by the time they entered the room in their slow, noisy way the money was just a green and silver mist on their grandmother's platter, and by the time they reached out for it, it was no longer there.

But he hardly cost them a penny. They could not even tell if he ate, because he took so little that it was as nothing to them, who were big eaters. He came out from somewhere at night and crept around the kitchen with a sharp razor in his white, fine-boned hand, shaving off slivers of meat, of nuts, of bread, until his plate, paper-thin, felt heavy to him. He filled his cup with milk, but the cup was so small that it held no more than an ounce or two.

He ate without a sound, and cleanly, he let no drop fall from his mouth. Where he wiped his lips on the napkin there was no mark. There was no stain on his plate, there was no crumb on his mat, there was no trace of milk in his cup.

He might have stayed on for years, if one winter had not been too severe for him. But he could not bear the cold, and began to dissipate. For a long time they were not sure if he was still in the house. There was no real way of knowing. But in the first days of spring they cleaned the guest room where, quite rightly, he had slept, and where he was by now no more than a sort of vapor. They shook him out of the mattress, brushed him over the floor, wiped him off the window-pane, and never knew what they had done.

—*1986*

A Second Chance

IF ONLY I had a chance to learn from my mistakes, I would, but there are too many things you don't do twice; in fact, the most important things are things you don't do twice, so you can't do them better the second time. You do something wrong, and see what the right thing would have been, and are ready to do it, should you have the chance again, but the next experience is quite different, and your judgment is wrong again, and though you are now prepared for this experience should it repeat itself, you are not prepared for the next experience. If only, for instance, you could get married at eighteen twice, then the second time you could make sure you were not too young to do this, because you have the perspective of being older, and would know that the person advising you to marry this man was giving you the wrong advice because his reasons were the same ones he gave you the last time he advised you to get married at eighteen. If you could bring a child from a first marriage into a second marriage a second time, you would know that generosity could turn to resentment if you did not do the right things and resentment back to kindness if you did, unless the man you married when you married a second time for the second time was quite different in temperament from the man you married when you married a second time for the first time, in which case you would have to marry that one twice also in order to learn just what the wisest course would be to take with a man of his temperament. If you could have your mother die a second time you might be prepared to fight for a private room that had no other person in it watching television while she died, but if you were prepared to fight for that, and did, you might have to lose your mother again in order to know enough to ask them to put her teeth in the right way and not the wrong way before you went into her room and saw her for the last time grinning so strangely, and then yet one more time to make sure her ashes were not buried again in that plain sort of airmail container in which she was sent north to the cemetery.

—*1997*

OCTAVIA BUTLER

Octavia Butler was an American author best known for psychologically re-alistic science fiction that examines racial, sexual, and environmental poli-tics. A leading figure of the Afrofuturism movement, Butler addressed the history, present concerns, and possible futures of Black Americans through her fiction. A creator of complex speculative worlds, Butler was, in her own words, "a pessimist, a feminist always, a Black, a quiet egoist, a former Baptist, and an oil-and-water combination of ambition, laziness, insecurity, certainty, and drive."

Born in Pasadena, California, Butler was raised by her mother and grand-mother. At the age of 10, she decided that writing was her vocation. After graduating from Pasadena Community College, Butler enrolled in a screen-writing workshop, where her talent was noticed by the established science-fiction writer Harlan Ellison, who would become her mentor. Butler's first novel, *Patternmaster* (1976), was well-received by critics, with Orson Scott Card describing the text as a "vibrant [study] of the ethics of power and submission." The novel became the first in a series employing concepts such as human selective breeding, genetic mutation, and social control though te-lepathy. As she worked on this series, Butler also published *Kindred* (1979), one of her most widely read novels, about a Black woman who is transported back in time to the era of slavery.

In the 1980s, as she published follow-ups to *Patternmaster* as well as other novels and short stories, Butler met with increasing critical and commercial success, winning two Hugo Awards and a Nebula Award. In the 1990s, she became the first science-fiction writer to receive a prestigious MacArthur "Genius Grant." Her last major works were the highly influential Earthseed books—*Parable of the Sower* (1993) and *Parable of the Talents* (1998)—in which she envisioned American society disintegrating as a result of extreme inequality and environmental degradation.

Through her penetrating engagement with racial, sexual, and social power structures, Butler challenged science fiction's domination by white men. "When I begin writing science fiction ... I wasn't in any of this stuff I read,"

Butler once remarked in an interview with *The New York Times*. "I wrote myself in."

Speech Sounds

THERE WAS trouble aboard the Washington Boulevard bus. Rye had expected trouble sooner or later in her journey. She had put off going until loneliness and hopelessness drove her out. She believed she might have one group of relatives left alive—a brother and his two children twenty miles away in Pasadena. That was a day's journey one-way, if she were lucky. The unexpected arrival of the bus as she left her Virginia Road home had seemed to be a piece of luck—until the trouble began.

Two young men were involved in a disagreement of some kind, or, more likely, a misunderstanding. They stood in the aisle, grunting and gesturing at each other, each in his own uncertain T stance as the bus lurched over the potholes. The driver seemed to be putting some effort into keeping them off balance. Still, their gestures stopped just short of contact—mock punches, hand games of intimidation to replace lost curses.

People watched the pair, then looked at one another and made small anxious sounds. Two children whimpered.

Rye sat a few feet behind the disputants and across from the back door. She watched the two carefully, knowing the fight would begin when someone's nerve broke or someone's hand slipped or someone came to the end of his limited ability to communicate. These things could happen anytime.

One of them happened as the bus hit an especially large pothole and one man, tall, thin, and sneering, was thrown into his shorter opponent.

Instantly, the shorter man drove his left fist into the disintegrating sneer. He hammered his larger opponent as though he neither had nor needed any weapon other than his left fist. He hit quickly enough, hard enough to batter his opponent down before the taller man could regain his balance or hit back even once.

People screamed or squawked in fear. Those nearby scrambled to get out of the way. Three more young men roared in excitement and gestured wildly. Then, somehow, a second dispute broke out between two of these three—probably because one inadvertently touched or hit the other.

As the second fight scattered frightened passengers, a woman shook the driver's shoulder and grunted as she gestured toward the fighting.

The driver grunted back through bared teeth. Frightened, the woman drew away.

Rye, knowing the methods of bus drivers, braced herself and held on to the crossbar of the seat in front of her. When the driver hit the brakes, she was ready and the combatants were not. They fell over seats and onto screaming passengers, creating even more confusion. At least one more fight started.

The instant the bus came to a full stop, Rye was on her feet, pushing the back door. At the second push, it opened and she jumped out, holding her pack in one arm. Several other passengers followed, but some stayed on the bus. Buses were rare and irregular now, people rode when they could, no matter what. There might not be another bus today—or tomorrow. People started walking, and if they saw a bus they flagged it down. People making intercity trips like Rye's from Los Angeles to Pasadena made plans to camp out, or risked seeking shelter with locals who might rob or murder them.

The bus did not move, but Rye moved away from it. She intended to wait until the trouble was over and get on again, but if there was shooting, she wanted the protection of a tree. Thus, she was near the curb when a battered blue Ford on the other side of the street made a U-turn and pulled up in front of the bus. Cars were rare these days—as rare as a severe shortage of fuel and of relatively unimpaired mechanics could make them. Cars that still ran were as likely to be used as weapons as they were to serve as transportation. Thus, when the driver of the Ford beckoned to Rye, she moved away warily. The driver got out—a big man, young, neatly bearded with dark, thick hair. He wore a long overcoat and a look of wariness that matched Rye's. She stood several feet from him, waiting to see what he would do. He looked at the bus, now rocking with the combat inside, at the small cluster of passengers who had gotten off. Finally he looked at Rye again.

She returned his gaze, very much aware of the old forty-five automatic her jacket concealed. She watched his hands.

He pointed with his left hand toward the bus. The dark tinted windows prevented him from seeing what was happening inside.

His use of the left hand interested Rye more than his obvious question. Left-handed people tended to be less impaired, more reasonable and comprehending, less driven by frustration, confusion, and anger.

She imitated his gesture, pointing toward the bus with her own left hand, then punching the air with both fists.

The man took off his coat revealing a Los Angeles Police Department uniform complete with baton and service revolver.

Rye took another step back from him. There was no more LAPD, no more *any* large organization, governmental or private. There were neighbourhood patrols and armed individuals. That was all.

The man took something from his coat pocket, then threw the coat into the car. Then he gestured Rye back, back toward the rear of the bus. He had something made of plastic in his hand. Rye did not understand what he wanted until he went to the rear door of the bus and beckoned her to stand there. She obeyed mainly out of curiosity. Cop or not, maybe he could do something to stop the stupid fighting.

He walked around the front of the bus, to the street side where the driver's window was open. There, she thought she saw him throw something into the bus. She was still trying to peer through the tinted glass when people began stumbling out the rear door, choking and weeping. Gas.

Rye caught an old woman who would have fallen, lifted two little children down when they were in danger of being knocked down and trampled. She could see the bearded man helping people at the front door. She caught a thin old man shoved out by one of the combatants. Staggered by the old man's weight, she was barely able to get out of the way as the last of the young men pushed his way out. This one, bleeding from nose and mouth, stumbled into another, and they grappled blindly, still sobbing from the gas.

The bearded man helped the bus driver out through the front door, though the driver did not seem to appreciate his help. For a moment, Rye thought there would be another fight. The bearded man stepped back and watched the driver gesture threateningly, watched him shout in wordless anger.

The bearded man stood still, made no sound, refused to respond to clearly obscene gestures. The least impaired people tended to do this—stand back unless they were physically threatened and let those with less control scream and jump around. It was as though they felt it beneath them to be as touchy as the less comprehending. This was an attitude of superiority, and that was the way people like the bus driver perceived it. Such "superiority" was frequently punished by beatings, even by death. Rye had had close calls of her own. As a result, she never went unarmed. And in this world where the only likely common language was body language, being armed was often enough. She had rarely had to draw her gun or even display it.

The bearded man's revolver was on constant display. Apparently that was enough for the bus driver. The driver spat in disgust, glared at the bearded man for a moment longer, then strode back to his gas-filled bus. He stared at it for a moment, clearly wanting to get in, but the gas was still too strong. Of the windows, only his tiny driver's window actually opened. The front door was open, but the rear door would not stay open unless someone held it. Of course, the air conditioning had failed long ago. The bus would take some time to clear. It was the driver's property, his livelihood. He had pasted old magazine pictures of items he would accept as fare on its sides. Then he would use what he collected to feed his family or to trade. If his bus did not run, he did not eat. On the other hand, if the inside of his bus was torn apart by senseless fighting, he would not eat very well either. He was apparently unable to perceive this. All he could see was that it would be some time before he could use his bus again. He shook his fist at the bearded man and shouted. There seemed to be words in his shout, but Rye could not understand them. She did not know whether this was his fault or hers. She had heard so little coherent human speech for the past three years, she was no longer certain how well she recognized it, no longer certain of the degree of her own impairment.

The bearded man sighed. He glanced toward his car, then beckoned to Rye. He was ready to leave, but he wanted something from her first. No. No, he wanted her to leave with him. Risk getting into his car when, in spite of his uniform, law and order were nothing—not even words any longer.

She shook her head in a universally understood negative, but the man continued to beckon.

She waved him away. He was doing what the less impaired rarely did—drawing potentially negative attention to another of his kind. People from the bus had begun to look at her.

One of the men who had been fighting tapped another on the arm, then pointed from the bearded man to Rye, and finally held up the first two fingers of his right hand as though giving two-thirds of a Boy Scout salute. The gesture was very quick, its meaning obvious even at a distance. She had been grouped with the bearded man. Now what?

The man who had made the gesture started toward her.

She had no idea what he intended, but she stood her ground. The man was half a foot taller than she was and perhaps ten years younger. She did not imagine she could outrun him. Nor did she expect anyone to help her if she needed help. The people around her were all strangers.

She gestured once—a clear indication to the man to stop. She did not intend to repeat the gesture. Fortunately, the man obeyed. He gestured obscenely and several other men laughed. Loss of verbal language had spawned a whole new set of obscene gestures. The man, with stark simplicity, had accused her of sex with the bearded man and had suggested she accommodate the other men present—beginning with him.

Rye watched him wearily. People might very well stand by and watch if he tried to rape her. They would also stand and watch her shoot him. Would he push things that far?

He did not. After a series of obscene gestures that brought him no closer to her, he turned contemptuously and walked away.

And the bearded man still waited. He had removed his service revolver, holster and all. He beckoned again, both hands empty. No doubt his gun was in the car and within easy reach, but his taking it off impressed her. Maybe he was all right. Maybe he was just alone. She had been alone herself for three years. The illness had stripped her, killing her children one by one, killing her husband, her sister, her parents ...

The illness, if it was an illness, had cut even the living off from one another. As it swept over the country, people hardly had time to lay blame on the Soviets[1] (though they were falling silent along with the rest of the world), on a new virus, a new pollutant, radiation, divine retribution ... The illness was stroke-swift in the way it cut people down and strokelike in some of its effects. But it was highly specific. Language was always lost or severely impaired. It was never regained. Often there was also paralysis, intellectual impairment, death.

Rye walked toward the bearded man, ignoring the whistling and applauding of two of the young men and their thumbs-up signs to the bearded man. If he had smiled at them or acknowledged them in any way, she would almost certainly have changed her mind. If she had let herself think of the possible deadly consequences of getting into a stranger's car, she would have changed her mind. Instead, she thought of the man who lived across the street from her. He rarely washed since his bout with the illness. And he had gotten into the habit of urinating wherever he happened to be. He had two women already—one tending each of his large gardens. They put up with him in exchange for his protection. He had made it clear that he wanted Rye to become his third woman.

She got into the car and the bearded man shut the door. She watched as he walked around to the driver's door—watched for his sake because his gun was on the seat beside her. And the bus driver and a pair of young men had come a few steps closer. They did nothing, though, until the bearded man was in the car. Then one of them threw a rock. Others followed his example, and as the car drove away, several rocks bounced off harmlessly.

When the bus was some distance behind them, Rye wiped sweat from her forehead and longed to relax. The bus would have taken her more than halfway to Pasadena. She would have had only ten miles to walk. She wondered how far she would have to walk now—and wondered if walking a long distance would be her only problem.

---

1   The second half of the twentieth century was characterized by political tensions between the United States and the Soviet Union, with continual threat of a nuclear war between the two nations. In 1991 the Soviet Union collapsed into Russia and other independent states.

At Figueroa and Washington where the bus normally made a left turn, the bearded man stopped, looked at her, and indicated that she should choose a direction. When she directed him left and he actually turned left, she began to relax. If he was willing to go where she directed, perhaps he was safe.

As they passed blocks of burned, abandoned buildings, empty lots, and wrecked or stripped cars, he slipped a gold chain over his head and handed it to her. The pendant attached to it was a smooth, glassy, black rock. Obsidian. His name might be Rock or Peter[2] or Black, but she decided to think of him as Obsidian. Even her sometimes useless memory would retain a name like Obsidian.

She handed him her own name symbol—a pin in the shape of a large golden stalk of wheat. She had bought it long before the illness and the silence began. Now she wore it, thinking it was as close as she was likely to come to Rye. People like Obsidian who had not known her before probably thought of her as Wheat. Not that it mattered. She would never hear her name spoken again.

Obsidian handed her pin back to her. He caught her hand as she reached for it and rubbed his thumb over her calluses.

He stopped at First Street and asked which way again. Then, after turning right as she had indicated, he parked near the Music Center. There, he took a folded paper from the dashboard and unfolded it. Rye recognized it as a street map, though the writing on it meant nothing to her. He flattened the map, took her hand again, and put her index finger on one spot. He touched her, touched himself, pointed toward the floor. In effect, "We are here." She knew he wanted to know where she was going. She wanted to tell him, but she shook her head sadly. She had lost reading and writing. That was her most serious impairment and her most painful. She had taught history at UCLA. She had done freelance writing. Now she could not even read her own manuscripts. She had a houseful of books that she could neither read nor bring herself to use as fuel. And she had a memory that would not bring back to her much of what she had read before.

She stared at the map, trying to calculate. She had been born in Pasadena, had lived for fifteen years in Los Angeles. Now she was near L.A. Civic Center. She knew the relative positions of the two cities, knew streets, directions, even knew to stay away from freeways, which might be blocked by wrecked cars and destroyed overpasses. She ought to know how to point out Pasadena even though she could not recognize the word.

Hesitantly, she placed her hand over a pale orange patch in the upper right corner of the map. That should be right. Pasadena.

Obsidian lifted her hand and looked under it, then folded the map and put it back on the dashboard. He could read, she realized belatedly. He could probably

---

2   The name Peter is derived from the Greek word for "stone."

write, too. Abruptly, she hated him—deep, bitter hatred. What did literacy mean to him—a grown man who played cops and robbers? But he was literate and she was not. She never would be. She felt sick to her stomach with hatred, frustration, and jealousy. And only a few inches from her hand was a loaded gun.

She held herself still, staring at him, almost seeing his blood. But her rage crested and ebbed and she did nothing.

Obsidian reached for her hand with hesitant familiarity. She looked at him. Her face had already revealed too much. No person still living in what was left of human society could fail to recognize that expression, that jealousy.

She closed her eyes wearily, drew a deep breath. She had experienced longing for the past, hatred of the present, growing hopelessness, purposelessness, but she had never experienced such a powerful urge to kill another person. She had left her home, finally, because she had come near to killing herself. She had found no reason to stay alive. Perhaps that was why she had gotten into Obsidian's car. She had never before done such a thing.

He touched her mouth and made chatter motions with thumb and fingers. Could she speak?

She nodded and watched his milder envy come and go. Now both had admitted what it was not safe to admit, and there had been no violence. He tapped his mouth and fore head and shook his head. He did not speak or comprehend spoken language. The illness had played with them, taking away, she suspected, what each valued most.

She plucked at his sleeve, wondering why he had decided on his own to keep the LAPD alive with what he had left. He was sane enough otherwise. Why wasn't he at home raising corn, rabbits, and children? But she did not know how to ask. Then he put his hand on her thigh and she had another question to deal with.

She shook her head. Disease, pregnancy, helpless, solitary agony ... no.

He massaged her thigh gently and smiled in obvious disbelief.

No one had touched her for three years. She had not wanted anyone to touch her. What kind of world was this to chance bringing a child into even if the father were willing to stay and help raise it? It was too bad, though. Obsidian could not know how attractive he was to her—young, probably younger than she was, clean, asking for what he wanted rather than demanding it. But none of that mattered. What were a few moments of pleasure measured against a lifetime of consequences?

He pulled her closer to him and for a moment she let herself enjoy the closeness. He smelled good—male and good. She pulled away reluctantly.

He sighed, reached toward the glove compartment. She stiffened, not knowing what to expect, but all he took out was a small box. The writing on it meant nothing to her. She did not understand until he broke the seal, opened the box, and took out a condom. He looked at her, and she first looked away in surprise. Then she giggled. She could not remember when she had last giggled.

He grinned, gestured toward the backseat, and she laughed aloud. Even in her teens, she had disliked backseats of cars. But she looked around at the empty streets and ruined buildings, then she got out and into the backseat. He let her put the condom on him, then seemed surprised at her eagerness.

Sometime later, they sat together, covered by his coat, unwilling to become clothed near strangers again just yet. He made rock-the-baby gestures and looked questioningly at her.

She swallowed, shook her head. She did not know how to tell him her children were dead.

He took her hand and drew a cross in it with his index finger, then made his baby-rocking gesture again.

She nodded, held up three fingers, then turned away, trying to shut out a sudden flood of memories. She had told herself that the children growing up now were to be pitied. They would run through the downtown canyons with no real memory of what the buildings had been or even how they had come to be. Today's children gathered books as well as wood to be burned as fuel. They ran through the streets chasing one another and hooting like chimpanzees. They had no future. They were now all they would ever be.

He put his hand on her shoulder, and she turned suddenly, fumbling for his small box, then urging him to make love to her again. He could give her forgetfulness and pleasure. Until now, nothing had been able to do that. Until now, every day had brought her closer to the time when she would do what she had left home to avoid doing: putting her gun in her mouth and pulling the trigger.

She asked Obsidian if he would come home with her, stay with her.

He looked surprised and pleased once he understood. But he did not answer at once. Finally, he shook his head as she had feared he might. He was probably having too much fun playing cops and robbers and picking up women.

She dressed in silent disappointment, unable to feel any anger toward him. Perhaps he already had a wife and a home. That was likely. The illness had been harder on men than on women—had killed more men, had left male survivors more severely impaired. Men like Obsidian were rare. Women either settled for less or stayed alone. If they found an Obsidian, they did what they could to keep him. Rye suspected he had someone younger, prettier keeping him.

He touched her while she was strapping her gun on and asked with a complicated series of gestures whether it was loaded.

She nodded grimly.

He patted her arm.

She asked once more if he would come home with her, this time using a different series of gestures. He had seemed hesitant. Perhaps he could be courted.

He got out and into the front seat without responding.

She took her place in front again, watching him. Now he plucked at his uniform and looked at her. She thought she was being asked something but did not know what it was.

He took off his badge, tapped it with one finger, then tapped his chest. Of course.

She took the badge from his hand and pinned her wheat stalk to it. If playing cops and robbers was his only insanity, let him play. She would take him, uniform and all. It occurred to her that she might eventually lose him to someone he would meet as he had met her. But she would have him for a while.

He took the street map down again, tapped it, pointed vaguely northeast toward Pasadena, then looked at her.

She shrugged, tapped his shoulder, then her own, and held up her index and second fingers tight together, just to be sure.

He grasped the two fingers and nodded. He was with her.

She took the map from him and threw it onto the dashboard. She pointed back southwest—back toward home. Now he did not have to go to Pasadena. Now she could go on having a brother there and two nephews—three right-handed males. Now she did not have to find out for certain whether she was as alone as she feared. Now she was not alone.

Obsidian took Hill Street south, then Washington west, and she leaned back, wondering what it would be like to have someone again. With what she had scavenged, what she had preserved, and what she grew, there was easily enough food for them. There was certainly room enough in a four-bedroom house. He could move his possessions in. Best of all, the animal across the street would pull back and possibly not force her to kill him.

Obsidian had drawn her closer to him, and she had put her head on his shoulder when suddenly he braked hard, almost throwing her off the seat. Out of the corner of her eye, she saw that someone had run across the street in front of the car. One car on the street and someone had to run in front of it.

Straightening up, Rye saw that the runner was a woman, fleeing from an old frame house to a boarded-up storefront. She ran silently, but the man who followed her a moment later shouted what sounded like garbled words as he ran. He had something in his hand. Not a gun. A knife, perhaps.

The woman tried a door, found it locked, looked around desperately, finally snatched up a fragment of glass broken from the storefront window. With this she turned to face her pursuer. Rye thought she would be more likely to cut her own hand than to hurt anyone else with the glass.

Obsidian jumped from the car, shouting. It was the first time Rye had heard his voice—deep and hoarse from disuse. He made the same sound over and over the way some speechless people did, "Da, da, da!"

Rye got out of the car as Obsidian ran toward the couple. He had drawn his gun. Fearful, she drew her own and released the safety. She looked around to see who else might be attracted to the scene. She saw the man glance at Obsidian, then suddenly lunge at the woman. The woman jabbed his face with her glass, but he caught her arm and managed to stab her twice before Obsidian shot him.

The man doubled, then toppled, clutching his abdomen. Obsidian shouted, then gestured Rye over to help the woman.

Rye moved to the woman's side, remembering that she had little more than bandages and antiseptic in her pack. But the woman was beyond help. She had been stabbed with a long, slender boning knife.

She touched Obsidian to let him know the woman was dead. He had bent to check the wounded man who lay still and also seemed dead. But as Obsidian looked around to see what Rye wanted, the man opened his eyes. Face contorted, he seized Obsidian's just-holstered revolver and fired. The bullet caught Obsidian in the temple and he collapsed.

It happened just that simply, just that fast. An instant later, Rye shot the wounded man as he was turning the gun on her.

And Rye was alone—with three corpses.

She knelt beside Obsidian, dry-eyed, frowning, trying to understand why everything had suddenly changed. Obsidian was gone. He had died and left her—like everyone else.

Two very small children came out of the house from which the man and woman had run—a boy and girl perhaps three years old. Holding hands, they crossed the street toward Rye. They stared at her, then edged past her and went to the dead woman. The girl shook the woman's arm as though trying to wake her.

This was too much. Rye got up, feeling sick to her stomach with grief and anger. If the children began to cry, she thought she would vomit.

They were on their own, those two kids. They were old enough to scavenge. She did not need any more grief. She did not need a stranger's children who would grow up to be hairless chimps.

She went back to the car. She could drive home, at least. She remembered how to drive.

The thought that Obsidian should be buried occurred to her before she reached the car, and she did vomit.

She had found and lost the man so quickly. It was as though she had been snatched from comfort and security and given a sudden, inexplicable beating. Her head would not clear. She could not think.

Somehow, she made herself go back to him, look at him. She found herself on her knees beside him with no memory of having knelt. She stroked his face, his beard. One of the children made a noise and she looked at them, at the woman who was probably their mother. The children looked back at her, obviously frightened. Perhaps it was their fear that reached her finally.

She had been about to drive away and leave them. She had almost done it, almost left two toddlers to die. Surely there had been enough dying. She would have to take the children home with her. She would not be able to live with any other decision. She looked around for a place to bury three bodies. Or two. She wondered if the murderer were the children's father. Before the silence, the police had always said some of the most dangerous calls they went out on were domestic disturbance calls. Obsidian should have known that—not that the knowledge would have kept him in the car. It would not have held her back either. She could not have watched the woman murdered and done nothing.

She dragged Obsidian toward the car. She had nothing to dig with her, and no one to guard for her while she dug. Better to take the bodies with her and bury them next to her husband and her children. Obsidian would come home with her after all.

When she had gotten him onto the floor in the back, she returned for the woman. The little girl, thin, dirty, solemn, stood up and unknowingly gave Rye a gift. As Rye began to drag the woman by her arms, the little girl screamed, "No!"

Rye dropped the woman and stared at the girl.

"No!" the girl repeated. She came to stand beside the woman. "Go away!" she told Rye.

"Don't talk," the little boy said to her. There was no blurring or confusing of sounds. Both children had spoken and Rye had understood. The boy looked at the dead murderer and moved further from him. He took the girl's hand. "Be quiet," he whispered.

Fluent speech! Had the woman died because she could talk and had taught her children to talk? Had she been killed by a husband's festering anger or by a stranger's jealous rage?

And the children ... they must have been born after the silence. Had the disease run its course, then? Or were these children simply immune? Certainly they had had time to fall sick and silent. Rye's mind leaped ahead. What if children of three or fewer years were safe and able to learn language? What if all they needed were teachers? Teachers and protectors.

Rye glanced at the dead murderer. To her shame, she thought she could understand some of the passions that must have driven him, whomever he was. Anger, frustration, hopelessness, insane jealousy ... how many more of him were there—people willing to destroy what they could not have?

Obsidian had been the protector, had chosen that role for who knew what reason. Perhaps putting on an obsolete uniform and patrolling the empty streets had been what he did instead of putting a gun into his mouth. And now that there was something worth protecting, he was gone.

She had been a teacher. A good one. She had been a protector, too, though only of herself. She had kept herself alive when she had no reason to live. If the illness let these children alone, she could keep them alive.

Somehow she lifted the dead woman into her arms and placed her on the backseat of the car. The children began to cry, but she knelt on the broken pavement and whispered to them, fearful of frightening them with the harshness of her long unused voice.

"It's all right," she told them. "You're going with us, too. Come on." She lifted them both, one in each arm. They were so light. Had they been getting enough to eat?

The boy covered her mouth with his hand, but she moved her face away. "It's all right for me to talk," she told him. "As long as no one's around, it's all right." She put the boy down on the front seat of the car and he moved over without being told to, to make room for the girl. When they were both in the car, Rye leaned against the window, looking at them, seeing that they were less afraid now, that they watched her with at least as much curiosity as fear.

"I'm Valerie Rye," she said, savoring the words. "It's all right for you to talk to me."

—1983

JAMAICA KINCAID

Elaine Potter Richardson—who publishes under the name of Jamaica Kincaid—was born in 1949 in St. Johns, Antigua. Until the age of nine, when she ceased to be an only child, she maintained an extremely close relationship with her mother. With the birth of her three brothers, however, her parents' attention turned away from her—and, while her parents focused on sending her brothers to university, Kincaid was sent to apprentice with a seamstress and her education plans were forgotten. When Kincaid was 13, her mother withdrew her from school to help to take care of her brothers and her ailing father. At 17, her parents sent her to work in the United States in order to help the family financially. Kincaid would not return to Antigua or see her mother again for almost 20 years.

Kincaid went to work as an *au pair* for an Upper East Side New York couple—an experience she would later draw from when writing her novel *Lucy* (1990). As Kincaid once said in an interview, the relationship between her life and what she writes is complex. "I write about myself for the most part, and about things that have happened to me. Everything I say is true, and everything I say is not true." Kincaid eventually began freelance writing for magazines such as *Ms*, *Ingenue*, and *The New Yorker*. In 1973, with her first publication, she changed her name to Jamaica Kincaid: "Part of the reason I changed my name was so that they wouldn't know I was writing. I was afraid I would be laughed at, though it would not have stopped me. Nothing has made me not do what I wanted to do." Many of the short stories that appear in her collection *At the Bottom of the River* developed from Kincaid's work in the "Talk of the Town" column in *The New Yorker*. As she states in an interview, writing for "Talk of the Town" "did two things. It showed me how to write, and it allowed me to write in my own voice.... I wrote many very weird 'Talk' stories that appeared in *The New Yorker*, very experimental 'Talk' stories, and it was from them that I learned how to do the stories in *At the Bottom of the River*."

At the Bottom of the River was published in 1983, went on to win the Morton Dauwen Zabel Award of the American Academy and Institute of Arts and Letters, and was nominated for the PEN/Faulkner Award. The collection launched Kincaid's writing career, and she has published several acclaimed works since then, including the novels *Annie John, Lucy,* and *See Now Then* and the memoirs *A Small Place* and *My Brother.* She worked at *The New Yorker* as a staff writer from 1976 until 1995; she is currently a Professor of African and African American Studies at Harvard University.

Girl

WASH THE white clothes on Monday and put them on the stone heap; wash the color clothes on Tuesday and put them on the clothesline to dry; don't walk barehead in the hot sun; cook pumpkin fritters in very hot sweet oil; soak your little cloths right after you take them off; when buying cotton to make yourself a nice blouse, be sure that it doesn't have gum on it, because that way it won't hold up well after a wash; soak salt fish overnight before you cook it; is it true that you sing benna[1] in Sunday school?; always eat your food in such a way that it won't turn someone else's stomach; on Sundays try to walk like a lady and not like the slut you are so bent on becoming; don't sing benna in Sunday school; you mustn't speak to wharf-rat boys, not even to give directions; don't eat fruits on the street—flies will follow you; *but I don't sing benna on Sundays at all and never in Sunday school*; this is how to sew on a button; this is how to make a button-hole for the button you have just sewed on; this is how to hem a dress when you see the hem coming down and so to prevent yourself from looking like the slut I know you are so bent on becoming; this is how you iron your father's khaki shirt so that it doesn't have a crease; this is how you iron your father's khaki pants so that they don't have a crease; this is how you grow okra—far from the house, because okra tree harbors red ants; when you are growing dasheen,[2] make sure it gets plenty of water or else it makes your throat itch when you are eating it; this is how you sweep a corner; this is how you sweep a whole house; this is how you sweep a yard; this is how you smile to someone you don't like too much; this is how you smile to someone you don't like at all; this is how you smile to someone you like completely; this is how you set a table for tea; this is how you set a table for dinner; this is how you set a table for dinner with an important guest; this is how you set a table for lunch; this is how you set a table for breakfast; this is how to behave in the presence of men who don't

---

1 A type of Calypso music.
2 Another name for taro, a type of edible root plant cultivated in the tropics.

know you very well, and this way they won't recognize immediately the slut I have warned you against becoming; be sure to wash every day even if it is with your own spit; don't squat down to play marbles—you are not a boy, you know; don't pick people's flowers—you might catch something; don't throw stones at blackbirds, because it might not be a blackbird at all; this is how to make a bread pudding; this is how to make doukona;[3] this is how to make pepper pot;[4] this is how to make a good medicine for a cold; this is how to make a good medicine to throw away a child before it even becomes a child; this is how to catch a fish; this is how to throw back a fish you don't like, and that way something bad won't fall on you; this is how to bully a man; this is how a man bullies you; this is how to love a man, and if this doesn't work there are other ways, and if they don't work don't feel too bad about giving up; this is how to spit up in the air if you feel like it, and this is how to move quick so that it doesn't fall on you; this is how to make ends meet; always squeeze bread to make sure it's fresh; *but what if the baker won't let me feel the bread?*; you mean to say that after all you are really going to be the kind of woman who the baker won't let near the bread?

—*1983*

---

3   Pudding made from plantains, a banana-like fruit.
4   Meat stew.

HARUKI MURAKAMI

Though he was born in Kyoto to two professors of Japanese literature, Haruki Murakami didn't consider a career in writing until the age of 29. In the introduction to *Wind/Pinball* (2015), the first English release of his two earliest novels, Murakami claims that he decided to become a writer, "for no reason and on no grounds whatsoever," during a baseball game in 1978. Over the following decades, Murakami has become probably the most widely read Japanese author outside Japan, as well as a literary celebrity in his native country—though his continual rejection of Japanese influences has rankled critics at home.

As a youth, Murakami immersed himself in Western culture, especially through jazz music and American crime novels. His first novel, *Hear the Wind Sing* (1979), was written during evenings after work at the jazz café he ran in Tokyo with his wife. *Norwegian Wood* (1987), named after the Beatles song beloved by one of the novel's characters, was Murakami's first truly popular success. It is also, somewhat unusually for him, written in the realist style: most of Murakami's other novels possess a surreal element that contrasts with the almost blandly ordinary characters his narratives tend to follow, resulting in what Sam Anderson of *The New York Times* has described as "a strange broth of ennui and exoticism."

Since the 1970s Murakami has published more than a dozen novels, several collections of short stories, and some works of nonfiction. Increasingly, with novels such as *The Wind-Up Bird Chronicle* (1995), his writing has also touched on the dark and violent aspects of Japan's recent history, including its role in World War II, of which he is very critical. While John Wray of *The Paris Review* has described Murakami as the "voice of his generation" in Japan, Murakami's own literary influences range far beyond his home country, including Raymond Chandler, Franz Kafka, Fyodor Dostoevsky, and Leo Tolstoy. His work has been recognized by many awards including the World Fantasy Award and the prestigious Japanese Yomiuri Prize.

On Seeing the 100% Perfect Girl One Beautiful April Morning[1]

ONE BEAUTIFUL April morning, on a narrow side street in Tokyo's fashionable Harajuku neighbourhood, I walk past the 100% perfect girl.

Tell you the truth, she's not that good-looking. She doesn't stand out in any way. Her clothes are nothing special. The back of her hair is still bent out of shape from sleep. She isn't young, either—must be near thirty, not even close to a "girl," properly speaking. But still, I know from fifty yards away: She's the 100% perfect girl for me. The moment I see her, there's a rumbling in my chest, and my mouth is as dry as a desert.

Maybe you have your own particular favourite type of girl—one with slim ankles, say, or big eyes, or graceful fingers, or you're drawn for no good reason to girls who take their time with every meal. I have my own preferences, of course. Sometimes in a restaurant I'll catch myself staring at the girl at the table next to mine because I like the shape of her nose.

But no one can insist that his 100% perfect girl correspond to some preconceived type. Much as I like noses, I can't recall the shape of hers—or even if she had one. All I can remember for sure is that she was no great beauty. It's weird.

"Yesterday on the street I passed the 100% perfect girl," I tell someone.

"Yeah?" he says. "Good-looking?"

"Not really."

"Your favourite type, then?"

"I don't know. I can't seem to remember anything about her—the shape of her eyes or the size of her breasts."

"Strange."

"Yeah. Strange."

"So anyhow," he says, already bored, "what did you do? Talk to her? Follow her?"

"Nah. Just passed her on the street."

She's walking east to west, and I west to east. It's a really nice April morning.

Wish I could talk to her. Half an hour would be plenty: just ask her about herself, tell her about myself, and—what I'd really like to do—explain to her the complexities of fate that have led to our passing each other on a side street in Harajuku on a beautiful April morning in 1981. This was something sure to be crammed full of warm secrets, like an antique clock built when peace filled the world.

---

1 Translated by Jay Rubin.

After talking, we'd have lunch somewhere, maybe see a Woody Allen[2] movie, stop by a hotel bar for cocktails. With any kind of luck, we might end up in bed.

Potentiality knocks on the door of my heart.

Now the distance between us has narrowed to fifteen yards.

How can I approach her? What should I say?

"Good morning, miss. Do you think you could spare half an hour for a little conversation?"

Ridiculous. I'd sound like an insurance salesman.

"Pardon me, but would you happen to know if there is an all-night cleaners in the neighbourhood?"

No, this is just as ridiculous. I'm not carrying any laundry, for one thing. Who's going to buy a line like that?

Maybe the simple truth would do. "Good morning. You are the 100% perfect girl for me."

No, she wouldn't believe it. Or even if she did, she might not want to talk to me. Sorry, she could say, I might be the 100% perfect girl for you, but you're not the 100% perfect boy for me. It could happen. And if I found myself in that situation, I'd probably go to pieces. I'd never recover from the shock. I'm thirty-two, and that's what growing older is all about.

We pass in front of a flower shop. A small, warm air mass touches my skin. The asphalt is damp, and I catch the scent of roses. I can't bring myself to speak to her. She wears a white sweater, and in her right hand she holds a crisp white envelope lacking only a stamp. So: She's written somebody a letter, maybe spent the whole night writing, to judge from the sleepy look in her eyes. The envelope could contain every secret she's ever had.

I take a few more strides and turn: She's lost in the crowd.

Now, of course, I know exactly what I should have said to her. It would have been a long speech, though, far too long for me to have delivered it properly. The ideas I come up with are never very practical.

Oh, well. It would have started "Once upon a time" and ended "A sad story, don't you think?"

Once upon a time, there lived a boy and a girl. The boy was eighteen and the girl sixteen. He was not unusually handsome, and she was not especially beautiful. They were just an ordinary lonely boy and an ordinary lonely girl, like all the others. But they believed with their whole hearts that somewhere in the world

---

2   American film director (b. 1935).

there lived the 100% perfect boy and the 100% perfect girl for them. Yes, they believed in a miracle. And that miracle actually happened.

One day the two came upon each other on the corner of a street.

"This is amazing," he said. "I've been looking for you all my life. You may not believe this, but you're the 100% perfect girl for me."

"And you," she said to him, "are the 100% perfect boy for me, exactly as I'd pictured you in every detail. It's like a dream."

They sat on a park bench, held hands, and told each other their stories hour after hour. They were not lonely anymore. They had found and been found by their 100% perfect other. What a wonderful thing it is to find and be found by your 100% perfect other. It's a miracle, a cosmic miracle.

As they sat and talked, however, a tiny, tiny sliver of doubt took root in their hearts: Was it really all right for one's dreams to come true so easily?

And so, when there came a momentary lull in their conversation, the boy said to the girl, "Let's test ourselves—just once. If we really are each other's 100% perfect lovers, then sometime, somewhere, we will meet again without fail. And when that happens, and we know that we are the 100% perfect ones, we'll marry then and there. What do you think?"

"Yes," she said, "that is exactly what we should do."

And so they parted, she to the east, and he to the west.

The test they had agreed upon, however, was utterly unnecessary. They should never have undertaken it, because they really and truly were each other's 100% perfect lovers, and it was a miracle that they had ever met. But it was impossible for them to know this, young as they were. The cold, indifferent waves of fate proceeded to toss them unmercifully.

One winter, both the boy and the girl came down with the season's terrible influenza; and after drifting for weeks between life and death they lost all memory of their earlier years. When they awoke, their heads were as empty as the young D.H. Lawrence's piggy bank.[3]

They were two bright, determined young people, however, and through their unremitting efforts they were able to acquire once again the knowledge and feeling that qualified them to return as full-fledged members of society. Heaven be praised, they became truly upstanding citizens who knew how to transfer from one subway line to another, who were fully capable of sending a special-delivery letter at the post office. Indeed, they even experienced love again, sometimes as much as 75% or even 85% love.

---

3   This reference has puzzled critics, but may simply refer to the childhood poverty of the novelist D.H. Lawrence (1885–1930).

Time passed with shocking swiftness, and soon the boy was thirty-two, the girl thirty.

One beautiful April morning, in search of a cup of coffee to start the day, the boy was walking from west to east, while the girl, intending to send a special-delivery letter, was walking from east to west, both along the same narrow street in the Harajuku neighbourhood of Tokyo. They passed each other in the very centre of the street. The faintest gleam of their lost memories glimmered for the briefest moment in their hearts. Each felt a rumbling in the chest. And they knew:

She is the 100% perfect girl for me.

He is the 100% perfect boy for me.

But the glow of their memories was far too weak, and their thoughts no longer had the clarity of fourteen years earlier. Without a word, they passed each other, disappearing into the crowd. Forever.

A sad story, don't you think?

Yes, that's it, that is what I should have said to her.

—1993

ROHINTON MISTRY

Despite apparently non-literary beginnings as a Mathematics and Economics graduate from the University of Bombay, Rohinton Mistry has had a writing life blessed with successes. He has received numerous awards, and his second novel, *Such a Long Journey*, was made into a critically acclaimed film of the same name.

Born in 1952 to Parsi parents in Bombay, India, Mistry emigrated to Toronto with his wife in 1975, primarily out of familial and cultural expectation. In Canada, he worked in a bank while studying English and Philosophy part-time at the University of Toronto. His literary career began in 1983 after he contributed a story to a literary competition and won—he remarked in an interview that the contest was important because, as he says, "I discovered I had talent. I had such a good time telling stories that I want[ed] to keep on doing it." Encouraged by the positive response to his work, Mistry began writing full-time in 1985. His first book, a short-story collection entitled *Tales from Firozsha Baag*, appeared in 1987 and was nominated for a Governor General's Award. He followed in 1991 with the novel *Such a Long Journey*, which was short-listed for the Booker Prize, won him a Governor General's Award, and won the first of his two Commonwealth Prizes. His next two books, *A Fine Balance* (1995) and *Family Matters* (2002), were both greeted with similar success and made him one of Canada's literary superstars. Mistry published his short novel *The Scream* in 2008 in support of World Literacy Canada. In 2012 he was awarded the Neustadt International Prize for Literature, and in 2015 he was inducted as a Member of the Order of Canada.

"Swimming Lessons" is the final story in *Tales from Firozsha Baag*, a collection of stories detailing the lives of a group of Parsi tenants living in a Bombay apartment building called Firozsha Baag; the collection's interlinked structure and setting have led critic Geoff Hancock to call it "the book as apartment building."

Swimming Lessons

THE OLD MAN'S wheelchair is audible today as he creaks by in the hallway: on some days it's just a smooth whirr. Maybe the way he slumps in it, or the way his weight rests has something to do with it. Down to the lobby he goes, and sits there most of the time, talking to people on their way out or in. That's where he first spoke to me a few days ago. I was waiting for the elevator, back from Eaton's with my new pair of swimming-trunks.

"Hullo," he said. I nodded, smiled.

"Beautiful summer day we've got."

"Yes," I said, "it's lovely outside."

He shifted the wheelchair to face me squarely. "How old do you think I am?" I looked at him blankly, and he said, "Go on, take a guess."

I understood the game; he seemed about seventy-five although the hair was still black, so I said, "Sixty-five?" He made a sound between a chuckle and a wheeze: "I'll be seventy-seven next month." Close enough.

I've heard him ask that question several times since, and everyone plays by the rules. Their faked guesses range from sixty to seventy. They pick a lower number when he's more depressed than usual. He reminds me of Grandpa as he sits on the sofa in the lobby, staring out vacantly at the parking lot. Only difference is, he sits with the stillness of stroke victims, while Grandpa's Parkinson's disease would bounce his thighs and legs and arms all over the place. When he could no longer hold the *Bombay Samachar* steady enough to read, Grandpa took to sitting on the veranda and staring emptily at the traffic passing outside Firozsha Baag. Or waving to anyone who went by in the compound: Rustomji, Nariman Hansotia in his 1932 Mercedes-Benz, the fat ayah[1] Jaakaylee with her shopping-bag, the *kuchrawalli*[2] with her basket and long bamboo broom.

The Portuguese woman across the hall has told me a little about the old man. She is the communicator for the apartment building. To gather and disseminate information, she takes the liberty of unabashedly throwing open her door when newsworthy events transpire. Not for Portuguese Woman the furtive peerings from thin cracks or spyholes. She reminds me of a character in a movie, *Barefoot in the Park* I think it was, who left empty beer cans by the landing for anyone passing to stumble and give her the signal. But PW does not need beer cans. The gutang-khutang of the elevator opening and closing is enough.

---

1   Hindi: a maidservant or nursemaid.
2   Hindi: a person employed as a house cleaner.

The old man's daughter looks after him. He was living alone till his stroke, which coincided with his youngest daughter's divorce in Vancouver. She returned to him and they moved into this low-rise in Don Mills. PW says the daughter talks to no one in the building but takes good care of her father.

Mummy used to take good care of Grandpa, too, till things became complicated and he was moved to the Parsi[3] General Hospital. Parkinsonism and osteoporosis laid him low. The doctor explained that Grandpa's hip did not break because he fell, but he fell because the hip, gradually growing brittle, snapped on that fatal day. That's what osteoporosis does, hollows out the bones and turns effect into cause. It has an unusually high incidence in the Parsi community, he said, but did not say why. Just one of those mysterious things. We are the chosen people where osteoporosis is concerned. And divorce. The Parsi community has the highest divorce rate in India. It also claims to be the most westernized community in India. Which is the result of the other? Confusion again, of cause and effect.

The hip was put in traction. Single-handed, Mummy struggled valiantly with bedpans and dressings for bedsores which soon appeared like grim spectres on his back. *Mamaiji*,[4] bent double with her weak back, could give no assistance. My help would be enlisted to roll him over on his side while Mummy changed the dressing. But after three months, the doctor pronounced a patch upon Grandpa's lungs, and the male ward of Parsi General swallowed him up. There was no money for a private nursing home. I went to see him once, at Mummy's insistence. She used to say that the blessings of an old person were the most valuable and potent of all, they would last my whole life long. The ward had rows and rows of beds; the din was enormous, the smells nauseating, and it was just as well that Grandpa passed most of his time in a less than conscious state.

But I should have gone to see him more often. Whenever Grandpa went out, while he still could in the days before parkinsonism, he would bring back pink and white sugar-coated almonds for Percy and me. Every time I remember Grandpa, I remember that; and then I think: I should have gone to see him more often. That's what I also thought when our telephone-owning neighbour, esteemed by all for that reason, sent his son to tell us the hospital had phoned that Grandpa died an hour ago.

---

3   The Parsis are a small religious community numbering approximately 60,000 in India. They have also settled throughout the world. The Parsis originally fled Iran (ancient Persia) in the seventh century because of religious persecution due to Islamic conquest. Parsis are followers of Zoroaster (or Zarathustra), a prophet born in the sixth or seventh century BCE, and the founder of Zoroastrianism.

4   "-ji" is a Hindi suffix placed after a person's name or title as a mark of respect. In this case the narrator is referring to his grandmother.

The postman rang the doorbell the way he always did, long and continuous; Mother went to open it, wanting to give him a piece of her mind but thought better of it, she did not want to risk the vengeance of postmen, it was so easy for them to destroy letters; workers nowadays thought no end of themselves, strutting around like peacocks, ever since all this Shiv Sena[5] agitation about Maharashtra[6] for Maharashtrians, threatening strikes and Bombay bundh[7] *all the time, with no respect for the public; bus drivers and conductors were the worst, behaving as if they owned the buses and were doing favours to commuters, pulling the bell before you were in the bus, the driver purposely braking and moving with big jerks to make the standees lose their balance, the conductor so rude if you did not have the right change.*

But when she saw the airmail envelope with a Canadian stamp her face lit up, she said wait to the postman, and went in for a fifty paisa[8] piece, a little bak-sheesh[9] *for you, she told him, then shut the door and kissed the envelope, went in running, saying my son has written, my son has sent a letter, and Father looked up from the newspaper and said, don't get too excited, first read it, you know what kind of letters he writes, a few lines of empty words, I'm fine, hope you are all right, your loving son—that kind of writing I don't call letter-writing.*

Then Mother opened the envelope and took out one small page and began to read silently, and the joy brought to her face by the letter's arrival began to ebb; Father saw it happening and knew he was right, he said read aloud, let me also hear what our son is writing this time, so Mother read: My dear Mummy and Daddy, Last winter was terrible, we had record-breaking low temperatures all through February and March, and the first official day of spring was colder than the first official day of winter had been, but it's getting warmer now. Looks like it will be a nice warm summer. You asked about my new apartment. It's small, but not bad at all. This is just a quick note to let you know I'm fine, so you won't worry about me. Hope everything is okay at home.

After Mother put it back in the envelope, Father said everything about his life is locked in silence and secrecy, I still don't understand why he bothered to visit us last year if he had nothing to say; every letter of his has been a quick note so we won't worry—what does he think we worry about, his health, in that country everyone eats well whether they work or not, he should be worrying about us with all the black market and rationing, has he forgotten already how he used to

---

5   A right-wing, Hindu political party founded in the 1960s.

.6   A state in west Central India of which Mumbai (formerly Bombay) is the capital.

7   A general strike (alternate spelling is *bandh*).

8   A monetary unit of India and Pakistan, worth one hundredth of a rupee.

9   Hindi: money given as a tip or present.

go to the ration-shop and wait in line every week; and what kind of apartment description is that, not bad at all; and if it is a Canadian weather report I need from him, I can go with Nariman Hansotia from A Block to the Cawasji Framji Memorial Library and read all about it, there they get newspapers from all over the world.

The sun is hot today. Two women are sunbathing on the stretch of patchy lawn at the periphery of the parking lot. I can see them clearly from my kitchen. They're wearing bikinis and I'd love to take a closer look. But I have no binoculars. Nor do I have a car to saunter out to and pretend to look under the hood. They're both luscious and gleaming. From time to time they smear lotion over their skin, on the bellies, on the inside of the thighs, on the shoulders. Then one of them gets the other to undo the string of her top and spread some there. She lies on her stomach with the straps undone. I wait. I pray that the heat and haze make her forget, when it's time to turn over, that the straps are undone.

But the sun is not hot enough to work this magic for me. When it's time to come in, she flips over, deftly holding up the cups, and reties the top. They arise, pick up towels, lotions and magazines, and return to the building.

This is my chance to see them closer. I race down the stairs to the lobby. The old man says hullo. "Down again?"

"My mailbox," I mumble.

"It's Saturday," he chortles. For some reason he finds it extremely funny. My eye is on the door leading in from the parking lot.

Through the glass panel I see them approaching. I hurry to the elevator and wait. In the dimly lit lobby I can see their eyes are having trouble adjusting after the bright sun. They don't seem as attractive as they did from the kitchen window. The elevator arrives and I hold it open, inviting them in with what I think is a gallant flourish. Under the fluorescent glare in the elevator I see their wrinkled skin, aging hands, sagging bottoms, varicose veins. The lustrous trick of sun and lotion and distance has ended.

I step out and they continue to the third floor. I have Monday night to look forward to, my first swimming lesson. The high school behind the apartment building is offering, among its usual assortment of macramé and ceramics and pottery classes, a class for non-swimming adults.

The woman at the registration desk is quite friendly. She even gives me the opening to satisfy the compulsion I have about explaining my non-swimming status.

"Are you from India?" she asks. I nod. "I hope you don't mind my asking, but I was curious because an Indian couple, husband and wife, also registered a few minutes ago. Is swimming not encouraged in India?"

"On the contrary," I say. "Most Indians swim like fish. I'm an exception to the rule. My house was five minutes walking distance from Chaupatty beach in Bombay. It's one of the most beautiful beaches in Bombay, or was, before the filth took over. Anyway, even though we lived so close to it, I never learned to swim. It's just one of those things."

"Well," says the woman, "that happens sometimes. Take me, for instance. I never learned to ride a bicycle. It was the mounting that used to scare me, I was afraid of falling." People have lined up behind me. "It's been very nice talking to you," she says, "hope you enjoy the course."

The art of swimming had been trapped between the devil and the deep blue sea. The devil was money, always scarce, and kept the private swimming clubs out of reach; the deep blue sea of Chaupatty beach was grey and murky with garbage, too filthy to swim in. Every so often we would muster our courage and Mummy would take me there to try and teach me. But a few minutes of paddling was all we could endure. Sooner or later something would float up against our legs or thighs or waists, depending on how deep we'd gone in, and we'd be revulsed and stride out to the sand.

Water imagery in my life is recurring. Chaupatty beach, now the high-school swimming pool. The universal symbol of life and regeneration did nothing but frustrate me. Perhaps the swimming pool will overturn that failure.

When images and symbols abound in this manner, sprawling or rolling across the page without guile or artifice, one is prone to say, how obvious, how skilless; symbols, after all, should be still and gentle as dewdrops, tiny, yet shining with a world of meaning. But what happens when, on the page of life itself, one encounters the ever-moving, all-engirdling sprawl of the filthy sea? Dewdrops and oceans both have their rightful places; Nariman Hansotia certainly knew that when he told his stories to the boys of Firozsha Baag.

The sea of Chaupatty was fated to endure the finales of life's everyday functions. It seemed that the dirtier it became, the more crowds it attracted: street urchins and beggars and beachcombers, looking through the junk that washed up. (Or was it the crowds that made it dirtier?—another instance of cause and effect blurring and evading identification.)

Too many religious festivals also used the sea as repository for their finales. Its use should have been rationed, like rice and kerosene. On Ganesh Chaturthi,[10] clay idols of the god Ganesh,[11] adorned with garlands and all manner of finery, were carried in processions to the accompaniment of drums and a variety of

---

10 A popular Hindu festival celebrating the birthday of Lord Ganesh.

11 The Hindu god of Beginnings and Fighter of Obstacles, represented as having an elephant's head.

wind instruments. The music got more frenzied the closer the procession got to Chaupatty and to the moment of immersion.

Then there was Coconut Day,[12] which was never as popular as Ganesh Chaturthi. From a bystander's viewpoint, coconuts chucked into the sea do not provide as much of a spectacle. We used the sea, too, to deposit the leftovers from Parsi religious ceremonies, things such as flowers, or the ashes of the sacred sandalwood fire, which just could not be dumped with the regular garbage but had to be entrusted to the care of Avan Yazad, the guardian of the sea. And things which were of no use but which no one had the heart to destroy were also given to Avan Yazad. Such as old photographs.

After Grandpa died, some of his things were flung out to sea. It was high tide; we always checked the newspaper when going to perform these disposals; an ebb would mean a long walk in squelchy sand before finding water. Most of the things were probably washed up on shore. But we tried to throw them as far out as possible, then waited a few minutes; if they did not float back right away we would pretend they were in the permanent safekeeping of Avan Yazad, which was a comforting thought. I can't remember everything we sent out to sea, but his brush and comb were in the parcel, his *kusti*,[13] and some Kemadrin pills, which he used to take to keep the parkinsonism under control.

Our paddling sessions stopped for lack of enthusiasm on my part. Mummy wasn't too keen either, because of the filth. But my main concern was the little guttersnipes, like naked fish with little buoyant penises, taunting me with their skills, swimming underwater and emerging unexpectedly all around me, or pretending to masturbate—I think they were too young to achieve ejaculation. It was embarrassing. When I look back, I'm surprised that Mummy and I kept going as long as we did.

I examine the swimming-trunks I bought last week. Surf King, says the label, Made in Canada-Fabriqué Au Canada. I've been learning bits and pieces of French from bilingual labels at the supermarket too. These trunks are extremely sleek and streamlined hipsters, the distance from waistband to pouch tip the barest minimum. I wonder how everything will stay in place, not that I'm boastful about my endowments. I try them on, and feel that the tip of my member lingers perilously close to the exit. Too close, in fact, to conceal the exigencies of my swimming lesson fantasy: a gorgeous woman in the class for non-swimmers, at whose sight I will be instantly aroused, and she, spying the shape of my desire, will look me straight in the eye with her intentions; she will come home with

---

12 A day dedicated to the celebration of the coconut's contribution to culture and the economy.

13 A sacred cord worn around the waist by Zoroastrians.

me, to taste the pleasures of my delectable Asian brown body whose strangeness has intrigued her and unleashed uncontrollable surges of passion inside her throughout the duration of the swimming lesson.

I drop the Eaton's bag and wrapper in the garbage can. The swimming-trunks cost fifteen dollars, same as the fee for the ten weekly lessons. The garbage bag is almost full. I tie it up and take it outside. There is a medicinal smell in the hallway; the old man must have just returned to his apartment.

PW opens her door and says, "Two ladies from the third floor were lying in the sun this morning. In bikinis."

"That's nice," I say, and walk to the incinerator chute. She reminds me of Najamai in Firozsha Baag, except that Najamai employed a bit more subtlety while going about her life's chosen work.

PW withdraws and shuts her door.

Mother had to reply because Father said he did not want to write to his son till his son had something sensible to write to him, his questions had been ignored long enough, and if he wanted to keep his life a secret, fine, he would get no letters from his father.

But after Mother started the letter he went and looked over her shoulder, telling her what to ask him, because if they kept on writing the same questions, maybe he would understand how interested they were in knowing about things over there; Father said go on, ask him what his work is at the insurance company, tell him to take some courses at night school, that's how everyone moves ahead over there, tell him not to be discouraged if his job is just clerical right now, hard work will get him ahead, remind him he is a Zoroastrian: manashni, gavashni, kunashni, better write the translation also: good thoughts, good words, good deeds—he must have forgotten what it means, and tell him to say prayers and do kusti[14] at least twice a day.

Writing it all down sadly, Mother did not believe he wore his sudra[15] and kusti anymore, she would be very surprised if he remembered any of the prayers; when she had asked him if he needed new sudras he said not to take any trouble because the Zoroastrian Society of Ontario imported them from Bombay for their members, and this sounded like a story he was making up, but she was leaving it in the hands of God, ten thousand miles away there was nothing she could do but write a letter and hope for the best.

Then she sealed it, and Father wrote the address on it as usual because his writing was much neater than hers, handwriting was important in the address and

---

14   The short ritual of untying and retying the *kusti*.

15   A sacred shirt worn by Zoroastrians.

she did not want the postman in Canada to make any mistake; she took it to the post office herself, it was impossible to trust anyone to mail it ever since the postage rates went up because people just tore off the stamps for their own use and threw away the letter, the only safe way was to hand it over the counter and make the clerk cancel the stamps before your own eyes.

Berthe, the building superintendent, is yelling at her son in the parking lot. He tinkers away with his van. This happens every fine-weathered Sunday. It must be the van that Berthe dislikes because I've seen mother and son together in other quite amicable situations.

Berthe is a big Yugoslavian with high cheekbones. Her nationality was disclosed to me by PW. Berthe speaks a very rough-hewn English, I've overheard her in the lobby scolding tenants for late rents and leaving dirty lint screens in the dryers. It's exciting to listen to her, her words fall like rocks and boulders, and one can never tell where or how the next few will drop. But her Slavic yells at her son are a different matter, the words fly swift and true, well-aimed missiles that never miss. Finally, the son slams down the hood in disgust, wipes his hands on a rag, accompanies mother Berthe inside.

Berthe's husband has a job in a factory. But he loses several days of work every month when he succumbs to the booze, a word Berthe uses often in her Slavic tirades on those days, the only one I can understand, as it clunks down heavily out of the tight-flying formation of Yugoslavian sentences. He lolls around in the lobby, submitting passively to his wife's tongue-lashings. The bags under his bloodshot eyes, his stringy moustache, stubbled chin, dirty hair are so vulnerable to the poison-laden barbs (poison works the same way in any language) emanating from deep within the powerful watermelon bosom. No one's presence can embarrass or dignify her into silence.

No one except the old man who arrives now. "Good morning," he says, and Berthe turns, stops yelling, and smiles. Her husband rises, positions the wheelchair at the favourite angle. The lobby will be peaceful as long as the old man is there.

It was hopeless. My first swimming lesson. The water terrified me. When did that happen, I wonder, I used to love splashing at Chaupatty, carried about by the waves. And this was only a swimming pool. Where did all that terror come from? I'm trying to remember.

Armed with my Surf King I enter the high school and go to the pool area. A sheet with instructions for the new class is pinned to the bulletin board. All students must shower and then assemble at eight by the shallow end. As I enter the showers three young boys, probably from a previous class, emerge. One of them holds his nose. The second begins to hum, under his breath: Paki Paki, smell like curry. The third says to the first two: pretty soon all the water's going to taste of curry. They leave.

It's a mixed class, but the gorgeous woman of my fantasy is missing. I have to settle for another, in a pink one-piece suit, with brown hair and a bit of a stomach. She must be about thirty-five. Plain-looking.

The instructor is called Ron. He gives us a pep talk, sensing some nervousness in the group. We're finally all in the water, in the shallow end. He demonstrates floating on the back, then asks for a volunteer. The pink one-piece suit wades forward. He supports her, tells her to lean back and let her head drop in the water.

She does very well. And as we all regard her floating body, I see what was not visible outside the pool: her bush, curly bits of it, straying out at the pink Spandex V. Tongues of water lapping against her delta, as if caressing it teasingly, make the brown hair come alive in a most tantalizing manner. The crests and troughs of little waves, set off by the movement of our bodies in a circle around her, dutifully irrigate her; the curls alternately wave free inside the crest, then adhere to her wet thighs, beached by the inevitable trough. I could watch this forever, and I wish the floating demonstration would never end.

Next we are shown how to grasp the rail and paddle, face down in the water. Between practising floating and paddling, the hour is almost gone. I have been trying to observe the pink one-piece suit, getting glimpses of her straying pubic hair from various angles. Finally, Ron wants a volunteer for the last demonstration, and I go forward. To my horror he leads the class to the deep end. Fifteen feet of water. It is so blue, and I can see the bottom. He picks up a metal hoop attached to a long wooden stick. He wants me to grasp the hoop, jump in the water, and paddle, while he guides me by the stick. Perfectly safe, he tells me. A demonstration of how paddling propels the body.

It's too late to back out; besides, I'm so terrified I couldn't find the words to do so even if I wanted to. Everything he says I do as if in a trance. I don't remember the moment of jumping. The next thing I know is, I'm swallowing water and floundering, hanging on to the hoop for dear life. Ron draws me to the rails and helps me out. The class applauds.

We disperse and one thought is on my mind: what if I'd lost my grip? Fifteen feet of water under me. I shudder and take deep breaths. This is it. I'm not coming next week. This instructor is an irresponsible person. Or he does not value the lives of non-white immigrants. I remember the three teenagers. Maybe the swimming pool is the hangout of some racist group, bent on eliminating all non-white swimmers, to keep their waters pure and their white sisters unogled.

The elevator takes me upstairs. Then gutang-khutang. PW opens her door as I turn the corridor of medicinal smells. "Berthe was screaming loudly at her husband tonight," she tells me.

"Good for her," I say, and she frowns indignantly at me.

The old man is in the lobby. He's wearing thick wool gloves. He wants to know how the swimming was, must have seen me leaving with my towel yesterday. Not bad, I say.

"I used to swim a lot. Very good for the circulation." He wheezes. "My feet are cold all the time. Cold as ice. Hands too."

Summer is winding down, so I say stupidly, "Yes, it's not so warm any more."

The thought of the next swimming lesson sickens me. But as I comb through the memories of that terrifying Monday, I come upon the straying curls of brown pubic hair. Inexorably drawn by them, I decide to go.

It's a mistake, of course. This time I'm scared even to venture in the shallow end. When everyone has entered the water and I'm the only one outside, I feel a little foolish and slide in.

Instructor Ron says we should start by reviewing the floating technique. I'm in no hurry. I watch the pink one-piece pull the swim-suit down around her cheeks and flip back to achieve perfect flotation. And then reap disappointment. The pink Spandex triangle is perfectly streamlined today, nothing strays, not a trace of fuzz, not one filament, not even a sign of post-depilation irritation. Like the airbrushed parts of glamour magazine models. The barrenness of her impeccably packaged apex is a betrayal. Now she is shorn like the other women in the class. Why did she have to do it?

The weight of this disappointment makes the water less manageable, more lung-penetrating. With trepidation, I float and paddle my way through the remainder of the hour, jerking my head out every two seconds and breathing deeply, to continually shore up a supply of precious, precious air without, at the same time, seeming too anxious and losing my dignity.

I don't attend the remaining classes. After I've missed three, Ron the instructor telephones. I tell him I've had the flu and am still feeling poorly, but I'll try to be there the following week.

He does not call again. My Surf King is relegated to an unused drawer. Total losses: one fantasy plus thirty dollars. And no watery rebirth. The swimming pool, like Chaupatty beach, has produced a stillbirth. But there is a difference. Water means regeneration only if it is pure and cleansing. Chaupatty was filthy, the pool was not. Failure to swim through filth must mean something other than failure of rebirth—failure of symbolic death? Does that equal success of symbolic life? death of a symbolic failure? death of a symbol? What is the equation?

The postman did not bring a letter but a parcel, he was smiling because he knew that every time something came from Canada his baksheesh was guaranteed, and this time because it was a parcel Mother gave him a whole rupee, she was quite excited, there were so many stickers on it besides the stamps, one for Small Parcel, another Printed Papers, a red sticker saying Insured; she showed it to Father, and opened it, then put both hands on her cheeks, not able to speak because the surprise and happiness was so great, tears came to her eyes and she could not stop smiling, till Father became impatient to know and finally got up and came to the table.

When he saw it he was surprised and happy too, he began to grin, then hugged Mother saying our son is a writer, and we didn't even know it, he never told us a thing, here we are thinking he is still clerking away at the insurance company, and he has written a book of stories, all these years in school and college he kept his talent hidden, making us think he was just like one of the boys in the Baag, shouting and playing the fool in the compound, and now what a surprise; then Father opened the book and began reading it, heading back to the easy chair, and Mother so excited, still holding his arm, walked with him, saying it was not fair him reading it first, she wanted to read it too, and they agreed that he would read the first story, then give it to her so she could also read it, and they would take turns in that manner.

Mother removed the staples from the padded envelope in which he had mailed the book, and threw them away, then straightened the folded edges of the envelope and put it away safely with the other envelopes and letters she had collected since he left.

The leaves are beginning to fall. The only ones I can identify are maple. The days are dwindling like the leaves. I've started a habit of taking long walks every evening. The old man is in the lobby when I leave, he waves as I go by. By the time I'm back, the lobby is usually empty.

Today I was woken up by a grating sound outside that made my flesh crawl. I went to the window and saw Berthe raking the leaves in the parking lot. Not in the expanse of patchy lawn on the periphery, but in the parking lot proper. She was raking the black tarred surface. I went back to bed and dragged a pillow over my head, not releasing it till noon.

When I return from my walk in the evening, PW, summoned by the elevator's gutang-khutang, says, "Berthe filled six big black garbage bags with leaves today."

"Six bags!" I say. "Wow!"

Since the weather turned cold, Berthe's son does not tinker with his van on Sundays under my window. I'm able to sleep late.

Around eleven, there's a commotion outside. I reach out and switch on the clock radio. It's a sunny day, the window curtains are bright. I get up, curious, and see a black Olds Ninety-Eight in the parking lot, by the entrance to the building. The old man is in his wheelchair, bundled up, with a scarf wound several times round his neck as though to immobilize it, like a surgical collar. His daughter and another man, the car-owner, are helping him from the wheelchair into the front seat, encouraging him with words like: that's it, easy does it, attaboy. From the open door of the lobby, Berthe is shouting encouragement too, but hers is confined to one word: yah, repeated at different levels of pitch and volume, with variations on vowel-length. The stranger could be the old man's son, he has the same jet black hair and piercing eyes.

Maybe the old man is not well, it's an emergency. But I quickly scrap that thought—this isn't Bombay, an ambulance would have arrived. They're probably taking him out for a ride. If he is his son, where has he been all this time, I wonder.

The old man finally settles in the front seat, the wheelchair goes in the trunk, and they're off. The one I think is the son looks up and catches me at the window before I can move away, so I wave, and he waves back.

In the afternoon I take down a load of clothes to the laundry room. Both machines have completed their cycles, the clothes inside are waiting to be transferred to dryers. Should I remove them and place them on top of a dryer, or wait? I decide to wait. After a few minutes, two women arrive, they are in bathrobes, and smoking. It takes me a while to realize that these are the two disappointments who were sunbathing in bikinis last summer.

"You didn't have to wait, you could have removed the clothes and carried on, dear," says one. She has a Scottish accent. It's one of the few I've learned to identify. Like maple leaves.

"Well," I say, "some people might not like strangers touching their clothes."

"You're not a stranger, dear," she says, "you live in this building, we've seen you before."

"Besides, your hands are clean," the other one pipes in. "You can touch my things any time you like."

Horny old cow. I wonder what they've got on under their bathrobes. Not much, I find, as they bend over to place their clothes in the dryers.

"See you soon," they say, and exit, leaving me behind in an erotic wake of smoke and perfume and deep images of cleavages. I start the washers and depart, and when I come back later, the dryers are empty.

PW tells me, "The old man's son took him out for a drive today. He has a big beautiful black car."

I see my chance, and shoot back: "Olds Ninety-Eight."

"What?"

"The car," I explain, "it's an Oldsmobile Ninety-Eight."

She does not like this at all, my giving her information. She is visibly nettled, and retreats with a sour face.

Mother and Father read the first five stories, and she was very sad after reading some of them, she said he must be so unhappy there, all his stories are about Bombay, he remembers every little thing about his childhood, he is thinking about it all the time even though he is ten thousand miles away, my poor son, I think he misses his home and us and everything he left behind, because if he likes it over there why would he not write stories about that, there must be so many new ideas that his new life could give him.

But Father did not agree with this, he said it did not mean that he was unhappy, all writers worked in the same way, they used their memories and experiences and made stories out of them, changing some things, adding some, imagining some, all writers were very good at remembering details of their lives.

Mother said, how can you be sure that he is remembering because he is a writer, or whether he started to write because he is unhappy and thinks of his past, and wants to save it all by making stories of it; and Father said that is not a sensible question, anyway, it is now my turn to read the next story.

The first snow has fallen, and the air is crisp. It's not very deep, about two inches, just right to go for a walk in. I've been told that immigrants from hot countries always enjoy the snow the first year, maybe for a couple of years more, then inevitably the dread sets in, and the approach of winter gets them fretting and moping. On the other hand, if it hadn't been for my conversation with the woman at the swimming registration desk, they might now be saying that India is a nation of non-swimmers.

Berthe is outside, shovelling the snow off the walkway in the parking lot. She has a heavy, wide pusher which she wields expertly.

The old radiators in the apartment alarm me incessantly. They continue to broadcast a series of variations on death throes, and go from hot to cold and cold to hot at will, there's no controlling their temperature. I speak to Berthe about it in the lobby. The old man is there too, his chin seems to have sunk deeper into his chest, and his face is a yellowish grey.

"Nothing, not to worry about anything," says Berthe, dropping rough-hewn chunks of language around me. "Radiator no work, you tell me. You feel cold, you come to me, I keep you warm," and she opens her arms wide, laughing. I step back, and she advances, her breasts preceding her like the gallant prows of two ice-breakers. She looks at the old man to see if he is appreciating the act: "You no feel scared, I keep you safe and warm."

But the old man is staring outside, at the flakes of falling snow. What thoughts is he thinking as he watches them? Of childhood days, perhaps, and snowmen with hats and pipes, and snowball fights, and white Christmases, and Christmas trees? What will I think of, old in this country, when I sit and watch the snow come down? For me, it is already too late for snowmen and snowball fights, and all I will have is thoughts about childhood thoughts and dreams, built around snowscapes and winter-wonderlands on the Christmas cards so popular in Bombay; my snowmen and snowball fights and Christmas trees are in the pages of Enid Blyton's[16] books, dispersed amidst the adventures of the Famous Five, and the Five Find-Outers, and the Secret Seven. My snowflakes are even less forgettable than the old man's, for they never melt.

It finally happened. The heat went. Not the usual intermittent coming and going, but out completely. Stone cold. The radiators are like ice. And so is everything else. There's no hot water. Naturally. It's the hot water that goes through the rads and heats them. Or is it the other way around? Is there no hot water because the rads have stopped circulating it? I don't care, I'm too cold to sort out the cause and effect relationship. Maybe there is no connection at all.

I dress quickly, put on my winter jacket, and go down to the lobby. The elevator is not working because the power is out, so I take the stairs. Several people are gathered, and Berthe has announced that she has telephoned the office, they are sending a man. I go back up the stairs. It's only one floor, the elevator is just a bad habit. Back in Firozsha Baag they were broken most of the time. The stairway enters the corridor outside the old man's apartment, and I think of his cold feet and hands. Poor man, it must be horrible for him without heat.

As I walk down the long hallway, I feel there's something different but can't pin it down. I look at the carpet, the ceiling, the wallpaper: it all seems the same. Maybe it's the freezing cold that imparts a feeling of difference.

PW opens her door: "The old man had another stroke yesterday. They took him to the hospital."

The medicinal smell. That's it. It's not in the hallway any more.

In the stories that he'd read so far Father said that all the Parsi families were poor or middle-class, but that was okay; nor did he mind that the seeds for the stories were picked from the sufferings of their own lives; but there should also have been something positive about Parsis, there was so much to be proud of the great Tatas[17] and their contribution to the steel industry, or Sir Dinshaw Petit in the textile

---

16   Enid Blyton (1897–1968): a British children's author.
17   A high-profile Parsi family that developed India's first steel industry.

industry who made Bombay the Manchester of the East,[18] *or Dadabhai Naoroji*[19] *in the freedom movement, where he was the first to use the word* swaraj,[20] *and the first to be elected to the British Parliament where he carried on his campaign; he should have found some way to bring some of these wonderful facts into his stories, what would people reading these stories think, those who did not know about Parsis—that the whole community was full of cranky bigoted people; and in reality it was the richest, most advanced and philanthropic community in India, and he did not need to tell his own son that Parsis had a reputation for being generous and family-oriented. And he could have written something also about the historic background, how Parsis came to India from Persia because of Islamic persecution in the seventh century, and were the descendants of Cyrus the Great and the magnificent Persian Empire. He could have made a story of all this, couldn't he?*

Mother said what she liked best was his remembering everything so well, how beautifully he wrote about it all, even the sad things, and though he changed some of it, and used his imagination, there was truth in it.

My hope is, Father said, that there will be some story based on his Canadian experience, that way we will know something about our son's life there, if not through his letters then in his stories; so far they are all about Parsis and Bombay, and the one with a little bit about Toronto, where a man perches on top of the toilet, is shameful and disgusting, although it is funny at times and did make me laugh, I have to admit, but where does he get such an imagination from, what is the point of such a fantasy; and Mother said that she would also enjoy some stories about Toronto and the people there; it puzzles me, she said, why he writes nothing about it, especially since you say that writers use their own experience to make stories out of.

Then Father said this is true, but he is probably not using his Toronto experience because it is too early; what do you mean, too early, asked Mother and Father explained it takes a writer about ten years time after an experience before he is able to use it in his writing, it takes that long to be absorbed internally and understood, thought out and thought about, over and over again, he haunts it and it haunts him if it is valuable enough, till the writer is comfortable with it to be

---

18 Sir Dinshaw (Manockjee) Petit, 1st Baronet (1823–1901): a Parsi entrepreneur who oversaw the development of Bombay's cotton textile industry and helped lay the foundation for Bombay's commercial prosperity. His contributions to Bombay's economy were so impressive that Bombay earned the title "Manchester of the East."

19 Dadabhai Naoroji (1825–1917): the first Indian person elected to British parliament (1892). He worked to improve the conditions for people in India and strongly advocated for Indian self-government.

20 Independence (in British India).

able to use it as he wants; but this is only one theory I read somewhere, it may or may not be true.

That means, said Mother, that his childhood in Bombay and our home here is the most valuable thing in his life just now, because he is able to remember it all to write about it, and you were so bitterly saying he is forgetting where he came from; and that may be true, said Father, but that is not what the theory means, according to the theory he is writing of these things because they are far enough in the past for him to deal with objectively, he is able to achieve what critics call artistic distance, without emotions interfering; and what do you mean emotions, said Mother, you are saying he does not feel anything for his characters, how can he write so beautifully about so many sad things without any feelings in his heart?

But before Father could explain more, about beauty and emotion and inspiration and imagination, Mother took the book and said it was her turn now and too much theory she did not want to listen to, it was confusing and did not make as much sense as reading the stories, she would read them her way and Father could read them his.

My books on the windowsill have been damaged. Ice has been forming on the inside ledge, which I did not notice, and melting when the sun shines in. I spread them in a corner of the living room to dry out.

The winter drags on. Berthe wields her snow pusher as expertly as ever, but there are signs of weariness in her performance. Neither husband nor son is ever seen outside with a shovel. Or anywhere else, for that matter. It occurs to me that the son's van is missing, too.

The medicinal smell is in the hall again, I sniff happily and look forward to seeing the old man in the lobby. I go downstairs and peer into the mailbox, see the blue and magenta of an Indian aerogramme with Don Mills, Ontario, Canada in Father's flawless hand through the slot.

I pocket the letter and enter the main lobby. The old man is there, but not in his usual place. He is not looking out through the glass door. His wheelchair is facing a bare wall where the wallpaper is torn in places. As though he is not interested in the outside world any more, having finished with all that, and now it's time to see inside. What does he see inside, I wonder? I go up to him and say hullo. He says hullo without raising his sunken chin. After a few seconds his grey countenance faces me. "How old do you think I am?" His eyes are dull and glazed; he is looking even further inside than I first presumed.

"Well, let's see, you're probably close to sixty-four."

"I'll be seventy-eight next August." But he does not chuckle or wheeze. Instead, he continues softly, "I wish my feet did not feel so cold all the time. And my hands." He lets his chin fall again.

In the elevator I start opening the aerogramme, a tricky business because a crooked tear means lost words. Absorbed in this while emerging, I don't notice PW occupying the centre of the hallway, arms folded across her chest: "They had a big fight. Both of them have left."

I don't immediately understand her agitation. "What ... who?"

"Berthe. Husband and son both left her. Now she is all alone."

Her tone and stance suggest that we should not be standing here talking but do something to bring Berthe's family back. "That's very sad," I say, and go in. I picture father and son in the van, driving away, driving across the snow-covered country, in the dead of winter, away from wife and mother; away to where? how far will they go? Not son's van nor father's booze can take them far enough. And the further they go, the more they'll remember, they can take it from me.

All the stories were read by Father and Mother, and they were sorry when the book was finished, they felt they had come to know their son better now, yet there was much more to know, they wished there were many more stories; and this is what they mean, said Father, when they say that the whole story can never be told, the whole truth can never be known; what do you mean, they say, asked Mother, who they, and Father said writers, poets, philosophers. I don't care what they say, said Mother, my son will write as much or as little as he wants to, and if I can read it I will be happy.

The last story they liked the best of all because it had the most in it about Canada, and now they felt they knew at least a little bit, even if it was a very little bit, about his day-to-day life in his apartment; and Father said if he continues to write about such things he will become popular because I am sure they are interested there in reading about life through the eyes of an immigrant, it provides a different viewpoint; the only danger is if he changes and becomes so much like them that he will write like one of them and lose the important difference.

The bathroom needs cleaning. I open a new can of Ajax and scour the tub. Sloshing with mug from bucket was standard bathing procedure in the bathrooms of Firozsha Baag, so my preference now is always for a shower. I've never used the tub as yet; besides, it would be too much like Chaupatty or the swimming pool, wallowing in my own dirt. Still, it must be cleaned.

When I've finished, I prepare for a shower. But the clean gleaming tub and the nearness of the vernal equinox give me the urge to do something different today. I find the drain plug in the bathroom cabinet and run the bath.

I've spoken so often to the old man, but I don't know his name. I should have asked him the last time I saw him, when his wheelchair was facing the bare wall because he had seen all there was to see outside and it was time to see what was inside. Well, tomorrow. Or better yet, I can look it up in the directory in the lobby. Why didn't I think of that before? It will only have an initial and a last name, but then I can surprise him with: hullo Mr. Wilson, or whatever it is.

The bath is full. Water imagery is recurring in my life: Chaupatty beach, swimming pool, bathtub. I step in and immerse myself up to the neck. It feels good. The hot water loses its opacity when the chlorine, or whatever it is, has cleared. My hair is still dry. I close my eyes, hold my breath, and dunk my head. Fighting the panic, I stay under and count to thirty. I come out, clear my lungs and breathe deeply.

I do it again. This time I open my eyes under water, and stare blindly without seeing, it takes all my will to keep the lids from closing. Then I am slowly able to discern the underwater objects. The drain plug looks different, slightly distorted; there is a hair trapped between the hole and the plug, it waves and dances with the movement of the water. I come up, refresh my lungs, examine quickly the overwater world of the washroom, and go in again. I do it several times, over and over. The world outside the water I have seen a lot of, it is now time to see what is inside.

The spring session for adult non-swimmers will begin in a few days at the high school. I must not forget the registration date.

The dwindled days of winter are now all but forgotten; they have grown and attained a respectable span. I resume my evening walks, it's spring, and a vigorous thaw is on. The snowbanks are melting, the sound of water on its gushing, gurgling journey to the drains is beautiful. I plan to buy a book of trees, so I can identify more than the maple as they begin to bloom.

When I return to the building, I wipe my feet energetically on the mat because some people are entering behind me, and I want to set a good example. Then I go to the board with its little plastic letters and numbers. The old man's apartment is the one on the corner by the stairway, that makes it number 201. I run down the list, come to 201, but there are no little white plastic letters beside it. Just the empty black rectangle with holes where the letters would be squeezed in. That's strange. Well, I can introduce myself to him, then ask his name.

However, the lobby is empty. I take the elevator, exit at the second floor, wait for the gutang-khutang. It does not come: the door closes noiselessly, smoothly. Berthe has been at work, or has made sure someone else has. PW's cue has been lubricated out of existence.

But she must have the ears of a cockroach. She is waiting for me. I whistle my way down the corridor. She fixes me with an accusing look. She waits till I stop whistling, then says: "You know the old man died last night."

I cease groping for my key. She turns to go and I take a step towards her, my hand still in my trouser pocket. "Did you know his name?" I ask, but she leaves without answering.

Then Mother said, the part I like best in the last story is about Grandpa, where he wonders if Grandpa's spirit is really watching him and blessing him, because you know I really told him that, I told him helping an old suffering person who is near death is the most blessed thing to do, because that person will ever after watch over you from heaven, I told him this when he was disgusted with Grandpa's urine-bottle and would not touch it, would not hand it to him even when I was not at home.

Are you sure, said Father, that you really told him this, or you believe you told him because you like the sound of it, you said yourself the other day that he changes and adds and alters things in the stories but he writes it all so beautifully that it seems true, so how can you be sure; this sounds like another theory, said Mother, but I don't care, he says I told him and I believe now I told him, so even if I did not tell him then it does not matter now.

Don't you see, said Father, that you are confusing fiction with facts, fiction does not create facts, fiction can come from facts, it can grow out of facts by compounding, transposing, augmenting, diminishing, or altering them in any way; but you must not confuse cause and effect, you must not confuse what really happened with what the story says happened, you must not loose your grasp on reality, that way madness lies.

Then Mother stopped listening because, as she told Father so often, she was not very fond of theories, and she took out her writing pad and started a letter to her son; Father looked over her shoulder telling her to say how proud they were of him and were waiting for his next book, he also said, leave a little space for me at the end, I want to write a few lines when I put the address on the envelope.

—1987

SANDRA CISNEROS

Born in 1954 as the only daughter in a family of seven children living in the Puerto Rican district of Chicago, Sandra Cisneros is part of an important wave of Chicana writers in the United States. Along with writers such as Gloria Anzaldúa, Ana Castillo, and Denise Chavez, she first attracted attention in the 1980s with work that explores the complexities of race and gender from a specifically Chicana perspective. Cisneros is a novelist, poet, and children's writer, as well as an author of short fiction. Her first book of interconnected short stories, *The House on Mango Street* (1984), won the Before Columbus Foundation's Book Award. Her other accolades include a Lannan Foundation Literary Award, an American Book Award, and fellowships from the National Endowment for the Arts and the MacArthur Foundation.

Cisneros graduated with a BA from Loyola University in 1976 and an MFA in Creative Writing from the Iowa Writers' Workshop in 1978. She says, "My consciousness of growing up, the consciousness of myself, the subjects that I write about, the voice that I write in—I suppose all of that began in Iowa in a seminar class.... I ceased to be ashamed because I realized that I knew something that they [the other students] could never learn at universities. It was all of a sudden that I realized something that I know that I was the authority on."

Drawing on her experience as a working-class Chicana and the inspiration she had found at Iowa, Cisneros wrote the pieces that would make up her first book, *The House on Mango Street*. Following her graduate work, she worked at a variety of jobs, including teacher to adult high-school students, poet-in-the-schools, college recruiter, and arts administrator. She has taught creative writing at the University of California at Berkeley, the University of California at Irvine, and the University of Michigan in Ann Arbor. She makes her home in the Southwestern United States.

Cisneros, born to a Spanish-speaking, Mexican father and an English-speaking, Mexican-American mother, has described herself as feeling "like this woman caught in mid-air with my own identity." Her first-hand experience with the interplay between cultures and languages manifests itself in her writing's poetic sensibility and her attention to language as a medium for play and message. Indeed, she regularly includes untranslated Spanish words in her English writing, because, as she observes, "incorporating the Spanish ... allows me to create new expressions in English—to say things in English that have never been said before."

My Lucy Friend Who Smells Like Corn

LUCY ANGUIANO, Texas girl who smells like corn, like Frito Bandito chips, like tortillas, something like that warm smell of *nixtamal*[1] or bread the way her head smells when she's leaning close to you over a paper cut-out doll or on the porch when we are squatting over marbles trading this pretty crystal that leaves a blue star on your hand for that giant cat-eye with a grasshopper green spiral in the center like the juice of bugs on the windshield when you drive to the border, like the yellow blood of butterflies.

Have you ever eaten dog food? I have. After crunching like ice, she opens her big mouth to prove it, only a pink tongue rolling around in there like a blind worm, and Janey looking in because she said Show me. But me I like that Lucy corn smell hair and aqua flipflops just like mine that we bought at the Kmart for only 79 cents same time.

I'm going to sit in the sun, don't care if it's a million trillion degrees outside, so my skin can get so dark it's blue where it bends like Lucy's. Her whole family like that. Eyes like knife slits. Lucy and her sisters. Norma, Margarita, Ofelia, Herminia, Nancy, Olivia, Cheli, *y la* Amber Sue.

Screen door with no screen. *Bang!* Little black dog biting his fur. Fat couch on the porch. Some of the windows painted blue, some pink, because her daddy got tired that day or forgot. Mama in the kitchen feeding clothes into the wringer washer and clothes rolling out all stiff and twisted and flat like paper. Lucy got her arm stuck once and had to yell Maaa! and her mama had to put the machine in reverse and then her hand rolled back, the finger black and later, her nail fell off. *But did your arm get flat like the clothes? What happened to your arm? Did they have to pump it with air?* No, only the finger, and she didn't cry neither.

Lean across the porch rail and pin the pink sock of the baby Amber Sue on top of Cheli's flowered T-shirt, and the blue jeans of *la* Ofelia over the inside seam of Olivia's blouse, over the flannel nightgown of Margarita so it don't

---

1   Ground corn mixture used to make tortillas.

stretch out, and then you take the work shirts of their daddy and hang them upside down like this, and this way all the clothes don't get so wrinkled and take up less space and you don't waste pins. The girls all wear each other's clothes, except Olivia, who is stingy. There ain't no boys here. Only girls and one father who is never home hardly and one mother who says *Ay! I'm real tired* and so many sisters there's no time to count them.

I'm sitting in the sun even though it's the hottest part of the day, the part that makes the streets dizzy, when the heat makes a little hat on the top of your head and bakes the dust and weed grass and sweat up good, all steamy and smelling like sweet corn.

I want to rub heads and sleep in a bed with little sisters, some at the top and some at the feets. I think it would be fun to sleep with sisters you could yell at one at a time or all together, instead of alone on the fold-out chair in the living room.

When I get home Abuelita[2] will say *Didn't I tell you?* and I'll get it because I was supposed to wear this dress again tomorrow. But first I'm going to jump off an old pissy mattress in the Anguiano yard. I'm going to scratch your mosquito bites, Lucy, so they'll itch you, then put Mercurochrome[3] smiley faces on them. We're going to trade shoes and wear them on our hands. We're going to walk over to Janey Ortiz's house and say *We're never ever going to be your friend again forever!* We're going to run home backwards and we're going to run home frontwards, look twice under the house where the rats hide and I'll stick one foot in there because you dared me, sky so blue and heaven inside those white clouds. I'm going to peel a scab from my knee and eat it, sneeze on the cat, give you three M & M's I've been saving for you since yesterday, comb your hair with my fingers and braid it into teeny-tiny braids real pretty. We're going to wave to a lady we don't know on the bus. Hello! I'm going to somersault on the rail of the front porch even though my *chones*[4] show. And cut paper dolls we draw ourselves, and color in their clothes with crayons, my arm around your neck.

And when we look at each other, our arms gummy from an orange Popsicle we split, we could be sisters, right? We could be, you and me waiting for our teeths to fall and money. You laughing something into my ear that tickles, and me going Ha Ha Ha Ha. Her and me, my Lucy friend who smells like corn.

—1991

---

2   A Spanish endearment for grandmother; literally, "little grandmother."
3   Antiseptic solution.
4   Underwear.

LORRIE MOORE

Novelist, critic, and short-fiction writer Marie Lorena Moore was born in 1957 in Glens Falls, New York, to an insurance executive and an ex-nurse turned homemaker. She attended St. Lawrence University, and, while still an undergraduate, won a short story contest in *Seventeen* magazine at the age of 19. Upon graduation, Moore worked as a paralegal for two years, and in 1980 she enrolled in Cornell's MFA program. As a graduate student, she published her work in magazines such as *Ms*, *Fiction International*, and *StoryQuarterly*. Her first collection of short stories, *Self-Help*, was released in 1985; it is primarily made up of the funny, caustic stories she wrote during her MFA. Moore's brand of humour is apparent in the opening line of the story "How to Become a Writer": "First, try to be something, anything, else."

Moore's first novel, *Anagrams*, was published in 1986 and was followed by the short story collection *Like Life* (1990) and the novel *Who Will Run the Frog Hospital?* (1994). These were well-received, and her stature as a major writer was firmly established with her next short story collection, *Birds of America* (1998), a bestseller that was named one of the year's best books by *The New York Times Book Review* and awarded the Irish Times International Fiction Prize. Moore's *Collected Stories* was published in 2008, and her 2009 novel, *A Gate at the Stairs*, was a finalist for the Pen/Faulkner award for fiction. Her next collection, *Bark* (2014), was praised in the *Guardian* as a continuation of Moore's signature style: "Offbeat and oblique, Moore has made a trademark of looking sidelong at contemporary behaviour in middle-class middle America; of sometimes witty and sometimes dreadful puns; of snippets of conversation that have the sense of 'found' art."

Moore spent two years as a lecturer at Cornell and three decades teaching creative writing at the University of Wisconsin before moving to Vanderbilt University in 2013. Her work has appeared in many periodicals, including *The New Yorker*, *Harper's*, *Granta*, *The Paris Review*, and *Rolling Stone*; a collection of her reviews and other periodical essays, *See What Can Be Done*, appeared in 2018. She has written juvenile fiction (*The Forgotten Helper*, 1987) and edited the anthology *I Know Some Things: Stories about Childhood*

303

by *Contemporary Writers* (1992). In 2006, Moore was welcomed into the prestigious American Academy of Arts and Letters.

You're Ugly, Too

YOU HAD to get out of them occasionally, those Illinois towns with the funny names: Paris, Oblong, Normal. Once, when the Dow Jones dipped two hundred points, a local paper boasted the banner headline "NORMAL MAN MARRIES OBLONG WOMAN." They knew what was important. They did! But you had to get out once in a while, even if it was just across the border to Terre Haute for a movie.

Outside of Paris, in the middle of a large field, was a scatter of brick buildings, a small liberal-arts college by the improbable name of Hilldale-Versailles. Zoë Hendricks had been teaching American history there for three years. She taught "The Revolution and Beyond" to freshmen and sophomores, and every third semester she had the senior seminar for majors, and although her student evaluations had been slipping in the last year and a half—*Professor Hendricks is often late for class and usually arrives with a cup of hot chocolate, which she offers the class sips of*—generally the department of nine men was pleased to have her. They felt she added some needed feminine touch to the corridors—that faint trace of Obsession and sweat, the light, fast clicking of heels. Plus they had had a sex-discrimination suit, and the dean had said, well, it was time.

The situation was not easy for her, they knew. Once, at the start of last semester, she had skipped into her lecture hall singing "Getting to Know You"—all of it. At the request of the dean, the chairman had called her into his office, but did not ask her for an explanation, not really. He asked her how she was and then smiled in an avuncular way. She said, "Fine," and he studied the way she said it, her front teeth catching on the inside of her lower lip. She was almost pretty, but her face showed the strain and ambition of always having been close but not quite. There was too much effort with the eyeliner, and her earrings, worn, no doubt, for the drama her features lacked, were a little frightening, jutting out the sides of her head like antennae.

"I'm going out of my mind," said Zoë to her younger sister, Evan, in Manhattan. *Professor Hendricks seems to know the entire soundtrack to "The King and I." Is this history?* Zoë phoned her every Tuesday.

"You always say that," said Evan, "but then you go on your trips and vacations and then you settle back into things and then you're quiet for a while and then you say you're fine, you're busy, and then after a while you say you're going crazy again, and you start all over." Evan was a part-time food designer for photo shoots. She cooked vegetables in green dye. She propped up beef stew with a bed of marbles and shopped for new kinds of silicone sprays and plastic ice cubes. She thought her life was O.K. She was living with her boyfriend of many years, who was independently wealthy and had an amusing little job in book publishing. They were five years out of college, and they lived in a luxury midtown high rise with a balcony and access to a pool. "It's not the same as having your own pool," Evan was always sighing, as if to let Zoë know that, as with Zoë, there were still things she, Evan, had to do without.

"Illinois. It makes me sarcastic to be here," said Zoë on the phone. She used to insist it was irony, something gently layered and sophisticated, something alien to the Midwest, but her students kept calling it sarcasm, something they felt qualified to recognize, and now she had to agree. It wasn't irony. "What is your perfume?" a student once asked her. "Room freshener," she said. She smiled, but he looked at her, unnerved.

Her students were by and large good Midwesterners, spacey with estrogen from large quantities of meat and eggs. They shared their parents' suburban values; their parents had given them things, things, things. They were complacent. They had been purchased. They were armed with a healthy vagueness about anything historical or geographic. They seemed actually to know very little about anything, but they were good-natured about it. "All those states in the East are so tiny and jagged and bunched up," complained one of her undergraduates the week she was lecturing on "The Turning Point of Independence: The Battle at Saratoga." "Professor Hendricks, you're from Delaware originally, right?" the student asked her.

"Maryland," corrected Zoë.

"Aw," he said, waving his hand dismissively. "New England."

Her articles—chapters toward a book called *Hearing the One About: Uses of Humor in the American Presidency*—were generally well received, though they came slowly for her. She liked her pieces to have something from every time of day in them—she didn't trust things written in the morning only—so she reread and rewrote painstakingly. No part of a day—its moods, its light—was allowed to dominate. She hung on to a piece for a year sometimes, revising at all hours, until the entirety of a day had registered there.

The job she'd had before the one at Hilldale-Versailles had been at a small college in New Geneva, Minnesota, Land of the Dying Shopping Mall. Everyone was so blond there that brunettes were often presumed to be from foreign countries. *Just because Professor Hendricks is from Spain doesn't give her the right to be so negative about our country.* There was a general emphasis on cheerfulness. In New Geneva you weren't supposed to be critical or complain. You weren't supposed to notice that the town had overextended and that its shopping malls were raggedy and going under. You were never to say you weren't "fine, thank you—and yourself?" You were supposed to be Heidi. You were supposed to lug goat milk up the hills and not think twice. Heidi did not complain. Heidi did not do things like stand in front of the new IBM photocopier saying, "If this fucking Xerox machine breaks on me one more time, I'm going to slit my wrists."

But now in her second job, in her fourth year of teaching in the Midwest, Zoë was discovering something she never suspected she had: a crusty edge, brittle and pointed. Once she had pampered her students, singing them songs, letting them call her at home even, and ask personal questions, but now she was losing sympathy. They were beginning to seem different. They were beginning to seem demanding and spoiled.

"You act," said one of her senior-seminar students at a scheduled conference, "like your opinion is worth more than everyone else's in the class."

Zoë's eyes widened. "I *am* the teacher," she said. "I do get paid to act like that." She narrowed her gaze at the student, who was wearing a big leather bow in her hair like a cowgirl in a TV ranch show. "I mean, otherwise *everybody* in the class would have little offices and office hours." *Sometimes Professor Hendricks will take up the class's time just talking about movies she's seen.* She stared at the student some more, then added, "I bet you'd like that."

"Maybe I sound whiny to you," said the girl, "but I simply want my history major to mean something."

"Well, there's your problem," said Zoë, and, with a smile, she showed the student to the door. "I like your bow," she said.

Zoë lived for the mail, for the postman—that handsome blue jay—and when she got a real letter with a real full-price stamp from someplace else, she took it to bed with her and read it over and over. She also watched television until all hours and had her set in the bedroom—a bad sign. *Professor Hendricks has said critical things about Fawn Hall, the Catholic religion, and the whole state of Illinois. It is unbelievable.* At Christmastime she gave twenty-dollar tips to the mailman and to Jerry, the only cabbie in town, whom she had gotten to know from all her rides to and from the Terre Haute airport, and who, since he realized such rides were an extravagance, often gave her cut rates.

"I'm flying in to visit you this weekend," announced Zoë.

"I was hoping you would," said Evan. "Charlie and I are having a party for Halloween. It'll be fun."

"I have a costume already. It's a bonehead. It's this thing that looks like a giant bone going through your head."

"Great," said Evan.

"It is, it's great."

"All I have is my moon mask from last year and the year before. I'll probably end up getting married in it."

"Are you and Charlie getting *married*?" Zoë felt slightly alarmed.

"Hmmmmmmmnnno, not immediately."

"Don't get married."

"Why?"

"Just not yet. You're too young."

"You're only saying that because you're five years older than I am and *you're* not married."

"*I'm* not married? Oh, my God," said Zoë, "I forgot to get married."

Zoë had been out with three men since she'd come to Hilldale-Versailles. One of them was a man in the municipal bureaucracy who had fixed a parking ticket she'd brought in to protest and then asked her out for coffee. At first, she thought he was amazing—at last, someone who did not want Heidi! But soon she came to realize that all men, deep down, wanted Heidi. Heidi with cleavage. Heidi with outfits. The parking-ticket bureaucrat soon became tired and intermittent. One cool fall day, in his snazzy, impractical convertible, when she asked him what was wrong he said, "You would not be ill served by new clothes, you know." She wore a lot of gray-green corduroy. She had been under the impression that it brought out her eyes, those shy stars. She flicked an ant from her sleeve.

"Did you have to brush that off in the car?" he said, driving. He glanced down at his own pectorals, giving first the left, then the right, a quick survey. He was wearing a tight shirt.

"Excuse me?"

He slowed down at an amber light and frowned. "Couldn't you have picked it up and thrown it outside?"

"The ant? It might have bitten me. I mean, what difference does it make?"

"It might have bitten you! Ha! How ridiculous! Now it's going to lay eggs in my car!"

The second guy was sweeter, lunkier, though not insensitive to certain paintings and songs, but too often, too, things he'd do or say would startle her. Once, in a restaurant, he stole the garnishes off her dinner plate and waited for her to notice. When she didn't, he finally thrust his fist across the table and said, "Look," and when he opened it, there was her parsley sprig and her orange slice crumpled to a wad. Another time, he described to her his recent trip to the Louvre. "And there I was in front of Delacroix's *The Barque of Dante*, and everyone else had wandered off, so I had my own private audience with it, all those agonized shades splayed in every direction, and there's this motion in that painting that starts at the bottom, swirling and building up into the red fabric of Dante's hood, swirling out into the distance, where you see these orange flames—" He was breathless in the telling. She found this touching, and smiled in encouragement. "A painting like that," he said, shaking his head. "It just makes you shit."

"I have to ask you something," said Evan. "I know every woman complains about not meeting men, but really, on my shoots I meet a lot of men. And they're not at all gay, either." She paused. "Not anymore."

"What are you asking?"

The third guy was a political-science professor named Murray Peterson, who liked to go out on double dates with colleagues whose wives he was attracted to. Usually, the wives would consent to flirt with him. Under the table sometimes there was footsie, and once there was even kneesie. Zoë and the husband would be left to their food, staring into their water glasses, chewing like goats. "Oh, Murray," said one wife, who had never finished her master's in physical therapy and wore great clothes. "You know, I know everything about you: your birthday, your license-plate number. I have everything memorized. But then that's the kind of mind I have. Once, at a dinner party, I amazed the host by getting up and saying goodbye to every single person there, first *and* last names."

"I knew a dog who could do that," said Zoë with her mouth full. Murray and the wife looked at her with vexed and rebuking expressions, but the husband seemed suddenly twinkling and amused. Zoë swallowed. "It was a talking Lab, and after about ten minutes of listening to the dinner conversation this dog knew everyone's name. You could say, 'Take this knife to Murray Peterson,' and it would."

"Really," said the wife, frowning, and Murray Peterson never called again.

"Are you seeing anyone?" said Evan. "I'm asking for a particular reason. I'm not just being like Mom."

"I'm seeing my house. I'm tending to it when it wets, when it cries, when it throws up." Zoë had bought a mint-green ranch house near campus, though now she was thinking that maybe she shouldn't have. It was hard to live in a house. She kept wandering in and out of the rooms, wondering where she had put things. She went downstairs into the basement for no reason at all except that it amused her to own a basement. It also amused her to own a tree.

Her parents, in Maryland, had been very pleased that one of their children had at last been able to afford real estate, and when she closed on the house they sent her flowers with a congratulations card. Her mother had even UPS'd a box of old decorating magazines saved over the years—photographs of beautiful rooms her mother used to moon over, since there never had been any money to redecorate. It was like getting her mother's pornography, that box, inheriting her drooled-upon fantasies, the endless wish and tease that had been her life. But to her mother it was a rite of passage that pleased her. "Maybe you will get some ideas from these," she had written. And when Zoë looked at the photographs, at the bold and beautiful living rooms, she was filled with longing. Ideas and ideas of longing.

Right now Zoë's house was rather empty. The previous owner had wallpapered around the furniture, leaving strange gaps and silhouettes on the walls, and Zoë hadn't done much about that yet. She had bought furniture, then taken it back, furnishing and unfurnishing, preparing and shedding, like a womb. She had bought several plain pine chests to use as love seats or boot boxes, but they came to look to her more and more like children's coffins, so she returned them. And she had recently bought an Oriental rug for the living room, with Chinese symbols on it she didn't understand. The salesgirl had kept saying she was sure they meant "Peace" and "Eternal Life," but when Zoë got the rug home she worried. What if they didn't mean "Peace" and "Eternal Life"? What if they meant, say, "Bruce Springsteen"? And the more she thought about it, the more she became convinced she had a rug that said "Bruce Springsteen," and so she returned that, too.

She had also bought a little baroque mirror for the front entryway, which, she had been told by Murray Peterson, would keep away evil spirits. The mirror, however, tended to frighten *her*, startling her with an image of a woman she never recognized. Sometimes she looked puffier and plainer than she remembered. Sometimes shifty and dark. Most times she just looked vague. "You look like someone I know," she had been told twice in the last year by strangers in restaurants in Terre Haute. In fact, sometimes she seemed not to have a look of her own, or any look whatsoever, and it began to amuse her that her students and colleagues were able to recognize her at all. How did they know? When she walked into a room, how did she look so that they knew it was she? Like this? Did she look like this? And so she returned the mirror.

"The reason I'm asking is that I know a man I think you should meet," said Evan. "He's fun. He's straight. He's single. That's all I'm going to say."

"I think I'm too old for fun," said Zoë. She had a dark bristly hair in her chin, and she could feel it now with her finger. Perhaps when you had been without the opposite sex for too long, you began to resemble them. In an act of desperate invention, you began to grow your own. "I just want to come, wear my bonehead, visit with Charlie's tropical fish, ask you about your food shoots."

She thought about all the papers on "Our Constitution: How It Affects Us" she was going to have to correct. She thought about how she was going in for ultrasound tests on Friday because, according to her doctor and her doctor's assistant, she had a large, mysterious growth in her abdomen. Gallbladder, they kept saying. Or ovaries or colon. "You guys practice medicine?" asked Zoë, aloud, after they had left the room. Once, as a girl, she brought her dog to a vet, who had told her, "Well, either your dog has worms or cancer or else it was hit by a car."

She was looking forward to New York.

"Well, whatever. We'll just play it cool. I can't wait to see you, hon. Don't forget your bonehead," said Evan.

"A bonehead you don't forget," said Zoë.

"I suppose," said Evan.

The ultrasound Zoë was keeping a secret, even from Evan. "I feel like I'm dying," Zoë had hinted just once on the phone.

"You're not dying," said Evan, "you're just annoyed."

"Ultrasound," Zoë now said jokingly to the technician who put the cold jelly on her bare stomach. "Does that sound like a really great stereo system or what?"

She had not had anyone make this much fuss over her bare stomach since her boyfriend in graduate school, who had hovered over her whenever she felt ill, waved his arms, pressed his hands upon her navel, and drawled evangelically, "Heal! Heal for thy Baby Jesus' sake!" Zoë would laugh and they would make love, both secretly hoping she would get pregnant. Later they would worry together, and he would sink a cheek to her belly and ask whether she was late, was she late, was she sure, she might be late, and when after two years she had not gotten pregnant they took to quarreling and drifted apart.

"O.K.," said the technician absently.

The monitor was in place, and Zoë's insides came on the screen in all their gray and ribbony hollowness. They were marbled in the finest gradations of black and white, like stone in an old church or a picture of the moon. "Do you suppose," she babbled at the technician, "that the rise in infertility among so many couples in this country is due to completely different species trying to reproduce?" The technician moved the scanner around and took more pictures. On one view in particular, on Zoë's right side, the technician became suddenly alert, the machine he was operating clicking away.

Zoë stared at the screen. "That must be the growth you found there," suggested Zoë.

"I can't tell you anything," said the technician rigidly. "Your doctor will get the radiologist's report this afternoon and will phone you then."

"I'll be out of town," said Zoë.

"I'm sorry," said the technician.

Driving home, Zoë looked in the rearview mirror and decided she looked—well, how would one describe it? A little wan. She thought of the joke about the guy who visits his doctor and the doctor says, "Well, I'm sorry to say you've got six weeks to live."

"I want a second opinion," says the guy. *You act like your opinion is worth more than everyone else's in the class.*

"You want a second opinion? O.K.," says the doctor. "You're ugly, too." She liked that joke. She thought it was terribly, terribly funny.

She took a cab to the airport. Jerry the cabbie was happy to see her.

"Have fun in New York," he said, getting her bag out of the trunk. He liked her, or at least he always acted as if he did. She called him Jare.

"Thanks, Jare."

"You know, I'll tell you a secret: I've never been to New York. I'll tell you two secrets: I've never been on a plane." And he waved at her sadly as she pushed her way in through the terminal door. "Or an escalator!" he shouted.

The trick to flying safely, Zoë always said, was to never buy a discount ticket and to tell yourself you had nothing to live for anyway, so that when the plane crashed it was no big deal. Then, when it didn't crash, when you succeeded in keeping it aloft with your own worthlessness, all you had to do was stagger off, locate your luggage, and, by the time a cab arrived, come up with a persuasive reason to go on living.

"You're here!" shrieked Evan over the doorbell, before she even opened the door. Then she opened it wide. Zoë set her bags on the hall floor and hugged Evan hard. When she was little, Evan had always been affectionate and devoted. Zoë had always taken care of her—advising, reassuring—until recently, when it seemed Evan had started advising and reassuring *her*. It startled Zoë. She suspected it had something to do with her being alone. It made people uncomfortable.

"How *are* you?"

"I threw up on the plane. Besides that, I'm O.K."

"Can I get you something? Here, let me take your suitcase. Sick on the plane. *Eeeyew.*"

"It was into one of those sickness bags," said Zoë, just in case Evan thought she'd lost it in the aisle. "I was very quiet."

The apartment was spacious and bright, with a view all the way downtown along the East Side. There was a balcony and sliding glass doors. "I keep forgetting how nice this apartment is. Twenty-first floor, doorman ..." Zoë could work her whole life and never have an apartment like this. So could Evan. It was Charlie's apartment. He and Evan lived in it like two kids in a dorm, beer cans and clothes strewn around. Evan put Zoë's bag away from the mess, over the fish tanks. "I'm so glad you're here," she said. "Now what can I get you?"

Evan made them lunch—soup from a can and saltines.

"I don't know about Charlie," she said after they had finished. "I feel like we've gone all sexless and middle-aged already."

"Hmmmm," said Zoë. She leaned back into Evan's sofa and stared out the window at the dark tops of the buildings. It seemed a little unnatural to live up in the sky like this, like birds that out of some wrong-headed derring-do had nested too high. She nodded toward the lighted fish tanks and giggled. "I feel like a bird," she said, "with my own personal supply of fish."

Evan sighed. "He comes home and just sacks out on the sofa, watching fuzzy football. He's wearing the psychic cold cream and curlers, if you know what I mean."

Zoë sat up, readjusted the sofa cushions. "What's fuzzy football?"

"We haven't gotten cable yet. Everything comes in fuzzy. Charlie just watches it that way."

"Hmm, yeah, that's a little depressing," Zoë said. She looked at her hands.

"Especially the part about not having cable."

"This is how he gets into bed at night." Evan stood up to demonstrate. "He whips all his clothes off, and when he gets to his underwear he lets it drop to one ankle. Then he kicks up his leg and flips the underwear in the air and catches it. I, of course, watch from the bed. There's nothing else. There's just that."

"Maybe you should just get it over with and get married."

"Really?"

"Yeah. I mean, you guys probably think living together like this is the best of both worlds, but—" Zoë tried to sound like an older sister; an older sister was supposed to be the parent you could never have, the hip, cool mom. "But I've always found that as soon as you think you've got the best of both worlds"—she thought now of herself, alone in her house, of the toad-faced cicadas that flew around like little men at night and landed on her screens, staring; of the size fourteen shoes she placed at the doorstep, to scare off intruders; of the ridiculous, inflatable blowup doll someone had told her to keep propped up at the breakfast table—"it can suddenly twist and become the worst of both worlds."

"Really?" Evan was beaming. "Oh, Zoë. I have something to tell you. Charlie and I *are* getting married."

"Really." Zoë felt confused.

"I didn't know how to tell you."

"Yeah, I guess the part about fuzzy football misled me a little."

"I was hoping you'd be my maid of honor," said Evan, waiting. "Aren't you happy for me?"

"Yes," said Zoë, and she began to tell Evan a story about an award-winning violinist at Hilldale-Versailles—how the violinist had come home from a competition in Europe and taken up with a local man who made her go to all his summer softball games, made her cheer for him from the stands, with the wives, until she later killed herself. But when Zoë got halfway through, to the part about cheering at the softball games, she stopped.

"What?" said Evan. "So what happened?"

"Actually, nothing," said Zoë lightly. "She just really got into softball. You should have seen her."

Zoë decided to go to a late afternoon movie, leaving Evan to chores she needed to do before the party—"I have to do them alone, really," she'd said, a little tense after the violinist story. Zoë thought about going to an art museum, but women alone in art museums had to look good. They always did. Chic and serious, moving languidly, with a great handbag. Instead, she walked down through Kips Bay, past an earring boutique called Stick It in Your Ear, past a hair salon called Dorian Gray. That was the funny thing about "beauty," thought Zoë. Look it up in the yellow pages and you found a hundred entries, hostile with wit, cutesy with warning. But look up "truth"—Ha! There was nothing at all.

Zoë thought about Evan getting married. Would Evan turn into Peter Pumpkin Eater's wife? Mrs. Eater? At the wedding, would she make Zoë wear some flouncy lavender dress, identical with the other maids'? Zoë hated uniforms, had even in the first grade refused to join Elf Girls because she didn't want to wear the same dress as everyone else. Now she might have to. But maybe she could distinguish it. Hitch it up on one side with a clothespin. Wear surgical gauze at the waist. Clip to her bodice one of those pins that say in loud letters "Shit Happens."

At the movie—*Death by Number*—she bought strands of red licorice to tug and chew. She took a seat off to one side in the theater. She felt strangely self-conscious sitting alone, and hoped for the place to darken fast. When it did, and the coming attractions came on, she reached inside her purse for her glasses. They were in a Baggie. Her Kleenex was also in a Baggie. So were her pen and her aspirin and her mints. Everything was in Baggies. This was what she'd become: *a woman alone at the movies with everything in a Baggie.*

At the Halloween party, there were about two dozen people. There were people with ape heads and large hairy hands. There was someone dressed as a leprechaun. There was someone dressed as a frozen dinner. Some man had brought his two small daughters: a ballerina and a ballerina's sister, also dressed as a ballerina. There was a gaggle of sexy witches—women dressed entirely in black, beautifully made up and jeweled. "I hate those sexy witches. It's not in the spirit of Halloween," said Evan. Evan had abandoned the moon mask and dolled herself up as hausfrau, in curlers and an apron, a decision she now regretted. Charlie, because he liked fish, because he owned fish and collected fish, had decided to go as a fish. He had fins, and eyes on the sides of his head. "Zoë! How are you! I'm sorry I wasn't here when you first arrived!" He spent the rest of his time chatting up the sexy witches.

"Isn't there something I can help you with here?" Zoë asked her sister. "You've been running yourself ragged." She rubbed her sister's arm, gently, as if she wished they were alone.

"Oh, God, not at all," said Evan, arranging stuffed mushrooms on a plate. The timer went off, and she pulled another sheetful out of the oven. "Actually, you know what you can do?"

"What?" Zoë put on her bonehead.

"Meet Earl. He's the guy I had in mind for you. When he gets here, just talk to him a little. He's nice. He's fun. He's going through a divorce."

"I'll try," Zoë groaned. "O.K.? I'll try." She looked at her watch.

When Earl arrived, he was dressed as a naked woman, steel wool glued strategically to a body stocking, and large rubber breasts protruding like hams.

"Zoë, this is Earl," said Evan.

"Good to meet you," said Earl, circling Evan to shake Zoë's hand. He stared at the top of Zoë's head. "Great bone."

Zoë nodded. "Great tits," she said. She looked past him, out the window at the city thrown glittering up against the sky; people were saying the usual things: how it looked like jewels, like bracelets and necklaces unstrung. You could see the clock of the Con Ed building, the orange-and-gold-capped Empire State, the Chrysler like a rocket ship dreamed up in a depression. Far west you could glimpse Astor Plaza, with its flying white roof like a nun's habit. "There's beer out on the balcony, Earl. Can I get you one?" Zoë asked.

"Sure, uh, I'll come along. Hey, Charlie, how's it going?"

Charlie grinned and whistled. People turned to look. "Hey, Earl," someone called from across the room. "Va-va-va-voom."

They squeezed their way past the other guests, past the apes and the sexy witches. The suction of the sliding door gave way in a whoosh, and Zoë and Earl stepped out onto the balcony, a bonehead and a naked woman, the night air roaring and smoky cool. Another couple were out there, too, murmuring privately. They were not wearing costumes. They smiled at Zoë and Earl. "Hi," said Zoë. She found the plastic-foam cooler, dug in and retrieved two beers.

"Thanks," said Earl. His rubber breasts folded inward, dimpled and dented, as he twisted open the bottle.

"Well," sighed Zoë anxiously. She had to learn not to be afraid of a man, the way, in your childhood, you learned not to be afraid of an earthworm or a bug. Often, when she spoke to men at parties, she rushed things in her mind. As the man politely blathered on, she would fall in love, marry, then find herself in a bitter custody battle with him for the kids and hoping for a reconciliation, so that despite all his betrayals she might no longer despise him, and, in the few minutes remaining, learn, perhaps, what his last name was and what he did for a living, though probably there was already too much history between them. She would nod, blush, turn away.

"Evan tells me you're a history professor. Where do you teach?"

"Just over the Indiana border into Illinois."

He looked a little shocked. "I guess Evan didn't tell me that part."

"She didn't?"

"No."

"Well, that's Evan for you. When we were kids we both had speech impediments."

"That can be tough," said Earl. One of his breasts was hidden behind his drinking arm, but the other shone low and pink, full as a strawberry moon.

"Yes, well, it wasn't a total loss. We used to go to what we called peach peara-py. For about ten years of my life, I had to map out every sentence in my mind, way ahead, before I said it. That was the only way I could get a coherent sentence out."

Earl drank from his beer. "How did you do that? I mean, how did you get through?"

"I told a lot of jokes. Jokes you know the lines to already. You can just say them. I love jokes. Jokes and songs."

Earl smiled. He had on lipstick, a deep shade of red, but it was wearing off from the beer. "What's your favorite joke?"

"Uh, my favorite joke is probably—O.K., all right. This guy goes into a doctor's office, and—"

"I think I know this one," interrupted Earl eagerly. He wanted to tell it himself. "A guy goes into a doctor's office, and the doctor tells him he's got some good news and some bad news—that one, right?"

"I'm not sure," said Zoë. "This might be a different version."

"So the guy says, 'Give me the bad news first,' and the doctor says, 'O.K. You've got three weeks to live.' And the guy cries, 'Three weeks to live! Doctor, what is the good news?' And the doctor says, 'Did you see that secretary out front? I finally fucked her.'"

Zoë frowned.

"That's not the one you were thinking of?"

"No." There was accusation in her voice. "Mine was different."

"Oh," said Earl. He looked away and then back again. "What kind of history do you teach?"

"I teach American, mostly—eighteenth- and nineteenth-century." In graduate school, at bars the pickup line was always, "So what's your century?"

"Occasionally, I teach a special theme course," she added. "Say, 'Humor and Personality in the White House.' That's what my book's on." She thought of something someone once told her about bowerbirds, how they build elaborate structures before mating.

"Your book's on *humor*?"

"Yeah, and, well, when I teach a theme course like that I do all the centuries." *So what's your century?*

"All three of them."

"Pardon?" The breeze glistened her eyes. Traffic revved beneath them. She felt high and puny, like someone lifted into heaven by mistake and then spurned.

"Three. There's only three."

"Well, four, really." She was thinking of Jamestown, and of the Pilgrims coming here with buckles and witch hats to say their prayers.

"I'm a photographer," said Earl. His face was starting to gleam, his rouge smearing in a sunset beneath his eyes.

"Do you like that?"

"Well, actually, I'm starting to feel it's a little dangerous."

"Really?"

"Spending all your time is a dark room with that red light and all those chemicals. There's links with Parkinson's, you know."

"No, I didn't."

"I suppose I should wear rubber gloves, but I don't like to. Unless I'm touching it directly, I don't think of it as real."

"Hmmm," said Zoë. Alarm buzzed mildly through her.

"Sometimes, when I have a cut or something, I feel the sting and think, *Shit*. I wash constantly and just hope. I don't like rubber over the skin like that."

"Really."

"I mean, the physical contact. That's what you want, or why bother?"

"I guess," said Zoë. She wished she could think of a joke, something slow and deliberate with the end in sight. She thought of gorillas, how when they had been kept too long alone in cages they would smack each other in the head instead of mating.

"Are you—in a relationship?" Earl suddenly blurted.

"Now? As we speak?"

"Well, I mean, I'm sure you have a relationship to your *work*." A smile, a little one, nestled in his mouth like an egg. She thought of zoos in parks, how when cities were under siege, during world wars, people ate the animals. "But I mean, with a *man*."

"No, I'm not in a relationship with a *man*." She rubbed her chin with her hand and could feel the one bristly hair there. "But my last relationship was with a very sweet man," she said. She made something up. "From Switzerland. He was a botanist—a weed expert. His name was Jerry. I called him Jare. He was so funny. You'd go to the movies with him and all he would notice was the plants. He would never pay attention to the plot. Once, in a jungle movie, he started rattling off all these Latin names, out loud. It was very exciting for him." She paused, caught her breath. "Eventually, he went back to Europe to, uh, study the edelweiss." She looked at Earl. "Are you involved in a relationship? With a *woman*?"

Earl shifted his weight and the creases in his body stocking changed, splintering outward like something broken. His pubic hair slid over to one hip, like a corsage on a saloon girl. "No," he said, clearing his throat. The steel wool in his underarms was inching down toward his biceps. "I've just gotten out of a marriage that was full of bad dialogue like 'You want more *space*? I'll give you more space!' *Clonk*. Your basic Three Stooges."

Zoë looked at him sympathetically. "I suppose it's hard for love to recover after that."

His eyes lit up. He wanted to talk about love. "But I keep thinking love should be like a tree. You look at trees and they've got bumps and scars from tumors, infestations, what have you, but they're still growing. Despite the bumps and bruises, they're—straight."

"Yeah, well," said Zoë, "where I'm from they're all married or gay. Did you see that movie *Death by Number*?"

Earl looked at her, a little lost. She was getting away from him. "No," he said. One of his breasts had slipped under his arm, tucked there like a baguette. She kept thinking of trees, of parks, of people in wartime eating the zebras. She felt a stabbing pain in her abdomen.

"Want some hors d'oeuvres?" Evan came pushing through the sliding door. She was smiling, though her curlers were coming out, hanging bedraggled at the ends of her hair like Christmas decorations, like food put out for the birds. She thrust forward a plate of stuffed mushrooms.

"Are you asking for donations or giving them away?" said Earl wittily. He liked Evan, and he put his arm around her.

"You know, I'll be right back," said Zoë.

"Oh," said Evan, looking concerned.

"Right back. I promise."

Zoë hurried inside, across the living room into the bedroom, to the adjoining bath. It was empty; most of the guests were using the half-bath near the kitchen. She flicked on the light and closed the door. The pain had stopped, and she didn't really have to go to the bathroom, but she stayed there anyway, resting. In the mirror above the sink, she looked haggard beneath her bonehead, violet-grays showing under the skin like a plucked and pocky bird's. She leaned closer, raising her chin a little to find the bristly hair. It was there, at the end of the jaw, sharp and dark as a wire. She opened the medicine cabinet, pawed through it until she found some tweezers. She lifted her head again and poked at her face with the metal tips, grasping and pinching and missing. Outside the door, she could hear two people talking low. They had come into the bedroom and were discussing something. They were sitting on the bed. One of them giggled in a false way. Zoë stabbed again at her chin, and it started to bleed a little. She pulled the skin tight along the jawbone, gripped the tweezers hard around what she hoped was the hair, and tugged. A tiny square of skin came away but the hair remained, blood bright at the root of it. Zoë clenched her teeth. "Come on," she whispered. The couple outside in the bedroom were now telling stories, softly and laughing. There was a bounce and squeak of mattress, and the sound of a chair being moved out of the way. Zoë aimed the tweezers carefully, pinched, then pulled gently, and this time the hair came, too, with a slight twinge of pain, and then a great flood of relief. "Yeah!" breathed Zoë. She grabbed some toilet paper and dabbed at her chin. It came away spotted with blood, and so she tore off some more and pressed hard until it stopped. Then she turned off the light, opened the door, and rejoined the party. "Excuse me," she said to the couple in the bedroom. They were the couple from the balcony, and they looked at her, a bit surprised. They had their arms around each other, and they were eating candy bars.

Earl was still out on the balcony, alone, and Zoë rejoined him there. "Hi," she said.

He turned around and smiled. He had straightened his costume out a bit, though all the secondary sex characteristics seemed slightly doomed, destined to shift and flip and zip around again any moment. "Are you O.K.?" he asked. He had opened another beer and was chugging.

"Oh, yeah. I just had to go to the bathroom." She paused. "Actually, I have been going to a lot of doctors recently."

"What's wrong?" asked Earl.

"Oh, probably nothing. But they're putting me through tests." She sighed. "I've had sonograms. I've had mammograms. Next week I'm going in for a candygram." He looked at her, concerned. "I've had too many gram words," she said.

"Here, I saved you these." He held out a napkin with two stuffed mushroom caps. They were cold and leaving oil marks on the napkin.

"Thanks," said Zoë, and pushed them both in her mouth. "Watch," she said with her mouth full. "With my luck it'll be a gallbladder operation."

Earl made a face. "So your sister's getting married," he said, changing the subject. "Tell me, really, what you think about love."

"*Love?*" Hadn't they done this already? "I don't know." She chewed thoughtfully and swallowed. "All right. I'll tell you what I think about love. Here is a love story. This friend of mine—"

"You've got something on your chin," said Earl, and he reached over to touch it.

"What?" said Zoë, stepping back. She turned her face away and grabbed at her chin. A piece of toilet paper peeled off it, like tape. "It's nothing," she said. "It's just—it's nothing."

Earl stared at her.

"At any rate," she continued, "this friend of mine was this award-winning violinist. She traveled all over Europe and won competitions; she made records, she gave concerts, she got famous. But she had no social life. So one day she threw herself at the feet of this conductor she had a terrible crush on. He picked her up, scolded her gently, and sent her back to her hotel room. After that, she came home from Europe. She went back to her old hometown, stopped playing the violin, and took up with a local boy. This was in Illinois. He took her to some Big Ten bar every night to drink with his buddies from the team. He used to say things like 'Katrina here likes to play the violin,' and then he'd pinch her cheek. When she once suggested that they go home, he said, 'What, you think you're too famous for a place like this? Well, let me tell you something. You may think you're famous, but you're not *famous* famous.' Two famouses. 'No one here's ever heard of you.' Then he went up and bought a round of drinks for everyone but her. She got her coat, went home, and shot a bullet through her head."

Earl was silent.

"That's the end of my love story," said Zoë.

"You're not at all like your sister," said Earl.

"Oh, really," said Zoë. The air had gotten colder, the wind singing minor and thick as a dirge.

"No." He didn't want to talk about love anymore. "You know, you should wear a lot of blue—blue and white—around your face. It would bring out your coloring." He reached an arm out to show her how the blue bracelet he was wearing might look against her skin, but she swatted it away.

"Tell me, Earl. Does the word 'fag' mean anything to you?"

He stepped back, away from her. He shook his head in disbelief. "You know, I just shouldn't try to go out with career women. You're all stricken. A guy can really tell what life has done to you. I do better with women who have part-time jobs."

"Oh, yes?" said Zoë. She had once read an article entitled "Professional Women and the Demographics of Grief." Or, no, it was a poem. *If there were a lake, the moonlight would dance across it in conniptions.* She remembered that line. But perhaps the title was "The Empty House: Aesthetics of Barrenness." Or maybe "Space Gypsies: Girls in Academe." She had forgotten.

Earl turned and leaned on the railing of the balcony. It was getting late. Inside, the party guests were beginning to leave. The sexy witches were already gone. "Live and learn," Earl murmured.

"Live and get dumb," replied Zoë. Beneath them on Lexington there were no cars, just the gold rush of an occasional cab. He leaned hard on his elbows, brooding.

"Look at those few people down there," he said. "They look like bugs. You know how bugs are kept under control? They're sprayed with bug hormones—female bug hormones. The male bugs get so crazy in the presence of this hormone they're screwing everything in sight—trees, rocks, everything but female bugs. Population control. That's what's happening in this country," he said drunkenly. "Hormones sprayed around, and now men are screwing rocks. Rocks!"

In the back, the Magic Marker line on his buttocks spread wide, a sketchy black on pink, like a funnies page. Zoë came up, slow, from behind, and gave him a shove. His arms slipped forward, off the railing, out over the street. Beer spilled out of his bottle, raining twenty stories down to the street.

"Hey, what are you doing!" he said, whipping around. He stood straight and readied, and moved away from the railing, sidestepping Zoë. "What the *hell* are you doing?"

"Just kidding," she said. "I was just kidding." But he gazed at her, appalled and frightened, his Magic Marker buttocks turned away now toward all of downtown, a naked pseudo-woman with a blue bracelet at the wrist, trapped out on a balcony with—with *what*? "Really, I was just kidding!" Zoë shouted. The wind lifted the hair up off her head, skyward in spines behind the bone. If there were a lake, the moonlight would dance across it in conniptions. She smiled at him and wondered how she looked.

—1989

GEORGE SAUNDERS

George Saunders is among the most acclaimed American writers of his generation. Born in Amarillo, Texas, in 1958, he was raised on the South Side of Chicago. Though interested in literature from a young age, he began his career as an exploration geophysicist after graduating from the Colorado School of Mines in 1981. Around this time, he became influenced by the pro-capitalist philosophy of Ayn Rand; he says that at this point he wanted "to be one of the earth movers, the scientific people who power the world ... not one of these lisping liberal artsy leeches." Following a year-and-a-half working in the oil industry in Sumatra—where he became severely ill following a swim in a polluted river—Saunders spent a period doing odd jobs around Texas, including working in a slaughterhouse. Of his unconventional history, Saunders has said, "any claim I might make to 'originality' in my fiction is really just the result of this odd background: basically, just me working inefficiently, with flawed tools, in a mode I don't have sufficient background to really understand."

With ample spare time to fill while in Sumatra, Saunders began to read more broadly, and he eventually rejected Rand's philosophy and began to think about writing his own stories. Saunders entered the creative writing MFA program at Syracuse University in 1986. Here he met and married future writer Paula Redick; after graduating he spent several years supporting their growing family by doing technical writing in a variety of industries, while also working steadily at beginning his own fiction-writing career.

Saunders's earliest stories were inspired by such writers as Ernest Hemingway, Kurt Vonnegut, and Jack Kerouac. He began publishing in periodicals such as *The New Yorker* in the early 1990s, and his first collection, *CivilWarLand in Bad Decline*, burst onto the literary scene to wide acclaim in 1996. Since then, Saunders has become known for fiction that is both bitingly satirical and emotionally heartfelt, earning him comparisons to Vonnegut and to Mark Twain; more recently, Saunders has emphasized the importance of Russian writers such as Anton Chekhov and Isaac Babel to his work. His later collections include *Pastoralia* (2000), *In Persuasion*

Nation (2006), and *Tenth of December* (2013), which have all received substantial praise.

A self-described "working-class" writer, Saunders highlights in many of his stories the everyday absurdities of modern-day capitalism, often blending the banal with fantastical and dystopian elements. Most of his narratives are in the first person, and reveal troubled, sometimes dysfunctional narrators trapped by terrible situations. Fellow writer Junot Díaz has praised Saunders for his critiques of the "dehumanizing parameters of our current culture of capital," noting that "the cool rigor of his fiction is counterbalanced by this enormous compassion. Just how capacious his moral vision is sometimes gets lost, because few people cut as hard or deep as Saunders does." In 2000, Saunders published a children's novel, *The Very Persistent Gappers of Frip* (2000), and in 2017 he received the Booker Prize for *Lincoln in the Bardo*, an experimental novel about the death of Abraham Lincoln's son. He continues to contribute both fiction and non-fiction to *The New Yorker*; his journalistic pieces have included an extensive and compassionate investigation of the phenomenon of Donald Trump support. Other accolades he has received include the PEN/Malamud Award, the National Book Award, and the World Fantasy Award.

Victory Lap

THREE DAYS shy of her fifteenth birthday, Alison Pope paused at the top of the stairs.

Say the staircase was marble. Say she descended and all heads turned. Where was {special one}? Approaching now, bowing slightly, he exclaimed, How can so much grace be contained in one small package? Oops. Had he said *small package*? And just stood there? Broad princelike face totally bland of expression? Poor thing! Sorry, no way, down he went, he was definitely not {special one}.

What about this guy, behind Mr. Small Package, standing near the home entertainment center? With a thick neck of farmer integrity yet tender ample lips, who, placing one hand on the small of her back, whispered, Dreadfully sorry you had to endure that bit about the small package just now. Let us go stand on the moon. Or, uh, in the moon. In the moonlight.

Had he said, *Let us go stand on the moon*? If so, she would have to be like, {eyebrows up}. And if no wry acknowledgment was forthcoming, be like, Uh, I am not exactly dressed for standing on the moon, which, as I understand it, is super-cold?

Come on, guys, she couldn't keep treading gracefully on this marble staircase in her mind forever! That dear old white-hair in the tiara was getting all like, Why are those supposed princes making that darling girl march in place ad nausea? Plus she had a recital tonight and had to go fetch her tights from the dryer.

Egads! One found oneself still standing at the top of the stairs.

Do the thing where, facing upstairs, hand on railing, you hop down the stairs one at a time, which was getting a lot harder lately, due to, someone's feet were getting longer every day, seemed like.

Pas de chat, pas de chat.[1]

Changement, changement.

Hop over thin metal thingie separating hallway tile from living-room rug.

Curtsy to self in entryway mirror.

Come on, Mom, get here. We do not wish to be castrigated by Ms. Callow again in the wings.

Although actually she loved Ms. C. So strict! Also loved the other girls in class. And the girls from school. *Loved* them. Everyone was so nice. Plus the boys at her school. Plus the teachers at her school. All of them were doing their best. Actually, she loved her whole town. That adorable grocer, spraying his lettuce! Pastor Carol, with her large comfortable butt! The chubby postman, gesticulating with his padded envelopes! It had once been a mill town. Wasn't that crazy? What did that even mean?

Also she loved her house. Across the creek was the Russian church. So ethnic! That onion dome had loomed in her window since her Pooh footie days. Also loved Gladsong Drive. Every house on Gladsong was a Corona del Mar. That was amazing! If you had a friend on Gladsong, you already knew where everything was in his or her home.

Jeté, jeté, rond de jambe.

Pas de bourrée.

On a happy whim, do front roll, hop to your feet, kiss the picture of Mom and Dad taken at Penney's back in the Stone Ages, when you were that little cutie right there {kiss} with a hair bow bigger than all outdoors.

Sometimes, feeling happy like this, she imagined a baby deer trembling in the woods.

Where's your mama, little guy?

I don't know, the deer said in the voice of Heather's little sister Becca.

Are you afraid? she asked it. Are you hungry? Do you want me to hold you?

O.K., the baby deer said.

---

1   These French terms all refer to ballet movements and poses.

Here came the hunter now, dragging the deer's mother by the antlers. Her guts were completely splayed. Jeez, that was nice! She covered the baby's eyes and was like, Don't you have anything better to do, dank hunter, than kill this baby's mom? You seem like a nice enough guy.

Is my mom killed? the baby said in Becca's voice.

No, no, she said. This gentleman was just leaving.

The hunter, captivated by her beauty, toffed or doffed his cap, and, going down on one knee, said, If I could will life back into this fawn, I would do so, in hopes you might defer one tender kiss upon our elderly forehead.

Go, she said. Only, for your task of penance do not eat her. Lay her out in a field of clover, with roses strewn about her. And bestow a choir, to softly sing of her foul end.

Lay who out? the baby deer said.

No one, she said. Never mind. Stop asking so many questions.

Pas de chat, pas de chat.

Changement, changement.

She felt hopeful that {special one} would hail from far away. The local boys possessed a certain *je ne sais quoi*, which, tell the truth, she was not *très* crazy about, such as: actually named their own nuts. She had overheard that! And aspired to work for County Power because the work shirts were awesome and you got them free.

So ixnay on the local boys. A special ixnay on Matt Drey, owner of the largest mouth in the land. Kissing him last night at the pep rally had been like kissing an underpass. Scary! Kissing Matt was like suddenly this cow in a sweater is bearing down on you, who will not take no for an answer, and his huge cow head is being flooded by chemicals that are drowning out what little powers of reason Matt actually did have.

What she liked was being in charge of her. Her body, her mind. Her thoughts, her career, her future.

That was what she liked.

So be it.

We might have a slight snack.

Un petit repas.

Was she special? Did she consider herself special? Oh, gosh, she didn't know. In the history of the world many had been more special than her. Helen Keller had been awesome; Mother Teresa was amazing; Mrs. Roosevelt was quite chipper in spite of her husband, who was handicapped, which, in addition, she had been gay, with those big old teeth, long before such time as being gay and First Lady was even conceptual. She, Alison, could not hope to compete in the category of those ladies. Not yet, anyway!

There was so much she didn't know! Like how to change the oil. Or even check the oil. How to open the hood. How to bake brownies. That was embarrassing, actually, being a girl and all. And what was a mortgage? Did it come with the house? When you breast-fed, did you have to like push the milk out?

Egads. Who was this wan figure, visible through the living-room window, trotting up Gladsong Drive? Kyle Boot, palest kid in all the land? Still dressed in his weird cross-country-running toggles?

Poor thing. He looked like a skeleton with a mullet. Were those cross-country shorts from the like "Charlie's Angels" days or *quoi*? How could he run so well when he seemed to have literally no muscles? Every day he ran home like this, shirtless with his backpack on, then hit the remote from down by the Fungs' and scooted into his garage without breaking stride.

You almost had to admire the poor goof.

They'd grown up together, been little beaners in that mutual sandbox down by the creek. Hadn't they bathed together when wee or some such crud? She hoped that never got out. Because in terms of friends Kyle was basically down to Tasso Slavko, who walked leaning way backward and was always retrieving things from between his teeth, announcing the name of the retrieved thing in Greek, then re-eating it. Kyle's mom and dad didn't let him do squat. He had to call home if the movie in World Culture might show bare boobs. Each of the items in his lunch box was clearly labelled.

Pas de bourrée.

And curtsy.

Pour quantity of Cheez Doodles into compartmentalized old-school Tupperware dealie.

Thanks, Mom, thanks, Dad. Your kitchen *rocks*.

Shake Tupperware dealie back and forth like panning for gold, then offer to some imaginary poor gathered round.

Please enjoy. Is there anything else I can do for you folks?

You have already done enough, Alison, by even deigning to speak to us.

That is so not true! Don't you understand, all people deserve respect? Each of us is a rainbow.

Uh, really? Look at this big open sore on my poor shrivelled flank.

Allow me to fetch you some Vaseline.

That would be much appreciated. This thing kills.

But as far as that rainbow idea? She believed that. People were amazing. Mom was awesome, Dad was awesome, her teachers worked so hard and had kids of their own, and some were even getting divorced, such as Mrs. Dees, but still always took time for their students. What she found especially inspiring about Mrs. Dees was that, even though Mr. Dees was cheating on Mrs. Dees with the lady who ran the bowling alley, Mrs. Dees was still teaching the best course ever in Ethics, posing such questions as: Can goodness win? Or do good people always get shafted, evil being more reckless? That last bit seemed to be Mrs. Dees taking a shot at the bowling-alley gal. But seriously! Is life fun or scary? Are people good or bad? On the one hand, that clip of those gauntish pale bodies being steamrolled while fat German ladies looked on chomping gum. On the other hand, sometimes rural folks, even if their particular farms were on hills, stayed up late filling sandbags.

In their straw poll she had voted for people being good and life being fun, with Mrs. Dees giving her a pitying glance as she stated her views: To do good, you just have to decide to do good. You have to be brave. You have to stand up for what's right. At that last, Mrs. Dees had made this kind of groan. Which was fine. Mrs. Dees had a lot of pain in her life, yet, interestingly? Still obviously found something fun about life and good about people, because otherwise why sometimes stay up so late grading you come in the next day all exhausted, blouse on backward, having messed it up in the early-morning dark, you dear discombobulated thing?

Here came a knock on the door. Back door. In-ter-est-ing. Who could it be? Father Dmitri from across the way? UPS? FedEx? With *un petit* check *pour Papa*?

Jeté, jeté, rond de jambe.

Pas de bourrée.

Open door, and—

Here was a man she did not know. Quite huge fellow, in one of those meter-reader vests.

Something told her to step back in, slam the door. But that seemed rude.

Instead she froze, smiled, did {eyebrow-raise} to indicate: May I help you?

Kyle Boot dashed through the garage, into the living area, where the big clock-like wooden indicator was set at All Out. Other choices included: Mom & Dad Out; Mom Out; Dad Out; Kyle Out; Mom & Kyle Out; Dad & Kyle Out; and All In.

Why did they even need All In? Wouldn't they know it when they were All In? Would he like to ask Dad that? Who, in his excellent, totally silent downstairs woodshop, had designed and built the Family Status Indicator?

Ha.

Ha ha.

On the kitchen island was a Work Notice.

Scout: New geode on deck. Place in yard per included drawing. No goofing. Rake area first, put down plastic as I have shown you. Then lay in white rock. THIS GEODE EXPENSIVE. Pls take seriously. No reason this should not be done by time I get home. This = five (5) Work Points.

Gar, Dad, do you honestly feel it fair that I should have to slave in the yard until dark, after a rigorous cross-country practice that included sixteen 440s, eight 880s, a mile-for-time, a kajillion Drake sprints, and a five-mile Indian relay?

Shoes off, mister.

Yoinks, too late. He was already at the TV. And had left an incriminating trail of micro-clods. Way verboten. Could the micro-clods be hand-plucked? Although, problem: if he went back to hand-pluck the micro-clods, he'd leave an incriminating new trail of micro-clods.

He took off his shoes and stood mentally rehearsing a little show he liked to call "*WHAT IF . . . RIGHT NOW*?"

WHAT IF they came home *RIGHT NOW*?

It's a funny story, Dad! I came in thoughtlessly! Then realized what I'd done! I guess, when I think about it, what I'm happy about? Is how quickly I self-corrected! The reason I came in so thoughtlessly was, I wanted to get right to work, Dad, per your note!

He raced in his socks to the garage, threw his shoes into the garage, ran for the vacuum, vacuumed up the micro-clods, then realized, holy golly, he had thrown his shoes into the garage rather than placing them on the Shoe Sheet as required, toes facing away from the door for ease of donnage later.

He stepped into the garage, placed his shoes on the Shoe Sheet, stepped back inside.

Scout, Dad said in his head, has anyone ever told you that even the most neatly maintained garage is going to have some oil on its floor, which is now on your socks, being tracked all over the tan Berber?

Oh gar, his ass was grass.

But no—celebrate good times, come on—no oil stain on rug.

He tore off his socks. It was absolutely verboten for him to be in the main living area barefoot. Mom and Dad coming home to find him Tarzaning around like some sort of white-trasher would not be the least fucking bit—

Swearing in your head? Dad said in his head. Step up, Scout, be a man. If you want to swear, swear aloud.

I don't want to swear aloud.

Then don't swear in your head.

Mom and Dad would be heartsick if they could hear the swearing he sometimes did in his head, such as crap-cunt shit-turd dick-in-the-ear butt-creamery. Why couldn't he stop doing that? They thought so highly of him, sending weekly braggy e-mails to both sets of grandparents, such as: Kyle's been super-busy keeping up his grades while running varsity cross-country though still a sophomore, while setting aside a little time each day to manufacture such humdingers as cunt-swoggle rear-fuck—

What was wrong with him? Why couldn't he be grateful for all that Mom and Dad did for him, instead of—

Cornhole the ear-cunt.

Flake-fuck the pale vestige with a proddering dick-knee.

You could always clear the mind with a hard pinch on your own minimal love handle.

Ouch.

Hey, today was Tuesday, a Major Treat day. The five (5) new Work Points for placing the geode, plus his existing two (2) Work Points, totalled seven (7) Work Points, which, added to his eight (8) accrued Usual Chore Points, made fifteen (15) Total Treat Points, which could garner him a Major Treat (for example, two handfuls of yogurt-covered raisins), plus twenty free-choice TV minutes, although the particular show would have to be negotiated with Dad at time of cash-in.

One thing you will not be watching, Scout, is "America's Most Outspoken Dirt Bikers."

Whatever.

Whatever, Dad.

Really, Scout? "Whatever"? Will it be "whatever" when I take away all your Treat Points and force you to quit cross-country, as I have several times threatened to do if a little more cheerful obedience wasn't forthcoming?

No, no, no. I don't want to quit, Dad. Please. I'm good at it. You'll see, first meet. Even Matt Drey said—

Who is Matt Drey? Some ape on the football team?

Yes.

Is his word law?

No.

What did he say?

Little shit can run.

Nice talk, Scout. Ape talk. Anyway, you may not make it to the first meet. Your ego seems to be overflowing its banks. And why? Because you can jog? Anyone can jog. Beasts of the field can jog.

I'm not quitting! Anal-cock shitbird rectum-fritz! Please, I'm begging you, it's the only thing I'm decent at! Mom, if he makes me quit I swear to God I'll—

Drama doesn't suit you, Beloved Only.

If you want the privilege of competing in a team sport, Scout, show us that you can live within our perfectly reasonable system of directives designed to benefit you.

Hello.

A van had just pulled up in the St. Mikhail's parking lot.

Kyle walked in a controlled, gentlemanly manner to the kitchen counter. On the counter was Kyle's Traffic Log, which served the dual purpose of (1) buttressing Dad's argument that Father Dmitri should build a soundproof retaining wall and (2) constituting a data set for a possible Science Fair project for him, Kyle, entitled, by Dad, "Correlation of Church Parking Lot Volume vs. Day of Week, with Ancillary Investigation of Sunday Volume Throughout Year."

Smiling agreeably as if he enjoyed filling out the Log, Kyle very legibly filled out the Log:

> Vehicle: VAN.
> Color: GRAY.
> Make: CHEVY.
> Year: UNKNOWN.

A guy got out of the van. One of the usual Rooskies. "Rooskie" was an allowed slang. Also "dang it." Also "holy golly." Also "crapper." The Rooskie was wearing a jean jacket over a hoodie, which, in Kyle's experience, was not unusual church-wear for the Rooskies, who sometimes came directly over from Jiffy Lube still wearing coveralls.

Under "Vehicle Driver" he wrote, PROBABLE PARISHIONER.

That sucked. Stank, rather. The guy being a stranger, he, Kyle, now had to stay inside until the stranger left the neighborhood. Which totally futzed up his geode placing. He'd be out there until midnight. What a detriment!

The guy put on a DayGlo vest. Ah, dude was a meter reader. The meter reader looked left, then right, leaped across the creek, entered the Pope back yard, passed between the soccer-ball rebounder and the in-ground pool, then knocked on the Pope door.

Good leap there, Boris.

The door swung open.

Alison.

Kyle's heart was singing. He'd always thought that was just a phrase. Alison was like a national treasure. In the dictionary under "beauty" there should be a picture of her in that jean skort. Although lately she didn't seem to like him all that much.

Now she stepped across her deck so the meter reader could show her something. Something electrical wrong on the roof? The guy seemed eager to show her. Actually, he had her by the wrist. And was like tugging.

That was weird. Wasn't it? Nothing had ever been weird around here before. So probably it was fine. Probably the guy was just a really new meter reader?

Somehow Kyle felt like stepping out onto the deck. He stepped out. The guy froze. Alison's eyes were scared-horse eyes. The guy cleared his throat, turned slightly to let Kyle see something.

A knife.

The meter reader had a knife.

Here's what you're doing, the guy said. Standing right there until we leave. Move a muscle, I knife her in the heart. Swear to God. Got it?

Kyle's mouth was so spitless all he could do was make his mouth do the shape it normally did when saying Yes.

Now they were crossing the yard. Alison threw herself to the ground. The guy hauled her up. She threw herself down. He hauled her up. It was odd seeing Alison tossed like a rag doll in the sanctuary of the perfect yard her dad had made for her. She threw herself down.

The guy hissed something and she rose, suddenly docile.

In his chest Kyle felt the many directives, Major and Minor, he was right now violating. He was on the deck shoeless, on the deck shirtless, was outside when a stranger was near, had engaged with that stranger.

Last week Sean Ball had brought a wig to school to more effectively mimic the way Bev Mirren chewed her hair when nervous. Kyle had briefly considered intervening. At Evening Meeting, Mom had said that she considered Kyle's decision not to intervene judicious. Dad had said, That was none of your business. You could have been badly hurt. Mom had said, Think of all the resources we've invested in you, Beloved Only. Dad had said, I know we sometimes strike you as strict but you are literally all we have.

They were at the soccer-ball rebounder now, Alison's arm up behind her back. She was making a low repetitive sound of denial, like she was trying to invent a noise that would adequately communicate her feelings about what she'd just this instant realized was going to happen to her.

He was a kid. There was nothing he could do. In his chest he felt the lush release of pressure that always resulted when he submitted to a directive. There at his feet was the geode. He should just look at that until they were gone. It was a great one. Maybe the greatest one ever. The crystals at the cutaway glistened in the sun. It would look nice in the yard. Once he'd placed it. He'd place it once they were gone. Dad would be impressed that even after what had occurred he'd remembered to place the geode.

That's the ticket, Scout.

We are well pleased, Beloved Only.

Super job, Scout.

Holy crap. It was happening. She was marching along all meek like the trooper he'd known she'd be. He'd had her in mind since the baptism of what's-his-name. Sergei's kid. At the Russian church. She'd been standing in her yard, her dad or some such taking her picture.

He'd been like, Hello, Betty.

Kenny had been like, Little young, bro.

He'd been like, For you, grandpa.

When you studied history, the history of cultures, you saw your own individual time as hidebound. There were various theories of acquiescence. In Bible days a king might ride through a field and go: That one. And she would be brought unto him. And they would duly be betrothed and if she gave birth unto a son, super, bring out the streamers, she was a keeper. Was she, that first night, digging it? Probably not. Was she shaking like a leaf? Didn't matter. What mattered was offspring and the furtherance of the lineage. Plus the exaltation of the king, which resulted in righteous kingly power.

Here was the creek.

He marched her right through.

The following bullet points remained in the decision matrix: take to side van door, shove in, follow in, tape wrists/mouth, hook to chain, make speech. He had the speech down cold. Had practiced it both in his head and on the recorder: *Calm your heart, darling, I know you're scared because you don't know me yet and didn't expect this today but give me a chance and you will see we will fly high. See I am putting the knife right over here and I don't expect I'll have to use it, right?*

If she wouldn't get in the van, punch hard in gut. Then pick up, carry to side van door, throw in, tape wrists/mouth, hook to chain, make speech, etc., etc.

Stop, pause, he said.

Gal stopped.

Fucksake. Side door of the van was locked. How undisciplined was that. Insuring that the van door was unlocked was clearly indicated on the pre-mission matrix. Melvin appeared in his mind. On Melvin's face was the look of hot disappointment that had always preceded an ass-whooping, which had always preceded the other thing. Put up your hands, Melvin said, defend yourself.

True, true. Little error there. Should have double-checked the pre-mission matrix.

No biggie.

Joy not fear.

Melvin was dead fifteen years. Mom dead twelve.

Little bitch was turned around now, looking back at the house. That will-fulness wouldn't stand. That was going to get nipped in the bud. He'd have to remember to hurt her early, establish a baseline.

Turn the fuck around, he said.

She turned around.

He unlocked the door, swung it open. Moment of truth. If she got in and let him use the tape, they were home free. He'd picked out a place in Sackett, big-ass cornfield, dirt road leading in. If fuckwise it went good they'd pick up the freeway from there. Basically steal the van. It was Kenny's van. He'd borrowed it for the day. Screw Kenny. Kenny had once called him stupid. Too bad, Kenny, that remark just cost you one van. If fuckwise it went bad and she didn't properly arouse him he'd abort the activity, truncate the subject, heave the thing out, clean van as necessary, go buy corn, return van to Kenny, say, Hey, bro, here's a shitload of corn, thanks for the van, I never could've bought a suitable quantity of corn in my car. Then lay low, watch the papers like he'd done with the non-arousing redhead out in—

Gal gave him an imploring look, like, Please don't.

Was this a good time? To give her one in the gut, knock the wind out of her sails?

It was.

He did.

The geode was beautiful. What a beautiful geode. What made it beautiful? What were the principal characteristics of a beautiful geode? Come on, think. Come on, concentrate.

She'll recover in time, Beloved Only.

None of our affair, Scout.

We're amazed by your good judgment, Beloved Only.

Dimly he noted that Alison had been punched. Eyes on the geode, he heard the little *oof*.

His heart dropped at the thought of what he was letting happen. They'd used goldfish snacks as coins. They'd made bridges out of rocks. Down by the creek. Back in the day. Oh God. He should've never stepped outside. Once they were gone he'd just go back inside, pretend he'd never stepped out, make the model-railroad town, still be making it when Mom and Dad got home. When eventually someone told him about it? He'd make a certain face. Already on his face he could feel the face he would make, like, What? Alison? Raped? Killed? Oh God.

Raped and killed while I innocently made my railroad town, sitting cross-legged and unaware on the floor like a tiny little—

No. No, no, no. They'd be gone soon. Then he could go inside. Call 911. Although then everyone would know he'd done nothing. All his future life would be bad. Forever he'd be the guy who'd done nothing. Besides, calling wouldn't do any good. They'd be long gone. The Parkway was just across Featherstone, with like a million arteries and cloverleafs or whatever sprouting out of it. So that was that. In he'd go. As soon as they left. Leave, leave, leave, he thought, so I can go inside, forget this ever—

Then he was running. Across the lawn. Oh God! What was he doing, what was he doing? Jesus, shit, the directives he was violating! Running in the yard (bad for the sod); transporting a geode without its protective wrapping; hopping the fence, which stressed the fence, which had cost a pretty penny; leaving the yard; leaving the yard barefoot; entering the Secondary Area without permission; entering the creek barefoot (broken glass, dangerous microorganisms), and, not only that, oh God, suddenly he saw what this giddy part of himself intended, which was to violate a directive so Major and absolute that it wasn't even a directive, since you didn't need a directive to know how totally verboten it was to—

He burst out of the creek, the guy still not turning, and let the geode fly into his head, which seemed to emit a weird edge-seep of blood even before the skull visibly indented and the guy sat right on his ass.

Yes! Score! It was fun! Fun dominating a grownup! Fun using the most dazzling gazelle-like leg speed ever seen in the history of mankind to dash soundlessly across space and master this huge galoot, who otherwise, right now, would be—

What if he hadn't?

God, what if he hadn't?

He imagined the guy bending Alison in two like a pale garment bag while pulling her hair and thrusting bluntly, as he, Kyle, sat cowed and obedient, tiny railroad viaduct grasped in his pathetic babyish—

Jesus! He skipped over and hurled the geode through the windshield of the van, which imploded, producing an inward rain of glass shards that made the sound of thousands of tiny bamboo wind chimes.

He scrambled up the hood of the van, retrieved the geode.

Really? Really? You were going to ruin her life, ruin my life, you cunt-probe dick-munch ass-gashing Animal? Who's bossing who now? Gash-ass, jiz-lips, turd-munch—

He'd never felt so strong/angry/wild. Who's the man? Who's your daddy? What else must he do? To insure that Animal did no further harm? You still moving, freak? Got a plan, stroke-dick? Want a skull gash on top of your existing skull gash, big man? You think I won't? You think I—

Easy, Scout, you're out of control.

Slow your motor down, Beloved Only.

Quiet. I'm the boss of me.

FUCK!

What the hell? What was he doing on the ground? Had he tripped? Did someone wonk him? Did a branch fall? God damn. He touched his head. His hand came away bloody.

The beanpole kid was bending. To pick something up. A rock. Why was that kid off his porch? Where was the knife?

Where was the gal?

Crab-crawling toward the creek.

Flying across her yard.

Going into her house.

Fuck it, everything was fucked. Better hit the road. With what, his good looks? He had eight bucks total.

Ah Christ! The kid had smashed the windshield! With the rock! Kenny was not going to like that one bit.

He tried to stand but couldn't. The blood was just pouring out. He was not going to jail again. No way. He'd slit his wrists. Where was the knife? He'd stab himself in the chest. That had nobility. Then the people would know his name. Which of them had the balls to samurai themselves with a knife in the chest?

None.

Nobody.

Go ahead, pussy. Do it.

No. The king does not take his own life. The superior man silently accepts the mindless rebuke of the rabble. Waits to rise and fight anew. Plus he had no idea where the knife was. Well, he didn't need it. He'd crawl into the woods, kill something with his bare hands. Or make a trap from some grass. Ugh. Was he going to barf? There, he had. Right on his lap.

Figures you'd blow the simplest thing, Melvin said.

Melvin, God, can't you see my head is bleeding so bad?

A kid did it to you. You're a joke. You got fucked by a kid.

Oh, sirens, perfect.

Well, it was a sad day for the cops. He'd fight them hand to hand. He'd sit until the last moment, watching them draw near, doing a silent death mantra that would centralize all his life power in his fists.

He sat thinking about his fists. They were huge granite boulders. They were a pit bull each. He tried to get up. Somehow his legs weren't working. He hoped the cops would get here soon. His head really hurt. When he touched up there, things moved. It was like he was wearing a gore-cap. He was going to need a bunch of stitches. He hoped it wouldn't hurt too much. Probably it would, though.

Where was that beanpole kid?

Oh, here he was.

Looming over him, blocking out the sun, rock held high, yelling something, but he couldn't tell what, because of the ringing in his ears.

Then he saw that the kid was going to bring the rock down. He closed his eyes and waited and was not at peace at all but instead felt the beginnings of a terrible dread welling up inside him, and if that dread kept growing at the current rate, he realized in a flash of insight, there was a name for the place he would be then, and it was Hell.

Alison stood at the kitchen window. She'd peed herself. Which was fine. People did that. When super-scared. She'd noticed it while making the call. Her hands had been shaking so bad. They still were. One leg was doing the Thumper thing. God, the things he'd said to her. He'd punched her. He'd pinched her. The mark on her arm was black. How could Kyle still be out there? But there he was, in those comical shorts, so confident he was goofing around, hands clenched over his head like a boxer from some cute alt universe where a kid that skinny could actually win a fight against a guy with a knife.

Wait.

His hands weren't clenched. He was holding the rock, shouting something down at the guy, who was on his knees, like the blindfolded Chinese fellow in that video they'd seen in History, about to get sword-killed by a formal dude in a helmet.

Kyle, don't, she whispered.

For months afterward she had nightmares in which Kyle brought the rock down. She was on the deck trying to scream his name but nothing was coming out. Down came the rock. Then the guy had no head. The blow just literally dissolved his head. Then his body tumped over and Kyle turned to her with this heartbroken look of, My life is over. I have killed a guy.

Why was it, she sometimes wondered, that in dreams we can't do the simplest things? Like a crying puppy is standing on some broken glass and you want to pick it up and brush the shards off its pads but you can't because you're balancing a ball on your head. Or you're driving and there's this old guy on crutches, and you go, to Mr. Feder, your Driver's Ed teacher, Should I swerve? And he's like, Uh, probably. But then you hear this big clunk and Feder makes a negative mark in his book.

Sometimes she'd wake up crying from the dream about Kyle. The last time, Mom and Dad were already there, going, That's not how it was. Remember, Allie? How did it happen? Say it. Say it out loud. Allie, can you tell Mommy and Daddy how it really happened?

I ran outside, she said. I shouted.

That's right, Dad said. You shouted. Shouted like a champ.

And what did Kyle do? Mom said.

Put down the rock, she said.

A bad thing happened to you kids, Dad said. But it could have been worse.

So much worse, Mom said.

But because of you kids, Dad said, it wasn't.

You did so good, Mom said.

Did beautiful, Dad said.

—2009

KATHY PAGE

Praised by *The Globe and Mail* as "as a consummate stylist, a master of craft," British-Canadian novelist and short story writer Kathy Page is known for writing that is emotionally evocative yet unsentimental, often with a current of biting humour. She was born in 1958 in London, England, and studied English literature at the University of York, but has also trained and worked as a carpenter and as a psychotherapist. Her first novel, *Back in the First Person*, was published in 1986, and she continued to work and write while obtaining her MA in Creative Writing at the University of East Anglia. Her varied career has included time spent as writer in residence at Nottingham Prison as well as at universities in England, Finland, and Estonia. In 2001, Page settled on Salt Spring Island, BC, where she writes in what she calls "a room of my own," a small solar-powered studio in the woods.

Page was, in her words, "disillusioned" by the publishing industry by the time she was in her thirties, and briefly wrote for film and television. She said in an interview, "I think writing is both a craft and a vocation. A privilege too—though I am still sometimes ambivalent about it, and have periodically tried to escape and do something different." Despite this ambivalence, she published three novels and a short story collection between 1987 and 1992, and later said that her experience with screenwriting improved the structure of her fiction. Her fifth novel, *The Story of My Face* (2002), was longlisted for the Orange Prize for Fiction. *Paradise and Elsewhere* and *The Two of Us*, short story collections, were longlisted for the Giller Prize, and her 2018 novel *Dear Evelyn* won the Rogers Writers' Trust Fiction Prize.

With some exceptions—among them the fairytale- and myth-inspired stories collected in *Paradise and Elsewhere*—Page often works in a realist mode. She often draws on real-life experiences for her work; *Dear Evelyn* was inspired in part by her parents' love letters, and her novel *Alphabet* is set in a high-security prison like the one where she briefly worked, though in both cases she says her memories are supplemented by extensive research. As one critic wrote of *Dear Evelyn*, the resulting narratives may be "familiar, even conventional, both formally and conceptually"—but also demonstrate that "the kind of fiction some consider old-fashioned can be both beautiful and valuable for its sympathetic insight into ordinary lives." Page's work often investigates the power of human relationships, especially difficult ones: "The kind," she says, "that a therapist perhaps might not recommend, but in which many or even most of us are passionately involved."

Different Lips

JESSICA, RIGHT at the front of the upper deck of the bus, gazed out past the ghost of her face in the window. She registered the dusty, sun-scoured streets, the Saturday shoppers—their stuffed bags, their trailing children—but most of her was taken up with remembering Simon. She was thinking especially about his lips, so very small in his face, the upper almost non-existent, the lower tiny, but plump and very pink. She was remembering how those lips met with a pucker, like a navel in the face, and were neither manly nor conventionally attractive. Yet this was precisely why she had liked them so much: few others would have the imagination to try them, to realize how very soft, yet also somehow resilient, they were and how, although they seemed narrow at first, there was always a shock of pleasure when his mouth opened up to her, wet and alive. And after this came another surprise: that such a tongue-tied and nervous man could be, in the flesh, so articulate.

She wore the pink linen dress and matching sandals she had bought with the last of her money. Her hands lay loosely in her lap. Her face showed no sign of the memories that preoccupied her. On the contrary, it had the appearance of a contemplative's face or a saint's: pale, oval, unlined, symmetrical. Behind the sunglasses, her eyes were large, slightly hooded and set wide apart beneath gently arched brows. Her nose was straight, and below it her lips were wide but not particularly plump. The impression was solemn and wise.

She had been told countless times by social workers, teachers, foster parents and even the occasional Justice of the Peace that without her looks, she would be in worse trouble than she was. Jessica had never minded trouble, but they unfailingly gave her the benefit of the doubt.

As a child, playing to the mirror, she'd wrinkle her nose, expose the rims of her eyes, turn her lips inside out to display the ridges of arteries shiny with saliva. As a woman, she had tried makeup, piercings, dirt, bad-girl haircuts—but somehow the wise, saintly mask shone through them all, pretending, it seemed to her, to know things she did not. Now, she avoided confronting it. There were other things she avoided also, and avoidance was, at least in part, why she was taking the bus that Saturday to visit Simon Stone, thinking that soon she would kiss those lips again, that it was almost certain.

The spark between them had lost some of its intensity by the time they parted, but would be easy to revive. They would hold each other and kiss—as she considered this, the inside of her own mouth flooded itself and her own neatly formed lips grew imperceptibly plumper. She imagined how kisses would lead to the undoing of a belt buckle, to the warm, velvety skin around the hard flesh of his cock. She wanted to have him for a long time, slowly, different ways. And afterwards, they would very likely go out for the friendly drink he had frequently suggested in the unreciprocated birthday and Christmas cards he had sent her over the years since they broke up. Though maybe she'd just leave, because when they were seeing each other she had often been bored with the talking side of things. Simon's voice—hesitant, high, but also loud—could be irritating. He repeated himself; he clung obstinately to his point. It would be better, under the present circumstances, to carry the good feeling straight back to the studio.

The bus lurched to another standstill, and Jessica peeled herself out of her seat, adjusted the pink linen dress and took the stairs down and out into the noise of the main road. Each step she took increased her desire until it bordered on a kind of misery. You'd better be there, she thought as she turned onto the neat, tree-lined street. The district, bordering on Notting Hill, was far better than where he had lived before. The buildings were spacious and Georgian, painted white and cream. There was a gate, a tiled path, a flight of four steps to a rather grand columned porch. There were wide double doors ranked with many bells. She stood with the sun on her back, searching for his name.

The doors unlocked with a click. It was cool inside. And there in the dimness of the first-floor landing was Simon: a tall, slightly lopsided figure.

"Jess!" he called out, gesturing for her to follow him through an unlit hall and into a large room at the front of the building. The room was shaded by venetian blinds. A fan whirred in the corner, turning slowly from side to side. A new drawing board, a stool and office paraphernalia were arranged by the far wall, a low glass table and piles of cushions in the bay window. On the table stood two glasses and a bottle of water, beaded from the fridge.

Seated, she looked at him properly for the first time. She judged his hair to be ever-so-slightly thinner on the crown of his head and cut shorter. She recognized his long-fingered hands with their baby-pink, neatly filed nails. But the lips she had crossed the city for, changing buses three times—those weren't here. Instead, a different pair of lips stood out on Simon's face, fissured, bloody, and swollen to almost twice their usual size. Skin blistered from them in bubbles and rags, as if they were being barbecued.

He raised his hand towards them, stopped halfway.

"Allergy," he told her. "Stress, pollution, take your pick. I'm keeping in for a while, to see if that helps. So"—a staccato laugh—"it was lucky you called."

Lucky? What am I going to do now? Jessica thought, heavy with disappointment. She called to mind the studio, empty, waiting. She should go straight back there but it felt far too hard; she needed something to lift her up beforehand. She found his gaze and held it. His eyes, brown, liquid, hadn't changed at all, but they were no use to her.

"It must be, what, two years now?" he was saying. "So, what are you up to? Still with that production company?" Jessica nodded, swallowed. There had been difficulties with the new boss and she'd ended up moving on to a smaller, less prestigious company. After a few more months, the new place had decided not to renew her contract. She couldn't find anything else and had refused to temp, so it was a matter of going freelance, which had meant moving to a run-down studio flat in Streatham. Freelancing didn't work out, and then the bank cancelled her credit card, so she couldn't even jump on an airplane and get away from it all for a few months, which for a long time had been in the back of her mind as a failsafe. Thailand, Mexico, India—somewhere cheap. But she sat still on the cushion and didn't explain any of this to Simon, nor did she tell him about the row she'd had two weeks ago with her longest-standing girl friend, Anna, concerning the dog Jessica had adopted from the Dogs' Home to keep her company when she started to freelance.

She'd liked the dog at first, but he just stared at her all day and made her feel even more down than she had been before: not the idea. She returned him a fortnight later.

"You can't just take a dog back, like a library book," Anna had said.

"He had a holiday," Jessica joked. "Or say I fostered him."

A dog was for life, Anna said.

"Anna, nothing is for life, let alone a dog."

"I do make allowances for your background," Anna told Jessica, "but there are limits."

"Did I ever ask you to?" Jessica replied, and at the time she felt as if she had won, but Anna hadn't answered her messages since.

It wasn't just about the dog. Nothing had worked out recently. For over a year, things had been going bad. It felt as if the absurd, fall-on-your-feet luck she had taken for granted until now had just run right out and that was it. Finite. Gone. But she certainly wasn't going to explain any of that to Simon Stone, and when he asked, "Why now, Jessica?" she shrugged and looked at him and hated his lips.

"Jessica," he chided her, "you must have wanted something!"

"I was coming over this way," she insisted, sitting straight-backed on her cushion.

"I thought," he said, "maybe she's feeling down? The world's not going her way, or someone's moved out of her life, so she wants to touch an old base? To be honest, I thought you might want, well—" He reached for the water bottle and it gasped faintly as he unscrewed its cap, and suddenly the room was full of other small sounds too: the fax machine behind him hummed and flicked a message through, a blind tapped against the window frame, bubbles in the two glasses fizzled, expired with tiny sighs.

She took her water, drank.

"You know, there's not been anyone else," he said.

No one? In the years since she'd seen him last, more people than she could think of had been all over and inside of her. There had been lips and hair, sweat, semen, hands grasping and stroking flesh, sucking, licking, biting. She couldn't imagine the loneliness of being without all that.

Stand up and walk out of here, she advised herself. Things could only get worse. But it was Simon who rose. He came around to her side of the table, settled himself next to her.

"You still look great," he told her. "Like a delinquent nun." He took her hand and her insides lurched; she pulled it away and he let go.

"Is it these lips?" he asked. "Do they bother you? We don't have to kiss. Can't, in fact." Again, his laugh set her teeth on edge. "They really hurt." He moved closer, leaned into her so that she lost her balance and found herself semi-prone in a drift of cushions.

"No, Simon," she told him.

"Why not?" he said, his hand on her breast. A moment later his other hand slid up her thigh, inside the burgundy lace underpants she'd bought at the same time as the dress; he felt her where she was still wet. A moment later he was on top of her—she could feel his heart race frantically, just as it used to, and his raw lips were inches away from her face, blood and scab in the cracks. She wrenched her head sideways.

"No!" she said again, but his hand was busy and she was half-responding, despite herself. Then he was inside her and she, Jessica, lay flat on her back, legs apart, while Simon Stone (of all people) took his pleasure from her, apparently indifferent as to her consent. But her hips were cooperating with his movements. She stopped them and then they started again. Nothing like this had happened to her before. It was almost funny, but then again, it was really not.

"There," he muttered, "there, there, there."

He made it last but finally pressed his face into the side of Jessica's neck, groaned, fell still. An answering quake passed through Jessica's body but she willed her mouth shut tight.

"Get off me!" she told him. "Simon, it's bloody well time you found someone else." He laughed, moved away to lie on his back among his cushions, post-coitally expansive.

"Don't worry," he told her. "I'm not fixated. It's just always been so easy with you because—well, because of how you are." His face broke into a grin. "Thanks."

"It wasn't what I wanted," she said pulling away. Though it so nearly was.

"You could have fooled me." Simon closed his eyes as if to sleep, and she went and cleaned herself up in his bathroom, then left. The door was on a closer and would not slam.

The homebound bus jerked forward in rough spurts, interspersed with long, throbbing pauses. Jessica, sitting in the exact same seat on the top of the bus, added what had occurred in Simon's flat to the list of things she would not think about. She focused her attention on the shoppers below, who seemed even more burdened and fretful than before. There were more of them, too—that last desperate surge before closing time. Street markets were winding down, cash machines emptying. Litter flooded the street. She noticed, tied to a railing outside Marks and Spencer, a short-haired dog with floppy ears and she was sure, absolutely sure, that it was her dog, the one she had sent back. It sat obediently but at the same time strained towards the automatic doors at the shop's entrance, every fibre of its body yearning for the person who had left it there. Who? Jessica twisted in her seat to keep the dog in sight, but the bus pulled away before anyone came out. Would Simon still send her cards? It seemed, all of a sudden, a very important thing. Nothing made sense—and that had not mattered before, but now it did.

The studio was empty. She had spent the last two weeks disposing of everything, from the futon to the computer and the TV. Laptop, phone, her collections of books, all the old CDs and shoes—all gone. She had sold what she could for whatever she could get, and then she had bought the dress and the shoes from Browns with the last of the cash: £350. *That's a good dress*, the saleswoman had said. Wearing it, Jessica walked into the windowless, damp-smelling bathroom, which automatically filled with the clatter of the extractor fan when she shut the door. She set the bath running. There was a tremor in her hands as she fumbled with the catch of the cabinet above the basin and felt along the upper shelf for the packet of razor blades. She slid one out, unwrapped it.

Then, holding it tight between forefinger and thumb, she glanced up into the mirror on the cabinet door. There was a moment during which she might have shifted her attention back to the running bath or to the blade. But it passed. She leaned forward, steadied herself by pressing the heels of both hands hard into the cool porcelain of the basin, and looked.

She saw the high forehead and even higher hairline, the wide jaw, the straight nose that held them together and apart at the same time. She weighed her eyebrows against each other, saw how the curve of the left was ever so slightly fuller than the right, and how that was balanced perfectly by the slight upward pull of her lips on the opposite side. She noted two very faint lines running parallel across her forehead, and others even fainter in the corners of grey-green eyes sunk in roomy sockets, and observed the delicacy of the ruffled skin on her lids. Finally, she met the eyes themselves and allowed them, their pupils wide with fear, to look back at her.

With a tiny clatter, the razor blade fell from between her finger and thumb and skittered itself still. And now there was no choice. Jessica understood, but to grow to fit this thing she had been born with, the unwanted gift from one or the other of her parents (or both: she'd never know). *A terrible process*, her smug saint's face seemed to advise her, its eyes glistening darkly with foreknowledge, with wisdom that had not been easily earned. It was too much. She strode out of the bathroom forgetting to turn off the bath water and left the empty flat, clattering down the dusty communal staircase and out into the street.

The four-lane road running alongside the park was solid with traffic. She set off uphill towards the bus stop where the payphone booths were. Her heart beat hard as she waited her turn.

The cheap restaurants and pubs nearby were filling up. People spilled out onto improvised terraces, or else just leaned on walls, glasses in hand. A few parents pushed slack-faced, sleeping children homewards, the older siblings, occupied with brightly coloured drinks and ice creams, trailing behind.

Fingering the two coins in her pocket, she closed her eyes a moment and saw Simon's face, his spoiled lips. Suppose he doesn't answer? she thought. What then?

Half a mile way in her abandoned flat, water gushed from the tap she had forgotten to close. In the phone booth, a punky boy in a studded jacket fed another coin into the slot.

—2016

EDEN ROBINSON

Eden Robinson's first collection of short stories, *Traplines* (1996), won the Winifred Holtby Prize for the best first work of fiction in the commonwealth, and was selected as a *New York Times* Editor's Choice and Notable Book of the Year. This attention, along with the enthusiastic critical reception for her novel *Monkey Beach* (2000)—nominated for Canada's illustrious Giller Prize and the Governor General's Award—quickly established Robinson as a major Canadian writer.

Robinson was born on January 19, 1968, the same date, she says, "as Edgar Allan Poe and Dolly Parton.... I am absolutely certain that this affects my writing in some way." Born to Haisla and Heiltsuk parents, she grew up in Haisla territory near Kitamaat, British Columbia. She earned her BFA from the University of Victoria, and then moved to Vancouver to pursue work that would give her time to write. She worked for several years at a variety of what she calls "McJobs," including janitor, mail clerk, and napkin ironer, but after she had a short story published in *Prism International* magazine, she returned to school.

Robinson graduated from the University of British Columbia in 1992 with an MFA in creative writing; the result was the manuscript for *Traplines*. Her 2006 novel, *Blood Sports*, is a sequel to a story from *Traplines*, picking up on the lives of the story's characters in five years' time. In 2010, she was invited to give the year's Henry Kreisel Memorial Lecture, held annually at the University of Alberta; the three-part personal essay she delivered was published as *The Sasquatch at Home: Traditional Protocols and Modern Storytelling* (2011). She has also been a writer-in-residence at the University of Calgary and the Whitehorse Public Library.

Much, though not all, of Robinson's work engages with the lives of First Nations people today and incorporates elements of traditional Haisla and Heiltsuk storytelling. However, Robinson, like so many writers, is suspicious of labels, including the label of "First Nations writer." As she has observed: "Once you've been put in the box of being a native writer, then it's hard to get out." It is difficult to fashion any sort of box to hold Robinson's fiction:

it is dark, disturbing, traversed by characters she describes as "flamboyant psychopaths," and yet full of humour. Robinson's novel *Son of a Trickster* (2017) was shortlisted for the Giller Prize; its sequel, *Trickster Drift*, was published in 2018.

Queen of the North

Frog Song

WHENEVER I see abandoned buildings, I think of our old house in the village, a rickety shack by the swamp where the frogs used to live. It's gone now. The council covered the whole area with rocks and gravel.

In my memory, the sun is setting and the frogs begin to sing. As the light shifts from yellow to orange to red, I walk down the path to the beach. The wind blows in from the channel, making the grass hiss and shiver around my legs. The tide is low and there's a strong rotting smell from the beach. Tree stumps that have been washed down the channel from the logged areas loom ahead—black, twisted silhouettes against the darkening sky.

The seiner coming down the channel is the *Queen of the North*, pale yellow with blue trim, Uncle Josh's boat. I wait on the beach. The water laps my ankles. The sound of the old diesel engine grows louder as the boat gets closer.

Usually I can will myself to move, but sometimes I'm frozen where I stand, waiting for the crew to come ashore.

The only thing my cousin Ronny didn't own was a Barbie Doll speedboat. She had the swimming pool, she had the Barbie-Goes-to-Paris carrying case, but she didn't have the boat. There was one left in Northern Drugs, nestling between the puzzles and the stuffed Garfields, but it cost sixty bucks and we were broke. I knew Ronny was going to get it. She'd already saved twenty bucks out of her allowance. Anyway, she always got everything she wanted because she was an only child and both her parents worked at the aluminum smelter. Mom knew how much I wanted it, but she said it was a toss-up between school supplies and paying bills, or wasting our money on something I'd get sick of in a few weeks.

We had a small Christmas tree. I got socks and underwear and forced a cry of surprise when I opened the package. Uncle Josh came in just as Mom was carving the turkey. He pushed a big box in my direction.

"Go on," Mom said, smiling. "It's for you."

Uncle Josh looked like a young Elvis. He had the soulful brown eyes and the thick black hair. He dressed his long, thin body in clothes with expensive labels—no Sears or Kmart for him. He smiled at me with his perfect pouty lips and bleached white teeth.

"Here you go, sweetheart," Uncle Josh said.

I didn't want it. Whatever it was, I didn't want it. He put it down in front of me. Mom must have wrapped it. She was never any good at wrapping presents. You'd think with two kids and a million Christmases behind her she'd know how to wrap a present.

"Come on, open it," Mom said.

I unwrapped it slowly, my skin crawling. Yes, it was the Barbie Doll speedboat.

My mouth smiled. We all had dinner and I pulled the wishbone with my little sister, Alice. I got the bigger piece and made a wish. Uncle Josh kissed me. Alice sulked. Uncle Josh never got her anything, and later that afternoon she screamed about it. I put the boat in my closet and didn't touch it for days.

Until Ronny came over to play. She was showing off her new set of Barbie-in-the-Ice-Capades clothes. Then I pulled out the speedboat and the look on her face was almost worth it.

My sister hated me for weeks. When I was off at soccer practice, Alice took the boat and threw it in the river. To this day, Alice doesn't know how grateful I was.

There's a dream I have sometimes. Ronny comes to visit. We go down the hallway to my room. She goes in first. I point to the closet and she eagerly opens the door. She thinks I've been lying, that I don't really have a boat. She wants proof.

When she turns to me, she looks horrified, pale and shocked. I laugh, triumphant. I reach in and stop, seeing Uncle Josh's head, arms, and legs squashed inside, severed from the rest of his body. My clothes are soaked dark red with his blood.

"Well, what do you know," I say. "Wishes do come true."

***

Me and five chug buddies are in the Tamitik arena, in the girls' locker room under the bleachers. The hockey game is in the third period and the score is tied. The yells and shouting of the fans drown out the girl's screaming. There are four of us against her. It doesn't take long before she's on the floor trying to crawl away. I want to say I'm not part of it, but that's my foot hooking her ankle and tripping her while Ronny takes her down with a blow to the temple. She grunts. Her head makes a hollow sound when it bounces off the sink. The lights make us all look green. A cheer explodes from inside the arena. Our team has scored.

The girl's now curled up under the sink and I punch her and kick her and smash her face into the floor.

My cuz Ronny had great connections. She could get hold of almost any drug you wanted. This was during her biker chick phase, when she wore tight leather skirts, teeny weeny tops, and many silver bracelets, rings, and studs. Her parents started coming down really hard on her then. I went over to her house to get high. It was okay to do it there, as long as we sprayed the living room with Lysol and opened the windows before her parents came home.

We toked up and decided to go back to my house to get some munchies. Ronny tagged along when I went up to my bedroom to get the bottle of Visine. There was an envelope on my dresser. Even before I opened it I knew it would be money. I knew who it was from.

I pulled the bills out. Ronny squealed.

"Holy sheep shit, how much is there?"

I spread the fifties out on the dresser. Two hundred and fifty dollars. I could get some flashy clothes or nice earrings with that money, if I could bring myself to touch it. Anything I bought would remind me of him.

"You want to have a party?" I said to Ronny.

"Are you serious?" she said, going bug-eyed.

I gave her the money and said make it happen. She asked who it came from, but she didn't really care. She was already making phone calls.

That weekend we had a house party in town. The house belonged to one of Ronny's biker buddies and was filled with people I knew by sight from school. As the night wore on, they came up and told me what a generous person I was. Yeah, that's me, I thought, Saint Karaoke of Good Times.

I took Ronny aside when she was drunk enough. "Ronny, I got to tell you something."

"What?" she said, blinking too fast, like she had something in her eye.

"You know where I got the money?"

She shook her head, lost her balance, blearily put her hand on my shoulder, and barfed out the window.

As I listened to her heave out her guts, I decided I didn't want to tell her after all. What was the point? She had a big mouth, and anything I told her I might as well stand on a street corner and shout to the world. What I really wanted was to have a good time and forget about the money, and after beating everyone hands down at tequila shots that's exactly what I did.

"Moooo." I copy the two aliens on *Sesame Street* mooing to a telephone. Me and Uncle Josh are watching television together. He smells faintly of the halibut he cooked for dinner. Uncle Josh undoes his pants. "Moo." I keep my eyes on the TV and say nothing as he moves toward me. I'm not a baby like Alice, who runs to Mommy about everything. When it's over he'll have treats for me. It's like when the dentist gives me extra suckers for not crying, not even when it really hurts.

I could have got my scorpion tattoo at The Body Hole, where my friends went. A perfectly groomed beautician would sit me in a black-leather dentist's chair and the tattoo artist would show me the tiny diagram on tracing paper. We'd choose the exact spot on my neck where the scorpion would go, just below the hairline where my hair comes to a point. Techno, maybe some funky remix of Abba, would blare through the speakers as he whirred the tattoo needle's motor.

But Ronny had done her own tattoo, casually standing in front of the bathroom mirror with a short needle and permanent blue ink from a pen. She simply poked the needle in and out, added the ink, and that was that. No fuss, no muss.

So I asked her to do it for me. After all, I thought, if she could brand six marks of Satan on her own breast, she could certainly do my scorpion.

Ronny led me into the kitchen and cleared off a chair. I twisted my hair up into a bun and held it in place. She showed me the needle, then dropped it into a pot of boiling water. She was wearing a crop top and I could see her navel ring, glowing bright gold in the slanting light of the setting sun. She was prone to lifting her shirt in front of complete strangers and telling them she'd pierced herself.

Ronny emptied the water into the sink and lifted the needle in gloved hands. I bent my head and looked down at the floor as she traced the drawing on my skin.

The needle was hot. It hurt more than I expected, a deep ache, a throbbing. I breathed through my mouth. I fought not to cry. I concentrated fiercely on not crying in front of her, and when she finished I lay very still.

"See?" Ronny said. "Nothing to it, you big baby."

When I opened my eyes and raised my head, she held one small mirror to my face and another behind me so I could see her work. I frowned at my reflection.

The scorpion looked like a smear.

"It'll look better when the swelling goes down," she said, handing me the two mirrors.

As Ronny went to start the kettle for tea, she looked out the window over the sink. "Star light, star bright, first star—"

I glanced out the window. "That's Venus."

"Like you'd know the difference."

I didn't want to argue. The skin on the back of my neck ached like it was sunburned.

I am singing Janis Joplin songs, my arms wrapped around the karaoke machine. I fend people off with a stolen switchblade. No one can get near until some kid from school has the bright idea of giving me drinks until I pass out.

Someone else videotapes me so my one night as a rock star is recorded forever. She tries to send it to *America's Funniest Home Videos,* but they reject it as unsuitable for family viewing. I remember nothing else about that night after I got my first hit of acid. My real name is Adelaine, but the next day a girl from school sees me coming and yells, "Hey, look, it's Karaoke!"

The morning after my sixteenth birthday I woke up looking down into Jimmy Hill's face. We were squashed together in the backseat of a car and I thought, God, I didn't.

I crawled around and found my shirt and then spent the next half hour vomiting beside the car. I vaguely remembered the night before, leaving the party with Jimmy. I remembered being afraid of bears.

Jimmy stayed passed out in the backseat, naked except for his socks. We were somewhere up in the mountains, just off a logging road. The sky was misty and gray. As I stood up and stretched, the car headlights went out.

Dead battery. That's just fucking perfect, I thought.

I checked the trunk and found an emergency kit. I got out one of those blankets that look like a large sheet of aluminum and wrapped it around myself. I searched the car until I found my jeans. I threw Jimmy's shirt over him. His jeans were hanging off the car's antenna. When I took them down, the antenna wouldn't straighten up.

I sat in the front seat. I had just slept with Jimmy Hill. Christ, he was practically a Boy Scout. I saw his picture in the local newspaper all the time, with these medals for swimming. Other than that, I never really noticed him. We went to different parties.

About midmorning, the sun broke through the mist and streamed to the ground in fingers of light, just like in the movies when God is talking to someone. The sun hit my face and I closed my eyes.

I heard the seat shift and turned. Jimmy smiled at me and I knew why I'd slept with him. He leaned forward and we kissed. His lips were soft and the kiss was gentle. He put his hand on the back of my neck. "You're beautiful."

I thought it was just a line, the polite thing to say after a one-night stand, so I didn't answer.

"Did you get any?" Jimmy said.

"What?" I said.

"Blueberries." He grinned. "Don't you remember?"

I stared at him.

His grin faded. "Do you remember anything?"

I shrugged.

"Well. We left the party, I dunno, around two, I guess. You said you wanted blueberries. We came out here—" He cleared his throat.

"Then we fucked, passed out, and now we're stranded." I finished the sentence. The sun was getting uncomfortable. I took off the emergency blanket. I had no idea what to say next. "Battery's dead."

He swore and leaned over me to try the ignition.

I got out of his way by stepping out of the car. Hastily he put his shirt on, not looking up at me. He had a nice chest, buff and tan. He blushed and I wondered if he had done this before.

"You cool with this?" I said.

He immediately became macho. "Yeah."

I felt really shitty then. God, I thought, he's going to be a bragger.

I went and sat on the hood. It was hot. I was thirsty and had a killer headache. Jimmy got out and sat beside me.

"You know where we are?" Jimmy said.

"Not a fucking clue."

He looked at me and we both started laughing.

"You were navigating last night," he said, nudging me.

"You always listen to pissed women?"

"Yeah," he said, looking sheepish. "Well. You hungry?"

I shook my head. "Thirsty."

Jimmy hopped off the car and came back with a warm Coke from under the driver's seat. We drank it in silence.

"You in any rush to get back?" he asked.

We started laughing again and then went hunting for blueberries. Jimmy found a patch not far from the car and we picked the bushes clean. I'd forgotten how tart wild blueberries are. They're smaller than store-bought berries, but their flavor is much more intense.

"My sister's the wilderness freak," Jimmy said. "She'd be able to get us out of this. Or at least she'd know where we are."

We were perched on a log. "You gotta promise me something."

"What?"

"If I pop off before you, you aren't going to eat me."

"What?"

"I'm serious," I said. "And I'm not eating any bugs."

"If you don't try them, you'll never know what you're missing." Jimmy looked at the road. "You want to pick a direction?"

The thought of trekking down the dusty logging road in the wrong direction held no appeal to me. I must have made a face because Jimmy said, "Me neither."

After the sun set, Jimmy made a fire in front of the car. We put the aluminum blanket under us and lay down. Jimmy pointed at the sky. "That's the Big Dipper."

"Ursa Major," I said. "Mother of all bears. There's Ursa Minor, Cassiopeia ..." I stopped.

"I didn't know you liked astronomy."

"It's pretty nerdy."

He kissed me. "Only if you think it is." He put his arm around me and I put my head on his chest and listened to his heart. It was a nice way to fall asleep.

Jimmy shook me awake. "Car's coming." He pulled me to my feet. "It's my sister."

"Mmm." Blurrily I focused on the road. I could hear birds and, in the distance, the rumble of an engine.

"My sister could find me in hell," he said.

When they dropped me off at home, my mom went ballistic. "Where the hell were you?"

"Out." I stopped at the door. I hadn't expected her to be there when I came in.

Her chest was heaving. I thought she'd start yelling, but she said very calmly, "You've been gone for two days."

You noticed? I didn't say it. I felt ill and I didn't want a fight. "Sorry. Should've called."

I pushed past her, kicked off my shoes, and went upstairs.

Still wearing my smelly jeans and shirt I lay down on the bed. Mom followed me to my room and shook my shoulder.

"Tell me where you've been."

"At Ronny's."

"Don't lie to me. What is wrong with you?"

God. Just get lost. I wondered what she'd do if I came out and said what we both knew. Probably have a heart attack. Or call me a liar.

"You figure it out," I said. "I'm going to sleep." I expected her to give me a lecture or something, but she just left.

Sometimes, when friends were over, she'd point to Alice and say, "This is my good kid." Then she'd point to me and say, "This is my rotten kid, nothing but trouble. She steals, she lies, she sleeps around. She's just no damn good."

Alice knocked on my door later.

"Fuck off," I said.

"You've got a phone call."

"Take a message. I'm sleeping."

Alice opened the door and poked her head in. "You want me to tell Jimmy anything else?"

I scrambled down the hallway and grabbed the receiver. I took a couple of deep breaths so it wouldn't sound like I'd rushed to the phone. "Hi."

"Hi," Jimmy said. "We just replaced the battery on the car. You want to go for a ride?"

"Aren't you grounded?"

He laughed. "So?"

I thought he just wanted to get lucky again, and then I thought, What the hell, at least this time I'll remember it.

"Pick me up in five minutes."

I'm getting my ass kicked by two sisters. They're really good. They hit solidly and back off quickly. I don't even see them coming anymore. I get mad enough to kick out. By sheer luck, the kick connects. One of the sisters shrieks and goes down. She's on the ground, her leg at an odd angle. The other one loses it and swings. The bouncer steps in and the crowd around us boos.

"My cousins'll be at a biker party. You want to go?"

Jimmy looked at me like he wasn't sure if I was serious.

"I'll be good," I said, crossing my heart then holding up my fingers in a scout salute.

"What fun would that be?" he said, revving the car's engine.

I gave him directions. The car roared away from our house, skidding a bit. Jimmy didn't say anything. I found it unnerving. He looked over at me, smiled, then turned back to face the road. I was used to yappy guys, but this was nice. I leaned my head back into the seat. The leather creaked.

Ronny's newest party house didn't look too bad, which could have meant it was going to be dead in there. It's hard to get down and dirty when you're worried you'll stain the carpet. You couldn't hear anything until someone opened the door and the music throbbed out. They did a good job with the soundproofing. We went up the steps just as my cousin Frank came out with some bar buddies.

Jimmy stopped when he saw Frank and I guess I could see why. Frank is on the large side, six-foot-four and scarred up from his days as a hard-core Bruce Lee fan, when he felt compelled to fight Evil in street bars. He looked down at Jimmy.

"Hey, Jimbo," Frank said. "Heard you quit the swim team."

"You betcha," Jimmy said.

"Fucking right!" Frank body-slammed him. He tended to be more enthusiastic than most people could handle, but Jimmy looked okay with it. "More time to party," he said. Now they were going to gossip forever so I went inside.

The place was half-empty. I recognized some people and nodded. They nodded back. The music was too loud for conversation.

"You want a drink?" Frank yelled, touching my arm.

I jumped. He quickly took his hand back. "Where's Jimmy?"

"Ronny gave him a hoot and now he's hacking up his lungs out back." Frank took off his jacket, closed his eyes, and shuffled back and forth. All he knew was the reservation two-step and I wasn't in the mood. I moved toward the porch but Frank grabbed my hand. "You two doing the wild thing?"

"He's all yours," I said.

"Fuck you," Frank called after me.

Jimmy was leaning against the railing, his back toward me, his hands jammed into his pockets. I watched him. His hair was dark and shiny, brushing his shoulders. I liked the way he moved, easily, like he was in no hurry to get anywhere. His eyes were light brown with gold flecks. I knew that in a moment he would turn and smile at me and it would be like stepping into sunlight.

In my dream Jimmy's casting a fishing rod. I'm afraid of getting hooked, so I sit at the bow of the skiff. The ocean is mildly choppy, the sky is hard blue, the air is cool. Jimmy reaches over to kiss me, but now he is soaking wet. His hands and lips are cold, his eyes are sunken and dull. Something moves in his mouth. It isn't his tongue. When I pull away, a crab drops from his lips and Jimmy laughs. "Miss me?"

I feel a scream in my throat but nothing comes out.

"What's the matter?" Jimmy tilts his head. Water runs off his hair and drips into the boat. "Crab got your tongue?"

This one's outside Hanky Panky's. The woman is so totally bigger than me it isn't funny. Still, she doesn't like getting hurt. She's afraid of the pain but can't back down because she started it. She's grabbing my hair, yanking it hard. I pull hers. We get stuck there, bent over, trying to kick each other, neither one of us willing to let go. My friends are laughing their heads off. I'm pissed at that but I'm too sloshed to let go. In the morning my scalp will throb and be so tender I won't be able to comb my hair. At that moment, a bouncer comes over and splits us apart. The woman tries to kick me but kicks him instead and he knocks her down. My friends grab my arm and steer me to the bus stop.

Jimmy and I lay down together on a sleeping bag in a field of fireweed. The forest fire the year before had razed the place and the weeds had only sprouted back up about a month earlier. With the spring sun and just the right sprinkling of rain, they were as tall as sunflowers, as dark pink as prize roses, swaying around us in the night breeze.

Jimmy popped open a bottle of Baby Duck. "May I?" he said, reaching down to untie my sneaker.

"You may," I said.

He carefully lifted the sneaker and poured in some Baby Duck. Then he raised it to my lips and I drank. We lay down, flattening fireweed and knocking over the bottle. Jimmy nibbled my ear. I drew circles in the bend of his arm. Headlights came up fast, then disappeared down the highway. We watched the fireweed shimmer and wave in the wind.

"You're quiet tonight," Jimmy said. "What're you thinking?"

I almost told him then. I wanted to tell him. I wanted someone else to know and not have it locked inside me. I kept starting and then chickening out. What was the point? He'd probably pull away from me in horror, disgusted, revolted.

"I want to ask you something," Jimmy whispered. I closed my eyes, feeling my chest tighten. "You hungry? I've got a monster craving for chicken wings."

Bloody Vancouver

When I got to Aunt Erma's the light in the hallway was going spastic, flickering like a strobe, little bright flashes then darkness so deep I had to feel my way along the wall. I stopped in front of the door, sweating, smelling myself through the thick layer of deodorant. I felt my stomach go queasy and wondered if I was going to throw up after all. I hadn't eaten and was still bleeding heavily.

Aunt Erma lived in east Van in a low-income government housing unit. Light showed under the door. I knocked. I could hear the familiar opening of *Star Trek*, the old version, with the trumpets blaring. I knocked again.

The door swung open and a girl with a purple Mohawk and Cleopatra eye-liner thrust money at me.

"Shit," she said. She looked me up and down, pulling the money back.

"Where's the pizza?"

"I'm sorry," I said. "I think I have the wrong house."

"Pizza, pizza, pizza!" teenaged voices inside screamed. Someone was banging the floor in time to the chant.

"You with Cola?" she asked me.

I shook my head. "No. I'm here to see Erma Williamson. Is she in?"

"In? I guess. Mom?" she screamed. "Mom? It's for you!"

A whoop rose up. "Erma and Marley sittin' in a tree, k-i-s-s-i-n-g. First comes lust—"

"Shut up, you social rejects!"

"—then comes humping, then comes a baby after all that bumping!"

"How many times did they boink last night!" a single voice yelled over the laughter.

"Ten!" the voices chorused enthusiastically. "Twenty! Thirty! Forty!"

"Hey! Who's buying the pizza, eh? No respect! I get no respect!"

Aunt Erma came to the door. She didn't look much different from her pictures, except she wasn't wearing her cat-eye glasses.

She stared at me, puzzled. Then she spread open her arms.

"Adelaine, baby! I wasn't expecting you! Hey, come on in and say hi to your cousins. Pepsi! Cola! Look who came by for your birthday!"

She gave me a tight bear hug and I wanted to cry.

Two girls stood at the entrance to the living room, identical right down to their lip rings. They had different colored Mohawks though—one pink, one purple.

"Erica?" I said, peering. I vaguely remembered them as having pigtails and making fun of Mr. Rogers. "Heather?"

"It's Pepsi," the purple Mohawk said. "Not, n-o-t, Erica."

"Oh," I said.

"Cola," the pink-Mohawked girl said, turning around and ignoring me to watch TV.

"What'd you bring us?" Pepsi said matter-of-factly.

"Excuse the fruit of my loins," Aunt Erma said, leading me into the living room and sitting me between two guys who were glued to the TV. "They've temporarily lost their manners. I'm putting it down to hormones and hoping the birth control pills turn them back into normal human beings."

Aunt Erma introduced me to everyone in the room, but their names went in one ear and out the other. I was so relieved just to be there and out of the clinic I couldn't concentrate on much else.

"How is he, Bones?" the guy on my right said, exactly in synch with Captain Kirk on TV. Captain Kirk was standing over McCoy and a prone security guard with large purple circles all over his face.

"He's dead, Jim," the guy on my left said.

"I wanna watch something else," Pepsi said. "This sucks."

She was booed.

"Hey, it's my birthday. I can watch what I want."

"Siddown," Cola said. "You're out-voted."

"You guys have no taste at all. This is crap. I just can't believe you guys are watching this—this cultural pabulum. I—"

A pair of panties hit her in the face. The doorbell rang and the pink-haired girl held the pizza boxes over her head and yelled, "Dinner's ready!"

"Eat in the kitchen," Aunt Erma said. "All of youse. I ain't scraping your cheese out of my carpet."

Everyone left except me and Pepsi. She grabbed the remote control and flipped through a bunch of channels until we arrived at one where an announcer for the World Wrestling Federation screamed that the ref was blind.

"Now this," Pepsi said, "is entertainment."

By the time the party ended, I was snoring on the couch. Pepsi shook my shoulder. She and Cola were watching Bugs Bunny and Tweety.

"If we're bothering you," Cola said. "You can go crash in my room."

"Thanks," I said. I rolled off the couch, grabbed my backpack, and found the bathroom on the second floor. I made it just in time to throw up in the sink. The cramps didn't come back as badly as on the bus, but I took three Extra-Strength Tylenols anyway. My pad had soaked right through and leaked all over my underwear. I put on clean clothes and crashed in one of the beds. I wanted a black hole to open up and suck me out of the universe.

When I woke, I discovered I should have put on a diaper. It looked like something had been hideously murdered on the mattress.

"God," I said just as Pepsi walked in. I snatched up the blanket and tried to cover the mess.

"Man," Pepsi said. "Who are you? Carrie?"

"Freaky," Cola said, coming in behind her. "You okay?"

I nodded. I wished I'd never been born.

Pepsi hit my hand when I touched the sheets. "You're not the only one with killer periods." She pushed me out of the bedroom. In the bathroom she started water going in the tub for me, poured some Mr. Bubble in, and left without saying anything. I stripped off my blood-soaked underwear and hid them in the bottom of the garbage. There would be no saving them. I lay back. The bubbles popped and gradually the water became cool. I was smelly and gross. I scrubbed hard but the smell wouldn't go away.

"You still alive in there?" Pepsi said, opening the door.

I jumped up and whisked the shower curtain shut.

"Jesus, don't you knock?"

"Well, excuuuse me. I brought you a bathrobe. Good thing you finally crawled out of bed. Mom told us to make you eat something before we left. We got Ichiban, Kraft, or hot dogs. You want anything else, you gotta make it yourself. What do you want?"

"Privacy."

"We got Ichiban, Kraft, or hot dogs. What do you want?"

"The noodles," I said, more to get her out than because I was hungry.

She left and I tried to lock the door. It wouldn't lock so I scrubbed myself off quickly. I stopped when I saw the bathwater. It was dark pink with blood. I crashed on the couch and woke when I heard sirens. I hobbled to the front window in time to see an ambulance pull into the parking lot. The attendants wheeled a man bound to a stretcher across the lot. He was screaming about the eyes in the walls that were watching him, waiting for him to fall asleep so they could come peel his skin from his body.

Aunt Erma, the twins, and I drove to the powwow at the Trout Lake community center in East Vancouver. I was still bleeding a little and felt pretty lousy, but Aunt Erma was doing fundraising for the Helping Hands Society and had asked me to work her bannock booth. I wanted to help her out.

Pepsi had come along just to meet guys, dressed up in her flashiest bracelets and most conservatively ripped jeans. Aunt Erma enlisted her too, when she found out that none of her other volunteers had showed up. Pepsi was disgusted.

Cola got out of working at the booth because she was one of the jingle dancers. Aunt Erma had made her outfit, a form-fitting red dress with silver jingles that flashed and twinkled as she walked. Cola wore a bobbed wig to cover her pink Mohawk. Pepsi bugged her about it, but Cola airily waved good-bye and said, "Have fun."

I hadn't made fry bread in a long time. The first three batches were already mixed. I just added water and kneaded them into shapes roughly the size of a large doughnut, then threw them in the electric frying pan. The oil spattered and crackled and steamed because I'd turned the heat up too high. Pepsi wasn't much better. She burned her first batch and then had to leave so she could watch Cola dance.

"Be right back," she said. She gave me a thumbs-up sign and disappeared into the crowd.

The heat from the frying pan and the sun was fierce. I wished I'd thought to bring an umbrella. One of the organizers gave me her baseball cap. Someone else brought me a glass of water. I wondered how much longer Pepsi was going to be. My arms were starting to hurt.

I flattened six more pieces of bread into shape and threw them in the pan, beyond caring anymore that none of them were symmetrical. I could feel the sun sizzling my forearms, my hands, my neck, my legs. A headache throbbed at the base of my skull.

The people came in swarms, buzzing groups of tourists, conventioneers on a break, families, and assorted browsers. Six women wearing HI! MY NAME IS tags stopped and bought all the fry bread I had. Another hoard came and a line started at my end of the table.

"Last batch!" I shouted to the cashiers. They waved at me.

"What are you making?" someone asked.

I looked up. A middle-aged red-headed man in a business suit stared at me. At the beginning, when we were still feeling spunky, Pepsi and I had had fun with that question. We said, Oh, this is fish-head bread. Or fried beer foam. But bullshitting took energy.

"Fry bread," I said. "This is my last batch."

"Is it good?"

"I don't think you'll find out," I said. "It's all gone."

The man looked at my tray. "There seems to be more than enough. Do I buy it from you?"

"No, the cashier, but you're out of luck, it's all sold." I pointed to the line of people.

"Do you do this for a living?" the man said.

"Volunteer work. Raising money for the Helping Hands," I said.

"Are you Indian then?"

A hundred stupid answers came to my head but like I said, bullshit is work.

"Haisla. And you?"

He blinked. "Is that a tribe?"

"Excuse me," I said, taking the fry bread out of the pan and passing it down to the cashier.

The man slapped a twenty-dollar bill on the table. "Make another batch."

"I'm tired," I said.

He put down another twenty.

"You don't understand. I've been doing this since this morning. You could put a million bucks on the table and I wouldn't change my mind."

He put five twenty-dollar bills on the table.

It was all for the Helping Hands, I figured, and he wasn't going to budge. I emptied the flour bag into the bowl. I measured out a handful of baking powder, a few fingers of salt, a thumb of lard. Sweat dribbled over my face, down the tip of my nose, and into the mix as I kneaded the dough until it was very soft but hard to shape. For a hundred bucks I made sure the pieces of fry bread were roughly the same shape.

"You have strong hands," the man said.

"I'm selling fry bread."

"Of course."

I could feel him watching me, was suddenly aware of how far my shirt dipped and how short my cutoffs were. In the heat, they were necessary. I was sweating too much to wear anything more.

"My name is Arnold," he said.

"Pleased to meet you, Arnold," I said. "Scuse me if I don't shake hands. You with the convention?"

"No. I'm here on vacation."

He had teeth so perfect I wondered if they were dentures. No, probably caps. I bet he took exquisite care of his teeth.

We said nothing more until I'd fried the last piece of bread. I handed him the plate and bowed. I expected him to leave then, but he bowed back and said, "Thank you."

"No," I said. "Thank you. The money's going to a good cause. It'll—"

"How should I eat these?" he interrupted me.

With your mouth, asshole. "Put some syrup on them, or jam, or honey. Anything you want."

"Anything?" he said, staring deep into my eyes.

Oh, barf. "Whatever."

I wiped sweat off my forehead with the back of my hand, reached down and unplugged the frying pan. I began to clean up, knowing that he was still standing there, watching.

"What's your name?" he said.

"Suzy," I lied.

"Why're you so pale?"

I didn't answer. He blushed suddenly and cleared his throat. "Would you do me a favor?"

"Depends."

"Would you—" he blushed harder, "shake your hair out of that baseball cap?"

I shrugged, pulled the cap off, and let my hair loose. It hung limply down to my waist. My scalp felt like it was oozing enough oil to cause environmental damage.

"You should keep it down at all times," he said.

"Good-bye, Arnold," I said, picking up the money and starting toward the cashiers. He said something else but I kept on walking until I reached Pepsi.

I heard the buzz of an electric razor. Aunt Erma hated it when Pepsi shaved her head in the bedroom. She came out of her room, crossed the landing, and banged on the door. "In the bathroom!" she shouted. "You want to get hair all over the rug?"

The razor stopped. Pepsi ripped the door open and stomped down the hall.

She kicked the bathroom door shut and the buzz started again.

I went into the kitchen and popped myself another Jolt. Sweat trickled down my pits, down my back, ran along my jaw and dripped off my chin.

"Karaoke?" Pepsi said. Then louder. "Hey! Are you deaf?"

"What?" I said.

"Get me my cell phone."

"Why don't you get it?"

"I'm on the can."

"So?" Personally, I hate it when you're talking on the phone with someone and then you hear the toilet flush.

Pepsi banged about in the bathroom and came out with her freshly coiffed Mohawk and her backpack slung over her shoulder. "What's up your butt?" she said.

"Do you want me to leave? Is that it?"

"Do what you want. This place is like an oven," Pepsi said. "Who can deal with this bullshit?" She slammed the front door behind her.

The apartment was quiet now, except for the chirpy weatherman on the TV promising another week of record highs. I moved out to the balcony. The headlights from the traffic cut into my eyes, bright and painful. Cola and Aunt Erma bumped around upstairs, then their bedroom doors squeaked shut and I was alone. I had a severe caffeine buzz. Shaky hands, fluttery heart, mild headache. It was still warm outside, heat rising from the concrete, stored up during the last four weeks of weather straight from hell. I could feel my eyes itching. This was the third night I was having trouble getting to sleep.

Tired and wired. I used to be able to party for days and days. You start to hallucinate badly after the fifth day without sleep. I don't know why, but I used to see leprechauns. These waist-high men would come and sit beside me, smiling with their brown wrinkled faces, brown eyes, brown teeth. When I tried to shoo them away, they'd leap straight up into the air, ten or twelve feet, their green clothes and long red hair flapping around them.

A low, gray haze hung over Vancouver, fuzzing the street lights. Air-quality bulletins on the TV were warning the elderly and those with breathing problems to stay indoors. There were mostly semis on the roads this late. Their engines rumbled down the street, creating minor earthquakes. Pictures trembled on the wall. I took a sip of warm, flat Jolt, let it slide over my tongue, sweet and harsh. It had a metallic twang, which meant I'd drunk too much, my stomach wanted to heave.

I went back inside and started to pack.

Home Again, Home Again, Jiggity-Jig

Jimmy and I lay in the graveyard, on one of my cousin's graves. We should have been creeped out, but we were both tipsy.

"I'm never going to leave the village," Jimmy said. His voice buzzed in my ears.

"Mmm."

"Did you hear me?" Jimmy said.

"Mmm."

"Don't you care?" Jimmy said, sounding like I should.

"This is what we've got, and it's not that bad."

He closed his eyes. "No, it's not bad."

I poured myself some cereal. Mom turned the radio up. She glared at me as if it were my fault the Rice Crispies were loud. I opened my mouth and kept chewing.

The radio announcer had a thick Nisga'a accent. Most of the news was about the latest soccer tournament. I thought, that's northern native broadcasting: sports or bingo.

"Who's this?" I said to Mom. I'd been rummaging through the drawer, hunting for spare change.

"What?"

It was the first thing she'd said to me since I'd come back. I'd heard that she'd cried to practically everyone in the village, saying I'd gone to Vancouver to become a hooker.

I held up a picture of a priest with his hand on a little boy's shoulder. The boy looked happy.

"Oh, that," Mom said. "I forgot I had it. He was Uncle Josh's teacher."

I turned it over. *Dear Joshua*, it read. *How are you? I miss you terribly. Please write. Your friend in Christ, Archibald.*

"Looks like he taught him more than just prayers."

"What are you talking about? Your Uncle Josh was a bright student. They were fond of each other."

"I bet," I said, vaguely remembering that famous priest who got eleven years in jail. He'd molested twenty-three boys while they were in residential school.

Uncle Josh was home from fishing for only two more days. As he was opening my bedroom door, I said, "Father Archibald?"

He stopped. I couldn't see his face because of the way the light was shining through the door. He stayed there a long time.

"I've said my prayers," I said.

He backed away and closed the door.

In the kitchen the next morning he wouldn't look at me. I felt light and giddy, not believing it could end so easily. Before I ate breakfast I closed my eyes and said grace out loud. I had hardly begun when I heard Uncle Josh's chair scrape the floor as he pushed it back.

I opened my eyes. Mom was staring at me. From her expression I knew that she knew. I thought she'd say something then, but we ate breakfast in silence.

"Don't forget your lunch," she said.

She handed me my lunch bag and went up to her bedroom.

I use a recent picture of Uncle Josh that I raided from Mom's album. I paste his face onto the body of Father Archibald and my face onto the boy. The montage looks real enough. Uncle Josh is smiling down at a younger version of me.

My period is vicious this month. I've got clots the size and texture of liver. I put one of them in a Ziploc bag. I put the picture and the bag in a hatbox. I tie it up with a bright red ribbon. I place it on the kitchen table and go upstairs to get a jacket. I think nothing of leaving it there because there's no one else at home. The note inside the box reads, "It was yours so I killed it."

"Yowtz!" Jimmy called out as he opened the front door. He came to my house while I was upstairs getting my jacket. He was going to surprise me and take me to the hot springs. I stopped at the top of the landing. Jimmy was sitting at the kitchen table with the present that I'd meant for Uncle Josh, looking at the note. Without seeing me, he closed the box, neatly folded the note, and walked out the door.

He wouldn't take my calls. After two days, I went over to Jimmy's house, my heart hammering so hard I could feel it in my temples. Michelle answered the door.

"Karaoke!" she said, smiling. Then she frowned. "He's not here. Didn't he tell you?"

"Tell me what?"

"He got the job," Michelle said.

My relief was so strong I almost passed out. "A job."

"I know. I couldn't believe it either. It's hard to believe he's going fishing, he's so spoiled. I think he'll last a week. Thanks for putting in a good word, anyways." She kept talking, kept saying things about the boat.

My tongue stuck in my mouth. My feet felt like two slabs of stone. "So he's on *Queen of the North*?"

"Of course, silly." Michelle said. "We know you pulled strings. How else could Jimmy get on with your uncle?"

The lunchtime buzzer rings as I smash this girl's face. Her front teeth crack. She screams, holding her mouth as blood spurts from her split lips. The other two twist my arms back and hold me still while the fourth one starts smacking my face, girl hits, movie hits. I aim a kick at her crotch. The kids around us cheer enthusiastically. She rams into me and I go down as someone else boots me in the kidneys.

I hide in the bushes near the docks and wait all night. Near sunrise, the crew starts to make their way to the boat. Uncle Josh arrives first, throwing his gear onto the deck, then dragging it inside the cabin. I see Jimmy carrying two heavy bags. As he walks down the gangplank, his footsteps make hollow thumping noises that echo off the mountains. The docks creak, seagulls circle overhead in the soft morning light, and the smell of the beach at low tide is carried on the breeze that ruffles the water. When the seiner's engines start, Jimmy passes his bags to Uncle Josh, then unties the rope and casts off. Uncle Josh holds out his hand, Jimmy takes it and is pulled on board. The boat chugs out of the bay and rounds the point. I come out of the bushes and stand on the dock, watching the *Queen of the North* disappear.

—*1996*

LEANNE BETASAMOSAKE SIMPSON

"When I think about my life as an Indigenous woman, one of the things that I circle back to is this feeling of being lost or fragmented which, I think, comes from the experience of the violence of colonialism," says Leanne Betasamosake Simpson, a Michi Saagiig Nishnaabeg writer, scholar, and musician. Simpson addresses Canadian colonialism not only in her nonfiction writing, teaching, and activism, but also in her short fiction, music, and poetry. The power of the land, including urban landscapes, is a recurring motif in her work; Simpson has written on the importance of land in Nishnaabeg education and epistemology. She positions her work in opposition to the racist narrative that justifies colonialism by suggesting that Indigenous thought "lack[s] theory, analysis, and intellect.... Naming our intelligence is important," she says, "because it is intervention, resistance and resurgence."

Though Simpson has taught at Ryerson University and the Dechinta Centre for Research and Learning, she has conducted much of her academic work as an independent scholar. In *Dancing on Our Turtle's Back: Stories of Nishnaabeg Re-Creation, Resurgence, and a New Emergence* (2011), she examines how Nishnaabeg people "can re-establish the processes by which we live who we are within the current context," and in so doing take "the first step in transforming our relationship with the state." In *As We Have Always Done: Indigenous Freedom through Radical Resistance* (2017), she goes further, envisioning possibilities for cultural and political resurgence that are not based on seeking recognition from the colonizing state but are instead founded in rebuilding Indigenous intellectual traditions and relationship to place.

Simpson published her first short story collection, *Islands of Decolonial Love*, in 2013. A major influence on her creative writing is traditional Indigenous fiction; its importance to her work is reflected in *The Gift Is in the Making* (2013), a collection of her retellings of Anishinaabeg stories. In her next fiction book, *This Accident of Being Lost* (2017), songs appear alongside

tightly constructed short stories, most only a few pages long; reviewer Mela-
nie Lefebvre has praised these stories as "incredibly economical, with each
word seemingly measured and weighed with great care, producing just the
right balance of sarcasm and the sacred." Simpson is also a musician; her
second album, *f(l)ight*, was released in 2016.

Akiden Boreal

THE BROCHURE for Akiden Boreal is cluttered with words, a pamphlet of the
kind that has too much information and in a font demanding a reader's commitment. But we all read it anyway, and saved it, and passed it around to our friends
who get what it's pushing and act nonchalant for those who don't. We hovered
over it while it was passed from sweaty hand to sweaty hand, babysitting it until
we could get it safely taped back onto the fridge, behind the magneted pile of
shit we can't lose and have nowhere else to put.

   Akiden means "vagina." Literally, I think it means "earth place" or "land
place," though I'm not completely confident about the meaning of the "den" part
of the word and there is no one left to ask. I think about that word a lot because I
approach my vagina as a decolonizing project and because metaphors are excellent hiding places. The brochure says that you can't take any expectations into
the Akiden. That whatever happens, happens. That this could be your first and
only time in the natural world, and you just have to accept whatever experience
you have. For some it's profoundly spiritual. For others it's just full-on traumatic,
and still others feel nothing. The brochure says that learning takes place either
way. That the teacher, the Akinomaaget, will teach whatever way it goes.

   I've read and re-read the Akiden Boreal brochure every night for the past
six months and so has Migizi. The words "last place of its kind" are seared into
my heart. A combination of fear verging on horror mixes with fleeting placidity
when I get to the "Tips for a Great Visit" section. I'm worried that I'll have a
panic attack or some sort of a meltdown and fuck up my only chance in this
place. The brochure warns in stilted legalese that there's a "sizable" percentage of
people who visit the Akiden network and never recover. They spend the rest of
their lives trying to get back in. This kind of desperation is a friend of mine and
I know myself well enough to know that it is perhaps better not to play russian
roulette with myself like this and with Migizi. I also know myself well enough
to know I will.

   When I asked Migizi to do this with me last year he said yes, seemingly without taking the time to feel the weight of "yes" on the decaying cartilage that

barely holds life together. People do all kinds of shit in the Akiden network, and in the tiny moment he said yes, it was unclear what he was saying yes to, exactly.

The network was initially set up for ceremony, but when people thought about it, there are all kinds of things we can't do anymore and all kinds of those things can be thought of as ceremony—having a fire, sharing food, making love, even just sitting with things for a few hours.

I decided ahead of time not to ask Migizi questions about our visit to the network or about anything else that I didn't want answers to. And you should know that I'm not sorry. We are from people that have been forced to give up everything and we have this one opportunity to give something to ourselves and we're going to take it. We are fucking taking it. Even though occupation anxiety has worn our self-worth down to frayed wires. Even though there is risk. After all, everything we are afraid of has already happened.

The confirmation number for my reservation at Akiden Boreal is written on a slip of paper, scotch-taped to the fridge, behind the brochure that is also taped to the fridge, hidden in plain sight. It is for three hours on June 21. I also memorized the confirmation number because I was confident I'd lose the slip, and on the same day I scratched it into the right front bumper of my car in case of early-onset dementia. I'm not good at looking after important pieces of paper so I also wrote it on the eavestrough on the left side of the house, because houses and cars are harder to lose than paper and no one will think to look there.

The number is ten years old now, booked on the blind faith of youth, in hopes that I'd have enough of a credit rating to borrow the money to pay for the three hours. Blind faith rarely pays off, but this time it did, and I do. Barely. The bank says it will take me the rest of my life to pay off the loan, but it doesn't matter. No one gives a shit about owing money anymore.

I arrived a day early in accordance to the anxiety-management plan I made, as was suggested in the brochure. I booked a massage at the hotel, spent some time in the sauna and steam room, ate leafy green vegetables, did yoga and cardio, just like a white lady. I was still carrying a lot of frightened that the two of us will just be caught up in awkwardness and we won't be able to relax into this place. The brochure suggested taking anxiety meds, and most people do because this is a more controlled strategy than self-medicating with drugs and alcohol. I wanted to be the kind of person that could melt into this experience fully present. I wanted to be that kind of person, but I knew in my core I'm not. I'm the kind of person that actually needs to self-medicate in order to not fuck up important things.

Migizi and I met at the hotel bar that night for a few drinks and to reconnect before the visit. It was graceless at first for sure. But after the first bottle of wine I could see him breathing more easily. He stretched out his legs under the table and let them touch mine. My eye contact was less jolted. He seemed more confident as the night went on, and the silently voiced "you're not good enough," which marinates in the bones of my inner ear and pricks at my edges, was a little quieter.

Now it's 10 a.m. and we've each had two cups of coffee, one at the hotel and one in the waiting room at the security check-in. You have to arrive two hours before your scheduled appointment to make sure there is ample time for the scanning process. Last year some activists burnt down the Cerrado, a tropical savannah habitat in Brazil, by sneaking in an old-style flint. They wanted open access, which I want too. But in the process, they disappeared the last members of the tropical savannah choir.

I'm watching to see if Migizi is nervous too, but he is good at holding his cards close to his chest. He drank three shots of whiskey from a silver flask just outside the scanning room before we came in. I had two because I'm desperate to be able to feel this place. I tell myself our Ancestors would be ok with that; after all, we're going to be someone's Ancestors some day, and I'd want my grandchildren to do whatever they had to do to experience this. Compassion and empathy have to win at some point.

We clear security and wait in the holding room until the Watcher comes in to unlock the door to the site. She does so at exactly noon. I walk inside and am immediately hit with the smell of cedar. It's real cedar, not synthetic, and according to the brochure that means it comes with a feeling, not just a smell. The brochure says to be prepared for feelings and to let them wash over you like the warm waves of the ocean. This is the key to a good visit, the brochure insists.

I feel my body relaxing in spite of myself. The space seems immense even though I know my Ancestors would think this is ridiculous. The idea of finding the smallest amount of habitat that could sustain itself and then putting it in a big glass jar without a lid. The glass dome. The edges.

I feel like crying. Actually I'm starting to cry and I know Migizi hates that and I hate that too and so I'm biting my lip but silent tears are falling all over my face anyway. Migizi licks the tears off my cheeks, takes my hand, and we walk to the centre of Akiden Boreal, where there is a circle of woven cedar, like our Ancestors might have done on the floor of a lodge. He opens his hand and he is holding two tiny dried red berries. I ask. He says they are from his Kobade, his great-grandmother, and they are called "raspberries." He says they are medicine and his family saved them. For nearly one hundred years in case one of them ever got into Akiden Boreal. I ask him if they are hallucinogens. He says he thinks so. I'm becoming overwhelmed in the same way the brochure warned us and so I decide to eat one. We both do. Within minutes, I'm more relaxed and happier than I've ever felt. I'm drowning in peacefulness and calm, and there is a knife of deep sadness being forcefully pulled out from deep in me.

Migizi reaches over and touches the skin on my lower back with just his fingertips. It feels like he's moving around the air very closest to my skin. I'm losing track of my body; the edges are dissolving and I'm a fugitive in a fragile vessel of feelings and smells and senses. My lungs draw in moist air to deeper reaches, my back is arching, my heart feels like it is floating out of my chest.

Then Migizi lies down on the cedar boughs, on his side, facing me. He puts his right hand on my cheek, and he kisses my lips. He's kissing my lips, and in doing so he is touching that part of me I've never shared with anyone, because I didn't know it was there. There is a yellow light around his body and I can feel it mixing with my light. Part of me is a pool of want. Part of me is a waterfall filling up that want almost faster than I can desire. At one point he stops and takes his clothes off, which he's never done before, because he's afraid I will see his self-hatred, the self-hatred we both share and pretend doesn't exist. And we're there, in the middle of Akiden Boreal. Naked. Embraced. Enmeshed. Crying. Convinced that being an Akiden addict for the rest of our lives is important, convinced that living as an addict, dying as an addict, is unconditionally worth it. Convinced that breaking all of our healthy connections to the city, the concrete and even the movement, for the chance to be here one more time before we die, is worth it. Because this is how our Ancestors would have wanted it.

—2017

SHEILA HETI

At age 23, Sheila Heti burst on to the North American literary scene when five of her short stories debuted in the prominent American literary quarterly *McSweeney's* in 2000. Those stories and many others would appear in her first collection, *The Middle Stories*, published by *McSweeney's* the following year. In 2005 she released her first novel, *Ticknor*. Her second novel, *How Should a Person Be?* followed in 2010 and made *The New Yorker's* list of the year's best books. Her autobiographical novel *Motherhood*, published in 2018, was shortlisted for the Scotiabank Giller Prize.

Of Jewish and Hungarian heritage, Heti was born in Toronto in 1976. She studied playwriting for a year at Montreal's National Theatre School and went on to study art history and philosophy at the University of Toronto. Her short fiction is notable for transporting contemporary malaise to the realm of fable or myth, rendering the banal extraordinary. In an interview with *McSweeney's*, Heti states, "Every good story names something. In the way that other languages have words for feelings or experiences for which we don't have equivalent words, a story should be like that word in another language for a feeling or an experience we don't yet have the name for."

Heti is known around her native Toronto as the founder of the popular Trampoline Hall Lecture Series, a monthly symposium that challenges guest speakers to present on topics they know little about. She is the author of the illustrated children's book *We Need a Horse* (2011) and co-wrote a philosophical handbook entitled *The Chairs Are Where the People Go* (2011) with Misha Glouberman.

The Raspberry Bush

A LITTLE old woman who never stopped smiling walked into her kitchen from her garden. She had been standing in the sun for twenty minutes, tears in her eyes, looking at her beautiful raspberry bush that had died overnight. Instead of perky red raspberries she had found them black and brittle, and they fell to the ground at the slightest touch.

The sun shone through the kitchen window and lit up everything with sparkles of gold as the little old woman who never stopped smiling called up her sister in such a sorrow. Her sister was eighty-eight and lived in California. She said into the phone, "The raspberries are dead."

Her sister replied, "Well, the grandchildren are flunking out of school and Martha is pregnant and Sam is divorcing his wife and his wife is taking up with a gypsy girl. The infant has the flu and she never stops coughing. I was over there the other day and all they talk about is money ever since Tom got fired from the plant. Not to mention that Timothy never stops dating and we all think he has AIDS or gonorrhea or something. The news, I saw it today, told about a hurricane in the Andes which, as you know, is where David and Sue went skiing last week. Everyone here is miserable with grief and worry."

The little old woman listened to her sister, and when she had finished the little old woman who never stopped smiling put down the phone and sat in her kitchen that was dotted with gold.

There was a knock.

"Hello?" called the woman, and she stood up and padded to the door and peeped through the peephole and saw a young man in a delivery cap holding a bouquet of flowers. She opened the door.

"Why," her lips curled up in a smile. "These can't be for me."

"Are you Miss Marcia—"

"No, young man. She's next door." And the little old woman who never stopped smiling closed the door and went to sit at her kitchen table. The day was long; there were eight more hours in it. She had planned to eat the raspberries, one by one, every last one of them. But overnight the bush had died and there wouldn't be raspberries ever again.

The little old woman laid down her head and started to cry. She cried at her table every day, but no one knew it.

—2001

My Life Is a Joke

WHEN I died, there was no one around to see it. I died all alone. It's fine. Some people think it's a great tragedy to die all alone, with no one around to see it. My high-school boyfriend wanted to marry me, because he thought the most important thing to have in life was a witness. To marry your high-school girl-friend, and have her with you all through life—that is a lot of witnessing. Every-thing important would be witnessed by one woman. I didn't like his idea of what a wife was for—someone to just hang around and watch your life unfold. But I understand him better now. It is no small thing to have someone who loves you see your life, and discuss it with you every night.

Instead of marrying him, I married no one. We broke up. I lived alone. I had no children. I was the only witness to my life, while he found a woman to marry, then had a child using fertility. Her family of origin is large and lives near them—same with his family of origin. I visited them one time, and at his birthday dinner there were thirty relatives and close friends, including their only child. We were at the home of his wife's parents, in the small coastal town where they were building their lives. He got exactly what he wanted. He has thirty reliable witnesses. Even if half of them die or move away or come to hate him, he still has fifteen. When he dies, he will be surrounded by a loving family, who will remember when he still had hair. Who will remember every night that he came home stinking drunk and yelling. Who will remember his every failure, and love him in spite of it all. When all his witnesses die, his life will be over. When his son is dead, and his son's wife is dead, and the children of his son are also dead, the life of my first boyfriend will be through.

When I drew my last breath, no one saw me. The car that hit me drove quick-ly away, and a driver stopped to carry me out of the center of the road. I was already dead when he carried me, so I can say I died alone.

Now, you can probably tell that I'm lying. If I really am O.K. with the fact that no one I loved witnessed my death, why did I come all the way back here from the dead? Why did I put on the flesh of my body, and the clothes I wore my last day on earth? Why did I resume the voice I spoke with when I was living, and return to the weight I was at the time of my death? I even washed the dirt out of my eyes and my hair, settled my teeth in the places in my mouth where they were before they got knocked out. Why did I bother doing that? It was a lot of work. I could have stayed in the ground for eternity. I could have stayed there, disintegrating, if I felt that my life was resolved. If there had not been a twinge of anxiety in me that something still needed to be said, I would still be in the ground.

Here is the thing: I was a joke, and my life was a joke. The last man I loved—not my high-school boyfriend—told me this during our final fight. I was thirty-four at the time. During the fight, as I was trying to explain my version of things, he shouted, "You are a joke, and your life is a joke!"

The night before, we loved each other still. We went to bed at the same time, and, as he read a popular crime novel on his phone, I fell asleep on my pillow, gently touching his arm. A few days later, I died. It has taken me since that time—four years—to understand the full significance of what he said: that I was a joke and my life was a joke. At the moment he said it, I didn't know how to reply. I was so hurt, I just began bawling. This only proved to him that he was correct. I stared at him with an open mouth. Of course, I was used to his cruelties by then, but still it hurt.

When I received your invitation to come speak here tonight—Didn't you know I had died? You did not—when I received your invitation, at first I thought, No, I cannot come. The truth is I had no reason to. But then a few months later I wrote you a note: I'll come if you'll pay to dig me up. If you'll pay to fly my corpse across North America, from where I am buried, and wheel me to the mike stand, then yes, I'll come. As I flew, I worked so hard to keep in my dead brain what I wanted to say—it was the whole reason I'd said yes. I had something important to declare. What was it? Have I said it already? Thoughts slip from a dead brain so quickly. I can't remember if I said it.

Lying there under the ground, salt and soil and sweat and worms and seedlings and saplings and the bones of dried birds collecting in my mouth, and my blood caked dry, and my toes curled up, and my brain filled with hair and the feathers of birds, and the little white balls of whatever it is that sometimes specks the soil—those little Styrofoam balls—and the shit of dogs, and the piss of skunks, and the seedlings and the saplings and the acorns and the raisins; it is so amazing I could think down there, in that total, wet darkness. You never know, lying in the ground, what your niggling thought will be. You can take only one thought with you to the grave, and invariably it is a thought that bugs you, something that must be thought all the way through to the end before you find your peace. The thought I took was of a man I loved saying, "You are a joke, and your life is a joke." It cleaved to my head and my muscles and my bones, until I was nothing but those words. When my life collapsed inward—which is what death is, life collapsing deep into itself—that phrase remained outside the collapsing; it became a thing separate from me. And, because it was separate from me, I could take it with me—it was the only thing I had.

Could I have a glass of water, please? Where is my water? I am parched and I am dead. Tomorrow I will be on an airplane home, down there with all the luggage, peace in my bones, having declared what I came here to declare—what I realized when I was underground. Then I will be dead for the rest of eternity, never having to brush myself off.

The man who said I was a joke and my life was a joke—he may not have been there in my final moments, witnessing my final breath, but what I realized was: he foretold my death. He could only have foretold it by seeing me to my core—by having been my soul's witness. When he said those awful words, he witnessed me into the future, a future he knew I would meet. During our fight, I tried to convince him that he was wrong. "I'm not a joke!" I cried. "You're the joke! You're the joke!"

When a person slips on a banana peel and dies, then her life is a joke. Slipping on a banana peel is not how I died. When a person walks into a bar with a rabbi, a priest, and a nun, and that is how she dies, then her life is a joke. That is not how I died. When a person is a chicken who crosses the road to get to the other side, and that is how she dies, then her life is a joke. Well, that is how I died—as a chicken crossing the road to get to the other side.

When I crossed the road that day, it was to the other side I was heading—that was how much despair I felt, our fight still in my mind. Why did the chicken cross the road? To get to the other side. A suicide. The other side is death. Everyone knows that, right?

I scurried out in front of that rusty old car, and smashed myself into the metal, my teeth pushed back into my throat by the fender, my chest completely run over.

I didn't come here to depress you. I came here to tell you a joke. Or, rather, to show you a joke. Me! And to brag that I was witnessed. That first boyfriend of mine—he doesn't live far from here. Perhaps he is in the audience, listening? Having a beer? I hope he's here! My life and death were witnessed, I tell you! Witnessed and foretold! You did not fare any better than me. It seems both of us won, in the end.

What a chicken I was. I couldn't bear any aspect of living. Especially that old custom: that you have to live a better life than everyone else.

What is the other side like, you may be wondering. Since I'm here, I might as well tell you: it's a ridiculous place where everyone is always laughing. It's like something I experienced once, on a transcontinental flight. This woman beside me laughed at every dumb joke in whatever show she was watching, literally every joke the show made. Then she watched another show, then another one. Her laughter filled our row of seats. She didn't stop laughing from takeoff to landing. How a person's laughter can make you hate her! Don't the laughers of the world know this? Do they think it makes them lovable? Who likes to hear someone laughing to herself, headphones on, while staring at a screen? Probably the same people who like to listen to strangers fuck behind a hotel wall.

Over there on the other side, it's like that all the time—the dogs laugh, the trees laugh, everyone laughs—whether there's anything funny or not. I practiced this speech on the other side, before an audience of sixteen people, and it took four hours, from beginning to end, as I waited after saying each sentence for the laughter to subside. Here on earth it is different, of course. The quiet of the living is one of the great reliefs. Is death the same for everyone, or is this laughing world a death made just for me? How can I know for sure?

Does anything I'm saying make any sense? I'm self-conscious about my speaking. Does my voice sound all right? When you are dead, it's difficult to carry a thought. My head feels stuffed with cotton batting; my eyes feel stuffed with cotton balls; my ears feel plugged up with cotton. It is hard to think, to string meaning to meaning. I did not come here to tell you I love you. Is that what you think I am saying? I only loved two men ever. One of them wanted to marry me, and the other thought my life was a joke. My first boyfriend found himself a witness, and I have come to declare that I found one, too. I won, you see? I won! I won the best thing a person can win—to be seen! I declare it here today. It's the only reason I crawled into my flesh to stand here before you—a joke on this stage. His words no longer hurt me. They make me feel so proud.

Why did the chicken cross the road? That's me. I am the chicken. And I got to the other side. He knew this would happen when he spoke those words. How beautiful to be seen.

—2015

DONAL RYAN

An Irish author whose novels have twice been long-listed for the Booker prize, Donal Ryan is renowned for his depictions of rural Ireland and its people. Born in the Irish village of Nenagh, Tipperary, he yearned from a young age to become a writer; he reports that during his childhood his parents "had no spare money but somehow we always had books." After graduating from the University of Limerick, he took a job as a civil servant, spending ten years in what he later described as "a creative wilderness." At age 30, while his wife Anne Marie was pregnant with their second child, Ryan decided to make a serious effort to pursue his dream. He began working on the manuscript that would eventually become the novel *That Thing About December*.

As Ireland's economy struggled in the wake of the 2008 recession, Ryan's family lost a quarter of its income. During this period of financial misfortune, unable to find a publisher for *That Thing About December*, he began work on another book. The resulting novel, *The Spinning Heart*, is an exploration of the frustrations and aspirations of a village ravaged by the downturn; each of the 21 chapters is narrated by a different character in the community. After almost 50 rejections, both of Ryan's novels were finally accepted by a small publisher, Lilliput Press. *The Spinning Heart* (2012) was released first and met with critical acclaim, praised for its "perceptive, intimate and darkly comic" style. It was followed two years later by *That Thing About December*, which is set in the same fictional village as *The Spinning Heart*. Both these novels, along with the 2015 short story collection *A Slanting of the Sun*, were commended for the psychological realism with which they, as one *Guardian* critic phrased it, "anatomise rural despair."

In 2017, Ryan released *All We Shall Know*, a novel about an affair between a 33-year-old teacher and her 17-year-old student. The following year, he left his civil service career to teach creative writing at the University of Limerick; he also completed *From a Low and Quiet Sea*, the story of a Syrian doctor forced to flee his war-torn homeland. On the subject of his work's political content, Ryan has said, "I don't think writers necessarily have a responsibility to address social issues, but to be clear-eyed and compassionate if they happen to do so. I don't mind being described or seen as a social commentator, but I hope it's obvious that my main interest lies in the chaos inside us all, in the terrible, beautiful humanity we're all afflicted with. Recession or no recession, the storms will rage on."

The Passion

SHE CRIES sometimes, without noise. I know not to talk, only to leave my hand under hers on the gearstick. Where were you all the time before the court case, she asked me once, early on. In my room, I said, I slept a lot. She said she'd heard I was seen below in the Ragg[1] and inside in Easy Street[2] in Nenagh as bould as you like. She wasn't accusing, just telling me what she'd heard. I said I wasn't, and that was enough. You'd hear lots of things, she said. People thinking they're helping. I look sometimes at the side of her face when she cries, the straightness of the line the tears make slowly on her cheek, the red of her lips, and I want to touch her cheek, to wipe away the mark of her sorrow. But I never do.

My mother and father don't know what to say to me. Will you go back training? My shoulder, Dad, I can hardly lift a hurl[3] with my right hand. Oh, ya, ya. Sure of course. More physio, maybe. And I say something along the lines of It's fucked for good, Dad. And he clenches his jaw and I'd say he thinks to himself He must have got that roughness in jail and God only knows what happened to him in jail and I'd say me in jail is all he thinks about ever since the day I was charged and still he won't ask me about it, never, ever. Would you not go out for a few pucks[4] below in the field maybe or against the wall beyond and maybe it'll come right? And I say nothing and he taps his forehead with his forefinger like he doesn't know he's doing it and asks will I eat another cut of fruitcake.

They make me fries in the morning and give me plates of tart and cream and cups of scalding tea for my elevenses,[5] as they call it, and we have dinner for lunch and dinner again for dinner and the leanness I got in jail is nearly gone. I'm melting out to fat. I'll have to do a bit of something soon that wouldn't call

---

1   Another name for Bouladuff, a village in Ireland.
2   Pub in Nenagh.
3   Wooden stick used in hurling, a popular sport in Ireland that has similarities to field hockey and lacrosse.
4   In hurling, striking the ball with the stick.
5   Light mid-morning meal.

too heavy on my shoulder, running or soccer or something. But Bonny's brother plays for the juniors and I'd see him at training and it wouldn't be fair on him.

My mother stands and twists tea-towels in her hands as she watches birds out the back window, and gives out about the way that oul bad bitch of a cat lies in wait for them, crouched on her haunches in behind the trees. A dead wren she left on the back porch step the other day and Mam cried at the sight of it. The little darling, she said. And she wouldn't give Puss her supper no matter how much yowling she did at the kitchen window and rubbing with her paw. She can go and shite now, the murdering little rap. Then she softened a bit when Dad said She killed that bird for you, Moll, and left it there for a present for you, because she's so stuck on you. But still Puss wasn't fed.

You'll have to call out to those people, my father had said once, long before the inquest or the court. While there was still bandages on me and a cast on my arm. Why will he, PJ? My mother exploded from silence, giving him a shock. He hadn't known she was there. To see to know can he make amends in some way, to let them know how sorry he is. Lord God almighty, she said. Sorry? Sorry? Sure for the love of Jesus Christ isn't it plain to see he's sorry? What do they want? Wasn't it an accident? Tisn't as if he meant it, is it? Is it? Is it? And he never repeated himself, and I stayed in my room for most of that year, clinging to the edge of my childhood bed. They have their pound of flesh well got now, that crowd, I heard my mother say after I got out. They can put away their wounded faces. My child was taken off of me as well and he was gave back different. Toughies, that crowd.

The first day in court I pled guilty and the judge looked at me for ages before she talked. Guilty, are you? Ya, yes miss, yes ma'am, yes your honour, then I remembered the solicitor said to call her Judge. Yes, Judge. When I looked up from the floor I could have sworn she was smiling a bit at me. There was more talk and a date was given to come back. My father put his hand on my arm walking back out. Jim Gildea had called up to our house in the squad that morning even though he's meant to be retired to say there was a wild uncle over from England, the mother's brother, he had two days given on the batter[6] inside in Limerick already, to watch out for him at the courthouse, a foxy[7] lad, butty,[8] wide across the shoulders. He said he'd ring the lads in Nenagh the way they'd be warned, but to be on the lookout all the same. Thanks, Jim, Dad said. Jim shook hands with me and wished me the best of luck.

---

6   Drinking, on a bender.
7   Red-haired.
8   Muscular.

It was Jim came on us that night, and he'd cried while we waited for the ambulance, and he'd held my hand and I'd whispered Bonny, Bonny, Bonny, and I couldn't move and Jim told me She's gone, son, she's gone, just keep looking, keep looking at me.

The uncle appeared from behind a pillar at the courthouse door. He had a suit on him, and he had no drink taken, the Nenagh boys said afterwards in mitigation of themselves. He even had a manila folder in his hand, as much as to say he was a lad with legitimate business with the court. He squeezed through a gap that was barely there between a cop and a solicitor, slashing sideways through the air; I felt the hot breeze of him before I properly saw him. He was a small red man with big fists and he had three digs in before I felt the first one. Four shades fell on the uncle and I was at the bottom of them and my back was flexed at an awful angle from the top step and my bad shoulder burned and when they dragged him off he was still kicking and Dad was sitting on the ground and trying to get up and there was a thin line of blood from his nose to his mouth and there was no one helping him.

The second day in court the judge made a speech about young men being in a hurry even when they were going nowhere and she asked about my apprenticeship and Bobby Mahon put up his hand and half stood with his face all red and said nearly in a whisper that I was in my third year with him and just about to get my papers and Pawsy Rogers went up to the stand and said I was a great lad and a fine hurler and a good worker and my people were the salt of the earth and he looked sideways in guilt and sorrow at Bonny's father and brother and sister and her aunts and uncles and her grandfather and still Pawsy went on that there'd be only more damage done if this boy was given a custodial sentence and there was a half a minute or so of shuffling and shouting and someone was crying and people were escorted out and the judge got a bit wicked then I think and her hammer near splintered the wood of her bench and she thanked Pawsy but she didn't sound a bit grateful and there was no mustard cut and a fella in a blue shirt and navy tie caught my elbow gently and asked into my ear did I want to go straight or go home first and I said I'd go straight and I called my mother Mammy and my father Daddy as they held me tight as pale as ghosts and the lad in the blue shirt said Okay, come on now, and as the van doors closed in the small car park at the back of the courthouse I felt a lightening inside me, a letting go, like I was stretched out flat and floating on a gentle swell.

I wasn't a week out of prison the first evening I drove out that way in the mother's Clio. I was only thinking about calling. Trying to test out the feeling I'd have if I was to call for definite, to see how much I'd shake and how sick I'd feel in my stomach. I had a jumble of words in my head, lines of things to say that wouldn't stand in any order for me. I'd thought maybe I'd write down some things and learn them off by heart, but then I had an image of myself in my head reeling off things, like a child saying tables, with my face red, getting stuck and shaking with fear and embarrassment and they all standing up looking at me, and they more embarrassed than me even and only wanting me to go away and stop reminding them of their agonies.

It was raining and she was standing by the pier of their gate wearing a mackintosh with a see-through hood pulled up over a headscarf like an oul one, waiting for a lift to town I suppose. I was shocked to see her there and slowed and stopped without thinking and wound the window down, and when I looked out and up into the rain where she stood I hadn't a word in me that was ever known and she was just as silent and her mouth shaped itself as if to speak and her green eyes widened a little bit and as mad and unexpected a thing as it was it didn't seem one bit wrong when she walked around to the passenger side. She gave a glance back to the house the way you might expect to see something or someone that might stop her or call her back to herself. But there was no one or what empty space was there didn't have enough pull on her, and she gave her head a small shake and sat in beside me and I saw she was wearing red shoes with a bit of heel and a skirt that was shorter than her loosely buttoned raincoat and she smelt like rain and cold air and perfume and soap and some other thing that made my heart beat like a madman at the wall of a padded cell. Drive out as far as the Lookout, she said, and I parked there on the hillside above the lake and we sat and looked across at the Clare Hills and the darkness falling across them. And all she said was Were you going too fast? And I said I was. And I tried not to move or make a sound as I cried and she put her hand on top of mine for the first time and something rose up inside in me, like bubbles in a bottle that was hard shook and opened too fast.

There was a prison officer who trained the Roscrea minors[9] and he used to work in the aluminium factory with my father years ago. He was in charge of maintenance in the prison. He'd give me jobs to do during the day, scraping paint or sweeping or picking up papers, or if he'd a complicated job going on he'd leave me in my cell and say Tip away there at your oul books like a good lad. He stayed back my first night in even though he was finished his shift and brought me over to the games room and came in with me and asked did I want to play a game of pool and he pointed at a few quare hawks[10] and said Look after this boy for me, all right? And I could hardly breathe for fear when he went away. But those lads were sound enough and I soon learned to look mostly at the floor and to stay out of things.

---

9   Hurling team.
10   Strange people.

I told her these stories over a good few drives, about the courthouse steps and what it was like in prison, and she listened without saying anything. She hadn't known the things that had happened, or even that her brother had been home. She'd been taking things the doctor gave her to stop her going mad and they'd made her lose herself for a good long while. I told her about the watery food, the hospital smell in the corridor, the wicked-looking fucker two cells down with the scar diagonal across his face, from his chin through his lips, along his nose as far as his forehead. Even on his eyelid it was. He screamed some nights and cried like a child and three or four screws would walk him away down to the infirmary with a blanket around his shoulders. She said How did his eye survive? I didn't know. I didn't ask him. It must have been closed tight when the knife went along it. I told her about the nights spent lying there in the half-light in a bunk bed underneath a man who wouldn't pay his television licence and farted and snorted all night and loved being in prison.

I sit there and she sits there and she puts her hand on mine and sometimes it feels cold if she's been waiting for me too long. She said once, You know the way Our Lord suffered His Passion[11] and the flesh flayed from Him? Well, that's the kind of pain I wish I felt and not this ... this ... And she had no name for it nor has she still. There's no words, I suppose. There's definitely none in my head, anyway. Some evenings she says nothing at all and I sit and look out through the windscreen at the lines of rain or at the sunlight that gets stuck on the smears on the glass that I keep meaning to wipe off. But her hand is always on mine and it's always warm after a minute or two and feels like it's a part of me.

She says things sometimes out of the silence suddenly, words on their own that make no sense, and then silence again. Sometimes she picks the words up again, like she's after thinking for a while about the idea that the first words represented. The heat, she said one day. Then nothing for miles. You have double it now, maybe. And Bonny has none. I can feel it off of you. Maybe it's the way you were given hers to carry. Maybe, maybe. I can feel it off you, coming from the bones of your hand, even when your hand is cold. It goes into me.

And that's all she ever said about heat. She says things now and again out of the blue that sound like questions but I can tell those days from the tone of her and the way her head is angled away from me that she's not asking anything of me. She mightn't even know she's talking out loud. I wonder what you know about me, she said one day. I wonder what Bonny had you told. Did ye talk at all

---

11 In Christianity, this refers to the last week of Jesus' life, right up until his death by crucifixion.

to one another, I don't know. Ye were always very quiet above in her bedroom. How long were ye doing a line?[12]

And I nearly answered her that it had been eleven and a bit months and she'd been impatient for it to be twelve and she'd wanted a Claddagh ring[13] for our one-year, she'd had it picked out and all below in Fitzgibbon's Jewellers, but she started again talking just as I opened my mouth, saying Oh ya, sure didn't ye start going out shortly after her debs?[14] How's it you didn't take her to her debs, I wonder. And she's wondering still because I offered no answer and nor do I think was one expected of me.

She's all I think about, all I have in my head, all day, every day. I count down the hours and minutes and seconds until I can ask for a lend of the car and lie that I'm only going for a spin or to meet the lads or to give someone a lift to training. I have a picture of her right thigh burnt into the inside of my eyes and the black tights on it and her skirt riding up along it as she sits in without a word and I feel shame at the ache in myself, I pray to God sometimes to take away the hardness, the wrongness. Sometimes we have miles driven before she speaks, if she speaks at all, or we're parked up in Castlelough looking out at the lake and the dark hills or we're in the car park of the shopping centre in Limerick or out at the Clare Glens surrounded by trees and the singing of birds. I think about her eyes and the greenness of them and her lips, swollen like they were stung by a bee. How she looks like she's crying even when she's not. About the straightness of the line the tears make slowly on her cheek, always that. About the feel of her hand on mine, the warmth of the blood pulsing through it.

Girls and their mothers are either the best of friends or else they can't bear one another as a rule, she told me. It's always either one or the other, there's no middle ground between the women. Not like the men, the way they can rub along with each other, never falling out nor being too wrapped in one another. It's all or nothing. She was only nineteen when Bonny was born. Bonny was two years younger than me. That mad bint we had for religion inside in the Brothers. She said something one day I often think of now. Mankind will evolve to the point of something. Something. Something. Apotheosis. Until then we're driven chiefly by animal wants. Is that all I am, an animal? Imagine doing these things and feeling nothing only worry about the day that's surely coming when I'll no longer be able to do these things. Sit in a car beside her, touching lightly

---

12 Dating.

13 Irish ring design, depicting two hands holding a heart wearing a crown. It represents love, friendship, and loyalty.

14 Graduation dance.

off her, filling up with some pain that's the sweetest thing I ever felt. A still, silent animal, waiting.

I never know until I see her standing still against the high wall at the unseen end of the old mill out past Ballinaclough Cross whether she'll be there or not. Some days she is and more she isn't. And I think I'll have someday to explain to someone somewhere how I could live with it, the awful wrongness of it all, the terrible, unforgivable joy I felt each time I saw her waiting there. And Bonny dead, lovely, lovely Bonny, her daughter, and I having killed her, and I hardly remembering her face any more. I'm going to scald for an eternity in hell and I don't care.

There's a kind of a peace now in the knowing of the routes I have lying stretched away before me, only two of them, and they as clear as if they were drawn in black marker on a white page, with my present life a dot in the fork of their meeting. One is death and one is life. I'll call up to Bobby Mahon and ask to see will he take me back on for six more months and I'll sign up for my final block release inside in Limerick and once I have my papers got I'll ask her to come away with me to Canada or New Zealand or one of them places and if she says Yes I'll never be sad a day again and if she says No I'll never be sad a day again and I'll take my chances with that Lord God above of supposed infinite mercy and my mother and father will be relieved for once and for all of the burden of the worry of me. Someday soon I'll lean across and kiss her on her lips and there'll surely then be no going back from that and all that went before will just be dust.

—2015

IAN WILLIAMS

Poet, short story writer, and literature professor Ian Williams has been shortlisted for several Canadian literature awards, including the Giller Prize and the Griffin Prize, and he is the winner of the 2012 Danuta Gleed Literary Award. Praised by critics as "radical" and "inventive," Williams experiments with space, time, and language, creating a world at once strange and recognizable: one of connection and conversation, yet also one of disconnection and isolation. As fellow Canadian writer David Chariadny has observed, "[t]he startling brilliance of Ian Williams stems from his restlessness with form. His ceaseless creativity susses out the right patterning of story, the right vernacular nuance, the right diagram and deftly dropped reference."

Born in Trinidad in 1979, Williams was raised and educated in Canada. A precocious student, he moved through high school quickly. As an undergraduate at the University of Toronto, he studied Psychology and English, with the intent of going into medicine. He decided, however, against becoming a doctor and instead pursued his studies in English literature. Though he was writing creatively, he did not take creative writing classes; he preferred to study literature and learn the tricks and formal innovations of earlier masters, particularly those of the Romantic and Modernist periods. Williams describes his writing as "inquisitive about the world, playful with audience, musical and mathematical in form, and lightly muscled in syntax."

Williams studied under the poet George Elliott Clarke and focused his PhD on twentieth-century poetry and theories of voice and tone. He finished his PhD at the age of 25 and then took a job as professor of American literature at Fitchburg State University. He is now at the University of British Columbia, where he continues to teach and write. He has held fellowships and residencies at Vermont Studio Center, Cave Canem, Kimmel Harding Nelson Center for the Arts, and Palazzo Rinaldi. His works include the poetry collections *You Know Who You Are* (2010) and *Personals* (2012), the short story collection *Not Anyone's Anything* (2011), and his debut novel *Reproduction* (2019), which won the Giller Prize.

Break-In

HOOP planned to get in and out as quickly as possible. Six to eight minutes is all it should take to storm a house. Treat it like a timed shopping spree, like a game show, like a shot clock speeding to 0:00 at the top of the screen. But the back bedroom with its otherworldly girliness threw him, and when he heard the garage door rumbling up, he ran down the stairs, then down one more level (he panicked) into the basement and hid under the stairs. He didn't even see the side entrance.

Late evening, a month into first semester, a guy and his girl walk from school to Phase 2 of The Houses. He leads her to a Siamese house, joined at the cheek. He leads her to the left twin and they enter through the mouth. Inside is a mess of exposed plumbing, wood, and wires. Orange codes are spray-painted on the walls.

He's been in houses like this before, in this situation or nearly.

This house—this whole subdivision—was five stops from Hoop's aging apartment complex. The balconies of his building were streaked with rust. So he was attracted to the new development, and from the back corner seat of the 41 bus, he tracked its progress over the spring like a seed growing in a paper cup. First the land was bulldozed, then mixer trucks planted cement into the patterns of an old civilization, then workers put up wooden walls, then plastic walls, then dark shingles, then various colours of brick. By the end of April some of the houses were almost ready to be occupied. Hoop—not for Hooper, but for his skills balling—and his friend Duane got off the bus early to explore what guys were calling, with bravado, The Houses.

Everyone knew that guys took girls to The Houses to get some, except for the ninth graders, who still preferred the mall for softcore, handholding, closed-mouthed action.

The day Hoop and Duane first explored The Houses, the front door of lot 23L was unlocked. There were beige ceramic tiles in the small front foyer, and a step up to a narrow hallway, then, in walking sequence, powder room, basement door, open-concept kitchen (with breakfast bar), dining and family rooms, and a small raised deck beyond the sliding glass patio doors.

The guy suggests they use the basement to avoid curious homeowners or kids looking for hide-and-seek territory. Those types usually stay on the main floor, or they go upstairs and check out the bedrooms.

"No one ever goes down to the basement," he says. What's there to see? Insulation, concrete floors, a drain, bare bulbs, support beams, maybe a rough-in for a bathroom.

"Look at this," Duane said. He was still at the entrance, one hand on the door, the other on the frame. "All you gotta do is knock and the whole thing'll fly apart."

"What are you talking about?" Hoop walked back to the foyer.

Duane closed the door and turned the lock. "See how this dead-bolt fits in here? The casing—the wood—all around the frame is really thin. The only thing holding it there is these nails. What? Half inch?"

"'Cause of the glass," Hoop said. There were panels on either side of the door, so the lock was barely longer than the door latch.

"Yeah. They can't nail the casing in any more." Duane pulled hard on the locked door and the frame seemed to give. "They best get an alarm up in here."

o o o

At the time *Not at night* At the time *Better in the afternoon when everyone's at work* Hoop had no plans to invade lot 23L *Dress normal—a hoody or a jersey and nobody'll look at you twice* But that little piece of information from Duane *With all the Blacks and Indians in the area you'll just look like somebody's kid* existed for

———————————————————————————

Close to her ear, he says, "We could get our *mmm* on down here" and puckers his lips slightly, cool, touches the brim of his hat.

She knows this is where girls come to let themselves be touched. The fur around her hood dusts her forehead. She's been to The Houses before, not since Phase I though, and then it wasn't with this guy.

Hoop *Who knows his neighbour anymore* like a theory to be proven *Bring a package, ring the doorbell, enter through the door inside the garage* But if it were possible simply to enter a house by kicking down the door *Easy as that* why weren't more houses robbed *Think of the cred, man* or why weren't more people robbing their neighbours?

Bus ride after bus ride *Only bag stuff small enough to fit in a knapsack* the thought swelled in his head *and not too much, laptop, MP3 player, camera* until he finally *If it don't fit you must acquit* finally he

o o o

tried to get in and out as quickly as possible. Six to eight minutes is enough to take. With seven minutes left, Hoop saw photos over the fireplace. To blue eyes, the girls in separate frames might look like the same girl or twins: each wore two thick plaits like upside down horns on the side of her head, a toothless thick-lipped smile, the same pink sweater though the turtlenecks worn underneath were different. But he could tell that they were not the same girl, not twins either. Just poor, at the time, and wearing hand-me-downs.

He makes a show of opening the basement door for her. She steps down carefully, holding her hair to the sides of her face. Behind her, the guy's arms swish against his bubble vest. This morning he only had style in mind, but during the last two afternoon periods, when he proposed the idea of hanging out after school, the vest turned into something else—padding.

Six left. Hoop saw a glasses case and telephone bill on the arm of the converted patio chair in the family room. The surname on the envelope was Pearson, like the airport.

Five left. Upstairs in the master bedroom, he caught himself, knapsack on one shoulder, in the mirror of the ensuite. On the counter, a bottle of baby oil, a tube of cut-open foundation, and a comb with hair curling in it stared back at him like three guard dogs. He heard for the first time the low growl of the refrigerator downstairs.

Four left. He arrived in the otherworldly back bedroom, the older girl's, wallpapered with posters, carpeted with skirts and dresses left where she stepped out of them. Three left, he didn't know what to take. His bag was still empty. Three left. He heard the 41 pass. Three left. He found an MP3 player with headphones still attached on the bed. Two left. The garage door opened. Two left. He inadvertently ran to the basement. Two left. The car doors closed. There should be two minutes left. He ducked his head under the comforter covering boxes under the stairs. Overtime.

For a gun he had a boxcutter.

o o o

Light slants downward through the small windows on one side of the basement. Flecks of dust turn somersaults in the smoky light. The girl started talking dirty into his ear during third or fourth period, and now she wishes she hadn't. In this hollowed house, its ribs showing like the inside of a cathedral or a half-eaten turkey, she feels both watched and abandoned.

Hoop was already hoping for an inaccurate suspect description, for a neighbour to say, *male black six feet between twenty and twenty-five at least two hundred pounds dark baggy clothes baseball cap with a hood pulled over it.* And that wouldn't be Hoop. He looked eighteen but was fifteen, black yes, tall yes, not wearing what she saw, but an oversized basketball jersey. He was long-necked and his arms had the definition of a woman who curled light weights.

And he was strong, though he didn't look it. Shaking his hand or escaping his headlock, you'd wonder where he stored all that strength. His bones must be made of metal.

o o o

Whatever happened upstairs happened in Hoop's head.

"Some wayward boy do this," the woman said. Her deep voice engorged Hoop's heart with rhythm. *Wayward* was his mother's word.

"Call the police." A teenaged voice.

"Him gone."

"Call the police. Don't touch anything. He could come back. What if he's still here?"

The patio door slid open.

"Let's go upstairs," she says, turning around with her arms folded.

"Hold up, hold up," he says. He takes both her hands in his, unfolds her arms. "Didn't you say you wanted—"

"It's dirty."

"Dirty, huh." He speaks into her lips. "You been talking dirt all day."

"Tasha. Tasha! Stay here."

Pattering, then a child's voice: "I wasn't going anywhere."

"Hello? Somebody break in my house. (From the mother's responses, Hoop could tell what the dispatcher was asking.) I'm at 12 Deerpass Lane. It don't have a number outside, lot 23L. [←Where do you live?] In the kitchen. [←Where are you now?] No, my two girls with me. [←Are you alone?] I don't know. I don't see anybody. The door was open when I come home. [←Is the suspect there?] The front door. [←Which door did you find open?] No, like the inside door from the garage. Him kick it down. [←The front door?] Please send somebody quick, the police. I live at twel—[←The officers will be there any minute.] I didn't look. I don't know. [←Is anything missing?] I think so. We in the kitchen. [←Are you all safe?] Okay. Okay. Mm. Okay. [←Here's what I want you to do …]."

There's no reason to be afraid of me, Hoop thought downstairs. He was a spider at the heel of a woman. *Three* females. It might be better to get out now, just run, up the stairs, out the front, wave the boxcutter. He could cover his face. When the police came, there'd be no waving the boxcutter. Lord Jesus. Straight to Juvy. And his mother. Lord God.

Isn't anything he says that makes her stay—he could have been on mute—but strobe flashes of him on the court with his wifebeater pulled up behind his neck, and his slow kiss near her locker, thumb on her chin, and girls everywhere razing her with their eyes. This guy was—*real* was the only word, so said his shining bottom lip, his peach breath, and hot hands. She would approach the next few minutes as a job to be done, a vegetable to be eaten.

"Police!" Boots clomped overhead.

"In the kitchen," said the mother, Ms. (there was no man on the mantle) Pearson.

In Hoop's head, and possibly upstairs, the officers were wearing fatigues and Stallone headbands. One of them, Goliath-sized, spoke mechanically into his shoulder-mounted walkie-talkie, which beeped back before emitting a voice hoarse with static. Another officer, shorter, unable to grow facial hair, wearing a too-big uniform, and carrying a bazooka, appeared behind the first like an echo. Goliath told Ms. Pearson and her girls to wait where they were. He told his walkie-talkie, not the family, that he had already searched the first floor, that Echo was proceeding into the basement, and that he would search upstairs.

Echo never seemed to be looking at anything in particular. His gaze darted around as if tracking a housefly. The kind of man who snaps. The soldier cops walked around, touching boxes on their hips or shoulders, and Ms. Pearson stood at a distance inside her house, as if it were the model, open for the public to inspect, to walk on the carpet in dirty shoes. At that moment, Hoop wanted Goliath slain and Echo silenced, for what they had turned her house into.

o o o

If she feels like it later she might talk to her girls—her real girls—that night. Right now, she doesn't think she'll feel like it.

He, on the other hand, has a breathy re-enactment all set for tomorrow: *She was like* Oh no no, *and I was like* Yeas, No oh, *Yeas,* Noh, *Yeeas,* Oh yeaaas yes! He only kneads her body for a few minutes. Then it starts to relax.

Every sense shut off except Hoop's hearing. First he heard footsteps descending, each foot a different pitch. The melody made him want to cry. The footsteps belonged to Echo—Echo in his fatigues of a thousand pockets, something deadly in each, bazooka cocked over his shoulder, hand gun held sideways, little red laser searching for Hoop's black forehead.

Then Hoop heard Echo pull a chain. He was so well-covered that he did not notice the light. Or were his eyes closed?

Next rubber across the floor. That was the cold cellar opening. Another chain being pulled. On then off. The door closed.

The feet passed him. The washer opened. The dryer. On the way back to the stairs, the footsteps stopped. The officer knocked some boxes under the stairs with his gun, then again with the bazooka. He was waiting for the thief to screw things up, to sneeze or cough or shuffle. Hoop thought his trembling was seismic. Wasn't he panting? Wasn't his heart drumming? He knew this story from Poe and Lisa Simpson. Now was the time to burst through the boxes, screaming something, throwing his backpack at the feet of the officer, compressing the sides of his head between his hands.

o o o

His cue comes from her knees, which bounce slowly as if in a pool, then her legs give way. He spits out his gum and kisses her neck, the side of her face. One of her hands slides on the bubble vest beneath her, the other pushes against his shoulder. Something feels sharp, the vest's zipper, maybe a loose nail. She thinks, irrationally and maybe foolishly, but she thinks it all the same: *I don't want to die like this.*

Whatever happened upstairs seemed to happen far away in a smoky, tropical place. Hoop saw them all standing ankle-deep in swampy water.

Goliath got Ms. Pearson's story. She was questioned only for information, as if her fear and sense of violation were extravagances. The girls didn't say anything. They just stood to one side of their mother in descending height, partially obscured by palm fronds. The older one watched the officer drill her mother first with his mouth, then with his eyes, then with something further back in his skull like a low frequency wave.

After each question, Hoop could fill in what Goliath was thinking.

Do you own this home? [←She's probably renting. We should speak to the owners.]

You were all off the premises—[←Dumb down your language, boy.] You were out shopping, you said, when the break-in occurred?

No one saw the suspect. True? [←Black on black crime.]

Goliath studied the woman's hairline. *Unsure*, he wrote, just to write something. He studied the curtains hanging by thumbtacks, the cushions on patio furniture, and wrote *new owners*.

Were these rooms empty before? [←What do you have to steal?]

_____

He backs away suddenly and sits on his heels, fumbling with his zipper now instead of with her. She distracts herself. Where did his hat go? Wasn't he wearing a hat?

He is saying something, but he is on mute again, reaching for his wallet. The sight of it, thick and brown, tips her mind. She looks at the wad of gum on the cement floor.

"Won't hurt."

Echo had been wading in circles around the kitchen, looking for that housefly. After a few moments, he announced his intention (to his walkie-talkie) to search the exterior of the premises.

The patio door opened and closed. Through a nearby basement window, Hoop saw Echo's combat boots walk back and forth. From the attitude of the boots, Hoop guessed Echo was smoking.

He heard, "Not much furniture. Looks like she was robbed before," followed by a rush of air out Echo's nostrils, not a laugh quite. And, most significantly, he heard a smile on the other end of the walkie-talkie.

o   o   o

When the police left, the upstairs part of the house started to collapse like a deflating air mattress. The conversation was flimsy and tremulous. Tasha didn't have to sleep alone if she didn't want to. The door from the garage needed to be secured until they could change the lock. The thug could come back. The thugs. A gang of them.

A moment after he tears open the package and unrolls the rubber the upstairs door opens. Footsteps patter. A woman's voice, *Too small, this foyer, but look they have a step up to the hallway.* The girl pulls her clothes close to her, straightens up. The guy stops her arm. No sound. *Oh and Kevin look at this kitchen, see I told you the island was necessary, and look looklooklooklook they upgraded the backsplash.*

He heard things being moved. Perhaps the Pearsons were making old-fashioned booby traps. Cans and bottles by the front foyer. A houseplant by the patio door.

Hoop looked at the time on his cell phone. 6:58. He'd been in the basement for hours, and he had hours more to go before the family went to sleep. When they were all in the bedrooms, he'd sneak out. Except for his knees, which had been too sharply bent for too long, he was fairly comfortable under the stairs. Earlier, he had completely removed the comforter from over his head so that his eyes could get adjusted to the dark. But there was nothing to see.

Upstairs, they were watching TV. Drawers and cupboards closed. The music for an entertainment tabloid came on.

"Ready," the mother called over the music. "Tasha, come and eat."

Hoop smelled fried sardines upstairs. He was hungry, and gassy. That was another reason he uncovered his head.

"Did they check the cold room in the basement?" Ms. Pearson asked.

The voices continue upstairs into the bedrooms. In the basement, the guy and the girl look upward, as if listening with their eyes.

When the voices finally leave, the girl says with her palms, *I can't do this. It's too risky.*

"They're gone," he says, but she is already off his vest, brushing shavings from her skirt.

"I don't know. You want me to go down?" The older girl volunteered herself. "Give me a broom or something."

"You don't have to go. Eat." Ms. Pearson sucked her teeth. "I thought I heard—It's the neighbour maybe. They build these houses too close."

"You can use my umbrella," said Tasha.

"Girl, go and sit down!" Ms. Pearson said. "That's your food from this morning."

"I'll check," said the teenaged voice.

The basement light went on. Through the slats in the stairs, Hoop saw her ripple down: one dry bare heel then another, the back of her knee, the fingers of one hand around a yellow and red, Pooh umbrella, the other hand must have been on the banister. She reached the bottom, and, like Echo, walked to the cold room.

"I don't see anything," she shouted up as if checking the hold of a grappling hook.

"Hurry up," a little voice came back.

Ms. Pearson: "Girl, don't make me talk to you again. Sit. Down."

"I said I can't, all right." She starts up the stairs. "Don't follow me right away."

No answer.

"I'll meet you by the site office."

"Whatever."

She squeezes her chin into her neck and looks down on him from the basement stairs. His boxers are showing, as always.

"Whatever," she echoes back.

The upstairs door closed and footsteps ran away from the door of the basement.

Hoop was trying to settle the cover over his head again, but his hand knocked the back of a stair. The sound was enough to alert the girl. She whirled around with the umbrella raised over her head, ready to throw or strike.

"JaniceIwon'thurtanyofyou," Hoop whispered before she could scream or run, before she knew who she was seeing—that wet forehead, those two dark eyes, which were vibrating, barely, like a tuning fork, from fear to fatigue to anger to madness. He was wrapped in her old comforter. He looked like an Old Testament prophet.

Hoop saw the next two hours in a second. His mother's agonized image, the lines from her nose to jaw, her overprocessed hair, the carpet of the eleventh floor hallway, flanked by two soldier cops, Echo's thousand pockets and bazooka, the door opening inward, his mother's heavy bottom lip, one hand on the door. And he could read inside her too. She'd think *don't answer* at the knock. She'd think of herself in church, *God give me strength to raise my child in this country.* And in a few months, in the winter, she

Looking through one of the back bedroom windows of an unfinished house, Hoop and Duane, girlfriendless, observe a girl outside crossing tread marks of hardened mud.

Duane looks to see if he'd hit that.

Hoop looks to see if he knows her.

would think of his deviance, his big, expensive feet, while riding the bus between jobs, double-socked, in white no-name sneakers, and she would curse the cold cold winters of this country, and remember her government job in Jamaica, then fall asleep with her head on the window in someone else's grease patch.

Tears came when Hoop blinked. "Please," he said.

o o o

Tasha ran back to the door and opened it when she heard Janice's footsteps approaching the top.

"Did you see the killer?"

"Uh uh."

"I just wasn't sure if they checked," said the mother from the kitchen. "Come eat."

"Girl, you look scared," said Tasha.

o o o

Moments later, a guy emerges from the same house, dusting the front of his vest, looking both ways, putting a thumb to a nostril and sniffing tough-man style, then he picks up a slight limp and exits the site.

Hoop wants to hurt him. Duane wants to check out the house they came from. He puts a fist to his mouth and *whoop whoop*s. Starting to limp himself, he walks from the bedroom and says, "That's what I'm talkin' 'bout."

Hoop could no longer hear them, only the zooming sounds of segments changing on the entertainment show. The volume was higher. Janice must have been whispering everything up there, then they'd barricade the basement door, call the cops, then there'd be a loudspeaker and handcuffs and dogs and a helicopter whirring and a camera and *Bad boys, bad boys, whatcha gonna do?*

He started making a deal with God. *Lord, if you, if You, could get me out by some miracle—*How had he known Janice's name? Was that her name? Her name had come so easily to him, though he didn't recall noticing it, unlike the mother's bills on the patio furniture. *God if You, if YOU, could find a way out of this situation for me, then I'll—*Her room, that's where. On the door she had stuck up *Janice's room Keep out!* like a white girl would, Hoop thought, but he had been so distracted by the poster of some glistening, thick-legged, R&B singer, hair blowing like a horse, that he didn't remember the sign.

Then I'll what? Anything you want, Lord Jesus. That's how his mother prayed, every time there was a pause, she would fill up the space with *Lord Jesus,* barely aware that she was saying it.

Hoop made God an offer. But He could refuse. So Hoop started planning his explanations. *It was somebody else's idea. This guy*

Doorbell. There's a security sign on the front glass. That's new.

"Who that could be? Tasha don't open."

"I'm not a baby."

"Tasha I said no."

Tasha opens anyway. Ms. Pearson is flapping her hands dry as she approaches the door.

at school, I heard him talking so I tried it. I wasn't looking for anything, I just wanted to see if I could do it. Play dumb, good. Or *I was curious about how the inside of The Houses looked now that they're finished. There wasn't any car in the driveway. I thought this one hadn't closed yet.* [Didn't you see the shoes and the mat, the furniture?] *Yeah, as soon as I saw all that, the people came and I got scared so I hid.* Better. [What about all the stuff in your bag?] Dang.

The basement door opened again and Janice stepped down to the landing to collect some plastic bags—that's where they kept them, stuffed in a garbage bag, and when she took one more step down from the landing (Hoop could have grabbed her ankle to plead again or just slit her tendon with the boxcutter), she called up with her grappling-hook voice, "I need some air. We should go out."

"So late?"

"It's not late." The plastic bags hissed. "I at least need some air, but I'm not walking around by myself with some crazy in the neighbourhood."

She was at the top of the stairs again, her ankle was out of reach. Light flossed through the crack in the door.

"All right, just now, after Tasha brush she teeth."

"Um," Hoop says. He scratches his nose. He'll have to lie. "I go to Janice's school. She left this behind and I just …"

"Janice!" her mother shouts.

"You don't have to call her. Here, just give it to—"

"Come inside. She coming. Janice!" Ms. Pearson hurries back to the kitchen, slapping her slippers against the tile.

o o o

Still Hoop didn't trust her completely. She was evacuating the house so they'd be safe to call the police and dogs, camera, helicopter, *bad boys, bad boys*, etc.

But then footsteps ran down the upper staircase, Tasha protested wearing a coat when Janice didn't have to, chairs were cleared from the entrance, and the front door closed loudly. Hoop waited a few moments in case someone had forgotten her keys or needed to come back to pee. His heart was accelerating again. When the upstairs was still, he came out of hiding, willed his sore knees up the stairs and out the side entrance. He walked to the back of the house, cut across the unfenced back lawns and came out on the main road. Not safe enough. He kept his eyes on the intersection, where the buses travelled more frequently. He pulled the intersection toward him with his eyes because he couldn't run. He had to walk as slowly as anyone watching would expect him to in those jeans and ball shoes.

Hoop steps inside. They've installed bolts on the front door and the one leading to the garage. At the end of the hallway he sees real furniture. Leather.

Janice comes down the stairs. Tasha walks back to the staircase and says *ooh* with her back to Hoop.

He holds out a baseball hat, then he takes his MP3 player from his pocket. "I found it, just now, back by The Houses." He points a thumb over his shoulder.

o o o

He should have left his stash behind, but his prints were all over everything. Not that he had a record. Pay them back. A thank-you note—just to the girl, Janice.

He wanted to go home directly and go to sleep, but he took the knapsack to Duane's place first, in the apartment building near his. He shook out the booty on Duane's bed, lied and said he found it in Phase 11 of The Houses. Duane photographed everything and put it online. Hoop didn't care for the items either—what, a charger, a small video game, a cheap MP3 player, two brand name baby tees. No laptop, no digital camera.

Only the baby tees didn't sell. Duane and Hoop split the money, unevenly, and spent it on cafeteria lunches, dumping the ones their mothers prepared.

For days, Hoop listened to the news on AM radio, but there was no mention of 23L. Thank God there was worse news. A carjack on the east end, subway evacuations, insurgents overseas. It would be old news after a day anyway, and really nothing worth mentioning was stolen.

It's not mine you best get the hell out of here who do you think you are coming to my mother's house with your broken guilt trying to be all hero acting like you know me you don't know me fool you think you got my back I said you best run before I call the police on your skinny wannabe gangsta self I take you on myself nigga is what Janice would say outside, but not in this house. On this floor.

Hoop had made a deal with God underneath the basement stairs that if He got him out of this one, he'd—it had taken Hoop a while to come up with something sufficiently attractive for God to say *deal*—go to church with his mother again, read the Bible cover to cover, pay back seven times the money. He had specified his end of the deal: to escape wasn't enough, he'd need a guarantee that he would never get caught, specifically that word would never get to his mother. For that, he'd have to throw down more promises. Does the Lord have a price? He'd give up ball. He'd give up balling. He wouldn't ever take a girl to The Houses, wouldn't touch a girl till he was eighteen, till he was married.

I can get you out, the Lord said, but there will always be someone on your back.

You have to guarantee, Lord Jesus.

Then no deal.

Ms. Pearson comes padding back in her slippers. She looks at Janice. She looks at Hoop. Hoop pulls up his pants with one hand and scratches the back of his neck with the other.

"You," she says.

—2011

JILLIAN TAMAKI

Canadian cartoonist and illustrator Jillian Tamaki has worked in many genres: children's books, web comics, freelance magazine illustration, video games, and animated television shows. Praised for a varied style that is "expressive, vibrant and precise all at once," she is perhaps best known for her visually ingenious and emotionally rich graphic novels, sometimes co-created with her cousin Mariko Tamaki.

Born in 1980 to Japanese-Canadian and Egyptian-American parents, Jillian Tamaki was raised in Calgary, Alberta; in her own words, she "grew up mixed race in a very, very white part of Canada." After graduating from the Alberta College of Art and Design, she began her career as a freelance illustrator and worked at a video game company before moving to New York in 2005 (she would eventually return to Canada, settling in Toronto). Her first collection, *Gilded Lilies*, was published in 2006. She began to be recognized as a significant artist in 2008, when Jillian and Mariko Tamaki's illustrated book *Skim* was nominated for the Governor General's Award for children's literature—though controversy followed when only Mariko, who wrote the text, was named in the nomination. The cousins' 2014 book for young adults, *This One Summer*, won numerous awards, including the Ignatz Award for comics and the Caldecott Medal. It also went on to become one of the most commonly censored young adult books in the following years, often challenged for its depiction of teen sexuality, drug use, and profanity. In 2015 Jillian Tamaki published a collection of her popular webcomic *SuperMutant Magic Academy*, about precocious teen mutants and supernatural beings in high school; the book won two Ignatz Awards.

Tamaki's 2017 collection *Boundless* moves away from realism and linear narrative into more surreal and clearly adult territory, exploring such contemporary topics as social media, multi-level marketing, and viral content. Critic and novelist Rowan Hisayo Buchanan calls the collection an argument for "the primacy of images in storytelling." Like much of Tamaki's work, the art in *Boundless* uses colour sparingly but to powerful effect, with shifts in colour marking new stories or shifts in mood or character. Though the stories vary widely in perspective and voice, including a story narrated by non-human animals, most of the protagonists in *Boundless* are women. When asked if she writes feminist books, Tamaki says, "I don't categorize my books as feminist—they do not explicitly declare themselves as such nor are they about feminist theory. But I'm a feminist and a lot of [my] stories are about women living autonomous lives."

Half-Life

My shoes feel a little loose.

But why worry about that? They're old, and old leather stretches out.

Have you lost weight?

What? No! I don't think so...

You look great!

Well, thank you.

I'm trying a new multi-vitamin.

Ah, maybe that's it.

I concentrate on the sensation of my clothes on my body. Do the jeans offer less resistance to the motion of my legs? Do my shoulders move more freely within my shirt? Maybe they do.

A week after Jo's comment, I pull out the Hawaiian dress from the guest bedroom closet to test definitively.

Ha!

It fits.

Martha!

Sis!

It's nice to have an extra set of hands in the kitchen and Martha is the perfect helper. Knowledgable but deferential.

Hey, wait a minute. Come here.

Martha...

Stand still.

Are you getting SHORTER?

Oh my god, I think you are!

Ha ha ha! My big sister is a little old lady!

Oh shut up.

Watch your mouth, old-timer! Ha ha!

I think I need to see a doctor.

Are my bones shrinking? Is that what osteoporosis is? I look on the computer but end up more confused.

I leave the office annoyed. Doctors never really listen to what you say. But I understand what he means.

I certainly *look* fine — not emaciated or sickly. Just somehow....*smaller.*

The doctor's scale confirms *something* is missing. I am mysteriously 19 pounds lighter but otherwise appear perfectly *normal.*

I suppose we could all stand to lose a few pounds, eh?

I have to buy some new shoes.

No, this is definitely not normal.

Slowly, objects start rejecting me.

That's a little harsh. It's not the spoon's fault that I can no longer use it with ease. I'm the uncalibrated one.

I take indefinite leave from work which, frankly, is fine by me.

GET WELL SOO

The paperwork is a pain, given I have no official diagnosis. Still, it's no problem convincing my supervisor.

We hope to see you back soon, Helen.

I adapt.

I'll admit, I don't leave the house much anymore. Too much bother.

Where's your mummy, little girl?

The government provides me with a live-in aide shortly after the hospital becomes involved. His name is Lindsay, despite being a man—a very strong-looking man at that.

I guess my case has become very interesting to certain people.

Well, obviously it *is* very interesting.

I've taken up watercolour painting.

Despite my protestations, Martha quits her job and eventually replaces Lindsay. I can tell she still feels bad for laughing at me.

She spends her first week sewing me some simple items. I insist it's not necessary, that perhaps I can wear doll clothes, but Martha won't have it.

Dignity, she says.

I try to co-operate with the hospital and government people (Martha and I call them the "HGPs") but I draw the line at medical equipment in my room. I like being surrounded by my own things even though, at this point, they're of no use to me.

The rate of shrinking has sped up.

The blue and white vase we picked up on our honeymoon in Paris.

We bought it in the morning and lugged it around the city all day. Didn't even consider how on earth we'd get it home to Canada.

I could probably fit
inside that thing now.

There comes a day when I can't paint anymore.
I am surprised how deeply this upsets me. It was a good
way to pass time and I was just getting good at mixing
greys. But I'm now too small to hold a single sable hair.

The family gathers,
as is proper.

Someone designs a special glass
enclosure for me. Who?
The hospital, I suppose. To prevent
me from being devoured by an
insect or swept up on a bit of
pollen. We give the cat away.

One morning I wake to a commotion. I figure I must have disappeared from human vision. The machinery is taken away.

Martha stays on for two weeks, replacing food and water, but eventually she also leaves, which is only right.

A few days later, without Martha's company, I grow bored and decide to leave the enclosure. As I can easily fit inside the grain of the wood table, escaping is not difficult.

Outside, I'm instantly picked up by the air, much like a dust mote: I drift, not unpleasantly, around the room, then out a small crack in a drafty window.

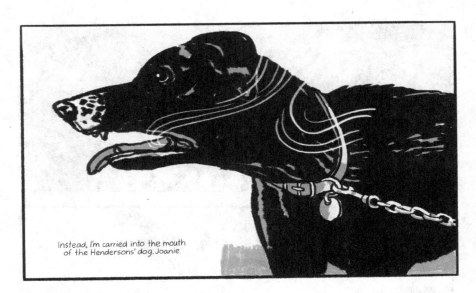

Instead, I'm carried into the mouth of the Hendersons' dog, Joanie.

Well, THIS must certainly be the end, I think. I still have eyes and hands and skin—real tissue, as tiny as it is. Surely they'll be broken apart by stomach acids. Or maybe I'll be snuffed out first.

The pain is blinding but very, very short. It doesn't take much.

My body dissolves but somehow I am still not completely gone.

I can no longer manipulate my environment in any way but, to my surprise, the emotional stimulus provided by Joanie affects me profoundly.

She feels elation and sadness, mostly. Not much nuance with dogs.

—*2017*

KRISTEN ROUPENIAN

Kristen Roupenian became a literary celebrity almost overnight in late 2017, when her story "Cat Person" was published by *The New Yorker*. The short piece, which centers on the brief relationship between a 20-year-old film student and a significantly older man, emerged at a key cultural moment, when the #MeToo movement had brought increased attention to matters of sexual consent and the power imbalance present in many relationships between men and women. By the end of the year, "Cat Person" had been shared online millions of times and eventually became one of the most-downloaded pieces in the *New Yorker*'s online history. While the story received a degree of popular attention—from passionate approval to indignant censure—rarely devoted to short fiction, it also received acclaim from literary critics and writers (Sheila Heti, for instance, selected the story for the 2017 edition of *The Best American Nonrequired Reading*). Many of Roupenian's readers were deeply affected by her penetrating depiction of the more destructive aspects of contemporary dating; indeed, many readers found the story so realistic that it was widely assumed to be memoir rather than fiction, an assumption that has itself generated heated debates about the ways in which fiction written by women is often interpreted.

Prior to the publication of "Cat Person," Roupenian had spent years considering both a life in literature and a life in foreign service. She received her PhD in English from Harvard in 2014, after which she spent a period volunteering for the Peace Corps in Kenya, the setting for her first (unpublished) novel—a thriller. Roupenian worked in various genres, especially horror and science fiction, before writing the realistic "Cat Person." Prior to 2017 these stories saw only limited success in a handful of relatively obscure online magazines—though her horror story "Don't Be Scarred" won the 2016 *Writer's Digest* Popular Fiction award. Roupenian's debut collection, *You Know You Want This* (2019), saw a return to the weird and grotesque, with some critics noting similarities to Stephen King and Angela Carter. The collection has received both criticism and praise for its frequent moral ambiguity, and for what one reviewer has called a commitment to "scampering across genres, and to showcasing evil in both male and female forms."

Cat Person

MARGOT MET Robert on a Wednesday night toward the end of her fall semester. She was working behind the concession stand at the artsy movie theatre downtown when he came in and bought a large popcorn and a box of Red Vines.

"That's an ... unusual choice," she said. "I don't think I've ever actually sold a box of Red Vines before."

Flirting with her customers was a habit she'd picked up back when she worked as a barista, and it helped with tips. She didn't earn tips at the movie theatre, but the job was boring otherwise, and she did think that Robert was cute. Not so cute that she would have, say, gone up to him at a party, but cute enough that she could have drummed up an imaginary crush on him if he'd sat across from her during a dull class—though she was pretty sure that he was out of college, in his mid-twenties at least. He was tall, which she liked, and she could see the edge of a tattoo peeking out from beneath the rolled-up sleeve of his shirt. But he was on the heavy side, his beard was a little too long, and his shoulders slumped forward slightly, as though he were protecting something.

Robert did not pick up on her flirtation. Or, if he did, he showed it only by stepping back, as though to make her lean toward him, try a little harder. "Well," he said. "O.K., then." He pocketed his change.

But the next week he came into the movie theatre again, and bought another box of Red Vines. "You're getting better at your job," he told her. "You managed not to insult me this time."

She shrugged. "I'm up for a promotion, so," she said.

After the movie, he came back to her. "Concession-stand girl, give me your phone number," he said, and, surprising herself, she did.

From that small exchange about Red Vines, over the next several weeks they built up an elaborate scaffolding of jokes via text, riffs that unfolded and shifted so quickly that she sometimes had a hard time keeping up. He was very clever, and she found that she had to work to impress him. Soon she noticed that when she texted him he usually texted her back right away, but if she took more than a few hours to respond his next message would always be short and wouldn't include a question, so it was up to her to re-initiate the conversation, which she always did. A few times, she got distracted for a day or so and wondered if the exchange would die out altogether, but then she'd think of something funny to tell him or she'd see a picture on the Internet that was relevant to their conversation, and they'd start up again. She still didn't know much about him, because they never talked about anything personal, but when they landed two or three good jokes in a row there was a kind of exhilaration to it, as if they were dancing.

Then, one night during reading period, she was complaining about how all the dining halls were closed and there was no food in her room because her roommate had raided her care package, and he offered to buy her some Red Vines to sustain her. At first, she deflected this with another joke, because she really did have to study, but he said, "No, I'm serious, stop fooling around and come now," so she put a jacket over her pajamas and met him at the 7-Eleven.

It was about eleven o'clock. He greeted her without ceremony, as though he saw her every day, and took her inside to choose some snacks. The store didn't have Red Vines, so he bought her a Cherry Coke Slurpee and a bag of Doritos and a novelty lighter shaped like a frog with a cigarette in its mouth.

"Thank you for my presents," she said, when they were back outside. Robert was wearing a rabbit-fur hat that came down over his ears and a thick, old-fashioned down jacket. She thought it was a good look for him, if a little dorky; the hat heightened his lumberjack aura, and the heavy coat hid his belly and the slightly sad slump of his shoulders.

"You're welcome, concession-stand girl," he said, though of course he knew her name by then. She thought he was going to go in for a kiss and prepared to duck and offer him her cheek, but instead of kissing her on the mouth he took her by the arm and kissed her gently on the forehead, as though she were something precious. "Study hard, sweetheart," he said. "I will see you soon."

On the walk back to her dorm, she was filled with a sparkly lightness that she recognized as the sign of an incipient crush.

While she was home over break, they texted nearly non-stop, not only jokes but little updates about their days. They started saying good morning and good night, and when she asked him a question and he didn't respond right away she felt a jab of anxious yearning. She learned that Robert had two cats, named Mu and Yan, and together they invented a complicated scenario in which her childhood cat, Pita, would send flirtatious texts to Yan, but whenever Pita talked to Mu she was formal and cold, because she was jealous of Mu's relationship with Yan.

"Why are you texting all the time?" Margot's stepdad asked her at dinner. "Are you having an affair with someone?"

"Yes," Margot said. "His name is Robert, and I met him at the movie theatre. We're in love, and we're probably going to get married."

"Hmm," her stepdad said. "Tell him we have some questions for him."

"My parents are asking about u," Margot texted, and Robert sent her back a smiley-face emoji whose eyes were hearts.

When Margot returned to campus, she was eager to see Robert again, but he turned out to be surprisingly hard to pin down. "Sorry, busy week at work," he replied. "I promise I will c u soon." Margot didn't like this; it felt as if the dynamic had shifted out of her favor, and when eventually he did ask her to go to a movie she agreed right away.

The movie he wanted to see was playing at the theatre where she worked, but she suggested that they see it at the big multiplex just outside town instead; students didn't go there very often, because you needed to drive. Robert came to pick her up in a muddy white Civic with candy wrappers spilling out of the cup holders. On the drive, he was quieter than she'd expected, and he didn't look at her very much. Before five minutes had gone by, she became wildly uncomfortable, and, as they got on the highway, it occurred to her that he could take her someplace and rape and murder her; she hardly knew anything about him, after all.

Just as she thought this, he said, "Don't worry, I'm not going to murder you," and she wondered if the discomfort in the car was her fault, because she was acting jumpy and nervous, like the kind of girl who thought she was going to get murdered every time she went on a date.

"It's O.K.—you can murder me if you want," she said, and he laughed and patted her knee. But he was still disconcertingly quiet, and all her bubbling attempts at making conversation bounced right off him. At the theatre, he made a joke to the cashier at the concession stand about Red Vines, which fell flat in a way that embarrassed everyone involved, but Margot most of all.

During the movie, he didn't hold her hand or put his arm around her, so by the time they were back in the parking lot she was pretty sure that he had changed his mind about liking her. She was wearing leggings and a sweatshirt, and that might have been the problem. When she got into the car, he'd said, "Glad to see you dressed up for me," which she'd assumed was a joke, but maybe she actually had offended him by not seeming to take the date seriously enough, or something. He was wearing khakis and a button-down shirt.

"So, do you want to go get a drink?" he asked when they got back to the car, as if being polite were an obligation that had been imposed on him. It seemed obvious to Margot that he was expecting her to say no and that, when she did, they wouldn't talk again. That made her sad, not so much because she wanted to continue spending time with him as because she'd had such high expectations for him over break, and it didn't seem fair that things had fallen apart so quickly.

"We could go get a drink, I guess?" she said.

"If you want," he said.

"If you want" was such an unpleasant response that she sat silently in the car until he poked her leg and said, "What are you sulking about?"

"I'm not sulking," she said. "I'm just a little tired."

"I can take you home."

"No, I could use a drink, after that movie." Even though it had been playing at the mainstream theatre, the film he'd chosen was a very depressing drama about the Holocaust, so inappropriate for a first date that when he suggested it she said, "Lol r u serious," and he made some joke about how he was sorry that he'd misjudged her taste and he could take her to a romantic comedy instead.

But now, when she said that about the movie, he winced a little, and a totally different interpretation of the night's events occurred to her. She wondered if perhaps he'd been trying to impress her by suggesting the Holocaust movie, because he didn't understand that a Holocaust movie was the wrong kind of "serious" movie with which to impress the type of person who worked at an artsy movie theatre, the type of person he probably assumed she was. Maybe, she thought, her texting "lol r u serious" had hurt him, had intimidated him and made him feel uncomfortable around her. The thought of this possible vulnerability touched her, and she felt kinder toward him than she had all night.

When he asked her where she wanted to go for a drink, she named the place where she usually hung out, but he made a face and said that it was in the student ghetto and he'd take her somewhere better. They went to a bar she'd never been to, an underground speakeasy type of place, with no sign announcing its presence. There was a line to get inside, and, as they waited, she grew fidgety trying to figure out how to tell him what she needed to tell him, but she couldn't, so when the bouncer asked to see her I.D. she just handed it to him. The bouncer hardly even looked at it; he just smirked and said, "Yeah, no," and waved her to the side, as he gestured toward the next group of people in line.

Robert had gone ahead of her, not noticing what was playing out behind him. "Robert," she said quietly. But he didn't turn around. Finally, someone in line who'd been paying attention tapped him on the shoulder and pointed to her, marooned on the sidewalk.

She stood, abashed, as he came back over to her. "Sorry!" she said. "This is so embarrassing."

"How old *are* you?" he demanded.

"I'm twenty," she said.

"Oh," he said. "I thought you said you were older."

"I told you I was a sophomore!" she said. Standing outside the bar, having been rejected in front of everyone, was humiliating enough, and now Robert was looking at her as if she'd done something wrong.

"But you did that—what do you call it? That gap year," he objected, as though this were an argument he could win.

"I don't know what to tell you," she said helplessly. "I'm twenty." And then, absurdly, she started to feel tears stinging her eyes, because somehow everything had been ruined and she couldn't understand why this was all so hard.

But, when Robert saw her face crumpling, a kind of magic happened. All the tension drained out of his posture; he stood up straight and wrapped his bearlike arms around her. "Oh, sweetheart," he said. "Oh, honey, it's O.K., it's all right. Please don't feel bad." She let herself be folded against him, and she was flooded with the same feeling she'd had outside the 7-Eleven—that she was a delicate, precious thing he was afraid he might break. He kissed the top of her head, and she laughed and wiped her tears away.

"I can't believe I'm crying because I didn't get into a bar," she said. "You must think I'm such an idiot." But she knew he didn't think that, from the way he was gazing at her; in his eyes, she could see how pretty she looked, smiling through her tears in the chalky glow of the streetlight, with a few flakes of snow coming down.

He kissed her then, on the lips, for real; he came for her in a kind of lunging motion and practically poured his tongue down her throat. It was a terrible kiss, shockingly bad; Margot had trouble believing that a grown man could possibly be so bad at kissing. It seemed awful, yet somehow it also gave her that tender feeling toward him again, the sense that even though he was older than her, she knew something he didn't.

When he was done kissing her, he took her hand firmly and led her to a different bar, where there were pool tables and pinball machines and sawdust on the floor and no one checking I.D.s at the door. In one of the booths, she saw the grad student who'd been her English T.A. her freshman year.

"Should I get you a vodka soda?" Robert asked, which she thought was maybe supposed to be a joke about the kind of drink college girls liked, though she'd never had a vodka soda. She actually was a little anxious about what to order; at the places she went to, they only carded people at the bar, so the kids who were twenty-one or had good fake I.D.s usually brought pitchers of P.B.R. or Bud Light back to share with the others. She wasn't sure if those brands were ones that Robert would make fun of, so, instead of specifying, she said, "I'll just have a beer."

With the drinks in front of him and the kiss behind him, and also maybe because she had cried, Robert became much more relaxed, more like the witty person she knew through his texts. As they talked, she became increasingly sure that what she'd interpreted as anger or dissatisfaction with her had, in fact, been nervousness, a fear that she wasn't having a good time. He kept coming back to her initial dismissal of the movie, making jokes that glanced off it and watching her closely to see how she responded. He teased her about her highbrow taste, and said how hard it was to impress her because of all the film classes she'd taken, even though he knew she'd taken only one summer class in film. He joked about how she and the other employees at the artsy theatre probably sat around and made fun of the people who went to the mainstream theatre, where they didn't even serve wine, and some of the movies were in IMAX 3-D.

Margot laughed along with the jokes he was making at the expense of this imaginary film-snob version of her, though nothing he said seemed quite fair, since she was the one who'd actually suggested that they see the movie at the Quality 16. Although now, she realized, maybe that had hurt Robert's feelings, too. She'd thought it was clear that she just didn't want to go on a date where she worked, but maybe he'd taken it more personally than that; maybe he'd suspected that she was ashamed to be seen with him. She was starting to think that she understood him—how sensitive he was, how easily he could be wounded—and that made her feel closer to him, and also powerful, because once she knew how to hurt him she also knew how he could be soothed. She asked him lots of questions about the movies he liked, and she spoke self-deprecatingly about the movies at the artsy theatre that she found boring or incomprehensible; she told him about how much her older co-workers intimidated her, and how she sometimes worried that she wasn't smart enough to form her own opinions on anything. The effect of this on him was palpable and immediate, and she felt as if she were petting a large, skittish animal, like a horse or a bear, skillfully coaxing it to eat from her hand.

By her third beer, she was thinking about what it would be like to have sex with Robert. Probably it would be like that bad kiss, clumsy and excessive, but imagining how excited he would be, how hungry and eager to impress her, she felt a twinge of desire pluck at her belly, as distinct and painful as the snap of an elastic band against her skin.

When they'd finished that round of drinks, she said, boldly, "Should we get out of here, then?," and he seemed briefly hurt, as if he thought she was cutting the date short, but she took his hand and pulled him up, and the look on his face when he realized what she was saying, and the obedient way he trailed her out of the bar, gave her that elastic-band snap again, as did, oddly, the fact that his palm was slick beneath hers.

Outside, she presented herself to him again for kissing, but, to her surprise, he only pecked her on the mouth. "You're drunk," he said, accusingly.

"No, I'm not," she said, though she was. She pushed her body against his, feeling tiny beside him, and he let out a great shuddering sigh, as if she were something too bright and painful to look at, and that was sexy, too, being made to feel like a kind of irresistible temptation.

"I'm taking you home, lightweight," he said, shepherding her to the car. Once they were inside it, though, she leaned into him again, and after a little while, by lightly pulling back when he pushed his tongue too far down her throat, she was able to get him to kiss her in the softer way that she liked, and soon after that she was straddling him, and she could feel the small log of his erection straining against his pants. Whenever it rolled beneath her weight, he let out these fluttery, high-pitched moans that she couldn't help feeling were a little melodramatic, and then suddenly he pushed her off him and turned the key in the ignition.

"Making out in the front seat like a teen-ager," he said, in mock disgust. Then he added, "I'd have thought you'd be too old for that, now that you're *twenty*."

She stuck her tongue out at him. "Where do you want to go, then?"

"Your place?"

"Um, that won't really work. Because of my roommate?"

"Oh, right. You live in the dorms," he said, as though that were something she should apologize for.

"Where do you live?" she asked.

"I live in a house."

"Can I ... come over?"

"You can."

The house was in a pretty, wooded neighborhood not too far from campus and had a string of cheerful white fairy lights across the doorway. Before he got out of the car, he said, darkly, like a warning, "Just so you know, I have cats."

"I know," she said. "We texted about them, remember?"

At the front door, he fumbled with his keys for what seemed a ridiculously long time and swore under his breath. She rubbed his back to try to keep the mood going, but that seemed to fluster him even more, so she stopped.

"Well. This is my house," he said flatly, pushing the door open.

The room they were in was dimly lit and full of objects, all of which, as her eyes adjusted, resolved into familiarity. He had two large, full bookcases, a shelf of vinyl records, a collection of board games, and a lot of art—or, at least, posters that had been hung in frames, instead of being tacked or taped to the wall.

"I like it," she said, truthfully, and, as she did, she identified the emotion she was feeling as relief. It occurred to her that she'd never gone to someone's house to have sex before; because she'd dated only guys her age, there had always been some element of sneaking around, to avoid roommates. It was new, and a little frightening, to be so completely on someone else's turf, and the fact that Robert's house gave evidence of his having interests that she shared, if only in their broadest categories—art, games, books, music—struck her as a reassuring endorsement of her choice.

As she thought this, she saw that Robert was watching her closely, observing the impression the room had made. And, as though fear weren't quite ready to release its hold on her, she had the brief wild idea that maybe this was not a room at all but a trap meant to lure her into the false belief that Robert was a normal person, a person like her, when in fact all the other rooms in the house were empty, or full of horrors: corpses or kidnap victims or chains. But then he was kissing her, throwing her bag and their coats on the couch and ushering her into the bedroom, groping her ass and pawing at her chest, with the avid clumsiness of that first kiss.

The bedroom wasn't empty, though it was emptier than the living room; he didn't have a bed frame, just a mattress and a box spring on the floor. There was a bottle of whiskey on his dresser, and he took a swig from it, then handed it to her and kneeled down and opened his laptop, an action that confused her, until she understood that he was putting on music.

Margot sat on the bed while Robert took off his shirt and unbuckled his pants, pulling them down to his ankles before realizing that he was still wearing his shoes and bending over to untie them. Looking at him like that, so awkwardly bent, his belly thick and soft and covered with hair, Margot recoiled. But the thought of what it would take to stop what she had set in motion was overwhelming; it would require an amount of tact and gentleness that she felt was impossible to summon. It wasn't that she was scared he would try to force her to do something against her will but that insisting that they stop now, after everything she'd done to push this forward, would make her seem spoiled and capricious, as if she'd ordered something at a restaurant and then, once the food arrived, had changed her mind and sent it back.

She tried to bludgeon her resistance into submission by taking a sip of the whiskey, but when he fell on top of her with those huge, sloppy kisses, his hand moving mechanically across her breasts and down to her crotch, as if he were making some perverse sign of the cross, she began to have trouble breathing and to feel that she really might not be able to go through with it after all.

Wriggling out from under the weight of him and straddling him helped, as did closing her eyes and remembering him kissing her forehead at the 7-Eleven. Encouraged by her progress, she pulled her shirt up over her head. Robert reached up and scooped her breast out of her bra, so that it jutted half in and half out of the cup, and rolled her nipple between his thumb and forefinger. This was uncomfortable, so she leaned forward, pushing herself into his hand. He got the hint and tried to undo her bra, but he couldn't work the clasp, his evident frustration reminiscent of his struggle with the keys, until at last he said, bossily, "Take that thing off," and she complied.

The way he looked at her then was like an exaggerated version of the expression she'd seen on the faces of all the guys she'd been naked with, not that there were that many—six in total, Robert made seven. He looked stunned and stupid with pleasure, like a milk-drunk baby, and she thought that maybe this was what she loved most about sex—a guy revealed like that. Robert showed her more open need than any of the others, even though he was older, and must have seen more breasts, more bodies, than they had—but maybe that was part of it for him, the fact that he was older, and she was young.

As they kissed, she found herself carried away by a fantasy of such pure ego that she could hardly admit even to herself that she was having it. Look at this beautiful girl, she imagined him thinking. She's so perfect, her body is perfect, everything about her is perfect, she's only twenty years old, her skin is flawless, I want her so badly, I want her more than I've ever wanted anyone else, I want her so bad I might die.

The more she imagined his arousal, the more turned-on she got, and soon they were rocking against each other, getting into a rhythm, and she reached into his underwear and took his penis in her hand and felt the pearled droplet of moisture on its tip. He made that sound again, that high-pitched feminine whine, and she wished there were a way she could ask him not to do that, but she couldn't think of any. Then his hand was inside her underwear, and when he felt that she was wet he visibly relaxed. He fingered her a little, very softly, and she bit her lip and put on a show for him, but then he poked her too hard and she flinched, and he jerked his hand away. "Sorry!" he said.

And then he asked, urgently, "Wait. Have you ever done this before?"

The night did, indeed, feel so odd and unprecedented that her first impulse was to say no, but then she realized what he meant and she laughed out loud.

She didn't mean to laugh; she knew well enough already that, while Robert might enjoy being the subject of gentle, flirtatious teasing, he was not a person who would enjoy being laughed at, not at all. But she couldn't help it. Losing her virginity had been a long, drawn-out affair preceded by several months' worth of intense discussion with her boyfriend of two years, plus a visit to the gynecologist and a horrifically embarrassing but ultimately incredibly meaningful conversation with her mom, who, in the end, had not only reserved her a room at a bed-and-breakfast but, after the event, written her a card. The idea that, instead of that whole involved, emotional process, she might have watched a pretentious Holocaust movie, drunk three beers, and then gone to some random house to lose her virginity to a guy she'd met at a movie theatre was so funny that suddenly she couldn't stop laughing, though the laughter had a slightly hysterical edge.

"I'm sorry," Robert said coldly. "I didn't know."

Abruptly, she stopped giggling.

"No, it was ... nice of you to check," she said. "I've had sex before, though. I'm sorry I laughed."

"You don't need to apologize," he said, but she could tell by his face, as well as by the fact that he was going soft beneath her, that she did.

"I'm sorry," she said again, reflexively, and then, in a burst of inspiration, "I guess I'm just nervous, or something?"

He narrowed his eyes at her, as though suspicious of this claim, but it seemed to placate him. "You don't have to be nervous," he said. "We'll take it slow."

Yeah, right, she thought, and then he was on top of her again, kissing her and weighing her down, and she knew that her last chance of enjoying this encounter had disappeared, but that she would carry through with it until it was over. When Robert was naked, rolling a condom onto a dick that was only half visible beneath the hairy shelf of his belly, she felt a wave of revulsion that she thought might actually break through her sense of pinned stasis, but then he shoved his finger in her again, not at all gently this time, and she imagined herself from above, naked and spread-eagled with this fat old man's finger inside her, and her revulsion turned to self-disgust and a humiliation that was a kind of perverse cousin to arousal.

During sex, he moved her through a series of positions with brusque efficiency, flipping her over, pushing her around, and she felt like a doll again, as she had outside the 7-Eleven, though not a precious one now—a doll made of rubber, flexible and resilient, a prop for the movie that was playing in his head. When she was on top, he slapped her thigh and said, "Yeah, yeah, you like that," with an intonation that made it impossible to tell whether he meant it as a question, an observation, or an order, and when he turned her over he growled in her ear, "I always wanted to fuck a girl with nice tits," and she had to smother her face in the pillow to keep from laughing again. At the end, when he was on top of her in missionary, he kept losing his erection, and every time he did he would say, aggressively, "You make my dick so hard," as though lying about it could make it true. At last, after a frantic rabbity burst, he shuddered, came, and collapsed on her like a tree falling, and, crushed beneath him, she thought, brightly, This is the worst life decision I have ever made! And she marvelled at herself for a while, at the mystery of this person who'd just done this bizarre, inexplicable thing.

After a short while, Robert got up and hurried to the bathroom in a bow-legged waddle, clutching the condom to keep it from falling off. Margot lay on the bed and stared at the ceiling, noticing for the first time that there were stickers on it, those little stars and moons that were supposed to glow in the dark.

Robert returned from the bathroom and stood silhouetted in the doorway. "What do you want to do now?" he asked her.

"We should probably just kill ourselves," she imagined saying, and then she imagined that somewhere, out there in the universe, there was a boy who would think that this moment was just as awful yet hilarious as she did, and that sometime, far in the future, she would tell the boy this story. She'd say, "And then he said, 'You make my dick so hard,'" and the boy would shriek in agony and grab her leg, saying, "Oh, my God, stop, please, no, I can't take it anymore," and the two of them would collapse into each other's arms and laugh and laugh—but of course there was no such future, because no such boy existed, and never would.

So instead she shrugged, and Robert said, "We could watch a movie," and he went to the computer and downloaded something; she didn't pay attention to what. For some reason, he'd chosen a movie with subtitles, and she kept closing her eyes, so she had no idea what was going on. The whole time, he was stroking her hair and trailing light kisses down her shoulder, as if he'd forgotten that ten minutes ago he'd thrown her around as if they were in a porno and growled, "I always wanted to fuck a girl with nice tits" in her ear.

Then, out of nowhere, he started talking about his feelings for her. He talked about how hard it had been for him when she went away for break, not knowing if she had an old high-school boyfriend she might reconnect with back home. During those two weeks, it turned out, an entire secret drama had played out in his head, one in which she'd left campus committed to him, to Robert, but at home had been drawn back to the high-school guy, who, in Robert's mind, was some kind of brutish, handsome jock, not worthy of her but nonetheless seductive by virtue of his position at the top of the hierarchy back home in Saline. "I was so worried you might, like, make a bad decision and things would be different between us when you got back," he said. "But I should have trusted you." My high-school boyfriend is gay, Margot imagined telling him. We were pretty sure of it in high school, but after a year of sleeping around at college he's definitely figured it out. In fact, he's not even a hundred per cent positive that he identifies as a man anymore; we spent a lot of time over break talking about what it would mean for him to come out as non-binary, so sex with him wasn't going to happen, and you could have asked me about that if you were worried; you could have asked me about a lot of things. But she didn't say any of that; she just lay silently, emanating a black, hateful aura, until finally Robert trailed off. "Are you still awake?" he asked, and she said yes, and he said, "Is everything O.K.?"

"How old are you, exactly?" she asked him.

"I'm thirty-four," he said. "Is that a problem?"

She could sense him in the dark beside her vibrating with fear.

"No," she said. "It's fine."

"Good," he said. "It was something I wanted to bring up with you, but I didn't know how you'd take it." He rolled over and kissed her forehead, and she felt like a slug he'd poured salt on, disintegrating under that kiss.

She looked at the clock; it was nearly three in the morning. "I should go home, probably," she said.

"Really?" he said. "But I thought you'd stay over. I make great scrambled eggs!"

"Thanks," she said, sliding into her leggings. "But I can't. My roommate would be worried. So."

"Gotta get back to the dorm room," he said, voice dripping with sarcasm.

"Yep," she said. "Since that's where I live."

The drive was endless. The snow had turned to rain. They didn't talk. Eventually, Robert switched the radio to late-night NPR. Margot recalled how, when they first got on the highway to go to the movie, she'd imagined that Robert might murder her, and she thought, Maybe he'll murder me now.

He didn't murder her. He drove her to her dorm. "I had a really nice time tonight," he said, unbuckling his seat belt.

"Thanks," she said. She clutched her bag in her hands. "Me, too."

"I'm so glad we finally got to go on a date," he said.

"A *date*," she said to her imaginary boyfriend. "He called that a *date*." And they both laughed and laughed.

"You're welcome," she said. She reached for the door handle. "Thanks for the movie and stuff."

"Wait," he said, and grabbed her arm. "Come here." He dragged her back, wrapped his arms around her, and pushed his tongue down her throat one last time. "Oh, my God, when will it end?" she asked the imaginary boyfriend, but the imaginary boyfriend didn't answer her.

"Good night," she said, and then she opened the door and escaped. By the time she got to her room, she already had a text from him: no words, just hearts and faces with heart eyes and, for some reason, a dolphin.

She slept for twelve hours, and when she woke up she ate waffles in the dining hall and binge-watched detective shows on Netflix and tried to envision the hopeful possibility that he would disappear without her having to do anything, that somehow she could just wish him away. When the next message from him did arrive, just after dinner, it was a harmless joke about Red Vines, but she deleted it immediately, overwhelmed with a skin-crawling loathing that felt vastly disproportionate to anything he had actually done. She told herself that she owed him at least some kind of breakup message, that to ghost on him would be inappropriate, childish, and cruel. And, if she did try to ghost, who knew how long it would take him to get the hint? Maybe the messages would keep coming and coming; maybe they would never end.

She began drafting a message—*Thank you for the nice time but I'm not interested in a relationship right now*—but she kept hedging and apologizing, attempting to close loopholes that she imagined him trying to slip through (*"It's O.K., I'm not interested in a relationship either, something casual is fine!"*), so that the message got longer and longer and even more impossible to send. Meanwhile, his texts kept arriving, none of them saying anything of consequence, each one more earnest than the last. She imagined him lying on his bed that was just a mattress, carefully crafting each one. She remembered that he'd talked a lot about his cats and yet she hadn't seen any cats in the house, and she wondered if he'd made them up.

Every so often, over the next day or so, she would find herself in a gray, daydreamy mood, missing something, and she'd realize that it was Robert she missed, not the real Robert but the Robert she'd imagined on the other end of all those text messages during break.

"Hey, so it seems like you're really busy, huh?" Robert finally wrote, three days after they'd fucked, and she knew that this was the perfect opportunity to send her half-completed breakup text, but instead she wrote back, "Haha sorry yeah" and "I'll text you soon," and then she thought, Why did I do that? And she truly didn't know.

"Just tell him you're not interested!" Margot's roommate, Tamara, screamed in frustration after Margot had spent an hour on her bed, dithering about what to say to Robert.

"I have to say more than that. We had *sex*," Margot said.

"*Do* you?" Tamara said. "I mean, really?"

"He's a nice guy, sort of," Margot said, and she wondered how true that was. Then, abruptly, Tamara lunged, snatching the phone out of Margot's hand and holding it far away from her as her thumbs flew across the screen. Tamara flung the phone onto the bed and Margot scrambled for it, and there it was, what Tamara had written: "Hi im not interested in you stop textng me."

"Oh, my God," Margot said, finding it suddenly hard to breathe.

"What?" Tamara said boldly. "What's the big deal? It's true."

But they both knew that it was a big deal, and Margot had a knot of fear in her stomach so solid that she thought she might retch. She imagined Robert picking up his phone, reading that message, turning to glass, and shattering to pieces.

"Calm down. Let's go get a drink," Tamara said, and they went to a bar and shared a pitcher, and all the while Margot's phone sat between them on the table, and though they tried to ignore it, when it chimed with an incoming message they screamed and clutched each other's arms.

"I can't do it—you read it," Margot said. She pushed the phone toward Tamara. "You did this. It's your fault."

But all the message said was "O.K., Margot, I am sorry to hear that. I hope I did not do anything to upset you. You are a sweet girl and I really enjoyed the time we spent together. Please let me know if you change your mind."

Margot collapsed on the table, laying her head in her hands. She felt as though a leech, grown heavy and swollen with her blood, had at last popped off her skin, leaving a tender, bruised spot behind. But why should she feel that way? Perhaps she was being unfair to Robert, who really had done nothing wrong, except like her, and be bad in bed, and maybe lie about having cats, although probably they had just been in another room.

But then, a month later, she saw him in the bar—her bar, the one in the student ghetto, where, on their date, she'd suggested they go. He was alone, at a table in the back, and he wasn't reading or looking at his phone; he was just sitting there silently, hunched over a beer.

She grabbed the friend she was with, a guy named Albert. "Oh, my God, that's him," she whispered. "The guy from the movie theatre!" By then, Albert had heard a version of the story, though not quite the true one; nearly all her friends had. Albert stepped in front of her, shielding her from Robert's view, as they rushed back to the table where their friends were. When Margot announced that Robert was there, everyone erupted in astonishment, and then they surrounded her and hustled her out of the bar as if she were the President and they were the Secret Service. It was all so over-the-top that she wondered if she was acting like a mean girl, but, at the same time, she truly did feel sick and scared.

Curled up on her bed with Tamara that night, the glow of the phone like a campfire illuminating their faces, Margot read the messages as they arrived:

"Hi Margot, I saw you out at the bar tonight. I know you said not to text you but I just wanted to say you looked really pretty. I hope you're doing well!"

"I know I shouldnt say this but I really miss you"

"Hey maybe I don't have the right to ask but I just wish youd tell me what it is I did wrog"

"*wrong"

"I felt like we had a real connection did you not feel that way or ..."

"Maybe I was too old for u or maybe you liked someone else"

"Is that guy you were with tonight your boyfriend"

"???"

"Or is he just some guy you are fucking"

"Sorry"

"When u laguehd when I asked if you were a virgin was it because youd fucked so many guys"

"Are you fucking that guy right now"

"Are you"

"Are you"

"Are you"

"Answer me"

"Whore."

—2017

DEBORAH WILLIS

Canadian short-story writer Deborah Willis was born in Calgary in 1982. She left her hometown to attend the University of Victoria, where she initially studied journalism, but soon moved to the creative writing department. There, she was taught and inspired by writers such as Lorna Crozier and Lorna Jackson. After graduation, Willis remained in Victoria, where she published her work in literary magazines and supported herself by working at Munro's Books, a prominent independent bookstore founded by Jim Munro and his first wife, the writer Alice Munro.

Willis's first story collection, *Vanishing and Other Stories* (2009), was short-listed for the Governor General's Award and praised by Alice Munro for its "emotional range and depth" and its "clarity and deftness." Willis's next book, *The Dark and Other Love Stories* (2017), was long-listed for the 2017 Giller Prize and won the Georges Bugnet Award for the best work of fiction published in Alberta. *The Times Colonist* applauded *The Dark*'s incisive style and offbeat subject matter: "A master of the sharply observed detail, Willis spins imaginative tales that are strange, beautiful and sometimes a bit frightening—just like real life."

Willis has named as literary influences Anton Chekhov, F. Scott Fitzgerald, and especially Alice Munro and Flannery O'Connor. "O'Connor and Munro are masters," she has written, "because they know how to make readers feel what their characters feel—and by feel, I truly mean feel in our bodies." Willis also credits her reading of popular novels by Elmore Leonard and Stephen King with impressing upon her the importance of a good plot, and it is one of her goals in writing that her work should have "movement and drama." Willis has been a writer-in-residence at Joy Kogawa House and at the University of Calgary, and she has published stories in such periodicals as *The Walrus*, *The Iowa Review*, and *Zoetrope*. She lives in Calgary, where she is submissions coordinator for Freehand Books, a publisher of Canadian literature.

Todd

WHEN EDDIE woke from alcohol-fueled dreams, the bird was on the edge of the mattress. Black feathers, black feet, black beak. Eddie figured he was dreaming. He closed his eyes—there was a heaviness behind them, an aftermath from the Jim Beam he drank last night—but when he opened them, the crow was still there. *A bird in the house*, but Eddie couldn't remember the rest.

It must have flown in the bedroom window—he left it open because he still slept best when he felt the cold air and heard the noise of the street.

The crow made a sound like a rusty hinge opening. Eddie reached for one of its brittle legs but his arm was too slow and the crow hopped easily away. "You fucker," he whispered. He liked animals, had a dog growing up until she got a tumor that hung heavily from her leg, but he hated crows. They were street birds. Dirty. Thieves.

"Listen, man." He sat up in bed. "You can't be here."

The crow cocked its head as though confused, as though Eddie were the intruder. Maybe he was. He'd only moved in yesterday, proud to sign the lease. Right now all he had was a mattress thrown on the floor, his patchwork quilt, a few mismatched dishes, and a scratched pot. The bathroom sink was rusty and two of the stove's burners didn't work, but he planned to buy a foldout couch for Abby when she came to stay.

The crow picked at a corner of the quilt, tugging a loose thread. Then made a low whine and watched him with a wary eye that reminded him of his daughter. The crow's eyes were blue like Abby's, something he'd never seen in a bird before. Maybe it wasn't a crow. Maybe it was a raven or a rook. But what was the difference? They all meant bad luck.

He spent the morning chasing the bird through the apartment, flicking a towel at it, and arrived late for work. His job was to install cable boxes and phone lines, and that meant he wore a name tag, rang doorbells, and slipped soft covers over his shoes before walking into strangers' homes—Yaletown high-rises, North Van mansions. He was quiet and polite and tried not to show his teeth when he smiled. He liked to tread over people's thick carpets and stand in their bright sunrooms. "Have a good one," he said each time he left.

When he finished work and got back to the apartment, he kicked off his shoes, heard them land with an echo against the door, then took a beer from the fridge. It was good to have his own place. If only he had a chair to sit on and maybe a CD player instead of that shitty tape deck. And a girlfriend, someone who found his jokes funny. Mostly he wished Abby were here, at the kitchen table. He didn't own a table yet, but when he did, she would sit there doing her homework.

What kind of homework would she do? He knew kids used computers now and he didn't have one. He also wasn't good at math and worried about how he'd help her. But these were small things—what was important was that he had cleaned himself up. And that his daughter still phoned him late at night, when her mom was asleep. "Hi," she'd say. "It's Abby." As though he might have forgotten.

No matter how bad things had gotten in his life, he always kept minutes on his phone so she could call to play the Question Game. It had no rules, no winner or loser, no beginning or end.

"What's your favorite fruit?" he might say, to start them off.

"Grapes. But only the green kind." She whispered so her mom wouldn't hear. "What vegetable do you hate most?"

"Cauliflower." That was an easy one. "What do you want to be when you grow up?"

"A bobsledder," she said. "What do you want to be?"

"A sea monster. Do you like sweaters or sweatshirts?"

"Sweatshirts. 'Cause they're not scratchy."

He collected this information, but knew nothing about the life she lived with Tara in Coquitlam. He was only a half-hour drive away but didn't own a car and, anyway, wouldn't have been welcome. So he didn't know the names of Abby's friends, or of the songs she listened to over and over, or even whether her hair was long or short now. And what could he tell her about his life? Not the part about sleeping in shelters or under cardboard. Not the part about buying drugs from a guy named Kit Kat. Not the part about emptying Tara's bank account.

So he and Abby played the Question Game, or they talked about the future: she was ten years old now and lived with her mom and grandparents, but she planned to move in with him when she was twelve and legally allowed to choose. "When I live with you, will we go to the aquarium?"

"Every day," he promised.

Now he poured Corn Pops into the same bowl he'd used for breakfast—Corn Pops were Abby's favorite. Or they had been a few years ago. When Tara was out, Eddie and Abby used to pour so much cereal into their bowls that the milk became thick and syrupy with sugar. This was one of their very-secret secrets.

He poured milk in now, and that's when he heard a grating sound from the bedroom, like a car driving over gravel. The crow. He'd forgotten about the crow. It flew into the kitchen and landed lightly on top of the fridge.

He banged his spoon on the counter and the bird fluttered to the other side of the room, then screeched at him—a sharp, startled squawk. Eddie threw a handful of Corn Pops at it, and they clattered over the counter and onto the floor. Then the crow picked one up and held it in his beak, as if to mock Eddie's inadequacy.

This couldn't be happening. Eddie was a human being—top of the food chain. Not only that, but he was a human being with a job and a debit card. A human being with a daughter who had his same blue eyes, a daughter who whispered into the phone that she missed him.

He strode to the entranceway and picked up one of his shoes. He would beat the thing to death.

But when he got back to the kitchen, he saw the crow stamping its small black foot to crush a Corn Pop to powder, then pecking the pieces off the floor. It ate quickly, nervously, watching Eddie with one of its blue eyes.

The fucking thing was hungry. And Eddie remembered being hungry.

He took the other bowl out of the cupboard, half filled it with cereal, poured in some milk. Did crows like milk? He would find out.

"Here." He set the bowl on the counter. "Have some."

For twenty minutes, the bird took tentative steps toward him, jumpy shuffles that reminded him of the meth-heads on Hastings—except the crow looked normal, looked right. Finally it settled on the bowl's rim, and, before eating, executed a little bow. Eddie was in an empty kitchen, eating Corn Pops from the box and drinking beer from a can, but suddenly felt like he was in another country, at a dinner with a sober and elegant guest. "*Bon appétit*," he said, using French he'd learned from his buddy Marc, a Quebecois who knew how to swallow swords. And the crow seemed to answer him. It gurgled like an old man gargling mouthwash.

Each night he came home from work with something new—apples, pepperoni—and the crow greeted him at the door, cawed, and curtsied. Eddie felt disoriented like when his daughter was born—five pounds seven ounces, with bright blue eyes and a head of dark hair. He'd been terrified to hold her, scared he'd drop her, worried that her quick, irregular breathing meant her lungs were collapsing. He was only eighteen when she was born and she was a creature he didn't understand at all. She seemed fragile as an egg. He vowed to do his best, to at least keep her alive, and he learned to change diapers and give her a bottle. He rocked her to sleep by holding her against his chest so she could feel his heartbeat.

After the curtsy, the crow took three prim steps to the left, its talons clicking on the floor. Then it bowed a second time, deeply and formally, and Eddie bowed back. Sometimes they greeted each other this way for five minutes, bowing back and forth. It reminded him of the first time Abby smiled. She was six weeks old, so small he could hold her with one arm. Just a week earlier, her eyes didn't focus properly, but suddenly she looked at his face and smiled. Christ, she looked so fucking cute, wrinkling up her face and showing those pink gums. He'd smiled back and she smiled a second time. They did that, smiling at each other, for what seemed like hours.

He learned that the crow liked banana but not avocado, cheddar but not Swiss. It devoured cans of Spam and of gray, mushy cat food. It loved raw eggs, rejected all fruit, left Doritos alone unless they were softened in water, and was fond of his culinary specialty, omelets with onion and bacon. Once Eddie brought home a grocery-store rotisserie chicken and the crow ate half the carcass, including the bones.

Over dinner, Eddie took one bite—of toast or pizza or whatever—and tossed one to the crow, who leapt and dove to catch the food in its mouth. "Hell, yeah!" Eddie found himself cheering like during a hockey game.

After dinner, while he hoped for Abby to call, they had tugsof-war with an elastic band. Or Eddie crumpled a piece of paper, rolled it along the floor, and the bird chased and pounced.

After about a week, Eddie gave the bird a name. He had no idea whether it was male or female, but he called it Todd, after his first roommate, a guy he'd worked with laying floors. Instead of tugof-war, they'd done a lot of coke, but living with avian Todd wasn't so different from living with human Todd.

As with any roommate, Todd did things that pissed Eddie off. Almost every evening he came home to find garbage—orange peels and coffee grounds and candy wrappers—scattered on the floor. And the bird liked to steal stuff: Eddie's watch, his nail clippers, even his nipple ring—once he woke to the bird pecking at it, trying to tear it out. He also found lettuce in his sock drawer and crackers in his shoes. And he couldn't figure out why Todd hated his leather wallet. The bird repeatedly bashed it on the floor as if to kill it.

And there was the bird shit. On the floors, in the shower, on the walls. Powdery white streaks on the legs of Eddie's jeans.

But now he knew that crows weren't black: they were iridescent blue and purple and pine green, like oil spilled on concrete. And it was calming to watch as Todd built a nest in the bedroom, busily and tenderly arranging scraps of paper, old receipts, Post-it notes, socks borrowed from the laundry pile.

They both liked the *White Album*, would shake their tails to "Ob-La-Di, Ob-La-Da." And at night, they slept side by side—Eddie on his back, Todd with his beak tucked under a wing. The bird gave off a dry, yeasty smell and trilled softly in his sleep. Do birds dream? It was a question for Abby the next time she called.

"Yeah," she answered. "But only half of their brain sleeps at a time. I did a project on it. They probably only have half a dream."

He wanted to tell her about the crow, wanted to say, *I have a very-secret secret.* But if Tara found out, she'd just use it as more evidence against him.

"Were you asleep?" Abby asked. "What were you dreaming about?"

"Not sure," he said. "Probably that I was flying."

"Maybe you were a velociraptor," she said. "I've dreamt that lots of times."

They talked this way until one or both of them drifted off. And in the mornings, Eddie woke with small, hot feet on his skin. Demanding breakfast, Todd stood on his shoulder and plucked out his hair, one strand at a time.

He went to the library and learned that crows mate for life, though some make brief forays with other partners. They have a language system, can count to six, and are able to see more colors than the human eye. To navigate they learn the layout of the stars, watch the sun's movement across the sky, sense the Earth's magnetic field. There's even a theory that they find their way by listening to the groan and crack of tectonic plates, the gathering of ocean waves, a volcano's underground rumble. They can hear the explosion of meteors in space.

He wanted to tell Abby this, but she hadn't called in weeks. Which was normal, he guessed, 'cause she must be busy. He knew she took dance classes and had schoolwork and sometimes had sleepovers at other girls' houses.

In those weeks, Todd grew bigger and walked with what Eddie thought of as a dealer's strut. The bird lost his downy feathers, and stiff, glossy ones grew in to replace them—once Eddie woke to find a spray of molted feathers through the bedsheets, as though he'd spent the night wrestling a dark angel.

Todd's blue eyes changed too, darkened to the color of the plums Eddie used to steal from a yard on East Twelfth. And a few weeks after that, Eddie came home from work to find that Todd had laid an egg.

It was the color of an olive, speckled with gray like it had been spray-painted. The crow sat lightly on top of it, eyes half closed, feathers puffed out.

"Todd." Eddie crouched down. "So you're a chick."

The bird snapped her beak at him, offended by his bad joke. Would the egg hatch? It needed to be fertilized—Eddie knew all about that—but maybe Todd had a boyfriend who flew in the open window and visited while Eddie was at work. And if it hatched, what was Eddie supposed to do? He shouldn't even have one crow living here—if the landlord found out, he could be evicted. If Tara found out, she'd say he was mentally ill.

He had to get rid of the bird. Take Todd outside, with her nest and her egg. Leave her in a park, maybe.

Todd snapped at him again, then opened her beak wide and showed her small pink tongue. She was hungry. She probably needed more calories now. Probably couldn't feed herself while keeping the egg warm.

He went to the kitchen, got one of the jars of applesauce he'd bought for her, and fed her with a spoon. She thanked him in her usual way: chattered and gurgled, as though cheerfully gossiping about people they both disliked.

"Yeah, okay." He settled in beside her. "You're welcome."

Abby called three days later, in the middle of the night. "What's your favorite song?" Her voice pulled him from sleep.

"Something by the Beatles. Maybe 'Here Comes the Sun.'"

Streetlight shone through the window and he could see Todd in her nest. She hadn't moved in days and there was a bare spot on her belly now, which she pressed to the egg. One of the bird's eyes was closed, the other open. Half of her brain was sleeping and he wished he could tell Abby. But he said, "What's your favorite color?"

"That's your question? You already know the answer."

He did. Yellow.

But he was tired of trying to keep the game going. "Guess what?" He would just say it. "I live with a crow."

"What?"

"A crow. You know, a bird."

"It's, like, alive?"

"Yeah," he said. "Alive." Then he told her about waking up with the bird on the mattress. He told her about the nest, the egg. "Her name is Todd," he said. "You'd like her. She's funny and she plays soccer."

Abby was so quiet that he thought she'd hung up. That she'd gone to tell her mom that he'd lost his mind. That she'd never call again.

But then she said, "They're descended from dinosaurs."

"What?"

"Birds," she said, "are dinosaurs that can fly."

"Do you know how they navigate?" he asked. "By looking up at the moon and the sun. By measuring the curve of the Earth."

"For real?"

And he felt like a parent. Like a person who knew things and could care for her.

"For real," he said. "And did you know they can hear earthquakes before they start?"

"No."

"They can hear tectonic plates moving. They can hear rain before it falls."

Todd spent each day warming the egg, her bare brood-patch pressed to its smooth surface, and Eddie had that easy feeling you get when you crack open a beer. Even when he was on his hands and knees in the alley behind his apartment, looking for worms and slugs because he'd read they were necessary to a crow's diet, he felt good.

This lasted until he got back from work one evening and saw that Todd had abandoned her nest. He found her wandering distractedly through the kitchen, her nails clicking on the counter.

"Hey," he said. "What's going on?"

He went into the bedroom: the egg was still there, nestled in the torn-up paper, but it had gone cold. He tucked it under his shirt, held it against his heart. It started to warm up but what was he supposed to do now? He couldn't take an egg with him to work.

He went into the kitchen and turned the oven on low—maybe he could use it as an incubator. But this was the first time he'd used the oven, and it gave off a smell like burning oil, sent gray smoke into the room. "Shit." He waved away the smoke, hoping the alarm wouldn't go off.

Todd was in the kitchen with a Triscuit in her mouth, hiding it under the dish-drainer mat. She stepped back, cocked her head while inspecting her work, then pulled the cracker out and started again.

"Todd?" He held the egg in front of her. "What the hell?"

She ignored him. Tucked the Triscuit under the mat again, and seemed satisfied that the cracker was well hidden now.

"Hey." He held the egg right under her face, but she looked away. She scratched her head with one of her talons.

She must have figured out that there was no point, that the thing wouldn't hatch. Eddie went back to the bedroom, swept up the nest, and put it and the egg in the garbage. But when Abby phoned that night, he didn't tell her any of this.

"What are you going to do?" she asked. "When the baby's born?"

"I'll look after it," he said. "And so will you, when you live here." He knew that she liked information, so told her that when the bird was born it would be called a "nestling," and when it learned to fly, a "fledgling." He said it would be smaller than her hand, bald and openmouthed. "Just like when you were born," he said. "You used to fit right in my pocket."

"No, I didn't!"

"Sure you did. And you had blue eyes that took up half your face."

He promised that she could name the new bird, and when she lived there, it would sleep in her bed.

"What about my friends?" she said. "Will I have to switch schools?"

"What do you mean?"

"If I move? Will I see Shyla anymore?"

He didn't know who Shyla was. Her best friend? A neighbor's dog? "Don't worry about that," he said. "You'll like it here."

"What will I tell Mom?"

"You'll tell her that you want to move in with me. That you're old enough to decide for yourself."

"But I mean, what will I tell her? She might be mad. Or kind of cry."

"That's why I got this apartment," he said. "So you could be here too."

"I know."

"Isn't that what you want!"

"I guess so."

"You guess so!"

"I don't know. Yeah. But—"

"But what?"

"It's just—"

Great. Now he'd made her cry.

"Christ, Abby," he said. "Forget it, okay!"

The next morning he called in sick to work and stayed in bed.

Todd flew up to him and tried to climb onto his shoulder, but he batted her away. "Leave me alone, buddy."

The bird flew into the kitchen and he heard a thud, then a sound like marbles scattering—she had spilled or broken something in a fit of hurt feelings. Eddie felt like he had a hangover and closed his eyes. When he opened them, the crow was on the mattress. Black feathers, black beak, black feet. She dropped something from her mouth. A Corn Pop.

"I'm not hungry, Todd."

But the bird made a disapproving *tsk-tsk* sound, then picked up the cereal in her beak. She used one of her long toes to scrape at his face—"Screw off," he said, and she dropped the Corn Pop into his open mouth.

Then she flew back to the kitchen, returned with more cereal, and he gave in this time. Opened his mouth and let her feed him. Her beak knocked his teeth and he tasted her bad, wild breath.

What the hell was he doing? Tara was right—there was something fucked up about him, something not normal.

"Go away." He swatted at the crow. "You can't be here." Which was what police officers and business owners and even librarians used to say to him. But the bird stayed, hopped closer.

"You can't be here." He slapped at her, his hand brushing her feathered face, and she croaked and stumbled on the mattress. Huddled and shivered like she was cold. "Come on, Todd." He climbed out of bed, picked her up, threw her toward the open window. "Get out."

But she flew back toward him, kept loving him like an idiot. So he smacked her for real this time, bent her wing feathers. "I said, get out." He slammed his fists against the wall, stamped his feet, and she puffed out her neck feathers, thrashed away from him. "Get out!" he screamed. "Out!" She shrieked and shrieked, circling his head—he heard the frantic flap of her wings. He swung with his fists and she slammed into the wall. Dropped to the floor.

Her wings beat the floorboards. Her eyes were open.

"Oh, Jesus." He fell to his knees. "Todd."

He crawled toward her and picked her up. She was so light—Abby had explained that the bones were hollow, and he pictured them made of delicate glass pipes. He'd fucked up; he'd fucked up. She seemed smaller, shrunken, and he held her to his heart.

"No," he said. "No."

Her quick, ragged heartbeat. Her crumpled feathers.

He couldn't even do this. Couldn't even care for a street bird. What would he tell Abby? That he was sorry. So sorry.

She shuddered in his hand. Then made a low, tuneless sound, like she was asking a question. And he tried not to cry, tried not to keen. Tried to quiet himself so she could listen for an answer, so she could find her way. He touched the bird's broken wingfeathers, settled her against his chest, and hoped this would calm her. Hoped she'd forgive him. Hoped she was listening to tectonic shifts, or meteors, or the hush of rain before it falls.

—2017

CHAVISA WOODS

Since the release of her first collection, *Love Does Not Make Me Gentle or Kind* (2008), Chavisa Woods has garnered praise for her skillful prose blending stark, brutal realism and eerie, sometimes grotesque surrealism; her work has been compared to that of writers such as Flannery O'Connor, Dorothy Allison, and Shirley Jackson. Woods's stories are set largely in the rural American Midwest and populated by outcasts of diverse sorts, struggling to cope with the boredom, poverty, and evangelical religious tyranny that frequently characterize the communities they inhabit. Woods, who has described her teenage self as a "queer punky goth," was born and raised in the small Midwestern town of Sandoval, Illinois, but has been based in New York City since 2003. Though many parallels can be identified between her own upbringing and personality and that of her characters, Woods has been careful to resist the idea that her fiction is ever autobiographical, only going so far as to say that some of her stories are "deeply personal, fictionalized retellings of some real-life experiences."

Woods's stories are often linked by motifs of conflict and violence; in her second collection, *Things to Do When You're Goth in the Country* (2017), in particular, allusions to international warfare are almost ubiquitous. "In a few of the stories," Woods has said, "this is at the forefront, but in most, it is peripheral, because that is how most Americans deal with the ongoing wars, peripherally.... I don't know how anyone can write a realist book about the United States of America without ever once bringing up the ongoing wars." Her work has also aimed to draw attention to US military recruiting strategies, which she points out disproportionately target poor and isolated communities. Writing for *The Rumpus*, Erin Wilcox has praised the way "Woods embraces the complex humanity of her characters even as she explores the tragedy of enculturation, identifying forces that divide us. Think of her as a literary exorcist." Her story "Take the Way Home That Leads Back to Sullivan Street" from *Things to Do* won the 2017 Shirley Jackson Award for best novelette, and she has been a finalist for the Lambda Literary Award three times. Aside from her short fiction collections, Woods has also written a novel—*The Albino Album* (2013)—and a nonfiction book, *100 Times: A Memoir of Sexism* (2019).

Things to Do When You're Goth in the Country

WHEN I WAS sixteen, I used to sit under the bell tower with my friends and smoke. Smoking was something to do. The little courtyard under the bell tower was like nothing else in the town. It looked European to us. A pointless enclave situated between three buildings with iron benches and a small stone fountain; that's all it was. Completely impractical and unlike anything else. There was never anyone there. We were the only ones in town who were in any way interested in that courtyard. It was a hip pocket where the universe opened up in the middle of that ugly rural town and allowed things to seem cosmopolitan for one hundred and fifty square feet. All we did there was smoke because no one could see us back there and we were too young to legally smoke cigarettes. Cigarettes tasted better there. That taste they have when you don't smoke often and it's new, that's what it was. The smell of Marlboros and Camels are two very different things, but both are savory when smoking is new to you, and taste like a fresh croissant in Paris your first day in town. That's how cigarettes tasted to me there under the bell tower when I was sixteen.

One time, I'd been smoking too much for a few days, and cigarettes didn't taste new anymore, they just tasted burning and sick. I was sitting on the ledge of the fountain under the bell tower, the fancy cobblestone under my boots, the thick foliage behind the fountain casting shade and a hot August sun at three o'clock. Sweat dripped down my nose. I pulled out a cigarette. My friends stood around preparing to do something: smoke. I said, "It's too hot to smoke." They all laughed and repeated what I'd said, "Too hot to smoke." I felt very cool. I knew in that moment that, whatever happened, I was going to be all right, we all were, because we could find a way to be hip, even there in the middle of nowhere: Bible Belt, cow country, abandoned train-town. I lit a cigarette and forced it down, making myself sick. The bell tower started gonging. We all looked up into the sunlight reflecting off the windows of the bell tower.

There's a girl I like to tell things to. She doesn't like to be called a woman, even though she is. I like to tell her these pointless things because they are prizes the trick claw of my brain catches and drops into her lap, worthless as purple stuffed elephants but celebrated in the moment because they got hooked against the odds and extracted. She gives me these things too. We keep passing quarters, piling up pretty plastic toys that look so different hanging in a difficult claw than they did on the worthless heap of memory.

She looks like trash to me, and I like it. I've spent years polishing it away, worrying that people could see right through my bag. My cow-shaped under-chin when I tilt my head might be a tell. I check skin tone for smoothness and pockmarks. My stomach is a dead giveaway. But I've been assured none of these things are trash markers to anyone other than me. I've been assured it's not visible to the outside world. Then I look at her, and it's so obvious. The trash signs are everywhere, even through her queerness. Queerness un-trashes people a little, or it can. (Sometimes it goes in the opposite direction, though.) Still, I can see what she would be without the good sex, weird haircut, and interesting clothes, clear as a dump truck at dawn. And I know also, when I look at her, for all my polishing, my face must be the same sort of obviousness and there was never anything I could have done about it. Trash gets into the body and forms it, molds speech and jawlines. It scars the skin with acne kisses from too many greasy-fry dinners. Just overhearing things like Guns N' Roses and Bon Jovi rots the teeth and yellows the eyes.

It's something about things. Things like things that hurt. Like whipped cream. $2.49. Something I did that became a thing for a moment. A thing for a moment because it abstracted everything and right then I wanted nothing to do with anything anymore that wasn't abstract and indecipherable; that wasn't a vague term.

Whippets turn the world into vague terms. My cousin and I had the same feeling about these days. So we went to the store at dusk all year and purchased cans of generic whipped cream, the aerosol kind. Then we went to the park. Then the sun would be setting. Then we laid down our sixteen-year-old trashy girl bodies on the merry-go-round. Then we pushed with our feet so that we were spinning. Then we tilted the jagged plastic nozzles of the whipped cream aerosol canisters to our lips. You don't shake the bottle. You don't want any cream to come out. Just the gas. We pushed the nozzle sideways and sucked. Inhaled. The nozzles have jagged tips for decorating. If you are dressing an ice cream sundae, the jagged edge makes the whipped cream wavy. It makes patterns, like stars. The gas creamed us. The gas cut stars out of our minds. Made us soft edges left over. The park was always blue-gray and empty just after dusk, and newly cool, and we spun, and everything hummed and became a vague terminology of dusk-glowing trees, cement, and swing sets. Our minds were creamy stars poking through the dusk, waving us goodbye.

It's something about things that hurt, how they stay and shape the body. Things that you seek pleasure in when you're trashy. It makes you tell stories like this. Like we were basically huffing glue, but it seemed sweet because it smelled like whipped cream. It makes vague terminology very appealing.

I looked different than my cousin while we were tripping from fumes on the merry-go-round. I looked better. Which meant I was. I liked to draw upside-down crosses below my eyes, like two sacrilegious tears ending above my cheeks. I wanted to draw Jesus there on them, a black silhouette of him hanging upside down. I drew upside-down crosses under my eyes and purchased a silver grill cut with upside-down crucifixes I wore on my three upper front teeth, and went around the country roads on my mountain bike when I was fifteen. I liked to go stand in the middle of cornfields in the autumn in a black bowler and trench coat and pretend I'd painted the sky, grinning my upside-down silver Jesus grill toward the pink sunset.

I was like a cat that way: staring at skylines, staring at ghosts. We liked to go to the haunted bridge in the next town over. Three towns away there was a haunted ditch, and in the country roads between Nashville and Hoyleton, Illinois, there was a haunted bump. You had to know exactly where that haunted bump was or you would never find it since it was on an unmarked black tar road with only trees on one side and a cornfield on the other, repeating for miles, and no markers. The knowledge of where that bump was got passed down to you from other people, and then you had to really memorize it before you showed anyone else, be taken there a few times, or else you'd end up at the wrong bump in the road late at night and try to do that haunted thing that we did at that bump, and it wouldn't work, because you weren't paying enough attention and parked your car on some other, ordinary, everyday, non-haunted bump in that road. And then nothing would happen. Then you would just be some kids sitting in a car near a bump in the road waiting in vain to be haunted.

I experienced the bump haunting three times. I went looking for it, seeking out a fourth haunted bump experience, but by myself for once, and instead I saw a UFO that I had to drive very fast to get away from, and I never went back to that haunted bump again.

The haunted bump haunting was a very mechanical kind of haunting. If you situated yourself just right, it would happen every time like ghostly clockwork. It wasn't as finicky as my haunted bridge. The ghost of the haunted bridge would only come out very sporadically, and even when she did, it was debatable what had actually happened. This bump's manner of haunting was not debatable.

The thing you had to do was park your car three yards past the bump and facing east. This situates your car sloping down a not very steep hill, front pointing downhill with the bump uphill behind you. It's very important that you understand exactly what I am saying about the situating of the car, or else it won't be obvious why what is about to happen when you do this is so scary.

Okay. So now you're sitting there. You're sloping downhill. Put the car in neutral. Turn it off. Leave it on. Either way. I usually turned it off so I could hear the cicadas for added effect. When the car is off and in neutral, it is natural that the car will roll forward, downhill. At first, it doesn't move at all. For several minutes, it just sits there. But then, it starts rolling, *backward, uphill*, gaining speed as it goes, faster and faster, backward, uphill, in the middle of the dark woods, until it gets over that bump, all the way over by a few yards, and then the car slides off to the side of the road into the dirt shoulder. Then it stops. Then you've experienced the haunted bump.

What's actually happening there is, a school bus crashed there in the sixties. Right there past that bump, and twenty kids died. The bus stalled in the middle of the road there and a drunk driver of a pickup truck crashed into it. The ghosts of those kids want to reverse their death over and over. Ghosts are very associative. So if you go there with any vehicle and stop where they crashed, which happens to be by that bump which is the only marker, they will come and push you back, then leave your car off to the side on the dirt shoulder, out of harm's way.

I wonder how anyone found out about that haunted bump in the first place. It must have taken a lot of sitting around. There's a lot of free time in the country.

My friends once tested the ghost children theory and went to the bump with bags of flour. They covered the car in flour and tossed it on the road there by that bump. Then they situated the car correctly for the haunting and sat in the car and waited. It rolled backward, uphill and all. The haunting worked as it did every time. Then they got out of the car and took out their flashlights, and they found children's handprints in the flour that covered the car. About twenty pairs of them, and footprints in the flour on the road as well. Then they all pissed their pants.

I've only pissed my pants three times in my entire life, and always when I was sleeping. Once when I was just out of diapers. Once when I was thirteen and had pneumonia with a fever of 104. And once when I was seventeen. It was just a very bad dream. But I'd been cutting myself all day the day before I went to sleep in that nightmare. (Cutting is also something to do, like smoking.) And then, in the summers especially, maintenance of cutting adds some other activities. Self-mutilation in the summer requires styling the legs of black panty hose to be worn like chic long-gloves over the blood-caked scabs. This way you can still wear T-shirts and be cool in the midwestern humidity.

There is nothing like pissing yourself from a nightmare, with scabs on your arms. Waking up, a year away from legal adulthood, to wet yellow sheets in the wavering sunlight below dust-drenched windows will make you understand your own fragility in a way only akin to suddenly realizing you are elderly. It's a gray happening.

Nearly, but not quite, as shocking as surprise exorcisms. If you are going to be Goth in the country and really go for it, I would highly recommend a nonconsensual, surprise Southern Baptist exorcism. There's just nothing else that can compete. That moment when your minister lays hands on you, and the faces of the congregation, people you thought you knew well, turn, doll-eyed and pitying, to begin praying some unknown demon out of you, their lips mouthing out whisperings of the same prayer in unison: that really is the pinnacle.

It's going to take a lot to cause this occurrence. You will have to commit yourself to a very particular type of disturbance in order to get an entire congregation of Southern Baptists to conspire with God against your soul. You don't have to do exactly what I did, but I'll share my experience as a template that can be reworked and altered, specifically tailored for your own personal CG (country Goth) experience.

Always begin with the Bible. I took advantage of my church duties. Wednesday night Bible study was a rotation. There were twelve regular members, myself included. Mine was an enforced attendance. Each week, a different Bible study member selected the text to be read and studied. Every twelfth week was my week to select the text, read it aloud to the congregation, and then sit through an hour-long discussion. For this, I utilized Halloween paint. It is very important to approach all unpleasant tasks in life as a performance art piece, especially if you are a teenager. On Wednesday nights, I dressed like I was going to kill a Marilyn Manson concert. I approached the pulpit with my big red Bible, held my hands out like an offering, and spread the Bible open, the thick, soft pages resting splayed and flowing out like a woman's thick paned thighs. My scabs healing underneath the hacked-up panty hose I wore on my arms. Chains rattling from my hips, and fucked-up Barbie doll-head necklaces hanging around my neck; Vietnam ear tokens honoring the violence of girlishness. There I stood before the congregation in the small steepled white church, under the empty cross, exposed rafters echoing barnyards, my eyes painted thick with black curlicues swirling up from my lids to around my temples, and upside-down black crosses resting like tears above my cheeks. My white powdered cheeks, sparkling fake-blood-red lips, and hot-pink dreadlocks sticking out from beneath a black bowler.

And I read them their Bible. I read the congregation their sacred text, dressed that way on their pulpit. I spoke in a booming, deep-throated voice that, at moments, devolved into a growl, echoing through their sanctuary like it was a black magic road show we were doing. I read them their Ezekiel. I read them their sacred book and I made it mine. I made their reverence my blasphemy, my sacrilege.

It was the word of the Lord I was reading, and more importantly, it was the word of *their* Lord saying through my horrible mouth, "*And I will lay the dead carcasses of the children before their idols; and I will scatter your bones round about your altars.*" And saying, "*I will drench the land with your flowing blood all the way to the mountains, and the ravines will be filled with your flesh.*" And saying, "*And they shall know that I am the LORD, and that I have not said in vain that I would do this evil.*"[1]

It was like a song I was singing to them, like low screamcore, like they'd never heard the words so crisp and clear before. *And the earth will become flesh and the birds will peck at the flesh until the rivers are rivers of blood, for I am the Lord your God*, sort of thing. It was my best performance piece ever. It was the best because it was happening in real time, in real space, on holy ground, making righteous people question and gawk and quake a little. I would go so far as to say there was some quaking. And there was a woman named Betty there. That made it really terrific.

It's things like this you will have to do to reach the pinnacle point (the pinnacle point being nonconsensual exorcism by people you have known all your life). Carving pentacles into your forehead with razor blades is always an option as well and requires less setup and performative skill. I prefer pentacles to pentagrams, as I find pentagrams to be a bit of an overkill, and rather silly as Satanism is so blasé and reactionary an endeavor. I also highly recommend being a homosexual. Rural Goth trash just reads better homo. If you are not already a homosexual, you can easily become one. I became one as young as the age of five, so it will be all the easier to do in adolescence at a time when most have a more developed aesthetic understanding of the libido.

Oh there are so many things to do.

You can harass military recruiters who set up tables in your school's lunchroom by brandishing neon feather boas and dancing around them singing Adam Ant's "You're Just Too Physical" as reworked by Trent Reznor, for instance. You will definitely want to spend a lot of time in the old part of the cemetery, just hanging out, then tell people about it. If you are very ambitious, write some poems there. I always did. Try some necromancy just for kicks, if you are wanting to be a true professional. Don't tell anyone about that. Some things we must keep to ourselves.

When I was very young, I had a voice in a well that I kept all to myself. As commanded by the voice in the well, our conversations were kept secret, and that was for the best, in retrospect, I am sure. The voice in the well was gray as

---

1   Bible verses from the book of Ezekiel.

the stone that housed it. It was a very grounded male voice of wisdom that told me many important things. It began telling me things when I was five years old; then when I was eight, my family cemented the well and it was covered then and I couldn't hear the voice anymore. But when I could it told me many important things. It told me to never grow up. It told me to always smell the grass. It told me the wind would guide and protect me and loved me unconditionally because I was exceptionally beautiful to the wind in my area. It told me where to find dead things.

I found many dead things guided by the voice in the well. One dead cow, legs pointing straight up toward the afternoon sky and stiff like Viagra meat. I found one dead dog gutted in the woods by a homeless man who'd been living there all summer. It was a golden retriever mix of something, and its belly was sliced open, full of maggots and flies so thick it looked like the thick love I had for the friend I found it with, and I would only have ever wanted to find something so perfectly fucked up with someone I loved as much as I loved that blond girl. The Air Force stole her perfect heart years later.

I found a nest of rabbits drowned in puddles; drowned by the bare hands of my six-year-old cousin who had spent the previous night glassy-eyed and babbling prophecies about stillborn kittens. So many dead birds fallen, innumerable deer, one dead squirrel I had known, and many dead classmates at funerals I attended during the summers when teenagers liked to have deadly wrecks or drown in lakes and flooded ponds. I found death in the eyes of friends who began enlisting in the military so they didn't have to become farmers and break the legs of chickens with hormones. It was a deep well of death in their eyes and there were voices there too, but they were not my voice.

My voice in the well was gray and kind. My voice in the well was also probably dead. The voice in my well told me the most important thing and the most difficult thing. It told me empathy. Repeatedly. It told me, "Empathy. Child. Be a child. Be an empathetic child. Always. All we kill is ourselves." It told me, "All we love is ourselves." It told me, "All. We. Kill. Is. Our. Selves."

The black helicopter's sonic booms are classified information and officially do not exist, but when they happened, everyone would come down off their porches and stand looking up. They would say, "Air Force base," and point west. When the swarms of black helicopters would pass over us in moments of bad consciousness I would remember the voice in the well saying, "Empathy. Child. All we kill is ourselves." I would look to the farmers saying, "Air Force," pointing their calloused fingers west and feel the wars which are endless and meant to be endless ripping open my guts with their flapping blades and I would know I was dead too. And I would know for a moment that it wasn't only me painting my eyes so black and my skin so pale. It wasn't something autonomous inside me making me need to look so dead. Dead as the kids dropping hands like bricks, and the carcasses of children God promised to spread around vain altars. Dead as the elite Republican Guard. Dead as Iraqi insurgents and people just trying to drive their cars home to dinner on the only road home that is awfully near a pipeline. Dead as oil and sand. Dead as the conscientiousness of this country that grew me up in vast cornfields jabbering with upside-down silver Jesus teeth at broken-egg-gone-bad sunsets that spill and spill and spill, as if there's nothing to lose, ever. You could find me wagging my crotch and scars at the warplanes that do not exist deafeningly in vast cornfields at sunset. Trench. Coat. Dread. Locks. Bowler.

Do not take the sky for granted. It falls all the time somewhere. And now there are kids wagging there at drones, wagging their fucked-up trash at no one, at video screens below the cracking sky spilling out orange paths for strange jets and helicopters. So many insects. Mosquitoes and fruit flies. If you want to do it right, let them suck on you. Don't smack anything painful away. The country itches. It eats you and burns. Always be prepared for the apocalypse. Or rather, be willing to see the apocalypse that is happening around you. Even when it is silent as glass and you can see nothing for miles except the miles stretching out to more miles. Know that it is out there, bred by where you are and so always present to you exploding the silence in silence.

Run through the fields in boots or barefooted in pressed suits and never comb your hair for any reason unless it is to be a dandy. Run through the fields to the woods and collect all the dead things. Curse all manifestations of monotheistic nation God. Masturbate to ghosts by the haunted creek and let your cumming flow long as time that stretches out and lasts so long in this place where people build things like scarecrows and pits and mud is a verb. Hang dolls in trees and let them blow in the wind. Return daily to watch their decay. Cut blood out of yourself and feed it in droplets to the creek like little boats the creek is always hungry for. Let the boats go to be devoured at the mouth or the bend. Let the boats go on like dead crows on the water of endless time that will rot to fertilize a more elaborate nothing of this land of dust and imbecilic violence concealed below the scent of earth, fresh cut wheat, and bleach for their fresh starched linens that glow on clotheslines at twilight like spectral flags. This is where you belong. There is much to be done.

—2017

CARMEN MARIA MACHADO

An American writer who has been praised for her surreal examinations of what one critic calls "the mundane horrors of female existence," Carmen Maria Machado is best known for her debut short story collection *Her Body and Other Parties* (2017). She was born in 1986 in Allentown, Pennsylvania; her mother was a homemaker from the Midwest, and her father was a descendant of Austrian and Cuban immigrants. Machado describes her upbringing as defined by rigid gender roles, though she also reports that her parents were accepting when, as an adult, she came out as bisexual. She wrote her first story at age five: a dark fantasy about a turkey who gets lost in the city and ends up being eaten for Thanksgiving. She continued writing throughout her childhood and college years and, in 2010, she enrolled in the Iowa Writers' Workshop, where she developed several stories that would later be incorporated into *Her Body and Other Parties*. After graduating, Machado worked as a retail associate at a luxury bath and beauty product store—work that left her "exhausted"—and credits writers' residencies with giving her the necessary psychological space to finish her short story collection.

In 2017, Machado released *Her Body and Other Parties* to widespread acclaim. *The New Yorker* characterized the text as a part of the "New Vanguard" of great literature written by women that is "shaping the way we read and write fiction in the 21st century." Critics remarked upon the collection's frank depictions of sex, as well as its innovative use of horror and dark fantasy. One story in the collection, "The Husband Stitch," is a retelling of the folk story "The Velvet Ribbon" that, like many of the pieces in the collection, plays with form—in this case, by giving the reader stage directions. "In my work, I think non-realism can be a way to insist on something different. It's a way to tap into aspects of being a woman that can be surreal or somehow liminal—certain experiences that can feel, even, like horror," Machado reflects. "Non-realism makes room for mythic expressions of the female experience." She also plays with genre in her 2019 memoir *In the Dream House*, which explores an abusive relationship through various genre lenses including erotica, sci-fi thriller, American Gothic, and "Choose Your Own Adventure." The same year, she authored a limited-run horror comic, *The Low, Low Woods*, published by DC.

Machado has published work in collections such as *Best American Science Fiction & Fantasy*, *Best Horror of the Year*, and *Best Women's Erotica*, as well as in periodicals such as the *New Yorker*, the *New York Times*, *Tin House*, and *Granta*. Her work often bridges the gap between highbrow and lowbrow fiction, sampling broadly from literature and popular culture—one story in *Her Body and Other Parties*, for example, consists entirely of surreal synopses of imagined episodes of *Law & Order: SVU*. Among her strongest influences, however, are macabre feminist writers such as Angela Carter and Shirley Jackson. On the importance of body horror in her own work, Machado has said, "Even the very basic metaphor inherent in monsters like werewolves, vampires, comes down to the question of what bodies can do and the ways bodies can fail and the ways they can hurt other people.... It's a really natural vehicle for exploring the marginalization of women and people of color and other marginalized groups." Machado serves as the Writer in Residence at the University of Pennsylvania and lives in Philadelphia with her wife.

Eight Bites

AS THEY PUT me to sleep, my mouth fills with the dust of the moon. I expect to choke on the silt but instead it slides in and out, and in and out, and I am, impossibly, breathing.

I have dreamt of inhaling underneath water and this is what it feels like: panic, and then acceptance, and then elation: I am going to die, I am not dying, I am doing a thing I never thought I could do.

Back on Earth, Dr. U is inside me. Her hands are in my torso, her fingers searching for something. She is loosening flesh from its casing, slipping around where she's been welcomed, talking to a nurse about her vacation to Chile. "We were going to fly to Antarctica," she says, "but it was too expensive."

"But the penguins," the nurse says.

"Next time," Dr. U responds.

Before this, it was January, a new year. I waded through two feet of snow on a silent street, and came to a shop where wind chimes hung silently on the other side of the glass, mermaid-shaped baubles and bits of driftwood and too-shiny seashells strung through with fishing line and unruffled by any wind.

The town was deep dead, a great distance from the late-season smattering of open shops that serve the day-trippers and the money-savers. Owners had fled to Boston or New York, or if they were lucky, further south. Businesses had shuttered for the season, leaving their wares in the windows like a tease. Underneath, a second town had opened up, familiar and alien at the same time. It's the same every year. Bars and restaurants made secret hours for locals, the rock-solid Cape Codders who've lived through dozens of winters. On any given night you could look up from your plate to see a round bundle stomp through the doorway; only when they peeled their outsides away could you see who was beneath. Even the ones you knew from the summer are more or less strangers in this perfunctory daylight; everyone was alone, even when they were with each other.

On this street, though, I might as well have been on another planet. The beach bunnies and art dealers would never see the town like this, I thought, when the streets are dark and liquid chill roils through the gaps and alleys. Silences and sound bumped up against each other but never intermingled; the jolly chaos of warm summer nights was as far away as it could be. It was hard to stop moving between doorways in this weather, but if you did you could hear life pricking the stillness: a rumble of voices from a local tavern, wind livening the buildings, sometimes even a muffled animal encounter in an alley: pleasure or fear, it was all the same noise.

Foxes wove through the streets at night. There was a white one among them, sleek and fast, and she looked like the ghost of the others.

I was not the first in my family to go through with it. My three sisters had gotten the procedure over the years, though they didn't say anything before showing up for a visit. Seeing them suddenly svelte after years of watching them grow organically, as I have, was like a palm to the nose; more painful than you'd expect. My first sister, well, I thought she was dying. Being sisters, I thought we all were dying, noosed by genetics. When confronted by my anxiety—"What disease is sawing off this branch of the family tree?" I asked, my voice crabwalking up an octave—my first sister confessed: a surgery.

Then, all of them, my sisters, a chorus of believers. Surgery. A surgery. As easy as when you broke your arm as a kid and had to get the pins in—maybe even easier. A band, a sleeve, a gut re-routed. *Re-routed*? But their stories—*it melts away, it's just gone*—were spring morning warm, when the sun makes the difference between happiness and shivering in a shadow.

When we went out, they ordered large meals and then said, "I couldn't possibly." They always said this, always, that decorous insistence that they *couldn't possibly*, but for once, they actually meant it—that bashful lie had been converted into truth vis-à-vis a medical procedure. They angled their forks and cut impossibly tiny portions of food—doll-sized cubes of watermelon, a slender stalk of peashoot, a corner of a sandwich as if they needed to feed a crowd loaves-and-fishes style[1] with that single serving of chicken salad—and swallowed them like a great decadence.

"I feel so good," they all said. Whenever I talk to them, that was what always came out of their mouths, or really, it was a mouth, a single mouth that once ate and now just says, "I feel really, really good."

Who knows where we got it from, though—the bodies that needed the surgery. It didn't come from our mother, who always looked normal, not hearty or curvy or Rubenesque or Midwestern or voluptuous, just normal. She always said eight bites are all you need, to get the sense of what you are eating. Even though she never counted out loud, I could hear the eight bites as clearly as if a game show audience was counting backwards, raucous and triumphant, and after *one* she would set her fork down, even if there was food left on her plate. She didn't mess around, my mother. No pushing food in circles or pretending. Iron will, slender waistline. Eight bites let her compliment the hostess. Eight bites lined her stomach like insulation rolled into the walls of houses. I wished she was still alive, to see the women her daughters had become.

And then, one day, not too soon after my third sister sashayed out of my house with more spring in her step than I'd ever seen, I ate eight bites and then stopped. I set the fork down next to the plate, more roughly than I intended, and took a chip of ceramic off the rim in the process. I pressed my finger into the shard and carried it to the trashcan. I turned and looked back at my plate, which had been so full before and was full still, barely a dent in the raucous mass of pasta and greens.

I sat down again, picked up my fork and had eight more bites. Not much more, still barely a dent, but now twice as much as necessary. But the salad leaves were dripping vinegar and oil and the noodles had lemon and cracked pepper and everything was just so beautiful, and I was still hungry, and so I had eight more. After, I finished what was in the pot on the stove and I was so angry I began to cry.

I don't remember getting fat. I wasn't a fat child or teenager; photos of those young selves are not embarrassing, or if they are, they're embarrassing in the right ways. Look how young I am! Look at my weird fashion! Saddle shoes—who

---

1   Reference to the Bible story in which Jesus miraculously feeds a "multitude" with five loaves of bread and two fish (see Matthew 14).

thought of those? Stirrup pants—are you joking? Squirrel barrettes? Look at those glasses, look at that face: mugging for the camera. Look at that expression, mugging for a future self who is holding those photos, sick with nostalgia. Even when I thought I was fat I wasn't; the teenager in those photos is very beautiful, in a wistful kind of way.

But then I had a baby. Then I had Cal—difficult, sharp-eyed Cal, who has never gotten me half as much as I have never gotten her—and suddenly everything was wrecked, like she was a heavy-metal rocker trashing a hotel room before departing. My stomach was the television set through the window. She was now a grown woman and so far away from me in every sense, but the evidence still clung to my body. It would never look right again.

As I stood over the empty pot, I was tired. I was tired of the skinny-minny women from church who cooed and touched each other's arms and told me I had beautiful skin, and having to rotate my hips sideways to move through rooms like crawling over someone at the movie theater. I was tired of flat, unforgiving dressing room lights; I was tired of looking into the mirror and grabbing the things that I hated and lifting them, claw-deep, and then letting them drop and everything aching. My sisters had gone somewhere else and left me behind, and as I always have, I wanted nothing more than to follow.

I could not make eight bites work for my body and so I would make my body work for eight bites.

Dr. U did twice-a-week consultations in an office a half an hour drive south on the Cape. I took a slow, circuitous route getting there. It had been snowing on and off for days, and the sleepy snowdrifts caught on every tree trunk and fencepost like blown-away laundry. I knew the way, because I'd driven past her office before—usually after a sister's departure—and so as I drove this time I daydreamed about buying clothes in the local boutiques, spending too much for a sundress taken off a mannequin, pulling it against my body in the afternoon sun as the mannequin stood, less lucky than I.

Then I was in her office, on her neutral carpet, and a receptionist was pushing open a door. The doctor was not what I expected. I suppose I had imagined that because of the depth of her convictions, as illustrated by her choice of profession, she should have been a slender woman: either someone with excessive self-control, or a sympathetic soul whose insides have also been rearranged to suit her vision of herself. But she was sweetly plump—why had I skipped over the phase where I was round and unthreatening as a panda, but still lovely? She smiled with all her teeth. What was she doing, sending me on this journey she herself had never taken?

She gestured, and I sat.

There were two Pomeranians running around her office. When they were separated—when one was curled up at Dr. U's feet and the other was decorously taking a shit in the hallway—they appeared identical but innocuous, but when one came near the other they were spooky, their heads twitching in sync, as if they were two halves of a whole. The doctor noticed the pile outside of the door and called for the receptionist. The door closed.

"I know what you're here for," she said, before I could open my mouth. "Have you researched bariatric surgery before?"

"Yes," I said. "I want the kind you can't reverse."

"I admire a woman of conviction," she said. She began pulling binders out of a drawer. "There are some procedures you'll have to go through. Visiting a psychiatrist, seeing another doctor, support groups—administrative nonsense, taking up a lot of time. But everything is going to change for you," she promised, shaking a finger at me with an accusing, loving smile. "It will hurt. It won't be easy. But when it's over, you're going to be the happiest woman alive."

My sisters arrived a few days before the surgery. They set themselves up in the house's many empty bedrooms, making up their side tables with lotions and crossword puzzles. I could hear them upstairs and they sounded like birds, distinct and luminously choral at the same time. I told them I was going out for a final meal.

"We'll come with you," said my first sister.

"Keep you company," said my second sister.

"Be supportive," said my third sister.

"No," I said, "I'll go alone. I need to be alone."

I walked to my favorite restaurant, Salt. It hadn't always been Salt, though, in name or spirit. It was Linda's, for a while, and then Family Diner, then The Table. The building remains the same, but it is always new and always better than before.

I thought about people on death row and their final meals, as I sat at a corner table, and for the third time that week I worried about my moral compass, or lack thereof. They aren't the same, I reminded myself as I unfolded the napkin over my lap. Those things are not comparable. Their last meal comes before death, mine comes before not just life, but a new life. *You are horrible*, I thought, as I lifted the menu to my face, higher than it needed to be.

I ordered a cavalcade of oysters. Most of them had been cut the way they were supposed to be, and they slipped down as easily as water, like the ocean, like nothing at all, but one fought me: anchored to its shell, a stubborn hinge of flesh. It resisted. It was resistance incarnate. Oysters are alive, I realized. They are nothing but muscle, they have no brains or insides, strictly speaking, but they are alive nonetheless. If there were any justice in the world, this oyster would grab hold of my tongue and choke me dead."

I almost gagged, but then I swallowed.

My third sister sat down across the table from me. Her dark hair reminded me of my mother's; almost too shiny and homogenous to be real, though it was. She smiled kindly at me, like she was about to give me some bad news.

"Why are you here?" I asked her.

"You look troubled," she said. She held her hands in a way that showed off her red nails, which were so lacquered they had horizontal depth, like a rose trapped in glass. She tapped them against her cheekbones, scraping them down her face with the very lightest touch. I shuddered. Then she picked up my water and drank deeply of it, until the water had filtered through the ice and the ice was nothing more than a fragile lattice and then the whole construction slid against her face as she tipped the glass higher and she chewed the slivers that landed in her mouth.

"Don't waste that stomach space on water," she said, *crunch crunch crunch*ing. "Come on now. What are you eating?"

"Oysters," I said, even though she could see the precarious pile of shells before me.

She nodded. "Are they good?" she asked.

"They are."

"Tell me about them."

"They are the sum of all healthy things: seawater and muscle and bone," I said. "Mindless protein. They feel no pain, have no verifiable thoughts. Very few calories. An indulgence without being an indulgence. Do you want one?"

I didn't want her to be there—I wanted to tell her to leave—but her eyes were glittering like she had a fever. She ran her fingernail lovingly along an oyster shell. The whole pile shifted, doubling down on its own mass.

"No," she said. "Then, have you told Cal? About the procedure?"

I bit my lip. "No," I said. "Did you tell your daughter, before you got it?"

"I did. She was so excited for me. She sent me flowers."

"Cal will not be excited," I said. "There are many daughter duties Cal does not perform, and this will be one, too."

"Do you think she needs the surgery, too? Is that why?"

"I don't know," I said. "I have never understood Cal's needs."

"Do you think it's because she will think badly of you?"

"I've also never understood her opinions," I said.

My sister nodded.

"She will not send me flowers," I concluded, even though this was probably not necessary.

I ordered a pile of hot truffle fries, which burned the roof of my mouth. It was only after the burn that I thought about how much I'd miss it all. I started to cry, and my sister put her hand over mine. I was jealous of the oysters. They never had to think about themselves.

At home, I called Cal, to tell her. My jaw was so tightly clenched, it popped when she answered the phone. On the other end I could hear another woman's voice, stopped short by a finger to the lips unseen; then a dog whined.

"Surgery?" she repeated.

"Yes," I said.

"Jesus Christ," she said.

"Don't swear," I told her, even though I was not a religious woman.

"What? That's not even a fucking swear," she yelled. "*That* was a fucking swear. And this. *Jesus Christ* is not a swear. It's a proper name. And if there's ever a time to swear, it's when your mom tells you she's getting half of one of her most important organs cut away for no reason—"

She was still talking, but it was growing into a yell. I shooed the words away like bees.

"—occur to you that you're never going to be able to eat like a normal human—"

"What is wrong with you?" I finally asked her.

"Mom, I just don't understand why you can't be happy with yourself. You've never been—"

She kept talking. I stared at the receiver. When did my child sour? I didn't remember the process, the top-down tumble from sweetness to curdled anger. She was furious constantly, she was all accusation. She had taken the moral high ground from me by force, time and time again. I had committed any number of sins: Why didn't I teach her about feminism? Why do I persist in not understanding anything? And *this*, this takes the cake, no, *don't* forgive the pun; language is infused with food like everything else, or at least like everything else should be. She was so angry I was glad I couldn't read her mind. I knew her thoughts would break my heart.

The line went dead. She'd hung up on me. I set the phone on the receiver and realized my sisters were watching me from the doorway, looking near tears, one sympathetic, the other smug.

I turned away. Why didn't Cal understand? Her body was imperfect but it was also fresh, pliable. She could sidestep my mistakes. She could have the release of a new start. I had no self-control, but tomorrow I would relinquish control and everything would be right again.

The phone rang. Cal, calling back? But it was my niece. She was selling knife sets so she could go back to school and become a—well, I missed that part, but she would get paid just for telling me about the knives, so I let her walk me through, step-by-step, and I bought a cheese knife with a special cut-out center—"So the cheese doesn't stick to the blade, see?" she said.

In the operating room, I was open to the world. Not that kind of open, not yet, everything was still sealed up inside, but I was naked except for a faintly patterned cloth gown that didn't quite wrap around my body.

"Wait," I said. I laid my hand upon my hip and squeezed a little. I trembled, though I didn't know why. There was an IV and the IV would relax me; soon I would be very far away.

Dr. U stared at me over her mask. Gone was the sweetness from her office; her eyes looked transformed. Icy.

"Did you ever read that picture book about Ping the duck?"[2] I asked her.

"No," she said.

"Ping the duck was always punished for being the last duck home. He'd get whacked across the back with a switch. He hated that. So he ran away. After he ran away he met some black fishing birds with metal bands around their necks. They caught fish for their masters but could not swallow the fish whole, because of the bands. When they brought fish back, they were rewarded with tiny pieces they could swallow. They were obedient, because they had to be. Ping, with no band, was always last and now was lost. I don't remember how it ends. It seems like a book you should read."

She adjusted her mask a little. "Don't make me cut out your tongue," she said.

"I'm ready," I told her.

The mask slipped over me and I was on the moon.

Afterwards, I sleep and sleep. It's been a long time since I've been so still. I stay on the couch because stairs, stairs are impossible. In the watery light of morning, dust motes drift through the air like plankton. I have never seen the living room so early. A new world.

I drink shaking sips of clear broth, brought to me by my first sister, who, silhouetted against the window, looks like a branch stripped bare by the wind. My second sister checks in on me every so often, opening the windows a crack despite the cold—to let some air in, she says softly. She does not say the house smells stale and like death but I can see it in her eyes as she fans the door open

---

2   From the children's book *The Story about Ping* by Marjorie Flack.

and shut and open and shut as patiently as a mother whose child has vomited. I can see her cheekbones, high and tight as cherries, and I smile at her as best I can.

My third sister observes me at night, sitting on a chair near the sofa, where she glances at me from above her book, her brows tightening and loosening with concern. She talks to her daughter—who loves her without judgment, I am sure—in the kitchen, so soft I can barely hear her, but then forgets herself and laughs loudly at some joke shared between them. I wonder if my niece has sold any more knives.

I am transformed but not yet, exactly. The transformation has begun—this pain, this excruciating pain, it is part of the process—and will not end until— well, I suppose I don't know when. Will I ever be done, transformed in the past tense, or will I always be transforming, better and better until I die?

Cal does not call. When she does I will remind her of my favorite memory of her: when I caught her with chemical depilatory in the bathroom in the wee hours of morning, creaming her little tan arms and legs and upper lip so the hair dissolved like snow. I will tell her, when she calls.

The shift, at first, is imperceptible, so small as to be a trick of the imagination. But then one day I button a pair of pants and they fall to my feet. I marvel at what is beneath. A pre-Cal body. A pre-me body. It is emerging, like the lie of snow withdrawing from the truth of the landscape. My sisters finally go home. They kiss me and tell me that I look beautiful.

I am finally well enough to walk along the beach. The weather has been so cold the water is thick with ice and the waves churn creamily, like soft serve. I take a photo and send it to Cal, but I know she won't respond.

At home, I cook a very small chicken breast and cut it into white cubes. I count the bites and when I reach eight I throw the rest of the food in the garbage. I stand over the can for a long while, breathing in the salt-pepper smell of chicken mixed in with coffee grounds and something older and closer to decay. I spray window cleaner into the garbage can so the food cannot be retrieved. I feel a little light but good; righteous, even. Before I would have been growling, climbing up the walls from want. Now I feel only slightly empty, and fully content.

That night, I wake up because something is standing over me, something small, and before I slide into being awake I think it's my daughter, up from a nightmare, or perhaps it's morning and I've overslept, except even as my hands exchange blanket-warmth for chilled air and it is so dark I remember my daughter is in her late twenties and lives in Portland with a roommate who is not really her roommate and she will not tell me and I don't know why.

But something is there, darkness blotting out darkness, a person-shaped out-line. It sits on the bed, and I feel the weight, the mattress' springs creaking and pinging. Is it looking at me? Away from me? Does it look, at all?

And then there is nothing, and I sit up alone.

As I learn my new diet—my forever diet, the one that will only end when I do—something is moving in the house. At first I think it is mice, but it is larger, more autonomous. Mice in walls scurry and drop through unexpected holes, and you can hear them scrabbling in terror as they plummet behind your family portraits. But this thing occupies the hidden parts of the house with purpose, and if I drop my ear to the wallpaper it breathes audibly.

After a week of this, I try to talk to it.

"Whatever you are, I say, please come out. I want to see you."

Nothing. I am not sure whether I am feeling afraid or curious or both.

I call my sisters. "It might be my imagination," I explain, "but did you also hear something, after? In the house? A presence?"

"Yes," says my first sister. "My joy danced around my house, like a child, and I danced with her. We almost broke two vases that way!"

"Yes," says my second sister. "My inner beauty was set free and lay around in patches of sunlight like a cat, preening itself."

"Yes," says my third sister. "My former shame slunk from shadow to shadow, as it should have. It will go away, after a while. You won't even notice and then one day it'll be gone."

After I hang up with her, I try and take a grapefruit apart with my hands, but it's an impossible task. The skin clings to the fruit, and between them is an intermediary skin, thick and impossible to separate from the meat.

Eventually I take a knife and lop off domes of rinds and cut the grapefruit into a cube before ripping it open with my fingers. It feels like I am dismantling a human heart. The fruit is delicious, slick. I swallow eight times, and when the ninth bite touches my lips I pull it back and squish it in my hand like I am crum-pling an old receipt. I put the remaining half of the grapefruit in a Tupperware. I close the fridge. Even now I can hear it. Behind me. Above me. Too large to perceive. Too small to see.

When I was in my twenties, I lived in a place with bugs and had the same sense of knowing invisible things moved, coordinated, in the darkness. Even if I flipped on the kitchen light in the wee hours and saw nothing, I would just wait. Then my eyes would adjust and I would see it: a cockroach who, instead of scut-tling two-dimensionally across the yawn of a white wall, was instead perched at the lip of a cupboard, probing the air endlessly with his antennae. He desired and feared in three dimensions. He was less vulnerable there, and yet somehow, more, I realized as I wiped his guts across the plywood.

In the same way, now, the house is filled with something else. It moves, restless. It does not say words but it breathes. I want to know it, and I don't know why.

"I've done research," Cal says. The line crackles like she is somewhere with a bad signal, so she is not calling from her house. I listen for the voice of the other woman who is always in the background, whose name I have never learned.

"Oh, you're back?" I say. I am in control, for once.

Her voice is clipped, but then softens. I can practically hear the therapist cooing to her. She is probably going through a list that she and the therapist created together. I feel a spasm of anger.

"I am worried because," she says, and then pauses.

"Because?"

"Sometimes there can be all of these complications—"

"It's done, Cal. It's been done for months. There's no point to this."

"Do you hate my body, Mom?" she says. Her voice splinters in pain, as if she is about to cry. "You hated yours, clearly, but mine looks just like yours used to, so—"

"Stop it."

"You think you're going to be happy but this is not going to make you happy," she says.

"I love you," I say.

"Do you love every part of me?"

It's my turn to hang up and then, after a moment's thought, disconnect the phone. Cal is probably calling back right now, but she won't be able to get through. I'll let her, when I'm ready.

I wake up because I can hear a sound like a vase breaking in reverse: thousands of shards of ceramic whispering along hardwood toward a reassembling form. From my bedroom, it sounds like it's coming from the hallway. From the hallway, it sounds like it's coming from the stairs. Down, down, foyer, dining room, living room, down deeper, and then I am standing at the top of the basement steps.

From below, from the dark, something shuffles. I wrap my fingers around the ball chain hanging from the naked lightbulb and I pull.

The thing is down there. At the light, it crumples to the cement floor, curls away from me.

It looks like my daughter, as a girl. That's my first thought. It's body-shaped. Pre-pubescent, boneless. It is 100 pounds, dripping wet.

And it does. Drip.

I descend to the bottom and up close it smells warm, like toast. It looks like the clothes stuffed with straw on someone's porch at Halloween; the vague person-shaped lump made from pillows to aid a midnight escape plan. I am afraid to step over it. I walk around it, admiring my unfamiliar face in the reflection of the water heater even as I hear its sounds: a gasping, arrested sob.

I kneel down next to it. It is a body with nothing it needs: no stomach or bones or mouth. Just soft indents. I crouch down and stroke its shoulder, or what I think is its shoulder.

It turns and looks at me. It has no eyes but still, it looks at me. *She* looks at me. She is awful but honest. She is grotesque but she is real.

I shake my head. "I don't know why I wanted to meet you," I say. "I should have known."

She curls a little tighter. I lean down and whisper where an ear might be.

"You are unwanted," I say. A tremor ripples her mass.

I do not know I am kicking her until I am kicking her. She has nothing and I feel nothing except she seems to solidify before my foot meets her, and so every kick is more satisfying than the last. I reach for a broom and I pull a muscle swinging back and in and back and in, and the handle breaks off in her and I kneel down and pull soft handfuls of her body out of herself, and I throw them against the wall, and I do not know I am screaming until I stop, finally.

I find myself wishing she would fight back, but she doesn't. Instead, she sounds like she is being deflated. A hissing, defeated wheeze.

I stand up and walk away. I shut the basement door. I leave her there until I can't hear her anymore.

***

Spring has come, marking the end of winter's long contraction.

Everyone is waking up. The first warm day, when light cardigans are enough, the streets begin to hum. Bodies move around. Not fast, but still: smiles. Neighbors suddenly recognizable after a season of watching their lumpy outlines walk past in the darkness.

"You look wonderful," says one.

"Have you lost weight?" asks another.

I smile. I get a manicure and tap my new nails along my face, to show them off. I go to Salt, which is now called "The Peppercorn," and eat three oysters.

I am a new woman. A new woman becomes best friends with her daughter. A new woman laughs with all of her teeth. A new woman does not just slough off her old self; she tosses it aside with force.

Summer will come next. Summer will come and the waves will be huge, the kind of waves that feel like a challenge. If you're brave, you'll step out of the bright-hot day and into the foaming roil of the water, moving toward where the waves break and might break you. If you're brave, you'll turn your body over to this water that is practically an animal, and so much larger than yourself.

Sometimes, if I sit very still, I can hear her gurgling underneath the floorboards. She sleeps in my bed when I'm at the grocery store, and when I come back and slam the door, loudly, there are padded footsteps above my head. I know she is around, but she never crosses my path. She leaves offerings on the coffee table: safety pins, champagne bottle corks, hard candies twisted in strawberry-patterned cellophane. She shuffles through my dirty laundry and leaves a trail of socks and bras all the way to the open window. The drawers and air are rifled through. She turns all the soup can labels forward and wipes up the constellations of dried coffee spatter on the kitchen tile. The perfume of her is caught on the linens. She is around, even when she is not around.

I will see her only one more time, after this.

I will die the day I turn seventy-nine. I will wake early because outside a neighbor is talking loudly to another neighbor about her roses, and because Cal is coming today with her daughter for our annual visit, and because I am a little hungry, and because a great pressure is on my chest. Even as it tightens and compresses I will perceive what is beyond my window: a cyclist bumping over concrete, a white fox loping through underbrush, the far roll of the ocean. I will think, *it is as my sisters prophesied*. I will think, *I miss them, still*. I will think, *here is where I learn if it's all been worth it*. The pain will be unbearable until it isn't anymore; until it loosens and I will feel better than I have in a long time.

There will be such a stillness, then, broken only by a honeybee's soft-winged stumble against the screen, and a floorboard's creak.

Arms will lift me from my bed—her arms. They will be mother-soft, like dough and moss. I will recognize the smell. I will flood with grief and shame.

I will look where her eyes would be. I will open my mouth to ask but then realize the question has answered itself: by loving me when I did not love her, by being abandoned by me, she has become immortal. She will outlive me by a hundred million years; more, even. She will outlive my daughter, and my daughter's daughter, and the earth will teem with her and her kind, their inscrutable forms and unknowable destinies.

She will touch my cheek like I once did Cal's, so long ago, and there will be no accusation in it. I will cry as she shuffles me away from myself, toward a door propped open into the salty morning. I will curl into her body, which was my body once, but I was a poor caretaker and she was removed from my charge.

"I'm sorry," I will whisper into her as she walks me toward the front door.

"I'm sorry," I will repeat. "I didn't know."

—2017

GLOSSARY

allegory A story with both a literal meaning and a second, less obvious meaning. This secondary narrative runs parallel to the action of the first (working as an extended **metaphor**) and presents a moral (religious or political) lesson. Characters often represent abstract concepts such as evil, justice, or faith. *See* **fable** and **parable**.

allusion A direct or indirect reference in a literary work to a person, place, object, event, or artistic work. This reference is not elaborated upon in the work; rather, its effect depends upon the reader's understanding of the reference. *See* **intertextuality**, **parody**, and **satire**.

ambiguity An "opening" of language created by the writer that allows for multiple meanings or differing interpretations. In literature, ambiguity may be deliberately employed to enrich meaning; this differs from any unintentional, unwanted ambiguity in non-literary prose.

analepsis *See* **flashback**.

archetype A **theme**, character, **symbol**, or event that recurs throughout literatures of different ages, cultures, and languages, and is therefore considered to reflect a conventional truth (or, sometimes, a stereotype) or a common human experience.

atmosphere *See* **tone**.

bathos In literature, an anticlimactic effect brought about by descending from elevated subject matter to the trivial or ordinary.

canon In literature, a collective term for those works that are commonly accepted as possessing authority or importance. In practice, "canonical" texts or authors are those that are discussed most frequently by scholars and taught most frequently in university courses.

characterization The means by which an author develops and presents a character's personality qualities, and distinguishing traits. A character may be established in the story by descriptive commentary or may be developed less directly—for example, through his or her words, actions, thoughts, and interactions with other characters.

chronology The way a story is organized in terms of time. Linear narratives run continuously from one point in time to a later point, while non-linear narratives are non-continuous and may jump forward and backward in time. A flashback, in which a story jumps to a scene previous in time, is an example of non-linearity.

closure The sense of completion evoked at the end of a story when all or most aspects of the major conflicts have been resolved. Not every story has a strong sense of closure.

comedy As a literary term, used originally to denote that class of ancient Greek drama in which the action ends happily. More broadly, the term has been used to describe a wide variety of literary forms of a light-hearted character. *See also* **tragedy**.

conflict Struggles between characters and opposing forces. Conflict can be internal (psychological) or external (conflict with another character, for instance, or with society or nature).

connotation The implied, often unspoken meaning(s) of a given word or phrase, as distinct from its denotation, or literal meaning.

denotation *See* **connotation**.

denouement That portion of a narrative which follows a dramatic crisis, in which conflicts are resolved and the narrative is brought to a close. Traditional accounts of narrative structure often posit a triangle or arc, with rising action followed by a crisis and then by a denouement. (Such accounts bear little relation, however, to the ways in which most actual narratives are structured—particularly most twentieth and twenty-first century literary fictions.)

dialogue The words spoken by characters in a story.

diction The author's choice of words. Different types of diction (for example, formal or informal, simple or elaborate, concrete or abstract) produce different effects, and an author may vary diction according to the character, context, or intended purpose of the work. The diction in "My Lucy Friend Who Smells Like Corn" is distinguished by colloquial language (slang, conversational usage) and helps establish the story's intimate **tone**. The story's seamless incorporation of Spanish words also evokes a particular cultural context.

embedded narrative A story contained within another story.

epiphany In literature, a moment at which matters of significance are suddenly illuminated for a literary character (or for the reader), typically triggered by something small and seemingly of little importance. The term first came into wide currency in connection with the fiction of James Joyce.

exposition In fiction, material that functions to provide information—to fill in background for the reader, to summarize parts of the story that have happened "off-stage," and/or to provide commentary on characters or situations.

fable A short **allegorical** tale that conveys an explicit moral lesson. The characters are often animals or objects with human speech and mannerisms. *See* **parable**.

fantasy In fiction, a sub-genre characterized by the presence of magical or miraculous elements—usually acknowledged as such by the characters and the narrative voice. In **magic realism**, by contrast, miraculous occurrences tend to be treated by the characters and/or the narrative voice as if they were entirely ordinary. In fantasy (also in contrast to magic realism), the fictional world generally has an internal consistency to it that precludes any sense of absurdity on the part of the reader; and the plot tends to build a strong sense of expectation in the reader.

fiction Imagined or invented narrative. In literature, the term is usually used to refer to prose narratives (such as novels and short stories).

first person narrative Narrative recounted using *I* and *me*. *See also* **narrative perspective**.

flashback In fiction, the inclusion in the primary thread of a story's narrative of a scene (or scenes) from an earlier point in time. Flashbacks may be used to revisit from a different viewpoint events that have already been recounted in the main thread of narrative; to present material that had been left out in the initial recounting; or to present relevant material from a time before the beginning of the main thread of narrative. The use of flashbacks in fiction is sometimes referred to as **analepsis**.

flashforward The inclusion in the primary thread of a story's narrative of a scene (or scenes) from a later point in time. *See also* **prolepsis**.

foreshadowing The inclusion of elements in a story that hint at some later development(s) in the same story. For example, in "A Good Man Is Hard to Find," the old family burying ground that the family sees on their drive foreshadows the violence that follows.

form Generally, form refers to the shape and structure of a work, which can be described by referring to (for example) its **genre**, and to the organization of its various components (such as **plot**, **diction**, **characters**, and **style**).

free indirect discourse In prose fiction, commentary in which a seemingly objective and omniscient narrative voice assumes the point of view of one or more characters. When we hear through the third person narrative voice of Jane Austen's *Pride and Prejudice*, for example, that Mr. Darcy "was the proudest, most disagreeable man in the world, and everybody hoped that he would never come there again," the narrative voice has assumed the point of view of "everybody in the community"; we as readers are not meant to take it that Mr. Darcy is indeed the most disagreeable man in the world.

The term "free indirect discourse" is also sometimes applied to situations in which it may not be entirely clear if the thoughts expressed emanate from the character, the narrator, or some combination of the two.

genre Class or type of literary work. The concept of genre may be used with different levels of generality. At the most general, poetry, drama, and prose fiction are distinguished as separate genres. At a lower level of generality various sub-genres are frequently distinguished, such as (within the genre of prose fiction) the novel, the novella, and the short story; and, at a still lower level of generality, the mystery novel, the detective novel, the novel of manners, and so on.

Gothic In architecture and the visual arts, a term used to describe styles prevalent from the twelfth to the fourteenth centuries, but in literature a term used to describe work with a sinister or grotesque tone that seeks to evoke a sense of terror on the part of the reader or audience. Gothic literature originated as a genre in the eighteenth century with works such as Horace Walpole's *The Castle of Otranto*. To some extent the notion of the medieval itself then carried with it associations of the dark and the grotesque, but from the beginning an element of intentional exaggeration (sometimes verging on self-parody) attached itself to the genre. The gothic trend of youth culture that began in the late twentieth century is less clearly associated with the medieval, but shares with gothic literature (from Walpole in the eighteenth century, to Bram Stoker in the early twentieth, to Stephen King and Anne Rice in the late twentieth) a fondness for the sensational and the grotesque, as well as a propensity to self-parody.

"The Cask of Amontillado" is one story in this anthology that incorporates many elements of the gothic.

grotesque Literature of the grotesque is characterized by a focus on extreme or distorted aspects of human characteristics. (The term can also refer particularly to a character who is odd or disturbing.) This focus can serve to comment on and challenge societal norms. The story "A Good Man Is Hard to Find" employs elements of the grotesque.

imagery Words or phrases about something within the physical world (an action, sight, sound, smell, taste, or touch) that illustrate something about a story's characters, settings, or situations. The imagery of spring (budding trees, rain, singing birds) in "The Story of an Hour" reinforces the suggestions of death and rebirth in the plot and theme.

implied author *See* **narrator**.

intertextuality The relationships between one literary work and other literary works. **Allusion**, imitation, **parody**, and **satire** are examples of intertextuality.

irony A discrepancy between an apparent reality or statement and its meaning. Three types of irony are verbal irony (in which there is an apparent discrepancy between what is said and what is meant), situational irony (when an event turns out very differently than expected), and dramatic irony (when the reader and sometimes other characters know something that one character does not know). *See also* **parody** and **satire**.

magic realism A style of fiction in which miraculous or bizarre things often happen but are treated in a matter-of-fact fashion by the characters and/or the narrative voice. There is often an element of the absurd to magic realist narratives, and they tend not to have any strong plot structure generating expectations in the reader's mind. *See also* **fantasy**.

melodrama Originally a term used to describe nineteenth-century plays featuring sensational story lines and a crude separation of characters into moral categories, with the pure and virtuous pitted against evil villains. Early melodramas employed background music throughout the action of the play as a means of heightening the emotional response of the audience. By extension, certain sorts of prose fictions or poems are often described as having melodramatic elements.

metafiction Fiction that calls attention to itself as fiction, in an effort to explore the relationships between fiction and reality. Examples of metafictional situations occur when the writing refers to the act of reading or writing, or an author seems to insert him or herself into the story as a character, or an author seems to address the reader directly or interrupt the narrative. In "The Yellow Wallpaper," the fictional situation of the narrator's relationship to her writing has implications for the significance of the story itself, because this suggests the possibility of certain relationships between "The Yellow Wallpaper," its author, and its reader.

metaphor A *figure of speech* (in this case, a **trope**) in which a comparison is made or identity is asserted between two unrelated things or actions without the use of "like" or "as." The primary subject is known as the *tenor*; to illuminate its nature, the writer links it to wholly different images, ideas, or actions (referred to as the *vehicle*). Unlike a **simile**, which is a direct comparison of two things, a metaphor "fuses" the separate qualities of two things, creating a new idea.

modernism In the history of literature, music, and the visual arts, a movement that began in the early twentieth century, characterized by a thoroughgoing rejection of the then-dominant conventions of literary plotting and characterization, of melody and harmony, and of perspective and other naturalistic forms of visual representation. In literature (as in music and the visual arts), Modernists endeavoured to represent the complexity of what seemed to them to be an increasingly fragmented world by adopting techniques of presenting story material, illuminating character, and employing imagery that emphasized (in the words of Virginia Woolf) "the spasmodic, the obscure, the fragmentary."

motif An idea, image, action, or plot element that recurs throughout a literary work, creating new levels of meaning and strengthening structural coherence. The term is taken from music, where it describes recurring melodies or themes. The recurring focus on blindness in "Cathedral" is suggestive of the narrator's isolation and lack of emotional bearings or direction.

motivation The forces that seem to cause characters to act, or why characters do what they do.

narration The process of storytelling.

narrative perspective In fiction, the point of view from which the story is narrated. A first-person narrative is recounted using *I* and me, whereas a third-person narrative is recounted using *he, she, they*, and so on. (Second-person narratives, in which the story is recounted using *you*, are extremely rare.) When a narrative is written in the third person and the narrative voice evidently "knows" all that is being done and thought, the story is typically described as being recounted by an "omniscient narrator." Third-person narratives may also present limited perspectives, however; whether writing in the third person or the first person, authors will sometimes intentionally present narrative perspectives that the reader will have grounds to interpret as unreliable. (*See also* **free indirect discourse, stream of consciousness**.)

narrator The voice (or voices) telling the story. The narrator is distinct from both the author (a real, historical person) and the implied author (whom the reader imagines the author to be). Narrators can be distinguished according to the degree to which they share the reality of the other characters in the story and the extent to which they participate in the action; according to how much information they are privy to (and how much of that information they are willing to share with the reader); and according to whether or not they are perceived by the reader as reliable or unreliable sources of information. *See also* **narrative perspective**.

omniscient narrator *See* **narrative perspective**.

parable A brief allegorical story that illustrates a moral or lesson. The term is religious in origin, referring to the stories told by Jesus in the New Testament. Unlike the characters in **fables**, the characters in parables are usually human. "The Raspberry Bush," because of its brevity, structural simplicity,

characterization (the folktale-like "little old woman"), and lesson in loneliness and sympathy, can be read as a parable.

parody Parody (a type of **satire**) is the imitation of another literary work or style in order to ridicule a target. Parody is recognizable by the extent to which the imitation differs from its original model in a ludicrous way; this difference is achieved by exaggerating or debasing (or otherwise making ridiculous) some aspect of the original. *See* **intertextuality**, **allusion**, and **satire**.

pathos An appeal to (or the technique of appealing to) the emotions of the reader or listener. In ancient Greece pathos was defined as one of the three methods through which persuasion might be accomplished (the others being logos—persuasion through words offering reasoned argument; and ethos—persuasion through the presentation of heroic or otherwise ethically admirable characters). In discussing literature the term pathos is most often applied to works (or scenes within works) that arouse feelings of pity or sorrow in the reader or audience through the presentation of narrative material concerning pain, suffering, or loss.

persona The assumed identity or "speaking voice" that a writer projects in a discourse. The term "persona" literally means "mask."

personification A figure of speech in which objects, ideas, or non-human animals are referred to as if they were human (or in which a human figure is created to represent abstract entities such as Wisdom or Peace).

plot The organization of story materials within a literary work. The order in which story material is presented; the inclusion of elements that allow or encourage the reader or audience to form expectations as to what is likely to happen; the decision to present story material directly to the reader as part of the narrative or to have it recounted in summary form through exposition—all these are matters of plotting.

"The Story of an Hour" may be used to illustrate the difference between story and plot. It is a story of the aftermath of a railway accident; it is also the story of a marriage. One might have plotted this story material in myriad different ways—showing husband and wife interacting with each other over a more extended period, for example, or narrating the accident directly (rather than having it reported as something that has happened "offstage"), or including material that encouraged the reader to be open to the possibility that the husband may have survived the accident. Instead the story's plot arranges the material so as to focus on only one hour, and on the thoughts and feelings during that hour of only one of the characters.

point of view *See* **narrative perspective**.

postmodernism In literature and the visual arts, a movement influential in the late twentieth and early twenty-first centuries. In some ways postmodernism represents a reaction to modernism, in others an extension of it. With roots in the work of French philosophers such as Jacques Derrida and Michel Foucault, it is deeply coloured by theory; indeed, it may be said to have begun at the "meta" level of theorizing rather than at the level of practice. It is notoriously resistant to definition—indeed, resistance to fixed definitions is itself a characteristic of postmodernism. Like modernism, postmodernism embraces difficulty and distrusts the simple and straightforward. More broadly, postmodernism is characterized by a rejection of absolute truth or value, of closed systems, of grand unified narratives.

Postmodernist fiction is characterized by a frequently ironic or playful tone in dealing with reality and illusion; by a willingness to combine different styles or forms in a single work (just as in architecture the postmodernist spirit embodies a willingness to borrow from seemingly disparate styles in designing a single structure); and by a highly attuned awareness of the problematized state of the writer, artist, or theorist as observer.

prolepsis Originally a rhetorical term used to refer to the anticipation of possible objections by someone advancing an argument, prolepsis is used in discussions of fiction to refer to elements in a narrative that anticipate the future of the story. The **flashforward** technique of storytelling is often described as a form of prolepsis; the inclusion in a narrative of material that foreshadows future developments is also sometimes treated as a form of prolepsis.

protagonist The central character in a literary work.

realism An approach to literature that endeavours to represent the world in ways that are true to real life. Just as notions of what constitutes "real life" may vary widely, so too has "realism" taken on a variety of meanings. The term "realism" originated in the nineteenth century to denote literature that eschewed romance and that did not shy away from presenting the grim, unpleasant, and ugly aspects of the real. In the twentieth century, social realism became a term used to convey very similar notions, while also suggesting that the most important defining conditions of reality are broad social conditions that are susceptible to political forces—and that can be changed by political activism. The term psychological realism, on the other hand, refers to fiction that endeavours to portray persuasively the perceptions of one or more individuals. (When the term "realistic" is used to refer to fiction that features plausible and consistent characters, settings, and situations, it is psychological realism that is being drawn attention to.) *See also* **magic realism**.

satire A literary work designed to make fun of (and, often, seriously criticize) human failings, social evils, and corrupt institutions. *See also* **parody**.

setting The time, place, and cultural environment in which a story takes place.

simile The comparison of one thing with another, using the words "as" or "like." The story "A Good Man Is Hard to Find," for example, includes the simile "the line of woods gaped like a dark open mouth." *See also* **metaphor**.

story Narrative material, independent of the manner in which it may be presented or the ways in which the narrative material may be organized. Story is thus distinct from **plot** (see above).

stream of consciousness A narrative technique that conveys the inner workings of a character's mind, in which a character's thoughts, feelings, memories, and impressions are related in an unbroken flow, without concern for **chronology** or coherence.

Some critics apply the term "stream of consciousness" only to passages which are written entirely in the first person. The term is also often used more loosely, though, to refer to any one of (or combination of) a range of techniques that attempt to convey in prose fiction a sense of the progression of thoughts and sensations occurring within a character's mind; extended passages of prose fiction written in **free indirect discourse**, for example, are often described as employing a stream of consciousness technique.

style A distinctive or specific use of language and form.

subtext Implicit or unstated meaning. There is a strong sense of subtext in "Hills Like White Elephants," where much of the story's meaning is suggested by the characters' silence.

symbol Something that represents another thing (an idea, quality, or another object, for example) beyond or in addition to itself.

theme A central idea, unifying principle, or underlying message of a story. A single work may have a number of themes.

third person narrative A narrative in which there is no *I* or *me* in the story; all the characters are seen "from the outside" as *he*, *she*, or *they*. *See also* **narrative perspective**.

tone The overall or most dominant impression produced by a work; its **atmosphere** or mood. For example, stories may be bleak, humorous, hopeful, romantic, alienating, wry, or suspenseful in tone.

tragedy In the traditional definition originating from discussions of ancient Greek drama, a serious narrative recounting the downfall of the protagonist. More loosely, the term has been applied to a wide variety of literary forms in which the tone is predominantly a dark one and the narrative does not end happily.

trope Any figure of speech that plays on our understanding of words to extend, alter, or transform "literal" meaning. Common tropes include **metaphor**, **simile**, **personification**, hyperbole, metonymy, oxymoron, and **irony**.

unreliable narrator *See* **narrative perspective**.

CONTENTS BY FORM AND THEME

Aging and Death

Childhood and Adolescence

Colonialism and Postcolonialism

Fable and Parable

Gender

Gothic and Ghost Stories

Indigenous Literature

LGBTQ Literature

Microfiction and Very Short Stories

Non-Human Animals

Race and Racism

Sexuality, Love, and Relationships

Social Class

Speculative Fiction and Magical Realism

Stories in Translation

War and Peace

PERMISSIONS ACKNOWLEDGEMENTS

From the Publisher

A name never says it all, but the word "Broadview" expresses a good deal of the philosophy behind our company. We are open to a broad range of academic approaches and political viewpoints. We pay attention to the broad impact book publishing and book printing has in the wider world; we began using recycled stock more than a decade ago, and for some years now we have used 100% recycled paper for most titles. Our publishing program is internationally oriented and broad-ranging. Our individual titles often appeal to a broad readership too; many are of interest as much to general readers as to academics and students.

Founded in 1985, Broadview remains a fully independent company owned by its shareholders—not an imprint or subsidiary of a larger multinational.

For the most accurate information on our books (including information on pricing, editions, and formats) please visit our website at www.broadviewpress.com. Our print books and ebooks are also available for sale on our site.

broadview press
www.broadviewpress.com